OXFORD W

SYLVIA

ELIZABETH GASKELL was born Elizabeth Cleghorn Stevenson in 1810. The daughter of a Unitarian, who was a civil servant and journalist, she was brought up after her mother's death by her aunt in Knutsford, Cheshire, which became the model not only for Cranford but also for Hollingford (in *Wives and Daughters*). In 1832 she married William Gaskell, a Unitarian minister in Manchester, with whom she lived very happily. Her first novel, *Mary Barton*, published in 1848, was immensely popular and brought her to the attention of Charles Dickens, who was looking for contributors to his new periodical, *Household Words*, for which she wrote the famous series of papers subsequently reprinted as *Cranford*. Her later novels include *Ruth* (1853), *North and South* (1854–5), *Sylvia's Lovers* (1863), and *Wives and Daughters* (1864–6). She also wrote many stories and her remarkable *Life of Charlotte Brontë*. She died in 1865.

ANDREW SANDERS is Professor of English at the University of Durham. He has edited George Eliot's *Romola* and Dickens's *Dombey and Son* for Penguin Classics and (in the Oxford World's Classics series) Elizabeth Gaskell's *Sylvia's Lovers*, Dickens's *David Copperfield* and *A Tale of Two Cities*, Thackeray's *Barry Lyndon* and *The Newcomes*, and Thomas Hughes's *Tom Brown's Schooldays*. He is the author of *The Victorian Historical Novel* (1978), *Charles Dickens: Resurrectionist* (1982), a companion to *A Tale of Two Cities*, *The Short Oxford History of English Literature* (1994), *Anthony Trollope* (Writers and their Work series) (1998), and *Dickens and the Spirit of the Age* (forthcoming). He was editor of *The Dickensian* from 1978 to 1986.

OXFORD WORLD'S CLASSICS

For almost 100 years Oxford World's Classics have brought readers closer to the world's great literature. Now with over 700 titles—from the 4,000-year-old myths of Mesopotamia to the twentieth century's greatest novels—the series makes available lesser-known as well as celebrated writing.

The pocket-sized hardbacks of the early years contained introductions by Virginia Woolf, T. S. Eliot, Graham Greene, and other literary figures which enriched the experience of reading. Today the series is recognized for its fine scholarship and reliability in texts that span world literature, drama and poetry, religion, philosophy and politics. Each edition includes perceptive commentary and essential background information to meet the changing needs of readers.

OXFORD WORLD'S CLASSICS

ELIZABETH GASKELL

Sylvia's Lovers

Edited with an Introduction and Notes by
ANDREW SANDERS

OXFORD
UNIVERSITY PRESS

OXFORD
UNIVERSITY PRESS

Great Clarendon Street, Oxford OX2 6DP

Oxford University Press is a department of the University of Oxford.
It furthers the University's objective of excellence in research, scholarship,
and education by publishing worldwide in

Oxford New York

Athens Auckland Bangkok Bogotá Buenos Aires Calcutta
Cape Town Chennai Dar es Salaam Delhi Florence Hong Kong Istanbul
Karachi Kuala Lumpur Madrid Melbourne Mexico City Mumbai
Nairobi Paris São Paulo Singapore Taipei Tokyo Toronto Warsaw

with associated companies in Berlin Ibadan

Oxford is a registered trade mark of Oxford University Press
in the UK and in certain other countries

Published in the United States
by Oxford University Press Inc., New York

First published as a World's Classics paperback 1982
Reissued as an Oxford World's Classics paperback 1999

British Library Cataloguing in Publication Data

Data available

Library of Congress Cataloging in Publication Data

Gaskell, Elizabeth Cleghorn, 1810–1865.
Sylvia's lovers.—(Oxford world's classics)
Bibliography.
I. Sanders, Andrew. II. Title.
PR4710.S9 1982 823'.8 81-18871

ISBN 0-19-283731-1

1 3 5 7 9 10 8 6 4 2

Printed in Great Britain by
Cox & Wyman Ltd.
Reading, Berkshire

CONTENTS

Introduction vii

Note on the Text xviii

Select Bibliography xix

A Chronology of Elizabeth Gaskell xxii

SYLVIA'S LOVERS 1

APPENDIX A 504

APPENDIX B 508

APPENDIX C 510

Explanatory Notes 516

INTRODUCTION

Sylvia's Lovers was inspired by a holiday visit to Whitby paid by Elizabeth Gaskell and her two daughters in November 1859. She spent only a fortnight in the town, and, despite the fact that she went out walking every day, she later explained the fact that there were minor topographical slips in the novel by recalling that 'it was such cloudy November weather that I might very easily be ignorant of the points of the compass if I did not look at a map'. Nevertheless, Whitby, its recent history, and its extraordinary setting, stirred her into writing her profoundest and saddest novel. We know from the preface to *Mary Barton* of 1848 that a story 'the period of which was more than a century ago, and the place on the borders of Yorkshire' had been contemplated before the novelist had embarked on her 'tale of Manchester life', but this Yorkshire story was abandoned and it would not seem to have contributed significantly to a mature masterpiece of the quality of *Sylvia's Lovers*. Whitby, or as it becomes in the novel, Monkshaven, is situated far from the 'borders' of Yorkshire and both the constant interaction of sea and land and the Napoleonic period in which it is set suggest a completely fresh idea. Almost certainly that idea had grown both out of a long-fostered fascination with the sea and out of a new and extended acquaintance with Yorkshire as a result of the researches involved in the composition of *The Life of Charlotte Brontë* between 1855 and 1857. The differences between land-locked Haworth and Whitby, and between the Brontë parsonage and the Robsons' farm at Haytersbank, are so striking as to discourage too easy a connection between the two.

The kind of investigation pursued at Haworth must, however, have added to Mrs Gaskell's pleasure and discrimination in discovering and recording anecdote, details of domestic life, and conversation marked by regional sounds and words. It would seem likely that one particular source of information concerning the Brontës, The Revd William Scoresby, sometime vicar of Bradford, also became a valuable influence on the genesis of *Sylvia's Lovers*. In 1820 Dr Scoresby had published his two-volume *An Account of the Arctic Regions, with a History and Description of the Northern Whale Fishery*, a full survey of contemporary whaling which drew on his own experience (his religious vocation came later) and on the life of his father, an Arctic navigator based in Whitby. Memories of Scoresby's book, and the germ of a Whitby story, may well have drawn the novelist to the town in 1859 to lodge with a family named Rose, and it is likely that it was there that she heard the story of a riot against the press-gang in 1793. Certainly all became elements in the scheme of the three-volume novel she proposed to her publisher, George Smith, in December 1859, a novel provisionally entitled 'the Specksioneer'.

A further interesting aspect of the Whitby holiday may also have influenced the idea for *Sylvia's Lovers*, and that was the reading matter that the Gaskells appear to have taken with them, Thackeray's rambling historical novel *The Virginians*, which had just completed its run in parts, and George Eliot's recently published *Scenes of Clerical Life* and *Adam Bede*. All three works are set in periods varying from the 1760s to the 1790s and both Thackeray's novel and *Adam Bede* tangentially consider the impact of war and military service on divided families and friends. Thackeray was an established novelist whose work was showing signs of strain; George Eliot, on the other hand, was a new star in the literary firmament and Mrs Gaskell's enthusiasm for her work was unequivocal. She wrote to her fellow-novelist from her Whitby lodgings fulsomely admitting how 'earnestly, fully, and humbly' she admired *Scenes of Clerical Life* and *Adam Bede*; a recent re-reading of both had confirmed the notion that she had never before read anything 'so complete, and beautiful in fiction'. In George Eliot's early fiction Elizabeth Gaskell found precisely the close observation of the lives and circumstances of ordinary men and women at which she herself had aimed, but she also found an acute historical sense which exhibited itself not in set-piece descriptions of the great events in the past but in an awareness that the passage of time conditions and changes perspectives. The balance of the 'then' against the 'now' which determines so much of the mood of *Adam Bede* and which informs the narrator's comments on, say, the village church or the attitudes and opinions of its incumbent, finds a determined echo in *Sylvia's Lovers*.

Although we have no record of the fact, it is very likely that Elizabeth Gaskell would also have known the third major novel of 1859 with an historical setting, Dickens's *A Tale of Two Cities*. It had begun its weekly run in *All the Year Round* at the end of April. Dickens, who had been so closely associated with the serialization of both *Cranford* and *North and South* in his earlier periodical, *Household Words*, had framed his new novel around the destinies of a single family and its associates caught up in a historical crisis and he had viewed the French Revolution from the point of view of its impact upon that family. Significantly, too, Dickens had dealt with a heroine loved by two men of widely differing character and he had moulded the crisis of his novel on the decisions of those two lovers. In *A Tale of Two Cities* we have another indication of the nature of *Sylvia's Lovers* as a historical novel, for both deal with private worlds touched and damaged by public events. Dickens is ambitious in dealing directly with the French Revolution; Elizabeth Gaskell, by contrast, looks steadily at provincial England and at war as a mirror of a private violence which has already disrupted the lives of her fictional characters.

It is scarcely surprising, therefore, that Mrs Gaskell's fifth novel should have a historical setting, a setting which serves to suggest something of the force with which war and the affairs of state impose themselves upon a provincial community. Whitby, with its whaling tradition and its memories of the violent incursions of the press-gang during the French Revolutionary Wars, had stirred a creative energy in the novelist. Although the seaport which she visited in the autumn of 1859 still retained its dramatic situation, with its ruined Abbey on the cliffs brooding over the harbour from which she coined the name 'Monkshaven', Whitby, like its fictional reflection, had experienced an important shift in its economic fortunes during the first half of the nineteenth century. This shift helps to explain the historical perspective offered in *Sylvia's Lovers*. The Monkshaven of Sylvia, Philip and Kinraid is a whaling-port shut in on the land side by 'the wild, bleak moors' almost as effectually 'as ever the waters did on the seaboard'. It is so cut off from the rest of England that the journey over the moors to York is arduous and Philip's quickest way to London proves to be via Hartlepool and Newcastle. The Monkshaven of the narrator, who writes looking back over the sixty years since the story of Sylvia and Philip ended, has changed; she hears their story outside the 'Public Baths' which symbolize a town which is now 'a rising bathing-place'. Even in Sylvia's time new houses are being built for visitors on the west side of the bridge and a 'grand new walk' is being formed round the cliffs to cater for promenaders. Like many similar, but less individual, seaside towns, Whitby was transformed by the nineteenth century. The whale-fishery, having risen to a peak in 1814 when eight ships took 172 whales, declined rapidly and ceased altogether in 1837; a new bridge replaced the old drawbridge across the river Esk in 1835, and the railway finally arrived in 1845, there having been a horse-drawn connection to the main line from 1836. Although Mrs Gaskell tells us at the opening of the novel that Monkshaven's population had doubled since the beginning of the century, that of Whitby seems to have remained constant, a constant explained by the decline of a stable industry and by its gradual transformation into a resort.

A play of 'now' against 'then' is as crucial an element in *Sylvia's Lovers* as it is in *Adam Bede* or *A Tale of Two Cities*. Elizabeth Gaskell is, however, far from being an apologist for self-satisfied Victorian notions of progress and improvement. She nevertheless looks back in her opening chapter with horror on the legalized 'tyranny' of the press-gang and wonders 'how it is that a nation submitted to it for so long', but she was able to look back from the mid-century over a period of fifty years of relative peace in which impressment had proved unnecessary. The French Revolutionary idea of conscription was also, as yet, unthinkable to liberal Englishmen. As A. W. Ward could confidently note in his introduction to the novel as late as 1906, there was 'no fear of their [the laws for regulating impressment's] repose being disturbed; and if now and then a recurrence of such cruel practices should be noted within the sphere of British administration – why, it is quite sure to be a long way off'. A later twentieth-century reader might react somewhat more uneasily to Elizabeth Gaskell's retrospect on the 'tyranny' of the state. The debate on the rights and wrongs of impressment is, however, extended into the story itself for the novelist gives us in Chapter 4 a spirited argument between the cautious, conventional respecter of authority, Philip Hepburn, and the headstrong upholder of individual rights, Daniel Robson, and we are later offered instances of both the propriety and the abuse of the state's powers and its laws. Mrs Gaskell is not being ambiguous; she is, with her customary tolerance, attempting to present two sides of a social and political argument while at the same time capturing the potency of an issue which might appear alien to her own contemporaries. Any ambiguity there might seem to be is, however, marvellously embodied in the dilemma of the vicar of Monkshaven, Dr Wilson. Wilson is a 'kindly, peaceable old man, hating strife and troubled waters above everything' but he is also 'a vehement Tory in theory'. Like George Eliot's Mr Irwine, Dr Wilson is a man of his time who holds opinions strange to Victorian readers and who acts in ways that Victorian (and for that matter, modern) readers might regard as inconsistent with his calling. His narrowness, Mrs Gaskell explains, is a product of his age and those who are separated from him by the passage of time risk being themselves judged if they judge him too harshly or too narrowly:

In looking back to the last century, it appears curious to see how little our ancestors had the power of putting two things together, and perceiving either the discord or harmony thus produced. Is it because we are farther off from those times, and have, consequently, a greater range of vision? Will our descendants have a wonder about us, such as we have about the inconsistency of our forefathers, or a surprise at our blindness that we do not perceive that, holding such and such opinions, our course of action must be so and so, or that the logical consequences of particular opinions must be convictions which at present we hold in abhorrence?

(Chapter 6, p. 68)

She then pauses to look back briefly once again on Dr Wilson's 'inconsistencies' and 'discrepancies' before addressing her readers with the ironic statement that 'it is well for us that we live at the present time, when everybody is logical and consistent'.

Time alters not only ideological, topographical, and cultural perspectives in *Sylvia's Lovers*, it is also seen changing characters both for bane and for blessing. For Daniel Robson, for Sylvia, and for Philip, time brings in his revenges. Daniel's tragedy is charted in the chapter-titles which describe his vigorous involvement in the sacking of the Randyvowse ('Retaliation'), an overflow of antipathy to the press-gang which, when recollected in tranquillity the morning after, gives occasion to a true but nonetheless 'Brief Rejoicing'. Daniel is the hero of the moment, able, at first, to confidently reject suggestions that he must suffer the consequences of having broken a seemingly unjust law. 'Coming Troubles' bring with them an awareness of the seriousness of his predicament and the probability of his arrest; once these troubles break upon him, his family keeps a 'Dreary Vigil', a vigil followed by 'Gloomy Days' and by the 'Ordeal' which marks his execution, and, for his family, the loss of a husband, a father and a home. Daniel's tragic fault, a stubbornness too often coupled with wilfulness, had led him earlier in his career to cut off a finger and the top joint of his thumb in order to spite and frustrate the press-gang; it finally stirs him to defy the law, but, even in his act of heroic defiance he shows an equally spontaneous generosity towards Simpson, the servant of the inn he is intent on destroying. Daniel Robson is one of Elizabeth Gaskell's most subtle portraits of upright, earnest, simple, if not always likeable, men caught up in circumstances which move beyond their control. The strengths of her characterization of him redeem any faults in her earlier study of John Barton.

From the beginning of *Sylvia's Lovers* we sense a clear distinction between men of Daniel's and Kinraid's stamp and the cautious, conventional Philip Hepburn. Philip too endures a decline which is tragic in the classical sense of the term. He knows himself too slenderly; he loves both unwisely and too well; he suffers and he dies. Philip adores Sylvia idolatrously, a fact which he sorrowingly admits on his death-bed. (Mrs Gaskell contemplated using 'Philip's Idol' as a provisional title for her novel.) Such idolatrous love seems to have been drawn from an emotion familiar enough to the novelist herself, for she had twice noted in the diary she had written some twenty years earlier a prayer that she might not turn her infant daughter, Marianne, into an 'idol'; the death of her infant son, Willie, in 1844 seems also to have brought home to her the agonies entailed in too exclusive a devotion. Philip craves for a love which Sylvia cannot return; he directs his prayers to the hope of gaining her, and he eventually persuades himself that even deception is proper to his ends. At the time of the great crisis in the affairs of the Robson family he acts, as it seems, selflessly, though really yet again it is in the desperate hope of earning Sylvia's love. When she finally submits, it is out of a sense of obligation both to her protector and to her increasingly senile mother. Philip's supererogatory goodness serves only to win him a bride who is outwardly muted by suffering and who is inwardly longing for the lost Kinraid; his idol takes refuge in a 'fortress of reserve' which he can neither storm nor take with stealth. While she dreams of a vanished lover, Philip frets over the possibility of the exposure of his lie, and, when it is exposed, he moves from a 'passive hopelessness' to an 'active despair' which drives him into an exile which is as much spiritual as it is emotional and physical. His self-abnegation becomes a kind of expiation.

However much some readers may detect signs of haste in the novel's last sixteen chapters, chapters which constituted the last of the original three volumes, their quickened pace can also be said to accentuate the sense we have of the changes effected by the passage of time. Philip returns to England an invalid, still restless and rootless, only to be drawn back to Monkshaven by the lodestone of his longing for Sylvia. It is in Monkshaven that Mrs Gaskell gives him a second, redeeming, act of heroism, the rescue of his daughter from the sea, but his action proves mortal to him. Only in his long drawn out death is he finally reconciled to his wife and forgiven by her, and in the reiterated pleas for forgiveness we guess that he is being prepared for a merciful heaven and the hope of another union in another time-scheme. Philip's tragedy ends as he dies smilingly. Sylvia, however, is left alone to continue the expiation of her own 'sin'.

The sadness of the novel's end lies partly in the silence with which Elizabeth Gaskell leaves us, wrenching us forward in time so that the story of Sylvia and Philip appears to fade into 'the memory of man' and to become little more than a local tradition which can be recounted to lady-visitors outside the Public Baths. Nevertheless, the passage of time, as Sylvia seems to experience it, brings with it a ripeness and a kind of wisdom. The novel as a whole delineates her development from a wilful, imaginative, but not particularly clever girl, to an alert woman who has been matured by a peculiarly acute suffering. Sylvia loses in turn a lover, a father, a home, a mother, and a husband. No other heroine of Mrs Gaskell's endures so painful a progress, articulates her suffering so little, or grasps the nature of what is happening to her so slowly. 'It is', the novelist later noted, 'the saddest story I ever wrote'.

The last third of the novel echoes and re-echoes Sylvia's determination 'niver' to forgive either those responsible for her father's downfall or the husband who had deceived her. When, in Chapter 29, Philip urges her to think more kindly on the dying, impoverished Simpson (who had testified against Daniel Robson) she rejects both mercy and Philip's suggestion that mercy is a Christian duty. She is aware, too, of an incompatibility between her nature and her husband's: 'Thee and me was niver meant to go together. It's not in me to forgive, – I sometimes think it's not in me to forget. I wonder,

Philip, if thy feyther had done a kind deed – and a right deed – and a merciful deed – and some one as he'd been good to, even i' t' midst of his just anger, had gone and let on about him to th' judge, as was trying to hang him, – and had getten him hanged, – hanged dead, so that his wife were a widow, and his child fatherless for ivermore, – I wonder if thy veins would run milk and water, so that thou could go and make friends, and speak soft wi' him as had caused thy feyther's death?

'It's said in t' Bible, Sylvie, that we're to forgive.'

'Ay, there's some things as I know I niver forgive; and there's others as I can't and I won't, either.'

Her awareness here of a distinction between Philip's moral notions and her own is as stark as her rejection of the doctrines of the Sermon on the Mount. Having drifted passively into marriage, however, a similar starkness and resolve readily emerge once Philip's lie is revealed. Chapter 33 ends dramatically with her vow never to forgive her husband and never to live with him again; it is a vow repeated in cooler blood to both Kester and Jeremiah Foster three chapters later. Sylvia is to find that she cannot live on vengeful passion alone: as her anger ebbs with time it is replaced by an emptiness which leaves her unfulfilled and by a growing awareness that the seemingly unforgiveable Philip loved her as passionately as she had once cursed him. When she again repeats her vow to Hester in Chapter 39, it is strangely softened by the knowledge that Kinraid has forgotten her. After hearing of Philip's heroism at the siege of Acre, she is prepared to admit to Kester in Chapter 43 that her husband 'had a deal o' good in him', and that, unlike Kinraid, he would not 'ha' gone and married another woman so soon'. Sylvia begins 'to wonder and to wonder' about the husband who poses an enigma to her, and she hopes 'to hear as he were doing well'. When Kester finally announces that it is Philip who has saved their daughter from drowning, she acknowledges his reappearance almost intuitively, and, in going penitently to his death-bed, she is able to retract her 'wicked words'. Time has brought the vow that the two shall never live together to a strange fulfilment, but it has also changed both of them and given them a mutual understanding which was so lacking before.

The spontaneity, the independence and the wildness which once linked Sylvia to Charley Kinraid appears to have vanished by the end of the story. It is also significant that Charley himself has receded into the background. He, the kind of self-helping, self-improving, self-made man of which the Victorians so approved, is not Elizabeth Gaskell's real hero. We end not with success, but with failure and death. The destinies of all the other main characters have proved darker than that of the northern specksioneer who ends up a lieutenant with a rich southern wife. After the close of the story we are told that the widowed Sylvia, always clad in black, is to die before her daughter is grown up; that Hester is to found almshouses in Philip's memory; and that Bella, enriched by the Fosters' fortune, is to emigrate. But though the novel ends thus sadly, its course has offered us so dense a representation of the variety and energy of ordinary life that it cannot be seen simply as tragic. For the novelist herself, the third volume of *Sylvia's Lovers* (originally containing Chapters 30–45) explored the 'crisis' to which all that had gone before had steadily 'worked up'. Many subsequent readers have felt, however, that the real triumphs of the novel lie not in its resolution, but in its first twenty-nine chapters, to Canon Ainger, quoted and endorsed by A. W. Ward in his introduction to the Knutsford Edition, 'the best thing Mrs Gaskell had ever done'. In its first stages *Sylvia's Lovers* meticulously, humorously and delicately observes that 'monotonous homely existence, which has been the fate of so many more among my fellow-mortals than a life of pomp or of absolute indigence, or tragic suffering or of world-stirring actions'. These words are from the celebrated opening chapter of the second book of *Adam Bede* and they serve to stress George Eliot's ideal of telling a 'simple story, without trying to make things seem better than they were'. It was an ideal that Elizabeth Gaskell shared and made her own.

ANDREW SANDERS

ACKNOWLEDGEMENTS

MY thanks are due to Mary Sanders for her assistance with the collation of texts, and to the following for help in various ways: Alexandra Artley; Winifred Bamforth; Michael Baron; Roy Bence; Angus Easson; Sarah Pearsall; Edwina Porter; Michael Slater; John Stephens; the staffs of Dr Williams' Library and the Vaughan Williams Memorial Library at Cecil Sharp House.

NOTE ON THE TEXT

THE text is that of the one-volume fourth, or *Illustrated Edition*, of *Sylvia's Lovers* published in December 1863. It has been checked against the three-volume first and second editions of the same year. The second edition contains a considerable number of revisions, the vast majority of which consist of changes in the dialect spoken by the characters (see Appendix C). The *Illustrated Edition* would appear to represent the novelist's final text, containing as it does several further revisions most of which are a response to criticisms of topographical or legal slips made in earlier editions. These final changes are detailed in footnotes. Any inconsistencies in Mrs Gaskell's spelling have been maintained, but printer's errors have been silently corrected.

SELECT BIBLIOGRAPHY

Sylvia's Lovers was first published in three volumes by Smith, Elder & Co. in February 1863. A second edition, also in three volumes, followed in March, and a third, a reprint of the second edition, in April. The second edition contains a considerable number of revisions. A fourth, or *Illustrated Edition*, was published in one volume in November or December 1863 with four plates and a pictorial title-page by George du Maurier. Two other English-language editions appeared in 1863: the two-volume Tauchnitz edition in Leipzig, and the New York edition, published by Harper & Brothers. *Sylvia's Lovers* was translated into German in 1863–4 and into French in 1865. The most notable later reprints are either those forming part of Collected Editions or those belonging to the Everyman Library with introductions by Esther Alice Chadwick (1911) and by Arthur Pollard (1965).

COLLECTED EDITIONS: *Novels and Tales by Mrs Gaskell*, illustr., 8 vols. (Smith, Elder, 1872–3; reissued 1887–92, 1889–93, 1894, 1897); *Works*, ed. Clement Shorter, World's Classics Series, with introduction and notes, 11 vols. (Oxford University Press, 1906–19); *Works*, ed. with introductions by A. W. Ward, 8 vols. (Smith, Elder: the 'Knutsford Edition' 1906).

BIBLIOGRAPHY: John Albert Green, *A Bibliographical Guide to the Gaskell Collection in the Moss Side Library* (Manchester, 1911); Michael Sadleir, *Excursions in Victorian Bibliography* (1922); Clark S. Northup in Gerald DeWitt Sanders, *Elizabeth Gaskell* (Cornell Studies in English, no. 14, 1929); Miriam Allott in the *New Cambridge Bibliography of English Literature*, vol. 3, ed. George Watson (1969); Jeffrey Welch, *Elizabeth Gaskell: An Annotated Bibliography 1929–1975* (1977). See also the studies by Edgar Wright and Angus Easson listed below.

BIOGRAPHY AND CRITICISM: The primary sources are Elizabeth Gaskell's *Letters*, eds. J. A. V. Chapple and Arthur

Pollard (1966), complemented by J. A. V. Chapple and John Geoffrey Sharps, *Elizabeth Gaskell: A Portrait in Letters* (1980). The most readable, critically alert and useful biography is now Jenny Uglow's *Elizabeth Gaskell: A Habit of Stories* (1993). Other important biographical studies include that by Gerald DeWitt Sanders (see above), Winifred Gérin's *Elizabeth Gaskell: A Biography* (1976), Mrs Ellis H. (Esther Alice) Chadwick's *Mrs Gaskell, Haunts, Homes, and Stories* (1910, revised 1913), and Elizabeth Haldane's, *Mrs Gaskell and her Friends* (1930).

A. W. Ward's introduction to the 'Knutsford Edition' (1906) vol. VI, is extremely helpful. Modern studies include: (*a*) Books: Arthur Pollard, *Mrs Gaskell: Novelist and Biographer* (1965); Edgar Wright, *Mrs Gaskell: The Basis for Reassessment* (1965); Graham Handley, *Sylvia's Lovers* (Notes on English Literature) (1968); John G. Sharps, *Mrs Gaskell's Observation and Invention: A Study of her Non-Biographic Works* (1970); W. A. Craik, *Elizabeth Gaskell and the English Provincial Novel* (1975); Angus Easson, *Elizabeth Gaskell* (1979); Andrew Sanders, *The Victorian Historical Novel 1840–1880* (1979); Enid L. Duthie, *The Themes of Elizabeth Gaskell* (1980); Hilary M. Schor, *Scheherezade in the Marketplace: Elizabeth Gaskell and the Victorian Novel* (1992); Felicia Bonaparte, *the Gypsy Batchelor of Manchester: The Life of Mrs Gaskell's Demon* (1992); Jane Spencer, *Elizabeth Gaskell* (Women Writers Series) (1993); Kate Flint, *Elizabeth Gaskell* (Writers and their Work) (forthcoming). (*b*) Articles: John McVeagh, 'The Making of *Sylvia's Lovers*', *MLR* LXV (April 1970); Terry Eagleton, '*Sylvia's Lovers* and Legality', *Essays in Criticism* XXVI (January 1976); Stephen Lee Schwartz, 'Sea and Land Symbolism in Mrs Gaskell's *Sylvia's Lovers*', *Estudos Anglo-Americanos* 7–8 (1983–4); Missy Kubitschek, 'Defying the Old Limits of Possibility: Unconventional Aspects of Two Gaskell Novels', *University of Mississippi Studies in English* 4 (1983); Andrew Sanders, 'Varieties of Religious Experience in *Sylvia's Lovers*', *The Gaskell Society Journal* 6 (1992).

Elizabeth Gaskell's likely sources for *Sylvia's Lovers* include: *The Annual Register* (1793, 1794, 1795, 1796, 1797, 1798, 1799, 1800); Revd George Young, *A History of Whitby and Streoneshalh Abbey; with a Statistical Survey of the Vicinity*, 2 vols. (1817); Revd George Young, *A Picture of Whitby and its Environs* (1824); William

Scoresby, *An Account of the Arctic Regions, with a History and Description of the Northern Whale-Fishery*, 2 vols. (1820); [Edward Howard] *Memoirs of Admiral Sir Sidney Smith KCB*, 2 vols. (1839); John Barrow, *The Life and Correspondence of Admiral Sir William Sidney Smith*, 2 vols. (1848); F. K. Robinson, *Whitby: its Abbey and the Principal Parts of the Neighbourhood* (1860).

A CHRONOLOGY OF ELIZABETH GASKELL

		Age
1810	Elizabeth Cleghorn Stevenson, second surviving child of William Stevenson and Elizabeth Holland, born in Chelsea 29 September	
1811	(November) After her mother's death, Elizabeth is taken to Knutsford to live with her Aunt Hannah Lumb	1
1822–7	Attends School at Misses Byerley's in Warwick and Stratford on Avon	12–16
1828–9	Her elder brother, John Stevenson (b. 1799), disappears while on a voyage to India. Elizabeth goes to Chelsea to live with her father and stepmother	17–18
1829	(22 March) Elizabeth's father dies; she goes to Newcastle upon Tyne, to the home of the Revd William Turner	18
1831	Spends much of this year in Edinburgh with Mr Turner's daughter. Visits Manchester	20–1
1832	(30 August) Marries the Revd William Gaskell, assistant Minister at Cross Street Chapel, Manchester, at St. John's Parish Church, Knutsford, They live at 14 Dover Street, Manchester	21
1833	Her first child, a daughter, born dead	22
1834	Her second daughter, Marianne, born	23
1837	A poem, 'Sketches among the Poor', by Mr and Mrs Gaskell, appears in *Blackwood's Magazine* (January). Her third daughter, Margaret Emily (Meta), born. Mrs Hannah Lumb dies	26
1840	Her description of Clopton Hall included by William Howitt in *Visits to Remarkable Places*	30
1841	Mr and Mrs Gaskell visit the Continent, touring the Rhine country	30–1
1842	Her fourth daughter, Florence Elizabeth, born. The family move to 121 Upper Rumford Street, Manchester	31–2
1844	Her only son, William, born; dies of scarlet fever at Ffestiniog, 1845	33–4
1846	Her fifth daughter, Julia Bradford, born	35

1847	'Libbie Marsh's Three Eras' published in *Howitt's Journal*	36
1848	'Christmas Storms and Sunshine' in *Howitt's Journal.* Her first novel, *Mary Barton*, published	37–8
1849	Visits London, where she meets Dickens and other literary figures. Meets Wordsworth while on holiday in Ambleside. 'Hand and Heart' published in the *Sunday School Penny Magazine*, 'The Last Generation in England' in *Sartain's Union Magazine*, America	38–9
1850	The family move to 84 Plymouth Grove, Manchester. Dickens invites Mrs Gaskell to contribute to *Household Words*: 'Lizzie Leigh' begins in first number, followed by 'The Well of Pen Morfa' and 'The Heart of John Middleton'. *The Moorland Cottage* published. First meets Charlotte Brontë in August	39–40
1851	'Mr Harrison's Confessions' appears in *The Ladies' Companion.* Continues to write for *Household Words,* the first episode of *Cranford* appearing in December. Visited by Charlotte Brontë in June. Her portrait, now in the National Portrait Gallery, painted by Richmond	40–1
1852	'The Schah's English Gardener' and 'The Old Nurse's Story' in *Household Words.* 'Bessy's Troubles at Home' in the *Sunday School Penny Magazine.* Gives Charlotte Brontë the outline of *Ruth* (April). Visited by Dickens (September)	41–2
1853	*Ruth* (January) and *Cranford* (June) published. 'Cumberland Sheep-Shearers', 'Traits and Stories of the Huguenots', 'Morton Hall', 'My French Master', 'The Squire's Story' all in *Household Words.* Begins *North and South.* Visits exchanged with Charlotte Brontë.	42–3
1854	'Modern Greek Songs', 'Company Manners' in *Household Words: North and South* begins to appear in September. Her husband succeeds as Minister of Cross Street Chapel, Manchester. Visits France with Marianne: meets Mme Mohl and William W. Story. Meets Florence Nightingale in London. Last meeting with Charlotte Brontë	43–4
1855	'An Accursed Race', 'Half a Lifetime Ago' in *Household Words. North and South* and *Lizzie Leigh and Other Stories* published. In June, Charlotte Brontë's father asks her to write his	44–5

	daughter's *Life*. She and Meta spend a month in Paris with Mme Mohl	
1856	'The Poor Clare' in *Household Words*	45–6
1857	*Life of Charlotte Brontë* published. Visits Paris and Rome with her two eldest daughters and Catherine Winkworth	46–7
1858	'My Lady Ludlow', 'Right at Last', and 'The Manchester Marriage' in *Household Words*. 'The Doom of the Griffiths' in *Harper's Magazine*	47–8
1859	*Round the Sofa and Other Tales* published. 'Lois the Witch' and 'The Crooked Branch' in *All the Year Round*. Visits Whitby where she collects material for *Sylvia's Lovers*. Takes her daughters Meta and Florence to Germany, returning via Paris	48–9
1860	*Right at Last and Other Tales* published. 'Curious if True' in *The Cornhill*. Visits to France	49–50
1861	'The Grey Woman' in *All the Year Round*	50–1
1862	Visits Paris, Normandy, and Britanny with Meta and a friend, returning to London for the Exhibition. Back in Manchester she over-exerts herself in relief work among the workmen, and has to recuperate. Writes a Preface to Vecchi's *Garibaldi*	51–2
1863	'A Dark Night's Work', 'An Italian Institution', 'The Cage at Cranford', and 'Crowley Castle' in *All the Year Round*. 'Cousin Phillis' in *The Cornhill*. *Sylvia's Lovers* published by Smith, Elder. Visits Mme Mohl in Paris, going on to Rome with three of her daughters. Her daughter Florence marries	52–3
1864	'French Life' in *Fraser's Magazine*. *Wives and Daughters* begins to appear in *The Cornhill*	53–4
1865	*Cousin Phillis and Other Tales* and *The Grey Woman and Other Tales* published. Visits Dieppe, and Mme Mohl in Paris. Buys a house, The Lawns, nr. Holybourne in Hampshire, and dies there suddenly on 12 November	54–5
1866	*Wives and Daughters* published posthumously	

SYLVIA'S LOVERS

Oh for thy voice to soothe and bless!
What hope of answer, or redress?
Behind the veil! Behind the veil!

TENNYSON*

This Book
is dedicated to

MY DEAR HUSBAND

by her
who best knows his value

CHAPTER I

MONKSHAVEN

On the north-eastern shores of England there is a town called Monkshaven,* containing at the present day about fifteen thousand inhabitants. There were, however, but half the number at the end of the last century, and it was at that period that the events narrated in the following pages occurred.

Monkshaven was a name not unknown in the history of England, and traditions of its having been the landing-place of a throneless queen* were current in the town. At that time there had been a fortified castle on the heights above it, the site of which was now occupied by a deserted manor-house; and at an even earlier date than the arrival of the queen, and coëval with the most ancient remains of the castle, a great monastery had stood on those cliffs, overlooking the vast ocean that blended with the distant sky. Monkshaven itself was built by the side of the Dee, just where the river falls into the German Ocean.* The principal street of the town ran parallel to the stream, and smaller lanes branched out of this, and straggled up the sides of the steep hill, between which and the river the houses were pent in. There was a bridge across the Dee, and consequently a Bridge Street running at right angles to the High Street; and on the south side of the stream there were a few houses of more pretension, around which lay gardens and fields. It was on this side of the town that the local aristocracy lived. And who were the great people of this small town? Not the younger branches of the county families that held hereditary state in their manor-houses on the wild bleak moors, that shut in Monkshaven almost as effectually on the land side as ever the waters did on the sea-board. No; these old families kept aloof from the unsavoury yet adventurous trade which brought wealth to generation after generation of certain families in Monkshaven.

The magnates of Monkshaven were those who had the

largest number of ships engaged in the whaling-trade. Something like the following was the course of life with a Monkshaven lad of this class: – He was apprenticed as a sailor to one of the great shipowners – to his own father, possibly – along with twenty other boys, or, it might be, even more. During the summer months he and his fellow apprentices made voyages to the Greenland seas, returning with their cargoes in the early autumn; and employing the winter months in watching the preparation of the oil from the blubber in the melting-sheds, and learning navigation from some quaint but experienced teacher, half schoolmaster, half sailor, who seasoned his instructions by stirring narrations of the wild adventures of his youth. The house of the shipowner to whom he was apprenticed was his home and that of his companions during the idle season between October and March. The domestic position of these boys varied according to the premium paid; some took rank with the sons of the family, others were considered as little better than servants. Yet once on board an equality prevailed, in which, if any claimed superiority, it was the bravest and brightest. After a certain number of voyages the Monkshaven lad would rise by degrees to be captain, and as such would have a share in the venture; all these profits, as well as all his savings, would go towards building a whaling vessel of his own, if he was not so fortunate as to be the child of a shipowner. At the time of which I write, there was but little division of labour in the Monkshaven whale fishery. The same man might be the owner of six or seven ships, any one of which he himself was fitted by education and experience to command; the master of a score of apprentices, each of whom paid a pretty sufficient premium; and the proprietor of the melting-sheds into which his cargoes of blubber and whalebone were conveyed to be fitted for sale. It was no wonder that large fortunes were acquired by these shipowners, nor that their houses on the south side of the river Dee were stately mansions, full of handsome and substantial furniture. It was also not surprising that the whole town had an amphibious appearance, to a degree unusual even in a seaport. Every one depended on the whale fishery, and almost every male inhabitant had been, or hoped to be, a sailor. Down by the river the smell was almost intolerable to any but Monkshaven people during certain seasons of the year; but on these unsavoury 'staithes'* the old men and children lounged for hours, almost as if they revelled in the odours of train-oil.

This is, perhaps, enough of a description of the town itself. I have said that the country for miles all around was moorland; high above the level of the sea towered the purple crags, whose summits were crowned with greensward that stole down the sides of the scaur* a little way in grassy veins. Here and there a brook forced its way from the heights down to the sea, making its channel into a valley more or less broad in long process of time. And in the moorland hollows, as in these valleys, trees and underwood grew and flourished; so that, while on the bare swells of the high land you shivered at the waste desolation of the scenery, when you dropped into these wooded 'bottoms' you were charmed with the nestling shelter which they gave. But above and around these rare and fertile vales there were moors for many a mile, here and there bleak enough, with the red freestone cropping out above the scanty herbage; then, perhaps, there was a brown tract of peat and bog, uncertain footing for the pedestrian who tried to make a short cut to his destination; then on the higher sandy soil there was the purple ling, or commonest species of heather growing in beautiful wild luxuriance. Tuffs of fine elastic grass were occasionally to be found, on which the little black-faced sheep browsed; but either the scanty food, or their goat-like agility, kept them in a lean condition that did not promise much for the butcher, nor yet was their wool of a quality fine enough to make them profitable in that way to their owners. In such districts there is little population at the present day; there was much less in the last century, before agriculture was sufficiently scientific to have a chance of contending with such natural disqualifications as the moors presented, and when there were no facilities of railroads to bring sportsmen from a distance to enjoy the shooting season, and make an annual demand for accommodation.

There were old stone halls in the valleys; there were bare farmhouses to be seen on the moors at long distances apart, with small stacks of coarse poor hay, and almost larger stacks of turf for winter fuel in their farmyards. The cattle in the pasture fields belonging to these farms looked half starved; but somehow there was an odd, intelligent expression in their faces, as well as in those of the black-visaged sheep, which is seldom seen in the placidly stupid countenances of well-fed animals. All the fences were turf banks, with loose stones piled into walls on the top of these.

There was comparative fertility and luxuriance down below in the rare green dales. The narrow meadows stretching along the brookside seemed as though the cows could really satisfy their hunger in the deep rich grass; whereas on the higher lands the scanty herbage was hardly worth the fatigue of moving about in search of it. Even in these 'bottoms' the piping sea-winds, following the current of the stream, stunted and cut low any trees; but still there was rich thick underwood, tangled and tied together with brambles, and brier-rose, and honeysuckle; and if the farmer in these comparatively happy valleys had had wife or daughter who cared for gardening, many a flower would have grown on the western or southern side of the rough stone house. But at that time gardening was not a popular art in any part of England; in the north it is not yet. Noblemen and gentlemen may have beautiful gardens; but farmers and day-labourers care little for them north of the Trent, which is all I can answer for. A few 'berry' bushes, a black currant tree or two (the leaves to be used in heightening the flavour of tea, the fruit as medicinal for colds and sore throats), a potato ground (and this was not so common at the close of the last century as it is now), a cabbage bed, a bush of sage, and balm, and thyme, and marjoram, with possibly a rose tree, and 'old man'* growing in the midst; a little plot of small strong coarse onions, and perhaps some marigolds, the petals of which flavoured the salt-beef broth; such plants made up a well-furnished garden to a farmhouse at the time and place to which my story belongs. But for twenty miles inland there was no forgetting the sea, nor the sea-trade; refuse shell-fish, sea-weed, the offal of the melting-houses, were the staple manure of the district; great ghastly whale-jaws, bleached bare and white, were the arches over the gate-posts to many a field or moorland stretch. Out of every family of several sons, however agricultural their position might be, one had gone to sea, and the mother looked wistfully seaward at the changes of the keep piping moorland winds. The holiday rambles were to the coast; no one cared to go inland to see aught, unless indeed it might be to the great annual horse-fairs held where the dreary land broke into habitation and cultivation.

Somehow in this country sea thoughts followed the thinker far inland; whereas in most other parts of the island, at five miles from the ocean, he has all but forgotten the existence of such an element as salt water. The great Greenland trade of the coasting towns was the main and primary cause of this, no doubt. But there was also a dread and an irritation in every one's mind, at the time of which I write, in connection with the neighbouring sea.

Since the termination of the American war, there had been nothing to call for any unusual energy in manning the navy; and the grants required by Government for this purpose diminished with every year of peace. In 1792 this grant touched its minimum for many years. In 1793 the proceedings of the French had set Europe on fire, and the English were raging with anti-Gallican excitement, fomented into action by every expedient of the Crown and its Ministers. We had our ships; but where were our men? The Admiralty had, however, a ready remedy at hand, with ample precedent for its use, and with common (if not statute) law to sanction its application. They issued 'press warrants,' calling upon the civil power throughout the country to support their officers in the discharge of their duty. The sea-coast was divided into districts, under the charge of a captain in the navy, who again delegated sub-districts to lieutenants; and in this manner all homeward-bound vessels were watched and waited for, all ports were under supervision; and in a day, if need were, a large number of men could be added to the forces of his

Majesty's navy. But if the Admiralty became urgent in their demands, they were also willing to be unscrupulous. Landsmen, if able-bodied, might soon be trained into good sailors; and once in the hold of the tender, which always awaited the success of the operations of the press-gang, it was difficult for such prisoners to bring evidence of the nature of their former occupations, especially when none had leisure to listen to such evidence, or were willing to believe it if they did listen, or would act upon it for the release of the captive if they had by possibility both listened and believed. Men were kidnapped, literally disappeared, and nothing was ever heard of them again. The street of a busy town was not safe from such press-gang captures, as Lord Thurlow* could have told, after a certain walk he took about this time on Tower Hill, when he, the attorney-general of England, was impressed, when the Admiralty had its own peculiar ways of getting rid of tiresome besiegers and petitioners. Nor yet were lonely inland dwellers more secure; many a rustic went to a statute fair or 'mop,' and never came home to tell of his hiring; many a stout young farmer vanished from his place by the hearth of his father, and was no more heard of by mother or lover; so great was the press for men to serve in the navy during the early years of the war with France, and after every great naval victory of that war.

The servants of the Admiralty lay in wait for all merchantmen and traders; there were many instances of vessels returning home after long absence, and laden with rich cargo, being boarded within a day's distance of land, and so many men pressed and carried off, that the ship, with her cargo, became unmanageable from the loss of her crew, drifted out again into the wild wide ocean, and was sometimes found in the helpless guidance of one or two infirm or ignorant sailors; sometimes such vessels were never heard of more. The men thus pressed were taken from the near grasp of parents or wives, and were often deprived of the hard earnings of years, which remained in the hands of the masters of the merchantman in which they had served, subject to all the chances of honesty or dishonesty, life or death. Now all this tyranny (for

I can use no other word) is marvellous to us; we cannot imagine how it is that a nation submitted to it for so long, even under any warlike enthusiasm, any panics of invasion, any amount of loyal subservience to the governing powers. When we read of the military being called in to assist the civil power in backing up the press-gang, of parties of soldiers patrolling the streets, and sentries with screwed bayonets placed at every door while the press-gang entered and searched each hole and corner of the dwelling; when we hear of churches being surrounded during divine service by troops, while the press-gang stood ready at the door to seize men as they came out from attending public worship, and take these instances as merely types of what was constantly going on in different forms, we do not wonder at Lord Mayors, and other civic authorities in large towns, complaining that a stop was put to business by the danger which the tradesmen and their servants incurred in leaving their houses and going into the streets, infested by press-gangs.

Whether it was that living in closer neighbourhood to the metropolis – the centre of politics and news – inspired the inhabitants of the southern counties with a strong feeling of that kind of patriotism which consists in hating all other nations; or whether it was that the chances of capture were so much greater at all the southern ports that the merchant sailors became inured to the danger; or whether it was that serving in the navy, to those familiar with such towns as Portsmouth and Plymouth, had an attraction to most men from the dash and brilliancy of the adventurous employment – it is certain that the southerners took the oppression of press-warrants more submissively than the wild north-eastern people. For with them the chances of profit beyond their wages in the whaling or Greenland trade extended to the lowest description of sailor. He might rise by daring and saving to be a shipowner himself. Numbers around him had done so; and this very fact made the distinction between class and class less apparent; and the common ventures and dangers, the universal interest felt in one pursuit, bound the inhabitants of that line of coast together with a strong tie, the severance of which by any violent extraneous measure, gave rise to passionate anger and thirst for vengeance. A Yorkshireman once said to me, 'My county folk are all alike. Their first thought is how to resist. Why! I myself, if I hear a man say it is a fine day, catch myself trying to find out that it is no such thing. It is so in thought; it is so in word; it is so in deed.'

So you may imagine the press-gang had no easy time of it on the Yorkshire coast. In other places they inspired fear, but here rage and hatred. The Lord Mayor of York was warned on 20th January, 1777, by an anonymous letter, that 'if those men were not sent from the city on or before the following Tuesday, his lordship's own dwelling, and the Mansion-house also, should be burned to the ground.'

Perhaps something of the ill-feeling that prevailed on the subject was owing to the fact which I have noticed in other places similarly situated. Where the landed possessions of gentlemen of ancient family but limited income surround a centre of any kind of profitable trade or manufacture, there is a sort of latent ill-will on the part of the squires to the tradesman, be he manufacturer, merchant, or shipowner, in whose hands is held a power of money-making, which no hereditary pride, or gentlemanly love of doing nothing, prevents him from using. This ill-will, to be sure, is mostly of a negative kind; its most common form of manifestation is in absence of speech or action, a sort of torpid and genteel ignoring all unpleasant neighbours; but really the whale-fisheries of Monkshaven had become so impertinently and obtrusively prosperous of late years at the time of which I write, the Monkshaven shipowners were growing so wealthy and consequential, that the squires, who lived at home at ease in the old stone manor-houses scattered up and down the surrounding moorland, felt that the check upon the Monkshaven trade likely to be inflicted by the press-gang, was wisely ordained by the higher powers (how high they placed these powers I will not venture to say), to prevent overhaste in getting rich, which was a scriptural fault, and they also thought that they were only doing their duty in backing up the Admiralty warrants by all the civil power at their disposal, whenever they were called upon, and whenever they could do so without taking too much trouble in affairs which did not after all much concern themselves.

There was just another motive in the minds of some provident parents of many daughters. The captains and lieutenants employed on this service were mostly agreeable bachelors, brought up to a genteel profession, at the least they were very pleasant visitors, when they had a day to spare; who knew what might come of it?

Indeed, these brave officers were not unpopular in Monkshaven itself, except at the time when they were brought into actual collision with the people. They had the frank manners of their profession; they were known to have served in those engagements, the very narrative of which at this day will warm the heart of a quaker, and they themselves did not come prominently forward in the dirty work which, nevertheless, was permitted and quietly sanctioned by them. So while few Monkshaven people passed the low public-house over which the navy blue-flag streamed, as a sign that it was the rendezvous of the press-gang, without spitting towards it in sign of abhorrence, yet, perhaps, the very same persons would give some rough token of respect to Lieutenant Atkinson if they met him in High Street. Touching their hats was an unknown gesture in those parts, but they would move their heads in a droll, familiar kind of way, neither a wag nor a nod, but meant all the same to imply friendly regard. The shipowners, too, invited him to an occasional dinner or supper, all the time looking forward to the chances of his turning out an active enemy, and not by any means inclined to give him 'the run of the house,' however many unmarried daughters might grace their table. Still as he could tell a rattling story, drink hard, and was seldom too busy to come at a short notice, he got on better than any one could have expected with the Monkshaven folk. And the principal share of the odium of his business fell on his subordinates, who were one and all regarded in the light of mean kidnappers and spies – 'varmint,' as the common people esteemed them: and as such they were ready at the first provocation to hunt and to worry them, and little cared the press-gang for this. Whatever else they were, they were brave and daring. They had law to back them, therefore their business was lawful. They were serving their king and country. They were using all their faculties, and that is always pleasant. There was plenty of scope for the glory and triumph of outwitting; plenty of adventure in their life. It was a lawful and loyal employment, requiring sense, readiness, courage, and besides it called out that strange love of the chase inherent in every man. Fourteen or fifteen miles at sea lay the *Aurora*, good man-of-war; and to her were conveyed the living cargoes of several tenders, which were stationed at likely places along the sea-coast. One, the *Lively Lady*, might be seen from the cliffs above Monkshaven, not so far away, but hidden by the angle of the high lands from the constant sight of the towns-people; and there was always the Randyvow-house (as the public-house with the navy blue-flag was called thereabouts) for the crew of the *Lively Lady* to lounge about, and there to offer drink to unwary passers-by. At present this was all that the press-gang had done at Monkshaven.

CHAPTER II

HOME FROM GREENLAND

ONE hot day, early in October of the year 1796,* two girls set off from their country homes to Monkshaven to sell their butter and eggs, for they were both farmers' daughters, though rather in different circumstances; for Molly Corney was one of a large family of children, and had to rough it accordingly; Sylvia Robson* was an only child, and was much made of in more people's estimation than Mary's by her elderly parents. They had each purchases to make after their sales were effected, as sales of butter and eggs were effected in those days by the market-women sitting on the steps of the great old mutilated cross till a certain hour in the afternoon, after which, if all their goods were not disposed of, they took them unwillingly to the shops and sold them at a lower price. But good housewives did not despise coming themselves to the Butter Cross, and, smelling and depreciating the articles they wanted, kept up a perpetual struggle of words, trying, often in vain, to beat down prices. A housekeeper of the last century would have thought that she did not know her business, if she had not gone through this preliminary process; and the farmers' wives and daughters treated it all as a matter of course, replying with a good deal of independent humour to the customer, who, once having discovered where good butter and fresh eggs were to be sold, came time after time to depreciate the articles she always ended in taking. There was leisure for all this kind of work in those days.

Molly had tied a knot on her pink-spotted handkerchief for each of the various purchases she had to make; dull but important articles needed for the week's consumption at home; if she forgot any one of them she knew she was sure of a good 'rating' from her mother. The number of them made her pocket-handkerchief look like one of the nine-tails of a 'cat;' but not a single thing was for herself, nor, indeed, for any one individual of her numerous family. There was neither much thought nor much money to spend for any but collective wants in the Corney family.

It was different with Sylvia. She was going to choose her first cloak, not to have an old one of her mother's, that had gone down through two sisters, dyed for the fourth time (and Molly would have been glad had even this chance been hers), but to buy a bran-new duffle cloak all for herself, with not even an elder authority to curb her as to price, only Molly to give her admiring counsel, and as much sympathy as was consistent with a little patient envy of Sylvia's happier circumstances. Every now and then they wandered off from the one grand subject of thought, but Sylvia, with unconscious art, soon brought the conversation round to the fresh consideration of the respective merits of gray and scarlet. These girls were walking bare-foot and carrying their shoes and stockings in their hands during the first part of their way; but as they were drawing near Monkshaven they stopped, and turned aside along a foot-path that led from the main-road down to the banks of the Dee. There were great stones in the river about here, round which the waters gathered and eddied and formed deep pools. Molly sate down on the grassy bank to wash her feet; but Sylvia, more active (or perhaps lighter-hearted with the notion of the cloak in the distance), placed her basket on a gravelly bit of shore, and, giving a long spring, seated herself on a stone almost in the middle of the stream. Then she began dipping her little rosy toes in the cool rushing water and whisking them out with childish glee.

'Be quiet, wi' the', Sylvia? Thou'st splashing me all ower, and my feyther'll noane be so keen o' giving me a new cloak as thine is, seemingly.'

Sylvia was quiet, not to say penitent, in a moment. She drew up her feet instantly; and, as if to take herself out of temptation, she turned away from Molly to that side of her stony seat on which the current ran shallow, and broken by pebbles. But once disturbed in her play, her thoughts reverted to the great subject of the cloak. She was now as still as a minute before she had been full of frolic and gambolling life. She had tucked herself up on the stone, as if it had been a cushion, and she a little sultana.*

Molly was deliberately washing her feet and drawing on her stockings, when she heard a sudden sigh, and her companion turned round so as to face her, and said,

'I wish mother hadn't spoken up for t' gray.'

'Why, Sylvia, thou wert saying as we topped t'brow, as she did nought but bid thee think twice afore settling on scarlet.'

'Ay! but mother's words are scarce, and weigh heavy. Feyther's liker me, and we talk a deal o' rubble; but mother's words are liker to hewn stone. She puts a deal o' meaning in 'em. And then,' said Sylvia, as if she was put out by the suggestion, 'she bid me ask cousin Philip for his opinion. I hate a man as has getten an opinion on such-like things.'

'Well! we shall niver get to Monkshaven this day, either for to sell our eggs and stuff, or to buy thy cloak, if we're sittin' here much longer. T' sun's for slanting low, so come along, lass, and let's be going.'

'But if I put on my stockings and shoon here, and jump back into yon wet gravel, I 'se not be fit to be seen,' said Sylvia, in a pathetic tone of bewilderment, that was funnily childlike. She stood up, her bare feet curved round the curving surface of the stone, her slight figure balancing as if in act to spring.

'Thou knows thou'll have just to jump back barefoot, and wash thy feet afresh, without making all that ado; thou shouldst ha' done it at first, like me, and all other sensible folk. But thou'st getten no gumption.'

Molly's mouth was stopped by Sylvia's hand. She was already on the river bank by her friend's side.

'Now dunnot lecture me; I'm none for a sermon hung on every peg o' words. I'm going to have a new cloak, lass, and I cannot heed thee if thou dost lecture. Thou shall have all the gumption, and I'll have my cloak.'

It may be doubted whether Molly thought this an equal division.

Each girl wore tightly-fitting stockings, knit by her own hands, of the blue worsted common in that country; they had on neat high-heeled black leather shoes, coming well over the instep, and fastened as well as ornamented with bright steel buckles. They did not walk so lightly and freely now as they did before they were shod, but their steps were still springy with the buoyancy of early youth; for neither of them was twenty, indeed I believe Sylvia was not more than seventeen at this time.

They clambered up the steep grassy path, with brambles catching at their kilted petticoats, through the copse-wood, till they regained the high road; and then they 'settled themselves,' as they called it; that is to say, they took off their black felt hats, and tied up their clustering hair afresh; they shook off every speck of wayside dust; straightened the little shawls (or large neck-kerchiefs, call them which you will) that were spread over their shoulders, pinned below the throat, and confined at the waist by their apron-strings; and then putting on their hats again, and picking up their baskets, they prepared to walk decorously into the town of Monkshaven.

The next turn of the road showed them the red peaked roofs of the closely packed houses lying almost directly below the hill on which they were. The full autumn sun brought out the ruddy colour of the tiled gables, and deepened the shadows in the narrow streets. The narrow harbour at the mouth of the river was crowded with small vessels of all descriptions, making an intricate forest of masts. Beyond lay the sea, like a flat pavement of sapphire, scarcely a ripple varying its sunny surface, that stretched out leagues away till it blended with the softened azure of the sky. On this blue trackless water floated scores of white-sailed fishing boats, apparently motionless, unless you measured their progress by some land-mark; but still, and silent, and distant as they seemed, the consciousness that there were men on board, each going forth into the great deep,* added unspeakably to the interest felt in watching them. Close to the bar of the river Dee a larger vessel lay to. Sylvia, who had only recently come into the neighbourhood, looked at this with the same quiet interest as she did at all the others; but Molly, as soon as her eye caught the build of it, cried out aloud—

'She's a whaler! she's a whaler home from t' Greenland seas! T' first this season! God bless her!' and she turned round and shook both Sylvia's hands in the fulness of her excitement. Sylvia's colour rose, and her eyes sparkled out of sympathy.

'Is ta sure?' she asked, breathless in her turn; for though she did not know by the aspect of the different ships on what trade they were bound, yet she was well aware of the paramount interest attached to whaling vessels.

'Three o'clock! and it's not high water till five!' said Molly. 'If we're sharp we can sell our eggs, and be down to the staithes before she comes into port. Be sharp, lass!'

And down the steep long hill they went at a pace that was almost a run. A run they dared not make it; and as it was, the rate at which they walked would have caused destruction among eggs less carefully packed. When the descent was ended, there was yet the long narrow street before them, bending and swerving from the straight line, as it followed the course of the river. The girls felt as if they should never come to the market-place, which was situated at the crossing of Bridge Street and High Street. There the old stone cross was raised by the monks long ago; now worn and mutilated, no one esteemed it as a holy symbol, but only as the Butter Cross, where market-women clustered on Wednesday, and whence the town crier made all his proclamations of household sales, things lost or found, beginning with 'Oh! yes, oh! yes, oh! yes!' and ending with 'God bless the king and the lord of this manor,' and a very brisk 'Amen,' before he went on his way and took off the livery-coat, the colours of which marked him as a servant of the Burnabys, the family who held manorial rights over Monkshaven.

Of course the much frequented space surrounding the Butter Cross was the favourite centre for shops; and on this day, a fine market-day, just when good housewives begin to look over their winter store of blankets and flannels, and discover their needs betimes, these shops ought to have had plenty of customers. But they were empty and of even quieter aspect than their every-day wont. The three-legged creepie-stools that were hired out at a penny an hour to such market-women as came too late to find room on the steps were unoccupied; knocked over here and there, as if people had passed by in haste.

Molly took in all at a glance, and interpreted the signs, though she had no time to explain their meaning, and her consequent course of action, to Sylvia, but darted into a corner shop.

'T' whalers is coming home! There's one lying outside t' bar!'

This was put in the form of an assertion; but the tone was that of eager cross-questioning.

'Ay!' said a lame man, mending fishing-nets behind a rough deal counter. 'She's come back airly, and she's brought good news o' t' others, as I've heered say. Time was I should ha' been on th' staithes throwing up my cap wit' t' best on 'em; but now it pleases t' Lord to keep me at home, and set me to mind other folks' gear. See thee, wench, there's a vast o' folk ha' left their skeps* o' things wi' me while they're away down to t' quay side. Leave me your eggs and be off wi' ye for t' see t' fun, for mebbe ye'll live to be palsied yet, and then ye'll be fretting ower spilt milk, and that ye didn't tak' all chances when ye was young. Ay, well! they're out o' hearin' o' my moralities; I'd better find a lamiter* like mysen to preach to, for it's not iverybody has t' luck t' clargy has of saying their say out whether folks likes it or not.'

He put the baskets carefully away with much of such talk as this addressed to himself while he did so. Then he sighed once or twice; and then he took the better course and began to sing over his tarry work.

Molly and Sylvia were far along the staithes by the time he got to this point of cheerfulness. They ran on, regardless of stitches and pains in the side; on along the river bank to where the concourse of people was gathered. There was no great length of way between the Butter Cross and the harbour; in five minutes the breathless girls were close together in the best place they could get for seeing, on the outside of the crowd; and in as short a time longer they were pressed inwards, by fresh arrivals, into the very midst of the throng. All eyes were directed to the ship, beating her anchor just outside the bar, not a quarter of a mile away. The custom-house officer was just gone aboard of her to receive the captain's report of his cargo, and make due examination. The men who had taken him out in his boat were rowing back to the shore, and brought small fragments of news when they landed a little distance from the crowd, which moved as one man to hear what was to be told. Sylvia took a hard grasp of the hand of the older and more experienced Molly, and listened open-mouthed to the answers she was extracting from a gruff old sailor she happened to find near her.

'What ship is she?'

'T' *Resolution** of Monkshaven!' said he, indignantly, as if any goose might have known that.

'An' a good *Resolution*, and a blessed ship she's been to me,' piped out an old woman, close at Mary's elbow. 'She's brought me home my ae' lad – for he shouted to yon boatman to bid him tell me he was well. 'Tell Peggy Christison,' says he (my name is Margaret Christison) – 'tell Peggy Christison as her son Hezekiah is come back safe and sound.' The Lord's name be praised! An' me a widow as never thought to see my lad again!'

It seemed as if everybody relied on every one else's sympathy in that hour of great joy.

'I ax pardon, but if you'd gie me just a bit of elbow-room for a minute like, I'd hold my babby up, so that he might see daddy's ship, and happen, my master might see him. He's four months old last Tuesday se'nnight, and his feyther's never clapt eyne on him yet, and he wi' a tooth through, an' another just breaking, bless him!'

One or two of the better end of the Monkshaven inhabitants stood a little before Molly and Sylvia; and as they moved in compliance with the young mother's request, they overheard some of the information these ship-owners had received from the boatman.

'Haynes says they'll send the manifest of the cargo ashore in twenty minutes, as soon as Fishburn has looked over the casks. Only eight whales, according to what he says.'

'No one can tell,' said the other, 'till the manifest comes to hand.'

'I'm afraid he's right. But he brings a good report of the *Good Fortune*. She's off St Abb's Head, with something like fifteen whales to her share.'

'We shall see how much is true, when she comes in.'

'That'll be by the afternoon-tide to-morrow.'

'That's my cousin's ship,' said Molly to Sylvia. He's specksioneer* on board the *Good Fortune*.'

An old man touched her as she spoke—

'I humbly make my manners, missus, but I'm stone blind; my lad's aboard yon vessel outside t' bar; and my old woman is bed-fast. Will she be long, think ye, in making t' harbour? Because, if so be as she were, I'd just make my way back, and speak a word or two to my missus, who'll be boiling o'er into some mak o' mischief now she knows he's so near. May I be so bold as to ax if t' Crooked Negro is covered yet?'

Molly stood on tip-toe to try and see the black stone thus named; but Sylvia, stooping and peeping through the glimpses afforded between the arms of the moving people, saw it first, and told the blind old man it was still above water.

'A watched pot,' said he, 'ne'er boils, I reckon. It's ta'en a vast o' watter t' cover that stone to-day. Anyhow, I'll have time to go home and rate my missus for worritin' hersen, as I'll be bound she's done, for all as I bade her not, but to keep easy and content.'

'We'd better be off too,' said Molly, as an opening was made through the press to let out the groping old man. 'Eggs and butter is yet to sell, and tha' cloak to be bought.'

'Well, I suppose we had!' said Sylvia, rather regretfully; for, though all the way into Monkshaven her head had been full of the purchase of this cloak, yet she was of that impressible nature that takes the tone of feeling from those surrounding; and though she knew no one on board the *Resolution*, she was just as anxious for the moment to see her come into harbour as any one in the crowd who had a dear relation on board. So she turned reluctantly to follow the more prudent Molly along the quay back to the Butter Cross.

It was a pretty scene, though it was too familiar to the eyes of all who then saw it for them to notice its beauty. The sun was low enough in the west to turn the mist that filled the distant valley of the river into golden haze. Above, on either bank of the Dee, there lay the moorland heights swelling one behind the other; the nearer, russet brown with the tints of the fading bracken; the more distant, gray and dim against the rich autumnal sky. The red and fluted tiles of the gabled houses rose in crowded irregularity on one side of the river, while the newer suburb was built in more orderly and less picturesque fashion on the opposite cliff. The river itself was swelling and chafing with the incoming tide till its vexed waters rushed over the very feet of the watching crowd on the staithes, as the great sea waves encroached more and more every minute. The quay-side was unsavourily ornamented with glittering fish-scales, for the hauls of fish were cleansed in the open air, and no sanitary arrangements existed for sweeping away any of the relics of this operation.

The fresh salt breeze was bringing up the lashing, leaping tide from the blue sea beyond the bar. Behind the returning girls there rocked the white-sailed ship, as if she were all alive with eagerness for her anchors to be heaved.

How impatient her crew of beating hearts were for that moment, how those on land sickened at the suspense, may be imagined, when you remember that for six long summer months those sailors had been as if dead from all news of those they loved; shut up in terrible, dreary Arctic seas from the hungry sight of sweethearts and friends, wives and mothers. No one knew what might have happened. The crowd on shore grew silent and solemn before the dread of the possible news of death that might toll in upon their hearts with this uprushing tide. The whalers went out into the Greenland seas full of strong, hopeful men; but the whalers never returned as they sailed forth. On land there are deaths among two or three hundred men to be mourned over in every half-year's space of time. Whose bones had been left to blacken on the gray and terrible icebergs? Who lay still until the sea should give up its dead? Who were those who should come back to Monkshaven never, no, never more?

Many a heart swelled with passionate, unspoken fear, as the first whaler lay off the bar on her return voyage.

Molly and Sylvia had left the crowd in this hushed suspense. But fifty yards along the staithe they passed five or six girls with flushed faces and careless attire, who had mounted a pile of timber, placed there to season for ship-building, from which, as from the steps of a ladder or staircase, they could command the harbour. They were wild and free in their gestures, and held each other by the hand, and swayed from side to side, stamping their feet in time, as they sang—

> Weel may the keel row, the keel row, the keel row,
> Weel may the keel row that my laddie's in!*

'What for are ye going off, now?' they called out to our

two girls. 'She'll be in in ten minutes!' and without waiting for the answer which never came, they resumed their song.

Old sailors stood about in little groups, too proud to show their interest in the adventures they could no longer share, but quite unable to keep up any semblance of talk on indifferent subjects.

The town seemed very quiet and deserted as Molly and Sylvia entered the dark, irregular Bridge Street, and the market-place was as empty of people as before. But the skeps and baskets and three-legged stools were all cleared away.

'Market's over for to-day,' said Molly Corney, in disappointed surprise. 'We mun make the best on't, and sell to t' huxters,* and a hard bargain they'll be for driving. I doubt mother'll be vexed.'

She and Sylvia went to the corner shop to reclaim their baskets. The man had his joke at them for their delay.

'Ay, ay! lasses as has sweethearts a-coming home don't care much what price they get for butter and eggs! I dare say, now, there's some un in yon ship that 'ud give as much as a shilling a pound for this butter if he only knowed who churned it!' This was to Sylvia, as he handed her back her property.

The fancy-free Sylvia reddened, pouted, tossed back her head, and hardly deigned a farewell word of thanks or civility to the lame man; she was at an age to be affronted by any jokes on such a subject. Molly took the joke without disclaimer and without offence. She rather liked the unfounded idea of her having a sweetheart, and was rather surprised to think how devoid of foundation the notion was. If she could have a new cloak as Sylvia was going to have, then, indeed, there might be a chance! Until some such good luck, it was as well to laugh and blush as if the surmise of her having a lover was not very far from the truth, and so she replied in something of the same strain as the lame net-maker to his joke about the butter.

'He'll need it all, and more too, to grease his tongue, if iver he reckons to win me for his wife!'

When they were out of the shop, Sylvia said, in a coaxing tone,—

'Molly, who is it? Whose tongue 'll need greasing? Just tell me, and I'll never tell!'

She was so much in earnest that Molly was perplexed. She did not quite like saying that she had alluded to no one in particular, only to a possible sweetheart, so she began to think what young man had made the most civil speeches to her in her life; the list was not a long one to go over, for her father was not so well off as to make her sought after for her money, and her face was rather of the homeliest. But she suddenly remembered her cousin, the specksioneer, who had given her two large shells, and taken a kiss from her half-willing lips before he went to sea the last time. So she smiled a little, and then said,—

'Well! I dunno. It's ill talking o' these things afore one has made up one's mind. And perhaps if Charley Kinraid behaves hissen, I might be brought to listen.'

'Charley Kinraid! who's he?'

'Yon specksioneer cousin o' mine, as I was talking on.'

'And do yo' think he cares for yo'?' asked Sylvia, in a low, tender tone, as if touching on a great mystery.

Molly only said, 'Be quiet wi' yo',' and Sylvia could not make out whether she cut the conversation so short because she was offended, or because they had come to the shop where they had to sell their butter and eggs.

'Now, Sylvia, if thou'll leave me thy basket, I'll make as good a bargain as iver I can on 'em; and thou can be off to choose this grand new cloak as is to be, afore it gets any darker. Where is ta going to?'

'Mother said I'd better go to Foster's,' answered Sylvia, with a shade of annoyance in her face. 'Feyther said just anywhere.'

'Foster's is t' best place; thou canst try anywhere afterwards. I'll be at Foster's in five minutes, for I reckon we mun hasten a bit now. It'll be near five o'clock.'

Sylvia hung her head and looked very demure as she walked off by herself to Foster's shop* in the market-place.

CHAPTER III

BUYING A NEW CLOAK

FOSTER'S shop was the shop of Monkshaven. It was kept by two Quaker brothers, who were now old men; and their father had kept it before them; probably his father before that. People remembered it as an old-fashioned dwelling-house, with a sort of supplementary shop with unglazed windows projecting from the lower story. These openings had long been filled with panes of glass that at the present day would be accounted very small, but which seventy years ago were much admired for their size. I can best make you understand the appearance of the place by bidding you think of the long openings in a butcher's shop, and then to fill them up in your imagination with panes about eight inches by six, in a heavy wooden frame. There was one of these windows on each side the door-place, which was kept partially closed through the day by a low gate about a yard high. Half the shop was appropriated to grocery; the other half to drapery, and a little mercery. The good old brothers gave all their known customers a kindly welcome; shaking hands with many of them, and asking all after their families and domestic circumstances before proceeding to business. They would not for the world have had any sign of festivity at Christmas, and scrupulously kept their shop open at that holy festival, ready themselves to serve sooner than tax the consciences of any of their assistants, only nobody ever came. But on New Year's Day they had a great cake, and wine, ready in the parlour behind the shop, of which all who came in to buy anything were asked to partake. Yet, though scrupulous in most things, it did not go against the consciences of these good brothers to purchase smuggled articles. There was a back way from the river side, up a covered entry, to the yard-door of the Fosters, and a peculiar kind of knock at this door always brought out either John or Jeremiah, or if not them, their shopman, Philip Hepburn; and the same cake and wine that the excise officer's wife might just have been tasting, was brought out in the back parlour to treat the smuggler. There was a little locking of doors, and drawing of the green silk curtain that was supposed to shut out the shop, but really all this was done very much for form's sake. Everybody in Monkshaven smuggled who could, and every one wore smuggled goods who could, and great reliance was placed on the excise officer's neighbourly feelings.

The story went that John and Jeremiah Foster were so rich that they could buy up all the new town across the bridge. They had certainly begun to have a kind of primitive bank in connection with their shop, receiving and taking care of such money as people did not wish to retain in their houses for fear of burglars. No one asked them for interest on the money thus deposited, nor did they give any; but, on the other hand, if any of their customers, on whose character they could depend, wanted a little advance, the Fosters, after due inquiries made, and in some cases due security given, were not unwilling to lend a moderate sum without charging a penny for the use of their money. All the articles they sold were as good as they knew how to choose, and for them they expected and obtained ready money. It was said that they only kept on the shop for their amusement. Others averred that there was some plan of a marriage running in the brothers' heads - a marriage between William Coulson, Mr Jeremiah's wife's nephew (Mr Jeremiah was a widower), and Hester Rose,* whose mother was some kind of distant relation, and who served in the shop along with William Coulson and Philip Hepburn. Again, this was denied by those who averred that Coulson was no blood relation, and that if the Fosters had intended to do anything considerable for Hester, they would never have allowed her and her mother to live in such a sparing way, ekeing out their small income by having Coulson and Hepburn for lodgers. No; John and Jeremiah would leave all their money to some hospital or to some charitable institution. But, of course, there was a reply to this; when are there not many sides to an argument about a possibility concerning which no facts are known? Part of the reply turned on this: the old gentlemen had, probably, some deep plan in their heads in permitting their cousin to take Coulson and Hepburn as lodgers, the one a kind of nephew, the other, though so young, the head man in the shop; if either of them took a fancy to Hester, how agreeably matters could be arranged!

All this time Hester is patiently waiting to serve Sylvia, who is standing before her a little shy, a little perplexed and distracted, by the sight of so many pretty things.

Hester was a tall young woman, sparely yet largely formed, of a grave aspect, which made her look older than she really was. Her thick brown hair was smoothly taken off her broad forehead, and put in a very orderly fashion, under her linen cap; her face was a little square, and her complexion sallow, though the texture of her skin was fine. Her gray eyes were very pleasant, because they looked at you so honestly and kindly; her mouth was slightly compressed, as most have it who are in the habit of restraining their feelings; but when she spoke you did not perceive this, and her rare smile slowly breaking forth showed her white even teeth, and when accompanied, as it generally was, by a sudden uplifting of her soft eyes, it made her countenance very winning. She was dressed in stuff of sober colours, both in accordance with her own taste, and in unasked compliance with the religious customs of the Fosters; but Hester herself was not a Friend.

Sylvia, standing opposite, not looking at Hester, but gazing at the ribbons in the shop window, as if hardly conscious that any one awaited the expression of her wishes, was a great contrast; ready to smile or to pout, or to show her feelings in any way, with a character as undeveloped as a child's, affectionate, wilful, naughty, tiresome, charming, anything, in fact, at present that the chances of an hour called out. Hester thought her customer the prettiest creature ever seen, in the moment she had for admiration before Sylvia turned round and, recalled to herself, began,—

'Oh, I beg your pardon, miss; I was thinking what may the price of yon crimson ribbon be?'

Hester said nothing, but went to examine the shop-mark.

'Oh! I did not mean that I wanted any, I only want some

stuff for a cloak. Thank you, miss, but I am very sorry – some duffle, please.'

Hester silently replaced the ribbon and went in search of the duffle. While she was gone Sylvia was addressed by the very person she most wished to avoid, and whose absence she had rejoiced over on first entering the shop, her cousin Philip Hepburn.

He was a serious-looking young man, tall, but with a slight stoop in his shoulders, brought on by his occupation. He had thick hair standing off from his forehead in a peculiar but not unpleasing manner; a long face, with a slightly aquiline nose, dark eyes, and a long upper lip, which gave a disagreeable aspect to a face that might otherwise have been good-looking.

'Good day, Sylvie,' he said; 'what are you wanting? How are all at home? Let me help you!'

Sylvia pursed up her red lips, and did not look at him as she replied,

'I'm very well, and so is mother; feyther's got a touch of rheumatiz, and there's a young woman getting what I want.'

She turned a little away from him when she had ended this sentence, as if it had comprised all she could possibly have to say to him. But he exclaimed,

'You won't know how to choose,' and, seating himself on the counter, he swung himself over after the fashion of shop-men.

Sylvia took no notice of him, but pretended to be counting over her money.

'What do you want, Sylvie?' asked he, at last annoyed at her silence.

'I don't like to be called "Sylvie;" my name is Sylvia; and I'm wanting duffle for a cloak, if you must know.'

Hester now returned, with a shop-boy helping her to drag along the great rolls of scarlet and gray cloth.

'Not that,' said Philip, kicking the red duffle with his foot, and speaking to the lad. 'It's the gray you want, is it not, Sylvie?' He used the name he had had the cousin's right to call her by since her childhood, without remembering her words on the subject not five minutes before; but she did, and was vexed.

'Please, miss, it is the scarlet duffle I want; don't let him take it away.'

Hester looked up at both their countenances, a little wondering what was their position with regard to each other; for this, then, was the beautiful little cousin about whom Philip had talked to her mother, as sadly spoilt, and shamefully ignorant; a lovely little dunce, and so forth. Hester had pictured Sylvia Robson, somehow, as very different from what she was: younger, more stupid, not half so bright and charming (for, though she was now both pouting and cross, it was evident that this was not her accustomed mood). Sylvia devoted her attention to the red cloth, pushing aside the gray.

Philip Hepburn was vexed at his advice being slighted; and yet he urged it afresh.

'This is a respectable, quiet-looking article that will go well with any colour; you niver will be so foolish as to take what will mark with every drop of rain.'

'I'm sorry you sell such good-for-nothing things,' replied Sylvia, conscious of her advantage, and relaxing a little (as little as she possibly could) of her gravity.

Hester came in now.

'He means to say that this cloth will lose its first brightness in wet or damp; but it will always be a good article, and the colour will stand a deal of wear. Mr Foster would not have had it in his shop else.'

Philip did not like that even a reasonable peace-making interpreter should come between him and Sylvia, so he held his tongue in indignant silence.

Hester went on:

'To be sure, this gray is the closer make, and would wear the longest.'

'I don't care,' said Sylvia, still rejecting the dull gray. 'I like this best. Eight yards, if you please, miss.'

'A cloak takes nine yards, at least,' said Philip, decisively.

'Mother told me eight,' said Sylvia, secretly conscious that her mother would have preferred the more sober colour; and feeling that as she had had her own way in that respect, she was bound to keep to the directions she had received as to the quantity. But, indeed, she would not have yielded to Philip in anything that she could help.

There was a sound of children's feet running up the street from the river-side, shouting with excitement. At the noise, Sylvia forgot her cloak and her little spirit of vexation, and ran to the half-door of the shop. Philip followed because she went. Hester looked on with passive, kindly interest, as soon as she had completed her duty of measuring. One of those girls whom Sylvia had seen as she and Molly left the crowd on the quay, came quickly up the street. Her face, which was handsome enough as to feature, was whitened with excess of passionate emotion, her dress untidy and flying, her movements heavy and free. She belonged to the lowest class of seaport inhabitants. As she came near, Sylvia saw that the tears were streaming down her cheeks, quite unconsciously to herself. She recognized Sylvia's face, full of interest as it was, and stopped her clumsy run to speak to the pretty, sympathetic creature.

'She's o'er t' bar! She's o'er t' bar! I'm boun' to tell mother!'

She caught at Sylvia's hand, and shook it, and went on breathless and gasping.

'Sylvia, how came you to know that girl?' asked Philip, sternly. 'She's not one for you to be shaking hands with. She's known all down t' quay-side as "Newcastle Bess."'

'I can't help it,' said Sylvia, half inclined to cry at his manner even more than his words. 'When folk are glad I can't help being glad too, and I just put out my hand, and she put out hers. To think o' yon ship come in at last! And if yo'd been down seeing all t' folk looking and looking their eyes out, as if they feared they should die afore she came in and brought home the lads they loved, yo'd ha' shaken hands wi' that lass too, and no great harm done. I never set eyne upon her till half an hour ago on th' staithes, and maybe I'll niver see her again.'

Hester was still behind the counter, but had moved so as to be near the window; so she heard what they were saying, and now put in her word:

'She can't be altogether bad, for she thought o' telling her mother first thing, according to what she said.'

Sylvia gave Hester a quick, grateful look. But Hester had resumed her gaze out of the window, and did not see the glance.

And now Molly Corney joined them, hastily bursting into the shop.

'Hech!' said she. 'Hearken! how they're crying and shouting down on t' quay. T' gang's among 'em like t' day of judgment. Hark!'

No one spoke, no one breathed, I had almost said no heart beat for listening. Not long; in an instant there rose the sharp simultaneous cry of many people in rage and despair. Inarticulate at that distance, it was yet an intelligible curse, and the roll, and the roar, and the irregular tramp came nearer and nearer.

'They're taking 'em to t' Randyvowse,'* said Molly. 'Eh! I wish I'd King George here just to tell him my mind.'

The girl clenched her hands, and set her teeth.

'It's terrible hard!' said Hester; 'there's mothers, and wives, looking out for 'em, as if they were stars dropt out o' t' lift.'

'But can we do nothing for 'em?' cried Sylvia. 'Let us go into t' thick of it and do a bit of help; I can't stand quiet and see 't!' Half crying, she pushed forwards to the door; but Philip held her back.

'Sylvie! you must not. Don't be silly; it's the law, and no one can do aught against it, least of all women and lasses.'

By this time the vanguard of the crowd came pressing up Bridge Street, past the windows of Foster's shop. It consisted of wild, half-amphibious boys, slowly moving backwards, as they were compelled by the pressure of the coming multitude to go on, and yet anxious to defy and annoy the gang by insults, and curses half choked with their indignant passion, doubling their fists in the very faces of the gang who came on with measured movement, armed to the teeth, their faces showing white with repressed and determined energy against the bronzed countenances of the half-dozen sailors, who were all they had thought it wise to pick out of the whaler's crew, this being the first time an Admiralty warrant had been used in Monkshaven for many years; not since the close of the American war, in fact. One of the men was addressing to his townspeople, in a high pitched voice, an exhortation which few could hear, for, pressing around this nucleus of cruel wrong, were women crying aloud, throwing up their arms in imprecation, showering down abuse as hearty and rapid as if they had been a Greek chorus. Their wild, famished eyes were strained on faces they might not kiss, their cheeks were flushed to purple with anger or else livid with impotent craving for revenge. Some of them looked scarce human; and yet an hour ago these lips, now tightly drawn back so as to show the teeth with the unconscious action of an enraged wild animal, had been soft and gracious with the smile of hope; eyes, that were fiery and bloodshot now, had been loving and bright; hearts, never to recover from the sense of injustice and cruelty, had been trustful and glad only one short hour ago.

There were men there, too, sullen and silent, brooding on remedial revenge; but not many, the greater proportion of this class being away in the absent whalers.

The stormy multitude swelled into the market-place and formed a solid crowd there, while the press-gang steadily forced their way on into High Street, and on to the rendezvous. A low, deep growl went up from the dense mass, as some had to wait for space to follow the others – now and then going up, as a lion's growl goes up, into a shriek of rage.

A woman forced her way up from the bridge. She lived some little way in the country, and had been late in hearing of the return of the whaler after her six months' absence; and on rushing down to the quay-side, she had been told by a score of busy, sympathizing voices, that her husband was kidnapped for the service of the Government.

She had need pause in the market-place, the outlet of which was crammed up. Then she gave tongue for the first time in such a fearful shriek, you could hardly catch the words she said.

'Jamié! Jamie! will they not let you to me?'

Those were the last words Sylvia heard before her own hysterical burst of tears called every one's attention to her.

She had been very busy about household work in the morning, and much agitated by all she had seen and heard since coming into Monkshaven; and so it ended in this.

Molly and Hester took her through the shop into the parlour beyond – John Foster's parlour, for Jeremiah, the elder brother, lived in a house of his own on the other side of the water. It was a low, comfortable room, with great beams running across the ceiling, and papered with the same paper as the walls – a piece of elegant luxury which took Molly's fancy mightily! This parlour looked out on the dark courtyard in which there grew two or three poplars, straining upwards to the light; and through an open door between the backs of two houses could be seen a glimpse of the dancing, heaving river, with such ships or fishing cobles* as happened to be moored in the waters above the bridge.

They placed Sylvia on the broad, old-fashioned sofa, and gave her water to drink, and tried to still her sobbing and choking. They loosed her hat, and copiously splashed her face and clustering chestnut hair, till at length she came to herself; restored, but dripping wet. She sate up and looked at them, smoothing back her tangled curls off her brow, as if to clear both her eyes and her intellect.

'Where am I? – oh, I know! Thank you. It was very silly, but somehow it seemed so sad!'

And here she was nearly going off again, but Hester said—

'Ay, it were sad, my poor lass – if I may call you so, for I don't rightly know your name – but it's best not think on it, for we can do no mak' o' good, and it'll mebbe set you off again. Yo're Philip Hepburn's cousin, I reckon, and yo' bide at Haytersbank Farm?'

'Yes; she's Sylvia Robson,' put in Molly, not seeing that Hester's purpose was to make Sylvia speak, and so to divert her attention from the subject which had set her off into hysterics. 'And we came in for market,' continued Molly, 'and for t' buy t' new cloak as her feyther's going to give her; and, for sure, I thought we was i' luck's way when we saw t' first whaler, and niver dreaming as t' press-gang 'ud be so marred.'

She, too, began to cry, but her little whimper was stopped by the sound of the opening door behind her. It was Philip, asking Hester by a silent gesture if he might come in.

Sylvia turned her face round from the light, and shut her eyes. Her cousin came close up to her on tip-toe, and looked anxiously at what he could see of her averted face; then he passed his hand so slightly over her hair that he could scarcely be said to touch it, and murmured—

'Poor lassie! it's a pity she came to-day, for it's a long walk in this heat!'

But Sylvia started to her feet, almost pushing him along. Her quickened senses heard an approaching step through the courtyard before any of the others were aware of the sound. In a minute afterwards, the glass-door at one corner of the parlour was opened from the outside, and Mr John* stood looking in with some surprise at the group collected in his usually empty parlour.

'It's my cousin,' said Philip, reddening a little; 'she came wi' her friend in to market, and to make purchases; and she's got a turn wi' seeing the press-gang go past carrying some of the crew of the whaler to the Randyvowse.'

'Ay, ay,' said Mr John, quickly passing on into the shop on tip-toe, as if he were afraid he were intruding in his own premises, and beckoning Philip to follow him there. 'Out of strife cometh strife. I guessed something of the sort was up from what I heard on t' bridge as I came across fra' brother Jeremiah's.' Here he softly shut the door between the parlour and the shop. 'It beareth hard on th' expectant women and childer; nor is it to be wondered at that they, being unconverted, rage together (poor creatures!) like the very heathen.* Philip,' he said, coming nearer to his 'head young man,' 'keep Nicholas and Henry at work in the ware-room upstairs until this riot be over, for it would grieve me if they were misled into violence.'

Philip hesitated.

'Speak out, man! Always ease an uneasy heart, and never let it get hidebound.'

'I had thought to convoy my cousin and the other young woman home, for the town is like to be rough, and it's getting dark.'

'And thou shalt, my lad,' said the good old man; 'and I myself will try and restrain the natural inclinations of Nicholas and Henry.'

But when he went to find the shop-boys with a gentle homily on his lips, those to whom it should have been addressed were absent. In consequence of the riotous state of things, all the other shops in the market-place had put their shutters up; and Nicholas and Henry, in the absence of their superiors, had followed the example of their neighbours, and, as business was over, they had hardly waited to put the goods away, but had hurried off to help their townsmen in any struggle that might ensue.

There was no remedy for it, but Mr John looked rather discomfited. The state of the counters, and of the disarranged goods, was such also as would have irritated any man as orderly but less sweet-tempered. All he said on the subject was: 'The old Adam! the old Adam!' but he shook his head long after he had finished speaking.

'Where is William Coulson?' he next asked. 'Oh! I remember. He was not to come back from York till the night closed in.'

Philip and his master arranged the shop in the exact order the old man loved. Then he recollected the wish of his subordinate, and turned round and said—

'Now go with thy cousin and her friend. Hester is here, and old Hannah. I myself will take Hester home, if need be. But for the present I think she had best tarry here, as it isn't many steps to her mother's house, and we may need her help if any of those poor creatures fall into suffering wi' their violence.'

With this, Mr John knocked at the door of the parlour, and waited for permission to enter. With old-fashioned courtesy he told the two strangers how glad he was that his room had been of service to them; that he would never have made so bold as to pass through it, if he had been aware how it was occupied. And then going to a corner cupboard, high up in the wall, he pulled a key out of his pocket and unlocked his little store of wine, and cake, and spirits; and insisted that they should eat and drink while waiting for Philip, who was taking some last measures for the security of the shop during the night.

Sylvia declined everything, with less courtesy than she ought to have shown to the offers of the hospitable old man. Molly took wine and cake, leaving a good half of both, according to the code of manners in that part of the country; and also because Sylvia was continually urging her to make haste. For the latter disliked the idea of her cousin's esteeming it necessary to accompany them home, and wanted to escape from him by setting off before he returned. But any such plans were frustrated by Philip's coming back into the parlour, full of grave content, which brimmed over from his eyes, with the parcel of Sylvia's obnoxious red duffle under his arm; anticipating so keenly the pleasure awaiting him in the walk, that he was almost surprised by the gravity of his companions as they prepared for it. Sylvia was a little penitent for her rejection of Mr John's hospitality, now she found out how unavailing for its purpose such rejection had been, and tried to make up by a modest sweetness of farewell, which quite won his heart, and made him praise her up to Hester in a way to which she, observant of all, could not bring herself fully to respond. What business had the pretty little creature to reject kindly-meant hospitality in the pettish way she did, thought Hester. And, oh! what business had she to be so ungrateful and to try and thwart Philip in his thoughtful wish of escorting them through the streets of the rough, riotous town? What did it all mean?

CHAPTER IV

PHILIP HEPBURN

THE coast on that part of the island to which this story refers is bordered by rocks and cliffs. The inland country immediately adjacent to the coast is level, flat, and bleak; it is only where the long stretch of dyke-enclosed fields terminates abruptly in a sheer descent, and the stranger sees the ocean creeping up the sands far below him, that he is aware on how great an elevation he has been. Here and there, as I have said, a cleft in the level land (thus running out into the sea in steep promontories) occurs – what they would call a 'chine' in the Isle of Wight; but instead of the soft south wind stealing up the woody ravine, as it does there, the eastern breeze comes piping shrill and clear along these northern chasms, keeping the trees that venture to grow on the sides down to the mere height of scrubby brushwood. The descent to the shore through these 'bottoms' is in most cases very abrupt, too much so for a cartway, or even a bridle-path; but people can pass up and down without difficulty, by the help of a few rude steps hewn here and there out of the rock.

Sixty or seventy years ago (not to speak of much later times) the farmers who owned or hired the land which lay directly on the summit of these cliffs were smugglers to the extent of their power, only partially checked by the coast-guard distributed, at pretty nearly equal interspaces of eight miles, all along the north-eastern seaboard. Still sea-wrack* was a good manure, and there was no law against carrying it up in great osier baskets for the purpose of tillage, and many a secret thing was lodged in hidden crevices in the rocks till the farmer sent trusty people down to the shore for a good supply of sand and seaweed for his land.

One of the farms on the cliff had lately been taken by Sylvia's father. He was a man who had roamed about a good deal – been sailor, smuggler, horse-dealer, and farmer in turns; a sort of fellow possessed by a spirit of adventure and love of change, which did him and his own family more harm than anybody else. He was just the kind of man that all his neighbours found fault with, and all his neighbours liked. Late in life (for such an imprudent man as he was, one of a class who generally wed, trusting to chance and luck for the provision for a family), farmer Robson married a woman whose only want of practical wisdom consisted in taking him for a husband. She was Philip Hepburn's aunt, and had had the charge of him until she married from her widowed brother's house. He it was who had let her know when Haytersbank Farm had been to let; esteeming it a likely piece of land for his uncle to settle down upon, after a somewhat unprosperous career of horse-dealing. The farmhouse lay in the shelter of a very slight green hollow scarcely scooped out of the pasture field by which it was surrounded; the short crisp turf came creeping up to the very door and windows, without any attempt at a yard or garden, or any nearer enclosure of the buildings than the stone dyke that formed the boundary of the field itself. The buildings were long and low, in order to avoid the rough violence of the winds that swept over that wild, bleak spot, both in winter and summer. It was well for the inhabitants of that house that coal was extremely cheap; otherwise a southerner might have imagined that they could never have survived the cutting of the bitter gales that piped all round, and seemed to seek out every crevice for admission into the house.

But the interior was warm enough when once you had mounted the long bleak lane, full of round rough stones, enough to lame any horse unaccustomed to such roads, and had crossed the field by the little dry, hard footpath, which tacked about so as to keep from directly facing the prevailing wind. Mrs Robson was a Cumberland woman, and as such, was a cleaner housewife than the farmers' wives of that north-eastern coast, and was often shocked at their ways, showing it more by her looks than by her words, for she was not a great talker. This fastidiousness in such matters made her own house extremely comfortable, but did not tend to render her popular among her neighbours. Indeed, Bell Robson piqued herself on her housekeeping generally, and once in-doors in the gray, bare stone house, there were plenty of comforts to be had besides cleanliness and warmth. The great rack of clap-bread* hung overhead, and Bell Robson's preference of this kind of oat-cake over the leavened and partly sour kind used in Yorkshire was another source of her unpopularity. Flitches of bacon and 'hands' (*i.e.*, shoulders of cured pork, the legs or hams being sold, as fetching a better price) abounded; and for any visitor who could stay, neither cream nor finest wheaten flour was wanting for 'turf cakes' and 'singing hinnies,'* with which it is the delight of the northern housewives to regale the honoured guest, as he sips their high-priced tea, sweetened with dainty sugar.

This night farmer Robson was fidgeting in and out of his house-door, climbing the little eminence in the field, and coming down disappointed in a state of fretful impatience. His quiet, taciturn wife was a little put out by Sylvia's non-appearance too; but she showed her anxiety by being shorter than usual in her replies to his perpetual wonders as to where the lass could have been tarrying, and by knitting away with extra diligence.

'I've a vast o' mind to go down to Monkshaven mysen, and see after t' child. It's well on for seven.'

'No, Dannel,' said his wife; 'thou'd best not. Thy leg has been paining thee this week past, and thou'rt not up to such a walk. I'll rouse Kester, and send him off, if thou think'st there's need on it.'

'A'll noan ha' Kester roused. Who's to go afield betimes after t' sheep in t' morn, if he's ca'ed up to-neet? He'd miss t' lass, and find a public-house, a reckon,' said Daniel, querulously.

'I'm not afeard o' Kester,' replied Bell. 'He's a good one for knowing folk i' th' dark. But if thou'd rather, I'll put on my hood and cloak and just go to th' end o' th' lane, if thou'lt have an eye to th' milk, and see as it does na' boil o'er, for she canna stomach it if it's bishopped* e'er so little.'

Before Mrs Robson, however, had put away her knitting, voices were heard at a good distance down the lane, but coming nearer every moment, and once more Daniel climbed the little brow to look and to listen.

'It's a' reet!' said he, hobbling quickly down. 'Niver fidget theesel' wi' gettin' ready to go search for her. I'll tak' thee a bet it's Philip Hepburn's voice, convoying her home, just as I said he would, an hour sin'.'

Bell did not answer, as she might have done, that this probability of Philip's bringing Sylvia home had been her own suggestion, set aside by her husband as utterly unlikely. Another minute and the countenances of both parents imperceptibly and unconsciously relaxed into pleasure as Sylvia came in.

She looked very rosy from the walk, and the October air, which began to be frosty in the evenings; there was a little cloud over her face at first, but it was quickly dispersed as she met the loving eyes of home. Philip, who followed her, had an excited, but not altogether pleased look about him. He received a hearty greeting from Daniel, and a quiet one from his aunt.

'Tak' off thy pan o' milk, missus, and set on t' kettle. Milk may do for wenches, but Philip and me is for a drop o' good Hollands* and watter this cold night. I'm a'most chilled to t' marrow wi' looking out for thee, lass, for t' mother was in a peck of troubles about thy none coming home i' t' dayleet, and I'd to keep hearkening out on t' browhead.'

This was entirely untrue, and Bell knew it to be so; but her husband did not. He had persuaded himself now, as he had done often before, that what he had in reality done for his own pleasure or satisfaction, he had done in order to gratify some one else.

'The town was rough with a riot between the press-gang and the whaling folk; and I thought I'd best see Sylvia home.'

'Ay, ay, lad; always welcome, if it's only as an excuse for t' liquor. But t' whalers, say'st ta? Why, is t' whalers in? There was none i' sight yesterday, when I were down on t' shore. It's early days for 'em as yet. And t' cursed old press-gang's agate again, doing its devil's work!'

His face changed as he ended his speech, and showed a steady passion of old hatred.

'Ay, missus, yo' may look. I wunnot pick and choose my words, noather for yo' nor for nobody, when I speak o' that daumed gang. I'm none ashamed o' my words. They're true, and I'm ready to prove 'em. Where's my forefinger? Ay! and as good a top-joint of a thumb as iver a man had? I wish I'd kept 'em i' sperits, as they done things at t' 'potticary's, just to show t' lass what flesh and bone I made away wi' to get free. I ups wi' a hatchet when I saw as I were fast a-board a man-o'-war standing out for sea – it were in t' time o' the war wi' Amerikay, an' I could na stomach the thought o' being murdered i' my own language – so I ups wi' a hatchet, and I says to Bill Watson, says I, "Now, my lad, if thou'll do me a kindness, I'll pay thee back, niver fear, and they'll be glad enough to get shut on us, and send us to old England again. Just come down with a will." Now, missus, why can't ye sit still and listen to me, 'stead o' pottering after pans and what not?' said he, speaking crossly to his wife, who had heard the story scores of times, and, it must be confessed, was making some noise in preparing bread and milk for Sylvia's supper.

Bell did not say a word in reply, but Sylvia tapped his shoulder with a pretty little authoritative air.

'It's for me, feyther. I'm just keen-set for my supper. Once let me get quickly set down to it, and Philip there to his glass o' grog, and you'll never have such listeners in your life, and mother's mind will be at ease too.'

'Eh! thou's a wilfu' wench,' said the proud father, giving her a great slap on her back. 'Well! set thee down to thy victual, and be quiet wi' thee, for I want to finish my tale to Philip. But, perhaps, I've telled it yo' afore?' said he, turning round to question Hepburn.

Hepburn could not say that he had not heard it, for he piqued himself on his truthfulness. But instead of frankly and directly owning this, he tried to frame a formal little speech, which would soothe Daniel's mortified vanity; and, of course, it had the directly opposite effect. Daniel resented being treated like a child, and yet turned his back on Philip with all the wilfulness of one. Sylvia did not care for her cousin, but hated the discomfort of having her father displeased; so she took up her tale of adventure, and told her father and mother of her afternoon's proceedings. Daniel pretended not to listen at first, and made ostentatious noises with his spoon and glass; but by-and-by he got quite warm and excited about the doings of the press-gang, and scolded both Philip and Sylvia for not having learnt more particulars as to what was the termination of the riot.

'I've been whaling mysel',' said he; 'and I've heerd tell as whalers wear knives, and I'd ha' gi'en t' gang a taste o' my whittle, if I'd been cotched up just as I'd set my foot a-shore.'

'I don't know,' said Philip; 'we're at war wi' the French, and we shouldn't like to be beaten; and yet if our numbers are not equal to theirs, we stand a strong chance of it.'

'Not a bit on't – so be d—d!' said Daniel Robson, bringing down his fist with such violence on the round deal table, that the glasses and eathenware shook again. 'Yo'd not strike a child or a woman, for sure! yet it 'ud be like it, if we did na' give the Frenchies some 'vantages – if we took 'em wi' equal numbers. It's not fair play, and that's one place where t' shoe pinches. It's not fair play two ways. It's not fair play to cotch up men as has no call for fightin' at another man's biddin', though they've no objection to fight a bit on their own account, and who are just landed, all keen after bread i'stead o' biscuit, and flesh-meat i'stead o' junk, and beds i'stead o' hammocks. (I make naught o' t' sentiment side, for I were niver gi'en up to such carnal-mindedness and poesies.) It's noane fair to cotch 'em up and put 'em in a stifling hole, all lined with metal for fear they should whittle their way out, and send 'em off to sea for years an' years to come. And again it's no fair play to t' French. Four o' them is rightly matched wi' one o' us; and if we go an' fight 'em four to four it's like as if yo' fell to beatin' Sylvie there, or little Billy Croxton, as isn't breeched. And that's my mind. Missus, where's t' pipe?'

Philip did not smoke, so took his turn at talking, a chance he seldom had with Daniel, unless the latter had his pipe between his lips. So after Daniel had filled it, and used Sylvia's little finger as a stopper to ram down the tobacco – a habit of his to which she was so accustomed that she laid her hand on the table by him, as naturally as she would have fetched him his spittoon when he began to smoke – Philip arranged his arguments, and began—

'I'm for fair play wi' the French, as much as any man, as long as we can be sure o' beating them; but, I say, make sure o' that, and then give them ivery advantage. Now I reckon Government is not sure as yet, for i' the papers it said as half th' ships i' th' Channel hadn't got their proper complement o' men; and all as I say is, let Government judge a bit for us; and if they say they're hampered for want o' men, why we must make it up somehow. John and Jeremiah Foster pay in taxes, and Militiaman pays in person; and if sailors cannot pay in taxes, and will not pay in person, why they must be made to pay; and that's what th' press-gang is for, I reckon. For my part, when I read o' the way those French chaps are going on, I'm thankful to be governed by King George and a British Constitution.'

Daniel took his pipe out of his mouth at this.

'And when did I say a word again King George and the Constitution? I only ax 'em to govern me as I judge best, and that's what I call representation. When I gived my vote* to Measter Cholmley to go up to t' Parliament House, I as good as said, 'Now yo' go up theer, sir, and tell 'em what I, Dannel Robson, think right, and what I, Dannel Robson, wish to have done.' Else I'd be darned if I'd ha' gi'en my vote to him or any other man. And div yo' think I want Seth Robson (as is my own brother's son, and mate to a collier) to be cotched up by a press-gang, and ten to one his wages all unpaid? Div yo' think I'd send up Measter Cholmley to speak up for that piece o' work? Not I.' He took up his pipe again, shook out the ashes, puffed it into a spark, and shut his eyes, preparatory to listening.

'But, asking pardon, laws is made for the good of the nation, not for your good or mine.'

Daniel could not stand this. He laid down his pipe, opened

his eyes, stared straight at Philip before speaking, in order to enforce his words, and then said slowly—

'Nation here! nation theere! I'm a man and yo're another, but nation's nowheere. If Measter Cholmley talked to me i' that fashion, he'd look long for another vote frae me. I can make out King George, and Measter Pitt, and yo' and me, but nation! nation, go hang!'

Philip, who sometimes pursued an argument longer than was politic for himself, especially when he felt sure of being on the conquering side, did not see that Daniel Robson was passing out of the indifference of conscious wisdom into that state of anger which ensues when a question becomes personal in some unspoken way. Robson had contested this subject once or twice before, and had the remembrance of former disputes to add to his present vehemence. So it was well for the harmony of the evening that Bell and Sylvia returned from the kitchen to sit in the house-place. They had been to wash up the pans and basins used for supper; Sylvia had privately shown off her cloak, and got over her mother's shake of the head at its colour with a coaxing kiss, at the end of which her mother had adjusted her cap with a 'There! there! ha' done wi' thee,' but had no more heart to show her disapprobation; and now they came back to their usual occupations until it should please their visitor to go; then they would rake the fire and be off to bed; for neither Sylvia's spinning nor Bell's knitting was worth candle-light, and morning hours are precious in a dairy.

People speak of the way in which harp-playing sets off a graceful figure; spinning is almost as becoming an employment. A woman stands at the great wool-wheel, one arm extended, the other holding the thread, her head thrown back to take in all the scope of her occupation; or if it is the lesser spinning-wheel for flax – and it was this that Sylvia moved forwards to-night – the pretty sound of the buzzing, whirring motion, the attitude of the spinner, foot and hand alike engaged in the business – the bunch of gay coloured ribbon that ties the bundle of flax on the rock – all make it into a picturesque piece of domestic business that may rival harp-playing any day for the amount of softness and grace which it calls out.

Sylvia's cheeks were rather flushed by the warmth of the room after the frosty air. The blue ribbon with which she had thought it necessary to tie back her hair before putting on her hat to go to market had got rather loose, and allowed her disarranged curls to stray in a manner which would have annoyed her extremely, if she had been upstairs to look at herself in the glass; but although they were not set in the exact fashion which Sylvia esteemed as correct, they looked very pretty and luxuriant. Her little foot, placed on the 'traddle,' was still encased in its smartly buckled shoe – not slightly to her discomfort, as she was unaccustomed to be shod in walking far; only as Philip had accompanied them home, neither she nor Molly had liked to go barefoot. Her round mottled arm and ruddy taper hand drew out the flax with nimble, agile motion, keeping time to the movement of the wheel. All this Philip could see; the greater part of her face was lost to him as she half averted it, with a shy dislike to the way in which she knew from past experience that cousin Philip always stared at her. And avert it as she would she heard with silent petulance the harsh screech of Philip's chair as he heavily dragged it on the stone floor, sitting on it all the while, and felt that he was moving round so as to look at her as much as was in his power, without absolutely turning his back on either her father or mother. She got herself ready for the first opportunity of contradiction or opposition.

'Well, wench! and has ta bought this grand new cloak?'

'Yes, feyther. It's a scarlet one.'

'Ay, ay! and what does mother say?'

'Oh, mother's content,' said Sylvia, a little doubting in her heart, but determined to defy Philip at all hazards.

'Mother 'll put up with it if it does na' spot would be nearer fact, I'm thinking,' said Bell, quietly.

'I wanted Sylvia to take the gray,' said Philip.

'And I chose the red; it's so much gayer, and folk can see me the farther off. Feyther likes to see me at first turn o' t' lane, don't yo', feyther? and I'll niver turn out when it's boun' for to rain, so it shall niver get a spot near it, mammy.'

'I reckoned it were to wear i' bad weather,' said Bell. 'Leastways that were the pretext for coaxing feyther out o' it.'

She said it in a kindly tone, though the words became a prudent rather than a fond mother. But Sylvia understood her better than Daniel did as it appeared.

'Hou'd thy tongue, mother. She niver spoke a pretext at all.'

He did not rightly know what a 'pretext' was: Bell was a touch better educated than her husband, but he did not acknowledge this, and made a particular point of differing from her whenever she used a word beyond his comprehension.

'She's a good lass at times; and if she liked to wear a yellow-orange cloak she should have it. Here's Philip here, as stands up for laws and press-gangs, I'll set him to find us a law again pleasing our lass; and she our only one. Thou dostn't think on that, mother!

Bell did think of that often; oftener than her husband, perhaps, for she remembered every day, and many times a day, the little one that had been born and had died while its father was away on some long voyage. But it was not her way to make replies.

Sylvia, who had more insight into her mother's heart than Daniel, broke in with a new subject.

'Oh! as for Philip, he's been preaching up laws all t' way home. I said naught, but let Molly hold her own; or else I could ha' told a tale about silks an' lace an' things.'

Philip's face flushed. Not because of the smuggling; every one did that, only it was considered polite to ignore it; but he was annoyed to perceive how quickly his little cousin had discovered that his practice did not agree with his preaching, and vexed, too, to see how delighted she was to bring out the fact. He had some little idea, too, that his uncle might make use of his practice as an argument against the preaching he had lately been indulging in, in opposition to Daniel; but Daniel was too far gone in his Hollands-and-water to do more than enunciate his own opinions, which he did with hesitating and laboured distinctness in the following sentence:

'What I think and say is this. Laws is made for to keep some folks fra' harming others. Press-gangs and coast-guards harm me i' my business, and keep me fra' getting what I want. Theerefore, what I think and say is this: Measter Cholmley should put down press-gangs and coast-guards. If that theere isn't reason I ax yo' to tell me what is? an' if Measter Cholmley don't do what I ax him, he may go whistle for my vote, he may.'

At this period in his conversation, Bell Robson interfered; not in the least from any feeling of disgust or annoyance, or dread of what he might say or do if he went on drinking, but simply as a matter of health. Sylvia, too, was in no way annoyed; not only with her father, but with every man whom she knew, excepting her cousin Philip, was it a matter of course to drink till their ideas became confused. So she simply put her wheel aside, as preparatory to going to bed, when her mother said, in a more decided tone than that which she had used on any other occasion but this, and similar ones—

'Come, measter, you've had as much as is good for you.'

'Let a' be! Let a' be,' said he, clutching at the bottle of spirits, but perhaps rather more good-humoured with what he had drunk than he was before; he jerked a little more into his glass before his wife carried it off, and locked it up in the cupboard, putting the key in her pocket, and then he said, winking at Philip—

'Eh! my man. Niver gie a woman t' whip hand o'er yo'! Yo' seen what it brings a man to; but for a' that I'll vote for Cholmley, an' d—— t' press-gang!'

He had to shout out the last after Philip, for Hepburn, really anxious to please his aunt, and disliking drinking habits himself by constitution, was already at the door, and setting out on his return home, thinking, it must be confessed, far more of the character of Sylvia's shake of the hand than of the parting words of either his uncle or aunt.

CHAPTER V

STORY OF THE PRESS-GANG

FOR a few days after the evening mentioned in the last chapter the weather was dull. Not in quick, sudden showers did the rain come down, but in constant drizzle, blotting out all colour from the surrounding landscape, and filling the air with fine gray mist, until people breathed more water than air. At such times the consciousness of the nearness of the vast unseen sea acted as a dreary depression to the spirits; but besides acting on the nerves of the excitable, such weather affected the sensitive or ailing in material ways. Daniel Robson's fit of rheumatism incapacitated him from stirring abroad; and to a man of his active habits, and somewhat inactive mind, this was a great hardship. He was not ill-tempered naturally, but this state of confinement made him more ill-tempered than he had ever been before in his life. He sat in the chimney-corner, abusing the weather and doubting the wisdom or desirableness of all his wife saw fit to do in the usual daily household matters. The 'chimney-corner' was really a corner at Haytersbank. There were two projecting walls on each side of the fire-place, running about six feet into the room, and a stout wooden settle was placed against one of these, while opposite was the circular-backed 'master's chair,' the seat of which was composed of a square piece of wood judiciously hollowed out, and placed with one corner to the front. Here, in full view of all the operations going on over the fire, sat Daniel Robson for four live-long days, advising and directing his wife in all such minor matters as the boiling of potatoes, the making of porridge, all the work on which she specially piqued herself, and on which she would have taken advice – no! not from the most skilled housewife in all the three Ridings. But, somehow, she managed to keep her tongue quiet from telling him, as she would have done any woman, and any other man, to mind his own business, or she would pin a dish-clout to his tail.

She even checked Sylvia when the latter proposed, as much for fun as for anything else, that his ignorant directions should be followed, and the consequences brought before his eyes and his nose.

'Na, na!' said Bell, 'th' feyther's feyther, and we mun respect him. But it's dree* work havin' a man i' th' house, nursing th' fire, an' such weather too, and not a soul coming near us, not even to fall out wi' him; for thee and me must na' do that, for th' Bible's sake, dear; and a good stand-up wordy quarrel would do him a power of good; stir his blood like. I wish Philip would turn up.'

Bell sighed, for in these four days she had experienced somewhat of Madame de Maintenon's* difficulty (and with fewer resources to meet it) of trying to amuse a man who was not amusable. For Bell, good and sensible as she was, was not a woman of resources. Sylvia's plan, undutiful as it was in her mother's eyes, would have done Daniel more good, even though it might have made him angry, than his wife's quiet, careful monotony of action, which, however it might conduce to her husband's comfort when he was absent, did not amuse him when present.

Sylvia scouted the notion of cousin Philip coming into their household in the character of an amusing or entertaining person, till she nearly made her mother angry at her ridicule of the good steady young fellow, to whom Bell looked up as the pattern of all that early manhood should be. But the moment Sylvia saw she had been giving her mother pain, she left off her wilful little jokes, and kissed her, and told her she would manage all famously, and ran out of the back-kitchen, in which mother and daughter had been scrubbing the churn and all the wooden implements of butter-making. Bell looked at the pretty figure of her little daughter, as, running past with her apron thrown over her head, she darkened the window beneath which her mother was doing her work. She paused just for a moment, and then said, almost unawares to herself, 'Bless thee, lass,' before resuming her scouring of what already looked almost snow-white.

Sylvia scampered across the rough farmyard in the wetting,

drizzling rain to the place where she expected to find Kester; but he was not there, so she had to retrace her steps to the cow-house, and, making her way up a rough kind of ladder-staircase fixed straight against the wall, she surprised Kester as he sat in the wool-loft, looking over the fleeces reserved for the home-spinning, by popping her bright face, swathed round with her blue woollen apron, up through the trap-door, and thus, her head the only visible part, she addressed the farm-servant, who was almost like one of the family.

'Kester, feyther's just tiring hissel' wi' weariness an' vexation, sitting by t' fireside wi' his hands afore him, an' nought to do. An' mother and me can't think on aught as 'll rouse him up to a bit of a laugh, or aught more cheerful than a scolding. Now, Kester, thou mun just be off, and find Harry Donkin th' tailor, and bring him here; it's gettin' on for Martinmas, an' he'll be coming his rounds, and he may as well come here first as last, and feyther's clothes want a deal o' mending up, and Harry's always full of his news, and anyhow he'll do for feyther to scold, an' be a new person too, and that's somewhat for all on us. Now go, like a good old Kester as yo' are.'

Kester looked at her with loving, faithful admiration. He had set himself his day's work in his master's absence, and was very desirous of finishing it, but, somehow, he never dreamed of resisting Sylvia, so he only stated the case.

'T' 'ool's a vast o' muck in 't, an' a thowt as a'd fettle it, an' do it up; but a reckon a mun do yo'r biddin'.'

'There's a good old Kester,' said she, smiling, and nodding her muffled head at him; then she dipped down out of his sight, then rose up again (he had never taken his slow, mooney eyes from the spot where she had disappeared) to say – 'Now, Kester, be wary and deep – thou mun tell Harry Donkin not to let on as we've sent for him, but just to come in as if he were on his round, and took us first; and he mun ask feyther if there is any work for him to do; and I'll answer for 't, he'll have a welcome and a half. Now, be deep and fause,* mind thee!'

'A'se deep an' fause enow wi' simple folk; but what can a

do i' Donkin be as fause as me – as happen he may be?'

'Ga way wi' thee! I' Donkin be Solomon, thou mun be t' Queen o' Sheba; and I'se bound for to say she outwitted him at last!'

Kester laughed so long at the idea of his being the Queen of Sheba, that Sylvia was back by her mother's side before the cachinnation* ended.

That night, just as Sylvia was preparing to go to bed in her little closet of a room, she heard some shot rattling at her window. She opened the little casement, and saw Kester standing below. He recommenced where he left off, with a laugh—

'He, he, he! A's been t' queen! A'se ta'en Donkin on t' reet side, an' he'll coom in to-morrow, just permiskus, an' ax for work, like as if 't were a favour; t' oud felley were a bit cross-grained at startin', for he were workin' at farmer Crosskey's up at t' other side o' t' town, wheer they puts a strike* an' a half of maut intil t' beer, when most folk put nobbut a strike, an t' made him ill to convince: but he'll coom, niver fear!'

The honest fellow never said a word of the shilling he had paid out of his own pocket to forward Sylvia's wishes, and to persuade the tailor to leave the good beer. All his anxiety now was to know if he had been missed, and if it was likely that a scolding awaited him in the morning.

'T' oud measter didn't set up his back, 'cause a didn't coom in t' supper?'

'He questioned a bit as to what thou were about, but mother didn't know, an' I held my peace. Mother carried thy supper in t' loft for thee.'

'A'll gang after 't, then, for a'm like a pair o' bellowses wi' t' wind out; just two flat sides wi' nowt betwixt.'

The next morning, Sylvia's face was a little redder than usual when Harry Donkin's bow-legs were seen circling down the path to the house door.

'Here's Donkin, for sure!' exclaimed Bell, when she caught sight of him a minute after her daughter. 'Well, I just call that lucky! for he'll be company for thee while Sylvia and me has to turn th' cheeses.'

This was too original a remark for a wife to make in Daniel's opinion, on this especial morning, when his rheumatism was twinging him more than usual, so he replied with severity—

'That's all t' women know about it. Wi' them it's "coompany, coompany, coompany," an' they think a man's no better than theirsels. A'd have yo' to know a've a vast o' thoughts in myself', as I'm noane willing to lay out for t' benefit o' every man. A've niver gotten time for meditation sin' a were married; leastways, sin' a left t' sea. Aboard ship, wi' niver a woman wi'n leagues o' hail, and upo' t' masthead, in special, a could.'

'Then I'd better tell Donkin as we've no work for him,' said Sylvia, instinctively managing her father by agreeing with him, instead of reasoning with or contradicting him.

'Now, theere you go!' wrenching himself round, for fear Sylvia should carry her meekly made threat into execution. 'Ugh! ugh!' as his limb hurt him. 'Come in, Harry, come in, and talk a bit o' sense to me, for a've been shut up wi' women these four days, and a'm a'most a nateral by this time. A'se bound for 't, they'll find yo' some wark, if 't's nought but for to save their own fingers.'

So Harry took off his coat, and seated himself professionalwise on the hastily-cleared dresser, so that he might have all the light afforded by the long, low casement window. Then he blew in his thimble, sucked his finger, so that they might adhere tightly together, and looked about for a subject for opening conversation, while Sylvia and her mother might be heard opening and shutting drawers and box-lids before they could find the articles that needed repair, or that were required to mend each other.

'Women's well enough i' their way,' said Daniel, in a philosophizing tone, 'but a man may have too much on 'em. Now there's me, leg-fast these four days, and a'll make free to say to yo', a'd rather a deal ha' been loading dung i' t' wettest weather; an' a reckon it's th' being wi' nought but women as tires me so: they talk so foolish it gets int' t' bones like. Now thou know'st thou'rt not called much of a man oather, but bless yo', t' ninth part's summut to be thankful for, after nought but women. An' yet, yo' seen, they were for sending yo' away i' their foolishness! Well! missus, and who's to pay for t' fettling* of all them clothes?' as Bell came down with her arms full. She was going to answer her husband meekly and literally according to her wont, but Sylvia, already detecting the increased cheerfulness of his tone, called out from behind her mother—

'I am, feyther. I'm going for to sell my new cloak as I bought Thursday, for the mending on your old coats and waistcoats.'

'Hearken till her,' said Daniel, chuckling. 'She's a true wench. Three days sin' noane so full as she o' t' new cloak that now she's fain t' sell.'

'Ay, Harry. If feyther won't pay yo' for making all these old clothes as good as new, I'll sell my new red cloak sooner than yo' shall go unpaid.'

'A reckon it's a bargain,' said Harry, casting sharp, professional eyes on the heap before him, and singling out the best article as to texture for examination and comment.

'They're all again these metal buttons,' said he. 'Silk weavers has been petitioning Ministers t' make a law to favour silk buttons;* and I did hear tell as there were informers goin' about spyin' after metal buttons, and as how they could haul yo' before a justice for wearing on 'em.

'A were wed in 'em, and a'll wear 'em to my dyin' day, or a'll wear noane at a'. They're for makking such a pack o' laws, they'll be for meddling wi' my fashion o' sleeping next, and taxing me for ivery snore a give. They've been after t' winders, and after t' vittle, and after t' very saut to 't; it's dearer by hauf an' more nor it were when a were a boy: they're a meddlesome set o' folks, law-makers is, an' a'll niver believe King George has ought t' do wi' 't. But mark my words; I were wed wi' brass buttons, and brass buttons a'll wear to my death, an' if they moither me about it, a'll wear brass buttons i' my coffin!'

By this time Harry had arranged a certain course of action

with Mrs Robson, conducting the consultation and agreement by signs. His thread was flying fast already, and the mother and daughter felt more free to pursue their own business than they had done for several days; for it was a good sign that Daniel had taken his pipe out of the square hollow in the fireside wall, where he usually kept it, and was preparing to diversify his remarks with satisfying interludes of puffing.

'Why, look ye; this very baccy had a run for 't. It came ashore sewed up neatly enough i' a woman's stays, as was wife to a fishing-smack down at t' bay yonder. She were a lean thing as iver you saw, when she went for t' see her husband aboard t' vessel; but she coom back lustier by a deal, an' wi' many a thing on her, here and theere, beside baccy. An' that were i' t' face o' coast-guard and yon tender, an' a'. But she made as though she were tipsy, an' so they did nought but curse her, an' get out on her way.'

'Speaking of t' tender, there's been a piece o' work i' Monkshaven this week wi' t' press-gang,' said Harry.

'Ay! ay! our lass was telling about 't; but, Lord bless ye! there's no gettin' t' rights on a story out on a woman – though a will say this for our Sylvie, she's as bright a lass as iver a man looked at.'

Now the truth was, that Daniel had not liked to demean himself, at the time when Sylvia came back so full of what she had seen at Monkshaven, by evincing any curiosity on the subject. He had then thought that the next day he would find some business that should take him down to the town, when he could learn all that was to be learnt, without flattering his womankind by asking questions, as if anything they might say could interest him. He had a strong notion of being a kind of domestic Jupiter.*

'It's made a deal o' work i' Monkshaven. Folk had gotten to think nought o' t' tender, she lay so still, an' t' leftenant paid such a good price for all he wanted for t' ship. But o' Thursday t' *Resolution*, first whaler back this season, came in port, and t' press-gang showed their teeth, and carried off four as good able-bodied seamen as iver I made trousers for; and t' place were all up like a nest o' wasps, when yo've set your foot in t' midst. They were so mad, they were ready for t' fight t' very pavin' stones.'

'A wish a'd been theere! A just wish a had! A've a score for t' reckon up wi' t' press-gang!'

And the old man lifted up his right hand – his hand on which the forefinger and thumb were maimed and useless – partly in denunciation, and partly as a witness of what he had endured to escape from the service, abhorred because it was forced. His face became a totally different countenance with the expression of settled and unrelenting indignation, which his words called out.

'G'on, man, g'on,' said Daniel, impatient with Donkin for the little delay occasioned by the necessity of arranging his work more fully.

'Ay! ay! all in good time; for a've a long tale to tell yet; an' a mun have some 'un to iron me out my seams, and look me out my bits, for there's none here fit for my purpose.'

'Dang thy bits! Here, Sylvie! Sylvie! come and be tailor's man, and let t' chap get settled sharp, for a'm fain t' hear his story.'

Sylvia took her directions, and placed her irons in the fire, and ran upstairs for the bundle which had been put aside by her careful mother for occasions like the present. It consisted of small pieces of various coloured cloth, cut out of old coats and waistcoats, and similar garments, when the whole had become too much worn for use, yet when part had been good enough to be treasured by a thrifty housewife. Daniel grew angry before Donkin had selected his patterns and settled the work to his own mind.

'Well,' said he at last; 'a mought be a young man a-goin' a wooin', by t' pains thou'st taken for t' match my oud clothes. I don't care if they're patched wi' scarlet, a tell thee; so as thou'lt work away at thy tale wi' thy tongue, same time as thou works at thy needle wi' thy fingers.'

'Then, as a were saying, all Monkshaven were like a nest o' wasps, flyin' hither and thither, and makin' sich a buzzin' and a talkin' as niver were; and each wi' his sting out, ready for t' vent his venom o' rage and revenge. And women cryin' and sobbin' i' t' streets – when, Lord help us! o' Saturday came a worse time than iver! for all Friday there had been a kind o' expectation an' dismay about t' *Good Fortune*, as t' mariners had said was off St Abb's Head o' Thursday, when t' *Resolution* came in; and there was wives and maids wi' husbands an' sweethearts aboard t' *Good Fortune* ready to throw their eyes out on their heads wi' gazin, gazin' nor'ards over t'sea, as were all one haze o' blankness wi' t' rain; and when t' afternoon tide comed in, an' niver a line on her to be seen, folk were oncertain as t' whether she were holding off for fear o' t' tender – as were out o' sight, too – or what were her mak' o' goin' on. An' t' poor wet draggled women folk came up t' town, some slowly cryin', as if their hearts was sick, an' others just bent their heads to t'wind, and went straight to their homes, nother looking nor speaking to ony one; but barred their doors, and stiffened theirsels up for a night o' waiting. Saturday morn – yo'll mind Saturday morn, it were stormy and gusty, downreet dirty weather – theere stood t' folk again by daylight, a watching an' a straining, and by that tide t' *Good Fortune* came o'er t' bar. But t' excisemen had sent back her news by t' boat as took 'em there. They'd a deal of oil, and a vast o' blubber. But for all that her flag was drooping i' t' rain, half mast high, for mourning and sorrow, an' they'd a dead man aboard – a dead man as was living and strong last sunrise. An' there was another as lay between life an' death, and there was seven more as should ha' been theere as wasn't, but was carried off by t' gang. T' frigate as we 'n a' heard tell on, as lying off Hartlepool, got tidings fra' t' tender as captured t' seamen o' Thursday: and t' *Aurora*, as they ca'ed her, made off for t' nor'ard; and nine leagues off St Abb's Head, t' *Resolution* thinks she were, she see'd t' frigate, and knowed by her build she were a man-o'-war, and guessed she were bound on king's kidnapping. I seen t' wounded man mysen wi' my own eyes; and he'll live! he'll live! Niver a man died yet, wi' such a strong purpose o' vengeance in him. He could barely speak, for he were badly shot, but his colour coome and went, as t' master's mate an' t' captain telled me and some others how t'

Aurora fired at 'em, and how t' innocent whaler hoisted her colours, but afore they were fairly run up, another shot coome close in t' shrouds, and then t' Greenland ship being t' windward, bore down on t' frigate; but as they knew she were an oud fox, and bent on mischief, Kinraid (that's he who lies a-dying, only he'll noane die, a'se bound), the specksioneer, bade t' men go down between decks, and fasten t' hatches well, an' he'd stand guard, he an' captain, and t' oud master's mate, being left upo' deck for t' give a welcome just skin-deep to t' boat's crew fra' t' *Aurora,* as they could see coming t'wards them o'er t' watter, wi' their reg'lar man-o'-war's rowing——'

'Damn 'em!' said Daniel, in soliloquy, and under his breath.

Sylvia stood, poising her iron, and listening eagerly, afraid to give Donkin the hot iron for fear of interrupting the narrative, unwilling to put it into the fire again, because that action would perchance remind him of his work, which now the tailor had forgotten, so eager was he in telling his story.

'Well! they coome on over t' watters wi' great bounds, and up t' sides they coome like locusts, all armed men; an' t' captain says he saw Kinraid hide away his whaling knife under some tarpaulin', and he knew he meant mischief, an' he would no more ha' stopped him wi' a word nor he would ha' stopped him fra' killing a whale. And when t' *Aurora*'s men were aboard, one on 'em runs to t' helm; and at that t' captain says, he felt as if his wife were kissed afore his face; but says he, "I bethought me on t' men as were shut up below hatches, an' I remembered t' folk at Monkshaven as were looking out for us even then; an' I said to mysel', I would speak fair as long as I could, more by token o' the whaling-knife, as I could see glinting bright under t' black tarpaulin." So he spoke quite fair and civil, though he see'd they was nearing t' *Aurora,* and t' *Aurora* was nearing them. Then t' navy captain hailed him thro' t' trumpet, wi' a great rough blast, and, says he, "Order your men to come on deck." And t' captain of t' whaler says, his men cried up from under t' hatches as they'd niver be gi'en up wi'out bloodshed, and he sees Kinraid take out his pistol, and look well to t' priming; so he says to t' navy captain. "We're protected Greenland-men, and you have no right t' meddle wi' us." But t' navy captain only bellows t' more, "Order your men t' come on deck. If they won't obey you, and you have lost the command of your vessel, I reckon you're in a state of mutiny, and you may come aboard t' *Aurora* and such men as are willing t' follow you and I'll fire int' the rest." Yo' see, that were t' depth o' the man: he were for pretending and pretexting as t' captain could na manage his own ship, and as he'd help him. But our Greenland captain were noâne so poor-spirited, and says he, "She's full of oil, and I ware you of consequences if you fire into her. Anyhow, pirate, or no pirate" (for t' word pirate stuck in his gizzard), "I'm a honest Monkshaven man, an' I come fra' a land where there's great icebergs and many a deadly danger, but niver a press-gang, thank God! and that's what you are, I reckon." Them's the words he told me, but whether he spoke 'em out so bold at t' time, I'se not so sure; they were in his mind for t' speak, only maybe prudence got t' better on him, for he said he prayed i' his heart to bring his cargo safe to t' owners, come what might. Well, t' *Aurora*'s men aboard t' *Good Fortune* cried out "might they fire down t' hatches, and bring t' men out that a way?" and then t' specksioneer, he speaks, an' he says he stands ower t' hatches, and he has two good pistols, and summut besides, and he don't care for his life, bein' a bachelor, but all below are men, yo' see, and he'll put an end to t' first two chaps as come near t' hatches. An' they say he picked two off as made for t' come near, and then, just as he were stooping for t' whaling knife, an' it's as big as a sickle——'

'Teach folk as don't know a whaling knife,' cried Daniel. 'I were a Greenland-man mysel'.'

'They shot him through t' side, and dizzied him, and kicked him aside for dead; and fired down t' hatches, and killed one man, and disabled two, and then t' rest cried for quarter, for life is sweet, e'en aboard a king's ship; and t' *Aurora* carried 'em off, wounded men, an' able men, an' all: leaving Kinraid for dead, as wasn't dead, and Darley* for dead, as was dead, an' t' captain and master's mate as were too old for work; and t' captain, as loves Kinraid like a brother, poured rum down his throat, and bandaged him up, and has sent for t' first doctor in Monkshaven for to get t' slugs out; for they say there's niver such a harpooner in a' t' Greenland seas; an' I can speak fra' my own seeing he's a fine young fellow where he lies theere, all stark and wan for weakness and loss o' blood. But Darley's dead as a door-nail; and there's to be such a burying of him as niver was seen afore i' Monkshaven, come Sunday. And now gi' us t' iron, wench, and let's lose no more time a-talking.'

'It's noane loss o' time,' said Daniel, moving himself heavily in his chair, to feel how helpless he was once more. 'If a were as young as once a were – nay, lad, if a had na these sore rheumatics, now – a reckon as t' press-gang 'ud find out as t' shouldn't do such things for nothing. Bless thee, man! it's waur nor i' my youth i' th' Ameriky war, and then 't were bad enough.'

'And Kinraid?' said Sylvia, drawing a long breath, after the effort of realizing it all; her cheeks had flushed up, and her eyes had glittered during the progress of the tale.

'Oh! he'll do. He'll not die. Life's stuff is in him yet.'

'He'll be Molly Corney's cousin, I reckon,' said Sylvia, bethinking her with a blush of Molly Corney's implication that he was more than a cousin to her, and immediately longing to go off and see Molly, and hear all the little details which women do not think it beneath them to give to women. From that time Sylvia's little heart was bent on this purpose. But it was not one to be openly avowed even to herself. She only wanted sadly to see Molly, and she almost believed herself that it was to consult her about the fashion of her cloak; which Donkin was to cut out, and which she was to make under his directions; at any rate, this was the reason she gave to her mother when the day's work was done, and a fine gleam came out upon the pale and watery sky towards evening.

CHAPTER VI

THE SAILOR'S FUNERAL

MOSS BROW, the Corneys' house, was but a disorderly, comfortless place. You had to cross a dirty farmyard, all puddles and dungheaps, on stepping-stones, to get to the door of the house-place. That great room itself was sure to have clothes hanging to dry at the fire, whatever day of the week it was; some one of the large irregular family having had what is called in the district a 'dab-wash' of a few articles, forgotten on the regular day. And sometimes these articles lay in their dirty state in the untidy kitchen, out of which a room, half parlour, half bedroom, opened on one side, and a dairy, the only clean place in the house, at the opposite. In face of you, as you entered the door, was the entrance to the working-kitchen, or scullery. Still, in spite of disorder like this, there was a well-to-do aspect about the place; the Corneys were rich in their way, in flocks and herds as well as in children; and to them neither dirt nor the perpetual bustle arising from ill-ordered work detracted from comfort. They were all of an easy, good-tempered nature; Mrs Corney and her daughters gave every one a welcome at whatever time of the day they came, and would just as soon sit down for a gossip at ten o'clock in the morning, as at five in the evening, though at the former time the house-place was full of work of various kinds which ought to be got out of hand and done with: while the latter hour was towards the end of the day, when farmers' wives and daughters were usually – 'cleaned' was the word then, 'dressed' is that in vogue now. Of course in such a household as this Sylvia was sure to be gladly received. She was young, and pretty, and bright, and brought a fresh breeze of pleasant air about her as her appropriate atmosphere. And besides, Bell Robson held her head so high that visits from her daughter were rather esteemed as a favour, for it was not everywhere that Sylvia was allowed to go.

'Sit yo' down, sit yo' down!' cried Dame Corney, dusting

a chair with her apron; 'a reckon Molly 'll be in i' no time. She's nobbut gone int' t' orchard, to see if she can find windfalls enough for t' make a pie or two for t' lads. They like nowt so weel for supper as apple-pies sweetened wi' treacle, crust stout and leathery, as stands chewing, and we hannot getten in our apples yet.'

'If Molly is in t' orchard, I'll go find her,' said Sylvia.

'Well! yo' lasses will have your conks' (private talks), 'a know; secrets 'bout sweethearts and such like,' said Mrs Corney, with a knowing look, which made Sylvia hate her for the moment. 'A've not forgotten as a were young mysen. Tak' care; there's a pool o' mucky watter just outside t' back-door.'

But Sylvia was half-way across the back-yard – worse, if possible, than the front as to the condition in which it was kept – and had passed through the little gate into the orchard. It was full of old gnarled apple-trees, their trunks covered with gray lichen, in which the cunning chaffinch built her nest in spring-time. The cankered branches remained on the trees, and added to the knotted interweaving overhead, if they did not to the productiveness; the grass grew in long tufts, and was wet and tangled under foot. There was a tolerable crop of rosy apples still hanging on the gray old trees, and here and there they showed ruddy in the green bosses of untrimmed grass. Why the fruit was not gathered, as it was evidently ripe, would have puzzled any one not acquainted with the Corney family to say; but to them it was always a maxim in practice, if not in precept, 'Do nothing to-day that you can put off till to-morrow,' and accordingly the apples dropped from the trees at any little gust of wind, and lay rotting on the ground until the 'lads' wanted a supply of pies for supper.

Molly saw Sylvia, and came quickly across the orchard to meet her, catching her feet in knots of grass as she hurried along.

'Well, lass!' said she, 'who'd ha' thought o' seeing yo' such a day as it has been?'

'But it's cleared up now beautiful,' said Sylvia, looking up at the soft evening sky, to be seen through the apple boughs.

It was of a tender, delicate gray, with the faint warmth of a promising sunset tinging it with a pink atmosphere. 'Rain is over and gone, and I wanted to know how my cloak is to be made; for Donkin 's working at our house, and I wanted to know all about – the news, yo' know.'

'What news?' asked Molly, for she had heard of the affair between the *Good Fortune* and the *Aurora* some days before; and, to tell the truth, it had rather passed out of her head just at this moment.

'Hannot yo' heard all about t' press-gang and t' whaler, and t' great fight, and Kinraid, as is your cousin, acting so brave and grand, and lying on his death-bed now?'

'Oh!' said Molly, enlightened as to Sylvia's 'news,' and half surprised at the vehemence with which the little creature spoke; 'yes; a heerd that days ago. But Charley's noane on his death-bed, he's a deal better; an' mother says as he's to be moved up here next week for nursin' and better air nor he gets i' t' town yonder.'

'Oh! I am so glad,' said Sylvia, with all her heart. 'I thought he'd maybe die, and I should niver see him.'

'A'll promise yo' shall see him; that's t' say if a' goes on well, for he's getten an ugly hurt. Mother says as there's four blue marks on his side as'll last him his life, an' t' doctor fears bleeding i' his inside; and then he'll drop down dead when no one looks for 't.'

'But you said he was better,' said Sylvia, blanching a little at this account.

'Ay, he's better, but life's uncertain, special after gun-shot wounds.'

'He acted very fine,' said Sylvia, meditating.

'A allays knowed he would. Many's the time a've heerd him say "honour bright," and now he's shown how bright his is.'

Molly did not speak sentimentally, but with a kind of proprietorship in Kinraid's honour, which confirmed Sylvia in her previous idea of a mutual attachment between her and her cousin. Considering this notion, she was a little surprised at Molly's next speech.

'An' about yer cloak, are you for a hood or a cape? a reckon that's the question.'

'Oh, I don't care! tell me more about Kinraid. Do yo' really think he'll get better?'

'Dear! how t' lass takes on about him. A'll tell him what a deal of interest a young woman taks i' him!'

From that time Sylvia never asked another question about him. In a somewhat dry and altered tone, she said, after a little pause—

'I think on a hood. What do you say to it?'

'Well; hoods is a bit old-fashioned, to my mind. If 't were mine, I'd have a cape cut i' three points, one to tie on each shoulder, and one to dip down handsome behind. But let yo' an' me go to Monkshaven church o' Sunday, and see Measter Fishburn's daughters, as has their things made i' York, and notice a bit how they're made. We needn't do it i' church, but just scan 'em o'er i' t' churchyard, and there'll be no harm done. Besides, there's to be this grand burryin' o' t' man t' press-gang shot, and 't will be like killing two birds at once.'

'I should like to go,' said Sylvia. 'I feel so sorry like for the poor sailors shot down and kidnapped just as they was coming home, as we see'd 'em o' Thursday last. I'll ask mother if she'll let me go.'

'Ay, do. I know my mother 'll let me, if she doesn't go hersen; for it 'll be a sight to see and to speak on for many a long year, after what I've heerd. And Miss Fishburns is sure to be theere, so I'd just get Donkin to cut out cloak itsel', and keep back yer mind fra' fixing o' either cape or hood till Sunday's turn'd.'

'Will yo' set me part o' t' way home?' said Sylvia, seeing the dying daylight become more and more crimson through the blackening trees.

'No; I can't. A should like it well enough, but somehow, there's a deal o' work to be done yet, for t' hours slip through one's fingers so as there's no knowing. Mind yo', then, o' Sunday. A'll be at t' stile one o'clock punctual; and we'll go slowly into t' town, and look about us as we go, and see folk's dresses; and go to t' church, and say wer prayers, and come out and have a look at t' funeral.'

And with this programme of proceedings settled for the following Sunday, the girls whom neighbourhood and parity of age had forced into some measure of friendship parted for the time.

Sylvia hastened home, feeling as if she had been absent long; her mother stood on the little knoll at the side of the house watching for her, with her hand shading her eyes from the low rays of the setting sun: but as soon as she saw her daughter in the distance, she returned to her work, whatever that might be. She was not a woman of many words, or of much demonstration; few observers would have guessed how much she loved her child; but Sylvia, without any reasoning or observation, instinctively knew that her mother's heart was bound up in her.

Her father and Donkin were going on much as when she had left them; talking and disputing, the one compelled to be idle, the other stitching away as fast as he talked. They seemed as if they had never missed Sylvia; no more did her mother for that matter, for she was busy and absorbed in her afternoon dairy-work to all appearance. But Sylvia had noted the watching not three minutes before, and many a time in her after life, when no one cared much for her out-goings and in-comings, the straight, upright figure of her mother, fronting the setting sun, but searching through its blinding rays for a sight of her child, rose up like a sudden-seen picture, the remembrance of which smote Sylvia to the heart with a sense of a lost blessing, not duly valued while possessed.

'Well, feyther, and how's a' wi' you?' asked Sylvia, going to the side of his chair, and laying her hand on his shoulder.

'Eh! harkee till this lass o' mine. She thinks as because she's gone galraverging* I maun ha' missed her and be ailing. Why, lass, Donkin and me has had t' most sensible talk a've had this many a day. A've gi'en him a vast o' knowledge, and he's done me a power o' good. Please God, to-morrow a'll tak' a start at walking, if t' weather holds up.'

'Ay!' said Donkin, with a touch of sarcasm in his voice;

'feyther and me has settled many puzzles; it's been a loss to Government as they hannot been here for profiting by our wisdom. We've done away wi' taxes and press-gangs, and many a plague, and beaten t' French – i' our own minds, that's to say.'

'It's a wonder t' me as those Lunnon folks can't see things clear,' said Daniel, all in good faith.

Sylvia did not quite understand the state of things as regarded politics and taxes – and politics and taxes were all one in her mind, it must be confessed – but she saw that her innocent little scheme of giving her father the change of society afforded by Donkin's coming had answered; and in the gladness of her heart she went out and ran round the corner of the house to find Kester, and obtain from him that sympathy in her success which she dared not ask from her mother.

'Kester, Kester, lad!' said she, in a loud whisper; but Kester was suppering the horses, and in the clamp of their feet on the round stable pavement, he did not hear her at first. She went a little farther into the stable. 'Kester! he's a vast better, he'll go out to-morrow; it's all Donkin's doing. I'm beholden to thee for fetching him, and I'll try and spare thee waistcoat fronts out o' t' stuff for my new red cloak. Thou'll like that, Kester, won't ta?'

Kester took the notion in slowly, and weighed it.

'Na, lass,' said he, deliberately, after a pause. 'A could na' bear to see thee wi' thy cloak scrimpit.* A like t' see a wench look bonny and smart, an' a tak' a kind o' pride in thee, an' should be a'most as much hurt i' my mind to see thee i' a pinched cloak as if old Moll's tail here were docked too short. Na, lass, a'se niver got a mirroring glass for t' see mysen in, so what's waistcoats to me? Keep thy stuff to thysen, theere's a good wench; but a'se main and glad about t' measter. Place isn't like itsen when he's shut up and cranky.'

He took up a wisp of straw and began rubbing down the old mare, and hissing over his work as if he wished to consider the conversation as ended. And Sylvia, who had strung herself up in a momentary fervour of gratitude to make the generous offer, was not sorry to have it refused, and went back planning what kindness she could show to Kester without its involving so much sacrifice to herself. For giving waistcoat fronts to him would deprive her of the pleasant power of selecting a fashionable pattern in Monkshaven churchyard next Sunday.

That wished-for day seemed long a-coming, as wished-for days most frequently do. Her father got better by slow degrees, and her mother was pleased by the tailor's good pieces of work; showing the neatly-placed patches with as much pride as many matrons take in new clothes now-a-days. And the weather cleared up into a dim kind of autumnal fineness, into anything but an Indian summer as far as regarded gorgeousness of colouring, for on that coast the mists and sea fogs early spoil the brilliancy of the foliage. Yet, perhaps, the more did the silvery grays and browns of the inland scenery conduce to the tranquillity of the time, – the time of peace and rest before the fierce and stormy winter comes on. It seems a time for gathering up human forces to encounter the coming severity, as well as of storing up the produce of harvest for the needs of winter. Old people turn out and sun themselves in that calm St. Martin's summer, without fear of 'the heat o' th' sun, or the coming winter's rages,'* and we may read in their pensive, dreamy eyes that they are weaning themselves away from the earth, which probably many may never see dressed in her summer glory again.

Many such old people set out betimes, on the Sunday afternoon to which Sylvia had been so looking forward, to scale the long flights of stone steps – worn by the feet of many generations – which led up to the parish church, placed on a height above the town, on a great green area at the summit of the cliff, which was the angle where the river and the sea met, and so overlooking both the busy crowded little town, the port, the shipping, and the bar on the one hand, and the wide illimitable tranquil sea on the other – types of life and eternity. It was a good situation for that church.* Homeward-bound sailors caught sight of the tower of St Nicholas, the first land object of all. They who went forth upon the great deep might carry solemn thoughts with them of the words they had heard there; not conscious thoughts, perhaps – rather a distinct if dim conviction that buying and selling, eating and marrying, even life and death, were not all the realities in existence. Nor were the words that came up to their remembrance words of sermons preached there, however impressive. The sailors mostly slept through the sermons; unless, indeed, there were incidents such as were involved in what were called 'funeral discourses' to be narrated. They did not recognize their daily faults or temptations under the grand aliases befitting their appearance from a preacher's mouth. But they knew the old, oft-repeated words praying for deliverance from the familiar dangers of lightning and tempest; from battle, murder, and sudden death;* and nearly every man was aware that he left behind him some one who would watch for the prayer for the preservation of those who travel by land or by water, and think of him, as God-protected the more for the earnestness of the response then given.

There, too, lay the dead of many generations; for St. Nicholas had been the parish church ever since Monkshaven was a town, and the large churchyard was rich in the dead. Masters, mariners, shipowners, seamen: it seemed strange how few other trades were represented in that great plain so full of upright gravestones. Here and there was a memorial stone, placed by some survivor of a large family, most of whom perished at sea: – 'Supposed to have perished in the Greenland seas,' 'Shipwrecked in the Baltic,' 'Drowned off the coast of Iceland.' There was a strange sensation, as if the cold sea-winds must bring with them the dim phantoms of those lost sailors, who had died far from their homes, and from the hallowed ground where their fathers lay.

Each flight of steps up to this churchyard ended in a small flat space, on which a wooden seat was placed. On this particular Sunday, all these seats were filled by aged people, breathless with the unusual exertion of climbing. You could see the church stair,* as it was called, from nearly every part of the town, and the figures of the numerous climbers, diminished by distance, looked like a busy ant-hill, long before the bell began to ring for afternoon service. All who could manage it had put on a bit of black in token of mourning; it might be very little; an old ribbon, a rusty piece of crape; but some sign of mourning was shown by every one down to the little child in its mother's arms, that innocently clutched the piece of rosemary to be thrown into the grave 'for remembrance.' Darley, the seaman shot by the press-gang, nine leagues off St. Abb's Head, was to be buried to-day, at the accustomed time for the funerals* of the poorer classes, directly after evening service, and there were only the sick and their nurse-tenders who did not come forth to show their feeling for the man whom they looked upon as murdered. The crowd of vessels in harbour bore their flags half-mast high; and the crews were making their way through the High Street. The gentlefolk of Monkshaven, full of indignation at this interference with their ships, full of sympathy with the family who had lost their son and brother almost within sight of his home, came in unusual numbers - no lack of patterns for Sylvia; but her thoughts were far otherwise and more suitably occupied. The unwonted sternness and solemnity visible on the countenances of all whom she met awed and affected her. She did not speak in reply to Molly's remarks on the dress or appearance of those who struck her. She felt as if these speeches jarred on her, and annoyed her almost to irritation; yet Molly had come all the way to Monkshaven Church in her service, and deserved forbearance accordingly. The two mounted the steps alongside of many people; few words were exchanged, even at the breathing places, so often the little centres of gossip. Looking over the sea there was not a sail to be seen; it seemed bared of life, as if to be in serious harmony with what was going on inland.

The church was of old Norman architecture; low and massive outside: inside, of vast space, only a quarter of which was filled on ordinary Sundays. The walls were disfigured by numerous tablets of black and white marble intermixed, and the usual ornamentation of that style of memorial as erected in the last century, of weeping willows, urns, and drooping figures, with here and there a ship in full sail, or an anchor, where the seafaring idea prevalent through the place had launched out into a little originality. There was no woodwork, the church had been stripped of that, most probably when the neighbouring monastery had been destroyed. There were large square pews, lined with green baize, with the names of the families of the most flourishing shipowners painted white on the doors; there were pews, not so large, and not lined at all, for the farmers and shopkeepers of the parish; and numerous heavy oaken benches which, by the united efforts of several men, might be brought within earshot of the pulpit.* These were being removed into the most convenient situations when Molly and Sylvia entered the church, and after two or three whispered sentences they took their seats on one of these.

The vicar of Monkshaven was a kindly, peaceable old man, hating strife and troubled waters above everything. He was a vehement Tory in theory, as became his cloth in those days. He had two bugbears to fear – the French and the Dissenters. It was difficult to say of which he had the worst opinion and the most intense dread. Perhaps he hated the Dissenters most, because they came nearer in contact with him than the French; besides, the French had the excuse of being Papists, while the Dissenters might have belonged to the Church of England if they had not been utterly depraved. Yet in practice Dr Wilson did not object to dine with Mr Fishburn, who was a personal friend and follower of Wesley,* but then, as the doctor would say, 'Wesley was an Oxford man, and that makes him a gentleman; and he was an ordained minister of the Church of England, so that grace can never depart from him.' But I do not know what excuse he would have alleged for sending broth and vegetables to old Ralph Thompson, a rabid Independent, who had been given to abusing the Church and the vicar, from a Dissenting pulpit, as long as ever he could mount the stairs. However, that inconsistency between Dr Wilson's theories and practice was not generally known in Monkshaven, so we have nothing to do with it.

Dr Wilson had had a very difficult part to play, and a still more difficult sermon to write, during this last week. The Darley who had been killed was the son of the vicar's gardener, and Dr Wilson's sympathies as a man had been all on the bereaved father's side. But then he had received, as the oldest magistrate in the neighbourhood, a letter from the captain of the *Aurora*, explanatory and exculpatory. Darley had been resisting the orders of an officer in his Majesty's service. What would become of due subordination and loyalty, and the interests of the service, and the chances of beating those confounded French, if such conduct as Darley's was to be encouraged? (Poor Darley! he was past all evil effects of human encouragement now!)

So the vicar mumbled hastily over a sermon on the text, 'In the midst of life we are in death;'* which might have done as well for a baby cut off in a convulsion-fit as for the strong man shot down with all his eager blood hot within him, by men as hot-blooded as himself. But once when the old doctor's eye caught the up-turned, straining gaze of the father Darley, seeking with all his soul to find a grain of holy comfort in the chaff of words, his conscience smote him. Had he nothing to say that should calm anger and revenge with spiritual power? no breath of the comforter to soothe repining into resignation? But again the discord between the laws of man and the laws of Christ stood before him; and he gave up the attempt to do more than he was doing, as beyond his power. Though the hearers went away as full of anger as they had entered the church, and some with a dull feeling of disappointment as to what they had got there, yet no one felt anything but kindly towards the old vicar. His simple, happy life led amongst them for forty years, and open to all men in its daily course; his sweet-tempered, cordial ways; his practical kindness, made him beloved by all; and neither he nor they thought much or cared much for admiration of his talents. Respect for his office was all the respect he thought of; and that was conceded to him from old traditional and hereditary association. In looking back to the last century, it appears curious to see how little our ancestors had the power of putting two things together, and perceiving either the discord or harmony thus produced. Is it because we are farther off from those times, and have, consequently, a greater range of vision? Will our descendants have a wonder about us, such as we have about the inconsistency of our forefathers, or a surprise at our blindness that we do not perceive that, holding such and such opinions, our course of action must be so and so, or that the logical consequence of particular opinions must be convictions which at present we hold in abhorrence? It seems puzzling to look back on men such as our vicar, who almost held the doctrine that the King could do no wrong, yet were ever ready to talk of the glorious Revolution,* and to abuse the Stuarts for having entertained the same doctrine, and tried to put it in practice. But such discrepancies ran through good men's lives in those days. It is well for us that we live at the present time, when everybody is logical and consistent. This little discussion must be taken in place of Dr Wilson's sermon, of which no one could remember more than the text half an hour after it was delivered. Even the doctor himself had the recollection of the words he had uttered swept out of his mind, as, having doffed his gown and donned his surplice, he came out of the dusk of his vestry and went to the church-door, looking into the broad light which came upon the plain of the churchyard on the cliffs; for the sun had not yet set, and the pale moon was slowly rising through the silvery mist that obscured the distant moors. There was a thick, dense crowd, all still and silent, looking away from the church and the vicar, who awaited the bringing of the dead. They were watching the slow black line winding up the long steps, resting their heavy burden here and there, standing in silent groups at each landing-place; now lost to sight as a piece of broken, overhanging ground intervened, now emerging suddenly nearer; and overhead the great church bell, with its mediæval inscription, familiar to the vicar, if to no one else who heard it,

I to the grave do summon all,

kept on its heavy booming monotone, with which no other sound from land or sea, near or distant, intermingled, except the cackle of the geese on some far-away farm on the moors, as they were coming home to roost; and that one noise from so great a distance seemed only to deepen the stillness. Then there was a little movement in the crowd; a little pushing from side to side, to make a path for the corpse and its bearers – an aggregate of the fragments of room.

With bent heads and spent strength, those who carried the coffin moved on; behind came the poor old gardener, a brown-black funeral cloak thrown over his homely dress, and supporting his wife with steps scarcely less feeble than her own. He had come to church that afternoon, with a promise to her that he would return to lead her to the funeral of her firstborn; for he felt, in his sore perplexed heart, full of indignation and dumb anger, as if he must go and hear something which should exorcise the unwonted longing for revenge that disturbed his grief, and made him conscious of that great blank of consolation which faithfulness produces. And for the time he was faithless. How came God to permit such cruel injustice of man? Permitting it, He could not be good. Then what was life, and what was death, but woe and despair? The beautiful solemn words of the ritual had done him good, and restored much of his faith. Though he could not understand why such sorrow had befallen him any more than before, he had come back to something of his childlike trust; he kept saying to himself in a whisper, as he mounted the weary steps, 'It is the Lord's doing;'* and the repetition soothed him unspeakably. Behind this old couple followed their children, grown men and women, come from distant place or farmhouse service; the servants at the vicarage, and many a neighbour, anxious to show their sympathy, and most of the sailors from the crews of the vessels in port, joined in procession, and followed the dead body into the church.

There was too great a crowd immediately within the door for Sylvia and Molly to go in again, and they accordingly betook themselves to the place where the deep grave was waiting, wide and hungry, to receive its dead. There, leaning against the headstones all around, were many standing – looking over the broad and placid sea, and turned to the soft salt air which blew on their hot eyes and rigid faces; for no one spoke of all that number. They were thinking of the violent death of him over whom the solemn words were now being said in the gray old church, scarcely out of their hearing, had not the sound been broken by the measured lapping of the tide far beneath.

Suddenly every one looked round towards the path from the churchyard steps. Two sailors were supporting a ghastly figure that, with feeble motions, was drawing near the open grave.

'It's t' specksioneer as tried to save him! It's him as was left for dead!' the people murmured round.

'It's Charley Kinraid, as I'm a sinner!' said Molly, starting forward to greet her cousin.

But as he came on, she saw that all his strength was needed for the mere action of walking. The sailors, in their strong sympathy, had yielded to his earnest entreaty, and carried him up the steps, in order that he might see the last of his messmate. They placed him near the grave, resting against a stone; and he was hardly there before the vicar came forth, and the great crowd poured out of the church, following the body to the grave.

Sylvia was so much wrapt up in the solemnity of the occasion, that she had no thought to spare at the first moment for the pale and haggard figure opposite; much less was she aware of her cousin Philip, who now singling her out for the first time from among the crowd, pressed to her side, with an intention of companionship and protection.

As the service went on, ill-checked sobs rose from behind the two girls, who were among the foremost in the crowd, and by-and-by the cry and the wail became general. Sylvia's tears rained down her face, and her distress became so evident that it attracted the attention of many in that inner circle. Among others who noticed it, the specksioneer's hollow eyes were caught by the sight of the innocent blooming childlike face opposite to him, and he wondered if she were a relation;

yet, seeing that she bore no badge of mourning, he rather concluded that she must have been a sweetheart of the dead man.

And now all was over: the rattle of the gravel on the coffin; the last long, lingering look of friends and lovers; the rosemary sprigs had been cast down by all who were fortunate enough to have brought them – and oh! how much Sylvia wished she had remembered this last act of respect – and slowly the outer rim of the crowd began to slacken and disappear.

Now Philip spoke to Sylvia.

'I never dreamt of seeing you here. I thought my aunt always went to Kirk Moorside.'

'I came with Molly Corney,' said Sylvia. 'Mother is staying at home with feyther.'

'How's his rheumatics?' asked Philip.

But at the same moment Molly took hold of Sylvia's hand, and said—

'A want t' get round and speak to Charley. Mother 'll be main and glad to hear as he's getten out; though, for sure, he looks as though he'd ha' been better in 's bed. Come, Sylvia.'

And Philip, fain to keep with Sylvia, had to follow the two girls close up to the specksioneer, who was preparing for his slow laborious walk back to his lodgings. He stopped on seeing his cousin.

'Well, Molly,' said he, faintly, putting out his hand, but his eye passing her face to look at Sylvia in the background, her tear-stained face full of shy admiration of the nearest approach to a hero she had ever seen.

'Well, Charley, a niver was so taken aback as when a saw yo' theere, like a ghost, a-standin' agin a gravestone. How white and wan yo' do look!'

'Ay!' said he, wearily, 'wan and weak enough.'

'But I hope you're getting better, sir,' said Sylvia, in a low voice, longing to speak to him, and yet wondering at her own temerity.

'Thank you, my lass. I'm o'er th' worst.'

He sighed heavily.

Philip now spoke.

'We're doing him no kindness a-keeping him standing here i' t' night-fall, and him so tired.' And he made as though he would turn away. Kinraid's two sailor friends backed up Philip's words with such urgency, that, somehow, Sylvia thought they had been to blame in speaking to him, and blushed excessively with the idea.

'Yo'll come and be nursed at Moss Brow, Charley,' said Molly; and Sylvia dropped her little maidenly curtsey, and said, 'Good-by;' and went away, wondering how Molly could talk so freely to such a hero; but then, to be sure, he was a cousin, and probably a sweetheart, and that would make a great deal of difference, of course.

Meanwhile her own cousin kept close by her side.

CHAPTER VII

TÊTE-À-TÊTE. – THE WILL

'AND now tell me all about t' folk at home,' said Philip, evidently preparing to walk back with the girls. He generally came to Haytersbank every Sunday afternoon, so Sylvia knew what she had to expect the moment she became aware of his neighbourhood in the churchyard.

'My feyther's been sadly troubled with his rheumatics this week past; but he's a vast better now, thank you kindly.' Then, addressing herself to Molly, she asked, 'Has your cousin a doctor to look after him?'

'Ay, for sure!' said Molly, quickly; for though she knew nothing about the matter, she was determined to suppose that her cousin had everything becoming an invalid as well as a hero. 'He's well-to-do, and can afford iverything as he needs,' continued she. 'His feyther's left him money, and he were a farmer out up i' Northumberland, and he's reckoned such a specksioneer as niver, niver was, and gets what wage he asks for and a share on every whale he harpoons beside.'

'I reckon he'll have to make himself scarce on this coast for awhile, at any rate,' said Philip.

'An' what for should he?' asked Molly, who never liked Philip at the best of times, and now, if he was going to disparage her cousin in any way, was ready to take up arms and do battle.

'Why, they do say as he fired the shot as has killed some o' the men-o'-war's men, and, of course, if he has, he'll have to stand his trial if he's caught.'

'What lies people do say!' exclaimed Molly. 'He niver killed nought but whales, a'll be bound; or, if he did, it were all right and proper as he should, when they were for stealing him an' all t' others, and did kill poor Darley as we come fra' seein' buried. A suppose, now yo're such a Quaker* that, if some one was to break through fra' t' other side o' this dyke, and offer for to murder Sylvia and me, yo'd look on wi' yo'r hands hanging by yo'r side.'

'But t' press-gang had law on their side, and were doing nought but what they'd warrant for.'

'Th' tender's gone away, as if she were ashamed o' what she'd done,' said Sylvia, 'and t' flag's down fra' o'er the Randyvowse. There 'll be no more press-ganging here awhile.'

'No; feyther says,' continued Molly, 'as they've made t' place too hot t' hold 'em, coming so strong afore people had getten used to their ways o' catchin' up poor lads just come fra' t' Greenland seas. T' folks ha' their blood so up they'd think no harm o' fighting 'em i' t' streets – ay, and o' killing 'em, too, if they were for using fire-arms, as t' *Aurora*'s men did.'

'Women is so fond o' bloodshed,' said Philip; 'for t' hear you talk, who'd ha' thought you'd just come fra' crying ower the grave of a man who was killed by violence? I should ha' thought you'd seen enough of what sorrow comes o' fighting. Why, them lads o' t' *Aurora* as they say Kinraid shot down had fathers and mothers, maybe, a looking out for them to come home.'

'I don't think he could ha' killed them,' said Sylvia; 'he looked so gentle.'

But Molly did not like this half-and-half view of the case.

'A dare say he did kill 'em dead; he's not one to do things by halves. And a think he served 'em reet, that's what a do.'

'Is na' this Hester, as serves in Foster's shop?' asked Sylvia, in a low voice, as a young woman came through a stile in the stone wall by the roadside, and suddenly appeared before them.

'Yes,' said Philip. 'Why, Hester, where have you been?' he asked, as they drew near.

Hester reddened a little, and then replied, in her slow, quiet way—

'I've been sitting with Betsy Darley – her that is bed-ridden. It were lonesome for her when the others were away at the burying.'

And she made as though she would have passed; but Sylvia, all her sympathies alive for the relations of the murdered man, wanted to ask more questions, and put her hand on Hester's arm to detain her a moment. Hester suddenly drew back a little, reddened still more, and then replied fully and quietly to all Sylvia asked.

In the agricultural counties, and among the class to which these four persons belonged, there is little analysis of motive or comparison of characters and actions, even at this present day of enlightenment. Sixty or seventy years ago there was still less. I do not mean that amongst thoughtful and serious people there was not much reading of such books as *Mason on Self-Knowledge*, and *Law's Serious Call*,* or that there were not the experiences of the Wesleyans, that were related at class-meeting for the edification of the hearers. But, taken as a general rule, it may be said that few knew what manner of men they were, compared to the numbers now who are fully conscious of their virtues, qualities, failings, and weaknesses, and who go about comparing others with themselves – not in a spirit of Pharisaism and arrogance, but with a vivid self-consciousness that more than anything else deprives characters of freshness and originality.

To return to the party we left standing on the high-raised footway that ran alongside of the bridle-road to Haytersbank.

Sylvia had leisure in her heart to think 'how good Hester is for sitting with the poor bed-ridden sister of Darley!' without having a pang of self-depreciation in the comparison of her own conduct with that she was capable of so fully appreciating. She had gone to church for the ends of vanity, and remained to the funeral for curiosity and the pleasure of the excitement. In this way a modern young lady would have condemned herself, and therefore lost the simple, purifying pleasure of admiration of another.

Hester passed onwards, going down the hill towards the town. The other three walked slowly on. All were silent for a few moments, then Sylvia said—

'How good she is!'

And Philip replied with ready warmth,—

'Yes, she is; no one knows how good but us, who live in the same house wi' her.'

'Her mother is an old Quakeress, bean't she?' Molly inquired.

'Alice Rose is a Friend, if that is what you mean,' said Philip.

'Well, well! some folk's so particular. Is William Coulson a Quaker, by which a mean a Friend?'

'Yes; they're all on 'em right-down good folk.'

'Deary me! What a wonder yo' can speak to such sinners as Sylvia and me, after keepin' company with so much goodness,' said Molly, who had not yet forgiven Philip for doubting Kinraid's power of killing men. 'Is na' it, Sylvia?'

But Sylvia was too highly strung for banter. If she had not been one of those who went to mock, but remained to pray, she had gone to church with the thought of the cloak-that-was-to-be uppermost in her mind, and she had come down the long church stair with life and death suddenly become real to her mind, the enduring sea and hills forming a contrasting background to the vanishing away of man. She was full of a solemn wonder as to the abiding-place of the souls of the dead, and a childlike dread lest the number of the elect* should be accomplished before she was included therein. How people could ever be merry again after they had been at a funeral, she could not imagine; so she answered gravely, and slightly beside the question:

'I wonder if I was a Friend if I should be good?'

'Gi' me your red cloak, that's all, when yo' turn Quaker; they'll none let thee wear scarlet, so it 'll be of no use t' thee.'

'I think thou'rt good enough as thou art,' said Philip, tenderly – at least as tenderly as he durst, for he knew by experience that it did not do to alarm her girlish coyness. Either one speech or the other made Sylvia silent; neither was accordant to her mood of mind, so perhaps both contributed to her quietness.

'Folk say William Coulson looks sweet on Hester Rose,' said Molly, always up in Monkshaven gossip. It was in the form of an assertion, but was said in the tone of a question, and as such Philip replied to it.

'Yes, I think he likes her a good deal; but he's so quiet, I never feel sure. John and Jeremiah would like the match, I've a notion.'

And now they came to the stile which had filled Philip's eye for some minutes past, though neither of the others had perceived they were so near it; the stile which led to Moss Brow from the road into the fields that sloped down to Haystersbank. Here they would leave Molly, and now would begin the delicious *tête-à-tête* walk, which Philip always tried to make as lingering as possible. To-day he was anxious to show his sympathy with Sylvia, as far as he could read what was passing in her mind; but how was he to guess the multitude of tangled thoughts in that unseen receptacle? A resolution to be good, if she could, and always to be thinking on death, so that what seemed to her now as simply impossible, might come true – that she might 'dread the grave as little as her bed;'* a wish that Philip were not coming home with her; a wonder if the specksioneer really had killed a man, an idea which made her shudder; yet from the awful fascination about it, her imagination was compelled to dwell on the tall, gaunt figure, and try to recall the wan countenance; a hatred and desire of revenge on the press-gang, so vehement that it sadly militated against her intention of trying to be good; all these notions, and wonders, and fancies, were whirling about in Sylvia's brain, and at one of their promptings she spoke,—

'How many miles away is t' Greenland seas? – I mean, how long do they take to reach?'

'I don't know; ten days or a fortnight, or more, maybe. I'll ask.'

'Oh! feyther 'll tell me all about it. He's been there many a time.'

'I say, Sylvie! My aunt said I were to give you lessons this winter i' writing and ciphering. I can begin to come up now, two evenings, maybe, a week. T' shop closes early after November comes in.'

Sylvia did not like learning, and did not want him for her teacher; so she answered in a dry little tone,—

'It'll use a deal o' candle-light; mother 'll not like that. I can't see to spell wi'out a candle close at my elbow.'

'Niver mind about candles. I can bring up a candle wi' me, for I should be burning one at Alice Rose's.'

So that excuse would not do. Sylvia beat her brains for another.

'Writing cramps my hand so, I can't do any sewing for a day after; and feyther wants his shirts very bad.'

'But, Sylvia, I'll teach you geography, and ever such a vast o' fine things about t' countries, on t' map.'

'Is t' Arctic seas down on t' map?' she asked, in a tone of greater interest.

'Yes! Arctics, and tropics, and equator, and equinoctial line; we'll take em turn and turn about; we'll do writing and ciphering one night, and geography t' other.'

Philip spoke with pleasure at the prospect, but Sylvia relaxed into indifference.

'I'm no scholard; it's like throwing away labour to teach me, I'm such a dunce at my book. Now there's Betsy Corney, third girl, her as is younger than Molly, she'd be a credit to you. There niver was such a lass for pottering ower books.'

If Philip had had his wits about him, he would have pretended to listen to this proposition of a change of pupils, and then possibly Sylvia might have repented making it. But he was too much mortified to be diplomatic.

'My aunt asked me to teach *you* a bit, not any neighbour's lass.'

'Well! if I mun be taught, I mun; but I'd raythr be whipped and ha' done with it,' was Sylvia's ungracious reply.

A moment afterwards, she repented of her little spirit of unkindness, and thought that she should not like to die that night without making friends. Sudden death was very present in her thoughts since the funeral. So she instinctively chose the best method of making friends again, and slipped her hand into his, as he walked a little sullenly at her side. She was half afraid, however, when she found it firmly held, and that she could not draw it away again without making what she called in her own mind a 'fuss.' So, hand in hand, they slowly and silently came up to the door of Haytersbank Farm; not unseen by Bell Robson, who sate in the window-seat, with her Bible open upon her knee. She had read her chapter aloud to herself, and now she could see no longer, even if she had wished to read more; but she gazed out into the darkening air, and a dim look of contentment came like moonshine over her face when she saw the cousins approach.

'That's my prayer day and night,' said she to herself.

But there was no unusual aspect of gladness on her face, as she lighted the candle to give them a more cheerful welcome.

'Wheere's feyther?' said Sylvia, looking round the room for Daniel.

'He's been to Kirk Moorside Church, for t' see a bit o' th' world, as he ca's it. And sin' then he's gone out to th' cattle; for Kester 's ta'en his turn of playing hissel', now that father's better.'

'I've been talking to Sylvia,' said Philip, his head still full of his pleasant plan, his hand still tingling from the touch of hers, 'about turning schoolmaster, and coming up here two nights a week for t' teach her a bit o' writing and ciphering.'

'And geography,' put in Sylvia; 'for,' thought she, 'if I'm to learn them things I don't care a pin about, anyhow I'll learn what I do care to know, if it 'll tell me about t' Greenland seas, and how far they're off.'

That same evening, a trio alike in many outward circumstances sate in a small neat room in a house opening out of a confined court on the hilly side of the High Street of Monkshaven – a mother, her only child, and the young man who silently loved that daughter, and was favoured by Alice Rose, though not by Hester.

When the latter returned from her afternoon's absence, she stood for a minute or two on the little flight of steep steps, whitened to a snowy whiteness; the aspect of the whole house partook of the same character of irreproachable cleanliness. It was wedged up into a space which necessitated all sorts of odd projections and irregularities in order to obtain sufficient light for the interior; and if ever the being situated in a dusky, confined corner might have been made an excuse for dirt, Alice Rose's house had that apology. Yet the small diamond panes of glass in the casement window were kept so bright and clear that a great sweet-scented-leaved geranium grew and flourished, though it did not flower profusely. The leaves seemed to fill the air with fragrance as soon as Hester summoned up energy enough to open the door. Perhaps that was because the young Quaker, William Coulson, was crushing one between his finger and thumb, while waiting to set down Alice's next words. For the old woman, who looked as if many years of life remained in her yet, was solemnly dictating her last will and testament.

It had been on her mind for many months; for she had something to leave beyond the mere furniture of the house. Something – a few pounds – in the hands of John and Jeremiah Foster, her cousins: and it was they who had suggested the duty on which she was engaged. She had asked William Coulson to write down her wishes, and he had consented, though with some fear and trepidation; for he had an idea that he was infringing on a lawyer's prerogative, and that, for aught he knew, he might be prosecuted for making a will without a licence, just as a man might be punished for selling wine and spirits without going through the preliminary legal forms that give permission for such a sale. But to his suggestion that Alice should employ a lawyer, she had replied—

'That would cost me five pounds sterling; and thee canst do it as well, if thee'll but attend to my words.'

Se he had bought, at her desire, a black-edged sheet of fine-wove paper, and a couple of good pens, on the previous Saturday; and while waiting for her to begin her dictation, and full serious thought himself, he had almost unconsciously made the grand flourish at the top of the paper which he had learnt at school, and which was there called a spread-eagle.

'What art thee doing there?' asked Alice, suddenly alive to his proceedings.

Without a word he showed her his handiwork.

'It's a vanity,' said she, 'and 't may make t' will not stand. Folk may think I were na' in my right mind, if they see such fly-legs and cob-webs a-top. Write, "This is my doing, William Coulson, and none of Alice Rose's, she being in her sound mind." '

'I don't think it's needed,' said William. Nevertheless he wrote down the words.

'Hast thee put that I'm in my sound mind and seven senses? Then make the sign of the Trinity, and write, "In the name of the Father, the Son, and the Holy Ghost." '

'Is that the right way o' beginning a will?' said Coulson, a little startled.

'My father, and my father's father, and my husband had it a-top of theirs, and I'm noane going for to cease fra' following after them, for they were godly men, though my husband were o' t' episcopal persuasion.'

'It's done,' said William.

'Hast thee dated it?' asked Alice.

'Nay.'

'Then date it third day, ninth month. Now, art ready?'

Coulson nodded.

'I, Alice Rose, do leave my furniture (that is, my bed and chest o' drawers, for thy bed and things is thine, and not mine), and settle, and saucepans, and dresser, and table, and kettle, and all the rest of my furniture, to my lawful and only daughter, Hester Rose. I think that's safe for her to have all, is 't not, William?'

'I think so, too,' said he, writing on all the time.

'And thee shalt have t' roller and paste-board, because thee's so fond o' puddings and cakes. It 'll serve thy wife after I'm gone, and I trust she'll boil her paste long enough, for that's been t' secret o' mine, and thee'll noane be so easy t' please.'

'I din't reckon on marriage,' said William.

'Thee'll marry,' said Alice. 'Thee likes to have thy victuals hot and comfortable; and there's noane many but a wife as'll look after that for t' please thee.'

'I know who could please me,' sighed forth William, 'but I can't please her.'

Alice looked sharply at him from over her spectacles, which she had put on the better to think about the disposal of her property.

'Thee art thinking on our Hester,' said she, plainly out.

He started a little, but looked up at her and met her eye.

'Hester cares noane for me,' said he, dejectedly.

'Bide a while, my lad,' said Alice, kindly. 'Young women don't always know their own minds. Thee and her would make a marriage after my own heart; and the Lord has been very good to me hitherto, and I think He'll bring it t' pass. But don't thee let on as thee cares for her so much. I sometimes think she wearies o' thy looks and thy ways. Show up thy manly heart, and make as though thee had much else to think on, and no leisure for to dawdle after her, and she'll think a deal more on thee. And now mend thy pen for a fresh start. I give and bequeath – did thee put "give and bequeath," at th' beginning?'

'Nay,' said William, looking back. 'Thee didst not tell me "give and bequeath!"'

'Then it won't be legal, and my bit o' furniture 'll be taken to London, and put into chancery, and Hester will have noane on it.'

'I can write it over,' said William.

'Well, write it clear then, and put a line under it to show

those are my special words. Hast thee done it? Then now start afresh. I give and bequeath my book o' sermons, as is bound in good calfskin, and lies on the third shelf o' corner cupboard at the right hand o' t' fire-place, to Philip Hepburn; for I reckon he's as fond o' reading sermons as thee art o' light, well-boiled paste, and I'd be glad for each on ye to have somewhat ye like for to remember me by. Is that down? There; now for my cousins John and Jeremiah. They are rich i' world's gear, but they'll prize what I leave 'em if I could only onbethink me what they would like. Hearken! Is na' that our Hester's step? Put it away, quick! I'm noane for grieving her wi' telling her what I've been about. We'll take a turn at t' will next First Day;* it will serve us for several Sabbaths to come, and maybe I can think on something as will suit cousin John and cousin Jeremiah afore then.'

Hester, as was mentioned, paused a minute or two before lifting the latch of the door. When she entered there was no unusual sign of writing about; only Will Coulson looking very red, and crushing and smelling at the geranium leaf.

Hester came in briskly, with the little stock of enforced cheerfulness she had stopped at the door to acquire. But it faded away along with the faint flush of colour in her cheeks; and the mother's quick eye immediately noted the wan heavy look of care.

'I have kept t' pot in t' oven; it'll have a'most got a' t' goodness out of t' tea by now, for it'll be an hour since I made it. Poor lass, thou look'st as if thou needed a good cup o' tea. It were dree work sitting wi' Betsy Darley, were it? And how does she look on her affliction?'

'She takes it sore to heart,' said Hester, taking off her hat, and folding and smoothing away her cloak, before putting them in the great oak chest (or 'ark,' as it was called), in which they were laid from Sunday to Sunday.

As she opened the lid a sweet scent of dried lavender and rose-leaves came out. William stepped hastily forwards to hold up the heavy lid for her. She lifted up her head, looked at him full with her serene eyes, and thanked him for his little service. Then she took a creepie-stool* and sate down on the side of the fireplace, having her back to the window.

The hearth was of the same spotless whiteness as the steps; all that was black about the grate was polished to the utmost extent; all that was of brass, like the handle of the oven, was burnished bright. Her mother placed the little black earthenware teapot, in which the tea had been stewing, on the table, where cups and saucers were already set for four, and a large plate of bread and butter cut. Then they sate round the table, bowed their heads, and kept silence for a minute or two.

When this grace was ended, and they were about to begin, Alice said, as if without premeditation, but in reality with a keen shrinking of heart out of sympathy with her child—

'Philip would have been in to his tea by now, I reckon, if he'd been coming.'

William looked up suddenly at Hester; her mother carefully turned her head another way. But she answered quite quietly—

'He'll be gone to his aunt's at Haytersbank. I met him at t' top o' t' Brow, with his cousin and Molly Corney.'

'He's a deal there,' said William.

'Yes,' said Hester. 'It's likely; him and his aunt come from Carlisle-way, and must needs cling together in these strange parts.'

'I saw him at the burying of yon Darley,' said William.

'It were a vast o' people went past th' entry end,' said Alice. 'It were a'most like election time; I were just come back fra' meeting when they were all going up th' church steps. I met yon sailor as, they say, used violence and did murder; he looked like a ghost, though whether it were his bodily wounds, or the sense of his sins stirring within him, it's not for me to say. And by t' time I was back here and settled to my Bible, t' folk were returning, and it were tramp, tramp, past th' entry end for better nor a quarter of an hour.'

'They say Kinraid has getten slugs and gun-shot in his side,' said Hester.

'He's niver one Charley Kinraid, for sure, as I knowed at Newcastle,' said William Coulson, roused to sudden and energetic curiosity.

'I don't know,' replied Hester; 'they call him just Kinraid; and Betsy Darley says he's t' most daring specksioneer of all that go off this coast to t' Greenland seas. But he's been in Newcastle, for I mind me she said her poor brother met with him there.'

'How didst thee come to know him?' inquired Alice.

'I cannot abide him if it is Charley,' said William. 'He kept company with my poor sister as is dead for better nor two year, and then he left off coming to see her and went wi' another girl, and it just broke her heart.'

'He don't look now as if he iver could play at that game again,' said Alice; 'he has had a warning fra' the Lord. Whether it be a call no one can tell. But to my eyne he looks as if he had been called, and was going.'

'Then he'll meet my sister,' said William, solemnly; 'and I hope the Lord will make it clear to him, then, how he killed her, as sure as he shot down yon sailors; an' if there's a gnashing o' teeth* for murder i' that other place, I reckon he'll have his share on't. He's a bad man yon.'

'Betsy said he were such a friend to her brother as niver was; and he's sent her word and promised to go and see her, first place he goes out to.'

But William only shook his head, and repeated his last words,—

'He's a bad man, he is.'

When Philip came home that Sunday night, he found only Alice up to receive him. The usual bedtime in the household was nine o'clock, and it was but ten minutes past the hour; but Alice looked displeased and stern.

'Thee art late, lad,' said she, shortly.

'I'm sorry; it's a long way from my uncle's, and I think clocks are different,' said he, taking out his watch to compare it with the round moon's face that told the time to Alice.

'I know nought about thy uncle's, but thee art late. Take thy candle, and begone.'

If Alice made any reply to Philip's 'good-night,' he did not hear it.

CHAPTER VIII

ATTRACTION AND REPULSION

A FORTNIGHT had passed over and winter was advancing with rapid strides. In bleak northern farmsteads there was much to be done before November weather should make the roads too heavy for half-fed horses to pull carts through. There was the turf, pared up on the distant moors, and left out to dry, to be carried home and stacked; the brown fern was to be stored up for winter bedding for the cattle; for straw was scarce and dear in those parts; even for thatching, heather (or rather ling) was used. Then there was meat to salt while it could be had; for, in default of turnips and mangold-wurzel, there was a great slaughtering of barren cows as soon as the summer herbage failed; and good housewives stored up their Christmas piece of beef in pickle before Martinmas* was over. Corn was to be ground while yet it could be carried to the distant mill; the great racks for oat-cake, that swung at the top of the kitchen, had to be filled. And last of all came the pig-killing, when the second frost set in. For up in the north there is an idea that the ice stored in the first frost will melt, and the meat cured then taint; the first frost is good for nothing but to be thrown away, as they express it.

There came a breathing-time after this last event. The house had had its last autumn cleaning, and was neat and bright from top to bottom, from one end to another. The turf was led; the coal carted up from Monkshaven; the wood stored; the corn ground; the pig killed, and the hams and head and hands lying in salt. The butcher had been glad to take the best parts of a pig of Dame Robson's careful feeding; but there was unusual plenty in the Haytersbank pantry; and as Bell surveyed it one morning, she said to her husband—

'I wonder if yon poor sick chap at Moss Brow would fancy some o' my sausages. They're something to crack on, for they are made fra' an old Cumberland receipt, as is not known i' Yorkshire yet.'

'Thou's allays so set upo' Cumberland ways!' said her husband, not displeased with the suggestion, however. 'Still, when folk's sick they han their fancies, and maybe Kinraid 'll be glad o' thy sausages. I ha' known sick folk tak' t' eating snails.'

This was not complimentary, perhaps. But Daniel went on to say that he did not mind if he stepped over with the sausages himself, when it was too late to do anything else. Sylvia longed to offer to accompany her father; but, somehow, she did not like to propose it. Towards dusk she came to her mother to ask for the key of the great bureau that stood in the house-place as a state piece of furniture, although its use was to contain the family's best wearing apparel, and stores of linen, such as might be supposed to be more needed upstairs.

'What for do yo' want my keys?' asked Bell.

'Only just to get out one of t' damask napkins.'

'The best napkins, as my mother span?'

'Yes!' said Sylvia, her colour heightening. 'I thought as how it would set off t' sausages.'

'A good clean homespun cloth will serve them better,' said Bell, wondering in her own mind what was come over the girl, to be thinking of setting off sausages that were to be eaten, not to be looked at like a picture-book. She might have wondered still more, if she had seen Sylvia steal round to the little flower border she had persuaded Kester to make under the wall at the sunny side of the house, and gather the two or three Michaelmas daisies, and the one bud of the China rose, that, growing against the kitchen chimney, had escaped the frost; and then, when her mother was not looking, softly open the cloth inside of the little basket that contained the sausages and a fresh egg or two, and lay her autumn blossoms in one of the folds of the towel.

After Daniel, now pretty clear of his rheumatism, had had his afternoon meal (tea was a Sunday treat), he prepared to set out on his walk to Moss Brow; but as he was taking his stick he caught the look on Sylvia's face, and unconsciously interpreted its dumb wistfulness.

'Missus,' said he, 't' wench has nought more t' do, has she? She may as well put on her cloak and step down wi' me, and see Molly a bit; she'll be company like.'

Bell considered.

'There's t' yarn for thy stockings as is yet to spin; but she can go, for I'll do a bit at 't mysel', and there's nought else agate.'

'Put on thy things in a jiffy, then, and let's be off,' said Daniel.

And Sylvia did not need another word. Down she came in a twinkling, dressed in her new red cloak and hood, her face peeping out of the folds of the latter, bright and blushing.

'Thou should'st na' ha' put on thy new cloak for a night walk to Moss Brow,' said Bell, shaking her head.

'Shall I go take it off, and put on my shawl?' asked Sylvia, a little dolefully.

'Na, na, come along! a'm noane goin' for t' wait o' women's chops and changes. Come along; come, Lassie!' (this last to his dog).

So Sylvia set off with a dancing heart and a dancing step, that had to be restrained to the sober gait her father chose. The sky above was bright and clear with the light of a thousand stars, the grass was crisping under their feet with the coming hoar frost; and as they mounted to the higher ground they could see the dark sea stretching away far below them. The night was very still, though now and then crisp sounds in the distant air sounded very near in the silence. Sylvia carried the basket, and looked like little Red Riding Hood. Her father had nothing to say, and did not care to make himself agreeable; but Sylvia enjoyed her own thoughts, and any conversation would have been a disturbance to her. The long monotonous roll of the distant waves, as the tide bore them in, the multitudinous rush* at last, and then the retreating rattle and trickle, as the baffled waters fell back over the shingle that skirted the sands, and divided them from the cliffs; her father's measured tread, and slow, even movement; Lassie's pattering – all lulled Sylvia into a reverie, of which she could not have given herself any definite account. But at length they arrived at Moss Brow, and with a sudden sigh she quitted the subjects of her dreamy meditations, and followed her father into the great house-place. It had a more comfortable aspect by night than by day. The fire was always kept up to a wasteful size, and the dancing blaze and the partial light of candles left much in shadow that was best ignored in such a disorderly family. But there was always a warm welcome to friends, however roughly given; and after the words of this were spoken, the next rose up equally naturally in the mind of Mrs Corney.

'And what will ye tak'? Eh! but t' measter 'll be fine and vexed at your comin' when he's away. He's off to Horncastle t' sell some colts, and he'll not be back till to-morrow's neet. But here's Charley Kinraid as we've getten to nurse up a bit, and' t' lads 'll be back fra' Monkshaven in a crack o' no time.'

All this was addressed to Daniel, to whom she knew that none but masculine company would be acceptable. Amongst uneducated people – whose range of subjects and interest do not extend beyond their daily life – it is natural that when the first blush and hurry of youth is over, there should be no great pleasure in the conversation of the other sex. Men have plenty to say to men, which in their estimation (gained from tradition and experience) women cannot understand; and farmers of a much later date than the one of which I am writing, would have contemptuously considered it as a loss of time to talk to women; indeed, they were often more communicative to the sheep-dog that accompanied them through all the day's work, and frequently became a sort of dumb confidant. Farmer Robson's Lassie now lay down at her master's feet, placed her nose between her paws, and watched with attentive eyes the preparations going on for refreshments – preparations which, to the disappointment of her canine heart, consisted entirely of tumblers and sugar.

'Where's t' wench?' said Robson, after he had shaken hands with Kinraid, and spoken a few words to him and to Mrs Corney. 'She's getten' a basket wi' sausages in 'em, as my missus has made, and she's a rare hand at sausages; there's noane like her in a' t' three Ridings, I'll be bound!'

For Daniel could praise his wife's powers in her absence, though he did not often express himself in an appreciative manner when she was by to hear. But Sylvia's quick sense caught up the manner in which Mrs Corney would apply the way in which her mother's housewifery had been exalted, and stepping forwards out of the shadow, she said,—

'Mother thought, maybe, you hadn't killed a pig yet, and sausages is always a bit savoury for any one who is na' well, and——'

She might have gone on but that she caught Kinraid's eyes looking at her with kindly admiration. She stopped speaking, and Mrs Corney took up the word—

'As for sausages, I ha' niver had a chance this year, else I stand again any one for t' making of 'em. Yorkshire hams 's a vast thought on, and I'll niver let another county woman say as she can make better sausages nor me. But, as I'm saying, I'd niver a chance; for our pig, as I were so fond on, and fed mysel', and as would ha' been fourteen stone by now if he were an ounce, and as knew me as well as any Christian, and a pig, as I may say, that I just idolized, went and took a fit a week after Michaelmas Day, and died, as if it had been to spite me; and t' next is na' ready for killing, nor wunnot be this six week. So I'm much beholden to your missus, and so's Charley, I'm sure; though he's ta'en a turn to betterin' sin' he came out here to be nursed.'

'I'm a deal better,' said Kinraid; 'a'most ready for t' press-gang to give chase to again.'

'But folk say they're gone off this coast for one while,' added Daniel.

'They're gone down towards Hull, as I've been told,' said Kinraid. 'But they're a deep set, they'll be here before we know where we are, some of these days.'

'See thee here!' said Daniel, exhibiting his maimed hand; 'a reckon a served 'em out time o' t' Ameriky war.' And he began the story Sylvia knew so well; for her father never made a new acquaintance but what he told him of his self-mutilation to escape the press-gang. It had been done, as he would himself have owned, to spite himself as well as them;

for it had obliged him to leave a sea-life, to which, in comparison, all life spent on shore was worse than nothing for dulness. For Robson had never reached that rank aboard ship which made his being unable to run up the rigging, or to throw a harpoon, or to fire off a gun, of no great consequence; so he had to be thankful that an opportune legacy enabled him to turn farmer, a great degradation in his opinion. But his blood warmed, as he told the specksioneer, towards a sailor, and he pressed Kinraid to beguile the time when he was compelled to be ashore, by coming over to see him at Haytersbank, whenever he felt inclined.

Sylvia, appearing to listen to Molly's confidences, was hearkening in reality to all this conversation between her father and the specksioneer; and at this invitation she became especially attentive.

Kinraid replied,—

'I'm much obliged to ye, I'm sure; maybe I can come and spend an ev'ning wi' you; but as soon as I'm got round a bit, I must go see my own people as live at Cullercoats, near Newcastle-upo'-Tyne.'

'Well, well!' said Daniel, rising to take leave, with unusual prudence as to the amount of his drink. 'Thou'lt see, thou'lt see! I shall be main glad to see thee, if thou'lt come. But I've na' lads to keep thee company, only one sprig of a wench. Sylvia, come here, an let's show thee to this young fellow!'

Sylvia came forwards, ruddy as any rose, and in a moment Kinraid recognized her as the pretty little girl he had seen crying so bitterly over Darley's grave. He rose up out of true sailor's gallantry, as she shyly approached and stood by her father's side, scarcely daring to lift her great soft eyes, to have one fair gaze at his face. He had to support himself by one hand rested on the dresser, but she saw he was looking far better – younger, less haggard – than he had seemed to her before. His face was short and expressive; his complexion had been weatherbeaten and bronzed, though now he looked so pale; his eyes and hair were dark, – the former quick, deep-set, and penetrating; the latter curly, and almost in ringlets. His teeth gleamed white as he smiled at her, a pleasant friendly smile of recognition; but she only blushed the deeper, and hung her head.

'I'll come, sir, and be thankful. I daresay a turn'll do me good, if the weather holds up, an' th' frost keeps on.'

'That's right, my lad,' said Robson, shaking him by the hand, and then Kinraid's hand was held out to Sylvia, and she could not avoid the same friendly action.

Molly Corney followed her to the door, and when they were fairly outside, she held Sylvia back for an instant to say,—

'Is na' he a fine likely man? I'm so glad as yo've seen him, for he's to be off next week to Newcastle and that neighbourhood.'

'But he said he'd come to us some night?' asked Sylvia, half in a fright.

'Ay, I'll see as he does; never fear. For I should like yo' for to know him a bit. He's a rare talker. I'll mind him o' coming to yo'.'

Somehow, Sylvia felt as if this repeated promise of reminding Kinraid of his promise to come and see her father took away part of the pleasure she had anticipated from his visit. Yet what could be more natural than that Molly Corney should wish her friend to be acquainted with the man whom Sylvia believed to be all but Molly's engaged lover?

Pondering these thoughts, the walk home was as silent as that going to Moss Brow had been. The only change seemed to be that now they faced the brilliant northern lights flashing up the sky, and that either this appearance or some of the whaling narrations of Kinraid had stirred up Daniel Robson's recollections of a sea ditty, which he kept singing to himself in a low, unmusical voice, the burden of which was, 'for I loves the tossin' say!'* Bell met them at the door.

'Well, and here ye are at home again! and Philip has been, Sylvie, to give thee thy ciphering lesson; and he stayed awhile, thinking thou'd be coming back.'

'I'm very sorry,' said Sylvia, more out of deference to her mother's tone of annoyance, than because she herself cared either for her lesson or her cousin's disappointment.

'He'll come again to-morrow night, he says. But thou must take care, and mind the nights he says he'll come, for it's a long way to come for nought.'

Sylvia might have repeated her 'I'm very sorry' at this announcement of Philip's intentions; but she restrained herself, inwardly and fervently hoping that Molly would not urge the fulfilment of the specksioneer's promise for to-morrow night, for Philip's being there would spoil all; and besides, if she sate at the dresser at her lesson, and Kinraid at the table with her father, he might hear all, and find out what a dunce she was.

She need not have been afraid. With the next night Hepburn came; and Kinraid did not. After a few words to her mother, Philip produced the candles he had promised, and some books and a quill or two.

'What for hast thou brought candles?' asked Bell, in a half-affronted tone.

Hepburn smiled.

'Sylvia thought it would take a deal of candle-light, and was for making it into a reason not to learn. I should ha' used t' candles if I'd stayed at home, so I just brought them wi' me.'

'Then thou may'st just take them back again,' said Bell, shortly, blowing out that which he had lighted, and placing one of her own on the dresser instead.

Sylvia caught her mother's look of displeasure, and it made her docile for the evening, although she owed her cousin a grudge for her enforced good behaviour.

'Now, Sylvia, here's a copy-book wi' t' Tower o' London on it, and we'll fill it wi' as pretty writing as any in t' North Riding.'

Sylvia sate quite still, unenlivened by this prospect.

'Here's a pen as 'll nearly write of itsel',' continued Philip, still trying to coax her out her sullenness of manner.

Then he arranged her in the right position.

'Don't lay your head down on your left arm, you'll ne'er see to write straight.'

The attitude was changed, but not a word was spoken.

Philip began to grow angry at such determined dumbness.

'Are you tired?' asked he, with a strange mixture of crossness and tenderness.

'Yes, very,' was her reply.

'But thou ought'st not to be tired,' said Bell, who had not yet got over the offence to her hospitality; who, moreover, liked her nephew, and had, to boot, a great respect for the learning she had never acquired.

'Mother!' said Sylvia, bursting out, 'what's the use on my writing "Abednego," "Abednego," "Abednego," all down a page? If I could see t' use on 't, I'd ha' axed father to send me t' school; but I'm none wanting to have learning.'

'It's a fine thing, tho', is learning. My mother and my grandmother had it: but th' family came down i' the world, and Philip's mother and me, we had none of it; but I ha' set my heart on thy having it, child.'

'My fingers is stiff,' pleaded Sylvia, holding up her little hand and shaking it.

'Let us take a turn at spelling, then,' said Philip.

'What's t' use on't?' asked captious Sylvia.

'Why, it helps one i' reading an' writing.'

'And what does reading and writing do for one?'

Her mother gave her another of the severe looks that, quiet woman as she was, she could occasionally bestow upon the refractory, and Sylvia took her book and glanced down the column Philip pointed out to her; but, as she justly considered, one man might point out the task, but twenty could not make her learn it, if she did not choose; and she sat herself down on the edge of the dresser, and idly gazed into the fire. But her mother came round to look for something in the drawers of the dresser, and as she passed her daughter she said in a low voice—

'Sylvie, be a good lass. I set a deal o' store by learning, and father 'ud never send thee to school, as has stuck by me sore.'

If Philip, sitting with his back to them, heard these words he was discreet enough not to show that he heard. And he had his reward; for in a very short time, Sylvia stood before him with her book in her hand, prepared to say her spelling.

At which he also stood up by instinct, and listened to her slow succeeding letters; helping her out, when she looked up at him with a sweet childlike perplexity in her face: for a dunce as to book-learning poor Sylvia was and was likely to remain; and, in spite of his assumed office of schoolmaster, Philip Hepburn could almost have echoed the words of the lover of Jess MacFarlane—*

I sent my love a letter,
But, alas! she canna read,
And I lo'e her a' the better.

Still he knew his aunt's strong wish on the subject, and it was very delightful to stand in the relation of teacher to so dear and pretty, if so wilful, a pupil.

Perhaps it was not very flattering to notice Sylvia's great joy when her lessons were over, sadly shortened as they were by Philip's desire not to be too hard upon her. Sylvia danced round to her mother, bent her head back, and kissed her face, and then said defyingly to Philip,—

'If iver I write thee a letter it shall just be full of nothing but "Abednego! Abednego! Abednego!"'

But at this moment her father came in from a distant expedition on the moors with Kester to look after the sheep he had pasturing there before the winter set fairly in. He was tired, and so was Lassie, and so, too, was Kester, who, lifting his heavy legs one after the other, and smoothing down his hair, followed his master into the house-place, and seating himself on a bench at the farther end of the dresser, patiently awaited the supper of porridge and milk which he shared with his master. Sylvia, meanwhile, coaxed Lassie – poor foot-sore dog – to her side, and gave her some food, which the creature was almost too tired to eat. Philip made as though he would be going, but Daniel motioned to him to be quiet.

'Sit thee down, lad. As soon as I've had my victual, I want t' hear a bit o' news.'

Sylvia took her sewing and sat at the little round table by her mother, sharing the light of the scanty dip-candle.* No one spoke. Every one was absorbed in what they were doing.

What Philip was doing was, gazing at Sylvia – learning her face off by heart.

When every scrap of porridge was cleared out of the mighty bowl, Kester yawned, and wishing good-night, withdrew to his loft over the cow-house. Then Philip pulled out the weekly York paper, and began to read the latest accounts of the war then raging. This was giving Daniel one of his greatest pleasures; for though he could read pretty well, yet the double effort of reading and understanding what he read was almost too much for him. He could read, or he could understand what was read aloud to him; reading was no pleasure, but listening was.

Besides, he had a true John Bullish interest in the war, without very well knowing what the English were fighting for. But in those days, so long as they fought the French for any cause, or for no cause at all, every true patriot was satisfied. Sylvia and her mother did not care for any such far-extended interest; a little bit of York news, the stealing of a few apples out of a Scarborough garden that they knew, was of far more interest to them than all the battles of Nelson and the North.

Philip read in a high-pitched and unnatural tone of voice, which deprived the words of their reality; for even familiar expressions can become unfamiliar and convey no ideas, if the utterance is forced or affected. Philip was somewhat of a pedant; yet there was a simplicity in his pedantry not always to be met with in those who are self-taught, and which might have interested any one who cared to know with what labour and difficulty he had acquired the knowledge which now he prized so highly; reading out Latin quotations as easily as if they were English, and taking a pleasure in rolling poly-syllables, until all at once looking askance at Sylvia, he saw that her head had fallen back, her pretty rosy lips open, her eyes fast shut; in short, she was asleep.

'Ay,' said Farmer Robson, 'and t' reading has a'most sent me off. Mother 'd look angry now if I was to tell yo' yo' had a right to a kiss; but when I was a young man I'd ha' kissed a pretty girl as I saw asleep, afore yo'd said Jack Robson.'

Philip trembled at these words, and looked at his aunt.

She gave him no encouragement, standing up, and making as though she had never heard her husband's speech, by extending her hand, and wishing him 'good-night.' At the noise of the chairs moving over the flag floor, Sylvia started up, confused and annoyed at her father's laughter.

'Ay, lass; it's iver a good time t' fall asleep when a young fellow is by. Here's Philip here as thou'rt bound t' give a pair o' gloves to.'*

Sylvia went like fire; she turned to her mother to read her face.

'It's only father's joke, lass,' said she. 'Philip knows manners too well.'

'He'd better,' said Sylvia, flaming round at him. 'If he'd a touched me, I'd niver ha' spoken to him no more.' And she looked even as it was as if she was far from forgiving him.

'Hoots, lass! wenches are brought up sa mim,* now-a-days; i' my time they'd ha' thought na' such great harm of a kiss.'

'Good-night, Philip,' said Bell Robson, thinking the conversation unseemly.

'Good-night, aunt, good-night, Sylvie!' But Sylvia turned her back on him, and he could hardly say 'good-night' to Daniel, who had caused such an unpleasant end to an evening that had at one time been going on so well.

CHAPTER IX

THE SPECKSIONEER

A FEW days after, farmer Robson left Haytersbank betimes on a longish day's journey, to purchase a horse. Sylvia and her mother were busied with a hundred household things, and the early winter's evening closed in upon them almost before they were aware. The consequences of darkness in the country even now are to gather the members of a family together into one room, and to make them settle to some sedentary employment; and it was much more the case at the period of my story, when candles were far dearer than they are at present, and when one was often made to suffice for a large family.

The mother and daughter hardly spoke at all when they sat down at last. The cheerful click of the knitting-needles made a pleasant home-sound; and in the occasional snatches of slumber that overcame her mother, Sylvia could hear the long-rushing boom of the waves, down below the rocks, for the Haytersbank gulley allowed the sullen roar to come up so far inland. It might have been about eight o'clock – though from the monotonous course of the evening it seemed much later – when Sylvia heard her father's heavy step cranching* down the pebbly path. More unusual, she heard his voice talking to some companion.

Curious to see who it could be, with a lively instinctive advance towards any event which might break the monotony she had begun to find somewhat dull, she sprang up to open the door. Half a glance into the gray darkness outside made her suddenly timid, and she drew back behind the door as she opened it wide to admit her father and Kinraid.

Daniel Robson came in bright and boisterous. He was pleased with his purchase, and had had some drink to celebrate his bargain. He had ridden the new mare into Monkshaven, and left her at the smithy there until morning, to have her feet looked at, and to be new shod. On his way from the town he had met Kinraid wandering about in search of Haytersbank Farm itself, so he had just brought him along with him; and here they were, ready for bread and cheese, and aught else the mistress would set before them.

To Sylvia the sudden change into brightness and bustle occasioned by the entrance of her father and the specksioneer was like that which you may effect any winter's night, when you come into a room where a great lump of coal lies hot and slumbering on the fire; just break it up with a judicious blow from the poker, and the room, late so dark, and dusk, and lone, is full of life, and light, and warmth.

She moved about with pretty household briskness, attending to all her father's wants. Kinraid's eye watched her as she went backwards and forwards, to and fro, into the pantry, the back-kitchen, out of light into shade, out of the shadow into the broad firelight where he could see and note her appearance. She wore the high-crowned linen cap of that day, surmounting her lovely masses of golden brown hair, rather than concealing them, and tied firm to her head by a broad blue ribbon. A long curl hung down on each side of her neck – her throat rather, for her neck was concealed by a little spotted handkerchief carefully pinned across at the waist of her brown stuff gown.

How well it was, thought the young girl, that she had doffed her bed-gown and linsey-woolsey petticoat, her working-dress, and made herself smart in her stuff gown, when she sate down to work with her mother.

By the time she could sit down again, her father and Kinraid had their glasses filled, and were talking of the relative merits of various kinds of spirits; that led on to tales of smuggling, and the different contrivances by which they or their friends had eluded the preventive service; the nightly relays of men to carry the goods inland; the kegs of brandy found by certain farmers whose horses had gone so far in the night, that they could do no work the next day; the clever way in which certain women managed to bring in prohibited goods; in fact, that when a woman did give her mind to smuggling, she was more full of resources, and tricks, and impudence, and energy than any man. There was no question of the morality of the affair; one of the greatest signs of the real progress we have made since those times seems to be that our daily concerns of buying and selling, eating and drinking, whatsoever we do, are more tested by the real practical standard of our religion than they were in the days of our grandfathers. Neither Sylvia nor her mother was in advance of their age. Both listened with admiration to the ingenious devices, and acted as well as spoken lies, that were talked about as fine and spirited things. Yet if Sylvia had attempted one tithe of this deceit in her every-day life, it would have half broken her mother's heart. But when the duty on salt* was strictly and cruelly enforced, making it penal to pick up rough dirty lumps containing small quantities that might be thrown out with the ashes of the brine-houses on the high-roads; when the price of this necessary was so increased by the tax upon it as to make it an expensive, sometimes an un-attainable, luxury to the working man, Government did more to demoralise the popular sense of rectitude and uprightness than heaps of sermons could undo. And the same, though in smaller measure, was the consequence of many other taxes. It may seem curious to trace up the popular standard of truth to taxation; but I do not think the idea would be so very far-fetched.

From smuggling adventures it was easy to pass on to stories of what had happened to Robson, in his youth a sailor in the Greenland seas, and to Kinraid, now one of the best harpooners in any whaler that sailed off the coast.

'There's three things to be afeared on,' said Robson, authoritatively: 'there's t' ice, that's bad; there's dirty weather, that's worse; and there's whales theirselves, as is t' worst of all; leastways, they was i' my days; t' darned brutes may ha' larnt better manners sin'. When I were young, they could niver be got to let theirsels be harpooned wi'out flounderin' and makin' play wi' their tales and their fins, till t' say were all in a foam, and t' boats' crews was all o'er wi' spray, which i' them latitudes is a kind o' shower-bath not needed.'

'Th' whales hasn't mended their manners, as you call it,' said Kinraid; 'but th' ice is not to be spoken lightly on. I were once in th' ship *John*, of Hull,* and we were in good green water, and were keen after whales; and ne'er thought harm of a great gray iceberg as were on our lee-bow, a mile or so off; it looked as if it had been there from the days of Adam, and were likely to see th' last man out, and it ne'er a bit bigger nor smaller in all them thousands and thousands o' years. Well, the fast-boats were out after a fish, and I were specksioneer in one; and we were so keen after capturing our whale, that none on us ever saw that we were drifting away from them right into deep shadow o' th' iceberg. But we were set upon our whale, and I harpooned it; and as soon as it were dead we lashed its fins together, and fastened its tail to our boat; and then we took breath and looked about us, and away from us a little space were th' other boats, wi' two other fish making play, and as likely as not to break loose, for I may say as I were th' best harpooner on board the *John*, wi'out saying great things o' mysel'. So I says, "My lads, one o' you stay i' th' boat by this fish," – the fins o' which, as I said, I'd reeved* a rope through mysel', and which was as dead as Noah's grandfather – "and th' rest on us shall go off and help th' other boats wi' their fish." For, you see, we had another boat close by in order to sweep th' fish. (I suppose they swept fish i' your time, master?)'

'Ay, ay!' said Robson; 'one boat lies still holding t' end o' t' line; t' other makes a circuit round t' fish.'

'Well! luckily for us we had our second boat, for we all got into it, ne'er a man on us was left i' th' fast-boat. And says I, "But who's to stay by t' dead fish?" And no man answered, for they were all as keen as me for to go and help our mates; and we thought as we could come back to our dead fish, as had a boat for a buoy, once we had helped our mates. So off we rowed, every man Jack on us, out o' the black shadow o' th' iceberg, as looked as steady as th' pole-star. Well! we had na' been a dozen fathoms away fra' th' boat as we had left, when crash! down wi' a roaring noise, and then a gulp of the deep waters, and then a shower o' blinding spray; and when we had wiped our eyes clear, and getten our hearts down agen fra' our mouths, there were never a boat nor a glittering belly o' e'er a great whale to be seen; but th' iceberg were there, still and grim, as if a hundred ton or more had fallen off all in a mass, and crushed down boat, and fish, and all, into th' deep water, as goes half through the earth in them latitudes. Th' coal-miners round about Newcastle way may come upon our good boat if they mine deep enough, else ne'er another man will see her. And I left as good a clasp-knife in her as ever I clapt eyes on.'

'But what a mercy no man stayed in her,' said Bell.

'Why, mistress, I reckon we a' must die some way; and I'd as soon go down into the deep waters as be choked up wi' moulds.'*

'But it must be so cold,' said Sylvia, shuddering and giving a little poke to the fire to warm her fancy.

'Cold!' said her father, 'what do ye stay-at-homes know about cold, a should like to know? If yo'd been where a were once, north latitude 81, in such a frost as ye ha' niver known, no, not i' deep winter, and it were June i' them seas, and a whale i' sight, and a were off in a boat after her: an' t' ill-mannered brute, as soon as she were harpooned, ups wi' her big awkward tail, and struck t' boat i' her stern, and chucks me out into t' watter. That were cold, a can tell the'! First, I smarted all ower me, as if my skin were suddenly stript off me: and next, ivery bone i' my body had getten t' toothache, and there were a great roar i' my ears, an' a great dizziness i' my eyes; an' t' boat's crew kept throwin' out their oars, an' a kept clutchin' at 'em, but a could na' make out where they was, my eyes dazzled so wi' t' cold, an' I thought I were bound for "kingdom come," an' a tried to remember t' Creed, as a might die a Christian. But all a could think on was, "What is your name, M or N?"* an' just as a were giving up both words and life, they heaved me aboard. But, bless ye, they had but one oar; for they'd thrown a' t' others after me; so yo' may reckon, it were some time afore we could reach t' ship; an', a've heerd tell, a were a precious sight to look on, for my clothes was just hard frozen to me, an' my hair a'most as big a lump o' ice as yon iceberg he was a-telling us on; they rubbed me as missus theere were rubbing t' hams yesterday, and gav' me brandy; an' a've niver getten t' frost out o' my bones for a' their rubbin', and a deal o' brandy as I 'ave ta'on sin'. Talk o' cold! it's little yo' women known o' cold!'

'But there's heat, too, i' some places,' said Kinraid. 'I was once a voyage i' an American. They goes for th' most part south, to where you come round to t' cold again; and they'll stay there for three year at a time, if need be, going into winter harbour i' some o' th' Pacific Islands. Well, we were i' th' southern seas, a-seeking for good whaling-ground; and, close on our larboard beam, there were a great wall o' ice, as much as sixty feet high. And says our captain – as were a dare-devil, if ever a man were – "There'll be an opening in yon dark gray wall, and into that opening I'll sail, if I coast along it till th' day o' judgment." But, for all our sailing, we never seemed to come nearer to th' opening. The waters were rocking beneath us, and the sky were steady above us; and th' ice rose out o' the waters, and seemed to reach up into the sky. We sailed on, and we sailed on, for more days nor I could count. Our captain were a strange, wild man, but once he looked a little pale when he came upo' deck after his turn-in, and saw the green-gray ice going straight up on our beam. Many on us thought as the ship were bewitched for th' captain's words; and we got to speak low, and to say our prayers o' nights, and a kind o' dull silence came into th' very air; our voices did na' rightly seem our own. And we sailed on, and we sailed on. All at once, th' man as were on watch gave a cry: he saw a break in the ice, as we'd begun to think were everlasting; and we all gathered towards the bows, and the captain called to th' man at the helm to keep her course, and cocked his head, and began to walk the quarter-deck jaunty again. And we came to a great cleft in th' long weary rock of ice; and the sides o' th' cleft were not jagged, but went straight sharp down into th' foaming waters. But we took but one look at what lay inside, for our captain, with a loud cry to God, bade the helmsman steer nor'ards away fra' th' mouth o' Hell. We all saw wi' our own eyes, inside that fearsome wall o' ice – seventy miles long, as we could swear to – inside that gray, cold ice, came leaping flames, all red and yellow wi' heat o' some unearthly kind out o' th' very waters o' the sea; making our eyes dazzle wi' their scarlet blaze, that shot up as high, nay, higher than th' ice around, yet never so much as a shred on 't was melted. They did say that some beside our captain saw the black devils dart hither and thither, quicker than the very flames themselves; anyhow, *he* saw them. And as he knew it were his own daring as had led him to have that peep at terrors forbidden to any on us afore our time, he just dwined* away, and we hadn't taken but one whale afore our captain died, and first mate took th' command. It were a prosperous voyage; but, for all that, I'll never sail those seas again, nor ever take wage aboard an American again.'

'Eh, dear! but it's awful t' think o' sitting wi' a man that has seen th' doorway into hell,' said Bell, aghast.

Sylvia had dropped her work, and sat gazing at Kinraid with fascinated wonder.

Daniel was just a little annoyed at the admiration which his own wife and daughter were bestowing on the specksioneer's wonderful stories, and he said—

'Ay, ay. If a'd been a talker, ye'd ha' thought a deal more on me nor ye've iver done yet. A've seen such things, and done such things.'

'Tell us, father!' said Sylvia, greedy and breathless.

'Some on 'em is past telling,' he replied, 'an some is not to be had for t' asking, seeing as how they might bring a man into trouble. But, as a said, if a had a fancy to reveal all as is on my mind a could make t' hair on your heads lift up your caps – well, we'll say an inch, at least. Thy mother, lass, has heerd one or two on 'em. Thou minds the story o' my ride on a whale's back, Bell? That'll maybe be within this young fellow's comprehension o' t' danger; thou's heerd me tell it, hastn't ta?'

'Yes,' said Bell; 'but it's a long time ago; when we was courting.'

'An' that's afore this young lass were born, as is a'most up to woman's estate. But sin' those days a ha' been o'er busy to tell stories to my wife, an' as a'll warrant she's forgotten it; an' as Sylvia here niver heerd it, if yo'll fill your glass, Kinraid, yo' shall ha' t' benefit o't.

'A were a specksioneer mysel, though, after that, a raything directed my talents int' t' smuggling branch o' my profession; but a were once a whaling aboord t' *Aimwell** of Whitby. An' we was anchored off t' coast o' Greenland one season; an' we'd getten a cargo o' seven whale; but our captain he were a keen-eyed chap, an' niver above doin' any man's work; an' once seein' a whale he throws himself int' a boat an' goes off to it, makin' signals to me, an' another specksioneer as were off for diversion i' another boat, for to come after him sharp.

Well, afore we comes alongside, captain had harpooned t' fish; an' says he, "Now, Robson, all ready! give into her again when she comes to t' top;" an' I stands up, right leg foremost, harpoon all ready, as soon as iver I cotched a sight o' t' whale, but niver a fin could a see. 'Twere no wonder, for she were right below t' boat in which a were; and when she wanted to rise, what does t' great ugly brute do but come wi' her head, as is like cast iron, up bang again t' bottom o' t' boat. I were thrown up in t' air like a shuttlecock, me an' my line an' my harpoon – up we goes, an' many a good piece o' timber wi' us, an' many a good fellow too; but a had t' look after mysel', an' a were up high i' t' air, afore I could say Jack Robison, an' a thowt a were safe for another dive int' saut water; but, i'stead a comes down plump on t' back o' t' whale. Ay! yo' may stare, master, but theere a were, an' main an' slippery it were, only a sticks my harpoon intil her an' steadies mysel', an' looks abroad o'er t' vast o' waves, and gets sea-sick in a manner, an' puts up a prayer as she mayn't dive, and it were as good a prayer for wishin' it might come true as iver t' clargyman an' t' clerk too puts up i' Monkshaven church. Well, a reckon it were heerd, for all a were i' them north latitudes, for she keeps steady, an' a does my best for t' keep steady; an' 'deed a was too steady, for a was fast wi' t' harpoon line, all knotted and tangled about me. T' captain, he sings out for me to cut it; but it's easy singin' out, and it's noane so easy fumblin' for your knife i' t' pocket o' your drawers, when yo've t' hold hard wi' t' other hand on t' back of a whale, swimmin' fourteen knots an hour. At last a thinks to mysel' a can't get free o' t' line, and t' line is fast to t' harpoon, and t' harpoon is fast to t' whale; and t' whale may go down fathoms deep wheniver t' maggot stirs i' her head; an' t' watter's cold, an' noane good for drownin' in; a can't get free o' t' line, and a connot get my knife out o' my breeches pocket though t' captain should ca' it mutiny to disobey orders, and t' line's fast to t' harpoon – let's see if t' harpoon's fast to t' whale. So a tugged, and a lugged, and t' whale didn't mistake it for ticklin', but she cocks up her tail, and throws out showers o' water as were ice or iver it touched me; but a pulls on at t' shank, an' a were only afeard as she wouldn't keep at t' top wi' it sticking in her; but at last t' harpoon broke, an' just i' time, for a reckon she was near as tired o' me as a were on her, and down she went; an' a had hard work to make for t' boats as was near enough to catch me; for what wi' t' whale's being but slippery an' t' watter being cold, an' me hampered wi' t' line an' t' piece o' harpoon, it's a chance, missus, as thou had stopped an oud maid.'

'Eh dear a' me!' said Bell, 'how well I mind yo'r telling me that tale! It were twenty-four year ago come October. I thought I never could think enough on a man as had rode on a whale's back!'

'Yo' may learn t' way of winnin' t' women,' said Daniel, winking at the specksioneer.

And Kinraid immediately looked at Sylvia. It was no premeditated action; it came as naturally as wakening in the morning when his sleep was ended; but Sylvia coloured as red as any rose at his sudden glance, – coloured so deeply that he looked away until he thought she had recovered her composure, and then he sat gazing at her again. But not for long, for Bell suddenly starting up, did all but turn him out of the house. It was late, she said, and her master was tired, and they had a hard day before them next day; and it was keeping Ellen Corney up; and they had had enough to drink, – more than was good for them, she was sure, for they had both been taking her in with their stories, which she had been foolish enough to believe. No one saw the real motive of all this almost inhospitable haste to dismiss her guest, how the sudden fear had taken possession of her that he and Sylvia were 'fancying each other.' Kinraid had said early in the evening that he had come to thank her for her kindness in sending the sausages, as he was off to his own home near Newcastle in a day or two. But now he said, in reply to Daniel Robson, that he would step in another night before long and hear some more of the old man's yarns.

Daniel had just had enough drink to make him very good-tempered, or else his wife would not have dared to have acted as she did; and this maudlin amiability took the shape of hospitable urgency that Kinraid should come as often as he liked to Haytersbank; come and make it his home when he was in these parts; stay there altogether, and so on, till Bell fairly shut the outer door to, and locked it before the specksioneer had well got out of the shadow of their roof.

All night long Sylvia dreamed of burning volcanoes springing out of icy southern seas. But, as in the specksioneer's tale the flames were peopled with demons, there was no human interest for her in the wondrous scene in which she was no actor, only a spectator. With daylight came wakening and little homely every-day wonders. Did Kinraid mean that he was going away really and entirely, or did he not? Was he Molly Corney's sweetheart, or was he not? When she had argued herself into certainty on one side, she suddenly wheeled about, and was just of the opposite opinion. At length she settled that it could not be settled until she saw Molly again; so, by a strong gulping effort, she resolutely determined to think no more about him, only about the marvels he had told. She might think a little about them when she sat at night, spinning in silence by the household fire. or when she went out in the gloaming to call the cattle home to be milked, and sauntered back behind the patient, slow-gaited creatures; and at times on future summer days, when, as in the past, she took her knitting out for the sake of the freshness of the faint sea-breeze, and dropping down from ledge to ledge of the rocks that faced the blue ocean, established herself in a perilous nook that had been her haunt ever since her parents had come to Haytersbank Farm. From thence she had often seen the distant ships pass to and fro, with a certain sort of lazy pleasure in watching their swift tranquillity of motion, but no thought as to where they were bound to, or what strange places they would penetrate to before they turned again, homeward bound.

CHAPTER X

A REFRACTORY PUPIL

SYLVIA was still full of the specksioneer and his stories, when Hepburn came up to give her the next lesson. But the prospect of a little sensible commendation for writing a whole page full of flourishing 'Abednegos,' had lost all the slight charm it had ever possessed. She was much more inclined to try and elicit some sympathy in her interest in the perils and adventures of the northern seas, than to bend and control her mind to the right formation of letters. Unwisely enough, she endeavoured to repeat one of the narratives that she had heard from Kinraid; and when she found that Hepburn (if, indeed, he did not look upon the whole as a silly invention) considered it only as an interruption to the real business in hand, to which he would try to listen as patiently as he could, in the hope of Sylvia's applying herself diligently to her copy-book when she had cleared her mind, she contracted her pretty lips, as if to check them from making any further appeals for sympathy, and set about her writing-lesson in a very rebellious frame of mind, only restrained by her mother's presence from spoken mutiny.

'After all,' said she, throwing down her pen, and opening and shutting her weary, cramped hand, 'I see no good in tiring myself wi' learning for t' write letters when I'se never got one in a' my life. What for should I write answers, when there's niver a one writes to me? and if I had one, I couldn't read it; it's bad enough wi' a book o' print as I've niver seen afore, for there's sure to be new-fangled words in 't. I'm sure I wish the man were farred* who plagues his brains wi' striking out new words. Why can't folks just ha' a set on 'em for good and a'?'

'Why! you'll be after using two or three hundred yoursel' every day as you live, Sylvie; and yet I must use a great many as you never think on about t' shop; and t' folks in t' fields want their set, let alone the high English that parsons and lawyers speak.'

'Well, it's weary work is reading and writing. Cannot you learn me something else, if we mun do lessons?'

'There's sums – and geography,' said Hepburn, slowly and gravely.

'Geography!' said Sylvia, brightening, and perhaps not pronouncing the word quite correctly, 'I'd like yo' to learn me geography. There's a deal o' places I want to hear all about.'

'Well, I'll bring up a book and a map next time. But I can tell you something now. There's four quarters in the globe.'

'What's that?' asked Sylvia.

'The globe is the earth; the place we live on.'

'Go on. Which quarter is Greenland?'

'Greenland is no quarter. It is only a part of one.'

'Maybe it's a half quarter.'

'No, not so much as that.'

'Half again?'

'No!' he replied, smiling a little.

She thought he was making it into a very small place in order to tease her; so she pouted a little, and then said,—

'Greenland is all t' geography I want to know. Except, perhaps, York. I'd like to learn about York, because of t' races, and London, because King George lives there.'

'But if you learn geography at all, you must learn 'bout all places: which of them is hot, and which is cold, and how many inhabitants is in each, and what's the rivers, and which is the principal towns.'

'I'm sure, Sylvie, if Philip will learn thee all that, thou'lt be such a sight o' knowledge as ne'er a one o' th' Prestons has been sin' my great-grandfather lost his property. I should be main proud o' thee; 'twould seem as if we was Prestons o' Slaideburn once more.'

'I'd do a deal to pleasure yo', mammy; but weary befa' riches and land, if folks that has 'em is to write, "Abednegos" by t' score, and to get hard words int' their brains, till they work like barm,* and end wi' cracking 'em.'

This seemed to be Sylvia's last protest against learning for the night, for after this she turned docile, and really took pains to understand all that Philip could teach her, by means of the not unskilful, though rude, map which he drew for her with a piece of charred wood on his aunt's dresser. He had asked his aunt's leave before beginning what Sylvia called his 'dirty work;' but by-and-by even she became a little interested in starting from a great black spot called Monkshaven, and in the shaping of land and sea around that one centre. Sylvia held her round chin in the palms of her hands, supporting her elbows on the dresser; looking down at the progress of the rough drawing in general, but now and then glancing up at him with sudden inquiry. All along he was not so much absorbed in his teaching as to be unconscious of her sweet proximity. She was in her best mood towards him; neither mutinous nor saucy; and he was striving with all his might to retain her interest, speaking better than ever he had done before (such brightness did love call forth!) – understanding what she would care to hear and to know; when, in the middle of an attempt at explaining the cause of the long polar days, of which she had heard from her childhood, he felt that her attention was no longer his; that a discord had come in between their minds; that she had passed out of his power. This certainty of intuition lasted out for an instant; he had no time to wonder or to speculate as to what had affected her so adversely to his wishes before the door opened and Kinraid came in. Then Hepburn knew that she must have heard his coming footsteps, and recognized them.

He angrily stiffened himself up into coldness of demeanour. Almost to his surprise, Sylvia's greeting to the new comer was as cold as his own. She stood rather behind him; so perhaps she did not see the hand which Kinraid stretched out towards her, for she did not place her own little palm in it, as she had done to Philip an hour ago. And she hardly spoke, but began to pore over the rough black map, as if seized with strong geographical curiosity, or determined to impress Philip's lesson deep on her memory.

Still Philip was dismayed by seeing the warm welcome

which Kinraid received from the master of the house, who came in from the back premises almost at the same time as the specksioneer entered at the front. Hepburn was uneasy, too, at finding Kinraid take his seat by the fireside, like one accustomed to the ways of the house. Pipes were soon produced. Philip disliked smoking. Possibly Kinraid did so too, but he took a pipe at any rate, and lighted it, though he hardly used it at all, but kept talking to farmer Robson on sea affairs. He had the conversation pretty much to himself. Philip sat gloomily by; Sylvia and his aunt were silent, and old Robson smoked his long clay pipe, from time to time taking it out of his mouth to spit into the bright copper spittoon, and to shake the white ashes out of the bowl. Before he replaced it, he would give a short laugh of relishing interest in Kinraid's conversation; and now and then he put in a remark. Sylvia perched herself sideways on the end of the dresser, and made pretence to sew; but Philip could see how often she paused in her work to listen.

By-and-by, his aunt spoke to him, and they kept up a little side conversation, more because Bell Robson felt that her nephew, her own flesh and blood, was put out, than for any special interest they either of them felt in what they were saying. Perhaps, also, they neither of them disliked showing that they had no great faith in the stories Kinraid was telling. Mrs Robson, at any rate, knew so little as to be afraid of believing too much.

Philip was sitting on that side of the fire which was nearest to the window and to Sylvia, and opposite to the specksioneer. At length he turned to his cousin and said in a low voice—

'I suppose we can't go on with our spell at geography till that fellow's gone?'

The colour came into Sylvia's cheek at the words 'that fellow;' but she only replied with a careless air—

'Well, I'm one as thinks enough is as good as a feast; and I've had enough of geography this one night, thank you kindly all the same.'

Philip took refuge in offended silence. He was maliciously pleased when his aunt made so much noise with her preparation for supper as quite to prevent the sound of the sailor's words from reaching Sylvia's ears. She saw that he was glad to perceive that her efforts to reach the remainder of the story were baulked! this nettled her, and, determined not to let him have his malicious triumph, and still more to put a stop to any attempt at private conversation, she began to sing to herself as she sat at her work; till, suddenly seized with a desire to help her mother, she dexterously slipped down from her seat, passed Hepburn, and was on her knees toasting cakes right in front of the fire, and just close to her father and Kinraid. And now the noise that Hepburn had so rejoiced in proved his foe. He could not hear the little merry speeches that darted backwards and forwards as the specksioneer tried to take the toasting-fork out of Sylvia's hand.

'How comes that sailor chap here?' asked Hepburn of his aunt. 'He's none fit to be where Sylvia is.'

'Nay, I dunnot know,' said she; 'the Corneys made us acquaint first, and my master is quite fain* of his company.'

'And do you like him, too, aunt?' asked Hepburn, almost wistfully; he had followed Mrs Robson into the dairy on pretence of helping her.

'I'm none fond on him; I think he tells us traveller's tales, by way o' seeing how much we can swallow. But the master and Sylvia think that there never was such a one.'

'I could show them a score as good as he down on the quay-side.'

'Well, laddie, keep a calm sough.* Some folk like some folk and others don't. Wherever I am there'll allays be a welcome for thee.'

For the good woman thought that he had been hurt by the evident absorption of her husband and daughter with their new friend, and wished to make all easy and straight. But do what she would, he did not recover his temper all evening: he was uncomfortable, put out, not enjoying himself, and yet he would not go. He was determined to assert his greater intimacy in that house by outstaying Kinraid. At length the latter got up to go; but before he went, he must needs bend over Sylvia and say something to her in so low a tone that

Philip could not hear it; and she, seized with a sudden fit of diligence, never looked up from her sewing; only nodded her head by way of reply. At last he took his departure, after many a little delay, and many a quick return, which to the suspicious Philip seemed only pretences for taking stolen glances at Sylvia. As soon as he was decidedly gone, she folded up her work, and declared that she was so much tired that she must go to bed there and then. Her mother, too, had been dozing for the last half-hour, and was only too glad to see signs that she might betake herself to her natural place of slumber.

'Take another glass, Philip,' said farmer Robson.

But Hepburn refused the offer rather abruptly. He drew near to Sylvia instead. He wanted to make her speak to him, and he saw that she wished to avoid it. He took up the readiest pretext. It was an unwise one as it proved, for it deprived him of his chances of occasionally obtaining her undivided attention.

'I don't think you care much for learning geography, Sylvie?'

'Not much to-night,' said she, making a pretence to yawn, yet looking timidly up at his countenance of displeasure.

'Nor at any time,' said he, with growing anger; 'nor for any kind of learning. I did bring some books last time I came, meaning to teach you many a thing – but now I'll just trouble you for my books; I put them on yon shelf by the Bible.'

He had a mind that she should bring them to him; that, at any rate, he should have the pleasure of receiving them out of her hands.

Sylvia did not reply, but went and took down the books with a languid, indifferent air.

'And so you won't learn any more geography,' said Hepburn.

Something in his tone struck her, and she looked up in his face. There were marks of stern offence upon his countenance, and yet in it there was also an air of wistful regret and sadness that touched her.

'Yo're niver angry with me, Philip? Sooner than vex yo',

I'll try and learn. Only, I'm just stupid; and it mun be such a trouble to you.'

Hepburn would fain have snatched at this half proposal that the lessons should be continued, but he was too stubborn and proud to say anything. He turned away from the sweet, pleading face without a word, to wrap up his books in a piece of paper. He knew that she was was standing quite still by his side, though he made as if he did not perceive her. When he had done he abruptly wished them all 'good-night,' and took his leave.

There were tears in Sylvia's eyes, although the feeling in her heart was rather one of relief. She had made a fair offer, and it had been treated with silent contempt. A few days afterwards, her father came in from Monkshaven market, and dropped out, among other pieces of news, that he had met Kinraid, who was bound for his own home at Cullercoats. He had desired his respects to Mrs Robson and her daughter; and had bid Robson say that he would have come up to Haytersbank to wish them good-by, but that as he was pressed for time, he hoped they would excuse him. But Robson did not think it worth while to give this long message of mere politeness. Indeed, as it did not relate to business, and was only sent to women, Robson forgot all about it, pretty nearly as soon as it was uttered. So Sylvia went about fretting herself for one or two days, at her hero's apparent carelessness of those who had at any rate treated him more like a friend than an acquaintance of only a few weeks' standing; and then, her anger quenching her incipient regard, she went about her daily business pretty much as though he had never been. He had gone away out of her sight into the thick mist of unseen life from which he had emerged – gone away without a word, and she might never see him again. But still there was a chance of her seeing him when he came to marry Molly Corney. Perhaps she should be bridesmaid, and then what a pleasant merry time the wedding-day would be! The Corneys were all such kind people, and in their family there never seemed to be the checks and restraints by which her own mother hedged her round. Then there came an overwhelming self-reproaching burst of love for that 'own mother;' a humiliation before her slightest wish, as penance for the moment's unspoken treason; and thus Sylvia was led to request her cousin Philip to resume his lessons in so meek a manner, that he slowly and graciously acceded to a request which he was yearning to fulfil all the time.

During the ensuing winter, all went on in monotonous regularity at Haytersbank Farm for many weeks. Hepburn came and went, and thought Sylvia wonderfully improved in docility and sobriety; and perhaps also he noticed the improvement in her appearance. For she was at that age when a girl changes rapidly, and generally for the better. Sylvia shot up into a tall young woman; her eyes deepened in colour, her face increased in expression, and a sort of consciousness of unusual good looks gave her a slight tinge of coquettish shyness with the few strangers whom she ever saw. Philip hailed her interest in geography as another sign of improvement. He had brought back his book of maps to the farm; and there he sat on many an evening teaching his cousin, who had strange fancies respecting the places about which she wished to learn, and was coolly indifferent to the very existence of other towns, and countries, and seas far more famous in story. She was occasionally wilful, and at times very contemptuous as to the superior knowledge of her instructor; but, in spite of it all, Philip went regularly on the appointed evenings to Haytersbank – through keen black east wind, or driving snow, or slushing thaw; for he liked dearly to sit a little behind her, with his arm on the back of her chair, she stooping over the outspread map, with her eyes, – could he have seen them, – a good deal fixed on one spot in the map, not Northumberland, where Kinraid was spending the winter, but those wild northern seas about which he had told them such wonders.

One day towards spring, she saw Molly Corney coming towards the farm. The companions had not met for many weeks, for Molly had been from home visiting her relations in the north. Sylvia opened the door, and stood smiling and shivering on the threshold, glad to see her friend again. Molly called out, when a few paces off,—

'Why, Sylvia, is that thee! Why, how thou'rt growed, to be sure! What a bonny lass thou is!'

'Dunnot talk nonsense to my lass,' said Bell Robson, hospitably leaving her ironing and coming to the door; but though the mother tried to look as if she thought it nonsense, she could hardly keep down the smile that shone out of her eyes, as she put her hand on Sylvia's shoulder, with a fond sense of proprietorship in what was being praised.

'Oh! but she is,' persisted Molly. 'She's grown quite a beauty sin' I saw her. And if I don't tell her so, the men will.'

'Be quiet wi' thee,' said Sylvia, more than half offended, and turning away in a huff at the open barefaced admiration.

'Ay; but they will,' persevered Molly. 'Yo'll not keep her long, Mistress Robson. And as mother says, yo'd feel it a deal more to have yer daughters left on hand.'

'Thy mother has many, I have but this one,' said Mrs Robson, with severe sadness; for now Molly was getting to talk as she disliked. But Molly's purpose was to bring the conversation round to her own affairs, of which she was very full.

'Yes! I tell mother that wi' so many as she has, she ought to be thankful to t' one as gets off quickest.'

'Who? which is it?' asked Sylvia, a little eagerly, seeing that there was news of a wedding behind the talk.

'Why! who should it be but me?' said Molly, laughing a good deal, and reddening a little. 'I've not gone fra' home for nought; I'se picked up a measter on my travels, leastways one as is to be.'

'Charley Kinraid,' said Sylvia smiling, as she found that now she might reveal Molly's secret, which hitherto she had kept sacred.

'Charley Kinraid be hung!' said Molly, with a toss of her head. 'Whatten good's a husband who's at sea half t' year? Ha ha, my measter is a canny Newcassel shopkeeper, on t' Side.* A reckon a've done pretty well for mysel', and a'll wish yo' as good luck, Sylvia. For yo' see,' (turning to Bell Robson, who, perhaps, she thought would more appreciate the substantial advantages of her engagement than Sylvia,) 'though Measter Brunton is near upon forty if he's a day, yet he turns over a matter of two hundred pound every year; an' he's a good-looking man of his years too, an' a kind, good-tempered feller int' t' bargain. He's been married once, to be sure; but his childer are dead a' 'cept one; an' I don't mislike childer either; an' a'll feed 'em well, an' get 'em to bed early, out o' t' road.'

Mrs Robson gave her her grave good wishes; but Sylvia was silent. She was disappointed; it was a coming down from the romance with the specksioneer for its hero. Molly laughed awkwardly, understanding Sylvia's thoughts better than the latter imagined.

'Sylvia's noane so well pleased. Why, lass! it's a' t' better for thee. There's Charley to t' fore now, which if a'd married him, he'd not ha' been; and he's said more nor once what a pretty lass yo'd grow into by-and-by.'

Molly's prosperity was giving her an independence and fearlessness of talk such as had seldom appeared hitherto; and certainly never before Mrs Robson. Sylvia was annoyed at Molly's whole tone and manner, which were loud, laughing, and boisterous; but to her mother they were positively repugnant. She said shortly and gravely,—

'Sylvia's none so set upo' matrimony; she's content to bide wi' me and her father. Let a be such talking, it's not i' my way.'

Molly was a little subdued; but still her elation at the prospect of being so well married kept cropping out of all the other subjects which were introduced; and when she went away, Mrs Robson broke out in an unwonted strain of depreciation.

'That's the way wi' some lasses. They're like a cock on a dunghill, when they've teased a silly chap into wedding 'em. It's cock-a-doodle-do, I've cotched a husband, cock-a-doodle-doo, wi' 'em. I've no patience wi' such like; I beg, Sylvie, thou'lt not get too thick wi' Molly. She's not pretty behaved, making such an ado about men-kind, as if they were two-headed calves to be run after.'

'But Molly's a good-hearted lass, mother. Only I never

dreamt but what she was troth-plighted wi' Charley Kinraid,' said Sylvia, meditatively.

'That wench 'll be troth-plight to th' first man as 'll wed her and keep her i' plenty; that's a' she thinks about,' replied Bell, scornfully.

CHAPTER XI

VISIONS OF THE FUTURE

BEFORE May was out, Molly Corney was married and had left the neighbourhood for Newcastle. Although Charley Kinraid was not the bridegroom, Sylvia's promise to be bridesmaid was claimed. But the friendship brought on by the circumstances of neighbourhood and parity of age had become very much weakened in the time that elapsed between Molly's engagement and wedding. In the first place, she herself was so absorbed in her preparations, so elated by her good fortune in getting married, and married, too, before her elder sister, that all her faults blossomed out full and strong. Sylvia felt her to be selfish; Mrs Robson thought her not maidenly. A year before she would have been far more missed and regretted by Sylvia; now it was almost a relief to the latter to be freed from the perpetual calls upon her sympathy, from the constant demands upon her congratulations, made by one who had no thought or feeling to bestow on others; at least, not in these weeks of 'cock-a-doodle-dooing,' as Mrs Robson persisted in calling it. It was seldom that Bell was taken with a humorous idea; but this once having hatched a solitary joke, she was always clucking it into notice – to go on with her own poultry simile.

Every time during that summer that Philip saw his cousin, he thought her prettier than she had ever been before; some new touch of colour, some fresh sweet charm, seemed to have been added, just as every summer day calls out new beauty in the flowers. And this was not the addition of Philip's fancy. Hester Rose, who met Sylvia on rare occasions, came back each time with a candid, sad acknowledgement in her heart that it was no wonder that Sylvia was so much admired and loved.

One day Hester had seen her sitting near her mother in the market-place; there was a basket by her, and over the clean cloth that covered the yellow pounds of butter, she had laid the hedge-roses and honeysuckles she had gathered on the way into Monkshaven; her straw hat was on her knee, and she was busy placing some of the flowers in the ribbon that went round it. Then she held it on her hand, and turned it round about, putting her head on one side, the better to view the effect; and all this time, Hester, peeping at her through the folds of the stuffs displayed in Foster's windows, saw her with admiring, wistful eyes; wondering, too, if Philip, at the other counter, were aware of his cousin's being there, so near to him. Then Sylvia put on her hat, and, looking up at Foster's windows, caught Hester's face of interest, and smiled and blushed at the consciousness of having been watched over her little vanities, and Hester smiled back, but rather sadly. Then a customer came in, and she had to attend to her business, which, on this as on all market days, was great. In the midst she was aware of Philip rushing bare-headed out of the shop, eager and delighted at something he saw outside. There was a little looking-glass hung against the wall on Hester's side, placed in that retired corner, in order that the good women who came to purchase head-gear of any kind might see the effect thereof before they concluded their bargain. In a pause of custom, Hester, half-ashamed, stole into this corner, and looked at herself in the glass. What did she see? a colourless face, dark soft hair with no light gleams in it, eyes that were melancholy instead of smiling, a mouth compressed with a sense of dissatisfaction. This was what she had to compare with the bright bonny face in the sunlight outside. She gave a gulp to check the sigh that was rising, and came back, even more patient than she had been before this disheartening peep, to serve all the whims and fancies of purchasers.

Sylvia herself had been rather put out by Philip's way of coming to her. 'It made her look so silly,' she thought; and 'what for must he make a sight of himself, coming among the market folk in that-a-way;' and when he took to admiring her hat, she pulled out the flowers in a pet, and threw them down, and trampled them under foot.

'What for art thou doing that, Sylvie?' said her mother. 'The flowers is well enough, though maybe thy hat might ha' been stained.'

'I don't like Philip to speak to me so,' said Sylvia, pouting.

'How?' asked her mother.

But Sylvia could not repeat his words. She hung her head, and looked red and pre-occupied, anything but pleased. Philip had addressed his first expression of personal admiration at an unfortunate time.

It just shows what different views different men and women take of their fellow-creatures, when I say that Hester looked upon Philip as the best and most agreeable man she had ever known. He was not one to speak of himself without being questioned on the subject, so his Haytersbank relations, only come into the neighbourhod in the last year or two, knew nothing of the trials he had surmounted, or the difficult duties he had performed. His aunt, indeed, had strong faith in him, both from partial knowledge of his character, and because he was of her own tribe and kin; but she had never learnt the small details of his past life. Sylvia respected him as her mother's friend, and treated him tolerably well as long as he preserved his usual self-restraint of demeanour, but hardly ever thought of him when he was absent.

Now Hester, who had watched him daily for all the years since he had first come as an errand-boy into Foster's shop – watching with quiet, modest, yet observant eyes – had seen how devoted he was to his master's interests, had known of his careful and punctual ministration to his absent mother's comforts, as long as she was living to benefit by his silent, frugal self-denial.

His methodical appropriation of the few hours he could call his own was not without its charms to the equally methodical Hester; the way in which he reproduced any lately acquired piece of knowledge – knowledge so wearisome to

Sylvia – was delightfully instructive to Hester – although, as she was habitually silent, it would have required an observer more interested in discovering her feelings than Philip was to have perceived the little flush on the pale cheek, and the brightness in the half-veiled eyes whenever he was talking. She had not thought of love on either side. Love was a vanity, a worldliness not to be spoken about, or even thought about. Once or twice before the Robsons came into the neighbourhood, an idea had crossed her mind that possibly the quiet, habitual way in which she and Philip lived together, might drift them into matrimony at some distant period; and she could not bear the humble advances which Coulson, Philip's fellow-lodger, sometimes made. They seemed to disgust her with him.

But after the Robsons settled at Haytersbank, Philip's evenings were so often spent there that any unconscious hopes Hester might, unawares, have entertained, died away. At first she had felt a pang akin to jealousy when she heard of Sylvia, the little cousin, who was passing out of childhood into womanhood. Once – early in those days – she had ventured to ask Philip what Sylvia was like. Philip had not warmed up at the question, and had given rather a dry catalogue of her features, hair, and height, but Hester, almost to her own surprise, persevered, and jerked out the final question.

'Is she pretty?'

Philip's sallow cheek grew deeper by two or three shades; but he answered with a tone of indifference,—

'I believe some folks think her so.'

'But do you?' persevered Hester, in spite of her being aware that he somehow disliked the question.

'There's no need for talking o' such things,' he answered, with abrupt displeasure.

Hester silenced her curiosity from that time. But her heart was not quite at ease, and she kept on wondering whether Philip thought his little cousin pretty until she saw her and him together, on that occasion of which we have spoken, when Sylvia came to the shop to buy her new cloak; and after that Hester never wondered whether Philip thought his cousin pretty or no, for she knew quite well. Bell Robson had her own anxieties on the subject of her daughter's increasing attractions. She apprehended the dangers consequent upon certain facts, by a mental process more akin to intuition than reason. She was uncomfortable, even while her motherly vanity was flattered, at the admiration Sylvia received from the other sex. This admiration was made evident to her mother in many ways. When Sylvia was with her at market, it might have been thought that the doctors had prescribed a diet of butter and eggs to all the men under forty in Monkshaven. At first it seemed to Mrs Robson but a natural tribute to the superior merit of her farm produce; but by degrees she perceived that if Sylvia remained at home, she stood no better chance than her neighbours of an early sale. There were more customers than formerly for the fleeces stored in the wool-loft; comely young butchers came after the calf almost before it had been decided to sell it; in short, excuses were seldom wanting to those who wished to see the beauty of Haytersbank Farm. All this made Bell uncomfortable, though she could hardly have told what she dreaded. Sylvia herself seemed unspoilt by it as far as her home relations were concerned. A little thoughtless she had always been, and thoughtless she was still; but, as her mother had often said, 'Yo' canna put old heads on young shoulders;' and if blamed for her carelessness by her parents, Sylvia was always as penitent as she could be for the time being. To be sure, it was only to her father and mother that she remained the same as she had been when an awkward lassie of thirteen. Out of the house there were the most contradictory opinions of her, especially if the voices of women were to be listened to. She was 'an ill-favoured, overgrown thing;' 'just as bonny as the first rose i' June, and as sweet i' her nature as t' honeysuckle a-climbing round it;' she was 'a vixen, with a tongue sharp enough to make yer very heart bleed;' she was 'just a bit o' sunshine wheriver she went;' she was sulky, lively, witty, silent, affectionate, or cold-hearted, according to the person who spoke about her. In fact, her peculiarity seemed to be this – that every one who knew her talked about her either in praise or blame; in church, or in market, she unconsciously attracted attention; they could not forget her presence, as they could that of other girls perhaps more personally attractive. Now all this was a cause of anxiety to her mother, who began to feel as if she would rather have had her child passed by in silence than so much noticed. Bell's opinion was, that it was creditable to a woman to go through life in the shadow of obscurity, – never named except in connexion with good housewifery, husband, or children. Too much talking about a girl, even in the way of praise, disturbed Mrs Robson's opinion of her; and when her neighbours told her how her own daughter was admired, she would reply coldly, 'She's just well enough,' and change the subject of conversation. But it was quite different with her husband. To his looser, less-restrained mind, it was agreeable to hear of, and still more to see, the attention which his daughter's beauty received. He felt it as reflecting consequence on himself. He had never troubled his mind with speculations as to whether he himself was popular, still less whether he was respected. He was pretty welcome wherever he went, as a jovial good-natured man, who had done adventurous and illegal things in his youth, which in some measure entitled him to speak out his opinions on life in general in the authoritative manner he generally used; but, of the two, he preferred consorting with younger men, to taking a sober stand of respectability with the elders of the place; and he perceived, without reasoning upon it, that the gay daring spirits were more desirous of his company when Sylvia was by his side than at any other time. One or two of these would saunter up to Haytersbank on a Sunday afternoon, and lounge round his fields with the old farmer. Bell kept herself from the nap which had been her weekly solace for years, in order to look after Sylvia, and on such occasions she always turned as cold a shoulder to the visitors as her sense of hospitality and of duty to her husband would permit. But if they did not enter the house, old Robson would always have Sylvia with him when he went the round of his land. Bell could see them from the upper window: the young men standing in the attitudes of listeners, while Daniel laid down the law on some point, enforcing his words by pantomimic actions with his thick stick; and Sylvia, half turning away as if from some too admiring gaze, was possibly picking flowers out of the hedgebank. These Sunday afternoon strolls were the plague of Bell's life that whole summer. Then it took as much of artifice as was in the simple woman's nature to keep Daniel from insisting on having Sylvia's company every time he went down to Monkshaven. And here, again, came a perplexity, the acknowledgement of which in distinct thought would have been an act of disloyalty, according to Bell's conscience. If Sylvia went with her father, he never drank to excess; and that was a good gain to health at any rate (drinking was hardly a sin against morals in those days, and in that place); so, occasionally, she was allowed to accompany him to Monkshaven as a check upon his folly; for he was too fond and proud of his daughter to disgrace her by any open excess. But one Sunday afternoon early in November, Philip came up before the time at which he usually paid his visits. He looked grave and pale; and his aunt began,—

'Why, lad! what's been ado? Thou'rt looking as peaked and pined as a Methody preacher after a love-feast,* when he's talked hisself to Death's door. Thee dost na' get good milk enow, that's what it is, – such stuff as Monkshaven folks put up wi'!'

'No, aunt; I'm quite well. Only I'm a bit put out – vexed like at what I've heerd about Sylvie.'

His aunt's face changed immediately.

'And whatten folk say of her, next thing?'

'Oh,' said Philip, struck by the difference of look and manner in his aunt, and subdued by seeing how instantly she took alarm. 'It were only my uncle; – he should na' take a girl like her to a public. She were wi' him at t' "Admiral's Head" upo' All Souls' Day – that were all. There were many a one there beside, – it were statute fair;* but such a one as our Sylvie ought not to be cheapened wi' t' rest.'

'And he took her there, did he?' said Bell, in severe meditation. 'I had never no opinion o' th' wenches as 'll set theirselves to be hired for servants i' th' fair; they're a bad lot, as cannot find places for theirselves – 'bout going and stannin' to be stared at by folk, and grinnin' wi' th' plough-lads when no one's looking; it's a bad look-out for t' missus as takes one o' these wenches for a servant; and dost ta mean to say as my Sylvie went and demeaned hersel' to dance and marlock* wi' a' th' fair-folk at th' "Admiral's Head?" '

'No, no, she did na' dance; she barely set foot i' th' room; but it were her own pride as saved her; uncle would niver ha' kept her from it, for he had fallen in wi' Hayley o' Seaburn and one or two others, and they were having a glass i' t' bar, and Mrs Lawson, t' landlady, knew how there was them who would come and dance among parish 'prentices if need were, just to get a word or a look wi' Sylvie! So she tempts her in, saying that the room were all smartened and fine wi' flags; and there was them in the room as told me that they never were so startled as when they saw our Sylvie's face peeping in among all t' flustered maids and men, rough and red wi' weather and drink; and Jem Macbean, he said she were just like a bit o' apple-blossom among peonies; and some man, he didn't know who, went up and spoke to her; an' either at that, or at some o' t' words she heard – for they'd got a good way on afore that time – she went quite white and mad, as if fire were coming out of her eyes, and then she turned red and left the room, for all t' landlady tried to laugh it off and keep her in.'

'I'll be down to Monkshaven before I'm a day older, and tell Margaret Lawson some on my mind as she'll not forget in a hurry.'

Bell moved as though she would put on her cloak and hood there and then.

'Nay, it's not in reason as a woman i' that line o' life shouldn't try to make her house agreeable,' said Philip.

'Not wi' my wench,' said Bell, in a determined voice.

Philip's information had made a deeper impression on his aunt than he intended. He himself had been annoyed more at the idea that Sylvia would be spoken of as having been at a rough piece of rustic gaiety – a yearly festival for the lower classes of Yorkshire servants, out-door as well as in-door –

than at the affair itself, for he had learnt from his informant how instantaneous her appearance had been. He stood watching his aunt's troubled face, and almost wishing that he had not spoken. At last she heaved a deep sigh, and stirring the fire, as if by this little household occupation to compose her mind, she said—

'It's a pity as wenches aren't lads, or married folk. I could ha' wished – but it were the Lord's will – It would ha' been summut to look to, if she'd had a brother. My master is so full on his own thoughts, yo' see, he's no mind left for thinking on her, what wi' th' oats, and th' wool, and th' young colt, and his venture i' th' *Lucky Mary*.'

She really believed her husband to have the serious and important occupation for his mind that she had been taught to consider befitting the superior intellect of the masculine gender; she would have taxed herself severely, if, even in thought, she had blamed him, and Philip respected her feelings too much to say that Sylvia's father ought to look after her more closely if he made such a pretty creature so constantly his companion; yet some such speech was only just pent within Philip's closed lips. Again his aunt spoke—

'I used to think as she and yo' might fancy one another, but thou'rt too old-fashioned like for her; ye would na' suit; and it's as well, for now I can say to thee, that I would take it very kindly if thou would'st look after her a bit.'

Philip's countenance fell into gloom. He had to gulp down certain feelings before he could make answer with discretion.

'How can I look after her, and me tied to the shop more and more every day?'

'I could send her on a bit of an errand to Foster's, and then, for sure, yo' might keep an eye upon her when she's in th' town; and just walk a bit way with her when she's in th' street, and keep t' other fellows off her – Ned Simpson, t' butcher, in 'special, for folks do say he means no good by any girl he goes wi' – and I'll ask father to leave her a bit more wi' me. They're coming down th' brow, and Ned Simpson wi' them. Now, Philip, I look to thee to do a brother's part by my wench, and warn off all as isn't fit.'

The door opened, and the coarse strong voice of Simpson made itself heard. He was a stout man, comely enough as to form and feature, but with a depth of colour in his face that betokened the coming on of the habits of the sot. His Sunday hat was in his hand, and he smoothed the long nap of it, as he said, with a mixture of shyness and familiarity—

'Sarvant, missus. Yo'r measter is fain that I should come in an' have a drop; no offence, I hope?'

Sylvia passed quickly through the house-place, and went upstairs without speaking to her cousin Philip or to any one. He sat on, disliking the visitor, and almost disliking his hospitable uncle for having brought Simpson into the house, sympathizing with his aunt in the spirit which prompted her curt answers, and in the intervals of all these feelings wondering what ground she had for speaking as if she had now given up all thought of Sylvia and him ever being married, and in what way he was too 'old-fashioned.'

Robson would gladly have persuaded Philip to join him and Simpson in their drink, but Philip was in no sociable mood, and sate a little aloof, watching the staircase down which sooner or later Sylvia must come, for, as perhaps has been already said, the stairs went up straight out of the kitchen. And at length his yearning watch was rewarded; first, the little pointed toe came daintily in sight, then the trim ankle in the tight blue stocking, the wool of which was spun and the web of which was knitted by her mother's careful hands; then the full brown stuff petticoat, the arm holding the petticoat back in decent folds, so as not to encumber the descending feet; the slender neck and shoulders hidden under the folded square of fresh white muslin; the crowning beauty of the soft innocent face radiant in colour, and with the light brown curls clustering around. She made her way quickly to Philip's side; how his heart beat at her approach! and even more when she entered into a low-voiced *tête-à-tête*.

'Isn't he gone yet?' said she. 'I cannot abide him; I could ha' pinched father when he asked him for t' come in.'

'Maybe, he'll not stay long,' said Philip, hardly understanding the meaning of what he said, so sweet was it to have her making her whispered confidences to him.

But Simpson was not going to let her alone in the dark corner between the door and the window. He began paying her some coarse country compliments – too strong in their direct flattery for even her father's taste, more especially as he saw by his wife's set lips and frowning brow how much she disapproved of their visitor's style of conversation.

'Come, measter, leave t' lass alone; she's set up enough a'ready, her mother makes such a deal on her. Yo' an' me's men for sensible talk at our time o' life. An', as I was saying, t' horse was a weaver if iver one was, as any one could ha' told as had come within a mile on him.'

And in this way the old farmer and the bluff butcher chatted on about horses, while Philip and Sylvia sate together, he turning over all manner of hopes and projects for the future, in spite of his aunt's opinion that he was too 'old-fashioned' for her dainty, blooming daughter. Perhaps, too, Mrs Robson saw some reason for changing her mind on this head as she watched Sylvia this night, for she accompanied Philip to the door, when the time came for him to start homewards, and bade him 'good-night' with unusual fervour, adding—

'Thou'st been a deal o' comfort to me, lad – a'most as one as if thou wert a child o' my own, as at times I could welly think thou art to be. Anyways, I trust to thee to look after the lile* lass, as has no brother to guide her among men – and men's very kittle* for a woman to deal wi; but if thou'lt have an eye on whom she consorts wi', my mind 'll be easier.'

Philip's heart beat fast, but his voice was as calm as usual when he replied—

'I'd just keep her a bit aloof from Monkshaven folks; a lass is always the more thought on for being chary of herself; and as for t' rest, I'll have an eye to the folks she goes among, and if I see that they don't befit her, I'll just give her a warning, for she's not one to like such chaps as yon Simpson there; she can see what's becoming in a man to say to a lass, and what's not.'

Philip set out on his two-mile walk home with a tumult of happiness in his heart. He was not often carried away by delusions of his own creating; to-night he thought he had good ground for believing that by patient self-restraint he might win Sylvia's love. A year ago he had nearly earned her dislike by obtruding upon her looks and words betokening his passionate love. He alarmed her girlish coyness, as well as wearied her with the wish he had then felt that she should take an interest in his pursuits. But, with unusual wisdom, he had perceived his mistake; it was many months now since he had betrayed, by word or look, that she was anything more to him than a little cousin to be cared for and protected when need was. The consequence was that she had become tamed, just as a wild animal is tamed; he had remained tranquil and impassive, almost as if he did not perceive her shy advances towards friendliness. These advances were made by her after the lessons had ceased. She was afraid lest he was displeased with her behaviour in rejecting his instructions, and was not easy till she was at peace with him; and now, to all appearance, he and she were perfect friends, but nothing more. In his absence she would not allow her young companions to laugh at his grave sobriety of character, and somewhat prim demeanour; she would even go against her conscience, and deny that she perceived any peculiarity. When she wanted it, she sought his advice on such small subjects as came up in her daily life; and she tried not to show signs of weariness when he used more words – and more difficult words – than were necessary to convey his ideas. But her ideal husband was different from Philip in every point, the two images never for an instant merged into one. To Philip she was the only woman in the world; it was the one subject on which he dared not consider, for fear that both conscience and judgment should decide against him, and that he should be convinced against his will that she was an unfit mate for him, that she never would be his, and that it was waste of time and life to keep her shrined in the dearest sanctuary of his being, to the exclusion of all the serious and religious aims which, in any other case, he would have been the first to acknowledge as the object he ought to pursue. For he had been brought up among the Quakers, and shared in their austere distrust of a self-seeking spirit; yet what else but self-seeking was his passionate prayer, 'Give me Sylvia, or else, I die?' No other vision had ever crossed his masculine fancy for a moment; his was a rare and constant love that deserved a better fate than it met with. At this time his hopes were high, as I have said, not merely as to the growth of Sylvia's feelings towards him, but as to the probability of his soon being in a position to place her in such comfort, as his wife, as she had never enjoyed before.

For the brothers Foster were thinking of retiring from business, and relinquishing the shop to their two shopmen, Philip Hepburn and William Coulson. To be sure, it was only by looking back for a few months, and noticing chance expressions and small indications, that this intention of theirs could be discovered. But every step they took tended this way, and Philip knew their usual practice of deliberation too well to feel in the least impatient for the quicker progress of the end which he saw steadily approaching. The whole atmosphere of life among the Friends at this date partook of this character of self-repression, and both Coulson and Hepburn shared in it. Coulson was just as much aware of the prospect opening before him as Hepburn; but they never spoke together on the subject, although their mutual knowledge might be occasionally implied in their conversation on their future lives. Meanwhile the Fosters were imparting more of the background of their business to their successors. For the present, at least, the brothers meant to retain an interest in the shop, even after they had given up the active management; and they sometimes thought of setting up a separate establishment as bankers. The separation of the business, – the introduction of their shopmen to the distant manufacturers who furnished their goods (in those days the system of 'travellers' was not so widely organized as it is at present), – all these steps were in gradual progress; and already Philip saw himself in imagination in the dignified position of joint master of the principal shop in Monkshaven, with Sylvia installed as his wife, with certainly a silk gown, and possibly a gig at her disposal. In all Philip's visions of future prosperity, it was Sylvia who was to be aggrandized by them; his own life was to be spent as it was now, pretty much between the four shop walls.

CHAPTER XII

NEW YEAR'S FÊTE

ALL this enlargement of interest in the shop occupied Philip fully for some months after the period referred to in the preceding chapter. Remembering his last conversation with his aunt, he might have been uneasy at his inability to perform his promise and look after his pretty cousin, but that about the middle of November Bell Robson had fallen ill of a rheumatic fever, and that her daughter had been entirely absorbed in nursing her. No thought of company or gaiety was in Sylvia's mind as long as her mother's illness lasted; vehement in all her feelings, she discovered in the dread of losing her mother how passionately she was attached to her. Hitherto she had supposed, as children so often do, that her parents would live for ever; and now when it was a question of days, whether by that time the following week her mother might not be buried out of her sight for ever, she clung to every semblance of service to be rendered, or affection shown, as if she hoped to condense the love and care of years into the few days only that might remain. Mrs Robson lingered on, began slowly to recover, and before Christmas was again sitting by the fireside in the house-place, wan and pulled down, muffled up with shawls and blankets, but still there once more, where not long before Sylvia had scarcely expected to see her again. Philip came up that evening and found Sylvia in wild spirits. She thought that everything was done, now that her mother had once come downstairs again; she laughed with glee; she kissed her mother; she shook hands with Philip, she almost submitted to a speech of more than usual tenderness from him; but, in the midst of his words, her mother's pillows wanted arranging and she went to her chair, paying no more heed to his words than if they had been addressed to the cat, that lying on the invalid's knee was purring out her welcome to the weak hand feebly stroking her back. Robson himself soon came in, looking older and more subdued since Philip had seen him last. He was very urgent that his wife should have some spirits and water; but on her refusal, almost as if she loathed the thought of the smell, he contented himself with sharing her tea, though he kept abusing the beverage as 'washing the heart out of a man,' and attributing all the degeneracy of the world, growing up about him in his old age, to the drinking of such slop. At the same time, his little self-sacrifice put him in an unusually good temper; and, mingled with his real gladness at having his wife once more on the way to recovery, brought back some of the old charm of tenderness combined with light-heartedness, which had won the sober Isabella Preston long ago. He sat by her side, holding her hand, and talking of old times to the young couple opposite; of his adventures and escapes, and how he had won his wife. She, faintly smiling at the remembrance of those days, yet half-ashamed at having the little details of her courtship revealed, from time to time kept saying,—

'For shame wi' thee, Dannel – I never did,' and faint denials of a similar kind.

'Niver believe her, Sylvie. She were a woman, and there's niver a woman but likes to have a sweetheart, and can tell when a chap's castin' sheep's-eyes at her; ay, an' afore he knows what he's about hissen. She were a pretty one then, was my old 'ooman, an' liked them as thought her so, though she did cock her head high, as bein' a Preston, which were a family o' standin' and means i' those parts aforetime. There's Philip there, I'll warrant, is as proud o' bein' Preston by t' mother's side, for it runs i' t' blood, lass. A can tell when a child of a Preston tak's to being proud o' their kin, by t' cut o' their nose. Now Philip's and my missus has a turn beyond common i' their nostrils, as if they was sniffin' at t' rest of us world, an' seein' if we was good enough for 'em to consort wi'.

Thee an' me, lass, is Robsons – oat-cake folk, while they's pie-crust. Lord! how Bell used to speak to me, as short as though a wasn't a Christian, an' a' t' time she loved me as her very life, an' well a knew it, tho' a'd to mak' as tho' a didn't. Philip, when thou goes courtin', come t' me, and a'll give thee many a wrinkle. A've shown, too, as a know well how t' choose a good wife by tokens an' signs, hannot a, missus? Come t' me, my lad, and show me t' lass, an' a'll just tak' a squint at her, an' tell yo' if she'll do or not; an' if she'll do, a'll teach yo' how to win her.'

'They say another o' yon Corney girls is going to be married,' said Mrs Robson, in her faint deliberate tones.

'By gosh, an' it's well thou'st spoke on 'em; a was as clean forgettin' it as iver could be. A met Nanny Corney i' Monkshaven last neet, and she axed me for t' let our Sylvia come o' New Year's Eve, an' see Molly an' her man, that 'n as is wed beyond Newcassel, they'll be over at her feyther's, for t' New Year, an' there's to be a merry-making.'

Sylvia's colour came, her eyes brightened, she would have liked to go; but the thought of her mother came across her, and her features fell. Her mother's eye caught the look and the change, and knew what both meant as well as if Sylvia had spoken out.

'Thursday se'nnight,' said she. 'I'll be rare and strong by then, and Sylvie shall go play hersen; she's been nurse-tending long enough.'

'You're but weakly yet,' said Philip shortly; he did not intend to say it, but the words seemed to come out in spite of himself.

'A said as our lass should come, God willin', if she only came and went, an' thee goin' on sprightly, old 'ooman. An' a'll turn nurse-tender mysen for t' occasion, 'special if thou can stand t' good honest smell o' whisky by then. So, my lass, get up thy smart clothes, and cut t' best on 'em out, as becomes a Preston. Maybe, a'll fetch thee home, an' maybe Philip will convoy thee, for Nanny Corney bade thee to t' merry-making, as well. She said her measter would be seein' thee about t' wool afore then.'

'I don't think as I can go,' said Philip, secretly pleased to know that he had the opportunity in his power; 'I'm half bound to go wi' Hester Rose and her mother to t' watch-night.'*

'Is Hester a Methodee?' asked Sylvia in surprise.

'No! she's neither a Methodee, nor a Friend, nor a Church person; but she's a turn for serious things, choose wherever they're found.'

'Well, then,' said good-natured farmer Robson, only seeing the surface of things, 'a'll make shift to fetch Sylvie back fra' t' merry-making, and thee an' thy young woman can go to t' prayer-makin'; it's every man to his taste, say I.'

But in spite of his half-promise, nay against his natural inclination, Philip was lured to the Corneys' by the thought of meeting Sylvia, of watching her and exulting in her superiority in pretty looks and ways to all the other girls likely to be assembled. Besides (he told his conscience) he was pledged to his aunt to watch over Sylvia like a brother. So in the interval before New Year's Eve, he silently revelled as much as any young girl in the anticipation of the happy coming time.

At this hour, all the actors in this story having played out their parts and gone to their rest, there is something touching in recording the futile efforts made by Philip to win from Sylvia the love he yearned for. But, at the time, any one who had watched him might have been amused to see the grave, awkward, plain young man studying patterns and colours for a new waistcoat, with his head a little on one side, after the meditative manner common to those who are choosing a new article of dress. They might have smiled could they have read in his imagination the frequent rehearsals of the coming evening, when he and she should each be dressed in their gala atire, to spend a few hours under a bright, festive aspect, among people whose company would oblige them to assume a new demeanour towards each other, not so familiar as their everyday manner, but allowing more scope for the expression of rustic gallantry. Philip had so seldom been to anything of the kind, that, even had Sylvia not been going, he would have felt a kind of shy excitement at the prospect of anything so unusual. But, indeed, if Sylvia had not been going, it is very probable that Philip's rigid conscience might have been aroused to the question whether such parties did not savour too much of the world for him to form one in them.

As it was, however, the facts to him were simply these. He was going and she was going. The day before, he had hurried off to Haytersbank Farm with a small paper parcel in his pocket – a ribbon with a little briar-rose pattern running upon it for Sylvia. It was the first thing he had ever ventured to give her – the first thing of the kind would, perhaps, be more accurate; for when he had first begun to teach her any lessons, he had given her Mavor's Spelling-book,* but that he might have done, out of zeal for knowledge, to any dunce of a little girl of his acquaintance. This ribbon was quite a different kind of present; he touched it tenderly, as if he were caressing it, when he thought of her wearing it; the briar-rose (sweetness and thorns) seemed to be the very flower for her; the soft, green ground on which the pink and brown pattern ran, was just the colour to show off her complexion. And she would in a way belong to him: her cousin, her mentor, her chaperon, her lover! While others only admired, he might hope to appropriate; for of late they had been such happy friends! Her mother approved of him, her father liked him. A few months, perhaps only a few weeks more of self-restraint, and then he might go and speak openly of his wishes, and what he had to offer. For he had resolved, with the quiet force of his character, to wait until all was finally settled between him and his masters, before he declared himself to either Sylvia or her parents. The interval was spent in patient, silent endeavours to recommend himself to her.

He had to give his ribbon to his aunt in charge for Sylvia, and that was a disappointment to his fancy, although he tried to reason himself into thinking that it was better so. He had not time to wait for her return from some errand on which she had gone, for he was daily more and more occupied with the affairs of the shop.

Sylvia made many a promise to her mother, and more to

herself, that she would not stay late at the party, but she might go as early as she liked; and before the December daylight had faded away, Sylvia presented herself at the Corneys'. She was to come early in order to help to set out the supper, which was arranged in the large old flagged parlour, which served as best bed-room as well. It opened out of the house-place, and was the sacred room of the house, as chambers of a similar description are still considered in retired farm-houses in the north of England. They are used on occasions like the one now described for purposes of hospitality; but in the state bed, overshadowing so large a portion of the floor, the births and, as far as may be, the deaths, of the household take place. At the Corneys', the united efforts of some former generation of the family had produced patchwork curtains and coverlet; and patchwork was patchwork in those days, before the early Yates and Peels had found out the secret of printing the parsley-leaf.* Scraps of costly Indian chintzes and palempours* were intermixed with commoner black and red calico in minute hexagons; and the variety of patterns served for the useful purpose of promoting conversation as well as the more obvious one of displaying the work-woman's taste. Sylvia, for instance, began at once to her old friend, Molly Brunton, who had accompanied her into this chamber to take off her hat and cloak, with a remark on one of the chintzes. Stooping over the counterpane, with a face into which the flush would come whether or no, she said to Molly,—

'Dear! I never seed this one afore – this – for all t' world like th' eyes in a peacock's tail.'

'Thou's seen it many a time and oft, lass. But weren't thou surprised to find Charley here? We picked him up at Shields, quite by surprise like; and when Brunton and me said as we was comin' here, nought would serve him but comin' with us, for t' see t' New Year in. It's a pity as your mother's ta'en this time for t' fall ill and want yo' back so early.'

Sylvia had taken off her hat and cloak by this time, and began to help Molly and a younger unmarried sister in laying out the substantial supper.

'Here,' continued Mrs Brunton; 'stick a bit o' holly i' yon

pig's mouth, that's the way we do things i' Newcassel; but folks is so behindhand in Monkshaven. It's a fine thing to live in a large town, Sylvia; an' if yo're looking out for a husband, I'd advise yo' to tak' one as lives in a town. I feel as if I were buried alive comin' back here, such an out-o'-t'-way place after t' Side, wheere there's many a hundred carts and carriages goes past in a day. I've a great mind for t' tak yo' two lassies back wi' me, and let yo' see a bit o' t' world; maybe, I may yet.'

Her sister Bessy looked much pleased with this plan, but Sylvia was rather inclined to take offence at Molly's patronizing ways, and replied,—

'I'm none so fond o' noise and bustle; why, yo'll not be able to hear yoursels speak wi' all them carts and carriages. I'd rayther bide at home; let alone that mother can't spare me.'

It was, perhaps, a rather ungracious way of answering Molly Brunton's speech, and so she felt it to be, although her invitation had been none of the most courteously worded. She irritated Sylvia still further by repeating her last words,—

' "Mother can't spare me;" why, mother 'll have to spare thee sometime, when t' time for wedding comes.'

'I'm none going to be wed,' said Sylvia; 'and if I were, I'd niver go far fra' mother.'

'Eh! what a spoilt darling it is. How Brunton will laugh when I tell him about yo'; Brunton's a rare one for laughin'. It's a great thing to have got such a merry man for a husband. Why! he has his joke for every one as comes into t' shop; and he'll ha' something funny to say to everything this evenin'.'

Bessy saw that Sylvia was annoyed, and, with more delicacy than her sister, she tried to turn the conversation.

'That's a pretty ribbon in thy hair, Sylvia; I'd like to have one o' t' same pattern. Feyther likes pickled walnuts stuck about t' round o' beef, Molly.'

'I know what I'm about,' replied Mrs Brunton, with a toss of her married head.

Bessy resumed her inquiry.

'Is there any more to be had wheere that come fra', Sylvia?'

'I don't know,' replied Sylvia. 'It come fra' Foster's, and yo' can ask.'

'What might it cost?' said Betsy, fingering an end of it to test its quality.

'I can't tell,' said Sylvia, 'it were a present.'

'Niver mak' ado about t' price,' said Molly; 'I'll gi'e thee enough on 't to tie up thy hair, just like Sylvia's. Only thou hastn't such wealth o' curls as she has; it'll niver look t' same i' thy straight locks. And who might it be as give it thee, Sylvia?' asked the unscrupulous, if good-natured Molly.

'My cousin Philip, him as is shopman at Foster's,' said Sylvia, innocently. But it was far too good an opportunity for the exercise of Molly's kind of wit for her to pass over.

'Oh, oh! our cousin Philip, is it? and he'll not be living so far away from your mother? I've no need be a witch to put two and two together. He's a coming here to-night, isn't he, Bessy?'

'I wish yo' wouldn't talk so, Molly,' said Sylvia; 'me and Philip is good enough friends, but we niver think on each other in that way; leastways, I don't——'

'(Sweet butter! now that's my mother's old-fashioned way; as if folks must eat sweet butter now-a-days, because her mother did!) That way,' continued Molly, in the manner that annoyed Sylvia so much, repeating her words as if for the purpose of laughing at them. '"That way?" and pray what is t' way yo're speaking on? I niver said nought about marrying, did I, that yo' need look so red and shamefaced about yo'r cousin Philip? But, as Brunton says, if t' cap fits yo', put it on. I'm glad he's comin' to-night tho', for as I'm done makin' love and courtin', it's next best t' watch other folks; an' yo'r face, Sylvia, has letten me into a secret, as I'd some glimpses on afore I was wed.'

Sylvia secretly determined not to speak a word more to Philip than she could help, and wondered how she could ever have liked Molly at all, much less have made a companion of her. The table was now laid out, and nothing remained but to criticise the arrangement a little.

Bessy was full of admiration.

'Theere, Molly!' said she. 'Yo' niver seed more vittle brought together i' Newcassel, I'll be bound; there'll be above half a hundredweight o' butcher's meat, beside pies and custards. I've eaten no dinner these two days for thinking on 't; it's been a weary burden on my mind, but it's off now I see how well it looks. I told mother not to come near it till we'd spread it all out, and now I'll go fetch her.'

Bessy ran off into the house-place.

'It's well enough in a country kind o' way,' said Molly, with the faint approbation of condescension. 'But if I'd thought on, I'd ha' brought 'em down a beast or two done i' sponge-cake, wi' currants for his eyes to give t' table an air.'

The door was opened, and Bessy came in smiling and blushing with proud pleasure. Her mother followed her on tip-toe, smoothing down her apron, and with her voice subdued to a whisper:—

'Ay, my lass, it *is* fine! But dunnot mak' an ado about it, let 'em think it's just our common way. If any one says aught about how good t' vittle is, tak' it calm, and say we'n better i' t' house, – it'll mak' 'em eat wi' a better appetite, and think the more on us. Sylvie, I'm much beholden t' ye for comin' so early, and helpin' t' lasses, but yo' mun come in t' house-place now, t' folks is gatherin', an' yo'r cousin's been asking after yo' a'ready.'

Molly gave her a nudge, which made Sylvia's face go all aflame with angry embarrassment. She was conscious that the watching which Molly had threatened her with began directly; for Molly went up to her husband, and whispered something to him which set him off in a chuckling laugh, and Sylvia was aware that his eyes followed her about with knowing looks all the evening. She would hardly speak to Philip, and pretended not to see his outstretched hand, but passed on to the chimney-corner, and tried to shelter herself behind the broad back of farmer Corney, who had no notion of relinquishing his customary place for all the young people who ever came to the house, – or for any old people either, for that matter. It was his household throne, and there he sat with no more idea of abdicating in favour of any comer than

King George at St James's. But he was glad to see his friends; and had paid them the unwonted compliment of shaving on a week-day, and putting on his Sunday coat. The united efforts of wife and children had failed to persuade him to make any farther change in his attire; to all their arguments on this head he had replied,—

'Them as doesn't like t' see me i' my work-a-day wescut and breeches may bide away.'

It was the longest sentence he said that day, but he repeated it several times over. He was glad enough to see all the young people, but they were not 'of his kidney,' as he expressed it to himself, and he did not feel any call upon himself to entertain them. He left that to his bustling wife, all smartness and smiles, and to his daughters and son-in-law. His efforts at hospitality consisted in sitting still, smoking his pipe; when any one came, he took it out of his mouth for an instant, and nodded his head in a cheerful friendly way, without a word of speech; and then returned to his smoking with the greater relish for the moment's intermission. He thought to himself:—

'They're a set o' young chaps as thinks more on t' lasses than on baccy; – they'll find out their mistake in time; give 'em time, give 'em time.'

And before eight o'clock, he went as quietly as a man of twelve stone can upstairs to bed, having made a previous arrangement with his wife that she should bring him up about two pounds of spiced beef, and a hot tumbler of stiff grog. But at the beginning of the evening he formed a good screen for Sylvia, who was rather a favourite with the old man, for twice he spoke to her.

'Feyther smokes?'

'Yes,' said Sylvia.

'Reach me t' baccy-box, my lass.'

And that was all the conversation that passed between her and her nearest neighbour for the first quarter of an hour after she came into company.

But, for all her screen, she felt a pair of eyes were fixed upon her with a glow of admiration deepening their honest brightness. Somehow, look in what direction she would, she caught the glance of those eyes before she could see anything else. So she played with her apron-strings, and tried not to feel so conscious. There were another pair of eyes, – not such beautiful, sparkling eyes, – deep-set, earnest, sad, nay, even gloomy, watching her every movement; but of this she was not aware. Philip had not recovered from the rebuff she had given him by refusing his offered hand, and was standing still, in angry silence, when Mrs Corney thrust a young woman just arrived upon his attention.

'Come, Measter Hepburn, here's Nancy Pratt wi'out ev'n a soul to speak t' her, an' yo' mopin' theere. She says she knows yo' by sight fra' having dealt at Foster's these six year. See if yo' can't find summut t' say t' each other, for I mun go pour out tea. Dixons, an' Walkers, an' Elliotts, an' Smiths is come,' said she, marking off the families on her fingers, as she looked round and called over their names; 'an' there's only Will Latham an' his two sisters, and Roger Harbottle, an' Taylor t' come! an' they'll turn up afore tea's ended.'

So she went off to her duty at the one table, which, placed alongside of the dresser, was the only article of furniture left in the middle of the room: all the seats being arranged as close to the four walls as could be managed. The candles of those days gave but a faint light compared to the light of the immense fire, which it was a point of hospitality to keep at the highest roaring, blazing pitch; the young women occupied the seats, with the exception of two or three of the elder ones, who, in an eager desire to show their capability, insisted on helping Mrs Corney in her duties, very much to her annoyance, as there were certain little contrivances for eking out cream, and adjusting the strength of the cups of tea to the worldly position of the intended drinkers, which she did not like every one to see. The young men, – whom tea did not embolden, and who had as yet had no chance of stronger liquor, – clustered in rustic shyness round the door, not speaking even to themselves, except now and then, when one, apparently the wag of the party, made some whispered remark, which set them all off laughing; but in a minute they checked themselves, and passed the back of their hands across their mouths to compose that unlucky feature, and then some would try to fix their eyes on the rafters of the ceiling, in a manner which was decorous if rather abstracted from the business in hand. Most of these were young farmers, with whom Philip had nothing in common, and from whom, in shy reserve, he had withdrawn himself when he first came in. But now he wished himself among them sooner than set to talk to Nancy Pratt, when he had nothing to say. And yet he might have had a companion less to his mind, for she was a decent young woman of a sober age, less inclined to giggle than many of the younger ones. But all the time that he was making commonplace remarks to her he was wondering if he had offended Sylvia, and why she would not shake hands with him, and this pre-occupation of his thoughts did not make him an agreeable companion. Nancy Pratt, who had been engaged for some years to a mate of a whaling-ship, perceived something of his state of mind, and took no offence at it; on the contrary, she tried to give him pleasure by admiring Sylvia.

'I've often heerd tell on her,' said she, 'but I niver thought she's be so pretty, and so staid and quiet-like too. T' most part o' girls as has looks like hers are always gape-gazing to catch other folks's eyes, and see what is thought on 'em; but she looks just like a child, a bit flustered wi' coming into company, and gettin' into as dark a corner and bidin' as still as she can.'

Just then Sylvia lifted up her long, dark lashes, and catching the same glance which she had so often met before – Charley Kinraid was standing talking to Brunton on the opposite side of the fire-place – she started back into the shadow as if she had not expected it, and in so doing spilt her tea all over her gown. She could almost have cried, she felt herself so awkward, and as if everything was going wrong with her; she thought that every one would think she had never been in company before, and did not know how to behave; and while she was thus fluttered and crimson, she saw through her tearful eyes Kinraid on his knees before her, wiping her gown with his silk pocket handkerchief, and heard him speaking through all the buzz of commiserating voices.

'Your cupboard handle is so much i' th' way – I hurt my elbow against it only this very afternoon.'

So perhaps it was no clumsiness of hers, – as they would all know, now, since he had so skilfully laid the blame somewhere else; and after all it turned out that her accident had been the means of bringing him across to her side, which was much more pleasant than having him opposite, staring at her; for now he began to talk to her, and this was very pleasant, although she was rather embarrassed at their *tête-à-tête* at first.

'I did not know you again when I first saw you,' said he, in a tone which implied a good deal more than was uttered in words.

'I knowed yo' at once,' she replied, softly, and then she blushed and played with her apron-string, and wondered if she ought to have confessed to the clearness of her recollection.

'You're grown up into – well, perhaps it's not manners to say what you're grown into – anyhow, I shan't forget yo' again.'

More playing with her apron-string, and head hung still lower down, though the corners of her mouth would go up in a shy smile of pleasure. Philip watched it all as greedily as if it gave him delight.

'Yo'r father, he'll be well and hearty, I hope?' asked Charley.

'Yes,' replied Sylvia, and then she wished she could originate some remark; he would think her so stupid if she just kept on saying such little short bits of speeches, and if he thought her stupid he might perhaps go away again to his former place.

But he was quite far enough gone in love of her beauty, and pretty modest ways, not to care much whether she talked or no, so long as she showed herself so pleasingly conscious of his close neighbourhood.

'I must come and see the old gentleman; and your mother, too,' he added more slowly, for he remembered that his visits last year had not been quite so much welcomed by Bell

Robson as by her husband; perhaps it was because of the amount of drink which he and Daniel managed to get through of an evening. He resolved this year to be more careful to please the mother of Sylvia.

When tea was ended there was a great bustle and shifting of places, while Mrs Corney and her daughters carried out trays full of used cups, and great platters of uneaten bread and butter into the back-kitchen, to be washed up after the guests were gone. Just because she was so conscious that she did not want to move, and break up the little conversation between herself and Kinraid, Sylvia forced herself to be as active in the service going on as became a friend of the house; and she was too much her mother's own daughter to feel comfortable at leaving all the things in the disorder which to the Corney girls was second nature.

'This milk mun go back to t' dairy, I reckon,' said she, loading herself with milk and cream.

'Niver fash thysel'* about it,' said Nelly Corney, 'Christmas comes but onest a year, if it does go sour; and mother said she'd have a game at forfeits first thing after tea to loosen folks's tongues, and mix up t' lads and lasses, so come along.'

But Sylvia steered her careful way to the cold chill of the dairy, and would not be satisfied till she had carried away all the unused provision into some fresher air than that heated by the fires and ovens used for the long day's cooking of pies and cakes and much roast meat.

When they came back a round of red-faced 'lads,' as young men up to five-and-thirty are called in Lancashire and Yorkshire if they are not married before, and lasses, whose age was not to be defined, were playing at some country game, in which the women were apparently more interested than the men, who looked shamefaced, and afraid of each other's ridicule. Mrs Corney, however, knew how to remedy this, and at a sign from her a great jug of beer was brought in. This jug was the pride of her heart, and was in the shape of a fat man in white knee-breeches, and a three-cornered hat; with one arm he supported the pipe in his broad, smiling mouth, and the other was placed akimbo and formed the handle. There was also a great china punch-bowl filled with grog made after an old ship-receipt current in these parts, but not too strong, because if their visitors had too much to drink at that early part of the evening 'it would spoil t' fun,' as Nelly Corney had observed. Her father, however, after the notions of hospitality prevalent at that time in higher circles, had stipulated that each man should have 'enough' before he left the house; enough meaning in Monkshaven parlance the liberty of getting drunk, if they thought fit to do it.

Before long one of the lads was seized with a fit of admiration for Toby – the name of the old gentleman who contained liquor – and went up to the tray for a closer inspection. He was speedily followed by other amateurs of curious earthenware; and by-and-by Mr Brunton (who had been charged by his mother-in-law with the due supplying of liquor – by his father-in-law that every man should have his fill, and by his wife and her sisters that no one should have too much, at any rate at the beginning of the evening,) thought fit to carry out Toby to be replenished; and a faster spirit of enjoyment and mirth began to reign in the room.

Kinraid was too well seasoned to care what amount of liquor he drank; Philip had what was called a weak head, and disliked muddling himself with drink because of the immediate consequence of intense feelings of irritability, and the more distant one of a racking headache next day; so both these two preserved very much the same demeanour they had held at the beginning of the evening.

Sylvia was by all acknowledged and treated as the belle. When they played at blind-man's-buff go where she would, she was always caught; she was called out repeatedly to do what was required in any game, as if all had a pleasure in seeing her light figure and deft ways. She was sufficiently pleased with this to have got over her shyness with all except Charley. When others paid her their rustic compliments she tossed her head, and made her little saucy repartees; but when he said something low and flattering, it was too honey-sweet to her heart to be thrown off thus. And, somehow, the more she yielded to this fascination the more she avoided Philip.

He did not speak flatteringly – he did not pay compliments – he watched her with discontented, longing eyes, and grew more inclined every moment, as he remembered his anticipation of a happy evening, to cry out in his heart *vanitas vanitatum.**

And now came crying the forfeits. Molly Brunton knelt down, her face buried in her mother's lap; the latter took out the forfeits one by one, and as she held them up, said the accustomed formula,—

'A fine thing and a very fine thing, what must he (or she) do who owns this thing.'

One or two had been told to kneel to the prettiest, bow to the wittiest, and kiss those they loved best; others had had to bite an inch off the poker, or such plays upon words. And now came Sylvia's pretty new ribbon that Philip had given her (he almost longed to snatch it out of Mrs Corney's hands and burn it before all their faces, so annoyed was he with the whole affair.)

'A fine thing and a very fine thing – a most particular fine thing – choose how she came by it. What must she do as owns this thing?'

'She must blow out t' candle and kiss t' candlestick.'

In one instant Kinraid had hold of the only candle within reach, all the others had been put up high on inaccessible shelves and other places. Sylvia went up and blew out the candle, and before the sudden partial darkness was over he had taken the candle into his fingers, and, according to the traditional meaning of the words, was in the place of the candlestick, and as such was to be kissed. Every one laughed at innocent Sylvia's face as the meaning of her penance came into it, every one but Philip, who almost choked.

'I'm candlestick,' said Kinraid, with less of triumph in his voice than he would have had with any other girl in the room.

'Yo' mun kiss t' candlestick,' cried the Corneys, 'or yo'll niver get yo'r ribbon back.'

'And she sets a deal o' store by that ribbon,' said Molly Brunton, maliciously.

'I'll none kiss t' candlestick, nor him either,' said Sylvia, in a low voice of determination, turning away, full of confusion.

'Yo'll not get yo'r ribbon if yo' dunnot,' cried one and all.

'I don't care for t' ribbon,' said she, flashing up with a look at her tormentors, now her back was turned to Kinraid. 'An' I wannot play any more at such like games,' she added, with fresh indignation rising in her heart as she took her old place in the corner of the room a little away from the rest.

Philip's spirits rose, and he yearned to go to her and tell her how he approved of her conduct. Alas, Philip! Sylvia, though as modest a girl as ever lived, was no prude, and had been brought up in simple, straightforward country ways; and with any other young man, excepting, perhaps, Philip's self, she would have thought no more of making a rapid pretence of kissing the hand or cheek of the temporary 'candlestick,' than our ancestresses did in a much higher rank on similar occasions. Kinraid, though mortified by his public rejection, was more conscious of this than the inexperienced Philip; he resolved not to be baulked, and watched his opportunity. For the time he went on playing as if Sylvia's conduct had not affected him in the least, and as if he was hardly aware of her defection from the game. As she saw others submitting, quite as a matter of course, to similar penances, she began to be angry with herself for having thought twice about it, and almost to dislike herself for the strange consciousness which had made it at the time seem impossible to do what she was told. Her eyes kept filling with tears as her isolated position in the gay party, the thought of what a fool she had made of herself, kept recurring to her mind; but no one saw her, she thought, thus crying; and, ashamed to be discovered when the party should pause in their game, she stole round behind them into the great chamber in which she had helped to lay out the supper, with the intention of bathing her eyes, and taking a drink of water. One instant Charley Kinraid was missing from the circle of which he was the life and soul; and then back he came with an air of satisfaction on his face, intelligible enough to those who had seen his game; but unnoticed by Philip, who, amidst the perpetual noise and movements around him, had not perceived Sylvia's leaving the room, until she came back at the end of about a quarter of an hour, looking lovelier than ever, her complexion brilliant, her eyes drooping, her hair neatly and freshly arranged, tied with a brown ribbon instead of that she was supposed to have forfeited. She looked as if she did not wish her return to be noticed, stealing softly behind the romping lads and lasses with noiseless motions, and altogether such a contrast to them in her cool freshness and modest neatness, that both Kinraid and Philip found it difficult to keep their eyes off her. But the former had a secret triumph in his heart which enabled him to go on with his merry-making as if it absorbed him; while Philip dropped out of the crowd and came up to where she was standing silently by Mrs Corney, who, arms akimbo, was laughing at the frolic and fun around her. Sylvia started a little when Philip spoke, and kept her soft eyes averted from him after the first glance; she answered him shortly, but with unaccustomed gentleness. He had only asked her when she would like him to take her home; and she, a little surprised at the idea of going home when to her the evening seemed only beginning, had answered—

'Go home? I don't know! It's New Year's Eve!'

'Ay! but yo'r mother 'll lie awake till yo' come home, Sylvie!'

But Mrs Corney, having heard his question, broke in with all sorts of upbraidings. 'Go home! Not see t' New Year in! Why, what should take 'em home these six hours? Wasn't there a moon as clear as day? and did such a time as this come often? And were they to break up the party before the New Year came in? And was there not supper, with a spiced round of beef that had been in pickle pretty nigh sin' Martinmas, and hams, and mince-pies, and what not? And if they thought any evil of her master's going to bed, or that by that early retirement he meant to imply that he did not bid his friends welcome, why he would not stay up beyond eight o'clock for King George upon his throne, as he'd tell them soon enough, if they'd only step upstairs and ask him. Well;

she knowed what it was to want a daughter when she was ailing, so she'd say nought more, but hasten supper.'

And this idea now took possession of Mrs Corney's mind, for she would not willingly allow one of her guests to leave before they had done justice to her preparations; and, cutting her speech short, she hastily left Sylvia and Philip together.

His heart beat fast; his feeling towards her had never been so strong or so distinct as since her refusal to kiss the 'candlestick.' He was on the point of speaking, of saying something explicitly tender, when the wooden trencher which the party were using at their play, came bowling between him and Sylvia, and spun out its little period right betwixt them. Every one was moving from chair to chair, and when the bustle was over Sylvia was seated at some distance from him, and he left standing outside the circle, as if he were not playing. In fact, Sylvia had unconsciously taken his place as actor in the game while he remained spectator, and, as it turned out, an auditor of a conversation not intended for his ears. He was wedged against the wall, close to the great eight-day clock, with its round moon-like smiling face forming a ludicrous contrast to his long, sallow, grave countenance, which was pretty much at the same level above the sanded floor. Before him sat Molly Brunton and one of her sisters, their heads close together in too deep talk to attend to the progress of the game. Philip's attention was caught by the words—

'I'll lay any wager he kissed her when he ran off into t' parlour.'

'She's so coy she'd niver let him,' replied Bessy Corney.

'She couldn't help hersel'; and for all she looks so demure and prim now' (and then both heads were turned in the direction of Sylvia), 'I'm as sure as I'm born that Charley is not t' chap to lose his forfeit; and yet yo' see he says nought more about it, and she's left off being 'feared of him.'

There was something in Sylvia's look, ay, and in Charley Kinraid's, too, that shot conviction into Philip's mind. He watched them incessantly during the interval before supper; they were intimate, and yet shy with each other, in a manner that enraged while it bewildered Philip. What was Charley saying to her in that whispered voice, as they passed each other? Why did they linger near each other? Why did Sylvia look so dreamily happy, so startled at every call of the game, as if recalled from some pleasant idea? Why did Kinraid's eyes always seek her while hers were averted, or downcast, and her cheeks all aflame? Philip's dark brow grew darker as he gazed. He, too, started when Mrs Corney, close at his elbow, bade him go in to supper along with some of the elder ones, who were not playing; for the parlour was not large enough to hold all at once, even with the squeezing and cramming, and sitting together on chairs, which was not at all out of etiquette at Monkshaven. Philip was too reserved to express his disappointment and annoyance at being thus arrested in his painful watch over Sylvia; but he had no appetite for the good things set before him, and found it hard work to smile a sickly smile when called upon by Josiah Pratt for applause at some country joke. When supper was ended, there was some little discussion between Mrs Corney and her son-in-law as to whether the different individuals of the company should be called upon for songs or stories, as was the wont at such convivial meetings. Brunton had been helping his mother-in-law in urging people to eat, heaping their plates over their shoulders with unexpected good things, filling the glasses at the upper end of the table, and the mugs which supplied the deficiency of glasses at the lower. And now, every one being satisfied, not to say stuffed to repletion, the two who had been attending to their wants stood still, hot and exhausted.

'They're a'most stawed,'* said Mrs Corney, with a pleased smile. 'It'll be manners t' ask some one as knows how to sing.'

'It may be manners for full men, but not for fasting,' replied Brunton. 'Folks in t' next room will be wanting their victual, and singing is allays out o' tune to empty bellies.'

'But there's them here as 'll take it ill if they're not asked. I heerd Josiah Pratt a-clearing his throat not a minute ago, an' he thinks as much on his singin' as a cock does on his crowin'.'

'If one sings I'm afeard all on 'em will like to hear their own pipes.'

But their dilemma was solved by Bessy Corney, who opened the door to see if the hungry ones outside might not come in for their share of the entertainment; and in they rushed, bright and riotous, scarcely giving the first party time to rise from their seats ere they took their places. One or two young men, released from all their previous shyness, helped Mrs Corney and her daughters to carry off such dishes as were actually empty. There was no time for changing or washing of plates; but then, as Mrs Corney laughingly observed,—

'We're a' on us friends, and some on us mayhap sweethearts; so no need to be particular about plates. Them as gets clean ones is lucky; and them as doesn't, and cannot put up wi' plates that has been used, mun go without.'

It seemed to be Philip's luck this night to be pent up in places; for again the space between the benches and the wall was filled up by the in-rush before he had time to make his way out; and all he could do was to sit quiet where he was. But between the busy heads and over-reaching arms he could see Charley and Sylvia, sitting close together, talking and listening more than eating. She was in a new strange state of happiness not to be reasoned about, or accounted for, but in a state of more exquisite feeling than she had ever experienced before; when, suddenly lifting her eyes, she caught Philip's face of extreme displeasure.

'Oh,' said she, 'I must go. There's Philip looking at me so.'

'Philip!' said Kinraid, with a sudden frown upon his face.

'My cousin,' she replied, instinctively comprehending what had flashed into his mind, and anxious to disclaim the suspicion of having a lover. 'Mother told him to see me home, and he's noan one for staying up late.'

'But you needn't go. I'll see yo' home.'

'Mother's but ailing,' said Sylvia, a little conscience-smitten at having so entirely forgotten everything in the delight of the present, 'and I said I wouldn't be late.'

'And do you allays keep to your word?' asked he, with a tender meaning in his tone.

'Allays; leastways I think so,' replied she, blushing.

'Then if I ask you not to forget me, and you give me your word, I may be sure you'll keep it.'

'It wasn't I as forgot you,' said Sylvia, so softly as not to be heard by him.

He tried to make her repeat what she had said, but she would not, and he could only conjecture that it was something more tell-tale than she liked to say again, and that alone was very charming to him.

'I shall walk home with you,' said he, as Sylvia at last rose to depart, warned by a further glimpse of Philip's angry face.

'No!' said she, hastily, 'I can't do with yo';' for somehow she felt the need of pacifying Philip, and knew in her heart that a third person joining their *tête-à-tête* walk would only increase his displeasure.

'Why not?' said Charley, sharply.

'Oh! I don't know, only please don't!'

By this time her cloak and hood were on, and she was slowly making her way down her side of the room followed by Charley, and often interrupted by indignant remonstrances against her departure, and the early breaking-up of the party. Philip stood, hat in hand, in the doorway between the kitchen and parlour, watching her so intently that he forgot to be civil, and drew many a jest and gibe upon him for his absorption in his pretty cousin.

When Sylvia reached him, he said,—

'Yo're ready at last, are yo'?'

'Yes,' she replied, in her little beseeching tone. 'Yo've not been wanting to go long, han yo'? I ha' but just eaten my supper.'

'Yo've been so full of talk, that's been the reason your supper lasted so long. That fellow's none going wi' us?' said he sharply, as he saw Kinraid rummaging for his cap in a heap of men's clothes, thrown into the back-kitchen.

'No,' said Sylvia, in affright at Philip's fierce look and passionate tone. 'I telled him not.'

But at that moment the heavy outer door was opened by Daniel Robson himself – bright, broad, and rosy, a jolly impersonation of Winter. His large drover's coat was covered with snow-flakes, and through the black frame of the doorway might be seen a white waste world of sweeping fell and field, with the dark air filled with the pure down-fall. Robson stamped his snow-laden feet and shook himself well, still standing on the mat, and letting a cold frosty current of fresh air into the great warm kitchen. He laughed at them all before he spoke.

'It's a coud New Year as I'm lettin' in though it's noan t' New Year yet. Yo'll a' be snowed up, as sure as my name's Dannel, if yo' stop for twel' o'clock. Yo'd better mak' haste and go whoam. Why, Charley, my lad! how beest ta? who'd ha' thought o' seeing thee i' these parts again! Nay, missus, nay, t' New Year mun find its way int' t' house by itsel' for me; for a ha' promised my oud woman to bring Sylvie whoam as quick as maybe; she's lyin' awake and frettin' about t' snow and what not. Thank yo' kindly, missus, but a'll tak' nought to eat; just a drop o' somethin' hot to keep out coud, and wish yo' a' the compliments o' the season. Philip, my man, yo'll not be sorry to be spared t' walk round by Haytersbank such a neet. My missus were i' such a way about Sylvie that a thought a'd just step off mysel', and have a peep at yo' a', and bring her some wraps. Yo'r sheep will be a' folded, a reckon, Measter Pratt, for there'll niver be a nibble o' grass to be seen this two month, accordin' to my readin'; and a've been at sea long enough, and on land long enough t' know signs and wonders. It's good stuff that, any way, and worth comin' for,' after he had gulped down a tumblerful of half-and-half grog. 'Kinraid, if ta doesn't come and see me afore thou'rt many days ouder, thee and me'll have words. Come, Sylvie, what art ta about, keepin' me here? Here's Mistress Corney mixin' me another jorum.* Well, this time a'll give "T' married happy, and t' single wed!"'

Sylvia was all this while standing by her father quite ready for departure, and not a little relieved by his appearance as her convoy home.

'I'm ready to see Haytersbank to-night, master!' said Kinraid, with easy freedom – a freedom which Philip envied, but could not have imitated, although he was deeply disappointed at the loss of his walk with Sylvia, when he had intended to exercise the power his aunt had delegated to him of remonstrance if her behaviour had been light or thoughtless, and of warning if he saw cause to disapprove of any of her associates.

After the Robsons had left, a blank fell upon both Charley and Philip. In a few minutes, however, the former, accustomed to prompt decision, resolved that she and no other should be his wife. Accustomed to popularity among women, and well versed in the incipient signs of their liking for him, he anticipated no difficulty in winning her. Satisfied with the past, and pleasantly hopeful about the future, he found it easy to turn his attention to the next prettiest girl in the room, and to make the whole gathering bright with his ready good temper and buoyant spirit.

Mrs Corney had felt it her duty to press Philip to stay, now that, as she said, he had no one but himself to see home, and the New Year so near coming in. To any one else in the room she would have added the clinching argument, 'A shall take it very unkind if yo' go now;' but somehow she could not say this, for in truth Philip's look showed that he would be but a wet blanket on the merriment of the party. So, with as much civility as could be mustered up between them, he took leave. Shutting the door behind him, he went out into the dreary night, and began his lonesome walk back to Monkshaven. The cold sleet almost blinded him as the sea-wind drove it straight in his face; it cut against him as it was blown with drifting force. The roar of the wintry sea came borne on the breeze; there was more light from the whitened ground than from the dark laden sky above. The field-paths would have been a matter of perplexity, had it not been for the well-known gaps in the dyke-side, which showed the whitened land beyond, between the two dark stone walls. Yet he went clear and straight along his way, having unconsciously left all guidance to the animal instinct which co-exists with the human soul, and sometimes takes strange charge of the human body, when all the nobler powers of the individual are absorbed in acute suffering. At length he was in the lane, toiling up the hill, from which, by day, Monkshaven might be seen. Now all features of the landscape before him were lost in the darkness of night, against which the white flakes came closer and nearer, thicker and faster. On a sudden, the bells of Monkshaven church rang out a welcome to the New Year, 1796.* From the direction of the wind, it seemed as if the sound was flung with strength and power right into Philip's face. He walked down the hill to its merry sound – its merry sound, his heavy heart. As he entered the long High Street of Monkshaven he could see the watching lights put out in parlour, chamber, or kitchen. The New Year had come, and expectation was ended. Reality had begun.

He turned to the right, into the court where he lodged with Alice Rose. There was a light still burning there, and cheerful voices were heard. He opened the door; Alice, her daughter, and Coulson stood as if awaiting him. Hester's wet cloak hung on a chair before the fire; she had her hood on, for she and Coulson had been to the watch-night.

The solemn excitement of the services had left its traces upon her countenance and in her mind. There was a spiritual light in her usually shadowed eyes, and a slight flush on her pale cheek. Merely personal and self-conscious feelings were merged in a loving good-will to all her fellow-creatures. Under the influence of this large charity, she forgot her habitual reserve, and came forward as Philip entered to meet him with her New Year's wishes – wishes that she had previously interchanged with the other two.

'A happy New Year to you, Philip, and may God have you in his keeping all the days thereof!'

He took her hand, and shook it warmly in reply. The flush on her cheek deepened as she withdrew it. Alice Rose said something curtly about the lateness of the hour and her being much tired; and then she and her daughter went upstairs to the front chamber, and Philip and Coulson to that which they shared at the back of the house.

CHAPTER XIII

PERPLEXITIES

Coulson and Philip were friendly, but not intimate. They never had had a dispute, they never were confidential with each other; in truth, they were both reserved and silent men, and, probably, respected each other the more for being so self-contained. There was a private feeling in Coulson's heart which would have made a less amiable fellow dislike Philip. But of this the latter was unconscious: they were not apt to exchange many words in the room which they occupied jointly.

Coulson asked Philip if he had enjoyed himself at the Corneys', and Philip replied,—

'Not much; such parties are noane to my liking.'

'And yet thou broke off from t' watch-night to go there.'

No answer; so Coulson went on, with a sense of the duty laid upon him, to improve the occasion – the first that had presented itself since the good old Methodist minister had given his congregation the solemn warning to watch over the opportunities of various kinds which the coming year would present.

'Jonas Barclay told us as the pleasures o' this world were like apples o' Sodom,* pleasant to look at, but ashes to taste.'

Coulson wisely left Philip to make the application for himself. If he did he made no sign, but threw himself on his bed with a heavy sigh.

'Are yo' not going to undress?' said Coulson, as he covered him up in bed.

There had been a long pause of silence. Philip did not answer him, and he thought he had fallen asleep. But he was roused from his first slumber by Hepburn's soft movements about the room. Philip had thought better of it, and, with some penitence in his heart for his gruffness to the unoffending Coulson, was trying not to make any noise while he undressed.

But he could not sleep. He kept seeing the Corneys' kitchen and the scenes that had taken place in it, passing like a pageant before his closed eyes. Then he opened them in angry weariness at the recurring vision, and tried to make out the outlines of the room and the furniture in the darkness. The white ceiling sloped into the whitewashed walls, and against them he could see the four rush-bottomed chairs, the looking-glass hung on one side, the old carved oak-chest (his own property, with the initials of forgotten ancestors cut upon it), which held his clothes; the boxes that belonged to Coulson, sleeping soundly in the bed in the opposite corner of the room; the casement window in the roof, through which the snowy ground on the steep hill-side could be plainly seen; and when he got so far as this in the catalogue of the room, he fell into a troubled feverish sleep, which lasted two or three hours; and then he awoke with a start, and a consciousness of uneasiness, though what about he could not remember at first.

When he recollected all that had happened the night before, it impressed him much more favourably than it had done at the time. If not joy, hope had come in the morning;* and, at any rate, he could be up and be doing, for the late wintry light was stealing down the hill-side, and he knew that, although Coulson lay motionless in his sleep, it was past their usual time of rising. Still, as it was New Year's Day, a time of some licence, Philip had mercy on his fellow-shopman, and did not waken him till just as he was leaving the room.

Carrying his shoes in his hand, he went softly downstairs, for he could see from the top of the flight that neither Alice nor her daughter was down yet, as the kitchen shutters were not unclosed. It was Mrs Rose's habit to rise early, and have all bright and clean against her lodgers came down; but then, in general, she went to rest before nine o'clock, whereas the last night she had not gone till past twelve. Philip went about undoing the shutters, and trying to break up the raking coal, with as little noise as might be, for he had compassion on the tired sleepers. The kettle had not been filled, probably because Mrs Rose had been unable to face the storm of the night before, in taking it to the pump just at the entrance of the court. When Philip came back from filling it, he found Alice and Hester both in the kitchen, and trying to make up for lost time by hastening over their work. Hester looked busy and notable with her gown pinned up behind her, and her hair all tucked away under a clean linen cap; but Alice was angry with herself for her late sleeping, and that and other causes made her speak crossly to Philip, as he came in with his snowy feet and well-filled kettle.

'Look the' there! droppin' and drippin' along t' flags as was cleaned last night, and meddlin' wi' woman's work as a man has no business wi'.'

Philip was surprised and annoyed. He had found relief from his own thoughts in doing what he believed would help others. He gave up the kettle to her snatching hands, and sate down behind the door in momentary ill-temper. But the kettle was better filled, and consequently heavier than the old woman expected, and she could not manage to lift it to the crook from which it generally hung suspended. She looked round for Hester, but she was gone into the back-kitchen. In a minute Philip was at her side, and had heaved it to its place for her. She looked in his face for a moment wistfully, but hardly condescended to thank him; at least the sound of the words did not pass the lips that formed them. Rebuffed by her manner, he went back to his old seat, and mechanically watched the preparations for breakfast; but his thoughts went back to the night before, and the comparative ease of his heart was gone. The first stir of a new day had made him feel as if he had had no sufficient cause for his annoyance and despondency the previous evening; but now, condemned to sit quiet, he reviewed looks and words, and saw just reason for his anxiety. After some consideration he resolved to go that very night to Haytersbank, and have some talk with either Sylvia or her mother; what the exact nature of this purposed conversation should be, he did not determine; much would depend on Sylvia's manner and mood, and on her mother's state of health; but at any rate something would be learnt.

During breakfast something was learnt nearer home; though not all that a man less unconscious and more vain than Philip might have discovered. He only found out that Mrs Rose was displeased with him for not having gone to the watch-night with Hester, according to the plan made some weeks before. But he soothed his conscience by remembering that he had made no promise; he had merely spoken of his wish to be present at the service, about which Hester was speaking; and although at the time and for a good while afterwards, he had fully intended going, yet as there had been William Coulson to accompany her, his absence could not have been seriously noticed. Still he was made uncomfortable by Mrs Rose's change of manner; once or twice he said to himself that she little knew how miserable he had been during his 'gay evening,' as she would persist in calling it, or she would not talk at him with such persevering bitterness this morning. Before he left for the shop, he spoke of his intention of going to see how his aunt was, and of paying her a New Year's Day visit.

Hepburn and Coulson took it in turns week and week about to go first home to dinner; the one who went first sate down with Mrs Rose and her daughter, instead of having his portion put in the oven to keep warm for him. To-day it was Hepburn's turn to be last. All morning the shop was full with customers, come rather to offer good wishes than to buy, and with an unspoken remembrance of the cake and wine which the two hospitable brothers Foster made a point of offering to all comers on New Year's Day. It was busy work for all – for Hester on her side, where caps, ribbons, and women's gear were exclusively sold – for the shopmen and boys in the grocery and drapery department. Philip was trying to do his business with his mind far away; and the consequence was that his manner was not such as to recommend him to the customers, some of whom recollected it as very different, courteous and attentive, if grave and sedate. One buxom farmer's wife noticed the change to him. She had a little girl with her, of about five years old, that she had lifted up on the counter, and who was watching Philip with anxious eyes, occasionally whispering in her mother's ear, and then hiding her face against her cloak.

'She's thought a deal o' coming to see yo', and a dunnot think as yo' mind her at all. My pretty, he's clean forgotten as how he said last New Year's Day, he'd gi' thee a barley-sugar stick, if thou'd hem him a handkercher by this.'

The child's face was buried in the comfortable breadth of of duffle at these words, while the little outstretched hand held a small square of coarse linen.

'Ay, she's noane forgotten it, and has done her five stitches a day, bless her; and a dunnot believe as yo' know her again. She's Phœbe Moorsom, and a'm Hannah, and a've dealt at t' shop reg'lar this fifteen year.'

'I'm very sorry,' said Philip. 'I was up late last night, and I'm a bit dazed to-day. Well! this is nice work, Phœbe, and I'm sure I'm very much beholden to yo'. And here's five sticks o' barley-sugar, one for every stitch, and thank you kindly, Mrs Moorsom, too.'

Philip took the handkerchief and hoped he had made honourable amends for his want of recognition. But the wee lassie refused to be lifted down, and whispered something afresh into her mother's ear, who smiled and bade her be quiet. Philip saw, however, that there was some wish ungratified on the part of the little maiden which he was expected to inquire into, and, accordingly, he did his duty.

'She's a little fool; she says yo' promised to gi'e her a kiss, and t' make her yo'r wife.'

The child burrowed her face closer into her mother's neck, and refused to allow the kiss which Philip willingly offered. All he could do was to touch the back of the little white fat neck with his lips. The mother carried her off only half satisfied, and Philip felt that he must try and collect his scattered wits, and be more alive to the occasion.

Towards the dinner-hour the crowd slackened; Hester began to replenish decanters and bottles, and to bring out a fresh cake before she went home to dinner; and Coulson and Philip looked over the joint present they always made to her on this day. It was a silk handkerchief of the prettiest colours they could pick out of the shop, intended for her to wear round her neck. Each tried to persuade the other to give it to her, for each was shy of the act of presentation. Coulson was, however, the most resolute; and when she returned from the parlour the little parcel was in Philip's hands.

'Here, Hester,' said he, going round the counter to her, just as she was leaving the shop. 'It's from Coulson and me; a handkerchief for yo' to wear; and we wish yo' a happy New Year, and plenty on 'em; and there's many a one wishes the same.'

He took her hand as he said this. She went a little paler, and her eyes brightened as though they would fill with tears as they met his; she could not have helped it, do what she would. But she only said, 'Thank yo' kindly,' and going up to Coulson she repeated the words and action to him; and then they went off together to dinner.

There was a lull of business for the next hour. John and Jeremiah were dining like the rest of the world. Even the elder errand-boy had vanished. Philip rearranged disorderly goods; and then sate down on the counter by the window; it was the habitual place for the one who stayed behind; for excepting on market-day there was little or no custom during the noon-hour. Formerly he used to move the drapery with which the window was ornamented, and watch the passers-by with careless eye. But now, though he seemed to gaze abroad, he saw nothing but vacancy. All the morning since he got up he had been trying to fight through his duties – leaning against a hope – a hope that first had bowed, and then had broke as soon as he really tried its weight. There was not a sign of Sylvia's liking for him to be gathered from the most careful recollection of the past evening. It was of no use thinking that there was. It was better to give it up altogether and at once. But what if he could not? What if the thought of her was bound up with his life; and that once torn out by his own free will, the very roots of his heart must come also?

No; he was resolved he would go on; as long as there was life there was hope; as long as Sylvia remained unpledged to any one else, there was a chance for him. He would remodel his behaviour to her. He could not be merry and light-hearted like other young men; his nature was not cast in that mould:

and the early sorrows that had left him a lonely orphan might have matured, but had not enlivened, his character. He thought with some bitterness on the power of easy talking about trifles which some of those he had met with at the Corneys' had exhibited. But then he felt stirring within him a force of enduring love which he believed to be unusual, and which seemed as if it must compel all things to his wish in the end. A year or so ago he had thought much of his own cleverness and his painfully acquired learning, and he had imagined that these were the qualities which were to gain Sylvia. But now, whether he had tried them and had failed to win even her admiration, or whether some true instinct had told him that a woman's love may be gained in many ways sooner than by mere learning, he was only angry with himself for his past folly in making himself her school – nay, her task-master. To-night, though, he would start off on a new tack. He would not even upbraid her for her conduct the night before; he had shown her his displeasure at the time; but she should see how tender and forgiving he could be. He would lure her to him rather than find fault with her. There had perhaps been too much of that already.

When Coulson came back Philip went to his solitary dinner. In general he was quite alone while eating it; but to-day Alice Rose chose to bear him company. She watched him with cold severe eye for some time, until he had appeased his languid appetite. Then she began with the rebuke she had in store for him; a rebuke the motives to which were not entirely revealed even to herself.

'Thou 're none so keen after thy food as common,' she began. 'Plain victuals goes ill down after feastin'.'

Philip felt the colour mount to his face; he was not in the mood for patiently standing the brunt of the attack which he saw was coming, and yet he had a reverent feeling for woman and for age. He wished she would leave him alone; but he only said – 'I had nought but a slice o' cold beef for supper, if you'll call that feasting.'

'Neither do godly ways savour delicately after the pleasures of the world,' continued she, unheeding his speech. 'Thou wert wont to seek the house of the Lord, and I thought well on thee; but of late thou'st changed, and fallen away, and I mun speak what is in my heart towards thee.'

'Mother,' said Philip, impatiently (both he and Coulson called Alice 'mother' at times), 'I don't think I am fallen away, and any way I cannot stay now to be – it's New Year's Day, and t' shop is throng.'*

But Alice held up her hand. Her speech was ready, and she must deliver it.

'Shop here, shop there. The flesh and the devil are gettin' hold on yo', and yo' need more nor iver to seek t' ways o' grace. New Year's Day comes and says, "Watch and pray," and yo' say, "Nay, I'll seek feasts and market-places, and let times and seasons come and go without heedin' into whose presence they're hastening me." Time was, Philip, when thou'd niver ha' letten a merry-making keep thee fra' t' watch-night, and t' company o' the godly.'

'I tell yo' it was no merry-making to me,' said Philip, with sharpness, as he left the house.

Alice sat down on the nearest seat, and leant her head on her wrinkled hand.

'He's tangled and snared,' said she; 'my heart has yearned after him, and I esteemed him as one o' the elect. And more nor me yearns after him. O Lord, I have but one child! O Lord, spare her! But o'er and above a' I would like to pray for his soul, that Satan might not have it, for he came to me but a little lad.'

At that moment Philip, smitten by his conscience for his hard manner of speech, came back; but Alice did not hear or see him till he was close by her, and then he had to touch her to recall her attention.

'Mother,' said he, 'I was wrong. I'm fretted by many things. I shouldn't ha' spoken so. It was ill-done of me.'

'Oh, my lad!' said she, looking up and putting her thin arm on his shoulder as he stooped, 'Satan is desiring after yo' that he may sift yo' as wheat. Bide at whoam, bide at whoam, and go not after them as care nought for holy things. Why need yo' go to Haytersbank this night?'

Philip reddened. He could not and would not give it up, and yet it was difficult to resist the pleading of the usually stern old woman.

'Nay,' said he, withdrawing himself ever so little from her hold; 'my aunt is but ailing, they're my own flesh and blood, and as good folks as needs be, though they mayn't be o' our – o' your way o' thinking in a' things.'

'Our ways – your ways o' thinking, says he, as if they were no longer his'n. And as good folks as need be,' repeated she, with returning severity. 'Them's Satan's words, tho' yo' spoke 'em, Philip. I can do nought again Satan, but I can speak to them as can; an' we'll see which pulls hardest, for it'll be better for thee to be riven and rent i' twain than to go body and soul to hell.'

'But don't think, mother,' said Philip, his last words of conciliation, for the clock had given warning for two, 'as I'm boun' for hell, just because I go t' see my own folks, all I ha' left o' kin.' And once more, after laying his hand with as much of a caress as was in his nature on hers, he left the house.

Probably Alice would have considered the first words that greeted Philip on his entrance into the shop as an answer to her prayer, for they were such as put a stop to his plan of going to see Sylvia that evening; and if Alice had formed her inchoate thoughts into words, Sylvia would have appeared as the nearest earthly representative of the spirit of temptation whom she dreaded for Philip.

As he took his place behind the counter, Coulson said to him in a low voice,—

'Jeremiah Foster has been round to bid us to sup wi' him to-night. He says that he and John have a little matter o' business to talk over with us.'

A glance from his eyes to Philip told the latter that Coulson believed the business spoken of had something to do with the partnership, respecting which there had been a silent intelligence for some time between the shopmen.

'And what did thou say?' asked Philip, doggedly unwilling, even yet, to give up his purposed visit.

'Say! why, what could a say, but that we'd come? There

was summat up, for sure; and summat as he thought we should be glad on. I could tell it fra' t' look on his face.'

'I don't think as I can go,' said Philip, feeling just then as if the long-hoped-for partnership was as nothing compared to his plan. It was always distasteful to him to have to give up a project, or to disarrange an intended order of things, such was his nature; but to-day it was absolute pain to yield his own purpose.

'Why, man alive?' said Coulson, in amaze at his reluctance.

'I didn't say I mightn't go,' said Philip, weighing consequences, until called off to attend to customers.

In the course of the afternoon, however, he felt himself more easy in deferring his visit to Haytersbank till the next evening. Charley Kinraid entered the shop, accompanied by Molly Brunton and her sisters; and though they all went towards Hester's side of the shop, and Philip and Coulson had many people to attend to, yet Hepburn's sharpened ears caught much of what the young women were saying. From that he gathered that Kinraid had promised them New Year's gifts, for the purchase of which they were come; and after a little more listening he learnt that Kinraid was returning to Shields the next day, having only come over to spend a holiday with his relations, and being tied with ship's work at the other end. They all talked together lightly and merrily, as if his going or staying was almost a matter of indifference to himself and his cousins. The principal thought of the young women was to secure the articles they most fancied; Charley Kinraid was (so Philip thought) especially anxious that the youngest and prettiest should be pleased. Hepburn watched him perpetually with a kind of envy of his bright, courteous manner, the natural gallantry of the sailor. If it were but clear that Sylvia took as little thought of him as he did of her, to all appearance, Philip could even have given him praise for manly good looks, and a certain kind of geniality of disposition which made him ready to smile pleasantly at all strangers, from babies upwards.

As the party turned to leave the shop they saw Philip, the guest of the night before; and they came over to shake hands with him across the counter; Kinraid's hand was proffered among the number. Last night Philip could not have believed it possible that such a demonstration of fellowship should have passed between them; and perhaps there was a slight hesitation of manner on his part, for some idea or remembrance crossed Kinraid's mind which brought a keen searching glance into the eyes which for a moment were fastened on Philip's face. In spite of himself, and during the very action of hand-shaking, Philip felt a cloud come over his face, not altering or moving his features, but taking light and peace out of his countenance.

Molly Brunton began to say something, and he gladly turned to look at her. She was asking him why he went away so early, for they had kept it up for four hours after he left, and last of all, she added (turning to Kinraid), her cousin Charley had danced a hornpipe among the platters on the ground.

Philip hardly knew what he said in reply, the mention of that *pas seul* lifted such a weight off his heart. He could smile now, after his grave fashion, and would have shaken hands again with Kinraid had it been required; for it seemed to him that no one, caring ever so little in the way that he did for Sylvia, could have borne four mortal hours of a company where she had been, and was not; least of all could have danced a hornpipe, either from gaiety of heart, or even out of complaisance. He felt as if the yearning after the absent one would have been a weight to his legs, as well as to his spirit; and he imagined that all men were like himself.

CHAPTER XIV

PARTNERSHIP

As darkness closed in, and the New Year's throng became scarce, Philip's hesitation about accompanying Coulson faded away. He was more comfortable respecting Sylvia, and his going to see her might be deferred; and, after all, he felt that the wishes of his masters ought to be attended to, and the honour of an invitation to the private house of Jeremiah not to be slighted for anything short of a positive engagement. Besides, the ambitious man of business existed strongly in Philip. It would never do to slight advances towards the second great earthly object in his life; one also on which the first depended.

So when the shop was closed, the two set out down Bridge Street to cross the river to the house of Jeremiah Foster. They stood a moment on the bridge to breathe the keen fresh sea air after their busy day. The waters came down, swollen full and dark, with rapid rushing speed from the snow-fed springs high up on the moorland above. The close-packed houses in the old town seemed a cluster of white roofs irregularly piled against the more unbroken white of the hill-side. Lights twinkled here and there in the town, and were slung from stern and bow of the ships in the harbour. The air was very still, settling in for a frost; so still that all distant sounds seemed near: the rumble of a returning cart in the High Street, the voices on board ship, the closing of shutters and barring of doors in the new town to which they were bound. But the sharp air was filled, as it were, with saline particles in a freezing state; little pungent crystals of sea salt burning lips and cheeks with their cold keenness. It would not do to linger here in the very centre of the valley up which passed the current of atmosphere coming straight with the rushing tide from the icy northern seas. Besides, there was the unusual honour of a supper with Jeremiah Foster awaiting them. He had asked each of them separately to a meal before now; but they had never gone together, and they felt that there was something serious in the conjuncture.

They began to climb the steep heights leading to the freshly-built rows of the new town of Monkshaven, feeling as if they were rising into aristocratic regions where no shop profaned the streets. Jeremiah Foster's house was one of six, undistinguished in size, or shape, or colour; but noticed in the daytime by all passers-by for its spotless cleanliness of lintel and doorstep, window and window frame. The very bricks seemed as though they came in for the daily scrubbing which brightened handle, knocker, all down to the very scraper.

The two young men felt as shy of the interview with their master under such unusual relations of guest and host, as a girl does of her first party. Each rather drew back from the decided step of knocking at the door; but with a rebuffing shake at his own folly, Philip was the one to give a loud single rap. As if they had been waited for, the door flew open, and a middle-aged servant stood behind, as spotless and neat as the house itself, and smiled a welcome to the familiar faces.

'Let me dust yo' a bit, William,' said she, suiting the action to the word. 'You've been leanin' again some whitewash, a'll be bound. Ay, Philip,' continued she, turning him round with motherly freedom, 'yo'll do if yo'll but gi' your shoon a polishin' wipe on yon other mat. This'n for takin' t' roughest mud off. Measter allays polishes on that.'

In the square parlour the same precise order was observed. Every article of furniture was free from speck of dirt or particle of dust; and everything was placed either in a parallel line, or at exact right-angles with every other. Even John and Jeremiah sat in symmetry on opposite sides of the fire-place; the very smiles on their honest faces seemed drawn to a line of exactitude.

Such formality, however admirable, was not calculated to promote ease: it was not until after supper – until a good quantity of Yorkshire pie had been swallowed, and washed down, too, with the best and most generous wine in Jeremiah's cellar – that there was the least geniality among them, in spite of the friendly kindness of the host and his brother. The long silence, during which mute thanks for the meal were given, having come to an end, Jeremiah called for pipes, and three of the party began to smoke.

Politics in those days were tickle subjects to meddle with, even in the most private company. The nation was in a state of terror against France, and against any at home who might be supposed to sympathise with the enormities she had just been committing. The oppressive act against seditious meetings* had been passed the year before; and people were doubtful to what extremity of severity it might be construed. Even the law authorities forgot to be impartial, but either their alarms or their interests made too many of them vehement partisans instead of calm arbiters, and thus destroyed the popular confidence in what should have been considered the supreme tribunal of justice. Yet for all this, there were some who dared to speak of reform of Parliament, as a preliminary step to fair representation of the people, and to a reduction of the heavy war-taxation that was imminent, if not already imposed. But these pioneers of 1830 were generally obnoxious. The great body of the people gloried in being Tories and haters of the French, with whom they were on tenter-hooks to fight, almost unaware of the rising reputation of the young Corsican warrior,* whose name would be used ere a dozen years had passed to hush English babies with a terror such as that of Marlborough once had for the French.

At such a place as Monkshaven all these opinions were held in excess. One or two might, for the mere sake of argument, dispute on certain points of history or government; but they took care to be very sure of their listeners before such arguments touched on anything of the present day; for it had been not unfrequently found that the public duty of prosecuting opinions not your own overrode the private duty of respecting confidence. Most of the Monkshaven politicians confined themselves, therefore, to such general questions as these: 'Could an Englishman lick more than four Frenchmen at a time?' 'What was the proper punishment for members of the Corresponding Society* (correspondence with the French directory), hanging and quartering, or burning?' 'Would the forthcoming child of the Princess of Wales be a boy or a girl? If a girl, would it be more loyal to call it Charlotte or Elizabeth?'

The Fosters were quite secure enough of their guests this evening to have spoken freely on politics had they been so inclined. And they did begin on the outrages which had been lately offered to the king in crossing St James's Park to go and open the House of Lords; but soon, so accustomed were their minds to caution and restraint, the talk dropped down to the high price of provisions. Bread at 1*s.* 3*d.* the quartern loaf, according to the London test. Wheat at 120*s.* per quarter,* as the home-baking northerners viewed the matter; and then the conversation died away to an ominous silence. John looked at Jeremiah, as if asking him to begin. Jeremiah was the host, and had been a married man. Jeremiah returned the look with the same meaning in it. John, though a bachelor, was the elder brother. The great church bell, brought from the Monkshaven monastery centuries ago, high up on the opposite hill-side, began to ring nine o'clock; it was getting late. Jeremiah began:

'It seems a bad time for starting any one on business, wi' prices and taxes and bread so dear; but John and I are getting into years, and we've no children to follow us: yet we would fain draw out of some of our worldly affairs. We would like to give up the shop, and stick to banking, to which there seemeth a plain path. But first there is the stock and goodwill of the shop to be disposed on.'

A dead pause. This opening was not favourable to the hopes of the two moneyless young men who had been hoping to succeed their masters by the more gradual process of partnership. But it was only the kind of speech that had been agreed upon by the two brothers with a view of impressing on Hepburn and Coulson the great and unusual responsibility of the situation into which the Fosters wished them to enter. In some ways the talk of many was much less simple and straightforward in those days than it is now. The study of effect shown in the London diners-out of the last generation, who prepared their conversation beforehand, was not without its parallel in humbler spheres, and for different objects than self-display. The brothers Foster had all but rehearsed the speeches they were about to make this evening. They were aware of the youth of the parties to whom they were going to make a most favourable proposal; and they dreaded that if that proposal was too lightly made, it would be too lightly considered, and the duties involved in it too carelessly entered upon. So the *rôle* of one brother was to suggest, that of the other to repress. The young men, too, had their reserves.

They foresaw, and had long foreseen, what was coming that evening. They were impatient to hear it in distinct words; and yet they had to wait, as if unconscious, during all the long preamble. Do age and youth never play the same parts now? To return. John Foster replied to his brother:

'The stock and goodwill! That would take much wealth. And there will be fixtures to be considered. Philip, canst thee tell me the exact amount of stock in the shop at present?'

It had only just been taken; Philip had it at his fingers' ends. 'One thousand nine hundred and forty-one pounds, thirteen shillings and twopence.'

Coulson looked at him in a little dismay, and could not repress a sigh. The figures put into words and spoken aloud seemed to indicate so much larger an amount of money than when quickly written down in numerals. But Philip read the countenances, nay, by some process of which he was not himself aware, he read the minds of the brothers, and felt no dismay at what he saw there.

'And the fixtures?' asked John Foster.

'The appraiser valued them at four hundred and thirty-five pounds three and sixpence when father died. We have added to them since, but we will reckon them at that. How much does that make with the value of the stock?'

'Two thousand one hundred and seventy-six pounds, sixteen shillings and eightpence,' said Philip.

Coulson had done the sum quicker, but was too much disheartened by the amount to speak.

'And the goodwill?' asked the pitiless John. 'What dost thee set that at?'

'I think, brother, that that would depend on who came forward with the purchase-money of the stock and fixtures. To some folks we might make it sit easy, if they were known to us, and those as we wished well to. If Philip and William here, for instance, said they'd like to purchase the business, I reckon thee and me would not ask 'em so much as we should ask Millers' (Millers was an upstart petty rival shop at the end of the bridge in the New Town).

'I wish Philip and William was to come after us,' said John.

'But that's out of the question,' he continued, knowing all the while that, far from being out of the question, it was the very question, and that it was as good as settled at this very time.

No one spoke. Then Jeremiah went on:

'It's out of the question, I reckon?'

He looked at the two young men. Coulson shook his head. Philip more bravely said,—

'I have fifty-three pounds seven and fourpence in yo'r hands, Master John, and it's all I have i' the world.'

'It's a pity,' said John, and again they were silent. Half-past nine struck. It was time to be beginning to make an end. 'Perhaps, brother, they have friends who could advance 'em the money. We might make it sit light to them, for the sake of their good service?'

Philip replied,—

'There's no one who can put forwards a penny for me: I have but few kin, and they have little to spare beyond what they need.'

Coulson said—

'My father and mother have nine on us.'

'Let alone, let alone!' said John, relenting fast; for he was weary of his part of cold, stern prudence. 'Brother, I think we have enough of this world's goods to do what we like wi' our own.'

Jeremiah was a little scandalized at the rapid melting away of assumed character, and took a good pull at his pipe before he replied—

'Upwards of two thousand pounds is a large sum to set on the well-being and well-doing of two lads, the elder of whom is not three-and-twenty. I fear we must look farther a-field.'

'Why, John,' replied Jeremiah, 'it was but yesterday thee saidst thee would rather have Philip and William than any men o' fifty that thee knowed. And now to bring up their youth again them.'

'Well, well! t' half on it is thine, and thou shall do even as thou wilt. But I think as I must have security for my moiety, for it's a risk – a great risk. Have ye any security to offer? any expectations? any legacies, as other folk have a life-interest in at present?'

No; neither of them had. So Jeremiah rejoined—

'Then, I suppose, I mun do as thee dost, John, and take the security of character. And it's a great security too, lads, and t' best o' all, and one that I couldn't ha' done without; no, not if yo'd pay me down five thousand for goodwill, and stock, and fixtures. For John Foster and Son has been a shop i' Monkshaven this eighty years and more; and I dunnot think there's a man living – or dead, for that matter – as can say Fosters wronged him of a penny, or gave short measure to a child or a Cousin Betty.'

They all four shook hands round with the same heartiness as if it had been a legal ceremony necessary to the completion of the partnership. The old men's faces were bright with smiles; the eyes of the young ones sparkled with hope.

'But, after all,' said Jeremiah, 'we've not told you particulars. Yo're thanking us for a pig in a poke; but we had more forethought, and we put all down on a piece o' paper.'

He took down a folded piece of paper from the mantel-shelf, put on his horn spectacles, and began to read aloud, occasionally peering over his glasses to note the effect on the countenances of the young men. The only thing he was in the habit of reading aloud was a chapter in the Bible daily to his housekeeper servant; and, like many, he reserved a peculiar tone for that solemn occupation – a tone which he unconsciously employed for the present enumeration of pounds, shillings, and pence.

'Average returns of the last three years, one hundred and twenty-seven pounds, three shillings, and seven penny and one-sixth a week. Profits thereupon thirty-four per cent. – as near as may be. Clear profits of the concern, after deducting all expenses except rent – for t' house is our own – one thousand two hundred and two pound a year.'

This was far more than either Hepburn or Coulson had imagined it to be; and a look of surprise, almost amounting to dismay, crept over their faces, in spite of their endeavour to keep simply motionless and attentive.

'It's a deal of money, lads, and the Lord give you grace to guide it,' said Jeremiah, putting down his paper for a minute.

'Amen,' said John, shaking his head to give effect to his word.

'Now what we propose is this,' continued Jeremiah, beginning afresh to refer to his paper: 'We will call t' value of stock and fixtures two thousand one hundred and fifty. You may have John Holden, appraiser and auctioneer, in to set a price on them if yo' will; or yo' may look over books and bills; or, better still, do both, and so check one again t'other; but for t' sake o' making the ground o' the bargain, I state the sum as above; and I reckon it so much capital left in yo'r hands for the use o' which yo're bound to pay us five per cent. quarterly – that's one hundred and seven pound ten per annum at least for t' first year; and after it will be reduced by the gradual payment on our money, which must be at the rate of twenty per cent., thus paying us our principal back in five years. And the rent, including all back yards, right of wharfage, warehouse, and premises, is reckoned by us to be sixty-five pound per annum. So yo' will have to pay us, John and Jeremiah Foster, brothers, six hundred and twelve pound ten out of the profits of the first year, leaving, at the present rate of profits, about five hundred and eighty-nine pound ten, for the share to be divided between yo'.'

The plan had, in all its details, been carefully arranged by the two brothers. They were afraid lest Hepburn and Coulson should be dazzled by the amount of profits, and had so arranged the sliding-scale of payment as to reduce the first year's income to what the elder men thought a very moderate sum, but what to the younger ones appeared an amount of wealth such as they, who had neither of them ever owned much more than fifty pounds, considered almost inexhaustible. It was certainly a remarkable instance of prosperity and desert meeting together so early in life.

For a moment or two the brothers were disappointed at not hearing any reply from either of them. Then Philip stood up, for he felt as if anything he could say sitting down would not be sufficiently expressive of gratitude, and William instantly followed his example. Hepburn began in a formal manner, something the way in which he had read in the York newspapers that honourable members returned thanks when their health was given.

'I can hardly express my feelings' (Coulson nudged him) 'his feelings, too – of gratitude. Oh, Master John! Master Jeremiah, I thought it might come i' time; nay, I've thought it might come afore long; but I niver thought as it would be so much, or made so easy. We've got good kind friends – we have, have we not, William? – and we'll do our best, and I hope as we shall come up to their wishes.'

Philip's voice quivered a little, as some remembrance passed across his mind; at this unusual moment of expansion out it came. 'I wish mother could ha' seen this day.'

'She shall see a better day, my lad, when thy name and William's is painted over t' shop-door, and J. and J. Foster blacked out.'

'Nay, master,' said William, 'that mun never be. I'd a'most sooner not come in for the business. Anyhow, it must be 'late J. and J. Foster,' and I'm not sure as I can stomach that.'

'Well, well, William,' said John Foster, highly gratified, 'there be time enough to talk over that. There was one thing more to be said, was there not, brother Jeremiah? We do not wish to have this talked over in Monkshaven until shortly before the time when yo' must enter on the business. We have our own arrangements to make wi' regard to the banking concern, and there'll be lawyer's work to do, after yo've examined books and looked over stock again together; maybe we've overstated it, or t' fixtures aren't worth so much as we said. Anyhow yo' must each on yo' give us yo'r word for to keep fra' naming this night's conversation to any one. Meantime, Jeremiah and I will have to pay accounts, and take a kind of farewell of the merchants and manufacturers with whom Fosters have had dealings this seventy or eighty year; and when and where it seems fitting to us we will take one of yo' to introduce as our successors and friends. But all that's to come. But yo' must each give us yo'r word not to name what has passed here to any one till further speech on the subject has passed between us.'

Coulson immediately gave the promise. Philip's assent came lagging. He had thought of Sylvia living, almost as much as of the dead mother, whose last words had been a committal of her child to the Father of the friendless; and now that a short delay was placed between the sight of the cup and his enjoyment of it, there was an impatient chafing in the mind of the composed and self-restrained Philip; and then repentance quick as lightning effaced the feeling, and he pledged himself to the secrecy which was enjoined. Some few more details as to their mode of procedure – of verifying the Fosters' statements, which to the younger men seemed a perfectly unnecessary piece of business – of probable journeys and introductions, and then farewell was bidden, and Hepburn and Coulson were in the passage donning their wraps, and rather to their indignation being assisted therein by Martha, who was accustomed to the office with her own master Suddenly they were recalled into the parlour.

John Foster was fumbling with the papers a little nervously: Jeremiah spoke—

'We have not thought it necessary to commend Hester Rose to you; if she had been a lad she would have had a third o' the business along wi' yo'. Being a woman, it's ill troubling her with a partnership; better give her a fixed salary till such time as she marries.'

He looked a little knowingly and curiously at the faces of the young men he addressed. William Coulson seemed sheepish and uncomfortable, but said nothing, leaving it as usual to Philip to be spokesman.

'If we hadn't cared for Hester for hersel', master, we should ha' cared for her as being forespoken by yo'. Yo' and Master John shall fix what we ought t' pay her; and I think I may make bold to say that, as our income rises, hers shall too – eh, Coulson?' (a sound of assent quite distinct enough); 'for we both look on her as a sister, and on Alice like a mother, as I told her only this very day.'

CHAPTER XV

A DIFFICULT QUESTION

PHILIP went to bed with that kind of humble penitent gratitude in his heart, which we sometimes feel after a sudden revulsion of feeling from despondency to hope. The night before it seemed as if all events were so arranged as to thwart him in his dearest wishes; he felt now as if his discontent and repining, not twenty-four hours before, had been almost impious, so great was the change in his circumstances for the better. Now all seemed promising for the fulfilment of what he most desired. He was almost convinced that he was mistaken in thinking that Kinraid had had anything more than a sailor's admiration for a pretty girl with regard to Sylvia; at any rate, he was going away to-morrow, in all probability not to return for another year (for Greenland ships left for the northern seas as soon as there was a chance of the ice being broken up), and ere then he himself might speak out openly, laying before her parents all his fortunate prospects, and before her all his deep passionate love.

So this night his prayers were more than the mere form that they had been the night before; they were a vehement expression of gratitude to God for having, as it were, interfered on his behalf, to grant him the desire of his eyes and the lust of his heart. He was like too many of us, he did not place his future life in the hands of God, and only ask for grace to do His will in whatever circumstances might arise; but he yearned in that terrible way after a blessing which, when granted under such circumstances, too often turns out to be equivalent to a curse. And that spirit brings with it the material and earthly idea that all events that favour our wishes are answers to our prayer; and so they are in one sense, but they need prayer in a deeper and higher spirit to keep us from the temptation to evil which such events invariably bring with them.

Philip little knew how Sylvia's time had been passed that

day. If he had, he would have laid down this night with even a heavier heart than he had done on the last.

Charley Kinraid accompanied his cousins as far as the spot where the path to Haytersbank Farm diverged. Then he stopped his merry talk, and announced his intention of going to see farmer Robson. Bessy Corney looked disappointed and a little sulky; but her sister Molly Brunton laughed, and said,—

'Tell truth, lad! Dannel Robson 'd niver have a call fra' thee if he hadn't a pretty daughter.'

'Indeed, but he would,' replied Charley, rather annoyed; 'when I've said a thing, I do it. I promised last night to go see him; besides, I like the old man.'

'Well! when shall we tell mother yo're comin' whoam?'

'Toward eight o'clock – maybe sooner.'

'Why it's bare five now! bless t' lad, does he think o' staying theere a' neet, and they up so late last night, and Mrs Robson ailing beside? Mother 'll not think it kind on yo' either, will she, Bess?'

'I dunno. Charley mun do as he likes; I daresay no one'll miss him if he does bide away till eight.'

'Well, well! I can't tell what I shall do; but yo'd best not stop lingering here, for it's getting on, and there'll be a keen frost by t' look o' the stars.'

Haytersbank was closed for the night as far as it ever was closed; there were no shutters to the windows, nor did they care to draw the inside curtains, so few were the passers-by. The house door was fastened; but the shippen* door a little on in the same long low block of building stood open, and a dim light made an oblong upon the snowy ground outside. As Kinraid drew near he heard talking there, and a woman's voice; he threw a passing glance through the window into the fire-lit house-place, and seeing Mrs Robson asleep by the fireside in her easy-chair, he went on.

There was the intermittent sound of the sharp whistling of milk into the pail, and Kester, sitting on a three-legged stool, cajoling a capricious cow into letting her fragrant burden flow. Sylvia stood near the farther window-ledge, on which a horn lantern was placed, pretending to knit at a gray worsted stocking, but in reality laughing at Kester's futile endeavours, and finding quite enough to do with her eyes, in keeping herself untouched by the whisking tail, or the occasional kick. The frosty air was mellowed by the warm and odorous breath of the cattle – breath that hung about the place in faint misty clouds. There was only a dim light; such as it was, it was not clearly defined against the dark heavy shadow in which the old black rafters and manger and partitions were enveloped.

As Charley came to the door, Kester was saying, 'Quiet wi' thee, wench! Theere now, she's a beauty, if she'll stand still. There's niver such a cow i' t' Riding, if she'll only behave hersel'. She's a bonny lass, she is; let down her milk, theere's a pretty!'

'Why, Kester,' laughed Sylvia, 'thou'rt asking her for her milk wi' as many pretty speeches as if thou wert wooing a wife!'

'Hey, lass!' said Kester, turning a bit towards her, and shutting one eye to cock the other the better upon her; an operation which puckered up his already wrinkled face into a thousand new lines and folds. 'An' how does thee know how a man woos a wife, that thee talks so knowin' about it? That's tellin'. Some un's been tryin' it on thee.'

'There's niver a one been so impudent,' said Sylvia, reddening and tossing her head a little; 'I'd like to see 'em try me!'

'Well, well!' said Kester, wilfully misunderstanding her meaning, 'thou mun be patient, wench; and if thou's a good lass, maybe thy turn 'll come and they 'll try it.'

'I wish thou'd talk of what thou's some knowledge on, Kester, i'stead of i' that silly way,' replied Sylvia.

'Then a mun talk no more 'bout women for they're past knowin', an' druv e'en King Solomon silly.'*

At this moment Charley stepped in. Sylvia gave a little start and dropped her ball of worsted. Kester made as though absorbed in his task of cajoling Black Nell; but his eyes and ears were both vigilant.

'I was going into the house, but I saw yo'r mother asleep,

and I didn't like to waken her, so I just came on here. Is yo'r father to the fore?'

'No,' said Sylvia, hanging down her head a little, wondering if he could have heard the way in which she and Kester had been talking, and thinking over her little foolish jokes with anger against herself. 'Father is gone to Winthrop about some pigs as he's heerd on. He'll not be back till seven o'clock or so.'

It was but half-past five, and Sylvia in the irritation of the moment believed that she wished Kinraid would go. But she would have been extremely disappointed if he had. Kinraid himself seemed to have no thought of the kind. He saw with his quick eyes, not unaccustomed to women, that his coming so unexpectedly had fluttered Sylvia, and anxious to make her quite at her ease with him, and not unwilling to conciliate Kester, he addressed his next speech to him, with the same kind of air of interest in the old man's pursuit that a young man of a different class sometimes puts on when talking to the chaperone of a pretty girl in a ball-room.

'That's a handsome beast yo've just been milking, master.'

'Ay; but handsome is as handsome does. It were only yesterday as she aimed her leg right at t' pail wi' t' afterings* in. She knowed it were afterings as well as any Christian, and t' more t' mischief t' better she likes it; an' if a hadn't been too quick for her, it would have a' gone swash down i' t' litter. This'n 's a far better cow i' t' long run, she's just a steady goer,' as the milky down-pour came musical and even from the stall next to Black Nell's.

Sylvia was knitting away vigorously, thinking all the while that it was a great pity she had not put on a better gown, or even a cap with brighter ribbon, and quite unconscious how very pretty she looked standing against the faint light, her head a little bent down; her hair catching bright golden touches, as it fell from under her little linen cap; her pink bedgown, confined by her apron-string, giving a sort of easy grace to her figure; her dark full linsey petticoat short above her trim ancles, looking far more suitable to the place where she was standing than her long gown of the night before would have done. Kinraid was wanting to talk to her, and to make her talk, but was uncertain how to begin. In the meantime Kester went on with the subject last spoken about.

'Black Nell's at her fourth calf now, so she ought to ha' left off her tricks and turned sober-like. But bless yo', there's some cows as 'll be skittish till they're fat for t' butcher. Not but what a like milking her better nor a steady goer; a man has allays summat to be watchin' for; and a'm kind o' set up when a've mastered her at last. T' young missus theere, she's mighty fond o' comin' t' see Black Nell at her tantrums. She'd niver come near me if a' cows were like this'n.'

'Do you often come and see the cows milked?' asked Kinraid,

'Many a time,' said Sylvia, smiling a little. 'Why, when we're throng, I help Kester; but now we've only Black Nell and Daisy giving milk. Kester knows as I can milk Black Nell quite easy,' she continued, half vexed that Kester had not named this accomplishment.

'Ay! when she's in a good frame o' mind, as she is sometimes. But t' difficulty is to milk her at all times.'

'I wish I'd come a bit sooner. I should like t' have seen you milk Black Nell,' addressing Sylvia.

'Yo'd better come to-morrow e'en, and see what a hand she'll mak' on her,' said Kester.

'To-morrow night I shall be far on my road back to Shields.'

'To-morrow!' said Sylvia, suddenly looking up at him, and then dropping her eyes, as she found he had been watching for the effect of his intelligence on her.

'I mun be back at t' whaler, where I'm engaged,' continued he. 'She's fitting up after a fresh fashion, and as I've been one as wanted new ways, I mun be on the spot for t' look after her. Maybe I shall take a run down here afore sailing in March. I'm sure I shall try.'

There was a good deal meant and understood by these last few words. The tone in which they were spoken gave them a tender intensity not lost upon either of the hearers. Kester cocked his eye once more, but with as little obtrusiveness as he could, and pondered the sailor's looks and ways. He remembered his coming about the place the winter before, and how the old master had then appeared to have taken to him; but at that time Sylvia had seemed to Kester too little removed from a child to have either art or part in Kinraid's visits; now, however, the case was different. Kester in his sphere – among his circle of acquaintance, narrow though it was – had heard with much pride of Sylvia's bearing away the bell at church* and at market, wherever girls of her age were congregated. He was a north countryman, so he gave out no further sign of his feelings than his mistress and Sylvia's mother had done on a like occasion.

'T' lass is weel enough,' said he; but he grinned to himself, and looked about, and listened to the hearsay of every lad, wondering who was handsome, and brave, and good enough to be Sylvia's mate. Now, of late, it had seemed to the canny farm-servant pretty clear that Philip Hepburn was 'after her;' and to Philip, Kester had an instinctive objection, a kind of natural antipathy such as has existed in all ages between the dwellers in a town and those in the country, between agriculture and trade. So, while Kinraid and Sylvia kept up their half-tender, half-jesting conversation, Kester was making up his slow persistent mind as to the desirability of the young man then present as a husband for his darling, as much from his being other than Philip in every respect, as from the individual good qualities he possessed. Kester's first opportunity of favouring Kinraid's suit consisted in being as long as possible over his milking; so never were cows that required such 'stripping,'* or were expected to yield such 'afterings,' as Black Nell and Daisy that night. But all things must come to an end; and at length Kester got up from his three-legged stool, on seeing what the others did not – that the dip-candle in the lantern was coming to an end – and that in two or three minutes more the shippen would be in darkness, and so his pails of milk be endangered. In an instant Sylvia had started out of her delicious dreamland, her drooping eyes were raised, and recovered their power of observation; her ruddy arms were freed from the apron in which she had enfolded them, as a protection from the gathering cold, and she had seized and adjusted the wooden yoke across her shoulders, ready to bear the brimming milk-pails to the dairy.

'Look yo' at her!' exclaimed Kester to Charley, as he adjusted the fragrant pails on the yoke. 'She thinks she's missus a'ready, and she's allays for carrying in t' milk since t' rhumatiz cotched my shouther i' t' back end; and when she says "Yea," it's as much as my heed's worth to say "Nay."'

And along the wall, round the corner, down the round slippery stones of the rambling farmyard, behind the buildings, did Sylvia trip, safe and well-poised, though the ground wore all one coating of white snow, and in many places was so slippery as to oblige Kinraid to linger near Kester, the lantern-bearer. Kester did not lose his opportunity, though the cold misty night air provoked his asthmatic cough whenever he breathed, and often interrupted his words.

'She's a good wench – a good wench as iver was – an' come on a good stock, an' that's summat, whether in a cow or a woman. A've known her from a babby; she's a reet down good un.'

By this time they had reached the back kitchen door, just as Sylvia had unladen herself, and was striking a light with flint and tinder. The house seemed warm and inviting after the piercing outer air, although the kitchen into which they entered contained only a raked and slumbering fire at one end, over which, on a crook, hung the immense pan of potatoes cooking for the evening meal of the pigs. To this pan Kester immediately addressed himself, swinging it round with ease, owing to the admirable simplicity of the old-fashioned machinery. Kinraid stood between Kester and the door into the dairy, through which Sylvia had vanished with the milk. He half wished to conciliate Kester by helping him, but he seemed also attracted, by a force which annihilated his will, to follow her wherever she went. Kester read his mind.

'Let alone, let alone,' said he; 'pigs' vittle takes noan such dainty carryin' as milk. A may set it down an' niver spill a drop; she's noan fit for t' serve swine, nor yo' other, mester; better help her t' teem* t' milk.'

So Kinraid followed the light – his light – into the icy chill of the dairy, where the bright polished tin cans were quickly dimmed with the warm, sweet-smelling milk, that Sylvia was emptying out into the brown pans. In his haste to help her, Charley took up one of the pails.

'Eh? that'n 's to be strained. Yo' have a' the cow's hair in. Mother's very particular, and cannot abide a hair.'

So she went over to her awkward dairymaid, and before she – but not before he — was aware of the sweet proximity, she was adjusting his happy awkward arms to the new office of holding a milk-strainer over the bowl, and pouring the white liquid through it.

'There!' said she, looking up for a moment, and half blushing; 'now yo'll know how to do it next time.'

'I wish next time was to come now,' said Kinraid; but she had returned to her own pail, and seemed not to hear him. He followed her to her side of the dairy. 'I've but a short memory, can yo' not show me again how t' hold t' strainer?'

'No,' said she, half laughing, but holding her strainer fast in spite of his insinuating efforts to unlock her fingers. 'But there's no need to tell me yo've getten a short memory.'

'Why? what have I done? how dun you know it?'

'Last night,' she began, and then she stopped, and turned away her head, pretending to be busy in her dairy duties of rinsing and such like.

'Well!' said he, half conjecturing her meaning, and flattered by it, if his conjecture were right. 'Last night – what?'

'Oh, yo' know!' said she, as if impatient at being both literally and metaphorically followed about, and driven into a corner.

'No; tell me,' persisted he.

'Well,' said she, 'if yo' will have it, I think yo' showed yo'd but a short memory when yo' didn't know me again, and yo' were five times at this house last winter, and that's not so long sin'. But I suppose yo' see a vast o' things on yo'r voyages by land or by sea, and then it's but natural yo' should forget.' She wished she could go on talking, but could not think of anything more to say just then; for, in the middle of her sentence, the flattering interpretation he might put upon her words, on her knowing so exactly the number of times he had been to Haytersbank, flashed upon her, and she wanted to lead the conversation a little farther afield – to make it a little less personal. This was not his wish, however. In a tone which thrilled through her, even in her own despite, he said,—

'Do yo' think that can ever happen again, Sylvia?'

She was quite silent; almost trembling. He repeated the question as if to force her to answer. Driven to bay, she equivocated.

'What happen again? Let me go, I dunno what yo're talking about, and I'm a'most numbed wi' cold.'

For the frosty air came sharp in through the open lattice window, and the ice was already forming on the milk. Kinraid would have found a ready way of keeping his cousins, or indeed most young women, warm; but he paused before he dared put his arm round Sylvia; she had something so shy and wild in her look and manner; and her very innocence of what her words, spoken by another girl, might lead to, inspired him with respect, and kept him in check. So he contented himself with saying,—

'I'll let yo' go into t' warm kitchen if yo'll tell me if yo' think I can ever forget yo' again.'

She looked up at him defiantly, and set her red lips firm. He enjoyed her determination not to reply to this question; it showed she felt its significance. Her pure eyes looked steadily into his; nor was the expression in his such as to daunt her or make her afraid. They were like two children defying each other; each determined to conquer. At last she unclosed her lips, and nodding her head as if in triumph, said, as she folded her arms once more in her check apron,—

'Yo'll have to go home sometime.'

'Not for a couple of hours yet,' said he; 'and yo'll be frozen first; so yo'd better say if I can ever forget yo' again, without more ado.'

Perhaps the fresh voices breaking on the silence, – perhaps

the tones were less modulated than they had been before, but anyhow Bell Robson's voice was heard calling Sylvia through the second door, which opened from the dairy to the house-place, in which her mother had been till this moment asleep. Sylvia darted off in obedience to the call; glad to leave him, as at the moment Kinraid resentfully imagined. Through the open door he heard the conversation between mother and daughter, almost unconscious of its meaning, so difficult did he find it to wrench his thoughts from the ideas he had just been forming with Sylvia's bright lovely face right under his eyes.

'Sylvia!' said her mother, 'who's yonder?' Bell was sitting up in the attitude of one startled out of slumber into intensity of listening; her hands on each of the chair-arms, as if just going to rise. 'There's a fremd* man i' t' house. I heerd his voice!'

'It's only – it's just Charley Kinraid; he was a-talking to me i' t' dairy.'

'I' t' dairy, lass! and how com'd he i' t' dairy?'

'He com'd to see feyther. Feyther asked him last night,' said Sylvia, conscious that he could overhear every word that was said, and a little suspecting that he was no great favourite with her mother.

'Thy feyther's out; how com'd he i' t' dairy?' persevered Bell.

'He com'd past this window, and saw yo' asleep, and didn't like for t' waken yo'; so he com'd on to t' shippen, and when I carried t' milk in——'

But now Kinraid came in, feeling the awkwardness of his situation a little, yet with an expression so pleasant and manly in his open face, and in his exculpatory manner, that Sylvia lost his first words in a strange kind of pride of possession in him, about which she did not reason nor care to define the grounds. But her mother rose from her chair somewhat formally, as if she did not intend to sit down again while he stayed, yet was too weak to be kept in that standing attitude long.

'I'm afeared, sir, Sylvie hasn't told yo' that my master's*

out, and not like to be in till late. He'll be main and sorry to have missed yo'.'

There was nothing for it after this but to go. His only comfort was that on Sylvia's rosy face he could read unmistakable signs of regret and dismay. His sailor's life, in bringing him suddenly face to face with unexpected events, had given him something of that self-possession which we consider the attribute of a gentleman; and with an apparent calmness which almost disappointed Sylvia, who construed it into a symptom of indifference as to whether he went or stayed, he bade her mother good-night, and only said, in holding her hand a minute longer than was absolutely necessary,—

'I'm coming back ere I sail, and then, maybe, you'll answer yon question.'

He spoke low, and her mother was rearranging herself in her chair, else Sylvia would have had to repeat the previous words. As it was, with soft thrilling ideas ringing through her, she could get her wheel, and sit down to her spinning by the fire; waiting for her mother to speak first, Sylvia dreamt her dreams.

Bell Robson was partly aware of the state of things, as far as it lay on the surface. She was not aware how deep down certain feelings had penetrated into the girl's heart who sat on the other side of the fire, with a little sad air diffused over her face and figure. Bell looked upon Sylvia as still a child, to be warned off forbidden things by threats of danger. But the forbidden thing was already tasted, and possible danger in its full acquisition only served to make it more precious-sweet.

Bell sat upright in her chair, gazing into the fire. Her milk-white linen mob-cap fringed round and softened her face, from which the usual apple-red was banished by illness, and the features, from the same cause, rendered more prominent and stern. She had a clean buff kerchief round her neck, and stuffed into the bosom of her Sunday woollen gown of dark blue, – if she had been in working-trim she would have worn a bedgown like Sylvia's. Her sleeves were pinned back at the elbows, and her brown arms and hard-working hands lay crossed in unwonted idleness on her check apron. Her knitting was by her side; and if she had been going through any accustomed calculation or consideration she would have had it busily clinking in her fingers. But she had something quite beyond common to think about, and, perhaps, to speak about; and for the minute she was not equal to knitting.

'Sylvie,' she began at length, 'did I e'er tell thee on Nancy Hartley as I knew when I were a child? I'm thinking a deal on her to-night; maybe it's because I've been dreaming on yon old times. She was a bonny lass as ever were seen, I've heerd folk say; but that were afore I knew her. When I knew her she were crazy, poor wench; wi' her black hair a-streaming down her back, and her eyes, as were a'most as black, allays crying out for pity, though never a word she spoke but "He once was here." Just that o'er and o'er again, whether she were cold or hot, full or hungry, "He once was here," were all her speech. She had been farm-servant to my mother's brother – James Hepburn, thy great-uncle as was; she were a poor, friendless wench, a parish 'prentice, but honest and gaum-like,* till a lad, as nobody knowed, come o'er the hills one sheep-shearing fra' Whitehaven; he had summat to do wi' th' sea, though not rightly to be called a sailor: and he made a deal on Nancy Hartley, just to beguile the time like; and he went away and ne'er sent a thought after her more. It's the way as lads have; and there's no holding 'em when they're fellows as nobody knows – neither where they come fro', nor what they've been doing a' their lives, till they come athwart some poor wench like Nancy Hartley. She were but a softy after all: for she left off doing her work in a proper manner. I've heerd my aunt say as she found out as summat was wrong wi' Nancy as soon as th' milk turned bingy,* for there ne'er had been such a clean lass about her milk-cans afore that; and from bad it grew to worse, and she would sit and do nothing but play wi' her fingers fro' morn till night, and if they asked her what ailed her, she just said, "He once was here;" and if they bid her go about her work, it were a' the same. And when they scolded her, and pretty sharp too, she would stand up and put her hair from her eyes, and look about her like a crazy thing searching for her wits, and ne'er finding them, for all she could think on was just, "He once was here." It were a caution to me again thinking a man t' mean what he says when he's a-talking to a young woman.'

'But what became on poor Nancy?' asked Sylvia.

'What should become on her or on any lass as gives hersel' up to thinking on a man who cares nought for her?' replied her mother, a little severely. 'She were crazed, and my aunt couldn't keep her on, could she? She did keep her a long weary time, thinking as she would, maybe, come to hersel', and, anyhow, she were a motherless wench. But at length she had for t' go where she came fro' – back to Keswick workhouse: and when last I heerd on her she were chained to th' great kitchen dresser i' t' workhouse; they'd beaten her till she were taught to be silent and quiet i' th' daytime, but at night, when she were left alone, she would take up th' oud cry, till it wrung their heart, so they'd many a time to come down and beat her again to get any peace. It were a caution to me, as I said afore, to keep fro' thinking on men as thought nought on me.'

'Poor crazy Nancy!' sighed Sylvia. The mother wondered if she had taken the 'caution' to herself, or was only full of pity for the mad girl, dead long before.

CHAPTER XVI

THE ENGAGEMENT

'As the day lengthens so the cold strengthens.' It was so that year; the hard frost which began on New Year's Eve lasted on and on into late February, black and bitter, but welcome enough to the farmers, as it kept back the too early growth of autumn-sown wheat, and gave them the opportunity of leading manure.* But it did not suit invalids as well, and Bell Robson, though not getting worse, did not make any progress towards amendment. Sylvia was kept very busy, notwithstanding that she had the assistance of a poor widow-woman in the neighbourhood on cleaning, or washing, or churning days. Her life was quiet and monotonous, although hard-working; and while her hands mechanically found and did their accustomed labour, the thoughts that rose in her head always centred on Charley Kinraid, his ways, his words, his looks, whether they all meant what she would fain believe they did, and whether, meaning love at the time, such a feeling was likely to endure. Her mother's story of crazy Nancy had taken hold of her; but not as a 'caution,' rather as a parallel case to her own. Like Nancy, and borrowing the poor girl's own words, she would say softly to herself, 'He once was here;' but all along she believed in her heart he would come back again to her, though it touched her strangely to imagine the agonies of forsaken love.

Philip knew little of all this. He was very busy with facts and figures, doggedly fighting through the necessary business, and only now and then allowing himself the delicious relaxation of going to Haytersbank in an evening, to inquire after his aunt's health, and to see Sylvia; for the two Fosters were punctiliously anxious to make their shopmen test all their statements; insisting on an examination of the stock, as if Hepburn and Coulson were strangers to the shop; having the Monkshaven auctioneer in to appraise the fixtures and necessary furniture; going over the shop books for the last twenty years with their successors, an employment which took up evening after evening; and not unfrequently taking one of the young men on the long commercial journeys which were tediously made in a gig. By degrees both Hepburn and Coulson were introduced to distant manufacturers and wholesale dealers. They would have been willing to take the Fosters' word for every statement the brothers had made on New Year's Day; but this, it was evident, would not have satisfied their masters, who were scrupulous in insisting that whatever advantage there were should always fall on the side of the younger men.

When Philip saw Sylvia she was always quiet and gentle; perhaps more silent than she had been a year ago, and she did not attend so briskly to what was passing around her. She was rather thinner and paler; but whatever change there was in her was always an improvement in Philip's eyes, so long as she spoke graciously to him. He thought she was suffering from long-continued anxiety about her mother, or that she had too much to do; and either cause was enough to make him treat her with a grave regard and deference which had a repressed tenderness in it, of which she, otherwise occupied, was quite unaware. She liked him better, too, than she had done a year or two before, because he did not show her any of the eager attention which teased her then, although its meaning was not fully understood.

Things were much in this state when the frost broke, and milder weather succeeded. This was the time so long looked forward to by the invalid and her friends, as favouring the doctor's recommendation of change of air. Her husband was to take her to spend a fortnight with a kindly neighbour, who lived near the farm they had occupied, forty miles or so inland, before they came to Haytersbank. The widow-woman was to come and stay in the house, to keep Sylvia company, during her mother's absence. Daniel, indeed, was to return home after conveying his wife to her destination; but there was so much to be done on the land at this time of the year, that Sylvia would have been alone all day had it not been for the arrangement just mentioned.

There was active stirring in Monkshaven harbour as well as on shore. The whalers were finishing their fittings-out for the Greenland seas. It was a 'close' season, that is to say, there would be difficulty in passing the barrier of ice which lay between the ships and the whaling-grounds; and yet these must be reached before June, or the year's expedition would be of little avail. Every blacksmith's shop rung with the rhythmical clang of busy hammers, beating out old iron, such as horseshoes, nails or stubs,* into the great harpoons; the quays were thronged with busy and important sailors, rushing hither and thither, conscious of the demand in which they were held at this season of the year. It was war time, too. Many captains unable to procure men in Monkshaven would have to complete their crews in the Shetlands. The shops in the town were equally busy; stores had to be purchased by the whaling-masters, warm clothing of all sorts to be provided. These were the larger wholesale orders; but many a man, and woman, too, brought out their small hoards to purchase extra comforts, or precious keepsakes for some beloved one. It was the time of the great half-yearly traffic of the place; another impetus was given to business when the whalers returned in the autumn, and the men were flush of money, and full of delight at once more seeing their homes and their friends.

There was much to be done in Fosters' shop, and later hours were kept than usual. Some perplexity or other was occupying John and Jeremiah Foster; their minds were not so much on the alert as usual, being engaged on some weighty matter of which they had as yet spoken to no one. But it thus happened that they did not give the prompt assistance they were accustomed to render at such times; and Coulson had been away on some of the new expeditions devolving on him and Philip as future partners. One evening after the shop was closed, while they were examining the goods, and comparing the sales with the entries in the day-book, Coulson suddenly inquired—

'By the way, Hester, does thee know where the parcel of best bandanas* is gone? There was four left, as I'm pretty sure, when I set off to Sandsend; and to-day Mark Alderson came in, and would fain have had one, and I could find none nowhere.'

'I sold t' last to-day, to yon sailor, the specksioneer, who fought the press-gang same time as poor Darley were killed. He took it, and three yards of yon pink ribbon wi' t' black and yellow crosses on it, as Philip could never abide. Philip has got 'em i' t' book, if he'll only look.'

'Is he here again?' said Philip; 'I didn't see him. What brings him here, where he's noan wanted?'

'T' shop were throng wi' folk,' said Hester, 'and he knew his own mind about the handkercher, and didn't tarry long. Just as he was leaving, his eye caught on t' ribbon, and he came back for it. It were when yo' were serving Mary Darby and there was a vast o' folk about yo'.'

'I wish I'd seen him,' said Coulson. 'I'd ha' gi'en him a word and a look he'd not ha' forgotten in a hurry.'

'Why, what's up?' said Philip, surprised at William's unusual manner, and, at the same time, rather gratified to find a reflection of his own feelings about Kinraid. Coulson's face was pale with anger, but for a moment or two he seemed uncertain whether he would reply or not.

'Up!' said he at length. 'It's just this: he came after my sister for better nor two year; and a better lass – no, nor a prettier i' my eyes – niver broke bread. And then my master saw another girl, that he liked better' – William almost choked in his endeavour to keep down all appearance of violent anger, and then went on, 'and that he played t' same game wi', as I've heerd tell.'

'And how did thy sister take it?' asked Philip, eagerly.

'She died in a six-month,' said William; '*she* forgived him, but it's beyond me. I thought it were him when I heerd of t' work about Darley; Kinraid – and coming fra' Newcassel, where Annie lived 'prentice – and I made inquiry, and it were t' same man. But I'll say no more about him, for it stirs t' old Adam more nor I like, or is fitting.'

Out of respect to him, Philip asked no more questions, although there were many things that he fain would have known. Both Coulson and he went silently and grimly through the remainder of their day's work. Independent of any personal interest which either or both of them had or might have in Kinraid's being a light o' love, this fault of his was one with which the two grave, sedate young men had no sympathy. Their hearts were true and constant, whatever else might be their failings; and it is no new thing to 'damn the faults we have no mind to.'* Philip wished that it was not so late, or that very evening he would have gone to keep guard over Sylvia in her mother's absence – nay, perhaps he might have seen reason to give her a warning of some kind. But, if he had done so, it would have been locking the stable-door after the steed was stolen. Kinraid had turned his steps towards Haytersbank Farm as soon as ever he had completed his purchases. He had only come that afternoon to Monkshaven, and for the sole purpose of seeing Sylvia once more before he went to fulfil his engagement as specksioneer in the

Urania, a whaling-vessel that was to sail from North Shields on Thursday morning, and this was Monday.

Sylvia sat in the house-place, her back to the long low window, in order to have all the light the afternoon hour afforded for her work. A basket of her father's unmended stockings was on the little round table beside her, and one was on her left hand, which she supposed herself to be mending; but from time to time she made long pauses, and looked in the fire; and yet there was but little motion of flame or light in it out of which to conjure visions. It was 'redd up' for the afternoon; covered with a black mass of coal, over which the equally black kettle hung on the crook. In the back-kitchen Dolly Reid, Sylvia's assistant during her mother's absence, chanted a lugubrious ditty, befitting her condition as a widow, while she cleaned tins, and cans, and milking-pails. Perhaps these bustling sounds prevented Sylvia from hearing approaching footsteps coming down the brow with swift advance; at any rate, she started and suddenly stood up as some one entered the open door. It was strange she should be so much startled, for the person who entered had been in her thoughts all during those long pauses. Charley Kinraid and the story of crazy Nancy had been the subjects for her dreams for many a day, and many a night. Now he stood there, bright and handsome as ever, with just that much timidity in his face, that anxiety as to his welcome, which gave his accost an added charm, could she but have perceived it. But she was so afraid of herself, so unwilling to show what she felt, and how much she had been thinking of him in his absence, that her reception seemed cold and still. She did not come forward to meet him; she went crimson to the very roots of her hair; but that, in the waning light, he could not see; and she shook so that she felt as if she could hardly stand; but the tremor was not visible to him. She wondered if he remembered the kiss that had passed between them on New Year's Eve – the words that had been spoken in the dairy on New Year's Day; the tones, the looks, that had accompanied those words. But all she said was—

'I didn't think to see yo'. I thought yo'd ha' sailed.'

'I told yo' I should come back, didn't I?' said he, still standing, with his hat in his hand, waiting to be asked to sit down; and she, in her bashfulness, forgetting to give the invitation, but, instead, pretending to be attentively mending the stocking she held. Neither could keep quiet and silent long. She felt his eyes were upon her, watching every motion, and grew more and more confused in her expression and behaviour. He was a little taken aback by the nature of his reception, and was not sure at first whether to take the great change in her manner, from what it had been when last he saw her, as a favourable symptom or otherwise. By-and-by, luckily for him, in some turn of her arm to reach the scissors on the table, she caught the edge of her work-basket, and down it fell. She stooped to pick up the scattered stockings and ball of worsted, and so did he; and when they rose up, he had fast hold of her hand, and her face was turned away, half ready to cry.

'What ails yo' at me?' said he, beseechingly. 'Yo' might ha' forgotten me; and yet I thought we made a bargain against forgetting each other.' No answer. He went on: 'Yo've never been out o' my thoughts, Sylvia Robson; and I'm come back to Monkshaven for nought but to see you once and again afore I go away to the northern seas. It's not two hour sin' I landed at Monkshaven, and I've been near neither kith nor kin as yet; and now I'm here you won't speak to me.'

'I don't know what to say,' said she, in a low, almost inaudible tone. Then hardening herself, and resolving to speak as if she did not understand his only half-expressed meaning, she lifted up her head, and all but looking at him – while she wrenched her hand out of his – she said: 'Mother's gone to Middleham for a visit, and feyther's out i' t' plough-field wi' Kester; but he'll be in afore long.'

Charley did not speak for a minute or so. Then he said—

'Yo're not so dull as to think I'm come all this way for t' see either your father or your mother. I've a great respect for 'em both; but I'd hardly ha' come all this way for to see 'em, and me bound to be back i' Shields, if I walk every step of the way, by Wednesday night. It's that yo' won't understand my meaning, Sylvia; it's not that yo' don't, or that yo' can't.' He made no effort to repossess himself of her hand. She was quite silent, but in spite of herself she drew long hard breaths. 'I may go back to where I came from,' he went on. 'I thought to go to sea wi' a blessed hope to cheer me up, and a knowledge o' some one as loved me as I'd left behind; some one as loved me half as much as I did her; for th' measure o' my love toward her is so great and mighty, I'd be content wi' half as much from her, till I'd taught her to love me more. But if she's a cold heart and cannot care for a honest sailor, why, then, I'd best go back at once.'

He made for the door. He must have been pretty sure from some sign or other, or he would never have left it to her womanly pride to give way, and for her to make the next advance. He had not taken two steps when she turned quickly towards him, and said something – the echo of which, rather than the words themselves, reached him.

'I didn't know yo' cared for me; yo' niver said so.' In an instant he was back at her side, his arm round her in spite of her short struggle, and his eager passionate voice saying, 'Yo' never knowed I loved you, Sylvia? say it again, and look i' my face while yo' say it, if yo' can. Why, last winter I thought yo'd be such a woman when yo'd come to be one as my een had never looked upon, and this year, ever sin' I saw yo' i' the kitchen corner sitting crouching behind my uncle, I as good as swore I'd have yo' for wife, or never wed at all. And it was not long ere yo' knowed it, for all yo' were so coy, and now yo' have the face – no, yo' have not the face – come, my darling, what is it?' for she was crying; and on his turning her wet blushing face towards him the better to look at it, she suddenly hid it in his breast. He lulled and soothed her in his arms, as if she had been a weeping child and he her mother; and then they sat down on the settle together, and when she was more composed they began to talk. He asked her about her mother; not sorry in his heart at Bell Robson's absence. He had intended if necessary to acknowledge his wishes and desires with regard to Sylvia to her parents; but for various reasons he was not sorry that circumstances had given him the chance of seeing her alone, and obtaining her promise to marry him without being obliged to tell either her father or her mother at present. 'I ha' spent my money pretty free,' he said, 'and I've ne'er a penny to the fore, and yo'r parents may look for something better for yo', my pretty: but when I come back fro' this voyage I shall stand a chance of having a share i' th' *Urania*, and maybe I shall be mate as well as specksioneer; and I can get a matter of from seventy to ninety pound a voyage, let alone th' half-guineas for every whale I strike, and six shilling a gallon on th' oil; and if I keep steady wi' Forbes and Company, they'll make me master i' time, for I've had good schooling, and can work a ship as well as any man; an' I leave yo' wi' yo'r parents, or take a cottage for yo' nigh at hand; but I would like to have something to the fore, and that I shall have, please God, when we come back i' th' autumn. I shall go to sea happy, now, thinking I've yo'r word. Yo're not one to go back from it, I'm sure, else it's a long time to leave such a pretty girl as yo', and ne'er a chance of a letter reaching yo' just to tell yo' once again how I love yo', and to bid yo' not forget yo'r true love.'

'There'll be no need o' that,' murmured Sylvia.

She was too dizzy with happiness to have attended much to his details of his worldly prospects, but at the sound of his tender words of love her eager heart was ready to listen.

'I don't know,' said he, wanting to draw her out into more confession of her feelings. 'There's many a one ready to come after yo'; and yo'r mother is not o'er captivated wi' me; and there's yon tall fellow of a cousin as looks black at me, for if I'm not mista'en he's a notion of being sweet on yo' hisself.'

Not he,' said Sylvia, with some contempt in her tone. 'He's so full o' business and t' shop, and o' makin' money, and gettin' wealth.'

'Ay, ay; but perhaps when he gets a rich man he'll come and ask my Sylvia to be his wife, and what will she say then?'

'He'll niver come asking such a foolish question,' said she, a little impatiently; 'he knows what answer he'd get if he did.'

Kinraid said, almost as if to himself, 'Yo'r mother favours him though.' But she, weary of a subject she cared nothing about, and eager to identify herself with all his interests, asked him about his plans almost at the same time that he said these last words; and they went on as lovers do, intermixing a great many tender expressions with a very little conversation relating to facts.

Dolly Reid came in, and went out softly, unheeded by them. But Sylvia's listening ears caught her father's voice, as he and Kester returned homewards from their day's work in the plough-field; and she started away, and fled upstairs in shy affright, leaving Charley to explain his presence in the solitary kitchen to her father.

He came in, not seeing that any one was there at first; for they had never thought of lighting a candle. Kinraid stepped forward into the firelight; his purpose of concealing what he had said to Sylvia quite melted away by the cordial welcome her father gave him the instant that he recognized him.

'Bless thee, lad! who'd ha' thought o' seein' thee? Why, if iver a thought on thee at all, it were half way to Davis' Straits.* To be sure, t' winter's been a dree season, and thou'rt, maybe, i' t' reet on 't to mak' a late start. Latest start as iver I made was ninth o' March, an' we struck thirteen whales that year.'

'I have something to say to you,' said Charley, in a hesitating voice, so different to his usual hearty way, that Daniel gave him a keen look of attention before he began to speak. And, perhaps, the elder man was not unprepared for the communication that followed. At any rate, it was not unwelcome. He liked Kinraid, and had strong sympathy not merely with what he knew of the young sailor's character, but with the life he led, and the business he followed. Robson listened to all he said with approving nods and winks, till Charley had told him everything he had to say; and then he turned and struck his broad horny palm into Kinraid's as if concluding a bargain, while he expressed in words his hearty consent to their engagement. He wound up with a chuckle, as the thought struck him that this great piece of business, of disposing of their only child, had been concluded while his wife was away.

'A'm noane so sure as t' missus 'll like it,' said he; 'tho' whativer she'll ha' to say again it, mischief only knows. But she's noane keen on matterimony; though a have made her as good a man as there is in a' t' Ridings. Anyhow, a'm master, and that she knows. But maybe, for t' sake o' peace an' quietness – tho' she's niver a scolding tongue, that a will say for her – we'n best keep this matter to ourselves till thou comes int' port again. T' lass upstairs 'll like nought better than t' curl hersel' round a secret, and purr o'er it, just as t' oud cat does o'er her blind kitten. But thou'll be wanting to see t' lass, a'll be bound. An oud man like me isn't as good company as a pretty lass.' Laughing a low rich laugh over his own wit, Daniel went to the bottom of the stairs, and called, 'Sylvie, Sylvie! come down, lass! a's reet; come down!'

For a time there was no answer. Then a door was unbolted, and Sylvia said,

'I can't come down again. I'm noane comin' down again to-night.'

Daniel laughed the more at this, especially when he caught Charley's look of disappointment.

'Hearken how she's bolted her door. She'll noane come near us this neet. Eh! but she's a stiff little 'un; she's been our only one, and we'n mostly let her have her own way. But we'll have a pipe and a glass; and that, to my thinking, is as good company as iver a woman i' Yorkshire.'

CHAPTER XVII

REJECTED WARNINGS

THE post arrived at Monkshaven three times in the week; sometimes, indeed, there were not a dozen letters in the bag, which was brought thither by a man in a light mail-cart, who took the better part of a day to drive from York; dropping private bags here and there on the moors, at some squire's lodge or roadside inn. Of the number of letters that arrived in Monkshaven, the Fosters, shopkeepers and bankers, had the largest share.

The morning succeeding the day on which Sylvia had engaged herself to Kinraid, the Fosters seemed unusually anxious to obtain their letters. Several times Jeremiah came out of the parlour in which his brother John was sitting in expectant silence, and, passing through the shop, looked up and down the market-place in search of the old lame woman, who was charitably employed to deliver letters, and who must have been lamer than ever this morning, to judge from the lateness of her coming. Although none but the Fosters knew the cause of their impatience for their letters, yet there was such tacit sympathy between them and those whom they employed, that Hepburn, Coulson, and Hester were all much relieved when the old woman at length appeared with her basket of letters.

One of these seemed of especial consequence to the good brothers. They each separately looked at the direction, and then at one another; and without a word they returned with it unread into the parlour, shutting the door, and drawing the green silk curtain close, the better to read it in privacy.

Both Coulson and Philip felt that something unusual was going on, and were, perhaps, as full of consideration as to the possible contents of this London letter, as of attention to their more immediate business. But fortunately there was little doing in the shop. Philip, indeed, was quite idle when John Foster opened the parlour-door, and, half doubtfully, called him into the room. As the door of communication shut the three in, Coulson felt himself a little aggrieved. A minute ago Philip and he were on a level of ignorance, from which the former was evidently going to be raised. But he soon returned to his usual state of acquiescence in things as they were, which was partly constitutional, and partly the result of his Quaker training.

It was apparently by John Foster's wish that Philip had been summoned. Jeremiah, the less energetic and decided brother, was still discusing the propriety of the step when Philip entered.

'No need for haste, John; better not call the young man till we have further considered the matter.'

But the young man was there in presence; and John's will carried the day.

It seemed from his account to Philip (explanatory of what he, in advance of his brother's slower judgment, thought to be a necessary step), that the Fosters had for some time received anonymous letters, warning them, with distinct meaning, though in ambiguous terms, against a certain silk-manufacturer in Spitalfields, with whom they had had straightforward business dealings for many years; but to whom they had latterly advanced money. The letters hinted at the utter insolvency of this manufacturer. They had urged their correspondent to give them his name in confidence, and this morning's letter had brought it; but the name was totally unknown to them, though there seemed no reason to doubt the reality of either it or the address, the latter of which was given in full. Certain circumstances were mentioned regarding the transactions between the Fosters and this manufacturer, which could be known only to those who were in the confidence of one or the other; and to the Fosters the man was, as has been said, a perfect stranger. Probably, they would have been unwilling to incur the risk they had done on this manufacturer Dickinson's account, if it had not been that he belonged to the same denomination as themselves, and was publicly distinguished for his excellent and philanthropic character; but these letters were provocative of anxiety, especially since this morning's post had brought out the writer's full name, and various particulars showing his intimate knowledge of Dickinson's affairs.

After much perplexed consultation, John had hit upon the plan of sending Hepburn to London to make secret inquiries respecting the true character and commercial position of the man whose creditors, not a month ago, they had esteemed it an honour to be.

Even now Jeremiah was ashamed of their want of confidence in one so good; he believed that the information they had received would all prove a mistake, founded on erroneous grounds, if not a pure invention of an enemy; and he had only been brought partially to consent to the sending of Hepburn, by his brother's pledging himself that the real nature of Philip's errand should be unknown to any human creature, save them three.

As all this was being revealed to Philip, he sat apparently unmoved and simply attentive. In fact, he was giving all his mind to understanding the probabilities of the case, leaving his own feelings in the background till his intellect should have done its work. He said little; but what he did say was to the point, and satisfied both brothers. John perceived that his messenger would exercise penetration and act with energy; while Jeremiah was soothed by Philip's caution in not hastily admitting the probability of any charge against Dickinson, and in giving full weight to his previous good conduct and good character.

Philip had the satisfaction of feeling himself employed on a mission which would call out his powers, and yet not exceed them. In his own mind he forestalled the instructions of his masters, and was silently in advance of John Foster's plans and arrangements, while he appeared to listen to all that was said with quiet business-like attention.

It was settled that the next morning he was to make his way northwards to Hartlepool, whence he could easily proceed either by land or sea to Newcastle, from which place smacks were constantly sailing to London. As to his personal conduct and behaviour there, the brothers overwhelmed him with directions and advice; nor did they fail to draw out of the strong box in the thick wall of their counting-house a more than sufficient sum of money for all possible expenses. Philip had never had so much in his hands before, and hesitated to take it, saying it was more than he should require; but they repeated, with fresh urgency, their warnings about the terrible high prices of London, till he could only resolve to keep a strict account, and bring back all that he did not expend, since nothing but his taking the whole sum would satisfy his employers.

When he was once more behind the counter, he had leisure

enough for consideration as far as Coulson could give it him. The latter was silent, brooding over the confidence which Philip had apparently received, but which was withheld from him. He did not yet know of the culminating point – of Philip's proposed journey to London; that great city of London, which, from its very inaccessibility fifty years ago, loomed so magnificent through the mist of men's imaginations. It is not to be denied that Philip felt exultant at the mere fact of 'going to London.' But then again, the thought of leaving Sylvia; of going out of possible daily reach of her; of not seeing her for a week – a fortnight; nay, he might be away for a month, – for no rash hurry was to mar his delicate negotiation, – gnawed at his heart, and spoilt any enjoyment he might have anticipated from gratified curiosity, or even from the consciousness of being trusted by those whose trust and regard he valued. The sense of what he was leaving grew upon him the longer he thought on the subject; he almost wished that he had told his masters earlier in the conversation of his unwillingness to leave Monkshaven for so long a time; and then again he felt that the gratitude he owed them quite prohibited his declining any task they might impose, especially as they had more than once said that it would not do for them to appear in the affair, and yet that to no one else could they entrust so difficult and delicate a matter. Several times that day, as he perceived Coulson's jealous sullenness, he thought in his heart that the consequence of the excessive confidence for which Coulson envied him was a burden from which he would be thankful to be relieved.

As they all sat at tea in Alice Rose's house-place, Philip announced his intended journey; a piece of intelligence he had not communicated earlier to Coulson because he had rather dreaded the increase of dissatisfaction it was sure to produce, and of which he knew the expression would be restrained by the presence of Alice Rose and her daughter.

'To Lunnon!' exclaimed Alice.

Hester said nothing.

'Well! some folks has the luck!' said Coulson.

'Luck!' said Alice, turning sharp round on him. 'Niver let

me hear such a vain word out o' thy mouth, laddie, again. It's the Lord's doing, and luck's the devil's way o' putting it. Maybe it's to try Philip he's sent there; happen it may be a fiery furnace to him; for I've heerd tell it's full o' temptations, and he may fall into sin – and then where'd be the "luck" on it? But why art ta going? and the morning, say's thou? Why, thy best shirt is in t' suds, and no time for t' starch and iron it. Whatten the great haste as should take thee to Lunnon wi'out thy ruffled shirt?'

'It's none o' my doing,' said Philip; 'there's business to be done, and John Foster says I'm to do it; and I'm to start to-morrow.'

'I'll not turn thee out wi'out thy ruffled shirt, if I sit up a' neet,' said Alice, resolutely.

'Niver fret thyself, mother, about t' shirt,' said Philip. 'If I need a shirt, London's not what I take it for if I can't buy mysel' one ready-made.'

'Hearken to him!' said Alice. 'He speaks as if buying o' ready-made shirts were nought to him, and he wi' a good half-dozen as I made mysel'. Eh, lad? but if that's the frame o' mind thou'rt in, Lunnon is like for to be a sore place o' temptation. There's pitfalls for men, and traps for money at ivery turn, as I've heerd say. It would ha' been better if John Foster had sent an older man on his business, whativer it be.'

'They seem to make a deal o' Philip all on a sudden,' said Coulson. 'He's sent for, and talked to i' privacy, while Hester and me is left i' t' shop for t' bear t' brunt o' t' serving.'

'Philip knows,' said Hester, and then, somehow, her voice failed her and she stopped.

Philip paid no attention to this half-uttered sentence; he was eager to tell Coulson, as far as he could do so without betraying his master's secret, how many drawbacks there were to his proposed journey, in the responsibility which it involved, and his unwillingness to leave Monkshaven: he said—

'Coulson, I'd give a deal it were thou that were going, and not me. At least, there is many a time I'd give a deal. I'll not deny but at other times I'm pleased at the thought on't. But, if I could I'd change places wi' thee at this moment.'

'It's fine talking,' said Coulson, half mollified, and yet not caring to show it. 'I make no doubt it were an even chance betwixt us two at first, which on us was to go; but somehow thou got the start and thou'st stuck to it till it's too late for aught but to say thou's sorry.'

'Nay, William,' said Philip, rising, 'it's an ill look-out for the future, if thee and me is to quarrel, like two silly wenches, o'er each bit of pleasure, or what thou fancies to be pleasure, as falls in t' way of either on us. I've said truth to thee, and played thee fair, and I've got to go to Haytersbank for to wish 'em good-by, so I'll not stay longer here to be misdoubted by thee.'

He took his cap and was gone, not heeding Alice's shrill inquiry as to his clothes and his ruffled shirt. Coulson sat still, penitent and ashamed; at length he stole a look at Hester. She was playing with her teaspoon, but he could see that she was choking down her tears; he could not choose but force her to speak with an ill-timed question.

'What's to do, Hester?' said he.

She lifted up those eyes, usually so soft and serene; now they were full of the light of indignation shining through tears.

'To do!' she said; 'Coulson, I'd thought better of thee, going and doubting and envying Philip, as niver did thee an ill turn, or said an ill word, or thought an ill thought by thee; and sending him away out o' t' house this last night of all, maybe, wi' thy envyings and jealousy.'

She hastily got up and left the room. Alice was away, looking up Philip's things for his journey. Coulson remained alone, feeling like a guilty child, but dismayed by Hester's words, even more than by his own regret at what he had said.

Philip walked rapidly up the hill-road towards Haytersbank. He was chafed and excited by Coulson's words, and the events of the day. He had meant to shape his life, and now it was, as it were, being shaped for him, and yet he was reproached for the course it was taking, as much as though he were an active agent; accused of taking advantage over Coulson, his intimate companion for years; he who esteemed himself above taking an unfair advantage over any man! His feeling on the subject was akin to that of Hazael,* 'Is thy servant a dog that he should do this thing?'

His feelings, disturbed on this one point, shook his judgment off its balance on another. The resolution he had deliberately formed of not speaking to Sylvia on the subject of his love till he could announce to her parents the fact of his succession to Fosters' business, and till he had patiently, with long-continuing and deep affection, worked his way into her regard, was set aside during the present walk. He would speak to her of his passionate attachment, before he left, for an uncertain length of time, and the certain distance of London. And all the modification on this point which his judgment could obtain from his impetuous and excited heart was, that he would watch her words and manner well when he announced his approaching absence, and if in them he read the slightest token of tender regretful feeling, he would pour out his love at her feet, not even urging the young girl to make any return, or to express the feelings of which he hoped the germ was already budding in her. He would be patient with her; he could not be patient himself. His heart beating, his busy mind rehearsing the probable coming scene, he turned into the field-path that led to Haytersbank. Coming along it, and so meeting him, advanced Daniel Robson, in earnest talk with Charley Kinraid. Kinraid, then, had been at the farm: Kinraid had been seeing Sylvia, her mother away. The thought of poor dead Annie Coulson flashed into Philip's mind. Could he be playing the same game with Sylvia? Philip set his teeth and tightened his lips at the thought of it. They had stopped talking; they had seen him already, or his impulse would have been to dodge behind the wall and avoid them; even though one of his purposes in going to Haytersbank had been to bid his uncle farewell.

Kinraid took him by surprise from the hearty greeting he gave him, and which Philip would fain have avoided. But the specksioneer was full of kindliness towards all the world, especially towards all Sylvia's friends, and, convinced of her great love towards himself, had forgotten any previous jealousy of Philip. Secure and exultant, his broad, handsome, weather-bronzed face was as great a contrast to Philip's long, thoughtful, sallow countenance, as his frank manner was to the other's cold reserve. It was some minutes before Hepburn could bring himself to tell the great event that was about to befall him before this third person whom he considered as an intrusive stranger. But as Kinraid seemed to have no idea of going on, and as there really was no reason why he and all the world should not know of Philip's intentions, he told his uncle that he was bound for London the next day on business connected with the Fosters.

Daniel was deeply struck with the fact that he was talking to a man setting off for London at a day's notice.

'Thou'll niver tell me this hasn't been brewin' longer nor twelve hours; thou's a sly close chap, and we hannot seen thee this se'nnight; thou'll ha' been thinkin' on this, and cogitating it, maybe, a' that time.'

'Nay,' said Philip, 'I knew nought about it last night; it's none o' my doing, going, for I'd liefer ha' stayed where I am.'

'Yo'll like it when once yo're there,' said Kinraid, with a travelled air of superiority, as Philip fancied.

'No, I shan't,' he replied, shortly. 'Liking has nought to do with it.'

'An' yo' knew nought about it last neet,' continued Daniel, musingly. 'Well, life's soon o'er; else when I were a young fellow, folks made their wills afore goin' to Lunnon.'

'Yet I'll be bound to say yo' niver made a will before going to sea,' said Philip, half smiling.

'Na, na; but that's quite another mak' o' thing; going' to sea comes natteral to a man, but goin' to Lunnon, – I were once there, and were near deafened wi' t' throng and t' sound. I were but two hours i' t' place, though our ship lay a fortneet off Gravesend.'

Kinraid now seemed in a hurry; but Philip was stung with curiosity to ascertain his movements, and suddenly addressed him:

'I heard yo' were i' these parts. Are you for staying here long?'

There was a certain abruptness in Philip's tone, if not in his words, which made Kinraid look in his face with surprise, and answer with equal curtness.

'I'm off i' th' morning; and sail for the north seas day after.'

He turned away, and began to whistle, as if he did not wish for any further conversation with his interrogator. Philip, indeed, had nothing more to say to him: he had learned all he wanted to know.

'I'd like to bid good-by to Sylvie. Is she at home?' he asked of her father.

'A'm thinking thou'll not find her. She'll be off to Yester-barrow t' see if she'd get a settin' o' their eggs; her grey speckled hen is cluckin', and nought 'll serve our Sylvia but their eggs to set her upon. But, for a' that, she mayn't be gone yet. Best go on and see for thysel'.'

So they parted; but Philip had not gone many steps before his uncle called him back, Kinraid slowly loitering on mean-while. Robson was fumbling among some dirty papers he had in an old leather case, which he had produced out of his pocket.

'Fact is, Philip, t' pleugh's in a bad way, gearin' and a', an' folk is talkin' on a new kind o' mak'; and if thou's bound for York——'

'I'm not going by York; I'm going by a Newcastle smack.'

'Newcassel – Newcassel – it's pretty much t' same. Here, lad, thou can read print easy; it's a bit as was cut out on a papper; there's Newcassel, and York, and Durham, and a vast more towns named, wheere folk can learn a' about t' new mak' o' pleugh.'

'I see,' said Philip: '"Robinson, Side, Newcastle, can give all requisite information."'

'Ay, ay,' said Robson; 'thou's hit t' marrow on t' matter. Now, if thou'rt i' Newcassel, thou can learn all about it; thou'rt little better nor a woman, for sure, bein' mainly acquaint wi' ribbons, but they'll tell thee – they'll tell thee, lad; and write down what they sayn, and what's to be t' price, and look sharp as to what kind o' folk they are as sells 'em, an' write and let me know. Thou'll be i' Newcassel to-morrow, maybe? Well, then, I'll reckon to hear fro' thee in a week, or, mayhap, less, – for t' land is backward, and I'd like to know about t' pleughs. I'd a month's mind to write to Brunton, as married Molly Corney, but writin' is more i' thy way an' t' parson's nor mine; and if thou sells ribbons, Brunton sells cheese, and that's no better.'

Philip promised to do his best, and to write word to Robson, who, satisfied with his willingness to undertake the commission, bade him go on and see if he could not find the lass. Her father was right in saying that she might not have set out for Yesterbarrow. She had talked about it to Kinraid and her father in order to cover her regret at her lover's accompanying her father to see some new kind of harpoon about which the latter had spoken. But as soon as they had left the house, and she had covertly watched them up the brow in the field, she sate down to meditate and dream about her great happiness in being beloved by her hero, Charley Kinraid. No gloomy dread of his long summer's absence; no fear of the cold, glittering icebergs bearing mercilessly down on the *Urania*, nor shuddering anticipation of the dark waves of evil import, crossed her mind. He loved her, and that was enough. Her eyes looked, trance-like, into a dim, glorious future of life; her lips, still warm and reddened by his kiss, were just parted in a happy smile, when she was startled by the sound of an approaching footstep – a footstep quite familiar enough for her to recognize it, and which was unwelcome now, as disturbing her in the one blessed subject of thought in which alone she cared to indulge.

'Well, Philip! an' what brings *yo'* here?' was her rather ungracious greeting.

'Why, Sylvie, are yo' sorry to see me?' asked Philip, reproachfully. But she turned it off with assumed lightness.

'Oh, yes,' said she. 'I've been wanting yo' this week past wi' t' match to my blue ribbon yo' said yo'd get and bring me next time yo' came.'

'I've forgotten it, Sylvie. It's clean gone out of my mind,' said Philip, with true regret. 'But I've had a deal to think on,' he continued, penitently, as if anxious to be forgiven. Sylvia did not want his penitence, did not care for her ribbon, was troubled by his earnestness of manner – but he knew nothing of all that; he only knew that she whom he loved had asked him to do something for her, and he had neglected it; so, anxious to be excused and forgiven, he went on with the apology she cared not to hear.

If she had been less occupied with her own affairs, less engrossed with deep feeling, she would have reproached him, if only in jest, for his carelessness. As it was, she scarcely took in the sense of his words.

'You see, Sylvie, I've had a deal to think on; before long I intend telling yo' all about it; just now I'm not free to do it. And when a man's mind is full o' business, most particular when it's other folk's as is trusted to him, he seems to lose count on the very things he'd most care for at another time.' He paused a little.

Sylvia's galloping thoughts were pulled suddenly up by his silence; she felt that he wanted her to say something, but she could think of nothing besides an ambiguous—

'Well?'

'And I'm off to London i' t' morning,' added he, a little wistfully, almost as if beseeching her to show or express some sorrow at a journey, the very destination of which showed that he would be absent for some time.

'To Lunnon!' said she, with some surprise. 'Yo're niver thinking o' going to live theere, for sure!'

Surprise, and curiosity, and wonder; nothing more, as Philip's instinct told him. But he reasoned that first correct impression away with ingenious sophistry.

'Not to live there: only to stay for some time. I shall be back, I reckon, in a month or so.'

'Oh! that's nought of a going away,' said she, rather petulantly. 'Them as goes to t' Greenland seas has to bide away for six months and more,' and she sighed.

Suddenly a light shone down into Philip's mind. His voice was changed as he spoke next.

'I met that good-for-nothing chap, Kinraid, wi' yo'r father just now. He'll ha' been here, Sylvie?'

She stooped for something she had dropped, and came up red as a rose.

'To be sure; what then?' And she eyed him defiantly, though in her heart she trembled, she knew not why.

'What then? and yo'r mother away. He's no company for such as thee, at no time, Sylvie.'

'Feyther and me chooses our own company, without iver asking leave o' yo',' said Sylvia, hastily arranging the things in the little wooden work-box that was on the table, preparatory to putting it away. At the time, in his agitation, he saw, but did not affix any meaning to it, that the half of some silver coin was among the contents thus turned over before the box was locked.

'But thy mother wouldn't like it, Sylvie; he's played false wi' other lasses, he'll be playing thee false some o' these days, if thou lets him come about thee. He went on wi' Annie Coulson, William's sister, till he broke her heart; and sin' then he's been on wi' others.'

'I dunnot believe a word on 't,' said Sylvia, standing up, all aflame.

'I niver telled a lie i' my life,' said Philip, almost choking with grief at her manner to him, and the regard for his rival which she betrayed. 'It were Willie Coulson as telled me, as solemn and serious as one man can speak to another; and he said it weren't the first nor the last time as he had made his own game with young women.'

'And how dare yo' come here to me wi' yo'r backbiting tales?' said Sylvia, shivering all over with passion.

Philip tried to keep calm, and to explain.

'It were yo'r own mother, Sylvia, as knowed yo' had no brother, or any one to see after yo'; and yo' so pretty, so pretty, Sylvia,' he continued, shaking his head, sadly, 'that men run after yo' against their will, as one may say; and yo'r mother bade me watch o'er ye and see what company yo' kept, and who was following after yo', and to warn yo', if need were.'

'My mother niver bade yo' to come spying after me, and blaming me for seeing a lad as my feyther thinks well on.

An' I don't believe a word about Annie Coulson; an' I'm not going to suffer yo' to come wi' yo'r tales to me; say 'em out to his face, and hear what he'll say to yo'.'

'Sylvie, Sylvie,' cried poor Philip, as his offended cousin rushed past him, and upstairs to her little bedroom, where he heard the sound of the wooden bolt flying into its place. He could hear her feet pacing quickly about through the unceiled rafters. He sate still in despair, his head buried in his two hands. He sate till it grew dusk, dark; the wood fire, not gathered together by careful hands, died out into gray ashes. Dolly Reid had done her work and gone home. There were but Philip and Sylvia in the house. He knew he ought to be going home, for he had much to do, and many arrangements to make. Yet it seemed as though he could not stir. At length he raised his stiffened body, and stood up, dizzy. Up the little wooden stairs he went, where he had never been before, to the small square landing, almost filled up with the great chest for oat-cake. He breathed hard for a minute, and then knocked at the door of Sylvia's room.

'Sylvie! I'm going away; say good-by.' No answer. Not a sound heard. 'Sylvie!' (a little louder, and less hoarsely spoken). There was no reply. 'Sylvie! I shall be a long time away; perhaps I may niver come back at all;' here he bitterly thought of an unregarded death. 'Say good-by.' No answer. He waited patiently. Can she be wearied out, and gone to sleep, he wondered. Yet once again – 'Good-by, Sylvie, and God bless yo'! I'm sorry I vexed yo'.'

No reply.

With a heavy, heavy heart he creaked down the stairs, felt for his cap, and left the house.

'She's warned, any way,' thought he. Just at that moment the little casement window of Sylvia's room was opened, and she said—

'Good-by, Philip!'

The window was shut again as soon as the words were spoken. Philip knew the uselessness of remaining; the need for his departure; and yet he stood still for a little time like one entranced, as if his will had lost all power to compel him to leave the place. Those two words of hers, which two hours before would have been so far beneath his aspirations, had now power to re-light hope, to quench reproach or blame.

'She's but a young lassie,' said he to himself; 'an' Kinraid has been playing wi' her, as such as he can't help doing, once they get among t' women. An' I came down sudden on her about Annie Coulson, and touched her pride. Maybe, too, it were ill advised to tell her how her mother was feared for her. I couldn't ha' left the place to-morrow if he'd been biding here; but he's off for half a year or so, and I'll be home again as soon as iver I can. In half a year such as he forgets, if iver he's thought serious about her; but in a' my lifetime, if I live to fourscore, I can niver forget. God bless her for saying, "Good-by, Philip."' He repeated the words aloud in fond mimicry of her tones: 'Good-by, Philip.'

CHAPTER XVIII

EDDY IN LOVE'S CURRENT

THE next morning shone bright and clear, if ever a March morning did. The beguiling month was coming in like a lamb, with whatever storms it might go raging out. It was long since Philip had tasted the freshness of the early air on the shore, or in the country, as his employment at the shop detained him in Monkshaven till the evening. And as he turned down the quays (or staithes) on the north side of the river, towards the shore, and met the fresh sea-breeze blowing right in his face, it was impossible not to feel bright and elastic. With his knapsack slung over his shoulder, he was prepared for a good stretch towards Hartlepool, whence a coach would take him to Newcastle before night. For seven or eight miles the level sands were as short and far more agreeable a road than the up and down land-ways. Philip walked on pretty briskly, unconsciously enjoying the sunny landscape before him; the crisp curling waves rushing almost up to his feet, on his right hand, and then swishing back over the fine small pebbles into the great swelling sea. To his left were the cliffs rising one behind another, having deep gullies here and there between, with long green slopes upward from the land, and then sudden falls of brown and red soil or rock deepening to a yet greater richness of colour at their base towards the blue ocean before him. The loud, monotonous murmur of the advancing and receding waters lulled him into dreaminess; the sunny look of everything tinged his day-dreams with hope. So he trudged merrily over the first mile or so; not an obstacle to his measured pace on the hard, level pavement; not a creature to be seen since he had left the little gathering of bare-legged urchins dabbling in the sea-pools near Monkshaven. The cares of land were shut out by the glorious barrier of rocks before him. There were some great masses that had been detached by the action of the weather, and lay half embedded in the sand, draperied over by the heavy pendent olive-green sea-weed. The waves were nearer at this point; the advancing sea came up with a mighty distant length of roar; here and there the smooth swell was lashed by the fret against unseen rocks into white breakers; but otherwise the waves came up from the German Ocean upon that English shore with a long steady roll that might have taken its first impetus far away, in the haunt of the sea-serpent on the coast of 'Norroway over the foam.'* The air was soft as May; right overhead the sky was blue, but it deadened into gray near the sea lines. Flocks of seagulls hovered about the edge of the waves, slowly rising and turning their white under-plumage to glimmer in the sunlight as Philip approached. The whole scene was so peaceful, so soothing, that it dispelled the cares and fears (too well founded in fact) which had weighed down on his heart during the dark hours of the past night.

There was Haytersbank gully opening down its green entrance among the warm brown bases of the cliffs. Below, in the sheltered brushwood, among the last year's withered leaves, some primroses might be found. He half thought of gathering Sylvia a posy of them, and rushing up to the farm to make a little farewell peace-offering. But on looking at his watch, he put all thoughts of such an action out of his head; it was above an hour later than he had supposed, and he must make all haste on to Hartlepool. Just as he was approaching this gully, a man came dashing down, and ran out some way upon the sand with the very force of his descent; then he turned to the left and took the direction of Hartlepool a hundred yards or so in advance of Philip. He never stayed to look round him, but went swiftly and steadily on his way. By the peculiar lurch in his walk – by everything – Philip knew it was the specksioneer, Kinraid.

Now the road up Haytersbank gully led to the farm, and nowhere else. Still any one wishing to descend to the shore might do so by first going up to the Robsons' house, and skirting the walls till they came to the little slender path down to the shore. But by the farm, by the very house-door they must of necessity pass. Philip slackened his pace, keeping under the shadow of the rock. By-and-by Kinraid, walking on the sunlight open sands, turned round and looked long and earnestly towards Haytersbank gully. Hepburn paused when he paused, but as intently as he looked at some object above, so intently did Hepburn look at him. No need to ascertain by sight towards whom his looks, his thoughts were directed. He took off his hat and waved it, touching one part of it as if with particular meaning. When he turned away at last, Hepburn heaved a heavy sigh, and crept yet more into the cold dank shadow of the cliffs. Each step was now a heavy task, his sad heart tired and weary. After a while he climbed up a few feet, so as to mingle his form yet more completely with the stones and rocks around. Stumbling over the uneven and often jagged points, slipping on the sea-weed, plunging into little pools of water left by the ebbing tide in some natural basins, he yet kept his eyes fixed as if in fascination on Kinraid, and made his way almost alongside of him. But the last hour had pinched Hepburn's features into something of the wan haggardness they would wear when he should first be lying still for ever.

And now the two men were drawing near a creek, about eight miles from Monkshaven. The creek was formed by a beck (or small stream) that came flowing down from the moors, and took its way to the sea between the widening rocks. The melting of the snows and running of the flooded water-springs above made this beck in the early spring-time both deep and wide. Hepburn knew that here they both must take a path leading inland to a narrow foot-bridge about a quarter of a mile up the stream; indeed from this point, owing to the jutting out of the rocks, the land path was the shortest; and this way lay by the water-side at an angle right below the cliff to which Hepburn's steps were leading him. He knew that on this long level field-path he might easily be seen by any one following; nay, if he followed any one at a short distance, for it was full of turnings; and he resolved, late as he was, to sit down for a while till Kinraid was far enough in advance for him to escape being seen. He came up to the last rock behind which he could be concealed; seven or eight feet above the stream he stood, and looked cautiously for the specksioneer. Up by the rushing stream he looked, then right below.

'It is God's providence,' he murmured. 'It is God's providence.'

He crouched down where he had been standing and covered his face with his hands. He tried to deafen as well as to blind himself, that he might neither hear nor see anything of the coming event of which he, an inhabitant of Monkshaven at that day, well understood the betokening signs.

Kinraid had taken the larger angle of the sands before turning up towards the bridge. He came along now nearing the rocks. By this time he was sufficiently buoyant to whistle to himself. It steeled Philip's heart to what was coming to hear his rival whistling, 'Weel may the keel row,' so soon after parting with Sylvia.

The instant Kinraid turned the corner of the cliff, the ambush was upon him. Four man-of-war's men sprang on him and strove to pinion him.

'In the King's name!' cried they, with rough, triumphant jeers.

Their boat was moored not a dozen yards above; they were sent by the tender of a frigate lying off Hartlepool for fresh water. The tender was at anchor just beyond the jutting rocks in face.

They knew that fishermen were in the habit of going to and from their nets by the side of the creek; but such a prize as this active, strong, and evidently superior sailor, was what they had not hoped for, and their endeavours to secure him were in proportion to the value of the prize.

Although taken by surprise, and attacked by so many, Kinraid did not lose his wits. He wrenched himself free, crying out loud:

'Avast, I'm a protected whaler. I claim my protection. I've my papers to show, I'm bonded specksioneer to the *Urania* whaler, Donkin captain, North Shields port.'

As a protected whaler, the press-gang had, by the 17th section of Act 26 Geo. III. no legal right to seize him, unless he had failed to return to his ship by the 10th March following the date of his bond. But of what use were the papers he hastily dragged out of his breast; of what use were laws in those days of slow intercourse with such as were powerful enough to protect, and in the time of popular panic against a French invasion?

'D—n your protection,' cried the leader of the press-gang; 'come and serve his Majesty, that's better than catching whales.'

'Is it though?' said the specksioneer, with a motion of his hand, which the swift-eyed sailor opposed to him saw and interpreted rightly.

'Thou wilt, wilt thou? Close with him, Jack; and ware the cutlass.'

In a minute his cutlass was forced from him, and it became a hand-to-hand struggle, of which, from the difference in numbers, it was not difficult to foretell the result. Yet Kinraid made desperate efforts to free himself; he wasted no breath in words, but fought, as the men said, 'like a very devil.'

Hepburn heard loud pants of breath, great thuds, the dull struggle of limbs on the sand, the growling curses of those who thought to have managed their affair more easily; the sudden cry of some one wounded, not Kinraid he knew, Kinraid would have borne any pain in silence at such a moment; another wrestling, swearing, infuriated strife, and then a strange silence. Hepburn sickened at the heart; was then his rival dead? had he left this bright world? lost his life – his love? For an instant Hepburn felt guilty of his death; he said to himself he had never wished him dead, and yet in the struggle he had kept aloof, and now it might be too late for ever. Philip could not bear the suspense; he looked stealthily round the corner of the rock behind which he had been hidden, and saw that they had overpowered Kinraid, and, too exhausted to speak, were binding him hand and foot to carry him to their boat.

Kinraid lay as still as any hedgehog: he rolled when they pushed him; he suffered himself to be dragged without any resistance, any motion; the strong colour brought into his face while fighting was gone now, his countenance was livid pale; his lips were tightly held together, as if it cost him more effort to be passive, wooden, and stiff in their hands than it had done to fight and struggle with all his might. His eyes seemed the only part about him that showed cognizance of what was going on. They were watchful, vivid, fierce as those of a wild cat brought to bay, seeking in its desperate quickened brain for some mode of escape not yet visible, and in all probability never to become visible to the hopeless creature in its supreme agony.

Without a motion of his head, he was perceiving and taking in everything while he lay bound at the bottom of the boat. A sailor sat by his side, who had been hurt by a blow from him. The man held his head in his hand, moaning; but every now and then he revenged himself by a kick at the prostrate specksioneer, till even his comrades stopped their cursing and swearing at their prisoner for the trouble he had given them, to cry shame on their comrade. But Kinraid never spoke, nor shrank from the outstretched foot.

One of his captors, with the successful insolence of victory, ventured to jeer him on the supposed reason for his vehement and hopeless resistance.

He might have said yet more insolent things; the kicks

might have hit harder; Kinraid did not hear or heed. His soul was beating itself against the bars of inflexible circumstance; reviewing in one terible instant of time what had been, what might have been, what was. Yet while these thoughts thus stabbed him, he was still mechanically looking out for chances. He moved his head a little, so as to turn towards Haytersbank, where Sylvia must be quickly, if sadly, going about her simple daily work; and then his quick eye caught Hepburn's face, blanched with excitement rather than fear, watching eagerly from behind the rock, where he had sat breathless during the affray and the impressment of his rival.

'Come here, lad!' shouted the specksioneer as soon as he saw Philip, heaving and writhing his body the while with so much vigour that the sailors started away from the work they were engaged in about the boat, and held him down once more, as if afraid he should break the strong rope that held him like withes of green flax. But the bound man had no such notion in his head. His mighty wish was to call Hepburn near that he might send some message by him to Sylvia. 'Come here, Hepburn,' he cried again, falling back this time so weak and exhausted that the man-of-war's men became sympathetic.

'Come down, peeping Tom, and don't be afeared,' they called out.

'I'm not afeared,' said Philip; 'I'm no sailor for yo' t' impress me: nor have yo' any right to take that fellow; he's a Greenland specksioneer, under protection, as I know and can testify.'

'Yo' and yo'r testify go hang. Make haste, man, and hear what this gem'man, as was in a dirty blubbery whale-ship, and is now in his Majesty's service, has got to say. I dare say, Jack,' went on the speaker, 'it's some message to his sweetheart, asking her to come for to serve on board ship along with he, like Billy Taylor's young woman.'

Philip was coming towards them slowly, not from want of activity, but because he was undecided what he should be called upon to do or to say by the man whom he hated and dreaded, yet whom just now he could not help admiring.

Kinraid groaned with impatience at seeing one, free to move with quick decision, so slow and dilatory.

'Come on then,' cried the sailors, 'or we'll take you too on board, and run you up and down the main-mast a few times. Nothing like life aboard ship for quickening a land-lubber.'

'Yo'd better take him and leave me,' said Kinraid, grimly. 'I've been taught my lesson; and seemingly he has his yet to learn.'

'His Majesty isn't a schoolmaster to need scholars; but a jolly good captain to need men,' replied the leader of the gang, eyeing Philip nevertheless, and questioning within himself how far, with only two other available men, they durst venture on his capture as well as the specksioneer's. It might be done, he thought, even though there was this powerful captive aboard, and the boat to manage too; but, running his eye over Philip's figure, he decided that the tall stooping fellow was never cut out for a sailor, and that he should get small thanks if he captured him, to pay him for the possible risk of losing the other. Or else the mere fact of being a landsman was of as little consequence to the press-gang, as the protecting papers which Kinraid had vainly showed.

'Yon fellow wouldn't have been worth his grog this many a day, and be d—d to you,' said he, catching Hepburn by the shoulder, and giving him a push. Philip stumbled over something in this, his forced run. He looked down; his foot had caught in Kinraid's hat, which had dropped off in the previous struggle. In the band that went round the low crown, a ribbon was knotted; a piece of that same ribbon which Philip had chosen out, with such tender hope, to give to Sylvia for the Corneys' party on New Year's Eve. He knew every delicate thread that made up the briar-rose pattern; and a spasm of hatred towards Kinraid contracted his heart. He had been almost relenting into pity for the man captured before his eyes; now he abhorred him.

Kinraid did not speak for a minute or two. The sailors, who had begun to take him into favour, were all agog with curiosity to hear the message to his sweetheart, which they believed he was going to send. Hepburn's perceptions, quickened with his vehement agitation of soul, were aware of this feeling of theirs; and it increased his rage against Kinraid, who had exposed the idea of Sylvia to be the subject of ribald whispers. But the specksioneer cared little what others said or thought about the maiden, whom he yet saw before his closed eyelids as she stood watching him, from the Haytersbank gully, waving her hands, her handkerchief, all in one passionate farewell.

'What do yo' want wi' me?' asked Hepburn at last, in a gloomy tone. If he could have helped it, he would have kept silence till Kinraid spoke first; but he could no longer endure the sailors' nudges, and winks, and jests among themselves.

'Tell Sylvia,' said Kinraid——

'There's a smart name for a sweetheart,' exclaimed one of the men; but Kinraid went straight on,—

'What yo've seen; how I've been pressed by this cursed gang.'

'Civil words, messmate, if you please. Sylvia can't abide cursing and swearing, I'm sure. We're gentlemen serving his Majesty on board the *Alcestis*, and this proper young fellow shall be helped on to more honour and glory than he'd ever get bobbing for whales. Tell Sylvia this, with my love; Jack Carter's love, if she's anxious about my name.'

One of the sailors laughed at this rude humour; another bade Carter hold his stupid tongue. Philip hated him in his heart. Kinraid hardly heard him. He was growing faint with the heavy blows he had received, the stunning fall he had met with, and the reaction from his dogged self-control at first.

Philip did not speak nor move.

'Tell her,' continued Kinraid, rousing himself for another effort, 'what yo've seen. Tell her I'll come back to her. Bid her not forget the great oath we took together this morning; she's as much my wife as if we'd gone to church; – I'll come back and marry her afore long.'

Philip said something inarticulately.

'Hurra!' cried Carter, 'and I'll be best man. Tell her, too, that I'll have an eye on her sweetheart, and keep him from running after other girls.'

'Yo'll have yo'r hands full, then,' muttered Philip, his passion boiling over at the thought of having been chosen out from among all men to convey such a mesage as Kinraid's to Sylvia.

'Make an end of yo'r d—d yarns, and be off,' said the man who had been hurt by Kinraid, and who had sate apart and silent till now.

Philip turned away; Kinraid raised himself and cried after him,—

'Hepburn, Hepburn! tell her——' what he added Philip could not hear, for the words were lost before they reached him in the outward noise of the regular splash of the oars and the rush of the wind down the gully, with which mingled the closer sound that filled his ears of his own hurrying blood surging up into his brain. He was conscious that he had said something in reply to Kinraid's adjuration that he would deliver his message to Sylvia, at the very time when Carter had stung him into fresh anger by the allusion to the possibility of the specksioneer's 'running after other girls,' for, for an instant, Hepburn had been touched by the contrast of circumstances. Kinraid an hour or two ago, – Kinraid a banished man; for in those days, an impressed sailor might linger out years on some foreign station, far from those he loved, who all this time remained ignorant of his cruel fate.

But Hepburn began to wonder what he himself had said – how much of a promise he had made to deliver those last passionate words of Kinraid's. He could not recollect how much, how little he had said; he knew he had spoken hoarsely and low almost at the same time as Carter had utttered his loud joke. But he doubted if Kinraid had caught his words.

And then the dread Inner Creature, who lurks in each of our hearts, arose and said, 'It is as well: a promise given is a fetter to the giver. But a promise is not given when it has not been received.'

At a sudden impulse, he turned again towards the shore when he had crossed the bridge, and almost ran towards the verge of the land. Then he threw himself down on the soft fine turf that grew on the margin of the cliffs overhanging the sea, and commanding an extent of view towards the north. His face supported by his hands, he looked down upon the blue rippling ocean, flashing here and there, into the sunlight in long, glittering lines. The boat was still in the distance, making her swift silent way with long regular bounds to the tender that lay in the offing.

Hepburn felt insecure, as in a nightmare dream, so long as the boat did not reach her immediate destination. His contracted eyes could see four minute figures rowing with ceaseless motion, and a fifth sate at the helm. But he knew there was a sixth, unseen, lying, bound and helpless, at the bottom of the boat; and his fancy kept expecting this man to start up and break his bonds, and overcome all the others, and return to the shore – free and triumphant.

It was by no fault of Hepburn's that the boat sped well away; that she was now alongside the tender, dancing on the waves; now emptied of her crew; now hoisted up to her place. No fault of his! and yet it took him some time before he could reason himself into the belief that his mad, feverish wishes not an hour before – his wild prayer to be rid of his rival, as he himself had scrambled onward over the rocks alongside of Kinraid's path on the sands – had not compelled the event.

'Anyhow,' thought he, as he rose up, 'my prayer is granted. God be thanked!'

Once more he looked out towards the ship. She had spread her beautiful great sails, and was standing out to sea in the glittering path of the descending sun.

He saw that he had been delayed on his road, and had lingered long. He shook his stiffened limbs, shouldered his knapsack, and prepared to walk on to Hartlepool as swiftly as he could.

CHAPTER XIX

AN IMPORTANT MISSION

PHILIP was too late for the coach he had hoped to go by, but there was another that left at night, and which reached Newcastle in the forenoon, so that, by the loss of a night's sleep, he might overtake his lost time. But, restless and miserable, he could not stop in Hartlepool longer than to get some hasty food at the inn from which the coach started. He acquainted himself with the names of the towns through which it would pass, and the inns at which it would stop, and left word that the coachman was to be on the look-out for him and pick him up at some one of these places.

He was thoroughly worn out before this happened – too much tired to gain any sleep in the coach. When he reached Newcastle, he went to engage his passage in the next London-bound smack, and then directed his steps to Robinson's, in the Side, to make all the inquiries he could think of respecting the plough his uncle wanted to know about.

So it was pretty late in the afternoon, indeed almost evening, before he arrived at the small inn on the quay-side, where he intended to sleep. It was but a rough kind of place, frequented principally by sailors; he had been recommended to it by Daniel Robson, who had known it well in former days. The accommodation in it was, however, clean and homely, and the people keeping it were respectable enough in their way.

Still Hepburn was rather repelled by the appearance of the sailors who sate drinking in the bar, and he asked, in a low voice, if there was not another room. The woman stared in surprise, and only shook her head. Hepburn went to a separate table, away from the roaring fire, which on this cold March evening was the great attraction, and called for food and drink. Then seeing that the other men were eyeing him with the sociable idea of speaking to him, he asked for pen and ink and paper, with the intention of defeating their purpose by pre-occupation on his part. But when the paper came, the new pen, the unused thickened ink, he hesitated long before he began to write; and at last he slowly put down the words,—

'DEAR AND HONOURED UNCLE,'——

There was a pause; his meal was brought and hastily swallowed. Even while he was eating it, he kept occasionally touching up the letters of these words. When he had drunk a glass of ale he began again to write: fluently this time, for he was giving an account of the plough. Then came another long stop; he was weighing in his own mind what he should say about Kinraid. Once he thought for a second of writing to Sylvia herself, and telling her—— how much? She might treasure up her lover's words like grains of gold, while they were lighter than dust in their meaning to Philip's mind; words which such as the specksioneer used as counters to beguile and lead astray silly women. It was for him to prove his constancy by action; and the chances of his giving such proof were infinitesimal in Philip's estimation. But should the latter mention the bare fact of Kinraid's impressment to Robson? That would have been the natural course of things, remembering that the last time Philip had seen either, they were in each other's company. Twenty times he put his pen to the paper with the intention of relating briefly the event that had befallen Kinraid; and as often he stopped, as though the first word would be irrevocable. While he thus sate pen in hand, thinking himself wiser than conscience, and looking on beyond the next step which she bade him take into an indefinite future, he caught some fragments of the sailors' talk at the other end of the room, which made him listen to their words. They were speaking of that very Kinraid, the thought of whom filled his own mind like an actual presence. In a rough, careless way they spoke of the specksioneer, with admiration enough for his powers as a sailor and harpooner; and from that they passed on to jesting mention of his power amongst women, and one or two girls' names were spoken of in connection with him. Hepburn silently added Annie Coulson and Sylvia Robson to this list, and his cheeks turned paler as he did so. Long after they had done speaking about Kinraid, after they had paid their shot, and gone away, he sate in the same attitude, thinking bitter thoughts.

The people of the house prepared for bed. Their silent guest took no heed of their mute signs. At length the landlord spoke to him, and he started, gathered his wits together with an effort, and prepared to retire with the rest. But before he did so, he signed and directed the letter to his uncle, leaving it still open, however, in case some sudden feeling should prompt him to add a postscript. The landlord volunteered the information that the letter his guest had been writing must be posted early the next morning if it was going south; as the mails in that direction only left Newcastle every other day.

All night long Hepburn wearied himself with passionate tossings, prompted by stinging recollection. Towards morning he fell into a dead sound sleep. He was roused by a hasty knocking at the door. It was broad full daylight; he had overslept himself, and the smack was leaving by the early tide. He was even now summoned on board. He dressed, wafered* his letter, and rushed with it to the neighbouring post-office; and, without caring to touch the breakfast for which he paid, he embarked. Once on board, he experienced the relief which it always is to an undecided man, and generally is at first to any one who has been paltering with duty, when circumstances decide for him. In the first case, it is pleasant to be relieved from the burden of decision; in the second, the responsibility seems to be shifted on to impersonal events.

And so Philip sailed out of the mouth of the Tyne on to the great open sea. It would be a week before the smack reached London, even if she pursued a tolerably straight course, but she had to keep a sharp look-out after possible impressment of her crew; and it was not until after many dodges and some adventures that, at the end of a fortnight from the time of his leaving Monkshaven, Philip found himself safely housed in London, and ready to begin the delicate piece of work which was given him to do.

He felt himself fully capable of unravelling each clue to information, and deciding on the value of the knowledge so gained. But during the leisure of the voyage he had wisely determined to communicate everything he learnt about Dickinson, in short, every step he took in the matter, by letter to his employers. And thus his mind both in and out of his lodgings might have appeared to have been fully occupied with the concerns of others.

But there were times when the miserable luxury of dwelling upon his own affairs was his – when he lay down in his bed till he fell into restless sleep – when the point to which his steps tended in his walks was ascertained. Then he gave himself up to memory, and regret which often deepened into despair, and but seldom was cheered by hope.

He grew so impatient of the ignorance in which he was kept – for in those days of heavy postage any correspondence he might have had on mere Monkshaven intelligence was very limited – as to the affairs at Haytersbank, that he cut out an advertisement respecting some new kind of plough, from a newspaper that lay in the chop-house where he usually dined, and rising early the next morning he employed the time thus gained in going round to the shop where these new ploughs were sold.

That night he wrote another letter to Daniel Robson, with a long account of the merits of the implements he had that day seen. With a sick heart and a hesitating hand, he wound up with a message of regard to his aunt and to Sylvia; an expression of regard which he dared not make as warm as he wished, and which, consequently, fell below the usual mark attained by such messages, and would have apeared to any one who cared to think about it as cold and formal.

When this letter was despatched, Hepburn began to wonder what he had hoped for in writing it. He knew that Daniel could write – or rather that he could make strange hieroglyphics, the meaning of which puzzled others and often himself; but these pen-and-ink signs were seldom employed by Robson, and never, so far as Philip knew, for the purpose of letter-writing. But still he craved so for news of Sylvia – even for a sight of paper which she had seen, and perhaps touched – that he thought all his trouble about the plough (to say nothing of the one-and-twopence postage which he had prepaid in order to make sure of his letter's reception in the frugal household at Haytersbank)* well lost for the mere chance of his uncle's caring enough for the intelligence to write in reply, or even to get some friend to write an answer; for in such case, perhaps, Philip might see her name mentioned in some way, even though it was only that she sent her duty to him.

But the post-office was dumb; no letter came from Daniel Robson. Philip heard, it is true, from his employers pretty frequently on business; and he felt sure they would have named it, if any ill had befallen his uncle's family, for they knew of the relationship and of his intimacy there. They generally ended their formal letters with as formal a summary of Monkshaven news; but there was never a mention of the Robsons, and that of itself was well, but it did not soothe Philip's impatient curiosity. He had never confided his attachment to his cousin to any one, it was not his way; but he sometimes thought that if Coulson had not taken his present appointment to a confidential piece of employment so ill, he would have written to him and asked him to go up to Haytersbank Farm, and let him know how they all were.

All this time he was transacting the affair on which he had been sent, with great skill; and, indeed, in several ways, he was quietly laying the foundation for enlarging the business in Monkshaven. Naturally grave and quiet, and slow to speak, he impressed those who saw him with the idea of greater age and experience than he really possessed. Indeed, those who encountered him in London, thought he was absorbed in the business of money-making. Yet before the time came when he could wind up affairs and return to Monkshaven, he would have given all he possessed for a letter from his uncle, telling him something about Sylvia. For he still hoped to hear from Robson, although he knew that he hoped against reason. But we often convince ourselves by good argument that what we wish for need never have been expected; and then, at the end of our reasoning, find that we might have saved ourselves the trouble, for that our wishes are untouched, and are as strong enemies to our peace of mind as ever. Hepburn's baulked hope was the Mordecai sitting in Haman's gate;* all his success in his errand to London, his well-doing in worldly affairs, was tasteless, and gave him no pleasure, because of this blank and void of all intelligence concerning Sylvia.

And yet he came back with a letter from the Fosters in his pocket, curt, yet expressive of deep gratitude for his discreet services in London; and at another time – in fact, if Philip's life had been ordered differently to what it was – it might have given this man a not unworthy pleasure to remember that, without a penny of his own, simply by diligence, honesty, and faithful quick-sightedness as to the interests of his masters, he had risen to hold the promise of being their successor, and to be ranked by them as a trusted friend.

As the Newcastle smack neared the shore on her voyage home, Hepburn looked wistfully out for the faint gray outline of Monkshaven Priory against the sky, and the well-known cliffs; as if the masses of inanimate stone could tell him any news of Sylvia.

In the streets of Shields, just after landing, he encountered a neighbour of the Robsons, and an acquaintance of his own. By this honest man, he was welcomed as a great traveller is welcomed on his return from a long voyage, with many hearty good shakes of the hand, much repetition of kind wishes, and offers to treat him to drink. Yet, from some insurmountable feeling, Philip avoided all mention of the family who were the principal bond between the honest farmer and himself. He did not know why, but he could not bear the shock of first hearing her name in the open street, or in the rough public-house. And thus he shrank from the intelligence he craved to hear.

Thus he knew no more about the Robsons when he returned to Monkshaven, than he had done on the day when he had last seen them; and, of course, his first task there was to give a long *vivá voce* account of all his London proceedings to the two brothers Foster, who, considering that they had heard the result of everything by letter, seemed to take an insatiable interest in details.

He could hardly tell why, but even when released from the

Fosters' parlour, he was unwilling to go to Haytersbank Farm. It was late, it is true, but on a May evening even country people keep up till eight or nine o'clock. Perhaps it was because Hepburn was still in his travel-stained dress; having gone straight to the shop on his arrival in Monkshaven. Perhaps it was because, if he went this night for the short half-hour intervening before bed-time, he would have no excuse for paying a longer visit on the following evening. At any rate, he proceeded straight to Alice Rose's, as soon as he had finished his interview with his employers.

Both Hester and Coulson had given him their welcome home in the shop, which they had, however, left an hour or two before him.

Yet they gave him a fresh greeting, almost one in which surprise was blended, when he came to his lodgings. Even Alice seemed gratified by his spending this first evening with them, as if she had thought it might have been otherwise. Weary though he was, he exerted himself to talk and to relate what he had done and seen in London, as far as he could without breaking confidence with his employers. It was something to see the pleasure he gave to his auditors, although there were several mixed feelings in their minds to produce the expression of it which gratified him. Coulson was sorry for his former ungenerous reception of the news that Philip was going to London; Hester and her mother each secretly began to feel as if this evening was like more happy evenings of old, before the Robsons came to Haytersbank Farm; and who knows what faint delicious hopes this resemblance may not have suggested?

While Philip, restless and excited, feeling that he could not sleep, was glad to pass away the waking hours that must intervene before to-morrow night, at times, he tried to make them talk of what had happened in Monkshaven during his absence, but all had gone on in an eventless manner, as far as he could gather; if they knew of anything affecting the Robsons, they avoided speaking of it to him; and, indeed, how little likely were they ever to have heard their names while he was away?

CHAPTER XX

LOVED AND LOST*

PHILIP walked towards the Robsons' farm like a man in a dream, who has everything around him according to his wish, and yet is conscious of a secret mysterious inevitable drawback to his enjoyment. Hepburn did not care to think – would not realize what this drawback, which need not have been mysterious in his case, was.

The May evening was glorious in light and shadow. The crimson sun warmed up the chilly northern air to a semblance of pleasant heat. The spring sights and sounds were all about; the lambs were bleating out their gentle weariness before they sank to rest by the side of their mothers; the linnets were chirping in every bush of golden gorse that grew out of the stone walls; the lark was singing her good-night in the cloudless sky, before she dropped down to her nest in the tender green wheat; all spoke of brooding peace – but Philip's heart was not at peace.

Yet he was going to proclaim his good fortune. His masters had that day publicly announced that Coulson and he were to be their successors, and he had now arrived at that longed-for point in his business, when he had resolved to openly speak of his love to Sylvia, and might openly strive to gain her love. But, alas! the fulfilment of that wish of his had lagged sadly behind. He was placed as far as he could, even in his most sanguine moments, have hoped to be as regarded business, but Sylvia was as far from his attainment as ever – nay, farther. Still the great obstacle was removed in Kinraid's impressment. Philip took upon himself to decide that, with such a man as the specksioneer, absence was equivalent to faithless forgetfulness. He thought that he had just grounds for this decision in the account he had heard of Kinraid's behaviour to Annie Coulson; to the other nameless young girl, her successor in his fickle heart; in the ribald talk of the sailors in the Newcastle public-house. It would be well for Sylvia if she could forget as quickly; and, to promote this oblivion, the name of her lover should never be brought up, either in praise or blame. And Philip would be patient and enduring; all the time watching over her, and labouring to win her reluctant love.

There she was! He saw her as he stood at the top of the little hill-path leading down to the Robsons' door. She was out of doors, in the garden, which, at some distance from the house, sloped up the bank on the opposite side of the gully; much too far off to be spoken to – not too far off to be gazed at by eyes that caressed her every movement. How well Philip knew that garden; placed long ago by some tenant of the farm on a southern slope; walled in with rough moorland stones; planted with berry-bushes for use, and southernwood and sweet-briar* for sweetness of smell. When the Robsons had first come to Haytersbank, and Sylvia was scarcely more than a pretty child, how well he remembered helping her with the arrangement of this garden; laying out his few spare pence in hen-and-chicken daisies* at one time, in flower-seeds at another; again in a rose-tree in a pot. He knew how his unaccustomed hands had laboured with the spade at forming a little primitive bridge over the beck in the hollow before winter streams should make it too deep for fording; how he had cut down branches of the mountain-ash and covered them over, yet decked with their scarlet berries, with sods of green turf, beyond which the brilliancy crept out; but now it was months and years since he had been in that garden, which had lost its charm for Sylvia, as she found the bleak sea-winds came up and blighted all endeavours at cultivating more than the most useful things – pot-herbs, marigolds, potatoes, onions, and such-like. Why did she tarry there now, standing quite motionless up by the highest bit of wall, looking over the sea, with her hand shading her eyes? Quite motionless; as if she were a stone statue. He began to wish she would move – would look at him – but any way that she would move, and not stand gazing thus over that great dreary sea.

He went down the path with an impatient step, and entered the house-place. There sat his aunt spinning, and apparently as well as ever. He could hear his uncle talking to

Kester in the neighbouring shippen; all was well in the household. Why was Sylvia standing in the garden in that strange quiet way?

'Why, lad! thou'rt a sight for sair een!' said his aunt, as she stood up to welcome him back. 'An' when didst ta come, eh? – but thy uncle will be glad to see thee, and to hear thee talk about yon pleughs; he's thought a deal o' thy letters. I'll go call him in.'

'Not yet,' said Philip, stopping her in her progress towards the door. 'He's busy talking to Kester. I'm in no haste to be gone. I can stay a couple of hours. Sit down, and tell me how you are yoursel' – and how iverything is. And I've a deal to tell you.'

'To be sure – to be sure. To think thou's been in Lunnon sin' I saw thee! – well to be sure! There's a vast o' coming and going i' this world. Thou'll mind yon specksioneer lad, him as was cousin to t' Corneys – Charley Kinraid?'

Mind him! As if he could forget him.

'Well! he's dead and gone.'

'Dead! Who told you? I don't understand,' said Philip, in strange bewilderment. Could Kinraid have tried to escape after all, and been wounded, killed in the attempt? If not, how should they know he was dead? Missing he might be, though how this should be known was strange, as he was supposed to be sailing to the Greenland seas. But dead! What did they mean? At Philip's worst moment of hatred he had hardly dared to wish him dead.

'Dunnot yo' mention it afore our Sylvie; we niver speak on him to her, for she takes it a deal to heart, though I'm thinkin' it were a good thing for her; for he'd got a hold of her – he had on Bessy Corney, too, as her mother telled me; – not that I iver let on to them as Sylvia frets after him, so keep a calm sough, my lad. It's a girl's fancy – just a kind o' calf-love; let it go by; and it's well for her he's dead, though it's hard to say so on a drowned man.'

'Drowned!' said Philip. 'How do yo' know?' half hoping that the poor drenched swollen body might have been found, and thus all questions and dilemmas solved. Kinraid might have struggled overboard with ropes or handcuffs on, and so have been drowned.

'Eh, lad! there's no misdoubtin' it. He were thought a deal on by t' captain o' t' *Urania*; and when he niver come back on t' day when she ought for to have sailed, he sent to Kinraid's people at Cullercoats, and they sent to Brunton's i' Newcassel, and they knew he'd been here. T' captain put off sailing for two or three days, that he might ha' that much law; but when he heard as Kinraid were not at Corneys', but had left 'em a'most on to a week, he went off to them northern seas wi' t' next best specksioneer he could find. For there's no use speaking ill on t' dead; an' though I couldn't abear his coming for iver about t' house, he were a rare good specksioneer, as I've been told.'

'But how do you know he was drowned?' said Philip, feeling guiltily disappointed at his aunt's story.

'Why, lad! I'm a'most ashamed to tell thee, I were sore put out mysel'; but Sylvia were so broken-hearted like I couldn't cast it up to her as I should ha' liked: th' silly lass had gone and gi'en him a bit o' ribbon, as many a one knowed, for it had been a vast noticed and admired that evenin' at th' Corneys' – New Year's Eve I think it were – and t' poor vain peacock had tied it on his hat, so that when t' tide——hist! there's Sylvie coming in at t' back-door; never let on,' and in a forced made-up voice she inquired aloud, for hitherto she had been speaking almost in a whisper,—

'And didst ta see King George an' Queen Charlotte?'

Philip could not answer – did not hear. His soul had gone out to meet Sylvia, who entered with quiet slowness quite unlike her former self. Her face was wan and white; her gray eyes seemed larger, and full of dumb tearless sorrow; she came up to Philip, as if his being there touched her with no surprise, and gave him a gentle greeting as if he were a familiar indifferent person whom she had seen but yesterday. Philip, who had recollected the quarrel they had had, and about Kinraid too, the very last time they had met, had expected some trace of this remembrance to linger in her looks and speech to him. But there was no such sign; her great sorrow had wiped away all anger, almost all memory. Her mother looked at her anxiously, and then said in the same manner of forced cheerfulness which she had used before,—

'Here's Philip, lass, a' full o' Lunnon; call thy father in, an' we'll hear a' about t' new-fangled pleughs. It'll be rare an' nice a' sitting together again.'

Sylvia, silent and docile, went out to the shippen to obey her mother's wish. Bell Robson leant forward towards Philip, misinterpreting the expression on his face, which was guilt as much as sympathy, and checked the possible repentance which might have urged him on at that moment to tell all he knew, by saying, 'Lad! it's a' for t' best. He were noane good enough for her; and I misdoubt me he were only playin' wi' her as he'd done by others. Let her a-be, let her a-be; she'll come round to be thankful.'

Robson bustled in with loud welcome; all the louder and more talkative because he, like his wife, assumed a cheerful manner before Sylvia. Yet he, unlike his wife, had many a secret regret over Kinraid's fate. At first, while merely the fact of his disappearance was known, Daniel Robson had hit on the truth, and had stuck to his opinion that the cursed press-gang were at the bottom of it. He had backed his words by many an oath, and all the more because he had not a single reason to give that applied to the present occasion. No one on the lonely coast had remarked any sign of the presence of the men-of-war, or the tenders that accompanied them, for the purpose of impressment on the King's ships. At Shields, and at the mouth of the Tyne, where they lay in greedy wait, the owners of the *Urania* had caused strict search to be made for their skilled and protected specksioneer, but with no success. All this positive evidence in contradiction to Daniel Robson's opinion only made him cling to it the more; until the day when the hat was found on the shore with Kinraid's name written out large and fair in the inside, and the tell-tale bit of ribbon knotted in the band. Then Daniel, by a sudden revulsion, gave up every hope; it never entered his mind that it could have fallen off by any accident. No! now Kinraid was dead and drowned, and it was a bad job, and the sooner it could be forgotten the better for all parties; and it was well no one knew how far it had gone with Sylvia, especially now since Bessy Corney was crying her eyes out as if he had been engaged to her. So Daniel said nothing to his wife about the mischief that had gone on in her absence, and never spoke to Sylvia about the affair; only he was more than usually tender to her in his rough way, and thought, morning, noon, and night, on what he could do to give her pleasure, and drive away all recollection of her ill-starred love.

To-night he would have her sit by him while Philip told his stories, or heavily answered questions put to him. Sylvia sat on a stool by her father's knee, holding one of his hands in both of hers; and presently she laid down her head upon them, and Philip saw her sad eyes looking into the flickering fire-light with long unwinking stare, showing that her thoughts were far distant. He could hardly go on with his tales of what he had seen, and what done, he was so full of pity for her. Yet, for all his pity, he had now resolved never to soothe her with the knowledge of what he knew, nor to deliver the message sent by her false lover. He felt like a mother with-holding something injurious from the foolish wish of her plaining child.

But he went away without breathing a word of his good fortune in business. The telling of such kind of good fortune seemed out of place this night, when the thought of death and the loss of friends seemed to brood over the household, and cast its shadow there, obscuring for the time all worldly things.

And so the great piece of news came out in the ordinary course of gossip, told by some Monkshaven friend to Robson the next market-day. For months Philip had been looking forward to the sensation which the intelligence would produce in the farm household, as a preliminary to laying his good fortune at Sylvia's feet. And they heard of it, and he away, and all chance of his making use of it in the manner he had intended vanished for the present.

Daniel was always curious after other people's affairs, and now was more than ever bent on collecting scraps of news which might possibly interest Sylvia, and rouse her out of the state of indifference as to everything into which she had fallen. Perhaps he thought that he had not acted altogether wisely in allowing her to engage herself to Kinraid, for he was a man apt to judge by results; and moreover he had had so much reason to repent of the encouragement which he had given to the lover whose untimely end had so deeply affected his only child, that he was more unwilling than ever that his wife should know of the length to which the affair had gone during her absence. He even urged secrecy upon Sylvia as a personal favour; unwilling to encounter the silent blame which he openly affected to despise.

'We'll noane fret thy mother by lettin' on how oft he came and went. She'll, maybe, be thinkin' he were for speakin' to thee, my poor lass; an' it would put her out a deal, for she's a woman of a stern mind towards matteremony. And she'll be noane so strong till summer-weather comes, and I'd be loath to give her aught to worrit hersel' about. So thee and me 'll keep our own counsel.'

'I wish mother had been here, then she'd ha' known all, without my telling her.'

'Cheer up, lass; it's better as it is. Thou'll get o'er it sooner for havin' no one to let on to. A myself am noane going to speak on 't again.'

No more he did; but there was a strange tenderness in his tones when he spoke to her; a half-pathetic way of seeking after her, if by any chance she was absent for a minute from the places where he expected to find her; a consideration for her, about this time, in his way of bringing back trifling presents, or small pieces of news that he thought might interest her, which sank deep into her heart.

'And what dun yo' think a' t' folks is talkin' on i' Monkshaven?' asked he, almost before he had taken off his coat, on the day when he had heard of Philip's promotion in the world. 'Why, missus, thy nephew, Philip Hepburn, has got his name up i' gold letters four inch long o'er Fosters' door! Him and Coulson has set up shop together, and Fosters is gone out!'

'That's t' secret of his journey t' Lunnon,' said Bell, more gratified than she chose to show.

'Four inch long if they're theere at all! I heerd on it at t' Bay Horse first; but I thought yo'd niver be satisfied 'bout I seed it wi' my own eyes. They do say as Gregory Jones, t' plumber, got it done i' York, for that nought else would satisfy old Jeremiah. It'll be a matter o' some hundreds a year i' Philip's pocket.'

'There'll be Fosters i' th' background, as one may say, to take t' biggest share on t' profits,' said Bell.

'Ay, ay, that's but as it should be, for I reckon they'll ha' to find t' brass the first, my lass!' said he, turning to Sylvia. 'A'm fain to tak' thee in to t' town next market-day, just for thee t' see 't. A'll buy thee a bonny ribbon for thy hair out o' t' cousin's own shop.'

Some thought of another ribbon which had once tied up her hair, and afterwards been cut in twain, must have crossed Sylvia's mind, for she answered, as if she shrank from her father's words,—

'I cannot go, I'm noane wantin' a ribbon; I'm much obliged, father, a' t' same.'

Her mother read her heart clearly, and suffered with her, but never spoke a word of sympathy. But she went on rather more quickly than she would otherwise have done to question her husband as to all he knew about this great rise of Philip's. Once or twice Sylvia joined in with languid curiosity; but presently she became tired and went to bed. For a few moments after she left, her parents sate silent. Then Daniel, in a tone as if he were justifying his daughter, and comforting himself as well as his wife, observed that it was almost on for nine; the evenings were light so long now. Bell said nothing in reply, but gathered up her wool, and began to arrange the things for night.

By-and-by Daniel broke the silence by saying,—

'A thowt at one time as Philip had a fancy for our Sylvie.'

For a minute or two Bell did not speak. Then, with deeper insight into her daughter's heart than her husband, in spite of his greater knowledge of the events that had happened to affect it, she said,—

'If thou's thinking on a match between 'em, it 'll be a long time afore th' poor sad wench is fit t' think on another man as sweetheart.'

'A said nought about sweethearts,' replied he, as if his wife had reproached him in some way. 'Woman's allays so full o' sweethearts and matteremony. A only said as a'd thowt once as Philip had a fancy for our lass, and a think so still; and he'll be worth his two hunder a year afore long. But a niver said nought about sweethearts.'

CHAPTER XXI

A REJECTED SUITOR

THERE were many domestic arrangements to be made in connection with the new commercial ones which affected Hepburn and Coulson.

The Fosters, with something of the busybodiness which is apt to mingle itself with kindly patronage, had planned in their own minds that the Rose household should be removed altogether to the house belonging to the shop; and that Alice, with the assistance of the capable servant, who, at present, managed all John's* domestic affairs, should continue as mistress of the house, with Philip and Coulson for her lodgers.

But arrangements without her consent did not suit Alice at any time, and she had very good reasons for declining to accede to this. She was not going to be uprooted at her time of life, she said, nor would she consent to enter upon a future which might be so uncertain. Why, Hepburn and Coulson were both young men, she said, and they were as likely to marry as not; and then the bride would be sure to wish to live in the good old-fashioned house at the back of the shop.

It was in vain she was told by every one concerned, that, in case of such an event, the first married partner should take a house of his own, leaving her in undisputed possession. She replied, with apparent truth, that both might wish to marry, and surely the wife of one ought to take possession of the house belonging to the business; that she was not going to trust herself to the fancies of young men, who were always, the best of them, going and doing the very thing that was most foolish in the way of marriage; of which state, in fact, she spoke with something of acrimonious contempt and dislike, as if young people always got mismatched, yet had not the sense to let older and wiser people choose for them.

'Thou'll not have been understanding why Alice Rose spoke as she did this morning,' said Jeremiah Foster to Philip, on the afternoon succeeding the final discussion of this plan. 'She was a-thinking of her youth, I reckon, when she was a well-favoured young woman, and our John was full of the thought of marrying her. As he could not have her, he has lived a bachelor all his days. But if I am not a vast mistaken, all that he has will go to her and to Hester, for all that Hester is the child of another man. Thee and Coulson should have a try for Hester, Philip. I have told Coulson this day of Hester's chances. I told him first because he is my nephew; but I tell thee now, Philip. It would be a good thing for the shop if one of ye was married.'

Philip reddened. Often as the idea of marriage had come into his mind, this was the first time it had been gravely suggested to him by another. But he replied quietly enough.

'I don't think Hester Rose has any thought of matrimony.'

'To be sure not; it is for thee, or for William Coulson, to make her think. She, maybe, remembers enough of her mother's life with her father to make her slow to think on such things. But it's in her to think on matrimony; it's in all of us.'

'Alice's husband was dead before I knew her,' said Philip, rather evading the main subject.

'It was a mercy when he were taken. A mercy to them who were left, I mean. Alice was a bonny young woman, with a smile for everybody, when he wed her – a smile for every one except our John, who never could do enough to try and win one from her. But, no! she would have none of him, but set her heart on Jack Rose, a sailor in a whale-ship. And so they were married at last, though all her own folks were against it. And he was a profligate sinner, and went after other women, and drank, and beat her. She turned as stiff and as grey as thou seest her now within a year of Hester's birth. I believe they'd have perished for want and cold many a time if it had not been for John. If she ever guessed where the money came from, it must have hurt her pride above a bit, for she was always a proud woman. But mother's love is stronger than pride.'

Philip fell to thinking; a generation ago something of the same kind had been going on as that which he was now living through, quick with hopes and fears. A girl beloved by two – nay, those two so identical in occupation as he and Kinraid were – Rose identical even in character with what he knew of the specksioneer; a girl choosing the wrong lover, and suffering and soured all her life in consequence of her youth's mistake; was that to be Sylvia's lot? – or, rather, was she not saved from it by the event of the impressment, and by the course of silence he himself had resolved upon? Then he went on to wonder if the lives of one generation were but a repetition of the lives of those who had gone before, with no variation but from the internal cause that some had greater capacity for suffering than others. Would those very circumstances which made the interest of his life now, return, in due cycle, when he was dead and Sylvia was forgotten?

Perplexed thoughts of this and a similar kind kept returning into Philip's mind whenever he had leisure to give himself up to consideration of anything but the immediate throng of business. And every time he dwelt on this complication and succession of similar events, he emerged from his reverie more and more satisfied with the course he had taken in withholding from Sylvia all knowledge of her lover's fate.

It was settled at length that Philip was to remove to the house belonging to the shop, Coulson remaining with Alice and her daughter. But in the course of the summer the latter told his partner that he had offered marriage to Hester on the previous day, and been refused. It was an awkward affair altogether, as he lived in their house, and was in daily companionship with Hester, who, however, seemed to preserve her gentle calmness, with only a tinge more of reserve in her manner to Coulson.

'I wish yo' could find out what she has again' me, Philip,' said Coulson, about a fortnight after he had made the proposal. The poor young man thought that Hester's composure of manner towards him since the event argued that he was not distasteful to her; and as he was now on very happy terms with Philip, he came constantly to him, as if the latter could interpret the meaning of all the little occurrences between him and his beloved. 'I'm o' right age, not two months betwixt us; and there's few in Monkshaven as would think on her wi' better prospects than me; and she knows my folks; we're kind o' cousins, in fact; and I'd be like a son to her mother; and there's noane i' Monkshaven as can speak again' my character. There's nought between yo' and her, is there, Philip?'

'I ha' telled thee many a time that she and me is like brother and sister. She's no more thought on me nor I have for her. So be content wi't, for I'se not tell thee again.'

'Don't be vexed, Philip; if thou knew what it was to be in love, thou'd be always fancying things, just as I am.'

'I might be,' said Philip; 'but I dunnut think I should be always talking about my fancies.'

'I wunnot talk any more after this once, if thou'll just find out fra' thysel', as it were, what it is she has again' me. I'd go to chapel for iver with her, if that's what she wants. Just ask her, Philip.'

'It's an awkward thing for me to be melling wi',\'* said Hepburn, reluctantly.

'But thou said thee and she were like brother and sister; and a brother would ask a sister, and niver think twice about it.'

'Well, well,' replied Philip, 'I'll see what I can do; but, lad, I dunnot think she'll have thee. She doesn't fancy thee, and fancy is three parts o' love, if reason is t' other fourth.'

But somehow Philip could not begin on the subject with Hester. He did not know why, except that, as he said, 'it was so awkward.' But he really liked Coulson so much as to be anxious to do what the latter wished, although he was almost convinced that it would be of no use. So he watched his opportunity, and found Alice alone and at leisure one Sunday evening.

She was sitting by the window, reading her Bible, when he went in. She gave him a curt welcome, hearty enough for her, for she was always chary in her expressions of pleasure or satisfaction. But she took off her horn spectacles and placed them in the book to keep her place; and then turning more fully round on her chair, so as to face him, she said,—

'Well, lad! and how does it go on? Though it's not a day for t' ask about worldly things. But I niver see thee now but on Sabbath day, and rarely then. Still we munnot speak o' such things on t' Lord's day. So thee mun just say how t' shop is doing, and then we'll leave such vain talk.'

'T' shop is doing main an' well, thank ye, mother. But Coulson could tell yo' o' that any day.'

'I'd a deal rayther hear fra' thee, Philip. Coulson doesn't know how t' manage his own business, let alone half the business as it took John and Jeremiah's heads – ay, and tasked 'em, too – to manage. I've no patience with Coulson.'

'Why? he's a decent young fellow as ever there is in Monkshaven.'

'He may be. He's noane cut his wisdom-teeth yet. But, for that matter, there's other folks as far fra' sense as he is.'

'Ay, and farther. Coulson mayn't be so bright at all times as he might be, but he's a steady-goer, and I'd back him again' any chap o' his age i' Monkshaven.'

'I know who I'd sooner back in many a thing, Philip!' She said it with so much meaning that he could not fail to understand that he himself was meant, and he replied, ingenuously enough,—

'If yo' mean me, mother, I'll noane deny that in a thing or two I may be more knowledgeable than Coulson. I've had a deal o' time on my hands i' my youth, and I'd good schooling as long as father lived.'

'Lad! it's not schooling, nor knowledge, nor book-learning

as carries a man through t' world. It's mother-wit. And it's noane schooling, nor knowledge, nor book-learning as takes a young woman. It's summat as cannot be put into words.'

'That's just what I told Coulson!' said Philip, quickly. 'He were sore put about because Hester had gi'en him the bucket, and came to me about it.'

'And what did thou say?' asked Alice, her deep eyes gleaming at him as if to read his face as well as his words. Philip, thinking he could now do what Coulson had begged of him in the neatest manner, went on,—

'I told him I'd help him all as I could——'

'Thou did, did thou? Well, well, there's nought sa queer as folks, that a will say,' muttered Alice, between her teeth.

'—but that fancy had three parts to do wi' love,' continued Philip, 'and it would be hard, maybe, to get a reason for her not fancying him. Yet I wish she'd think twice about it; he so set upon having her, I think he'll do himself a mischief wi' fretting, if it goes on as it is.'

'It'll noane go on as it is,' said Alice, with gloomy oracularness.

'How not?' asked Philip. Then, receiving no answer, he went on, 'He loves her true, and he's within a month or two on her age, and his character will bear handling on a' sides; and his share on t' shop will be worth hundreds a year afore long.'

Another pause. Alice was trying to bring down her pride to say something, which she could not with all her efforts.

'Maybe yo'll speak a word for him, mother,' said Philip, annoyed at her silence.

'I'll do no such thing. Marriages are best made wi'out melling. How do I know but what she likes some one better?'

'Our Hester's not th' lass to think on a young man unless he's been a-wooing on her. And yo' know, mother, as well as I do – and Coulson does too – she's niver given any one a chance to woo her; living half her time here, and t' other half in t' shop, and niver speaking to no one by t' way.'

'I wish thou wouldn't come here troubling me on a Sabbath day wi' thy vanity and thy worldly talk. I'd liefer by far be i' that world wheere there's neither marrying nor giving in marriage, for it's all a moithering* mess here.' She turned to the closed Bible lying on the dresser, and opened it with a bang. While she was adjusting her spectacles on her nose, with hands trembling with passion, she heard Philip say,—

'I ask yo'r pardon, I'm sure. I couldn't well come any other day.'

'It's a' t' same – I care not. But thou might as well tell truth. I'll be bound thou's been at Haytersbank Farm some day this week?'

Philip reddened; in fact, he had forgotten how he had got to consider his frequent visits to the farm as a regular piece of occupation. He kept silence.

Alice looked at him with a sharp intelligence that read his silence through.

'I thought so. Next time thou thinks to thyself, 'I'm more knowledgeable than Coulson,' just remember Alice Rose's words and they are these:—If Coulson's too thick-sighted to see through a board, thou'rt too blind to see through a window. As for comin' and speakin' up for Coulson, why, he'll be married to some one else afore t' year's out, for all he thinks he's so set upon Hester now. Go thy ways, and leave me to my Scripture, and come no more on Sabbath days wi' thy vain babbling.'

So Philip returned from his mission rather crestfallen, but quite as far as ever from 'seeing through a glass window.'

Before the year was out, Alice's prophecy was fulfilled. Coulson, who found the position of a rejected lover in the same house with the girl who had refused him, too uncomfortable to be endured, as soon as he was convinced that his object was decidedly out of his reach, turned his attention to some one else. He did not love his new sweetheart as he had done Hester: there was more of reason and less of fancy in his attachment. But it ended successfully; and before the first snow fell, Philip was best man at his partner's wedding.

CHAPTER XXII

DEEPENING SHADOWS

But before Coulson was married, many small events happened – small events to all but Philip. To him they were as the sun and moon. The days when he went up to Haytersbank and Sylvia spoke to him, the days when he went up and she had apparently no heart to speak to any one, but left the room as soon as he came, or never entered it at all, although she must have known that he was there – these were his alternations from happiness to sorrow.

From her parents he always had a welcome. Oppressed by their daughter's depression of spirits, they hailed the coming of any visitor as a change for her as well as for themselves. The former intimacy with the Corneys was in abeyance for all parties, owing to Bessy Corney's out-spoken grief for the loss of her cousin, as if she had had reason to look upon him as her lover, whereas Sylvia's parents felt this as a slur upon their daughter's cause of grief. But although at this time the members of the two families ceased to seek after each other's society, nothing was said. The thread of friendship might be joined afresh at any time, only just now it was broken; and Philip was glad of it. Before going to Haytersbank he sought each time for some little present with which to make his coming welcome. And now he wished even more than ever that Sylvia had cared for learning; if she had he could have taken her many a pretty ballad, or story-book, such as were then in vogue. He did try her with the translation of the *Sorrows of Werther*,* so popular at the time that it had a place in all pedlars' baskets, with Law's *Serious Call*,* the *Pilgrim's Progress*, Klopstock's *Messiah** and *Paradise Lost*. But she could not read it for herself; and after turning the leaves languidly over, and smiling a little at the picture of Charlotte cutting bread and butter in a left-handed manner, she put it aside on the shelf by the *Complete Farrier*;* and there Philip saw it, upside down and untouched, the next time he came to the farm.

Many a time during that summer did he turn to the few verses in Genesis in which Jacob's twice seven years' service for Rachel* is related, and try and take fresh heart from the reward which came to the patriarch's constancy at last. After trying books, nosegays, small presents of pretty articles of dress, such as suited the notions of those days, and finding them all received with the same languid gratitude, he set himself to endeavour to please her in some other way. It was time that he should change his tactics; for the girl was becoming weary of the necessity for thanking him, every time he came, for some little favour or other. She wished he would let her alone and not watch her continually with such sad eyes. Her father and mother hailed her first signs of impatient petulance towards him as a return to the old state of things before Kinraid had come to disturb the tenour of their lives; for even Daniel had turned against the specksioneer, irritated by the Corneys' loud moans over the loss of the man to whom their daughter said that she was attached. If Daniel wished for him to be alive again, it was mainly that the Corneys might be convinced that his last visit to the neighbourhood of Monkshaven was for the sake of the pale and silent Sylvia, and not for that of Bessy, who complained of Kinraid's untimely death rather as if by it she had been cheated of a husband than for any overwhelming personal love towards the deceased.

'If he were after her he were a big black scoundrel, that's what he were; and a wish he were alive again to be hung. But a dunnot believe it; them Corney lasses were allays a-talkin' an' a-thinking on sweethearts, and niver a man crossed t' threshold but they tried him on as a husband. An' their mother were no better: Kinraid has spoken civil to Bessy as became a lad to a lass, and she makes an ado over him as if they'd been to church together not a week sin'.'

'I dunnot uphold t' Corneys; but Molly Corney – as is Molly Brunton now – used to speak on this dead man to our Sylvie as if he were her sweetheart in old days. Now there's no smoke without fire, and I'm thinking it's likely enough he were one of them fellows as is always after some lass or another, and, as often as not, two or three at a time. Now look at Philip, what a different one he is! He's niver thought on a woman but our Sylvie, I'll be bound. I wish he wern't so old-fashioned and faint-hearted.'

'Ay! and t' shop's doin' a vast o' business, I've heard say. He's a deal better company, too, nor he used to be. He'd a way o' preaching wi' him as a couldn't abide; but now he tak's his glass, an' holds his tongue, leavin' room for wiser men to say their say.'

Such was a conjugal colloquy about this time. Philip was gaining ground with Daniel, and that was something towards winning Sylvia's heart; for she was unaware of her father's change of feeling towards Kinraid, and took all his tenderness towards herself as if they were marks of his regard for her lost lover and his sympathy in her loss, instead of which he was rather feeling as if it might be a good thing after all that the fickle-hearted sailor was dead and drowned. In fact, Daniel was very like a child in all the parts of his character. He was strongly affected by whatever was present, and apt to forget the absent. He acted on impulse, and too often had reason to be sorry for it; but he hated his sorrow too much to let it teach him wisdom for the future. With all his many faults, however, he had something in him which made him be dearly loved, both by the daughter whom he indulged, and the wife who was in fact superior to him, but whom he imagined that he ruled with a wise and absolute sway.

Love to Sylvia gave Philip tact. He seemed to find out that to please the women of the household he must pay all possible attention to the man; and though he cared little in comparison for Daniel, yet this autumn he was continually thinking of how he could please him. When he had said or done anything to gratify or amuse her father, Sylvia smiled and was kind. Whatever he did was right with his aunt; but even she was unusually glad when her husband was pleased. Still his progress was slow towards his object; and often he sighed himself to sleep with the words, 'seven years, and maybe seven years more.' Then in his dreams he saw Kinraid again, sometimes struggling, sometimes sailing towards land, the only one on board a swift advancing ship, alone on deck, stern and avenging; till Philip awoke in remorseful terror.

Such and similar dreams returned with the greater frequency when, in the November of that year, the coast between Hartlepool and Monkshaven was overshadowed by the presence of guard-ships, driven south from their station at North Shields by the resolution which the sailors of that port had entered into to resist the press-gang, and the energy with which they had begun to carry out their determination. For on a certain Tuesday evening yet remembered by old inhabitants of North Shields, the sailors in the merchant service met together and overpowered the press-gang, dismissing them from the town with the highest contempt, and with their jackets reversed. A numerous mob went with them to Chirton Bar; gave them three cheers at parting, but vowed to tear them limb from limb should they seek to re-enter North Shields. But a few days afterwards some fresh cause of irritation arose, and five hundred sailors, armed with such swords and pistols as they could collect, paraded through the town in the most riotous manner, and at last attempted to seize the tender *Eleanor*, on some pretext of the ill-treatment of the impressed men aboard. This endeavour failed, however, owing to the energetic conduct of the officers in command. Next day this body of sailors set off for Newcastle; but learning, before they reached the town, that there was a strong military and civil force prepared to receive them there, they dispersed for the time; but not before the good citizens had received a great fright, the drums of the North Yorkshire militia beating to arms, and the terrified people rushing out into the streets to learn the reason of the alarm, and some of them seeing the militia, under the command of the Earl of Fauconberg, marching from the guard-house adjoining New Gate to the house of rendezvous for impressed seamen in the Broad Chase.

But a few weeks after, the impressment service took their

revenge for the insults they had been subjected to in North Shields. In the dead of night a cordon was formed round that town by a regiment stationed at Tynemouth barracks; the press-gangs belonging to armed vessels lying off Shields harbour were let loose; no one within the circle could escape, and upwards of two hundred and fifty men, sailors, mechanics, labourers of every description, were forced on board the armed ships. With that prize they set sail, and wisely left the place, where deep passionate vengeance was sworn against them. Not all the dread of an invasion by the French could reconcile the people of these coasts to the necessity of impressment. Fear and confusion prevailed after this to within many miles of the sea-shore. A Yorkshire gentleman of rank said that his labourers dispersed like a covey of birds, because a press-gang was reported to have established itself so far inland as Tadcaster; and they only returned to work on the assurance from the steward of his master's protection, but even then begged leave to sleep on straw in the stables or outhouses belonging to their landlord, not daring to sleep at their own homes. No fish was caught, for the fishermen dared not venture out to sea; the markets were deserted, as the press-gangs might come down on any gathering of men; prices were raised, and many were impoverished; many others ruined. For in the great struggle in which England was then involved, the navy was esteemed her safeguard; and men must be had at any price of money, or suffering, or of injustice. Landsmen were kidnapped and taken to London; there, in too many instances, to be discharged without redress and penniless, because they were discovered to be useless for the purpose for which they had been taken.

Autumn brought back the whaling-ships. But the period of their return was full of gloomy anxiety, instead of its being the annual time of rejoicing and feasting; of gladdened households, where brave steady husbands or sons returned; of unlimited and reckless expenditure, and boisterous joviality among those who thought that they had earned unbounded licence on shore by their six months of compelled abstinence.

In other years this had been the time for new and handsome winter clothing; for cheerful if humble hospitality; for the shopkeepers to display their gayest and best; for the public-houses to be crowded; for the streets to be full of blue jackets, rolling along with merry words and open hearts. In other years the boiling-houses had been full of active workers, the staithes crowded with barrels, the ship-carpenters' yards thronged with seamen and captains; now a few men, tempted by high wages, went stealthily by back lanes to their work, clustering together, with sinister looks, glancing round corners, and fearful of every approaching footstep, as if they were going on some unlawful business, instead of true honest work. Most of them kept their whaling-knives about them ready for bloody defence if they were attacked. The shops were almost deserted; there was no unnecessary expenditure by the men; they dared not venture out to buy lavish presents for the wife or sweetheart or little children. The public-houses kept scouts on the look-out; while fierce men drank and swore deep oaths of vengeance in the bar – men who did not maunder in their cups, nor grow foolishly merry, but in whom liquor called forth all the desperate, bad passions of human nature.

Indeed, all along the coast of Yorkshire, it seemed as if a blight hung over the land and the people. Men dodged about their daily business with hatred and suspicion in their eyes, and many a curse went over the sea to the three fatal ships lying motionless at anchor three miles off Monkshaven. When first Philip had heard in his shop that these three-men-of-war might be seen lying fell and still on the gray horizon, his heart sank, and he scarcely dared to ask their names. For if one should be the *Alcestis;* if Kinraid should send word to Sylvia; if he should say he was living, and loving, and faithful; if it should come to pass that the fact of the undelivered message sent by her lover through Philip should reach Sylvia's ears: what would be the position of the latter, not merely in her love – that, of course, would be hopeless – but in her esteem? All sophistry vanished; the fear of detection awakened Philip to a sense of guilt; and, besides, he found out, that, in spite of all idle talk and careless slander, he could not help believing that Kinraid was in terrible earnest when he uttered those passionate words, and entreated that they might be borne to Sylvia. Some instinct told Philip that if the specksioneer had only flirted with too many, yet that for Sylvia Robson his love was true and vehement. Then Philip tried to convince himself that, from all that was said of his previous character, Kinraid was not capable of an enduring constant attachment; and with such poor opiate to his conscience as he could obtain from this notion Philip was obliged to remain content, until, a day or two after the first intelligence of the presence of those three ships, he learned, with some trouble and pains, that their names were the *Megœra*, the *Bellerophon*, and the *Hanover*.

Then he began to perceive how unlikely it was that the *Alcestis* should have been lingering on this shore all these many months. She was, doubtless, gone far away by this time; she had, probably, joined the fleet on the war station. Who could tell what had become of her and her crew? she might have been in battle before now, and if so——

So his previous fancies shrank to nothing, rebuked for their improbability, and with them vanished his self-reproach. Yet there were times when the popular attention seemed totally absorbed by the dread of the press-gang; when no other subject was talked about – hardly, in fact, thought about. At such flows of panic, Philip had his own private fears lest a flash of light should come upon Sylvia, and she should suddenly see that Kinraid's absence might be accounted for in another way besides death. But when he reasoned, this seemed unlikely. No man-of-war had been seen off the coast, or, if seen, had never been spoken about, at the time of Kinraid's disappearance. If he had vanished this winter time, every one would have been convinced that the press-gang had seized upon him. Philip had never heard any one breathe the dreaded name of the *Alcestis*. Besides, he went on to think, at the farm they are out of hearing of this one great weary subject of talk. But it was not so, as he became convinced one evening. His aunt caught him a little aside while Sylvia was in the diary, and her husband talking in the shippen with Kester.

'For good's sake, Philip, dunnot thee bring us talk about t' press-gang. It's a thing as has got hold on my measter, till thou'd think him possessed. He's speaking perpetual on it i' such a way, that thou'd think he were itching to kill 'em a' afore he tasted bread again. He really trembles wi' rage and passion; an' a' night it's just as bad. He starts up i' his sleep, swearing and cursing at 'em, till I'm sometimes afeared he'll mak' an end o' me by mistake. And what mun he do last night but open out on Charley Kinraid, and tell Sylvie he thought m'appen t' gang had got hold on him. It might make her cry a' her saut tears o'er again.'

Philip spoke, by no wish of his own, but as if compelled to speak.

'An' who knows but what it's true?'

The instant these words had come out of his lips he could have bitten his tongue off. And yet afterwards it was a sort of balm to his conscience that he had so spoken.

'What nonsense, Philip!' said his aunt; 'why, these fearsome ships were far out o' sight when he went away, good go wi' him, and Sylvie just getting o'er her trouble so nicely, and even my master went on for to say if they'd getten hold on him, he were not a chap to stay wi' 'em; he'd gi'en proofs on his hatred to 'em, time on. He either ha' made off – an' then sure enough we should ha' heerd on him somehow – them Corneys is full on him still and they've a deal to wi' his folk beyond Newcassel – or, as my master says, he were just t' chap to hang or drown hissel, sooner nor do aught against his will.'

'What did Sylvie say?' asked Philip, in a hoarse low voice.

'Say? why, a' she could say was to burst out crying, and after a bit, she just repeated her feyther's words, and said anyhow he was dead, for he'd niver live to go to sea wi' a press-gang. She knowed him too well for that. Thou sees she thinks a deal on him for a spirited chap, as can do what he will. I belie' me she first began to think on him time o' t' fight aboard th' *Good Fortune*, when Darley were killed, and he would seem tame-like to her if he couldn't conquer press-gangs, and men-o'-war. She's sooner think on him drowned, as she's ne'er to see him again.'

'It's best so,' said Philip, and then, to calm his unusually excited aunt, he promised to avoid the subject of the press-gang as much as possible.

But it was a promise very difficult of performance, for Daniel Robson was, as his wife said, like one possessed. He could hardly think of anything else, though he himself was occasionally weary of the same constantly recurring idea, and would fain have banished it from his mind. He was too old a man to be likely to be taken by them; he had no son to become their victim; but the terror of them, which he had braved and defied in his youth, seemed to come back and take possession of him in his age; and with the terror came impatient hatred. Since his wife's illness the previous winter he had been a more sober man until now. He was never exactly drunk, for he had a strong, well-seasoned head; but the craving to hear the last news of the actions of the press-gang drew him into Monkshaven nearly every day at this dead agricultural season of the year; and a public-house is generally the focus from which gossip radiates; and probably the amount of drink thus consumed weakened Robson's power over his mind, and caused the concentration of thought on one subject. This may be a physiological explanation of what afterwards was spoken of as a supernatural kind of possession, leading him to his doom.

CHAPTER XXIII

RETALIATION

The public-house that had been chosen by the leaders of the press-gang in Monkshaven at this time, for their rendezvous (or 'Randyvowse,' as it was generally pronounced), was an inn of poor repute, with a yard at the back which opened on to the staithe or quay nearest to the open sea. A strong high stone wall bounded this grass-grown mouldy yard on two sides; the house, and some unused out-buildings, formed the other two. The choice of the place was good enough, both as to situation, which was sufficiently isolated, and yet near to the widening river; and as to the character of the landlord, John Hobbs was a failing man, one who seemed as if doomed to be unfortunate in all his undertakings, and the consequence of all this was that he was envious of the more prosperous, and willing to do anything that might bring him in a little present success in life. His household consisted of his wife, her niece, who acted as servant, and an out-of-doors man, a brother of Ned Simpson, the well-doing butcher, who at one time had had a fancy for Sylvia. But the one brother was prosperous, the other had gone on sinking in life, like him who was now his master. Neither Hobbs nor his man Simpson were absolutely bad men; if things had gone well with them they might each have been as scrupulous and conscientious as their neighbours, and even now, supposing the gain in money to be equal, they would sooner have done good than evil; but a very small sum was enough to turn the balance. And in a greater degree than in most cases was the famous maxim of Rochefoucault* true with them; for in the misfortunes of their friends they seemed to see some justification of their own. It was blind fate dealing out events, not that the events themselves were the inevitable consequences of folly or misconduct. To such men as these the large sum offered by the lieutenant of the press-gang for the accommodation of the Mariners' Arms was simply and immediately irresistible. The best room in the dilapidated house was put at the service of the commanding officer of the impress service, and all other arrangements made at his desire, irrespective of all the former unprofitable sources of custom and of business. If the relatives both of Hobbs and of Simpson had not been so well known and so prosperous in the town, they themselves would have received more marks of popular ill opinion than they did during the winter the events of which are now being recorded. As it was, people spoke to them when they appeared at kirk or at market, but held no conversation with them; no, not although they each appeared better dressed than they had either of them done for years past, and although their whole manner showed a change, inasmuch as they had been formerly snarling and misanthropic, and were now civil almost to deprecation.

Every one who was capable of understanding the state of feeling in Monkshaven at this time must have been aware that at any moment an explosion might take place; and probably there were those who had judgment enough to be surprised that it did not take place sooner than it did. For until February there were only occasional cries and growls of rage, as the press-gang made their captures first here, then there; often, apparently, tranquil for days, then heard of at some distance along the coast, then carrying off a seaman from the very heart of the town. They seemed afraid of provoking any general hostility, such as that which had driven them from Shields, and would have conciliated the inhabitants if they could; the officers on the service and on board the three men-of-war coming often into the town, spending largely, talking to all with cheery friendliness, and making themselves very popular in such society as they could obtain access to at the houses of the neighbouring magistrates or at the rectory. But this, however agreeable, did not forward the object the impress service had in view; and, accordingly, a more decided step was taken at a time when, although there was no apparent evidence as to the fact, the town was full of the Greenland mariners coming quietly in to renew their yearly engagements, which, when done, would legally entitle them to protection from impressment. One night – it was on a Saturday, February 23rd, when there was a bitter black frost, with a north-east wind sweeping through the streets, and men and women were close shut in their houses – all were startled in their household content and warmth by the sound of the firebell busily swinging, and pealing out for help. The fire-bell was kept in the market-house where High Street and Bridge Street met; every one knew what it meant. Some dwelling, or maybe a boiling-house was on fire, and neighbourly assistance was summoned with all speed, in a town where no water was laid on, nor fire-engines kept in readiness. Men snatched up their hats, and rushed out, wives following, some with the readiest wraps they could lay hands on, with which to clothe the over-hasty husbands, others from that mixture of dread and curiosity which draws people to the scene of any disaster. Those of the market people who were making the best of their way homewards, having waited in the town till the early darkness concealed their path, turned back at the sound of the ever-clanging fire-bell, ringing out faster and faster as if the danger became every instant more pressing.

As men ran against or alongside of each other, their breathless question was ever, 'Where is it?' and no one could tell; so they pressed onwards into the market-place, sure of obtaining the information desired there, where the fire-bell kept calling out with its furious metal tongue.

The dull oil-lamps in the adjoining streets only made darkness visible in the thronged market-place, where the buzz of many men's unanswered questions was rising louder and louder. A strange feeling of dread crept over those nearest to the closed market-house. Above them in the air the bell was still clanging; but before them was a door fast shut and locked; no one to speak and tell them why they were summoned – where they ought to be. They were at the heart of the mystery, and it was a silent blank! Their unformed dread took shape at the cry from the outside of the crowd, from where men were still coming down the eastern side of Bridge Street. 'The gang! the gang!' shrieked out some one. 'The gang are upon us! Help! help!' Then the fire-bell had been a decoy; a sort of seething the kid in its mother's milk, leading men into a snare through their kindliest feelings. Some dull sense of this added to utter dismay, and made them struggle and strain to get to all the outlets save that in which a fight was now going on; the swish of heavy whips, the thud of bludgeons, the groans, the growls of wounded or infuriated men, coming with terrible distinctness through the darkness to the quickened ear of fear.

A breathless group rushed up the blackness of a narrow entry to stand still awhile, and recover strength for fresh running. For a time nothing but heavy pants and gasps were heard amongst them. No one knew his neighbour, and their good feeling, so lately abused and preyed upon, made them full of suspicion. The first who spoke was recognized by his voice.

'Is it thee, Daniel Robson?' asked his neighbour, in a low tone.

'Ay! Who else should it be?'

'A dunno.'

'If a am to be any one else, I'd like to be a chap of nobbut eight stun. A'm welly done for!'

'It were as bloody a shame as iver I heerd on. Who's to go t' t' next fire, a'd like to know!'

'A tell yo' what, lads,' said Daniel, recovering his breath, but speaking in gasps. 'We were a pack o' cowards to let 'em carry off yon chaps as easy as they did, a'm reckoning!'

'A think so, indeed,' said another voice.

Daniel went on—

'We was two hunder, if we was a man; an' t' gang has niver numbered above twelve.'

'But they was armed. A seen t' glitter on their cutlasses,' spoke out a fresh voice.

'What then!' replied he who had latest come, and who stood at the mouth of the entry. 'A had my whalin' knife wi' me i' my pea-jacket* as my missus threw at me, and a'd ha' ripped 'em up as soon as winkin', if a could ha' thought what was best to do wi' that d——d bell makin' such a din reet above us. A man can but die onest, and we was ready to go int' t' fire for t' save folks' lives, and yet we'd none on us t' wit to see as we might ha' saved yon poor chaps as screeched out for help.'

'They'll ha' getten 'em to t' Randyvowse by now,' said some one.

'They cannot tak' 'em aboard till morning; t' tide won't serve,' said the last speaker but one.

Daniel Robson spoke out the thought that was surging up into the brain of every one there.

'There's a chance for us a'. How many be we?' By dint of touching each other the numbers were counted. Seven. 'Seven. But if us seven turns out and rouses t' town, there'll be many a score ready to gang t' Mariners' Arms, and it'll be easy work reskyin' them chaps as is pressed. Us seven, each man jack on us, go and seek up his friends, and get him as well as he can to t' church steps; then, mebbe, there'll be some theere as'll not be so soft as we was, lettin' them poor chaps be carried off from under our noses, just becase our ears was busy listenin' to yon confounded bell, whose clip-clappin' tongue a'll tear out afore this week is out.'

Before Daniel had finished speaking, those nearest to the entrance muttered their assent to his project, and had stolen off, keeping to the darkest side of the streets and lanes, which they threaded in different directions; most of them going straight as sleuth-hounds to the haunts of the wildest and most desperate portion of the seafaring population of Monkshaven. For, in the breasts of many, revenge for the misery and alarm of the past winter took a deeper and more ferocious form than Daniel had thought of when he made his proposal of a rescue. To him it was an adventure like many he had been engaged in in his younger days; indeed, the liquor he had drunk had given him a fictitious youth for the time; and it was more in the light of a rough frolic of which he was to be the leader, that he limped along (always lame from old attacks of rheumatism), chuckling to himself at the apparent stillness of the town, which gave no warning to the press-gang at the Rendezvous of anything in the wind. Daniel, too, had his friends to summon; old hands like himself, but 'deep uns,' also, like himself, as he imagined.

It was nine o'clock when all who were summoned met at the church steps; and by nine o'clock, Monkshaven, in those days, was more quiet and asleep than many a town at present is at midnight. The church and churchyard above them were flooded with silver light, for the moon was high in the heavens: the irregular steps were here and there in pure white clearness, here and there in blackest shadow. But more than half way up to the top, men clustered like bees; all pressing so as to be near enough to question those who stood nearest to the planning of the attack. Here and there, a woman, with wild gestures and shrill voice, that no entreaty would hush down to the whispered pitch of the men, pushed her way through the crowd – this one imploring immediate action, that adjuring those around her to smite and spare not those who had carried off her 'man,' – the father, the bread-winner. Low down in the darkened silent town were many whose hearts went with the angry and excited crowd, and who would bless them and caress them for that night's deeds. Daniel soon found himself a laggard in planning, compared to some of those around him. But when, with the rushing sound of many steps and but few words, they had arrived at the blank, dark, shut-up Mariners' Arms, they paused in surprise at the uninhabited look of the whole house: it was Daniel once more who took the lead.

'Speak 'em fair,' said he; 'try good words first. Hobbs 'll mebbe let 'em out quiet, if we can catch a word wi' him. A say, Hobbs,' said he, raising his voice, 'is a' shut up for t' neet; for a'd be glad of a glass. A'm Dannel Robson, thou knows.'

Not one word in reply, any more than from the tomb; but his speech had been heard nevertheless. The crowd behind him began to jeer and to threaten; there was no longer any keeping down their voices, their rage, their terrible oaths. If doors and windows had not of late been strengthened with bars of iron in anticipation of some such occasion, they would have been broken in with the onset of the fierce and now yelling crowd who rushed against them with the force of a battering-ram, to recoil in baffled rage from the vain assault. No sign, no sound from within, in that breathless pause.

'Come away round here! a've found a way to t' back o'

behint, where belike it's not so well fenced,' said Daniel, who had made way for younger and more powerful men to conduct the assault, and had employed his time meanwhile in examining the back premises. The men rushed after him, almost knocking him down, as he made his way into the lane into which the doors of the outbuildings belonging to the inn opened. Daniel had already broken the fastening of that which opened into a damp, mouldy-smelling shippen, in one corner of which a poor lean cow shifted herself on her legs, in an uneasy, restless manner, as her sleeping-place was invaded by as many men as could cram themselves into the dark hold. Daniel, at the end farthest from the door, was almost smothered before he could break down the rotten wooden shutter, that, when opened, displayed the weedy yard of the old inn, the full clear light defining the outline of each blade of grass, by the delicate black shadow behind.

This hole, used to give air and light to what had once been a stable, in the days when horse travellers were in the habit of coming to the Mariners' Arms, was large enough to admit the passage of a man; and Daniel, in virtue of its discovery, was the first to get through. But he was larger and heavier than he had been; his lameness made him less agile, and the impatient crowd behind him gave him a helping push that sent him down on the round stones with which the yard was paved, and for the time disabled him so much that he could only just crawl out of the way of leaping feet and heavy nailed boots, which came through the opening till the yard was filled with men, who now set up a fierce, derisive shout, which, to their delight, was answered from within. No more silence, no more dead opposition: a living struggle, a glowing, raging fight; and Daniel thought he should be obliged to sit there still, leaning against the wall, inactive, while the strife and the action were going on in which he had once been foremost.

He saw the stones torn up; he saw them used with good effect on the unguarded back-door; he cried out in useless warning as he saw the upper windows open, and aim taken among the crowd; but just then the door gave way, and there was an involuntary forward motion in the throng, so that no one was so disabled by the shots as to prevent his forcing his way in* with the rest. And now the sounds came veiled by the walls as of some raging ravening beast growling over his prey; the noise came and went – once utterly ceased; and Daniel raised himself with difficulty to ascertain the cause, when again the roar came clear and fresh, and men poured into the yard again, shouting and rejoicing over the rescued victims of the press-gang. Daniel hobbled up, and shouted, and rejoiced, and shook hands with the rest, hardly caring to understand that the lieutenant and his gang had quitted the house by a front window, and that all had poured out in search of them; the greater part, however, returning to liberate the prisoners, and then glut their vengeance on the house and its contents.

From all the windows, upper and lower, furniture was now being thrown into the yard. The smash of glass, the heavier crash of wood, the cries, the laughter, the oaths, all excited Daniel to the utmost; and, forgetting his bruises, he pressed forwards to lend a helping hand. The wild, rough success of his scheme almost turned his head. He hurraed at every flagrant piece of destruction; he shook hands with every one around him, and, at last, when the destroyers inside paused to take breath, he cried out,—

'If a was as young as onest a was, a'd have t' Randyvowse down, and mak' a bonfire on it. We'd ring t' fire-bell then t' some purpose.'*

No sooner said than done. Their excitement was ready to take the slightest hint of mischief; old chairs, broken tables, odd drawers, smashed chests, were rapidly and skilfully heaped into a pyramid, and one, who at the first broaching of the idea had gone for live coals the speedier to light up the fire, came now through the crowd with a large shovelful of red-hot cinders. The rioters stopped to take breath and look on like children at the uncertain flickering blaze, which sprang high one moment, and dropped down the next only to creep along the base of the heap of wreck, and make secure of its future work. Then the lurid blaze darted up wild, high, and irrepressible; and the men around gave a cry of fierce exultation, and in rough mirth began to try and push each other in. In one of the pauses of the rushing, roaring noise of the flames, the moaning low and groan of the poor alarmed cow fastened up in the shippen caught Daniel's ear, and he understood her groans as well as if they had been words. He limped out of the yard through the now deserted house, where men were busy at the mad work of destruction, and found his way back to the lane into which the shippen opened. The cow was dancing about at the roar, and dazzle, and heat of the fire; but Daniel knew how to soothe her, and in a few minutes he had a rope round her neck, and led her gently out from the scene of her alarm. He was still in the lane when Simpson, the man-of-all-work at the Mariners' Arms, crept out of some hiding-place in the deserted outbuilding, and stood suddenly face to face with Robson.

The man was white with fear and rage.

'Here, tak' thy beast, and lead her wheere she'll noane hear yon cries and shouts. She's fairly moithered wi' heat an' noise.'

'They're brennin' ivery rag I have i' t' world,' gasped out Simpson: 'I niver had much, and now I'm a beggar.'

'Well! thou shouldn't ha' turned again' thine own town-folks, and harboured t' gang. Sarves thee reet. A'd noane be here leadin' beasts if a were as young as a were; a'd be in t' thick on it.'

'It was thee set 'm on – a heerd thee – a see'd thee a helping on 'em t' break in; they'd niver ha' thought on attackin' t' house, and settin' fire to yon things, if thou hadn't spoken on it.' Simpson was now fairly crying. But Daniel did not realize what the loss of all the small property he had in the world was to the poor fellow (rapscallion though he was, broken down, unprosperous ne'er-do-weel!) in his pride at the good work he believed he had set on foot.

'Ay,' said he; 'it's a great thing for folk to have a chap for t' lead 'em wi' a head on his shouthers. A misdoubt me if there were a felly theere as would ha' thought o' routling out yon wasps' nest; it tak's a deal a' mother-wit to be up to things. But t' gang'll niver harbour theere again, one while. A only wish we'd cotched 'em. An' a should like t' ha' gi'en Hobbs a bit o' my mind.'

'He's had his sauce,' said Simpson, dolefully. 'Him and me is ruined.'

'Tut, tut, thou's got thy brother, he's rich enough. And Hobbs 'll do a deal better; he's had his lesson now, and he'll stick to his own side time to come. Here, tak' thy beast an' look after her, for my bones is achin'. An' mak' thysel' scarce, for some o' them fellys has getten their blood up, an' wunnot be for treating thee o'er well if they fall in wi' thee.'

'Hobbs ought to be served out; it were him as made t' bargain wi' lieutenant; and he's off safe wi' his wife and his money bag, and a'm left a beggar this neet i' Monkshaven street. My brother and me has had words, and he'll do nought for me but curse me. A had three crown-pieces, and a good pair o' breeches, and a shirt, and a dare say better nor two pair o' stockings. A wish t' gang, and thee, and Hobbs and them mad folk up yonder, were a 'down i' hell, a do.'

'Coom, lad,' said Daniel, noways offended at his companion's wish on his behalf. 'A'm noane flush myself', but here's half-a-crown and tuppence; it's a' a've getten wi' me, but it'll keep thee and t' beast i' food and shelter to-neet, and get thee a glass o' comfort, too. A had thought o' takin' one mysel', but a shannot ha' a penny left, so a'll just toddle whoam to my missus.'

Daniel was not in the habit of feeling any emotion at actions not directly affecting himself; or else he might have despised the poor wretch who immediately clutched at the money, and overwhelmed that man with slobbery thanks whom he had not a minute before been cursing. But all Simpson's stronger passions had been long ago used up; now he only faintly liked and disliked, where once he loved and hated; his only vehement feeling was for himself; that cared for, other men might wither or flourish as best suited them.

Many of the doors which had been close shut when the crowd went down the High Street, were partially open as Daniel slowly returned; and light streamed from them on the otherwise dark road. The news of the successful attempt at rescue had reached those who had sate in mourning and in desolation an hour or two ago, and several of these pressed forwards as from their watching corner they recognized Daniel's approach; they pressed forward into the street to shake him by the hand, to thank him (for his name had been bruited abroad as one of those who had planned the affair), and at several places he was urged to have a dram – urgency that he was loath for many reasons to refuse, but his increasing uneasiness and pain made him for once abstinent, and only anxious to get home and rest. But he could not help being both touched and flattered at the way in which those who formed his 'world' looked upon him as a hero; and was not insensible to the words of blessing which a wife, whose husband had been impressed and rescued this night, poured down upon him as he passed.

'Theere, theere, – dunnot crack thy throat wi' blessin'. Thy man would ha' done as much for me, though mebbe he mightn't ha' shown so much gumption and capability; but them's gifts, and not to be proud on.'

When Daniel reached the top of the hill on the road home, he turned to look round; but he was lame and bruised, he had gone along slowly, the fire had pretty nearly died out, only a red hue in the air about the houses at the end of the long High Street, and a hot lurid mist against the hill-side beyond where the Mariners' Arms had stood, were still left as signs and token of the deed of violence.

Daniel looked and chuckled. 'That comes o' ringin' t' fire-bell,' said he to himself; 'it were shame for it to be tellin' a lie, poor oud story-teller.'

CHAPTER XXIV

BRIEF REJOICING

DANIEL'S unusually late absence from home disturbed Bell and Sylvia not a little. He was generally at home between eight and nine on market-days. They expected to see him the worse for liquor at such times; but this did not shock them; he was no worse than most of his neighbours, indeed better than several, who went off once or twice a year, or even oftener, on drinking bouts of two or three days' duration, returning pale, sodden, and somewhat shame-faced, when all their money was gone;* and, after the conjugal reception was well over, settling down into hard-working and decently sober men until the temptation again got power over them. But, on market days, every man drank more than usual; every bargain or agreement was ratified by drink; they came from greater or less distances, either afoot or on horseback, and the 'good accommodation for man and beast' (as the old inn-signs expressed it) always included a considerable amount of liquor to be drunk by the man.

Daniel's way of announcing his intention of drinking more than ordinary was always the same. He would say at the last moment, 'Missus, I've a mind to get fuddled to-neet,' and be off, disregarding her look of remonstrance, and little heeding the injunctions she would call after him to beware of such and such companions, or to attend to his footsteps on his road home.

But this night he had given no such warning. Bell and Sylvia put the candle on the low window-seat at the usual hour to guide him through the fields – it was a habit kept up even on moonlight nights like this – and sate on each side of the fire, at first scarcely caring to listen, so secure were they of his return. Bell dozed, and Sylvia sate gazing at the fire with abstracted eyes, thinking of the past year and of the anniversary which was approaching of the day when she had last seen the lover whom she believed to be dead, lying somewhere fathoms deep beneath the surface of that sunny sea on which she looked day by day without ever seeing his up-turned face through the depths, with whatsoever heart-sick longing for just one more sight she yearned and inwardly cried. If she could set her eyes on his bright, handsome face, that face which was fading from her memory, overtasked in the too frequent efforts to recall it; if she could but see him once again, coming over the waters beneath which he lay with supernatural motion, awaiting her at the stile, with the evening sun shining ruddy into his bonny eyes, even though, after that one instant of vivid and visible life, he faded into mist; if she could but see him now, sitting in the faintly flickering fire-light in the old, happy, careless way, on a corner of the dresser, his legs dangling, his busy fingers playing with some of her woman's work; – she wrung her hands tight together as she implored some, any Power, to let her see him just once again – just once – for one minute of passionate delight. Never again would she forget that dear face, if but once more she might set her eyes upon it.

Her mother's head fell with a sudden jerk, and she roused herself up; and Sylvia put by her thought of the dead, and her craving after his presence, into that receptacle of her heart where all such are kept closed and sacred from the light of common day.

'Feyther's late,' said Bell.

'It's gone eight,' replied Sylvia.

'But our clock is better nor an hour forrard,' answered Bell.

'Ay, but t' wind brings Monkshaven bells clear to-night. I heerd t' eight o'clock bell ringing not five minutes ago.'

It was the fire-bell, but she had not distinguished the sound.

There was another long silence; both wide awake this time.

'He'll have his rheumatics again,' said Bell.

'It's cold for sartin,' said Sylvia. 'March weather come afore its time. But I'll make him a treacle-posset;* it's a famous thing for keeping off hoasts.'*

The treacle-posset was entertainment enough for both while it was being made. But once placed in a little basin in the oven, there was again time for wonder and anxiety.

'He said nought about having a bout, did he, mother?' asked Sylvia at length.

'No,' said Bell, her face a little contracting. After a while she added, 'There's many a one as has husbands that goes off drinking without iver saying a word to their wives. My master is none o' that mak'.'

'Mother,' broke in Sylvia again, 'I'll just go and get t' lantern out of t' shippen, and go up t' brow, and mebbe to t' ash-field end.'

'Do, lass,' said her mother. 'I'll get my wraps and go with thee.'

'Thou shall do niver such a thing,' said Sylvia. 'Thou's too frail to go out i' t' night air such a night as this.'

'Then call Kester up.'

'Not I. I'm noane afraid o' t' dark.'

'But of what thou mayst meet i' t' dark, lass?'

Sylvia shivered all over at the sudden thought, suggested by this speech of her mother's, that the idea that had flashed into her own mind of going to look for her father might be an answer to the invocation to the Powers which she had made not long ago, that she might indeed meet her dead lover at the ash-field stile; but though she shivered as this superstitious fancy came into her head, her heart beat firm and regular; not from darkness nor from the spirits of the dead was she going to shrink; her great sorrow had taken away all her girlish nervous fear.

She went; and she came back. Neither man nor spirit had she seen; the wind was blowing on the height enough to sweep all creatures before it; but no one was coming.

So they sate down again to keep watch. At length his step was heard close to the door; and it startled them even in their state of expectation.

'Why, feyther!' cried Sylvia as he entered; while his wife stood up trembling, but not saying a word.

'A'm a'most done up,' said he, sitting heavily down on the chair nearest the door.

'Poor old feyther!' said Sylvia, stooping to take off his heavy clogged shoes; while Bell took the posset out of the oven.

'What's this? posset? what creatures women is for slops,' said he; but he drank it all the same, while Sylvia fastened the door, and brought the flaring candle from the window-seat. The fresh arrangement of light displayed his face blackened with smoke, and his clothes disarranged and torn.

'Who's been melling wi' thee?' asked Bell.

'No one has melled wi' me; but a've been mellin' wi' t' gang at last.'

'Thee: they niver were for pressing thee!' exclaimed both the women at once.

'No! they knowed better. They'n getten their belly-full as it is. Next time they try it on, a reckon they'll ax if Daniel Robson is wi'in hearin'. A've led a resky this neet, and saved nine or ten honest chaps as was pressed, and carried off to t' Randyvowse. Me and some others did it. And Hobbs' things and t' lieutenant's is a' burnt; and by this time a reckon t' Randyvowse is pretty nigh four walls, ready for a parish-pound.'

'Thou'rt niver for saying thou burnt it down wi' t' gang in it, for sure?' asked Bell.

'Na, na, not this time. T' gang fled up t' hill like coneys; and Hobbs and his folks carried off a bag o' money; but t' oud tumbledown place is just a heap o' brick and mortar; an' t' furniture is smoulderin' int' ashes; and, best of a', t' men is free, and will niver be cotched wi' a fire-bell again.'

And so he went on to tell of the ruse by which they had been enticed into the market-place; interrupted from time to time by their eager questions, and interrupting himself every now and then with exclamations of weariness and pain, which made him at last say,—

'Now a'm willing to tell yo' a' about it to-morrow, for it's not ivery day a man can do such great things; but to-neet a mun go to bed, even if King George were wantin' for to know how a managed it a'.'

He went wearily upstairs, and wife and daughter both strove their best to ease his aching limbs, and make him comfortable. The warming-pan, only used on state occasions, was taken down and unpapered for his service; and as he got between the warm sheets, he thanked Sylvia and her mother in a sleepy voice, adding,—

'It's a vast o' comfort to think on yon poor lads as is sleepin' i' their own homes this neet,' and then slumber fell upon him, and he was hardly roused by Bell's softly kissing his weather-beaten cheek, and saying low,—

'God bless thee, my man! Thou was allays for them that was down and put upon.'

He murmured some monosyllabic reply, unheard by his wife, who stole away to undress herself noiselessly, and laid herself down on her side of the bed as gently as her stiffened limbs would permit.

They were late in rising the next morning. Kester was long since up and at his work among the cattle before he saw the house-door open to admit the fresh chill morning air; and even then Sylvia brushed softly, and went about almost on tip-toe. When the porridge was ready, Kester was called in to his breakfast, which he took sitting at the dresser with the family. A large wooden platter stood in the middle; and each had a bowl of the same material filled with milk. The way was for every one to dip his pewter spoon into the central dish, and convey as much or as little as he liked at a time of the hot porridge into his pure fresh milk. But to-day Bell told Kester to help himself all at once, and to take his bowl up to the master's room and keep him company. For Daniel was in bed, resting from his weariness, and bemoaning his painful bruises whenever he thought of them. But his mind was still so much occupied with the affair of the previous night, that Bell judged rightly that a new listener would give ease to his body as well as to his mind, and her proposal of Kester's carrying up his breakfast had been received by Daniel with satisfaction.

So Kester went up slowly, carrying his over-full basin tenderly, and seated himself on the step leading down into the bed-room (for levels had not been calculated when the old house was built) facing his master, who, half sitting up in the blue check bed, not unwillingly began his relation again; to which Kester listened so attentively, that his spoon was often arrested in its progress from the basin to his mouth, open ready to receive it, while he gazed with unwinking eyes at Daniel narrating his exploits.

But after Daniel had fought his battle o'er again to every auditor within his reach, he found the seclusion of his chamber rather oppressive, without even the usual week-days' noises below; so after dinner, though far from well, he came down and wandered about the stable and the fields nearest to the house, consulting with Kester as to crops and manure for the most part; but every now and then breaking out into an episodical chuckle over some part of last night's proceedings. Kester enjoyed the day even more than his master, for he had no bruises to remind him that, although a hero, he was also flesh and blood.

When they returned to the house they found Philip there, for it was already dusk. It was Kester's usual Sunday plan to withdraw to bed at as early an hour as he could manage to sleep, often in winter before six; but now he was too full of interest in what Philip might have to tell of Monkshaven news to forego his Sabbath privilege of spending the evening sitting on the chair at the end of the dresser behind the door.

Philip was as close to Sylvia as he could possibly get without giving her offence, when they came in. Her manner was listless and civil; she had lost all that active feeling towards him which made him positively distasteful, and had called out her girlish irritation and impertinence. She now was rather glad to see him than otherwise. He brought some change into the heavy monotony of her life – monotony so peaceful until she had been stirred by passion out of that content with the small daily events which had now become burdensome recurrences. Insensibly to herself she was becoming dependent on his timid devotion, his constant attention; and he, lover-like, once so attracted, in spite of his judgment, by her liveliness and piquancy, now doted on her languor, and thought her silence more sweet than words.

He had only just arrived when master and man came in. He had been to afternoon chapel; none of them had thought of going to the distant church; worship with them was only an occasional duty, and this day their minds had been too full of the events of the night before. Daniel sate himself heavily down in his accustomed chair, the three-cornered arm-chair in the fireside corner, which no one thought of anybody else ever occupying on any occasion whatever. In a minute or two he interrupted Philip's words of greeting and inquiry by breaking out into the story of the rescue of last night. But to the mute surprise of Sylvia, the only one who noticed it, Philip's face, instead of expressing admiration and pleasant wonder, lengthened into dismay; once or twice he began to interrupt, but stopped himself as if he would consider his words again. Kester was never tired of hearing his master talk; by long living together they understood every fold of each other's minds, and small expressions had much significance to them. Bell, too, sate thankful that her husband should have done such deeds. Only Sylvia was made uneasy by Philip's face and manner. When Daniel had ended there was a great silence, instead of the questions and compliments he looked to receive. He became testy, and turning to Bell, said,—

'My nephew looks as though he was a-thinking more on t' little profit he has made on his pins an' bobs, than as if he was heeding how honest men were saved from being haled out to yon tender, an' carried out o' sight o' wives and little 'uns for iver. Wives an' little 'uns may go t' workhouse or clem* for aught he cares.'

Philip went very red, and then more sallow than usual. He had not been thinking of Charley Kinraid, but of quite another thing, while Daniel had told his story; but this last speech of the old man's brought up the remembrance that was always quick, do what he would to smother or strangle it. He did not speak for a moment or two, then he said,—

'To-day has not been like Sabbath in Monkshaven. T' rioters, as folks call 'em, have been about all night. They wanted to give battle to t' men-o'-war's men; and it were taken up by th' better end, and they've sent to my Lord Malton for t' militia; and they're come into t' town, and they're hunting for a justice for t' read th' act; folk do say there'll be niver a shop opened to-morrow.'

This was rather a more serious account of the progress of the affair than any one had calculated upon. They looked grave upon it awhile, then Daniel took heart and said,—

'A think we'd done a'most enough last neet; but men's not to be stopped wi' a straw when their blood is up; still it's hard lines to call out t' sojers, even if they be but militia. So what we seven hatched in a dark entry has ta'en a lord to put a stop to 't!' continued he, chuckling a little, but more faintly this time.

Philip went on, still graver than before, boldly continuing to say what he knew would be discordant to the family he loved so well.

'I should ha' telled yo' all about it; I thought on it just as a bit o' news; I'd niver thought on such a thing as uncle there having been in it, and I'm main sorry to hear on it, I am.'

'Why?' said Sylvia, breathlessly.

'It's niver a thing to be sorry on. I'm proud and glad,' said Bell.

'Let-a-be, let-a-be,' said Daniel, in much dudgeon. 'A were a fool to tell him o' such-like doings, they're noane i' his line; we'll talk on yard measures now.'

Philip took no notice of this poor attempt at sarcasm: he seemed as if lost in thought, then he said, —

'I'm vexed to plague yo', but I'd best say all I've got i' my mind. There was a vast o' folk at our chapel speaking about it – last night's doings and this morning's work – and how them as set it afoot was assured o' being clapt int' prison and tried for it; and when I heered uncle say as he was one, it like ran through me; for they say as as t' justices will be all on t' Government side, and mad for vengeance.'

For an instant there was dead silence. The women looked at each other with blank eyes, as if they were as yet unable to take in the new idea that the conduct which had seemed to them a subject for such just pride could be regarded by any one as deserving of punishment or retribution. Daniel spoke before they had recovered from their amazement.

'A'm noane sorry for what a did, an' a'd do it again to-neet, if need were. So theere's for thee. Thou may tell t' justices fra' me that a reckon a did righter nor them, as letten poor fellys be carried off i' t' very midst o' t' town they're called justices for.'

Perhaps Philip had better have held his tongue; but he

believed in the danger, which he was anxious to impress upon his uncle, in order that, knowing what was to be apprehended, the latter might take some pains to avert it.

He went on.

'But they're making a coil* about the Randyvowse being all destroyed!'

Daniel had taken down his pipe from the shelf in the chimney corner, and was stuffing tobacco into the bowl. He went on pretending to do this a little while after it was filled; for, to tell the truth, he was beginning to feel uncomfortable at the new view of his conduct presented to him. Still he was not going to let this appear, so lifting up his head with an indifferent air he lighted the pipe, blew into it, took it out and examined it as something were wrong about it, and until that was put to rights he was unable to attend to anything else; all the while the faithful three who hung upon his well-being, gazing, breathless, at his proceedings, and anxious for his reply.

'Randyvowse!' said he at length, 'it were a good job it were brenned down, for such a harbour for vermin a never seed: t' rats ran across t' yard by hunders an' thousands; an' it were no man's property as a've heerd tell, but belonged to Chancery, up i' Lunnon; so wheere's t' harm done, my fine felly?'

Philip was silent. He did not care to brave any further his uncle's angry frown and contracted eye. If he had only known of Daniel Robson's part in the riot before he had left the town, he would have taken care to have had better authority for the reality of the danger which he had heard spoken about, and in which he could not help believing. As it was, he could only keep quiet until he had ascertained what was the legal peril overhanging the rioters, and how far his uncle had been recognized.

Daniel went on puffing angrily. Kester sighed audibly, and then was sorry he had done so, and began to whistle. Bell, full of her new fear, yet desirous to bring all present into some kind of harmony, said,—

'It'll ha' been a loss to John Hobbs – all his things burnt, or trampled on. Mebbe he desarved it all, but one's a kind o' tender feeling to one's tables and chairs, special if one's had t' bees-waxing on 'em.'

'A wish he'd been burnt on t' top on 'em, a do,' growled out Daniel, shaking the ash out of his pipe.

'Don't speak so ill o' thysel',' said his wife. 'Thou'd ha' been t' first t' pluck him down if he'd screeched out.'

'An' a'll warrant if they come about wi' a paper asking for feyther's name to make up for what Hobbs has lost by t' fire, feyther 'll be for giving him summut,' said Sylvia.

'Thou knows nought about it,' said Daniel. 'Hold thy tongue next time till thou's axed to speak, my wench.'

His sharp irritated way of speaking was so new to Sylvia, that the tears sprang to her eyes, and her lip quivered. Philip saw it all, and yearned over her. He plunged headlong into some other subject to try and divert attention from her; but Daniel was too ill at ease to talk much, and Bell was obliged to try and keep up the semblance of conversation, with an occasional word or two from Kester, who seemed instinctively to fall into her way of thinking, and to endeavour to keep the dark thought in the background.

Sylvia stole off to bed; more concerned at her father's angry way of speaking than at the idea of his being amenable to law for what he had done; the one was a sharp present evil, the other something distant and unlikely. Yet a dim terror of this latter evil hung over her, and once upstairs she threw herself on her bed and sobbed. Philip heard her where he sate near the bottom of the short steep staircase, and at every sob the cords of love round his heart seemed tightened, and he felt as if he must there and then do something to console her.

But, instead, he sat on talking of nothings, a conversation in which Daniel joined with somewhat of surliness, while Bell, grave and anxious, kept wistfully looking from one to the other, desirous of gleaning some further information on the subject, which had begun to trouble her mind. She hoped some chance would give her the opportunity of privately questioning Philip, but it seemed to be equally her husband's wish to thwart any such intention of hers. He remained in the house-place, till after Philip had left, although he was evidently so much fatigued as to give some very distinct, though unintentional, hints to his visitor to be gone.

At length the house-door was locked on Philip, and then Daniel prepared to go to bed. Kester had left for his loft above the shippen more than an hour before. Bell had still to rake the fire, and then she would follow her husband upstairs.

As she was scraping up the ashes, she heard, intermixed with the noise she was making, the sound of some one rapping gently at the window. In her then frame of mind she started a little; but on looking round, she saw Kester's face pressed against the glass, and, reassured, she softly opened the door. There he stood in the dusk outer air, distinct against the grey darkness beyond, and in his hand something which she presently perceived was a pitchfork.

'Missus!' whispered he, 'a've watched t' maister t' bed; an' now a'd be greatly beholden to yo' if yo'd let me just lay me down i' t' house-place. A'd warrant niver a constable i' a' Monkshaven should get sight o' t' maister, an' me below t' keep ward.'*

Bell shivered a little.

'Nay, Kester,' she said, patting her hand kindly on his shoulder; 'there's nought for t' fear. Thy master is not one for t' hurt nobody; and I dunnot think they can harm him for setting yon poor chaps free, as t' gang catched i' their wicked trap.'

Kester stood still; then he shook his head slowly.

'It's t' work at t' Randyvowse as a'm afeared on. Some folks thinks such a deal o' a bonfire. Then a may lay me down afore t' fire, missus?' said he, beseechingly.

'Nay, Kester—' she began; but suddenly changing, she said, 'God bless thee, my man; come in and lay thee down on t' settle, and I'll cover thee up wi' my cloak as hangs behind t' door. We're not many on us that love him, an' we'll be all on us under one roof, an' niver a stone wall or a lock betwixt us.'

So Kester took up his rest in the house-place that night, and none knew of it besides Bell.

CHAPTER XXV

COMING TROUBLES

THE morning brought more peace if it did not entirely dissipate fear. Daniel seemed to have got over his irritability, and was unusually kind and tender to wife and daughter, especially striving by silent little deeds to make up for the sharp words he had said the night before to the latter.

As if by common consent, all allusion to the Saturday night's proceedings was avoided. They spoke of the day's work before them; of the crops to be sown; of the cattle; of the markets; but each one was conscious of a wish to know more distinctly what were the chances of the danger that, to judge from Philip's words, hung over them, falling upon them and cutting them off from all these places for the coming days.

Bell longed to send Kester down into Monkshaven as a sort of spy to see how the land lay; but she dared not manifest her anxiety to her husband, and could not see Kester alone. She wished that she had told him to go to the town, when she had had him to herself in the house-place the night before; now it seemed as though Daniel were resolved not to part from him, and as though both had forgotten that any peril had been anticipated. Sylvia and her mother, in like manner, clung together, not speaking of their fears, yet each knowing that it was ever present in the other's mind.

So things went on till twelve o'clock – dinner-time. If at any time that morning they had had the courage to speak together on the thought which was engrossing all their minds, it is possible that some means might have been found to avert the calamity that was coming towards them with swift feet. But among the uneducated – the partially educated – nay, even the weakly educated – the feeling exists which prompted the futile experiment of the well-known ostrich. They imagine that, by closing their own eyes to apprehended evil, they avert it. The expression of fear is supposed to accelerate the coming of its cause. Yet, on the other hand, they shrink from acknowledging the long continuance of any blessing, in the idea that when unusual happiness is spoken about, it disappears. So, although perpetual complaints of past or present grievances and sorrows are most common among this class, they shrink from embodying apprehensions for the future in words, as if it then took shape and drew near.

They all four sate down to dinner, but not one of them was inclined to eat. The food was scarcely touched on their plates, yet they were trying to make talk among themselves as usual; they seemed as though they dared not let themselves be silent, when Sylvia, sitting opposite to the window, saw Philip at the top of the brow, running rapidly towards the farm. She had been so full of the anticipation of some kind of misfortune all the morning that she felt now as if this was the very precursive circumstance she had been expecting; she stood up, turning quite white, and, pointing with her finger, said,—

'There he is!'

Every one at table stood up too. An instant afterwards, Philip, breathless, was in the room.

He gasped out, 'They're coming! the warrant is out. You must go. I hoped you were gone.'

'God help us!' said Bell, and sate suddenly down, as if she had received a blow that made her collapse into helplessness; but she got up again directly.

Sylvia flew for her father's hat. He really seemed the most unmoved of the party.

'A'm noane afeared,' said he. 'A'd do it o'er again, a would; an' a'll tell 'em so. It's a fine time o' day when men's to be trapped and carried off, an' them as lays traps to set 'em free is to be put i' t' lock-ups for it.'

'But there was rioting, beside the rescue; t' house was burnt,' continued eager, breathless Philip.

'An' a'm noane goin' t' say a'm sorry for that, neyther; tho', mebbe, a wouldn't do it again.'

Sylvia had his hat on his head by this time; and Bell, wan and stiff, trembling all over, had his over-coat, and his leather purse with the few coins she could muster, ready for him to put on.

He looked at these preparations, at his wife and daughter, and his colour changed from its ruddy brown.

'A'd face lock-ups, an' a fair spell o' jail, but for these,' said he, hesitating.

'Oh!' said Philip, 'for God's sake, lose no time, but be off.'

'Where mun he go?' asked Bell, as if Philip must decide all.

'Anywhere, anywhere, out of this house – say Haverstone. This evening, I'll go and meet him there and plan further; only be off now.' Philip was so keenly eager, he hardly took note at the time of Sylvia's one vivid look of unspoken thanks, yet he remembered it afterwards.

'A'll dang* 'em dead,' said Kester, rushing to the door, for he saw what the others did not – that all chance of escape was over; the constables were already at the top of the little field-path not twenty yards off.

'Hide him, hide him,' cried Bell, wringing her hands in terror; for she, indeed they all, knew that flight would now be impossible. Daniel was heavy, rheumatic, and, moreover, had been pretty severely bruised on that unlucky night.

Philip, without another word, pushed Daniel before him upstairs, feeling that his own presence at Haytersbank Farm at that hour of the day would be a betrayal. They had just time to shut themselves up in the larger bed-room, before they heard a scuffle and the constables' entry downstairs.

'They're in,' said Philip, as Daniel squeezed himself under the bed; and then they held quite still, Philip as much concealed by the scanty, blue-check curtain as he could manage to be. They heard a confusion of voices below, a hasty moving of chairs, a banging of doors, a further parley, and then a woman's scream, shrill and pitiful; then steps on the stairs.

'That screech spoiled all,' sighed Philip.

In one instant the door was opened, and each of the hiders was conscious of the presence of the constables, although at first the latter stood motionless, surveying the apparently empty room with disappointment. Then in another moment they had rushed at Philip's legs, exposed as these were. They drew him out with violence, and then let him go.

'Measter Hepburn!' said one in amaze. But immediately they put two and two together; for in so small a place as Monkshaven every one's relationships and connections, and even likings, were known; and the motive of Philip's coming out to Haytersbank was perfectly clear to these men.

'T' other 'll not be far off,' said the other constable. 'His plate were downstairs, full o' victual; a seed Measter Hepburn a-walking briskly before me as a left Monkshaven.'

'Here he be, here be be,' called out the other man, dragging Daniel out by his legs, 'we've getten him.'

Daniel kicked violently, and came out from his hiding-place in a less ignominious way than by being pulled out by his heels.

He shook himself, and then turned, facing his captors.

'A wish a'd niver hidden mysel'; it were his doing,' jerking his thumb toward Philip: 'a'm ready to stand by what a've done. Yo've getten a warrant a'll be bound, for them justices is grand at writin' when t' fight's over.'

He was trying to carry it off with bravado, but Philip saw that he had received a shock, from his sudden look of withered colour and shrunken feature.

'Don't handcuff him,' said Philip, putting money into the constable's hand. 'You'll be able to guard him well enough without them things.'

Daniel turned round sharp at this whisper.

'Let-a-be, let-a-be, my lad,' he said. 'It 'll be summut to think on i' t' lock-up how two able-bodied fellys were so afeared on t' chap as reskyed them honest sailors o' Saturday neet, as they mun put him i' gyves, and he sixty-two come Martinmas, and sore laid up wi' t' rheumatics.'

But it was difficult to keep up this tone of bravado when he was led a prisoner through his own house-place, and saw his poor wife quivering and shaking all over with her efforts to keep back all signs of emotion until he was gone; and Sylvia standing by her mother, her arm round Bell's waist and stroking the poor shrunken fingers which worked so perpetually and nervously in futile unconscious restlessness. Kester was in a corner of the room, sullenly standing.

Bell quaked from head to foot as her husband came downstairs a prisoner. She opened her lips several times with an uneasy motion, as if she would fain say something, but knew not what. Sylvia's passionate swollen lips and her beautiful defiant eyes gave her face quite a new aspect; she looked a helpless fury.

'A may kiss my missus, a reckon,' said Daniel, coming to a standstill as he passed near her.

'Oh, Dannel, Dannel!' cried she, opening her arms wide to receive him. 'Dannel, Dannel, my man!' and she shook with her crying, laying her head on his shoulder, as if he was all her stay and comfort.

'Come, missus! come, missus!' said he, 'there couldn't be more ado if a'd been guilty of murder, an' yet a say again, as a said afore, a'm noane ashamed o' my doings. Here, Sylvie, lass, tak' thy mother off me, for a cannot do it mysel'; it like sets me off.' His voice was quavering as he said this. But he cheered up a little and said, 'Now, good-by, oud wench' (kissing her), 'and keep a good heart, and let me see thee lookin' lusty and strong when a come back. Good-by, my lass; look well after mother, and ask Philip for guidance if it's needed.'

He was taken out of his home, and then arose the shrill cries of the women; but in a minute or two they were checked by the return of one of the constables, who, cap in hand at the sight of so much grief, said,—

'He wants a word wi' his daughter.'

The party had come to a halt about ten yards from the house. Sylvia, hastily wiping her tears on her apron, ran out and threw her arms round her father, as if to burst out afresh on his neck.

'Nay, nay, my wench, it's thee as mun be a comfort to mother: nay, nay, or thou'll niver hear what a've got to say. Sylvie, my lass, a'm main and sorry a were so short wi' thee last neet; a ax thy pardon, lass, a were cross to thee, and sent thee to thy bed wi' a sore heart. Thou munnot think on it again, but forg'e me, now a'm leavin' thee.'

'Oh, feyther! feyther!' was all Sylvia could say; and at last they had to make as though they would have used force to separate her from their prisoner. Philip took her hand, and softly led her back to her weeping mother.

For some time nothing was to be heard in the little farm-house kitchen but the sobbing and wailing of the women. Philip stood by silent, thinking, as well as he could, for his keep sympathy with their grief, what had best be done next. Kester, after some growls at Sylvia for having held back the uplifted arm which he thought might have saved Daniel by a well-considered blow on his captors as they entered the house, went back into his shippen – his cell for meditation and consolation, where he might hope to soothe himself before going out to his afternoon's work; labour which his master had planned for him that very morning, with a strange foresight, as Kester thought, for the job was one which would take him two or three days without needing any further directions than those he had received, and by the end of that time he thought that his master would be at liberty again. So he – so they all thought in their ignorance and inexperience.

Although Daniel himself was unreasoning, hasty, impulsive – in a word, often thinking and acting very foolishly – yet, somehow, either from some quality in his character, or from the loyalty of nature in those with whom he had to deal in his every-day life, he had made his place and position clear as the arbiter and law-giver of his household. On his decision, as that of husband, father, master, perhaps superior natures waited. So now that he was gone and had left them in such strange new circumstances so suddenly, it seemed as though neither Bell nor Sylvia knew exactly what to do when their grief was spent, so much had every household action and plan been regulated by the thought of him. Meanwhile Philip had slowly been arriving at the conclusion that he was more wanted at Monkshaven to look after Daniel's interests, to learn what were the legal probabilities in consequence of the old man's arrest, and to arrange for his family accordingly, than standing still and silent in the Haytersbank kitchen, too full of fellow-feeling and heavy foreboding to comfort, awkwardly unsympathetic in appearance from the very aching of his heart.

So when his aunt, with instinctive sense of regularity and propriety, began to put away the scarcely tasted dinner, and Sylvia, blinded with crying, and convulsively sobbing, was yet trying to help her mother, Philip took his hat, and brushing it round and round with the sleeve of his coat, said,—

'I think I'll just go back, and see how matters stand.' He had a more distinct plan in his head than these words implied, but it depended on so many contingencies of which he was ignorant that he said only these few words; and with a silent resolution to see them again that day, but a dread of being compelled to express his fears, so far beyond theirs, he went off without saying anything more. Then Sylvia lifted up her voice with a great cry. Somehow she had expected him to do something – what, she did not know, but he was gone, and they were left without stay or help.

'Hush thee, hush thee,' said her mother, trembling all over herself; 'it's for the best. The Lord knows.'

'But I niver thought he'd leave us,' moaned Sylvia, half in her mother's arms, and thinking of Philip. Her mother took the words as applied to Daniel.

'And he'd niver ha' left us, my wench, if he could ha' stayed.'

'Oh, mother, mother, it's Philip as has left us, and he could ha' stayed.'

'He'll come back, or mebbe send, I'll be bound. Leastways he'll be gone to see feyther, and he'll need comfort most on all, in a fremd place – in Bridewell* – and niver a morsel of victual or a piece o' money.' And now she sate down, and wept the dry hot tears that come with such difficulty to the eyes of the aged. And so – first one grieving, and then the other, and each draining her own heart of every possible hope by way of comfort, alternately trying to cheer and console – the February afternoon passed away; the continuous rain closing in the daylight even earlier than usual, and adding to the dreariness, with the natural accompaniments of wailing winds, coming with long sweeps over the moors, and making the sobbings at the windows that always sound like the gasps of some one in great agony. Meanwhile Philip had hastened back to Monkshaven. He had no umbrella, he had to face the driving rain for the greater part of the way; but he was thankful to the weather, for it kept men indoors, and he wanted to meet no one, but to have time to think and mature his plans. The town itself was, so to speak, in mourning. The rescue of the sailors was a distinctly popular movement; the subsequent violence (which had, indeed, gone much further than has been described, after Daniel left it) was, in general, considered as only a kind of due punishment inflicted in wild justice on the press-gang and their abettors. The feeling of the Monkshaven people was, therefore, in decided opposition to the vigorous steps taken by the county magistrates, who, in consequence of an appeal from the naval officers in charge of the impressment service, had called out the militia (from a distant and inland county) stationed within a few miles, and had thus summarily quenched the riots that were continuing on the Sunday morning after a somewhat languid fashion; the greater part of the destruction of property having been accomplished during the previous night. Still there was little doubt but that the violence would have been renewed as evening drew on, and the more desperate part of the population and the enraged sailors had had the Sabbath leisure to brood over their wrongs, and to encourage each other in a passionate attempt at redress, or revenge. So the authorities were quite justified in the decided steps they had taken, both in their own estimation then, and now, in ours, looking back on the affair in cold blood. But at the time feeling ran strongly against them; and all means of expressing itself in action being prevented, men brooded sullenly in their own houses. Philip, as the representative of the family, the head of which was now suffering for his deeds in the popular cause, would have met with more sympathy, ay, and more respect than he imagined, as he went along the streets, glancing from side to side, fearful of meeting some who would shy him as the relation of one who had been ignominiously taken to Bridewell a few hours before. But in spite of this wincing of Philip's from observation and remark, he never dreamed of acting otherwise than as became a brave true friend. And this he did, and would have done, from a natural faithfulness and constancy of disposition, without any special regard for Sylvia.

He knew his services were needed in the shop; business which he had left at a moment's warning awaited him, unfinished; but at this time he could not bear the torture of giving explanations, and alleging reasons to the languid intelligence and slow sympathies of Coulson.

He went to the offices of Mr Donkin, the oldest established and most respected attorney in Monkshaven – he who had been employed to draw up the law papers and deeds of partnership consequent on Hepburn and Coulson succeeding to the shop of John and Jeremiah Foster, Brothers.

Mr Donkin knew Philip from this circumstance. But, indeed, nearly every one in Monkshaven knew each other; if not enough to speak to, at least enough to be acquainted with the personal appearance and reputation of most of those whom they met in the streets. It so happened that Mr Donkin had a favourable opinion of Philip; and perhaps for this reason the latter had a shorter time to wait before he obtained an interview with the head of the house, than many of the clients who came for that purpose from town or country for many miles round.

Philip was ushered in. Mr Donkin sate with his spectacles pushed up on his forehead, ready to watch his countenance and listen to his words.

'Good afternoon, Mr Hepburn!'

'Good afternoon, sir.' Philip hesitated how to begin. Mr Donkin became impatient, and tapped with the fingers of his left hand on his desk. Philip's sensitive nerves felt and rightly interpreted the action.

'Please, sir, I'm come to speak to you about Daniel Robson, of Haytersbank Farm.'

'Daniel Robson?' said Mr Donkin, after a short pause, to try and compel Philip into speed in his story.

'Yes, sir. He's been taken up on account of this affair, sir, about the press-gang on Saturday night.'

'To be sure! I thought I knew the name.' And Mr Donkin's face became graver, and the expression more concentrated. Looking up suddenly at Philip, he said, 'You are aware that I am the clerk to the magistrates?'

'No, sir,' in a tone that indicated the unexpressed 'What then?'

'Well, but I am. And so of course, if you want my services or advice in favour of a prisoner whom they have committed, or are going to commit, you can't have them, that's all.'

'I am very sorry – very!' said Philip; and then he was again silent for a period; long enough to make the busy attorney impatient.

'Well, Mr Hepburn, have you anything else to say to me?'

'Yes, sir. I've a deal to ask of you; for you see I don't rightly understand what to do; and yet I'm all as Daniel's wife and daughter has to look to; and I've their grief heavy on my heart. You could not tell me what is to be done with Daniel, could you, sir?'

'He'll be brought up before the magistrates to-morrow morning for final examination, along with the others, you know, before he's sent to York Castle to take his trial at the spring assizes.'

'To York Castle, sir?'

Mr Donkin nodded, as if words were too precious to waste.

'And when will he go?' asked poor Philip, in dismay.

'To-morrow: most probably as soon as the examination is over. The evidence is clear as to his being present, aiding and abetting, – indicted on the 4th section of 1 George I., statute 1, chapter 5.* I'm afraid it's a bad look-out. Is he a friend of yours, Mr Hepburn?'

'Only an uncle, sir,' said Philip, his heart getting full; more from Mr Donkin's manner than from his words. 'But what can they do to him, sir?'

'Do?' Mr Donkin half smiled at the ignorance displayed. 'Why, hang him, to be sure; if the judge is in a hanging mood. He's been either a principal in the offence, or a principal in the second degree, and, as such, liable to the full punishment. I drew up the warrant myself this morning, though I left the exact name to be filled up by my clerk.'

'Oh, sir! can you do nothing for me?' asked Philip, with sharp beseeching in his voice. He had never imagined that it was a capital offence; and the thought of his aunt's and Sylvia's ignorance of the possible fate awaiting him whom they so much loved, was like a stab to his heart.

'No, my good fellow. I'm sorry; but, you see, it's my duty to do all I can to bring criminals to justice.'

'My uncle thought he was doing such a fine deed.'

'Demolishing and pulling down, destroying and burning dwelling-houses and outhouses,' said Mr Donkin. 'He must have some peculiar notions.'

'The people is so mad with the press-gang, and Daniel has been at sea hisself, and took it so to heart when he heard of mariners and seafaring folk being carried off, and just cheated into doing what was kind and helpful – leastways, what would have been kind and helpful, if there had been a fire. I'm against violence and riots myself, sir, I'm sure; but I cannot help thinking as Daniel had a deal to justify him on Saturday night, sir.'

'Well; you must try and get a good lawyer to bring out all that side of the question. There's a good deal to be said on it; but it's my duty to get up all the evidence to prove that he and others were present on the night in question; so, as you'll perceive, I can give you no help in defending him.'

'But who can, sir? I came to you as a friend who, I thought, would see me through it. And I don't know any other lawyer; leastways, to speak to.'

Mr Donkin was really more concerned for the misguided rioters than he was aware; and he was aware of more interest than he cared to express. So he softened his tone a little, and tried to give the best advice in his power.

'You'd better go to Edward Dawson on the other side of the river; he that was articled clerk with me two years ago, you know. He's a clever fellow, and has not too much practice; he'll do the best he can for you. He'll have to be at the court-house, tell him, to-morrow morning at ten, when the justices meet. He'll watch the case for you; and then he'll give you his opinion, and tell you what to do. You can't do better than follow his advice. I must do all I can to collect evidence for a conviction, you know.'

Philip stood up, looked at his hat, and then came forward and laid down six and eightpence on the desk in a blushing, awkward way.

'Pooh! pooh!' said Mr Donkin, pushing the money away. 'Don't be a fool; you'll need it all before the trial's over. I've done nothing, man. It would be a pretty thing for me to be feed by both parties.'

Philip took up the money, and left the room. In an instant he came back again, glanced furtively at Mr Donkin's face, and then, once more having recourse to brushing his hat, he said, in a low voice—

'You'll not be hard upon him, sir, I hope?'

'I must do my duty,' replied Mr Donkin, a little sternly, 'without any question of hardness.'

Philip, discomfited, left the room; an instant of thought and Mr Donkin had jumped up, and hastening to the door he opened it and called after Philip.

'Hepburn – Hepburn – I say, he'll be taken to York as soon as may be to-morrow morning; if any one wants to see him before then, they'd better look sharp about it.'

Philip went quickly along the streets towards Mr Dawson's, pondering upon the meaning of all that he had heard, and what he had better do. He had made his plans pretty clearly out by the time he arrived at Mr Dawson's smart door in one of the new streets on the other side of the river. A clerk as smart as the door answered Philip's hesitating knock, and replied to his inquiry as to whether Mr Dawson was at home, in the negative, adding, after a moment's pause—

'He'll be at home in less than an hour; he's only gone to

make Mrs Dawson's will – Mrs Dawson, of Collyton – she's not expected to get better.'

Probably the clerk of an older-established attorney would not have given so many particulars as to the nature of his master's employment; but, as it happened it was of no consequence, the unnecessary information made no impression on Philip's mind; he thought the matter over, and then said—

'I'll be back in an hour, then. It's gone a quarter to four; I'll be back before five, tell Mr Dawson.'

He turned on his heel and went back to the High Street as fast as he could, with a far more prompt and decided step than before. He hastened through the streets, emptied by the bad weather, to the principal inn of the town, the George – the sign of which was fastened to a piece of wood stretched across the narrow street; and going up to the bar with some timidity (for the inn was frequented by the gentry of Monkshaven and the neighbourhood, and was considered as a touch above such customers as Philip), he asked if he could have a tax-cart* made ready in a quarter of an hour, and sent up to the door of his shop.

'To be sure he could; how far was it to go?'

Philip hesitated before he replied—

'Up the Knotting Lane, to the stile leading down to Haytersbank Farm; they'll have to wait there for some as are coming.'

'They must not wait long such an evening as this; standing in such rain and wind as there'll be up there, is enough to kill a horse.'

'They shan't wait long,' said Philip, decisively: 'in a quarter of an hour, mind.'

He now went back to the shop, beating against the storm, which was increasing as the tide came in and the night hours approached.

Coulson had no word for him, but he looked reproachfully at his partner for his long, unexplained absence. Hester was putting away the ribbons and handkerchiefs, and bright-coloured things which had been used to deck the window;

for no more customers were likely to come this night through the blustering weather to a shop dimly lighted by two tallow candles and an inefficient oil-lamp. Philip came up to her, and stood looking at her with unseeing eyes; but the strange consciousness of his fixed stare made her uncomfortable, and called the faint flush to her pale cheeks, and at length compelled her, as it were, to speak, and break the spell of the silence. So, curiously enough, all three spoke at once. Hester asked (without looking at Philip)—

'Yo're sadly wet, I'm feared?'

Coulson said—

'Thou might have a bit o' news to tell one after being on the gad all afternoon.'

Philip whispered to Hester—

'Wilt come into t'. parlour? I want a word wi' thee by oursel's.'

Hester quietly finished rolling up the ribbon she had in her hands when he spoke, and then followed him into the room behind the shop before spoken of.

Philip set down on the table the candle which he had brought out of the shop, and turning round to Hester, took her trembling hand into both of his, and gripping it nervously, said—

'Oh! Hester, thou must help me – thou will, will not thou?'

Hester gulped down something that seemed to rise in her throat and choke her, before she answered.

'Anything, thou knows, Philip.'

'Yes, yes, I know. Thou sees the matter is this: Daniel Robson – he who married my aunt – is taken up for yon riot on Saturday night at t' Mariners' Arms——'

'They spoke on it this afternoon; they said the warrant was out,' said Hester, filling up the sentence as Philip hesitated, lost for an instant in his own thoughts.

'Ay! the warrant is out, and he's in t' lock-up, and will be carried to York Castle to-morrow morn; and I'm afeared it will go bad with him; and they at Haytersbank is not prepared, and they must see him again before he goes. Now,

Hester, will thou go in a tax-cart as will be here in less than ten minutes from t' George, and bring them back here, and they must stay all night for to be ready to see him to-morrow before he goes? It's dree weather for them, but they'll not mind that.'

He had used words as if he was making a request to Hester; but he did not seem to await her answer, so sure was he that she would go. She noticed this, and noticed also that the rain was spoken of in reference to them, not to her. A cold shadow passed over her heart, though it was nothing more than she already knew – that Sylvia was the one centre of his thoughts and his love.

'I'll go put on my things at once,' said she, gently.

Philip pressed her hand tenderly, a glow of gratitude overspread him.

'Thou's a real good one, God bless thee!' said he. 'Thou must take care of thyself, too,' continued he; 'there's wraps and plenty i' th' house, and if there are not, there's those i' the shop as 'll be none the worse for once wearing at such a time as this; and wrap thee well up, and take shawls and cloaks for them, and mind as they put 'em on. Thou'll have to get out at a stile, I'll tell t' driver where; and thou must get over t' stile and follow t' path down two fields, and th' house is right before ye, and bid 'em make haste and lock up th' house, for they mun stay all night here. Kester 'll look after things.'

All this time Hester was hastily putting on her hat and cloak, which she had fetched from the closet where they usually hung through the day; now she stood listening, as it were, for final directions.

'But suppose they will not come,' said she; 'they dunnot know me, and mayn't believe my words.'

'They must,' said he, impatiently. 'They don't know what awaits 'em,' he continued. 'I'll tell thee, because thou 'll not let out, and it seems as if I mun tell some one – it were such a shock – he's to be tried for 's life. They know not it's so serious; and, Hester,' said he, going on in his search after sympathy, 'she's like as if she was bound up in her father.'

His lips quivered as he looked wistfully into Hester's face at these words. No need to tell her who was *she*. No need to put into words the fact, told plainer than words could have spoken it, that his heart was bound up in Sylvia.

Hester's face, instead of responding to his look, contracted a little, and, for the life of her, she could not have helped saying,—

'Why don't yo' go yourself, Philip?'

'I can't, I can't,' said he, impatiently. 'I'd give the world to go, for I might be able to comfort her; but there's lawyers to see, and iver so much to do, and they've niver a man friend but me to do it all. You'll tell her,' said Philip, insinuatingly, as if a fresh thought had struck him, 'as how I would ha' come. I would fain ha' come for 'em, myself, but I couldn't, because of th' lawyer – mind yo' say because of th' lawyer. I'd be loath for her to think I was minding any business of my own at this time; and, whatever yo' do, speak hopeful, and, for t' life of yo', don't speak of th' hanging, it's likely it's a mistake o' Donkin's; and anyhow – there's t' cart – anyhow I should perhaps not ha' telled thee, but it's a comfort to make a clean breast to a friend at times. God bless thee, Hester. I don't know what I should ha' done without thee,' said he, as he wrapped her well up in the cart, and placed the bundles of cloaks and things by her side.

Along the street, in the jolting cart, as long as Hester could see the misty light streaming out of the shop door, so long was Philip standing bareheaded in the rain looking after her. But she knew that it was not her own poor self that attracted his lingering gaze. It was the thought of the person she was bound to.

CHAPTER XXVI

A DREARY VIGIL

THROUGH the dark rain, against the cold wind, shaken over the rough stones, went Hester in the little tax-cart. Her heart kept rising against her fate; the hot tears came unbidden to her eyes. But rebellious heart was soothed, and hot tears were sent back to their source before the time came for her alighting.

The driver turned his horse in the narrow lane, and shouted after her an injunction to make haste as, with her head bent low, she struggled down to the path to Haytersbank Farm. She saw the light in the window from the top of the brow, and involuntarily she slackened her pace. She had never seen Bell Robson, and would Sylvia recollect her? If she did not, how awkward it would be to give the explanation of who she was, and what her errand was, and why she was sent. Nevertheless, it must be done; so on she went, and standing within the little porch, she knocked faintly at the door; but in the bluster of the elements the sound was lost. Again she knocked, and now the murmur of women's voices inside was hushed, and some one came quickly to the door, and opened it sharply.

It was Sylvia. Although her face was completely in shadow, of course Hester knew her well; but she, if indeed she would have recognized Hester less disguised, did not know in the least who the woman, muffled up in a great cloak, with her hat tied down with a silk handkerchief, standing in the porch at this time of night, could be. Nor, indeed, was she in a mood to care or to inquire. She said hastily, in a voice rendered hoarse and arid with grief:

'Go away. This is no house for strangers to come to. We've enough on our own to think on;' and she hastily shut the door in Hester's face, before the latter could put together the right words in which to explain her errand. Hester stood outside in the dark, wet porch discomfited, and wondering how next to obtain a hearing through the shut and bolted door. Not long did she stand, however; some one was again at the door, talking in a voice of distress and remonstrance, and slowly unbarring the bolts. A tall, thin figure of an elderly woman was seen against the warm fire-light inside as soon as the door was opened; a hand was put out, like that which took the dove into the ark, and Hester was drawn into the warmth and the light, while Bell's voice went on speaking to Sylvia before addressing the dripping stranger—

'It's not a night to turn a dog fra' t' door; it's ill letting our grief harden our hearts. But oh! missus' (to Hester), 'yo' mun forgive us, for a great sorrow has fallen upon us this day, an' we're like beside ourselves wi' crying an' plaining.'

Bell sate down, and threw her apron over her poor worn face, as if decently to shield the signs of her misery from a stranger's gaze. Sylvia, all tear-swollen, and looking askance and almost fiercely at the stranger who had made good her intrusion, was drawn, as it were, to her mother's side, and, kneeling down by her, put her arms round her waist, and almost lay across her lap, still gazing at Hester with cold, distrustful eyes, the expression of which repelled and daunted that poor, unwilling messenger, and made her silent for a minute or so after her entrance. Bell suddenly put down her apron.

'Yo're cold and drenched,' said she. 'Come near to t' fire and warm yo'rsel'; yo' mun pardon us if we dunnot think on everything at onest.'

'Yo're very kind, very kind indeed,' said Hester, touched by the poor woman's evident effort to forget her own grief in the duties of hospitality, and loving Bell from that moment.

'I'm Hester Rose,' she continued, half addressing Sylvia, who she thought might remember the name, 'and Philip Hepburn has sent me in a tax-cart to t' stile yonder, to fetch both on yo' back to Monkshaven.' Sylvia raised her head and looked intently at Hester. Bell clasped her hands tight together and leant forwards.

'It's my master as wants us?' said she, in an eager, questioning tone.

'It's for to see yo'r master,' said Hester. 'Philip says he'll be sent to York to-morrow, and yo'll be fain to see him before he goes; and if you'll come down to Monkshaven to-night, yo'll be on t' spot again' the time comes when t' justices will let ye.'

Bell was up and about, making for the place where she

kept her out-going things, almost before Hester had begun to speak. She hardly understood about her husband's being sent to York, in the possession of the idea that she might go and see him. She did not understand or care how, in this wild night, she was to get to Monkshaven; all she thought of was, that she might go and see her husband. But Sylvia took in more points than her mother, and, almost suspiciously, began to question Hester.

'Why are they sending him to York? What made Philip leave us? Why didn't he come hissel'?'

'He couldn't come hissel', he bade me say; because he was bound to be at the lawyer's at five, about yo'r father's business. I think yo' might ha' known he would ha' come for any business of his own; and, about York, it's Philip as telled me, and I never asked why. I never thought on yo'r asking me so many questions. I thought yo'd be ready to fly on any chance o' seeing your father.' Hester spoke out the sad reproach that ran from her heart to her lips. To distrust Philip! to linger when she might hasten!

'Oh!' said Sylvia, breaking out into a wild cry, that carried with it more conviction of agony than much weeping could have done. 'I may be rude and hard, and I may ask strange questions, as if I cared for t' answers yo' may gi' me; an', in my heart o' hearts, I care for nought but to have father back wi' us, as love him so dear. I can hardly tell what I say, much less why I say it. Mother is so patient, it puts me past mysel', for I could fight wi' t' very walls, I'm so mad wi' grieving. Sure, they'll let him come back wi' us to-morrow, when they hear from his own sel' why he did it?'

She looked eagerly at Hester for an answer to this last question, which she had put in a soft, entreating tone, as if with Hester herself the decision rested. Hester shook her head. Sylvia came up to her and took her hands, almost fondling them.

'Yo' dunnot think they'll be hard wi' him when they hear all about it, done yo'? Why, York Castle's t' place they send a' t' thieves and robbers to, not honest men like feyther.'

Hester put her hand on Sylvia's shoulder with a soft, caressing gesture.

'Philip will know,' she said, using Philip's name as a kind of spell – it would have been so to her. 'Come away to Philip,' said she again, urging Sylvia, by her looks and manner, to prepare for the little journey. Sylvia moved away for this purpose, saying to herself,—

'It's going to see feyther: he will tell me all.'

Poor Mrs. Robson was collecting a few clothes for her husband with an eager, trembling hand, so trembling that article after article fell to the floor, and it was Hester who picked them up; and at last, after many vain attempts by the grief-shaken woman, it was Hester who tied the bundle, and arranged the cloak, and fastened down the hood; Sylvia standing by, not unobservant, though apparently absorbed in her own thoughts.

At length, all was arranged, and the key given over to Kester. As they passed out into the storm, Sylvia said to Hester,—

'Thou's a real good wench. Thou's fitter to be about mother than me. I'm but a cross-patch at best, an' now it's like as if I was no good to nobody.'

Sylvia began to cry, but Hester had no time to attend to her, even had she the inclination: all her care was needed to help the hasty, tottering steps of the wife who was feebly speeding up the wet and slippery brow to her husband. All Bell thought of was that 'he' was at the end of her toil. She hardly understood when she was to see him; her weary heart and brain had only received one idea – that each step she was now taking was leading her to him. Tired and exhausted with her quick walk up hill, battling all the way with wind and rain, she could hardly have held up another minute when they reached the tax-cart in the lane, and Hester had almost to lift her on to the front seat by the driver. She covered and wrapped up the poor old woman, and afterwards placed herself in the straw at the back of the cart, packed up close by the shivering, weeping Sylvia. Neither of them spoke a word at first; but Hester's tender conscience smote her for her silence before they had reached Monkshaven. She wanted to say some kind word to Sylvia, and yet knew not how to begin. Somehow, without knowing why, or reasoning upon it, she hit upon Philip's message as the best comfort in her power to give. She had delivered it before, but it had been apparently little heeded.

'Philip bade me say it was business as kept him from fetchin' yo' hissel' – business wi' the lawyer, about – about yo'r father.'

'What do they say?' said Sylvia, suddenly, lifting her bowed head, as though she would read her companion's face in the dim light.

'I dunnot know,' said Hester, sadly. They were now jolting over the paved streets, and not a word could be spoken. They were now at Philip's door, which was opened to receive them even before they arrived, as if some one had been watching and listening. The old servant, Phœbe, the fixture in the house, who had belonged to it and to the shop for the last twenty years, came out, holding a candle and sheltering it in her hand from the weather, while Philip helped the tottering steps of Mrs Robson as she descended behind. As Hester had got in last, so she had now to be the first to move. Just as she was moving, Sylvia's cold little hand was laid on her arm.

'I am main* and thankful to yo'. I ask yo'r pardon for speaking cross, but, indeed, my heart's a'most broken wi' fear about feyther.'

The voice was so plaintive, so full of tears, that Hester could not but yearn towards the speaker. She bent over and kissed her cheek, and then clambered unaided down by the wheel on the dark side of the cart. Wistfully she longed for one word of thanks or recognition from Philip, in whose service she had performed this hard task; but he was otherwise occupied, and on casting a further glance back as she turned the corner of the street, she saw Philip lifting Sylvia carefully down in his arms from her footing on the top of the wheel, and then they all went into the light and the warmth, the door was shut, the lightened cart drove briskly away, and

Hester, in rain, and cold, and darkness, went homewards with her tired sad heart.

Philip had done all he could, since his return from lawyer Dawson's, to make his house bright and warm for the reception of his beloved. He had a strong apprehension of the probable fate of poor Daniel Robson; he had a warm sympathy with the miserable distress of the wife and daughter; but still at the back of his mind his spirits danced as if this was to them a festal occasion. He had even taken unconscious pleasure in Phœbe's suspicious looks and tones, as he had hurried and superintended her in her operations. A fire blazed cheerily in the parlour, almost dazzling to the travellers brought in from the darkness and the rain; candles burned – two candles, much to Phœbe's discontent. Poor Bell Robson had to sit down almost as soon as she entered the room, so worn out was she with fatigue and excitement; yet she grudged every moment which separated her, as she thought, from her husband.

'I'm ready now,' said she, standing up, and rather repulsing Sylvia's cares; 'I'm ready now,' said she, looking eagerly at Philip, as if for him to lead the way.

'It's not to-night,' replied he, almost apologetically. 'You can't see him to-night; it's to-morrow morning before he goes to York; it was better for yo' to be down here in town ready; and beside I didn't know when I sent for ye that he was locked up for the night.'

'Well-a-day, well-a-day,' said Bell, rocking herself backwards and forwards, and trying to soothe herself with these words. Suddenly she said,—

'But I've brought his comforter* wi' me – his red woollen comforter as he's allays slept in this twelvemonth past; he'll get his rheumatiz again; oh, Philip, cannot I get it to him?'

'I'll send it by Phœbe,' said Philip, who was busy making tea, hospitable and awkward.

'Cannot I take it mysel'?' repeated Bell. 'I could make surer nor anybody else; they'd maybe not mind yon woman – Phœbe d'ye call her?'

'Nay, mother,' said Sylvia, 'thou's not fit to go.'

'Shall I go?' asked Philip, hoping she would say 'no,' and be content with Phœbe, and leave him where he was.

'Oh, Philip, would yo'?' said Sylvia, turning round.

'Ay,' said Bell, 'if thou would take it they'd be minding yo'.'

So there was nothing for it but for him to go, in the first flush of his delightful rites of hospitality.

'It's not far,' said he, consoling himself rather than them. 'I'll be back in ten minutes, the tea is maskit,* and Phœbe will take yo'r wet things and dry 'em by t' kitchen fire; and here's the stairs,' opening a door in the corner of the room, from which the stairs immediately ascended. 'There's two rooms at the top; that to t' left is all made ready, t' other is mine,' said he, reddening a little as he spoke. Bell was busy undoing her bundle with trembling fingers.

'Here,' said she; 'and oh, lad, here's a bit o' peppermint cake; he's main and fond on it, and I catched sight on it by good luck just t' last minute.'

Philip was gone, and the excitement of Bell and Sylvia flagged once more, and sank into wondering despondency. Sylvia, however, roused herself enough to take off her mother's wet clothes, and she took them timidly into the kitchen and arranged them before Phœbe's fire.

Phœbe opened her lips once or twice to speak in remonstrance, and then, with an effort, gulped her words down; for her sympathy, like that of all the rest of the Monkshaven world, was in favour of Daniel Robson; and his daughter might place her dripping cloak this night wherever she would, for Phœbe.

Sylvia found her mother still sitting on the chair next the door, where she had first placed herself on entering the room.

'I'll gi'e you some tea, mother,' said she, struck with the shrunken look of Bell's face.

'No, no' said her mother. 'It's not manners for t' help oursel's.'

'I'm sure Philip would ha' wished yo' for to take it,' said Sylvia, pouring out a cup.

Just then he returned, and something in his look, some

dumb expression of delight at her occupation, made her blush and hesitate for an instant; but then she went on, and made a cup of tea ready, saying something a little incoherent all the time about her mother's need of it. After tea Bell Robson's weariness became so extreme, that Philip and Sylvia urged her to go to bed. She resisted a little, partly out of 'manners,' and partly because she kept fancying, poor woman, that somehow or other her husband might send for her. But about seven o'clock Sylvia persuaded her to come upstairs. Sylvia, too, bade Philip good-night, and his look followed the last wave of her dress as she disappeared up the stairs; then leaning his chin on his hand, he gazed at vacancy and thought deeply – for how long he knew not, so intent was his mind on the chances of futurity.

He was aroused by Sylvia's coming downstairs into the sitting-room again. He started up.

'Mother is so shivery,' said she. 'May I go in there,' indicating the kitchen, 'and make her a drop of gruel?'

'Phœbe shall make it, not you,' said Philip, eagerly preventing her, by going to the kitchen door and giving his orders. When he turned round again, Sylvia was standing over the fire, leaning her head against the stone mantel-piece for the comparative coolness. She did not speak at first, or take any notice of him. He watched her furtively, and saw that she was crying, the tears running down her cheeks, and she too much absorbed in her thoughts to wipe them away with her apron.

While he was turning over in his mind what he could best say to comfort her (his heart, like hers, being almost too full for words), she suddenly looked him full in the face, saying,—

'Philip! won't they soon let him go? what can they do to him?' Her open lips trembled while awaiting his answer, the tears came up and filled her eyes. It was just the question he had most dreaded; it led to the terror that possessed his own mind, but which he had hoped to keep out of hers. He hesitated. 'Speak, lad!' said she, impatiently, with a little passionate gesture. 'I can see thou knows!'

He had only made it worse by consideration; he rushed blindfold at a reply.

'He's ta'en up for felony.'

'Felony,' said she. 'There thou're out; he's in for letting yon men out; thou may call it rioting if thou's a mind to set folks again' him, but it's too bad to cast such hard words at him as yon – felony,' she repeated, in a half-offended tone.

'It's what the lawyers call it,' said Philip, sadly; 'it's no word o' mine.'

'Lawyers is allays for making the worst o' things,' said she, a little pacified, 'but folks shouldn't allays believe them.'

'It's lawyers as has to judge i' t' long run.'

'Cannot the justices, Mr Harter and them as is no lawyers, give him a sentence to-morrow, wi'out sending him to York?'

'No!' said Philip, shaking his head. He went to the kitchen door and asked if the gruel was not ready, so anxious was he to stop the conversation at this point; but Phœbe, who held her young master in but little respect, scolded him for a stupid man, who thought, like all his sex, that gruel was to be made in a minute, whatever the fire was, and bade him come and make it for himself if he was in such a hurry.

He had to return discomfited to Sylvia, who meanwhile had arranged her thoughts ready to return to the charge.

'And say he's sent to York, and say he's tried theere, what's t' worst they can do again' him?' asked she, keeping down her agitation to look at Philip the more sharply. Her eyes never slackened their penetrating gaze at his countenance, until he replied, with the utmost unwillingness, and most apparent confusion,—

'They may send him to Botany Bay.'*

He knew that he held back a worse contingency, and he was mortally afraid that she would perceive this reserve. But what he did say was so much beyond her utmost apprehension, which had only reached to various terms of imprisonment, that she did not imagine the dark shadow lurking behind. What he had said was too much for her. Her eyes dilated, her lips blanched, her pale cheeks grew yet paler. After a minute's look into his face, as if fascinated by some horror, she stumbled backwards into the chair in the chimney corner, and covered her face with her hands, moaning out some inarticulate words.

Philip was on his knees by her, dumb from excess of sympathy, kissing her dress, all unfelt by her; he murmured half-words, he began passionate sentences that died away upon his lips; and she – she thought of nothing but her father, and was possessed and rapt out of herself by the dread of losing him to that fearful country which was almost like the grave to her, so all but impassable was the gulf. But Philip knew that it was possible that the separation impending might be that of the dark, mysterious grave – that the gulf between the father and child might indeed be that which no living, breathing, warm human creature can ever cross.

'Sylvie, Sylvie!' said he, – and all their conversation had to be carried on in low tones and whispers, for fear of the listening ears above, – 'don't – don't, thou'rt rending my heart. Oh, Sylvie, hearken. There's not a thing I'll not do; there's not a penny I've got, – th' last drop of blood that's in me, – I'll give up my life for his.'

'Life,' said she, putting down her hands, and looking at him as if her looks could pierce his soul; 'who talks o' touching his life? Thou're going crazy, Philip, I think;' but she did not think so, although she would fain have believed it. In her keen agony she read his thoughts as though they were an open page; she sate there, upright and stony, the conviction creeping over her face like the grey shadow of death. No more tears, no more trembling, almost no more breathing. He could not bear to see her, and yet she held his eyes, and he feared to make the effort necessary to move or to turn away, lest the shunning motion should carry conviction to her heart. Alas! conviction of the probable danger to her father's life was already there: it was that that was calming her down, tightening her muscles, bracing her nerves. In that hour she lost all her early youth.

'Then he may be hung,' said she, low and solemnly, after a long pause. Philip turned away his face, and did not utter a word. Again deep silence, broken only by some homely sound in the kitchen. 'Mother must not know on it,' said Sylvia, in the same tone in which she had spoken before.

'It's t' worst as can happen to him,' said Philip. 'More likely he'll be transported: maybe he'll be brought in innocent after all.'

'No,' said Sylvia, heavily, as one without hope – as if she were reading some dreadful doom in the tablets of the awful future. 'They'll hang him. Oh, feyther! feyther!' she choked out, almost stuffing her apron into her mouth to deaden the sound, and catching at Philip's hand, and wringing it with convulsive force, till the pain that he loved was nearly more than he could bear. No words of his could touch such agony; but irrepressibly, and as he would have done it to a wounded child, he bent over her, and kissed her with a tender, trembling kiss. She did not repulse it, probably she did not even perceive it.

At that moment Phœbe came in with the gruel. Philip saw her, and knew, in an instant, what the old woman's conclusion must needs be; but Sylvia had to be shaken by the now standing Philip, before she could be brought back to the least consciousness of the present time. She lifted up her white face to understand his words, then she rose up like one who slowly comes to the use of her limbs.

'I suppose I mun go,' she said: 'but I'd sooner face the dead. If she asks me, Philip, what mun I say?'

'She'll not ask yo',' said he, 'if yo' go about as common. She's never asked yo' all this time, an' if she does, put her on to me. I'll keep it from her as long as I can; I'll manage better nor I've done wi' thee, Sylvie,' said he, with a sad, faint smile, looking with fond penitence at her altered countenance.

'Thou mustn't blame thysel',' said Sylvia, seeing his regret. 'I brought it on me mysel'; I thought I would ha' t' truth, whativer came on it, and now I'm not strong enough to stand it, God help me!' she continued, piteously.

'Oh, Sylvie, let me help yo'! I cannot do what God can, – I'm not meaning that, but I can do next to Him of any man. I have loved yo' for years an' years, in a way it's terrible to think on, if my love can do nought now to comfort yo' in your sore distress.'

'Cousin Philip,' she replied, in the same measured tone in which she had always spoken since she had learnt the extent of her father's danger, and the slow stillness of her words was in harmony with the stony look of her face, 'thou's a comfort to me, I couldn't bide my life without thee; but I cannot take in the thought o' love, it seems beside me quite; I can think on nought but them that is quick and them that is dead.'

CHAPTER XXVII

GLOOMY DAYS

PHILIP had money in the Fosters' bank, not so much as it might have been if he had not had to pay for the furniture in his house. Much of this furniture was old, and had belonged to the brothers Foster, and they had let Philip have it at a very reasonable rate; but still the purchase of it had diminished the amount of his savings. But on the sum which he possessed he drew largely – he drew all – nay, he overdrew his account somewhat, to his former master's dismay, although the kindness of their hearts overruled the harder arguments of their heads.

All was wanted to defend Daniel Robson at the approaching York assizes. His wife had handed over to Philip all the money or money's worth she could lay her hands upon. Daniel himself was not one to be much beforehand with the world; but to Bell's thrifty imagination the round golden guineas, tied up in the old stocking-foot against rent-day, seemed a mint of money on which Philip might draw infinitely. As yet she did not comprehend the extent of her husband's danger. Sylvia went about like one in a dream, keeping back the hot tears that might interfere with the course of life she had prescribed for herself in that terrible hour when she first learnt all. Every penny of money either she or her mother could save went to Philip. Kester's hoard, too, was placed in Hepburn's hands at Sylvia's earnest entreaty; for Kester had no great opinion of Philip's judgment, and would rather have taken his money straight himself to Mr Dawson, and begged him to use it for his master's behoof.

Indeed, if anything, the noiseless breach between Kester and Philip had widened of late. It was seed-time, and Philip, in his great anxiety for every possible interest that might affect Sylvia, and also as some distraction from his extreme anxiety about her father, had taken to study agriculture of an evening in some old books which he had borrowed – *The Farmer's Complete Guide*,* and such like; and from time to time he came down upon the practical dogged Kester with directions gathered from the theories in his books. Of course the two fell out, but without many words. Kester persevered in his old ways, making light of Philip and his books in manner and action, till at length Philip withdrew from the contest. 'Many a man may lead a horse to water, but there's few can make him drink,' and Philip certainly was not one of those few. Kester, indeed, looked upon him with jealous eyes on many accounts. He had favoured Charley Kinraid as a lover of Sylvia's; and though he had no idea of the truth – though he believed in the drowning of the specksioneer as much as any one – yet the year which had elapsed since Kinraid's supposed death was but a very short while to the middle-aged man, who forgot how slowly time passes with the young; and he could often have scolded Sylvia, if the poor girl had been a whit less heavy at heart than she was, for letting Philip come so much about her – come, though it was on her father's business. For the darkness of their common dread drew them together, occasionally to the comparative exclusion of Bell and Kester, which the latter perceived and resented. Kester even allowed himself to go so far as to wonder what Philip could want with all the money, which to him seemed unaccountable; and once or twice the ugly thought crossed his mind, that shops conducted by young men were often not so profitable as when guided by older heads, and that some of the coin poured into Philip's keeping might have another destination than the defence of his master. Poor Philip! and he was spending all his own, and more than all his own money, and no one ever knew it, as he had bound down his friendly bankers to secrecy.

Once only Kester ventured to speak to Sylvia on the subject of Philip. She had followed her cousin to the field just in front of their house, just outside the porch, to ask him some question she dared not put in her mother's presence – (Bell, indeed, in her anxiety, usually absorbed all the questions when Philip came) – and stood, after Philip had bid her good-by, hardly thinking about him at all, but looking unconsciously after him as he ascended the brow; and at the top he had turned to take a last glance at the place his love inhabited, and, seeing her, he had waved his hat in gratified farewell. She, meanwhile, was roused from far other thoughts than of him, and of his now acknowledged love, by the motion against the sky, and was turning back into the house when she heard Kester's low hoarse call, and saw him standing at the shippen door.

'Come hither, wench,' said he, indignantly; 'is this a time for courtin'?'

'Courting?' said she, drawing up her head, and looking back at him with proud defiance.

'Ay, courtin'! what other mak' o' thing is't when thou's gazin' after yon meddlesome chap, as if thou'd send thy eyes after him, and he making marlocks back at thee? It's what we ca'ed courtin' i' my young days anyhow. And it's noane a time for a wench to go courtin' when her feyther's i' prison,' said he, with a consciousness as he uttered these last words that he was cruel and unjust and going too far, yet carried on to say them by his hot jealousy against Philip.

Sylvia continued looking at him without speaking: she was too much offended for expression.

'Thou may glower an' thou may look, lass,' said he, 'but a'd thought better on thee. It's like last week thy last sweetheart were drowned; but thou's not one to waste time i' rememberin' them as is gone – if, indeed, thou iver cared a button for yon Kinraid – if it wasn't a make-believe.'

Her lips were contracted and drawn up, showing her small glittering teeth, which were scarcely apart as she breathed out—

'Thou thinks so, does thou, that I've forgetten *him?* Thou'd better have a care o' thy tongue.'

Then, as if fearful that her self-command might give way, she turned into the house; and going through the kitchen like a blind person, she went up to her now unused chamber, and threw herself, face downwards, flat on her bed, almost smothering herself.

Ever since Daniel's committal, the decay that had imperceptibly begun in his wife's bodily and mental strength during her illness of the previous winter, had been making quicker progress. She lost her reticence of speech, and often talked to herself. She had not so much forethought as of old; slight differences, it is true, but which, with some others of the same description, gave foundation for the homely expression which some now applied to Bell, 'She'll never be t' same woman again.'

This afternoon she had cried herself to sleep in her chair after Philip's departure. She had not heard Sylvia's sweeping passage through the kitchen; but half an hour afterwards she was startled up by Kester's abrupt entry.

'Where's Sylvie?' asked he.

'I don't know,' said Bell, looking scared, and as if she was ready to cry. 'It's no news about him?' said she, standing up, and supporting herself on the stick she was now accustomed to use.

'Bless yo', no, dunnot be afeared, missus; it's only as a spoke hasty to t' wench, an' a want t' tell her as a'm sorry,' said Kester, advancing into the kitchen, and looking round for Sylvia.

'Sylvie, Sylvie!' shouted he; 'she mun be i' t' house.'

Sylvia came slowly down the stairs, and stood before him. Her face was pale, her mouth set and determined; the light of her eyes veiled in gloom. Kester shrank from her look, and even more from her silence.

'A'm come to ax pardon,' said he, after a little pause.

She was still silent.

'A'm noane above axing pardon, though a'm fifty and more, and thee's but a silly wench, as a've nursed i' my arms. A'll say before thy mother as a ought niver to ha' used them words, and as how a'm sorry for 't.'

'I don't understand it all,' said Bell, in a hurried and perplexed tone. 'What has Kester been saying, my lass?' she added, turning to Sylvia.

Sylvia went a step or two nearer to her mother, and took hold of her hand as if to quieten her; then facing once more round, she said deliberately to Kester,—

'If thou wasn't Kester, I'd niver forgive thee. Niver,' she added, with bitterness, as the words he had used recurred to her mind. 'It's in me to hate thee now, for saying what thou did; but thou're dear old Kester after all, and I can't help mysel', I mun needs forgive thee,' and she went towards him. He took her little head between his horny hands and kissed it. She looked up with tears in her eyes, saying softly,—

'Niver say things like them again. Niver speak on——'

'A'll bite my tongue off first,' he interrupted.

He kept his word.

In all Philip's comings and goings to and from Haytersbank Farm at this time, he never spoke again of his love. In look, words, manner, he was like a thoughtful, tender brother; nothing more. He could be nothing more in the presence of the great dread which loomed larger upon him after every conversation with the lawyer.

For Mr Donkin had been right in his prognostication. Government took up the attack on the Rendezvous with a high and heavy hand. It was necessary to assert authority which had been of late too often braved. An example must be made, to strike dismay into those who opposed and defied the press-gang; and all the minor authorities who held their powers from Government were in a similar manner severe and relentless in the execution of their duty. So the attorney, who went over to see the prisoner in York Castle, told Philip. He added that Daniel still retained his pride in his achievement, and could not be brought to understand the dangerous position in which he was placed; that when pressed and questioned as to circumstances that might possibly be used in his defence, he always wandered off to accounts of previous outrages committed by the press-gang, or to passionate abuse of the trick by which men had been lured from their homes on the night in question to assist in putting out an imaginary fire, and then seized and carried off. Some of this very natural indignation might possibly have some effect on the jury; and this seemed the only ground of hope, and was indeed a slight one, as the judge was likely to warn the jury against allowing their natural sympathy in such a case to divert their minds from the real question.*

Such was the substance of what Philip heard, and heard repeatedly, during his many visits to Mr Dawson. And now the time of trial drew near; for the York assizes opened on March the twelfth; not much above three weeks since the offence was committed which took Daniel from his home and placed him in peril of death.

Philip was glad that, the extremity of his danger never having been hinted to Bell, and travelling some forty miles* being a most unusual exertion at that time to persons of her class, the idea of going to see her husband at York had never suggested itself to Bell's mind. Her increasing feebleness made this seem a step only to be taken in case of the fatal extreme necessity; such was the conclusion that both Sylvia and he had come to; and it was the knowledge of this that made Sylvia strangle her own daily longing to see her father. Not but that her hopes were stronger than her fears. Philip never told her the causes for despondency; she was young, and she, like her father, could not understand how fearful sometimes is the necessity for prompt and severe punishment of rebellion against authority.

Philip was to be in York during the time of the assizes; and it was understood, almost without words, that if the terrible worst occurred, the wife and daughter were to come to York as soon as might be. For this end Philip silently made all the necessary arrangements before leaving Monkshaven. The sympathy of all men was with him; it was too large an occasion for Coulson to be anything but magnanimous. He urged Philip to take all the time requisite; to leave all business cares to him. And as Philip went about pale and sad, there was another cheek that grew paler still, another eye that filled with quiet tears as his heaviness of heart became more and more apparent. The day for opening the assizes came on. Philip was in York Minster, watching the solemn antique procession in which the highest authority in the county accompanies the judges to the House of the Lord, to be there admonished as to the nature of their duties. As Philip listened to the sermon with a strained and beating heart, his hopes rose higher than his fears for the first time, and that evening he wrote his first letter to Sylvia.

'Dear Sylvia,

'It will be longer first than I thought for. Mr Dawson says Tuesday in next week. But keep up your heart. I have been hearing the sermon to-day which is preached to the judges; and the clergyman said so much in it about mercy and forgiveness, I think they cannot fail to be lenient this assize. I have seen uncle, who looks but thin, but is in good heart: only he will keep saying he would do it over again if he had the chance, which neither Mr Dawson nor I think is wise in him, in especial as the gaoler is by and hears every word as is said. He was very fain of hearing all about home; and wants you to rear Daisy's calf, as he thinks she will prove a good one. He bade me give his best love to you and my aunt, and his kind duty to Kester.

'Sylvia, will you try and forget how I used to scold you about your writing and spelling, and just write me two or three lines. I think I would rather have them badly spelt than not, because then I shall be sure they are yours. And never mind about capitals; I was a fool to say such a deal about them, for a man does just as well without them. A letter from you would do a vast to keep me patient all these days till Tuesday. Direct—

'Mr Philip Hepburn,
'Care of Mr Fraser, Draper,
'Micklegate, York.

'My affectionate duty to my aunt.

'Your respectful cousin and servant,

'PHILIP HEPBURN.

'P.S. The sermon was grand. The text was Zechariah vii. 9, "Execute true judgment and show mercy." God grant it may have put mercy into the judge's heart as is to try my uncle.'

Heavily the days passed over. On Sunday Bell and Sylvia went to church, with a strange, half-superstitious feeling, as if they could propitiate the Most High to order the events in their favour by paying Him the compliment of attending to duties in their time of sorrow which they had too often neglected in their prosperous days.

But He 'who knoweth our frame, and remembereth that we are dust,'* took pity upon His children, and sent some of His blessed peace into their hearts, else they could scarce have endured the agony of suspense of those next hours. For as they came slowly and wearily home from church, Sylvia could no longer bear her secret, but told her mother of the peril in which Daniel stood. Cold as the March wind blew, they had not felt it, and had sate down on a hedgebank for Bell to rest. And then Sylvia spoke, trembling and sick for fear, yet utterly unable to keep silence any longer. Bell heaved up her hands, and let them fall down on her knees before she replied.

'The Lord is above us,' said she, solemnly. 'He has sent a fear o' this into my heart afore now. I niver breathed it to thee, my lass——'

'And I niver spoke on it to thee, mother, because——'

Sylvia choked with crying, and laid her head on her mother's lap, feeling that she was no longer the strong one, and the protector, but the protected. Bell went on, stroking her head,

'The Lord is like a tender nurse as weans a child to look on and to like what it lothed once. He has sent me dreams as has prepared me for this, if so be it comes to pass.'

'Philip is hopeful,' said Sylvia, raising her head and looking through her tears at her mother.

'Ay, he is. And I cannot tell, but I think it's not for nought as the Lord has ta'en away all fear o' death out o' my heart. I think He means as Daniel and me is to go hand-in-hand through the valley – like as we walked up to our wedding in Crosthwaite Church. I could never guide th' house without Daniel, and I should be feared he'd take a deal more nor is good for him without me.'

'But me, mother, thou's forgetting me,' moaned out Sylvia. 'Oh, mother, mother, think on me!'

'Nay, my lass, I'm noane forgetting yo'. I'd a sore heart a' last winter a-thinking on thee, when that chap Kinraid were hanging about thee. I'll noane speak ill on the dead, but I were uneasylike. But sin' Philip and thee seem to ha' made it up——'

Sylvia shivered, and opened her mouth to speak, but did not say a word.

'And sin' the Lord has been comforting me, and talking to me many a time when thou's thought I were asleep, things has seemed to redd theirselves up,* and if Daniel goes, I'm ready to follow. I could niver stand living to hear folks say he'd been hung; it seems so unnatural and shameful.'

'But, mother, he won't! – he shan't be hung!' said Sylvia, springing to her feet. 'Philip says he won't.'

Bell shook her head. They walked on, Sylvia both disheartened and almost irritated at her mother's despondency. But before they went to bed at night Bell said things which seemed as though the morning's feelings had been but temporary, and as if she was referring every decision to the period of her husband's return. 'When father comes home,' seemed a sort of burden at the beginning or end of every sentence, and this reliance on his certain coming back to them was almost as great a trial to Sylvia as the absence of all hope had been in the morning. But that instinct told her that her mother was becoming incapable of argument, she would have asked her why her views were so essentially changed in so few hours. This inability of reason in poor Bell made Sylvia feel very desolate.

Monday passed over – how, neither of them knew, for

neither spoke of what was filling the thoughts of both. Before it was light on Tuesday morning, Bell was astir.

'It's very early, mother,' said weary, sleepy Sylvia, dreading returning consciousness.

'Ay, lass!' said Bell, in a brisk, cheerful tone; 'but he'll, maybe, be home to-night, and I'se bound to have all things ready for him.'

'Anyhow,' said Sylvia, sitting up in bed, 'he couldn't come home to-night.'

'Tut, lass! thou doesn't know how quick a man comes home to wife and child. I'll be a' ready at any rate.'

She hurried about in a way which Sylvia wondered to see; till at length she fancied that perhaps her mother did so to drive away thought. Every place was cleaned; there was scarce time allowed for breakfast; till at last, long before mid-day, all the work was done, and the two sat down to their spinning-wheels. Sylvia's spirits sank lower and lower at each speech of her mother's, from whose mind all fear seemed to have disappeared, leaving only a strange restless kind of excitement.

'It's time for t' potatoes,' said Bell, after her wool had snapped many a time from her uneven tread.

'Mother,' said Sylvia, 'it's but just gone ten!'

'Put 'em on,' said Bell, without attending to the full meaning of her daughter's words. 'It'll, maybe, hasten t' day on if we get dinner done betimes.'

'But Kester is in t' Far Acre field, and he'll not be home till noon.'

This seemed to settle matters for a while; but then Bell pushed her wheel away, and began searching for her hood and cloak. Sylvia found them for her, and then asked sadly—

'What does ta want 'em for, mother?'

'I'll go up t' brow and through t' field, and just have a look down t' lane.'

'I'll go wi' thee,' said Sylvia, feeling all the time the uselessness of any looking for intelligence from York so early in the day. Very patiently did she wait by her mother's side during the long half-hour which Bell spent in gazing down the road for those who never came.

When they got home Sylvia put the potatoes on to boil; but when dinner was ready and the three were seated at the dresser, Bell pushed her plate away from her, saying it was so long after dinner time that she was past eating. Kester would have said something about its being only half-past twelve, but Sylvia gave him a look beseeching silence, and he went on with his dinner without a word, only brushing away the tears from his eyes with the back of his hand from time to time.

'A'll noane go far fra' home t' rest o' t' day,' said he, in a whisper to Sylvia, as he went out.

'Will this day niver come to an end?' cried Bell, plaintively.

'Oh, mother! it'll come to an end some time, never fear. I've heerd say—

> "Be the day weary or be the day long,
> At length it ringeth to even-song." '*

'To even-song – to even-song,' repeated Bell. 'D'ye think now that even-song means death, Sylvie?'

'I cannot tell – I cannot bear it. Mother,' said Sylvia, in despair, 'I'll make some clap-bread: that's a heavy job, and will while away t' afternoon.'

'Ay, do!' replied the mother. 'He'll like it fresh – he'll like it fresh.'

Murmuring and talking to herself, she fell into a doze, from which Sylvia was careful not to disturb her.

The days were now getting long, although as cold as ever; and at Haytersbank Farm the light lingered, as there was no near horizon to bring on early darkness. Sylvia had all ready for her mother's tea against she wakened; but she slept on and on, the peaceful sleep of a child, and Sylvia did not care to waken her. Just after the sun had set, she saw Kester outside the window making signs to her to come out. She stole out on tip-toe by the back-kitchen, the door of which was standing open. She almost ran against Philip, who did not perceive her, as he was awaiting her coming the other way round the corner of the house, and who turned upon her a face whose import she read in an instant. 'Philip!' was all she said, and then she fainted at his feet, coming down with a heavy bang on the round paving stones of the yard.

'Kester! Kester!' he cried, for she looked like one dead, and with all his strength the wearied man could not lift her and carry her into the house.

With Kester's help she was borne into the back-kitchen, and Kester rushed to the pump for some cold water to throw over her.

While Philip, kneeling at her head, was partly supporting her in his arms, and heedless of any sight or sound, the shadow of some one fell upon him. He looked up and saw his aunt; the old dignified, sensible expression on her face, exactly like her former self, composed, strong, and calm.

'My lass,' said she, sitting down by Philip, and gently taking her out of his arms into her own. 'Lass, bear up! we mun bear up, and be agait on our way to him, he'll be needing us now. Bear up, my lass! the Lord will give us strength. We mun go to him; ay, time's precious; thou mun cry thy cry at after!'

Sylvia opened her dim eyes, and heard her mother's voice; the ideas came slowly into her mind, and slowly she rose up, standing still, like one who has been stunned, to regain her strength; and then, taking hold of her mother's arm, she said, in a soft, strange voice—

'Let's go. I'm ready.'

CHAPTER XXVIII

THE ORDEAL

It was the afternoon of an April day in that same year, and the sky was blue above, with little sailing white clouds catching the pleasant sunlight. The earth in that northern country had scarcely yet put on her robe of green. The few trees grew near brooks running down from the moors and the higher ground. The air was full of pleasant sounds prophesying of the coming summer. The rush, and murmur, and tinkle of the hidden watercourses; the song of the lark poised high up in the sunny air; the bleat of the lambs calling to their mothers – everything inanimate was full of hope and gladness.

For the first time for a mournful month the front door of Haytersbank Farm was open; the warm spring air might enter, and displace the sad dark gloom, if it could. There was a newly-lighted fire in the unused grate; and Kester was in the kitchen, with his clogs off his feet, so as not to dirty the spotless floor, stirring here and there, and trying in his awkward way to make things look home-like and cheerful. He had brought in some wild daffodils which he had been to seek in the dawn, and he placed them in a jug on the dresser. Dolly Reid, the woman who had come to help Sylvia during her mother's illness a year ago, was attending to something in the back-kitchen, making a noise among the milk-cans, and singing a ballad to herself as she worked; yet every now and then she checked herself in her singing, as if a sudden recollection came upon her that this was neither the time nor the place for songs. Once or twice she took up the funeral psalm which is sung by the bearers of the body in that country—

Our God, our help in ages past.*

But it was of no use: the pleasant April weather out of doors, and perhaps the natural spring in the body, disposed her nature to cheerfulness, and insensibly she returned to her old ditty.

Kester was turning over many things in his rude honest mind as he stood there, giving his finishing touches every now and then to the aspect of the house-place, in preparation for the return of the widow and daughter of his old master.

It was a month and more since they had left home; more than a fortnight since Kester, with three halfpence in his pocket, had set out after his day's work to go to York – to walk all night long, and to wish Daniel Robson his last farewell.

Daniel had tried to keep up and had brought out one or two familiar, thread-bare, well-worn jokes, such as he had made Kester chuckle over many a time and oft, when the two had been together afield or in the shippen at the home which he should never more see. But no 'Old Grouse in the gunroom'* could make Kester smile, or do anything except groan in but a heart-broken sort of fashion, and presently the talk had become more suitable to the occasion, Daniel being up to the last the more composed of the two; for Kester, when turned out of the condemned cell, fairly broke down into the heavy sobbing he had never thought to sob again on earth. He had left Bell and Sylvia in their lodging at York, under Philip's care; he dared not go to see them; he could not trust himself; he had sent them his duty, and bade Philip tell Sylvia that the game-hen had brought out fifteen chickens at a hatch.

Yet although Kester sent this message through Philip – although he saw and recognized all that Philip was doing in their behalf, in the behalf of Daniel Robson, the condemned felon, his honoured master – he liked Hepburn not a whit better than he had done before all this sorrow had come upon them.

Philip had, perhaps, shown a want of tact in his conduct to Kester. Acute with passionate keenness in one direction, he had a sort of dull straightforwardness in all others. For instance, he had returned Kester the money which the latter had so gladly advanced towards the expenses incurred in defending Daniel. Now the money which Philip gave him back was part of an advance which Foster Brothers had made on Philip's own account. Philip had thought that it was hard on Kester to lose his savings in a hopeless cause, and had made a point of repaying the old man; but Kester would far rather have felt that the earnings of the sweat of his brow had gone in the attempt to save his master's life than have had twice ten times as many golden guineas.

Moreover, it seemed to take his action in lending his hoard

out of the sphere of love, and make it but a leaden common loan, when it was Philip who brought him the sum, not Sylvia, into whose hands he had given it.

With these feelings Kester felt his heart shut up as he saw the long-watched-for two coming down the little path with a third person; with Philip holding up the failing steps of poor Bell Robson, as, loaded with her heavy mourning, and feeble from the illness which had detained her in York ever since the day of her husband's execution, she came faltering back to her desolate home. Sylvia was also occupied in attending to her mother; one or twice, when they paused a little, she and Philip spoke, in the familiar way in which there is no coyness nor reserve. Kester caught up his clogs, and went quickly out through the back-kitchen into the farmyard, not staying to greet them, as he had meant to do; and yet it was dull-sighted of him not to have perceived that whatever might be the relations between Philip and Sylvia, he was sure to have accompanied them home; for, alas! he was the only male protector of their blood remaining in the world. Poor Kester, who would fain have taken that office upon himself, chose to esteem himself cast off, and went heavily about the farmyard, knowing that he ought to go in and bid such poor welcome as he had to offer, yet feeling too much to like to show himself before Philip.

It was long, too, before any one had leisure to come and seek him. Bell's mind had flashed up for a time, till the fatal day, only to be reduced by her subsequent illness into complete and hopeless childishness. It was all Philip and Sylvia could do to manage her in the first excitement of returning home; her restless inquiry for him who would never more be present in the familiar scene, her feverish weariness and uneasiness, all required tender soothing and most patient endurance of her refusals to be satisfied with what they said or did.

At length she took some food, and, refreshed by it, and warmed by the fire, she sank asleep in her chair. Then Philip would fain have spoken with Sylvia before the hour came at which he must return to Monkshaven, but she eluded him, and went in search of Kester, whose presence she had missed.

She had guessed some of the causes which kept him from greeting them on their first return. But it was not as if she had shaped these causes into the definite form of words. It is astonishing to look back and find how differently constituted were the minds of most people fifty or sixty years ago; they felt, they understood, without going through reasoning or analytic processes, and if this was the case among the more educated people, of course it was still more so in the class to which Sylvia belonged. She knew by some sort of intuition that if Philip accompanied them home (as, indeed, under the circumstances, was so natural as to be almost unavoidable), the old servant and friend of the family would absent himself; and so she slipped away at the first possible moment to go in search of him. There he was in the farm-yard, leaning over the gate that opened into the home-field, apparently watching the poultry that scratched and pecked at the new-springing grass with the utmost relish. A little farther off were the ewes with their new-dropped lambs, beyond that the great old thorn-tree with its round fresh clusters of buds, again beyond that there was a glimpse of the vast sunny rippling sea; but Sylvia knew well that Kester was looking at none of these things. She went up to him and touched his arm. He started from his reverie, and turned round upon her with his dim eyes full of unshed tears. When he saw her black dress, her deep mourning, he had hard work to keep from breaking out, but by dint of a good brush of his eyes with the back of his hand, and a moment's pause, he could look at her again with tolerable calmness.

'Why, Kester: why didst niver come to speak to us?' said Sylvia, finding it necessary to be cheerful if she could.

'A dun know; niver ax me. A say, they'n gi'en Dick Simpson' (whose evidence had been all material against poor Daniel Robson at the trial) 'a' t' rotten eggs and fou' things they could o' Saturday, they did,' continued he, in a tone of satisfaction; 'ay, and they niver stopped t' see whether t' eggs were rotten or fresh when their blood was up – nor whether stones was hard or soft,' he added, in a lower tone, and chuckling a little.

Sylvia was silent. He looked at her now, chuckling still. Her face was white, her lips tightened, her eyes aflame. She drew a long breath.

'I wish I'd been theere! I wish I could do him an ill turn,' sighed she, with some kind of expression on her face that made Kester quail a little.

'Nay, lass! he'll get it fra' others. Niver fret thysel' about sich rubbish. A'n done ill to speak on him.'

'No! thou hasn't. Then as was friends o' father's I'll love for iver and iver; them as helped for t' hang him' (she shuddered from head to foot – a sharp irrepressible shudder!) 'I'll niver forgive – niver!'

'Niver's a long word,' said Kester, musingly. 'A could horsewhip him, or cast stones at him, or duck him mysel'; but, lass! niver's a long word!'

'Well! niver heed if it is – it's me as said it, and I'm turned savage late days. Come in, Kester, and see poor mother.'

'A cannot,' said he, turning his wrinkled puckered face away, that she might not see the twitchings of emotion on it. 'There's kine to be fetched up, and what not, and he's theere, isn't he, Sylvie?' facing round upon her with inquisitiveness. Under his peering eyes she reddened a little.

'Yes, if it's Philip thou means; he's been all we've had to look to sin'.' Again the shudder.

'Well, now he'll be seein' after his shop, a reckon?'

Sylvia was calling to the old mare nibbling tufts of early-springing grass here and there, and half unconsciously coaxing the creature to come to the gate to be stroked. But she heard Kester's words well enough, and so he saw, although she made this excuse not to reply. But Kester was not to be put off.

'Folks is talkin' about thee and him; thou'll ha' to mind lest thee and him gets yo'r names coupled together.'

'It's right down cruel on folks, then,' said she, crimsoning from some emotion. 'As if any man as was a man wouldn't do all he could for two lone women at such a time – and he a cousin, too! Tell me who said so,' continued she, firing round at Kester, 'and I'll niver forgive 'em – that's all.'

'Hoots!' said Kester, a little conscious that he himself was the principal representative of that name of multitude folk. 'Here's a pretty lass; she's got "a'll niver forgi'e" at her tongue's end wi' a vengeance.'

Sylvia was a little confused.

'Oh, Kester, man,' said she, 'my heart is sore again' every one, for feyther's sake.'

And at length the natural relief of plentiful tears came; and Kester, with instinctive wisdom, let her weep undisturbed; indeed, he cried not a little himself. They were interrupted by Philip's voice from the back-door.

'Sylvie, your mother's awake, and wants you!'

'Come, Kester, come,' and taking hold of him she drew him with her into the house.

Bell rose as they came in, holding by the arms of the chair. At first she received Kester as though he had been a stranger.

'I'm glad to see yo', sir; t' master's out, but he'll be in afore long. It'll be about t' lambs yo're come, mebbe?'

'Mother!' said Sylvia, 'dunnot yo' see? it's Kester, – Kester, wi' his Sunday clothes on.'

'Kester! ay, sure it is; my eyes have getten so sore and dim of late; just as if I'd been greeting.* I'm sure, lad, I'm glad to see thee! It's a long time I've been away, but it were not pleasure-seeking as took me, it were business o' some mak' – tell him, Sylvie, what it were, for my head's clean gone. I only know I wouldn't ha' left home if I could ha' helped it; for I think I should ha' kept my health better if I'd bided at home wi' my master. I wonder as he's not comed in for t' bid me welcome? Is he far afield, think ye, Kester?'

Kester looked at Sylvia, mutely imploring her to help him out in the dilemma of answering, but she was doing all she could to help crying. Philip came to the rescue.

'Aunt,' said he, 'the clock has stopped; can you tell me where t' find t' key, and I'll wind it up.'

'T' key,' said she, hurriedly, 't' key, it's behind th' big Bible on yon shelf. But I'd raythar thou wouldn't touch it, lad; it's t' master's work, and he distrusts folk meddling wi' it.'

Day after day there was this constant reference to her dead husband. In one sense it was a blessing; all the circumstances attendant on his sad and untimely end were swept out of her mind along with the recollection of the fact itself. She referred to him as absent, and had always some plausible way of accounting for it, which satisfied her own mind; and, accordingly they fell into the habit of humouring her, and speaking of him as gone to Monkshaven, or afield, or wearied out, and taking a nap upstairs, as her fancy led her to believe for the moment. But this forgetfulness, though happy for herself, was terrible for her child. It was a constant renewing of Sylvia's grief, while her mother could give her no sympathy, no help, or strength in any circumstances that arose out of this grief. She was driven more and more upon Philip; his advice and his affection became daily more necessary to her.

Kester saw what would be the end of all this more clearly than Sylvia did herself; and, impotent to hinder what he feared and disliked, he grew more and more surly every day. Yet he tried to labour hard and well for the interests of the family, as if they were bound up in his good management of the cattle and land. He was out and about by the earliest dawn, working all day long with might and main. He bought himself a pair of new spectacles, which might, he fancied, enable him to read the *Farmer's Complete Guide*, his dead master's *vade-mecum*. But he had never learnt more than his capital letters, and had forgotten many of them; so the spectacles did him but little good. Then he would take the book to Sylvia, and ask her to read to him the instructions he needed; instructions, be it noted, that he would formerly have despised as mere book-learning: but his present sense of responsibility had made him humble.

Sylvia would find the place with all deliberation: and putting her finger under the line to keep the exact place of the word she was reading, she would strive in good earnest to read out the directions given; but when every fourth word had to be spelt, it was rather hopeless work, especially as all these words were unintelligible to the open-mouthed listener, however intent he might be. He had generally to fall back on his own experience: and, guided by that, things were not doing badly in his estimation, when, one day, Sylvia said to him, as they were in the hay-field, heaping up the hay into cocks with Dolly Reid's assistance –

'Kester – I didn't tell thee – there were a letter from Measter Hall, Lord Malton's steward, that came last night and that Philip read me.'

She stopped for a moment.

'Ay lass! Philip read it thee, and whatten might it say?'

'Only that he had an offer for Haytersbank Farm, and would set mother free to go as soon as t' crops was off t' ground.'

She sighed a little as she said this.

'"Only!" sayst ta? Whatten business has he for to go an' offer to let t' farm afore iver he were told as yo' wished to leave it?' observed Kester, in high dudgeon.

'Oh!' replied Sylvia, throwing down her rake, as if weary of life. 'What could we do wi' t' farm and land? If it were all dairy I might ha' done, but wi' so much on it arable.'

'And if 'tis arable is not I allays to t' fore?'

'Oh, man, dunnot find fault wi' me! I'm just fain to lie down and die, if it were not for mother.'

'Ay! thy mother will be sore unsettled if thou's for quitting Haytersbank,' said merciless Kester.

'I cannot help it; I cannot help it! What can I do? It would take two pair o' men's hands to keep t' land up as Measter Hall likes it; and beside——'

'Beside what?' said Kester, looking up at her with his sudden odd look, one eye shut, the other open: there she stood, her two hands clasped tight together, her eyes filling with tears, her face pale and sad. 'Beside what?' he asked again, sharply.

'T' answer's sent to Measter Hall – Philip wrote it last

night; so there's no use planning and fretting, it were done for t' best, and mun be done.' She stooped and picked up her rake, and began tossing the hay with energy, the tears streaming down her cheeks unheeded. It was Kester's turn to throw down his rake. She took no notice, he did not feel sure that she had observed his action. He began to walk towards the field gate; this movement did catch her eye, for in a minute her hand was on his arm, and she was stooping forward to look into his face. It was working and twitching with emotion. 'Kester! oh, man! speak out, but dunnot leave me a this-ns. What could I ha' done? Mother is gone dateless* wi' sorrow, and I am but a young lass, i' years I mean; for I'm old enough wi' weeping.'

'I'd ha' put up for t' farm mysel', sooner than had thee turned out,' said Kester, in a low voice; then working himself up into a passion, as a new suspicion crossed his mind, he added, 'An' what for didn't yo' tell me on t' letter? Yo' were in a mighty hurry to settle it a', and get rid on t' oud place.'

'Measter Hall had sent a notice to quit on Midsummer day; but Philip had answered it hisself. Thou knows I'm not good at reading writing, 'special when a letter's full o' long words, and Philip had ta'en it in hand to answer.'

'Wi'out asking thee?'

Sylvia went on without minding the interruption.

'And Measter Hall makes a good offer, for t' man as is going to come in will take t' stock and a' t' implements; and if mother – if we – if I – like, th' furniture and a'——'

'Furniture!' said Kester, in grim surprise. 'What's to come o' t' missus and thee, that yo'll not need a bed to lie on, or a pot to boil yo'r vittel in?'

Sylvia reddened, but kept silence.

'Cannot yo' speak?'

'Oh, Kester, I didn't think thou'd turn again' me, and me so friendless. It's as if I'd been doin' something wrong, and I have so striven to act as is best; there's mother as well as me to be thought on.'

'Cannot yo' answer a question?' said Kester, once more.

'Whatten's up that t' missus and yo'll not need bed and table, pots and pans?'

'I think I'm going to marry Philip,' said Sylvia, in so low a tone, that if Kester had not suspected what her answer was to be, he could not have understood it.

After a moment's pause he recommenced his walk towards the field gate. But she went after him and held him tight by the arm, speaking rapidly.

'Kester, what could I do? What can I do? He's my cousin, and mother knows him, and likes him; and he's been so good to us in a' this time o' trouble and heavy grief, and he'll keep mother in comfort all t' rest of her days.'

'Ay, and thee in comfort. There's a deal in a well-filled purse in a wench's eyes, or one would ha' thought it weren't so easy forgettin' yon lad as loved thee as t' apple on his eye.'

'Kester, Kester,' she cried, 'I've niver forgotten Charley; I think on him, I see him ivery night lying drowned at t' bottom o' t' sea. Forgetten him! Man! it's easy talking!' She was like a wild creature that sees its young, but is unable to reach it without a deadly spring, and yet is preparing to take that fatal leap. Kester himself was almost startled, and yet it was as if he must go on torturing her.

'An' who telled thee so sure and certain as he were drowned? He might ha' been carried off by t' press-gang as well as other men.'

'Oh! if I were but dead that I might know all!' cried she, flinging herself down on the hay.

Kester kept silence. Then she sprang up again, and looking with eager wistfulness into his face, she said,—

'Tell me t' chances. Tell me quick! Philip's very good, and kind, and he says he shall die if I will not marry him, and there's no home for mother and me, – no home for her, for as for me I dunnot care what becomes on me; but if Charley's alive I cannot marry Philip – no, not if he dies for want o' me – and as for mother, poor mother, Kester, it's an awful strait; only first tell me if there's a chance, just one in a thousand, only one in a hundred thousand, as Charley were ta'en by t' gang?' She was breathless by this time, what with her hurried words, and what with the beating of her heart. Kester took time to answer. He had spoken before too hastily, this time he weighed his words.

'Kinraid went away from this here place t' join his ship. An' he niver joined it no more; an' t' captain an' all his friends at Newcassel as iver were, made search for him, on board t' king's ships. That's more nor fifteen month ago, an' nought has iver been heerd on him by any man. That's what's to be said on one side o' t' matter. Then on t' other there's this as is known. His hat were cast up by t' sea wi' a ribbon in it, as there's reason t' think as he'd not ha' parted wi' so quick if he'd had his own will.'

'But yo' said as he might ha' been carried off by t' gang – yo' did, Kester, tho' now yo're a' for t' other side.'

'My lass, a'd fain have him alive, an' a dunnot fancy Philip for thy husband; but it's a serious judgment as thou's put me on, an' a'm trying it fair. There's allays one chance i' a thousand as he's alive, for no man iver saw him dead. But t' gang were noane about Monkshaven then: there were niver a tender on t' coast nearer than Shields, an' those theere were searched.'

He did not say any more, but turned back into the field, and took up his hay-making again.

Sylvia stood quite still, thinking, and wistfully longing for some kind of certainty.

Kester came up to her.

'Sylvie, thou knows Philip paid me back my money, and it were eight pound fifteen and three-pence; and t' hay and stock 'll sell for summat above t' rent; and a've a sister as is a decent widow-woman, tho' but badly off, livin' at Dale End; and if thee and thy mother 'll go live wi' her, a'll give thee well on to all a can earn, and it'll be a matter o' five shilling a week. But dunnot go and marry a man as thou's noane taken wi', and another as is most like for t' be dead, but who, mebbe, is alive, havin' a pull on thy heart.'

Sylvia began to cry as if her heart was broken. She had promised herself more fully to Philip the night before than she had told Kester; and, with some pains and much patience, her cousin, her lover, alas! her future husband, had made the fact clear to the bewildered mind of her poor mother, who had all day long shown that her mind and heart were full of the subject, and that the contemplation of it was giving her as much peace as she could ever know. And now Kester's words came to call up echoes in the poor girl's heart. Just as she was in this miserable state, wishing that the grave lay open before her, and that she could lie down, and be covered up by the soft green turf from all the bitter sorrows and carking cares and weary bewilderments of this life; wishing that her father was alive, that Charlie was once more here; that she had not repeated the solemn words by which she had promised herself to Philip only the very evening before, she heard a soft, low whistle, and, looking round unconsciously, there was her lover and affianced husband, leaning on the gate, and gazing into the field with passionate eyes, devouring the fair face and figure of her, his future wife.

'Oh, Kester,' said she once more, 'what mun I do? I'm pledged to him as strong as words can make it, and mother blessed us both wi' more sense than she's had for weeks. Kester, man, speak! Shall I go and break it all off? – say.'

'Nay, it's noane for me t' say; m'appen thou's gone too far. Them above only knows what is best.'

Again that long, cooing whistle. 'Sylvie!'

'He's been very kind to us all,' said Sylvie, laying her rake down with slow care, 'and I'll try t' make him happy.'

CHAPTER XXIX

WEDDING RAIMENT

PHILIP and Sylvia were engaged. It was not so happy a state of things as Philip had imagined. He had already found that out, although it was not twenty-four hours since Sylvia had promised to be his. He could not have defined why he was dissatisfied; if he had been compelled to account for his feeling, he would probably have alleged as a reason that Sylvia's manner was so unchanged by her new position towards him. She was quiet and gentle; but no shyer, no brighter, no coyer, no happier, than she had been for months before. When she joined him at the field-gate, his heart was beating fast, his eyes were beaming out love at her approach. She neither blushed nor smiled, but seemed absorbed in thought of some kind. But she resisted his silent effort to draw her away from the path leading to the house, and turned her face steadily homewards. He murmured soft words, which she scarcely heard. Right in their way was the stone trough for the fresh bubbling water, that, issuing from a roadside spring, served for all the household purposes of Haytersbank Farm. By it were the milk-cans, glittering and clean. Sylvia knew she should have to stop for these, and carry them back home in readiness for the evening's milking; and at this time, during this action, she resolved to say what was on her mind.

They were there. Sylvia spoke.

'Philip, Kester has been saying as how it might ha' been——'

'Well!' said Philip.

Sylvia sate down on the edge of the trough, and dipped her hot little hand in the water. Then she went on quickly, and lifting her beautiful eyes to Philip's face, with a look of inquiry – 'He thinks as Charley Kinraid may ha' been took by t' press-gang.'

It was the first time she had named the name of her former lover to her present one since the day, long ago now, when they had quarrelled about him; and the rosy colour flushed her all over; but her sweet, trustful eyes never flinched from their steady, unconscious gaze.

Philip's heart stopped beating; literally, as if he had come to a sudden precipice, while he had thought himself securely walking on sunny greensward. He went purple all over from dismay; he dared not take his eyes away from that sad, earnest look of hers, but he was thankful that a mist came before them and drew a veil before his brain. He heard his own voice saying words he did not seem to have framed in his own mind.

'Kester's a d—d fool,' he growled.

'He says there's mebbe but one chance i' a hundred,' said Sylvia, pleading, as it were, for Kester; 'but oh! Philip, think yo' there's just that one chance?'

'Ay, there's a chance, sure enough,' said Philip, in a kind of fierce despair that made him reckless what he said or did. 'There's a chance, I suppose, for iverything i' life as we have not seen with our own eyes as it may not ha' happened. Kester may say next as there's a chance as your father is not dead, because we none on us saw him——'

'Hung,' he was going to have said, but a touch of humanity came back into his stony heart. Sylvia sent up a little sharp cry at his words. He longed at the sound to take her in his arms and hush her up, as a mother hushes her weeping child. But the very longing, having to be repressed, only made him more beside himself with guilt, anxiety, and rage. They were quite still now. Sylvia looking sadly down into the bubbling, merry, flowing water: Philip glaring at her, wishing that the next word were spoken, though it might stab him to the heart. But she did not speak.

At length, unable to bear it any longer, he said, 'Thou sets a deal o' store on that man, Sylvie.'

If 'that man' had been there at the moment, Philip would have grappled with him, and not let go his hold till one or the other were dead. Sylvia caught some of the passionate meaning of the gloomy, miserable tone of Philip's voice as he said these words. She looked up at him.

'I thought yo' knowed that I cared a deal for him.'

There was something so pleading and innocent in her pale, troubled face, so pathetic in her tone, that Philip's anger, which had been excited against her, as well as against all the rest of the world, melted away into love; and once more he felt that have her for his own he must, at any cost. He sate down by her, and spoke to her in quite a different manner to that which he had used before, with a ready tact and art which some strange instinct or tempter 'close at his ear'* supplied.

'Yes, darling, I knew yo' cared for him. I'll not say ill of him that is – dead – ay, dead and drowned – whativer Kester may say – before now; but if I chose I could tell tales.'

'No! tell no tales; I'll not hear them,' said she, wrenching herself out of Philip's clasping arm. 'They may misca' him for iver, and I'll not believe 'em.'

'I'll niver miscall one who is dead,' said Philip; each new unconscious sign of the strength of Sylvia's love for her former lover only making him the more anxious to convince her that he was dead, only rendering him more keen at deceiving his own conscience by repeating to it the lie that long ere this Kinraid was in all probability dead – killed by either the chances of war or tempestuous sea; that, even if not, he was as good as dead to her; so that the word 'dead' might be used in all honest certainty, as in one of its meanings Kinraid was dead for sure.

'Think yo' that if he were not dead he wouldn't ha' written ere this to some one of his kin, if not to thee? Yet none of his folk Newcassel-way but believe him dead.'

'So Kester says,' sighed Sylvia.

Philip took heart. He put his arm softly round her again, and murmured—

'My lassie, try not to think on them as is gone, as is dead, but t' think a bit more on him as loves yo' wi' heart, and soul, and might, and has done iver sin' he first set eyes on yo'. Oh, Sylvie, my love for thee is just terrible.'

At this moment Dolly Reid was seen at the back-door of the farmhouse, and catching sight of Sylvia, she called out—

'Sylvia, thy mother is axing for thee, and I cannot make her mind easy.'

In a moment Sylvia had sprung up from her seat, and was running in to soothe and comfort her mother's troubled fancies.

Philip sate on by the well-side, his face buried in his two hands. Presently he lifted himself up, drank some water eagerly out of his hollowed palm, sighed, and shook himself, and followed his cousin into the house. Sometimes he came unexpectedly to the limits of his influence over her. In general she obeyed his expressed wishes with gentle indifference, as if she had no preferences of her own; once or twice he found that she was doing what he desired out of the spirit of obedience, which, as her mother's daughter, she believed to be her duty towards her affianced husband. And this last motive for action depressed her lover more than anything. He wanted the old Sylvia back again; captious, capricious, wilful, haughty, merry, charming. Alas! that Sylvia was gone for ever.

But once especially his power, arising from whatever cause, was stopped entirely short – was utterly of no avail.

It was on the occasion of Dick Simpson's mortal illness. Sylvia and her mother kept aloof from every one. They had never been intimate with any family but the Corneys, and even this friendship had considerably cooled since Molly's marriage, and most especially since Kinraid's supposed death, when Bessy Corney and Sylvia had been, as it were, rival mourners. But many people, both in Monkshaven and the country round about, held the Robson family in great respect, although Mrs Robson herself was accounted 'high' and 'distant;' and poor little Sylvia, in her heyday of beautiful youth and high spirits, had been spoken of as 'a bit flighty,' and 'a set-up lassie.' Still, when their great sorrow fell upon them, there were plenty of friends to sympathize deeply with them; and, as Daniel had suffered in a popular cause, there were even more who, scarcely knowing them personally, were ready to give them all the marks of respect and friendly feeling in their power. But neither Bell nor Sylvia were aware of this. The former had lost all perception of what was not immediately before her; the latter shrank from all encounters of any kind with a sore heart, and sensitive avoidance of everything that could make her a subject of remark. So the poor afflicted people at Haytersbank knew little of Monkshaven news. What little did come to their ears came through Dolly Reid, when she returned from selling the farm produce of the week; and often, indeed, even then she found Sylvia too much absorbed in other cares or thoughts to listen to her gossip. So no one had ever named that Simpson was supposed to be dying till Philip began on the subject one evening. Sylvia's face suddenly flashed into glow and life.

'He's dying, is he? t' earth is well rid on such a fellow!'

'Eh, Sylvie, that's a hard speech o' thine!' said Philip; 'it gives me but poor heart to ask a favour of thee!'

'If it's aught about Simpson,' replied she, and then she interrupted herself. 'But say on; it were ill-mannered in me for t' interrupt yo'.'

'Thou would be sorry to see him, I think, Sylvie. He cannot get over the way, t' folk met him, and pelted him when he came back fra' York, – and he's weak and faint, and beside himself at times; and he'll lie a dreaming, and a-fancying they're all at him again, hooting, and yelling, and pelting him.'

'I'm glad on 't,' said Sylvia; 'it's t' best news I've heered for many a day, – he, to turn again' feyther, who gave him money fo t' get a lodging that night, when he'd no place to go to. It were his evidence as hung feyther; and he's rightly punished for it now.'

'For a' that, – and he's done a vast o' wrong beside, he's dying now, Sylvie!'

'Well! let him die – it's t' best thing he could do!'

'But he's lying i' such dree poverty, – and niver a friend to go near him, – niver a person to speak a kind word t' him.'

'It seems as yo've been speaking wi' him, at any rate,' said Sylvia, turning round on Philip.

'Ay. He sent for me by Nell Manning, th' old beggar-woman, who sometimes goes in and makes his bed for him, poor wretch, – he's lying in t' ruins of th' cow-house of th' Mariners' Arms, Sylvie.'

'Well!' said she, in the same hard, dry tone.

'And I went and fetched th' parish doctor, for I thought he'd ha' died before my face, – he was so wan, and ashen-grey, so thin, too, his eyes seem pushed out of his bony face.'

'That last time – feyther's eyes were starting, wild-like, and as if he couldn't meet ours, or bear the sight on our weeping.'

It was a bad look-out for Philip's purpose; but after a pause he went bravely on.

'He's a poor dying creature, anyhow. T' doctor said so, and told him he hadn't many hours, let alone days, to live.'

'And he'd shrink fra' dying wi' a' his sins on his head?' said Sylvia, almost exultingly.

Philip shook his head. 'He said this world had been too strong for him, and men too hard upon him; he could niver do any good here, and he thought he should, maybe, find folks i' t' next place more merciful.'

'He'll meet feyther theere,' said Sylvia, still hard and bitter.

'He's a poor ignorant creature, and doesn't seem to know rightly who he's like to meet; only he seems glad to get away fra' Monkshaven folks; he were really hurt, I am afeared, that night, Sylvie, – and he speaks as if he'd had hard times of it ever since he were a child, – and he talks as if he were really grieved for t' part t' lawyers made him take at th' trial, – they made him speak, against his will, he says.'

'Couldn't he ha' bitten his tongue out?' asked Sylvia. 'It's fine talking o' sorrow when the thing is done!'

'Well, anyhow he's sorry now; and he's not long for to live. And, Sylvie, he bid me ask thee, if, for the sake of all that is dear to thee both here, and i' th' world to come, thou'd go wi' me, and just say to him that thou forgives him his part that day.'

'He sent thee on that errand, did he? And thou could come and ask me? I've a mind to break it off for iver wi' thee, Philip.' She kept gasping, as if she could not say any more. Philip watched and waited till her breath came, his own half choked.

'Thee and me was niver meant to go together. It's not in me to forgive, – I sometimes think it's not in me to forget. I wonder, Philip, if thy feyther had done a kind deed – and a right deed – and a merciful deed – and some one as he'd been good to, even i' t' midst of his just anger, had gone and let on about him to th' judge, as was trying to hang him, – and had getten him hanged, – hanged dead, so that his wife were a widow, and his child fatherless for ivermore, – I wonder if thy veins would run milk and water, so that thou could go and make friends, and speak soft wi' him as had caused thy feyther's death?'

'It's said in t' Bible, Sylvie, that we're to forgive.'

'Ay, there's some things as I know I niver forgive; and there's others as I can't – and I won't, either.'

'But, Sylvie, yo' pray to be forgiven your trespasses, as you forgive them as trespass against you.'

'Well, if I'm to be taken at my word, I'll noane pray at all, that's all. It's well enough for them as has but little to forgive to use them words; and I don't reckon it's kind, or pretty behaved in yo', Philip, to bring up Scripture again' me. Thou may go about thy business.'

'Thou'rt vexed with me, Sylvie; and I'm not meaning but that it would go hard with thee to forgive him; but I think it would be right and Christian-like i' thee, and that thou'd find thy comfort in thinking on it after. If thou'd only go, and see his wistful eyes – I think they'd plead wi' thee more than his words, or mine either.'

'I tell thee my flesh and blood wasn't made for forgiving and forgetting. Once for all, thou must take my word. When I love I love, and when I hate I hate; and him as has done hard to me, or to mine, I may keep fra' striking or murdering, but I'll niver forgive. I should be just a monster, fit to be shown at a fair, if I could forgive him as got feyther hanged.'

Philip was silent, thinking what more he could urge.

'Yo'd better be off,' said Sylvia, in a minute or two. 'Yo' and me has got wrong, and it'll take a night's sleep to set us right. Yo've said all yo' can for him; and perhaps it's not yo' as is to blame, but yo'r nature. But I'm put out wi' thee, and want thee out o' my sight for awhile.'

One or two more speeches of this kind convinced him that it would be wise in him to take her at her word. He went back to Simpson, and found him, though still alive, past the understanding of any words of human forgiveness. Philip had almost wished he had not troubled or irritated Sylvia by urging the dying man's request: the performance of this duty seemed now to have been such a useless office.

After all, the performance of a duty is never a useless office, though we may not see the consequences, or they may be quite different to what we expected or calculated on. In the pause of active work, when daylight was done, and the evening shades came on, Sylvia had time to think; and her heart grew sad and soft, in comparison to what it had been when Philip's urgency had called out all her angry opposition. She thought of her father – his sharp passions, his frequent forgiveness, or rather his forgetfulness that he had even been injured. All Sylvia's persistent or enduring qualities were derived from her mother, her impulses from her father. It was her dead father whose example filled her mind this evening in the soft and tender twilight. She did not say to herself that she would go and tell Simpson that she forgave him; but she thought that if Philip asked her again that she should do so.

But when she saw Philip again he told her that Simpson was dead; and passed on from what he had reason to think would be an unpleasant subject to her. Thus he never learnt how her conduct might have been more gentle and relenting than her words – words which came up into his memory at a future time, with full measure of miserable significance.

In general, Sylvia was gentle and good enough; but Philip wanted her to be shy and tender with him, and this she was not. She spoke to him, her pretty eyes looking straight and composedly at him. She consulted him like the family friend that he was: she met him quietly in all the arrangements for the time of their marriage, which she looked upon more as a change of home, as the leaving of Haytersbank, as it would affect her mother, than in any more directly personal way. Philip was beginning to feel, though not as yet to acknowledge, that the fruit he had so inordinately longed for was but of the nature of an apple of Sodom.

Long ago, lodging in widow Rose's garret, he had been in the habit of watching some pigeons that were kept by a neighbour; the flock disported themselves on the steep tiled roofs just opposite to the attic window, and insensibly Philip grew to know their ways, and one pretty, soft little dove was somehow perpetually associated in his mind with his idea of his cousin Sylvia. The pigeon would sit in one particular place, sunning herself, and puffing out her feathered breast, with all the blue and rose-coloured lights gleaming in the morning rays, cooing softly to herself as she dressed her plumage. Philip fancied that he saw the same colours in a certain piece of shot silk – now in the shop; and none other seemed to him so suitable for his darling's wedding-dress. He carried enough to make a gown, and gave it to her one evening, as she sate on the grass just outside the house, half attending to her mother, half engaged in knitting stockings for her scanty marriage outfit. He was glad that the sun was not gone down, thus allowing him to display the changing colours in fuller light. Sylvia admired it duly; even Mrs. Robson was pleased and attracted by the soft yet brilliant hues. Philip whispered to Sylvia – (he took delight in whispers, – she, on the contrary, always spoke to him in her usual tone of voice)—

'Thou'lt look so pretty in it, sweetheart, – o' Thursday fortnight!'

'Thursday fortnight. On the fourth yo're thinking on. But I cannot wear it then, – I shall be i' black.'

'Not on that day, sure!' said Philip.

'Why not? There's nought t' happen on that day for t' make me forget feyther. I couldn't put off my black, Philip, – no, not to save my life! Yon silk is just lovely, far too good for the likes of me, – and I'm sure I'm much beholden to yo'; and I'll have it made up first of any gown after last April come two years, – but, oh, Philip, I cannot put off my mourning!'

'Not for our wedding-day!' said Philip, sadly.

'No, lad, I really cannot. I'm just sorry about it, for I see thou'rt set upon it; and thou'rt so kind and good, I sometimes think I can niver be thankful enough to thee. When I think on what would ha' become of mother and me if we hadn't had thee for a friend i' need, I'm noane ungrateful, Philip; tho' I sometimes fancy thou'rt thinking I am.'

'I don't want yo' to be grateful, Sylvie,' said poor Philip, dissatisfied, yet unable to explain what he did want; only knowing that there was something he lacked, yet fain would have had.

As the marriage-day drew near, all Sylvia's care seemed to be for her mother; all her anxiety was regarding the appurtenances of the home she was leaving. In vain Philip tried to interest her in details of his improvements or contrivances in the new home to which he was going to take her. She did not tell him; but the idea of the house behind the shop was associated in her mind with two times of discomfort and misery. The first time she had gone into the parlour about which Philip spoke so much was at the time of the press-gang riot, when she had fainted from terror and excitement; the second was on that night of misery when she and her mother had gone in to Monkshaven, to bid her father farewell before he was taken to York; in that room, on that night, she had first learnt something of the fatal peril in which he stood. She could not show the bright shy curiosity about her future dwelling that is common enough with girls who are going to be married. All she could do was to restrain herself from sighing, and listen patiently, when he talked on the subject. In time he saw that she shrank from it; so he held his peace, and planned and worked for her in silence, – smiling to himself as he looked on each completed arrangement for her pleasure or comfort; and knowing well that her happiness was involved in what fragments of peace and material comfort might remain to her mother.

The wedding-day drew near apace. It was Philip's plan that after they had been married in Kirk Moorside church, he and his Sylvia, his cousin, his love, his wife, should go for the day to Robin Hood's Bay, returning in the evening to the house behind the shop in the market-place. There they were to find Bell Robson installed in her future home; for Haytersbank Farm was to be given up to the new tenant on the very day of the wedding. Sylvia would not be married any sooner; she said that she must stay there till the very last; and had said it with such determination that Philip had desisted from all urgency at once.

He had told her that all should be settled for her mother's comfort during their few hours' absence; otherwise Sylvia would not have gone at all. He told her he should ask Hester, who was always so good and kind – who never yet had said him nay, to go to church with them as bridesmaid – for Sylvia would give no thought or care to anything but her mother – and that they would leave her at Haytersbank as they returned from church; she would manage Mrs Robson's removal – she would do this – do that – do everything. Such friendly confidence had Philip in Hester's willingness and tender skill. Sylvia acquiesced at length, and Philip took upon himself to speak to Hester on the subject.

'Hester,' said he, one day when he was preparing to go home after the shop was closed; 'would yo' mind stopping a bit? I should like to show yo' the place now it's done up; and I've a favour to ask on yo' besides.' He was so happy he did not see her shiver all over. She hesitated just a moment before she answered, —

'I'll stay, if thou wishes it, Philip. But I'm no judge o' fashions and such like.'

'Thou'rt a judge o' comfort, and that's what I've been aiming at. I were niver so comfortable in a' my life as when I were a lodger at thy house,' said he, with brotherly tenderness in his tone. 'If my mind had been at ease I could ha' said I niver were happier in all my days than under thy roof; and I know it were thy doing for the most part. So come along, Hester, and tell me if there's aught more I can put in for Sylvie.'

It might not have been a very appropriate text, but such as it was the words, 'From him that would ask of thee turn not thou away,'* seemed the only source of strength that could have enabled her to go patiently through the next half-hour. As it was, she unselfishly brought all her mind to bear upon the subject; admired this, thought and decided upon that, as one by one Philip showed her all his alterations and improvements. Never was such a quiet little bit of unconscious and unrecognized heroism. She really ended by such a conquest of self that she could absolutely sympathize with the proud expectant lover, and had quenched all envy of the beloved, in sympathy with the delight she imagined Sylvia must experience when she discovered all these proofs of Philip's fond consideration and care. But it was a great strain on the heart, that source of life; and when Hester returned into the parlour, after her deliberate survey of the house, she felt as weary and depressed in bodily strength as if she had gone through an illness of many days. She sate down on the nearest chair, and felt as though she never could rise again. Philip, joyous and content, stood near her talking.

'And, Hester,' said he, 'Sylvie has given me a message for thee – she says thou must be her bridesmaid – she'll have none other.'

'I cannot,' said Hester, with sudden sharpness.

'Oh, yes, but yo' must. It wouldn't be like my wedding if thou wasn't there: why I've looked upon thee as a sister iver since I came to lodge with thy mother.'

Hester shook her head. Did her duty require her not to turn away from this asking, too? Philip saw her reluctance, and, by intuition rather than reason, he knew that what she would not do for gaiety or pleasure she would consent to, if by so doing she could render any service to another. So he went on.

'Besides, Sylvie and me has planned to go for our wedding jaunt to Robin Hood's Bay. I ha' been to engage a shandry* this very morn, before t' shop was opened; and there's no one to leave wi' my aunt. Th' poor old body is sore crushed with sorrow; and is, as one may say, childish at times; she's to come down here, that we may find her when we come back at night; and there's niver a one she'll come with so willing and so happy as with thee, Hester. Sylvie and me has both said so.'

Hester looked up in his face with her grave honest eyes.

'I cannot go to church wi' thee, Philip; and thou must not ask me any further. But I'll go betimes to Haytersbank Farm, and I'll do my best to make the old lady happy, and to follow out thy directions in bringing her here before night-fall.'

Philip was on the point of urging her afresh to go with them to church; but something in her eyes brought a thought across his mind, as transistory as a breath passes over a looking-glass, and he desisted from his entreaty, and put away his thought as a piece of vain coxcombry, insulting to Hester. He passed rapidly on to all the careful directions rendered necessary by her compliance with the latter part of his request, coupling Sylvia's name with his perpetually; so that Hester looked upon her as a happy girl, as eager in planning all the details of her marriage as though no heavy shameful sorrow had passed over her head not many months ago.

Hester did not see Sylvia's white, dreamy, resolute face, that answered the solemn questions of the marriage service in a voice that did not seem her own. Hester was not with them to notice the heavy abstraction that made the bride as if unconscious of her husband's loving words, and then start and smile, and reply with a sad gentleness of tone. No! Hester's duty lay in conveying the poor widow and mother down from Haytersbank to the new home in Monkshaven; and for all Hester's assistance and thoughtfulness, it was a dreary, painful piece of work – the poor old woman crying like a child, with bewilderment at the confused bustle which, in spite of all Sylvia's careful forethought, could not be avoided on this final day, when her mother had to be carried away from the homestead over which she had so long presided. But all this was as nothing to the distress which overwhelmed poor Bell Robson when she entered Philip's house; the parlour – the whole place so associated with the keen agony she had undergone there, that the stab of memory penetrated through her deadened senses, and brought her back to misery. In vain Hester tried to console her by telling her the fact of Sylvia's marriage with Philip in every form of words that occurred to her. Bell only remembered her husband's fate, which filled up her poor wandering mind, and coloured everything; insomuch that Sylvia not being at hand to reply to her mother's cry for her, the latter imagined that her child, as well as her husband, was in danger of trial and death, and refused to be comforted by any endeavour of the patient sympathizing Hester. In a pause of Mrs Robson's sobs, Hester heard the welcome sound of the wheels of the returning shandry, bearing the bride and bridegroom home. It stopped at the door – an instant, and Sylvia, white as a sheet at the sound of her mother's wailings, which she had caught while yet at a distance, with the quick ears of love, came running in; her mother feebly rose and tottered towards her, and fell into her arms, saying, 'Oh! Sylvie, Sylvie, take me home, and away from this cruel place!'

Hester could not but be touched with the young girl's manner to her mother – as tender, as protecting as if their relation to each other had been reversed, and she was lulling and tenderly soothing a wayward, frightened child. She had neither eyes nor ears for any one till her mother was sitting in trembling peace, holding her daughter's hand tight in both of hers, as if afraid of losing sight of her: then Sylvia turned to Hester, and, with the sweet grace which is a natural gift to some happy people, thanked her; in common words enough she thanked her, but in that nameless manner, and with that strange, rare charm which made Hester feel as if she had never been thanked in all her life before; and from that time forth she understood, if she did not always yield to, the unconscious fascination which Sylvia could exercise over others at times.

Did it enter into Philip's heart to perceive that he had wedded his long-sought bride in mourning raiment, and that the first sounds which greeted them as they approached their home were those of weeping and wailing?

CHAPTER XXX

HAPPY DAYS

AND now Philip seemed as prosperous as his heart could desire. The business flourished, and money beyond his moderate wants came in. As for himself he required very little; but he had always looked forward to placing his idol in a befitting shrine; and means for this were now furnished to him. The dress, the comforts, the position he had desired for Sylvia were all hers. She did not need to do a stroke of household work if she preferred to 'sit in her parlour and sew up a seam.'* Indeed Phœbe resented any interference in the domestic labour, which she had performed so long, that she looked upon the kitchen as a private empire of her own. 'Mrs Hepburn' (as Sylvia was now termed) had a good dark silk gown-piece in her drawers, as well as the poor dove-coloured, against the day when she chose to leave off mourning; and stuff for either gray or scarlet cloaks was hers at her bidding.

What she cared for far more were the comforts with which it was in her power to surround her mother. In this Philip vied with her; for besides his old love, and new pity for his aunt Bell, he never forgot how she had welcomed him to Haytersbank, and favoured his love to Sylvia, in the yearning days when he little hoped he should ever win his cousin to be his wife. But even if he had not had these grateful and affectionate feelings towards the poor woman, he would have done much for her if only to gain the sweet, rare smiles which his wife never bestowed upon him so freely as when she saw him attending to 'mother,' for so both of them now called Bell. For her creature comforts, her silk gowns, and her humble luxury, Sylvia did not care; Philip was almost annoyed at the indifference she often manifested to all his efforts to surround her with such things. It was even a hardship to her to leave off her country dress, her uncovered hair, her linsey petticoat, and loose bed-gown, and to don a stiff and stately gown for her morning dress. Sitting in the dark parlour at the back of the shop, and doing 'white work,'* was much more wearying to her than running out into the fields to bring up the cows, or spinning wool, or making up butter. She sometimes thought to herself that it was a strange kind of life where there were no out-door animals to look after; the 'ox and the ass'* had hitherto come into all her ideas of humanity; and her care and gentleness had made the dumb creatures round her father's home into mute friends with loving eyes, looking at her as if wistful to speak in words the grateful regard that she could read without the poor expression of language.

She missed the free open air, the great dome of sky above the fields; she rebelled against the necessity of 'dressing' (as she called it) to go out, although she acknowledged that it was a necessity where the first step beyond the threshold must be into a populous street.

It is possible that Philip was right at one time when he had thought to win her by material advantages; but the old vanities had been burnt out of her by the hot iron of acute suffering. A great deal of passionate feeling still existed, concealed and latent; but at this period it appeared as though she were indifferent to most things, and had lost the power of either hoping or fearing much. She was stunned into a sort of temporary numbness on most points; those on which she was sensitive being such as referred to the injustice and oppression of her father's death, or anything that concerned her mother.

She was quiet even to passiveness in all her dealings with Philip; he would have given not a little for some of the old bursts of impatience, the old pettishness, which, naughty as they were, had gone to form his idea of the former Sylvia. Once or twice he was almost vexed with her for her docility; he wanted her so much to have a will of her own, if only that he might know how to rouse her to pleasure by gratifying it. Indeed he seldom fell asleep at nights without his last thoughts being devoted to some little plan for the morrow, that he fancied she would like; and when he wakened in the early dawn he looked to see if she were indeed sleeping by his side, or whether it was not all a dream that he called Sylvia 'wife.'

He was aware that her affection for him was not to be spoken of in the same way as his for her, but he found much happiness in only being allowed to love and cherish her; and with the patient perseverance that was one remarkable feature in his character, he went on striving to deepen and increase her love when most other men would have given up the endeavour, made themselves content with half a heart, and turned to some other object of attainment. All this time Philip was troubled by a dream that recurred whenever he was over-fatigued, or otherwise not in perfect health. Over and over again in this first year of married life he dreamt this dream; perhaps as many as eight or nine times, and it never varied. It was always of Kinraid's return; Kinraid was full of life in Philip's dream, though in his waking hours he could and did convince himself by all the laws of probability that his rival was dead. He never remembered the exact sequence of events in that terrible dream after he had roused himself, with a fight and a struggle, from his feverish slumbers. He was generally sitting up in bed when he found himself conscious, his heart beating wildly, with a conviction of Kinraid's living presence somewhere near him in the darkness. Occasionally Sylvia was disturbed by his agitation, and would question him about his dreams, having, like most of her class at that time, great faith in their prophetic interpretation; but Philip never gave her any truth in his reply.

After all, and though he did not acknowledge it even to himself, the long-desired happiness was not so delicious and perfect as he had anticipated. Many have felt the same in their first year of married life; but the faithful, patient nature that still works on, striving to gain love, and capable itself of steady love all the while, is a gift not given to all.

For many weeks after their wedding, Kester never came near them: a chance word or two from Sylvia showed Philip that she had noticed this and regretted it; and, accordingly, he made it his business at the next leisure opportunity to go to Haytersbank (never saying a word to his wife of his purpose), and seek out Kester.

All the whole place was altered! It was new white-washed, new thatched: the patches of colour in the surrounding ground were changed with altered tillage; the great geraniums were gone from the window, and instead, was a smart knitted blind. Children played before the house door; a dog lying on the step flew at Philip; all was so strange, that it was even the strangest thing of all for Kester to appear where everything else was so altered!

Philip had to put up with a good deal of crabbed behaviour on the part of the latter before he could induce Kester to promise to come down into the town and see Sylvia in her new home.

Somehow, the visit when paid was but a failure; at least, it seemed so at the time, though probably it broke the ice of restraint which was forming over the familiar intercourse between Kester and Sylvia. The old servant was daunted by seeing Sylvia in a strange place, and stood, sleeking his hair down, and furtively looking about him, instead of seating himself on the chair Sylvia had so eagerly brought forward for him.

Then his sense of the estrangement caused by their new positions infected her, and she began to cry pitifully, saying,—

'Oh, Kester! Kester! tell me about Haytersbank! Is it just as it used to be in feyther's days?'

'Well, a cannot say as it is,' said Kester, thankful to have a subject started. 'They'n pleughed up t' oud pasture-field, and are settin' it for 'taters. They're not for much cattle, isn't Higginses. They'll be for corn in t' next year, a reckon, and they'll just ha' their pains for their payment. But they're allays so pig-headed, is folk fra' a distance.'

So they went on discoursing on Haytersbank and the old days, till Bell Robson, having finished her afternoon nap, came slowly downstairs to join them; and after that the conversation became so broken up, from the desire of the other two to attend and reply as best they could to her fragmentary and disjointed talk, that Kester took his leave before long; falling, as he did so, into the formal and unnaturally respectful manner which he had adopted on first coming in.

But Sylvia ran after him, and brought him back from the door.

'To think of thy going away, Kester, without either bit or drink; nay, come back wi' thee, and taste wine and cake.'

Kester stood at the door, half shy, half pleased, while Sylvia, in all the glow and hurry of a young housekeeper's hospitality, sought for the decanter of wine, and a wine-glass in the corner cupboard, and hastily cut an immense wedge of cake, which she crammed into his hand in spite of his remonstrances; and then she poured him out an over-flowing glass of wine, which Kester would far rather have gone without, as he knew manners too well to suppose that he might taste it without having gone through the preliminary ceremony of wishing the donor health and happiness. He stood red and half smiling, with his cake in one hand, his wine in the other, and then began,—

'Long may ye live,
Happy may ye be,
And blest with a num'rous
Pro-ge-ny.'*

'Theere, that's po'try for yo' as I larnt i' my youth. But there's a deal to be said as cannot be put int' po'try, an' yet a cannot say it, somehow. It 'd tax a parson t' say a' as a've getten i' my mind. It's like a heap o' woo' just after shearin' time; it's worth a deal, but it tak's a vast o' combin,' an' cardin', an' spinnin' afore it can be made use on. If a were up to t' use o' words, a could say a mighty deal; but somehow a'm tongue-teed when a come to want my words most, so a'll only just mak' bold t' say as a think yo've done pretty well for yo'rsel', getten a house-full o' furniture' (looking around him as he said this), 'an' vittle an' clothin' for t' axing, belike, an' a home for t' missus in her time o' need; an' mebbe not such a bad husband as a once thought yon man 'ud mak'; a'm not above sayin' as he's, mebbe, better nor a took him for; – so here's to ye both, and wishin' ye health and happiness, ay, and money to buy yo' another, as country folk say.'

Having ended his oration, much to his own satisfaction, Kester tossed off his glass of wine, smacked his lips, wiped his mouth with the back of his hand, pocketed his cake, and made off.

That night Sylvia spoke of his visit to her husband. Philip never said how he himself had brought it to pass, nor did he name the fact that he had heard the old man come in just as he himself had intended going into the parlour for tea, but had kept away, as he thought Sylvia and Kester would most enjoy their interview undisturbed. And Sylvia felt as if her husband's silence was unsympathizing, and shut up the feelings that were just beginning to expand towards him. She sank again into the listless state of indifference from which nothing but some reference to former days, or present consideration for her mother, could rouse her.

Hester was almost surprised at Sylvia's evident liking for her. By slow degrees Hester was learning to love the woman, whose position as Philip's wife she would have envied so keenly had she not been so truly good and pious. But Sylvia seemed as though she had given Hester her whole affection all at once. Hester could not understand this, while she was touched and melted by the trust it implied. For one thing Sylvia remembered and regretted – her harsh treatment of Hester the rainy, stormy night on which the latter had come to Haytersbank to seek her and her mother, and bring them into Monkshaven to see the imprisoned father and husband. Sylvia had been struck with Hester's patient endurance of her rudeness, a rudeness which she was conscious that she herself should have immediately and vehemently resented. Sylvia did not understand how a totally different character from hers might immediately forgive the anger she could not forget; and because Hester had been so meek at the time, Sylvia, who knew how passing and transitory was her own anger, thought that all was forgotten; while Hester believed that the words, which she herself could not have uttered except under deep provocation, meant much more than they did, and admired and wondered at Sylvia for having so entirely conquered her anger against her.

Again, the two different women were divergently affected by the extreme fondness which Bell had shown towards Hester ever since Sylvia's wedding-day. Sylvia, who had always received more love from others than she knew what to do with, had the most entire faith in her own supremacy in her mother's heart, though at times Hester would do certain things more to the poor old woman's satisfaction. Hester, who had craved for the affection which had been withheld from her, and had from that one circumstance become distrustful of her own power of inspiring regard, while she exaggerated the delight of being beloved, feared lest Sylvia should become jealous of her mother's open display of great attachment and occasional preference for Hester. But such a thought never entered Sylvia's mind. She was more thankful than she knew how to express towards any one who made her mother happy; as has been already said, the contributing to Bell Robson's pleasures earned Philip more of his wife's smiles than anything else. And Sylvia threw her whole heart into the words and caresses she lavished on Hester whenever poor Mrs Robson spoke of the goodness and kindness of the latter. Hester attributed more virtue to these sweet words and deeds of gratitude than they deserved; they did not imply in Sylvia any victory over evil temptation, as they would have done in Hester.

It seemed to be Sylvia's fate to captivate more people than she cared to like back again. She turned the heads of John and Jeremiah Foster, who could hardly congratulate Philip enough on his choice of a wife.

They had been prepared to be critical on one who had interfered with their favourite project of a marriage between Philip and Hester; and, though full of compassion for the cruelty of Daniel Robson's fate, they were too completely men of business not to have some apprehension that the connection of Philip Hepburn with the daughter of a man who was hanged, might injure the shop over which both his and their name appeared. But all the possible proprieties demanded that they should pay attention to the bride of their former shopman and present successor; and the very first visitors whom Sylvia had received after her marriage had been John and Jeremiah Foster, in their Sabbath-day clothes. They found her in the parlour (so familiar to both of them!) clear-starching her mother's caps, which had to be got up in some particular fashion that Sylvia was afraid of dictating to Phœbe.

She was a little disturbed at her visitors discovering her at this employment; but she was on her own ground, and that gave her self-possession; and she welcomed the two old men so sweetly and modestly, and looked so pretty and feminine, and, besides, so notable in her handiwork, that she conquered all their prejudices at one blow; and their first thought on leaving the shop was how to do her honour, by inviting her to a supper party at Jeremiah Foster's house.

Sylvia was dismayed when she was bidden to this wedding feast, and Philip had to use all his authority, though tenderly, to make her consent to go at all. She had been to merry country parties like the Corneys', and to bright hay-making romps in the open air; but never to a set stately party at a friend's house.

She would fain have made attendance on her mother an excuse; but Philip knew he must not listen to any such plea, and applied to Hester in the dilemma, asking her to remain with Mrs Robson while he and Sylvia went out visiting; and Hester had willingly, nay, eagerly consented – it was much more to her taste than going out.

So Philip and Sylvia set out, arm-in-arm, down Bridge Street, across the bridge, and then clambered up the hill. On the way he gave her the directions she asked for about her behaviour as bride and most honoured guest; and altogether succeeded, against his intention and will, in frightening her so completely as to the grandeur and importance of the occasion, and the necessity of remembering certain set rules, and making certain set speeches and attending to them when the right time came, that, if any one so naturally graceful could have been awkward, Sylvia would have been so that night.

As it was, she sate, pale and weary-looking, on the very edge of her chair; she uttered the formal words which Philip had told her were appropriate to the occasion, and she heartily wished herself safe at home and in bed. Yet she left but one unanimous impression on the company when she went away, namely, that she was the prettiest and best-behaved woman they had ever seen, and that Philip Hepburn had done well in choosing her, felon's daughter though she might be.

Both the hosts had followed her into the lobby to help Philip in cloaking her, and putting on her pattens.* They were full of old-fashioned compliments and good-wishes; one speech of theirs came up to her memory in future years:—

'Now, Sylvia Hepburn,' said Jeremiah, 'I've known thy husband long, and I don't say but what thou hast done well in choosing him; but if he ever neglects or ill-uses thee, come to me, and I'll give him a sound lecture on his conduct. Mind, I'm thy friend from this day forrards, and ready to take thy part against him!'

Philip smiled as if the day would never come when he should neglect or ill-use his darling; Sylvia smiled a little, without much attending to, or caring for, the words that were detaining her, tired as she was; John and Jeremiah chuckled over the joke; but the words came up again in after days, as words idly spoken sometimes do.

Before the end of that first year, Philip had learnt to be jealous of his wife's new love for Hester. To the latter, Sylvia gave the free confidence on many things which Philip fancied she withheld from him. A suspicion crossed his mind, from time to time, that Sylvia might speak of her former lover to Hester. It would be not unnatural, he thought, if she did so, believing him to be dead; but the idea irritated him.

He was entirely mistaken, however; Sylvia, with all her apparent frankness, kept her deep sorrows to herself. She never mentioned her father's name, though he was continually present to her mind. Nor did she speak of Kinraid to human being, though, for his sake, her voice softened when, by chance, she spoke to a passing sailor; and for his sake her eyes lingered on such men longer than on others, trying to discover in them something of the old familiar gait; and partly for his dead sake, and partly because of the freedom of the outlook and the freshness of the air, she was glad occasionally to escape from the comfortable imprisonment of her 'parlour,' and the close streets around the market-place, and to mount the cliffs and sit on the turf, gazing abroad over the wide still expanse of the open sea; for, at that height, even breaking waves only looked like broken lines of white foam on the blue watery plain.

She did not want any companion on these rambles, which had somewhat of the delight of stolen pleasures; for all the other respectable matrons and town-dwellers whom she knew were content to have always a business object for their walk, or else to stop at home in their own households; and Sylvia was rather ashamed of her own yearnings for solitude and open air, and the sight and sound of the mother-like sea. She used to take off her hat, and sit there, her hands clasping her knees, the salt air lifting her bright curls, gazing at the distant horizon over the sea, in a sad dreaminess of thought; if she had been asked on what she meditated, she could not have told you.

But, by-and-by, the time came when she was a prisoner in the house; a prisoner in her room, lying in bed with a little baby by her side – her child, Philip's child. His pride, his delight knew no bounds; this was a new fast tie between them; this would reconcile her to the kind of life that, with all its respectability and comfort, was so different from what she had lived before, and which Philip had often perceived that she felt to be dull and restraining. He already began to trace in the little girl, only a few days old, the lovely curves that he knew so well by heart in the mother's face. Sylvia, too, pale, still, and weak, was very happy; yes, really happy for the first time since her irrevocable marriage. For its irrevocableness had weighed much upon her with a sense of dull hopelessness; she felt all Philip's kindness, she was grateful to him for his tender regard towards her mother, she was learning to love him as well as to like and respect him. She did not know what else she could have done but marry so true a friend, and she and her mother so friendless; but, at the same time, it was like lead on her morning spirits when she awoke and remembered that the decision was made, the dead was done, the choice taken which comes to most people but once in their lives. Now the little baby came in upon this state of mind like a ray of sunlight into a gloomy room.

Even her mother was rejoiced and proud; even with her crazed brain and broken heart, the sight of sweet, peaceful infancy brought light to her. All the old ways of holding a baby, of hushing it to sleep, of tenderly guarding its little limbs from injury, came back, like the habits of her youth, to Bell; and she was never so happy or so easy in her mind, or so sensible and connected in her ideas, as when she had Sylvia's baby in her arms.

It was a pretty sight to see, however familiar to all of us such things may be – the pale, worn old woman, in her quaint, old-fashioned country dress, holding the little infant on her knees, looking at its open, unspeculative eyes, and talking the little language to it as though it could understand; the father on his knees, kept prisoner by a small, small finger curled round his strong and sinewy one, and gazing at the tiny creature with wondering idolatry; the young mother, fair, pale, and smiling, propped up on pillows in order that she, too, might see the wonderful babe; it was astonishing how the doctor could come and go without being drawn into the admiring vortex, and look at this baby just as if babies came into the world every day.

'Philip,' said Sylvia, one night, as he sate as still as a mouse in her room, imagining her to be asleep. He was by her bedside in a moment.

'I've been thinking what she's to be called. Isabella, after mother; and what were yo'r mother's name?'

'Margaret,' said he.

'Margaret Isabella; Isabella Margaret. Mother's called Bell. She might be called Bella.'

'I could ha' wished her to be called after thee.'

She made a little impatient movement.

'Nay; Sylvia's not a lucky name. Best be called after thy mother and mine. And I want for to ask Hester to be godmother.'

'Anything thou likes, sweetheart. Shall we call her Rose, after Hester Rose?'

'No, no!' said Sylvia; 'she mun be called after my mother, or thine, or both. I should like her to be called Bella, after mother, because she's so fond of baby.'

'Anything to please thee, darling.'

'Don't say that as if it didn't signify; there's a deal in having a pretty name,' said Sylvia, a little annoyed. 'I ha' allays hated being called Sylvia. It were after father's mother, Sylvia Steele.'

'I niver thought any name in a' the world so sweet and pretty as Sylvia,' said Philip, fondly; but she was too much absorbed in her own thoughts to notice either his manner or his words.

'There, yo'll not mind if it is Bella, because yo' see my mother is alive to be pleased by its being named after her, and Hester may be godmother, and I'll ha' t' dove-coloured silk as yo' gave me afore we were married made up into a cloak for it to go to church in.'

'I got it for thee,' said Philip, a little disappointed. 'It'll be too good for the baby.'

'Eh! but I'm so careless, I should be spilling something on it? But if thou got it for me I cannot find i' my heart for t' wear it on baby, and I'll have it made into a christening gown for mysel'. But I'll niver feel at my ease in it, for fear of spoiling it.'

'Well! an' if thou does spoil it, love, I'll get thee another. I make account of riches only for thee; that I may be able to get thee whativer thou's a fancy for, for either thysel', or thy mother.'

She lifted her pale face from her pillow, and put up her lips to kiss him for these words.

Perhaps on that day Philip reached the zenith of his life's happiness.

CHAPTER XXXI

EVIL OMENS

THE first step in Philip's declension happened in this way. Sylvia had made rapid progress in her recovery; but now she seemed at a stationary point of weakness; wakeful nights succeeding to languid days. Occasionally she caught a little sleep in the afternoons, but she usually awoke startled and feverish.

One afternoon Philip had stolen upstairs to look at her and his child; but the efforts he made at careful noiselessness made the door creak on its hinges as he opened it. The woman employed to nurse her had taken the baby into another room that no sound might rouse her from her slumber; and Philip would probably have been warned against entering the chamber where his wife lay sleeping had he been perceived by the nurse. As it was, he opened the door, made a noise, and Sylvia started up, her face all one flush, her eyes wild and uncertain; she looked about her as if she did not know where she was; pushed the hair off her hot forehead; all which actions Philip saw, dismayed and regretful. But he kept still, hoping that she would lie down and compose herself. Instead she stretched out her arms imploringly, and said, in a voice full of yearning and tears,—

'Oh! Charley! come to me – come to me!' and then as she more fully became aware of the place where she was, her actual situation, she sank back and feebly began to cry. Philip's heart boiled within him; any man's would under the circumstances, but he had the sense of guilty concealment to aggravate the intensity of his feelings. Her weak cry after another man, too, irritated him, partly through his anxious love, which made him wise to know how much physical harm she was doing herself. At this moment he stirred, or unintentionally made some sound: she started up afresh, and called out,—

'Oh, who's theere? Do, for God's sake, tell me who yo' are!'

'It's me,' said Philip, coming forwards, striving to keep down the miserable complication of love and jealousy, and remorse and anger, that made his heart beat so wildly, and almost took him out of himself. Indeed, he must have been quite beside himself for the time, or he could never have gone on to utter the unwise, cruel words he did. But she spoke first, in a distressed and plaintive tone of voice.

'Oh, Philip, I've been asleep, and yet I think I was awake! And I saw Charley Kinraid as plain as iver I see thee now, and he wasn't drowned at all. I'm sure he's alive somewheere; he were so clear and life-like. Oh! what shall I do? what shall I do?'

She wrung her hands in feverish distress. Urged by passionate feelings of various kinds, and also by his desire to quench the agitation which was doing her harm, Philip spoke, hardly knowing what he said.

'Kinraid's dead, I tell yo', Sylvie! And what kind of a woman are yo' to go dreaming of another man i' this way, and taking on so about him; when yo're a wedded wife, with a child as yo've borne to another man?'

In a moment he could have bitten out his tongue. She looked at him with the mute reproach which some of us see (God help us!) in the eyes of the dead, as they come before our sad memories in the night-season; looked at him with such a solemn, searching look, never saying a word of reply or defence. Then she lay down, motionless and silent. He had been instantly stung with remorse for his speech; the words were not beyond his lips when an agony had entered his heart; but her steady, dilated eyes had kept him dumb and motionless as if by a spell.

Now he rushed to the bed on which she lay, and half knelt, half threw himself upon it, imploring her to forgive him; regardless for the time of any evil consequences to her, it seemed as if he must have her pardon – her relenting – at any price, even if they both died in the act of reconciliation. But she lay speechless, and, as far as she could be, motionless, the bed trembling under her with the quivering she could not still.

Philip's wild tones caught the nurse's ears, and she entered full of the dignified indignation of wisdom.

'Are yo' for killing yo'r wife, measter?' she asked. 'She's noane so strong as she can bear flytin'* and scoldin', nor will she be for many a week to come. Go down wi' ye, and leave her i' peace if yo're a man as can be called a man!'

Her anger was rising as she caught sight of Sylvia's averted face. It was flushed crimson, her eyes full of intense emotion of some kind, her lips compressed; but an involuntary twitching overmastering her resolute stillness from time to time. Philip, who did not see the averted face, nor understand the real danger in which he was placing his wife, felt as though he must have one word, one responsive touch of the hand which lay passive in his, which was not even drawn away from the kisses with which he covered it, any more than if it had been an impassive stone. The nurse had fairly to take him by the shoulders, and turn him out of the room.

In half an hour the doctor had to be summoned. Of course, the nurse gave him her version of the events of the afternoon, with much *animus* against Philip; and the doctor thought it his duty to have some very serious conversation with him.

'I do assure you, Mr Hepburn, that, in the state your wife has been in for some days, it was little less than madness on your part to speak to her about anything that could give rise to strong emotion.'

'It was madness, sir!' replied Philip, in a low, miserable tone of voice. The doctor's heart was touched, in spite of the nurse's accusations against the scolding husband. Yet the danger was now too serious for him to mince matters.

'I must tell you that I cannot answer for her life, unless the greatest precautions are taken on your part, and unless the measures I shall use have the effect I wish for in the next twenty-four hours. She is on the verge of a brain fever. Any allusion to the subject which has been the final cause of the state in which she now is must be most cautiously avoided, even to a chance word which may bring it to her memory.'

And so on; but Philip seemed to hear only this: then he might not express contrition, or sue for pardon, he must go on unforgiven through all this stress of anxiety; and even if she recovered the doctor warned him of the undesirableness of recurring to what had passed!

Heavy miserable times of endurance and waiting have to be passed through by all during the course of their lives; and Philip had had his share of such seasons, when the heart, and the will, and the speech, and the limbs, must be bound down with strong resolution to patience.

For many days, nay, for weeks, he was forbidden to see Sylvia, as the very sound of his footstep brought on a recurrence of the fever and convulsive movement. Yet she seemed, from questions she feebly asked the nurse, to have forgotten all that had happened on the day of her attack from the time when she dropped off to sleep. But how much she remembered of after occurrences no one could ascertain. She was quiet enough when, at length, Philip was allowed to see her. But he was half jealous of his child, when he watched how she could smile at it, while she never changed a muscle of her face at all he could do or say.

And of a piece with this extreme quietude and reserve was her behaviour to him when at length she had fully recovered, and was able to go about the house again. Philip thought many a time of the words she had used long before – before their marriage. Ominous words they were.

'It's not in me to forgive; I sometimes think it's not in me to forget.'

Philip was tender even to humility in his conduct towards her. But nothing stirred her from her fortress of reserve. And he knew she was so different; he knew how loving, nay, passionate, was her nature – vehement, demonstrative – oh! how could he stir her once more into expression, even if the first show or speech she made was of anger? Then he tried being angry with her himself; he was sometimes unjust to her consciously and of a purpose, in order to provoke her into defending herself, and appealing against his unkindness. He only seemed to drive her love away still more.

If any one had known all that was passing in that household, while yet the story of it was not ended, nor, indeed, come to its crisis, their hearts would have been sorry for the man who lingered long at the door of the room in which his wife sate cooing and talking to her baby, and sometimes laughing back to it, or who was soothing the querulousness of failing age with every possible patience of love; sorry for the poor listener who was hungering for the profusion of tenderness thus scattered on the senseless air, yet only by stealth caught the echoes of what ought to have been his.

It was so difficult to complain, too; impossible, in fact. Everything that a wife could do from duty she did; but the love seemed to have fled, and, in such cases, no reproaches or complaints can avail to bring it back. So reason outsiders, and are convinced of the result before the experiment is made. But Philip could not reason, or could not yield to reason; and so he complained and reproached. She did not much answer him; but he thought that her eyes expressed the old words,—

'It's not in me to forgive; I sometimes think it's not in me to forget.'

However, it is an old story, an ascertained fact, that, even in the most tender and stable masculine natures, at the supremest season of their lives, there is room for other thoughts and passions than such as are connected with love. Even with the most domestic and affectionate men, their emotions seem to be kept in a cell distinct and away from their actual lives. Philip had other thoughts and other occupations than those connected with his wife during all this time.

An uncle of his mother's, a Cumberland 'statesman,'* of whose existence he was barely conscious, died about this time, leaving to his unknown great-nephew four or five hundred pounds, which put him at once in a different position with regard to his business. Henceforward his ambition was roused,

– such humble ambition as befitted a shopkeeper in a country town sixty or seventy years ago. To be respected by the men around him had always been an object with him, and was, perhaps, becoming more so than ever now, as a sort of refuge from his deep, sorrowful mortification in other directions. He was greatly pleased at being made a sidesman; and, in preparation for the further honour of being churchwarden, he went regularly twice a day to church on Sundays. There was enough religious feeling in him to make him disguise the worldly reason for such conduct from himself. He believed that he went because he thought it right to attend public worship in the parish church whenever it was offered up; but it may be questioned of him, as of many others, how far he would have been as regular in attendance in a place where he was not known. With this, however, we have nothing to do. The fact was that he went regularly to church, and he wished his wife to accompany him to the pew, newly painted, with his name on the door, where he sate in full sight of the clergyman and congregation.

Sylvia had never been in the habit of such regular church-going, and she felt it as a hardship, and slipped out of the duty as often as ever she could. In her unmarried days, she and her parents had gone annually to the mother-church of the parish in which Haytersbank was situated: on the Monday succeeding the Sunday next after the Romish Saint's Day, to whom the church was dedicated, there was a great feast or wake held, and, on the Sunday, all the parishioners came to church from far and near. Frequently, too, in the course of the year, Sylvia would accompany one or other of her parents to Scarby Moorside* afternoon service, – when the hay was got in, and the corn not ready for cutting, or the cows were dry and there was no afternoon milking. Many clergymen were languid in those days, and did not too curiously inquire into the reasons which gave them such small congregations in country parishes.

Now she was married, this weekly church-going which Philip seemed to expect from her, became a tie and a small hardship, which connected itself with her life of respectability and prosperity. 'A crust of bread and liberty'* was much more accordant to Sylvia's nature than plenty of creature comforts and many restraints. Another wish of Philip's, against which she said no word, but constantly rebelled in thought and deed, was his desire that the servant he had engaged during the time of her illness to take charge of the baby, should always carry it whenever it was taken out for a walk. Sylvia often felt, now she was strong, as if she would far rather have been without the responsibility of having this nursemaid, of whom she was, in reality, rather afraid. The good side of it was that it set her at liberty to attend to her mother at times when she would have been otherwise occupied with her baby; but Bell required very little from any one: she was easily pleased, unexacting, and methodical even in her dotage; preserving the quiet, undemonstrative habits of her earlier life now that the faculty of reason, which had been at the basis of the formation of such habits, was gone. She took great delight in watching the baby, and was pleased to have it in her care for a short time; but she dozed so much that it prevented her having any strong wish on the subject.

So Sylvia contrived to get her baby as much as possible to herself, in spite of the nursemaid; and, above all, she would carry it out, softly cradled in her arms, warm pillowed on her breast, and bear it to the freedom and solitude of the sea-shore on the west side of the town,* where the cliffs were not so high, and there was a good space of sand and shingle at all low tides.

Once here, she was as happy as she ever expected to be in this world. The fresh sea-breeze restored something of the colour of former days to her cheeks, the old buoyancy to her spirits; here she might talk her heart-full of loving nonsense to her baby; here it was all her own; no father to share in it, no nursemaid to dispute the wisdom of anything she did with it. She sang to it, she tossed it; it crowed and it laughed back again, till both were weary; and then she would sit down on a broken piece of rock, and fall to gazing on the advancing waves catching the sunlight on their crests, advancing, receding, for ever and for ever, as they had done all her life long – as they did when she had walked with them that once by the side of Kinraid; those cruel waves that, forgetful of the happy lovers' talk by the side of their waters, had carried one away, and drowned him deep till he was dead. Every time she sate down to look at the sea, this process of thought was gone through up to this point; the next step would, she knew, bring her to the question she dared not, must not ask. He was dead; he must be dead; for was she not Philip's wife? Then came up the recollection of Philip's speech, never forgotten, only buried out of sight: 'What kind of a woman are yo' to go on dreaming of another man, and yo' a wedded wife?' She used to shudder as if cold steel had been plunged into her warm, living body as she remembered these words; cruel words, harmlessly provoked. They were too much associated with physical pains to be dwelt upon; only their memory was always there. She paid for these happy rambles with her baby by the depression which awaited her on her re-entrance into the dark, confined house that was her home; its very fulness of comfort was an oppression. Then, when her husband saw her pale and fatigued, he was annoyed, and sometimes upbraided her for doing what was so unnecessary as to load herself with her child. She knew full well it was not that that caused her weariness. By-and-by, when he inquired and discovered that all these walks were taken in one direction, out towards the sea, he grew jealous of her love for the inanimate ocean. Was it connected in her mind with the thought of Kinraid? Why did she so perseveringly, in wind or cold, go out to the sea-shore; the western* side, too, where, if she went but far enough, she would come upon the mouth of the Haytersbank gully, the point at which she had last seen Kinraid? Such fancies haunted Philip's mind for hours after she had acknowledged the direction of her walks. But he never said a word that could distinctly tell her he disliked her going to the sea, otherwise she would have obeyed him in this, as in everything else; for absolute obedience to her husband seemed to be her rule of life at this period – obedience to him who would so gladly have obeyed her smallest wish had she but expressed it! She never knew that Philip had any painful association with the particular point on the sea-shore that she instinctively avoided, both from a consciousness of wifely duty, and also because the sight of it brought up so much sharp pain.

Philip used to wonder if the dream that preceded her illness was the suggestive cause that drew her so often to the shore. Her illness consequent upon that dream had filled his mind, so that for many months he himself had had no haunting vision of Kinraid to disturb his slumbers. But now the old dream of Kinraid's actual presence by Philip's bedside began to return with fearful vividness. Night after night it recurred; each time with some new touch of reality, and close approach; till it was as if the fate that overtakes all men were then, even then, knocking at his door.

In his business Philip prospered. Men praised him because he did well to himself. He had the perseverence, the capability for head-work and calculation, the steadiness and general forethought which might have made him a great merchant if he had lived in a large city. Without any effort of his own, almost, too, without Coulson's being aware of it, Philip was now in the position of superior partner; the one to suggest and arrange, while Coulson only carried out the plans that emanated from Philip. The whole work of life was suited to the man: he did not aspire to any different position, only to the full development of the capabilities of that which he already held. He had originated several fresh schemes with regard to the traffic of the shop; and his old masters, with all their love of tried ways, and distrust of everything new, had been candid enough to confess that their successors' plans had resulted in success. 'Their successors.' Philip was content with having the power when the exercise of it was required, and never named his own important share in the new improvements. Possibly, if he had, Coulson's vanity might have taken the alarm, and he might not have been so acquiescent for the future. As it was, he forgot his own subordinate share, and always used the imperial 'we,' 'we thought,' 'it struck us,' &c.

CHAPTER XXXII

RESCUED FROM THE WAVES

MEANWHILE Hester came and went as usual; in so quiet and methodical a way, with so even and undisturbed a temper, that she was almost forgotten when everything went well in the shop or household. She was a star, the brightness of which was only recognized in times of darkness. She herself was almost surprised at her own increasing regard for Sylvia. She had not thought she should ever be able to love the woman who had been such a laggard in acknowledging Philip's merits; and from all she had ever heard of Sylvia before she came to know her, from the angry words with which Sylvia had received her when she had first gone to Haytersbank Farm, Hester had intended to remain on friendly terms, but to avoid intimacy. But her kindness to Bell Robson had won both the mother's and daughter's hearts; and in spite of herself, certainly against her own mother's advice, she had become the familiar friend and welcome guest of the household.

Now the very change in Sylvia's whole manner and ways, which grieved and vexed Philip, made his wife the more attractive to Hester. Brought up among Quakers, although not one herself, she admired and respected the staidness and outward peacefulness common amongst the young women of that sect. Sylvia, whom she had expected to find volatile, talkative, vain, and wilful, was quiet and still, as if she had been born a Friend: she seemed to have no will of her own; she served her mother and child for love; she obeyed her husband in all things, and never appeared to pine after gaiety or pleasure. And yet at times Hester thought, or rather a flash came across her mind, as if all things were not as right as they seemed. Philip looked older, more care-worn; nay, even Hester was obliged to allow to herself that she had heard him speak to his wife in sharp, aggrieved tones. Innocent Hester! she could not understand how the very qualities she so admired in Sylvia were just what were so foreign to her nature that the husband, who had known her from a child, felt what an unnatural restraint she was putting upon herself, and would have hailed petulant words or wilful actions with an unspeakable thankfulness for relief.

One day – it was in the spring of 1798 – Hester was engaged to stay to tea with the Hepburns, in order that after that early meal she might set to again in helping Philip and Coulson to pack away the winter cloths and flannels, for which there was no longer any use. The tea-time was half-past four; about four o'clock a heavy April shower came on, the hail pattering against the window-panes so as to awaken Mrs Robson from her afternoon's nap. She came down the corkscrew stairs, and found Phœbe in the parlour arranging the tea-things.

Phœbe and Mrs Robson were better friends than Phœbe and her young mistress; and so they began to talk a little together in a comfortable, familiar way. Once or twice Philip looked in, as if he would be glad to see the tea-table in readiness; and then Phœbe would put on a spurt of busy bustle, which ceased almost as soon as his back was turned, so eager was she to obtain Mrs Robson's sympathy in some little dispute that had occurred between her and the nurse-maid. The latter had misappropriated some hot water, prepared and required by Phœbe, to the washing of the baby's clothes; it was a long story, and would have tired the patience of any one in full possession of their senses; but the details were just within poor Bell's comprehension, and she was listening with the greatest sympathy. Both the women were unaware of the lapse of time; but it was of consequence to Philip, as the extra labour was not to be begun until after tea, and the daylight hours were precious.

At a quarter to five Hester and he came in, and then Phœbe began to hurry. Hester went up to sit by Bell and talk to her. Philip spoke to Phœbe in the familiar words of country-folk. Indeed, until his marriage, Phœbe had always called him by his Christian name, and had found it very difficult to change it into 'master.'

'Where's Sylvie?' said he.

'Gone out wi' t' babby,' replied Phœbe.

'Why can't Nancy carry it out?' asked Philip.

It was touching on the old grievance: he was tired, and he spoke with sharp annoyance. Phœbe might easily have told him the real state of the case; Nancy was busy at her washing, which would have been reason enough. But the nursemaid had vexed her, and she did not like Philip's sharpness, so she only said,—

'It's noane o' my business; it's yo' t' look after yo'r own wife and child; but yo'r but a lad after a'.'

This was not conciliatory speech, and just put the last stroke to Philip's fit of ill-temper.

'I'm not for my tea to-night,' said he, to Hester, when all was ready. 'Sylvie's not here, and nothing is nice, or as it should be. I'll go and set to on t' stock-taking. Don't yo' hurry, Hester; stop and chat a bit with th' old lady.'

'Nay, Philip,' said Hester, 'thou's sadly tired; just take this cup o' tea; Sylvia 'll be grieved if yo' haven't something.'

'Sylvia doesn't care whether I'm full or fasting,' replied he, impatiently putting aside the cup. 'If she did she'd ha' taken care to be in, and ha' seen to things being as I like them.'

Now in general Philip was the least particular of men about meals; and to do Sylvia justice, she was scrupulously attentive to every household duty in which old Phœbe would allow her to meddle, and always careful to see after her husband's comforts. But Philip was too vexed at her absence to perceive the injustice of what he was saying, nor was he aware how Bell Robson had been attending to what he said. But she was sadly discomfited by it, understanding just enough of the grievance in hand to think that her daughter was neglectful of those duties which she herself had always regarded as paramount to all others; nor could Hester convince her that Philip had not meant what he said; neither could she turn the poor old woman's thoughts from the words which had caused her distress.

Presently Sylvia came in, bright and cheerful, although breathless with hurry.

'Oh,' said she, taking off her wet shawl, 'we've had to shelter from such a storm of rain, baby and me – but see! she's none the worse for it, as bonny as iver, bless her.'

Hester began some speech of admiration for the child in order to prevent Bell from delivering the lecture she felt sure was coming down on the unsuspecting Sylvia; but all in vain.

'Philip's been complaining on thee, Sylvie,' said Bell, in the way in which she had spoken to her daughter when she was a little child; grave and severe in tone and look, more than in words. 'I forget justly what about, but he spoke on thy neglecting him continual. It's not right, my lass, it's not right; a woman should – but my head's very tired, and all I can think on to say is, it's not right.'

'Philip been complaining of me, and to mother!' said Sylvia, ready to burst into tears, so grieved and angry was she.

'No!' said Hester, 'thy mother has taken it a little too strong; he were vexed like at his tea not being ready.'

Sylvia said no more, but the bright colour faded from her cheek, and the contraction of care returned to her brow. She occupied herself with taking off her baby's walking things. Hester lingered, anxious to soothe and make peace; she was looking sorrowfully at Sylvia, when she saw tears dropping on the baby's cloak, and then it seemed as if she must speak a word of comfort before going to the shop-work, where she knew she was expected by both Philip and Coulson. She poured out a cup of tea, and coming close up to Sylvia, and kneeling down by her, she whispered,—

'Just take him this into t' ware-room; it'll put all to rights if thou'll take it to him wi' thy own hands.'

Sylvia looked up, and Hester then more fully saw how she had been crying. She whispered in reply, for fear of disturbing her mother,—

'I don't mind anything but his speaking ill on me to mother. I know I'm for iver trying and trying to be a good wife to him, an' it's very dull work; harder than yo' think on, Hester, – an' I would ha' been home for tea to-night only I was afeared of baby getting wet wi' t' storm o' hail as we had down on t' shore; and we sheltered under a rock. It's a weary coming home to this dark place, and to find my own mother set against me.'

'Take him his tea, like a good lassie. I'll answer for it he'll be all right. A man takes it hardly when he comes in tired, a-thinking his wife 'll be there to cheer him up a bit, to find her off, and niver know nought of t' reason why.'

'I'm glad enough I've getten a baby,' said Sylvia, 'but for aught else I wish I'd niver been married, I do!'

'Hush thee, lass!' said Hester, rising up indignant; 'now that is a sin. Eh! if thou only knew the lot o' some folk. But let's talk no more on that, that cannot be helped; go, take him his tea, for it's a sad thing to think on him fasting all this time.'

Hester's voice was raised by the simple fact of her change of position; and the word fasting caught Mrs Robson's ear, as she sate at her knitting by the chimney-corner.

'Fasting? he said thou didn't care if he were full or fasting. Lassie! it's not right in thee, I say; go, take him his tea at once.'

Sylvia rose, and gave up the baby, which she had been suckling, to Nancy, who having done her washing, had come for her charge, to put it to bed. Sylvia kissed it fondly, making a little moan of sad, passionate tenderness as she did so. Then she took the cup of tea; but she said, rather defiantly, to Hester,—

'I'll go to him with it, because mother bids me, and it'll ease her mind.'

Then louder to her mother, she added,—

'Mother, I'll take him his tea, though I couldn't help the being out.'

If the act itself was conciliatory, the spirit in which she was going to do it was the reverse. Hester followed her slowly into the ware-room, with intentional delay, thinking that her presence might be an obstacle to their mutually understanding one another. Sylvia held the cup and plate of bread and butter out to Philip, but avoided meeting his eye, and said not a word of explanation, or regret, or self-justification. If she had spoken, though ever so crossly, Philip would have been relieved, and would have preferred it to her silence. He wanted to provoke her to speech, but did not know how to begin.

'Thou's been out again wandering on that sea-shore!' said he. She did not answer him. 'I cannot think what's always taking thee there, when one would ha' thought a walk up to Esdale would be far more sheltered, both for thee and baby in such weather as this. Thou'll be having that baby ill some of these days.'

At this, she looked up at him, and her lips moved as though she were going to say something. Oh, how he wished she would, that they might come to a wholesome quarrel, and a making friends again, and a tender kissing, in which he might whisper penitence for all his hasty words, or unreasonable vexation. But she had come resolved not to speak, for fear of showing too much passion, too much emotion. Only as she was going away she turned and said,—

'Philip, mother hasn't many more years to live; dunnot grieve her, and set her again' me by finding fault wi' me afore her. Our being wed were a great mistake; but before t' poor old widow-woman let us make as if we were happy.'

'Sylvie! Sylvie!' he called after her. She must have heard, but she did not turn. He went after her, and seized her by the arm rather roughly; she had stung him to the heart with her calm words, which seemed to reveal a long-formed conviction.

'Sylvie!' said he, almost fiercely, 'what do yo' mean by what you've said? Speak! I will have an answer.'

He almost shook her: she was half frightened by his vehemence of behaviour, which she took for pure anger, while it was the outburst of agonized and unrequited love.

'Let me go! Oh, Philip, yo' hurt me!'

Just at this moment Hester came up; Philip was ashamed of his passionate ways in her serene presence, and loosened his grasp of his wife, and she ran away; ran into her mother's empty room, as to a solitary place, and there burst into that sobbing, miserable crying which we instinctively know is too surely lessening the length of our days on earth to be indulged in often.

When she had exhausted that first burst and lay weak and quiet for a time, she listened in dreading expectation of the sound of his footstep coming in search of her to make friends. But he was detained below on business, and never came. Instead, her mother came clambering up the stairs; she was now in the habit of going to bed between seven and eight, and to-night she was retiring at even an earlier hour.

Sylvia sprang up and drew down the window-blind, and made her face and manner as composed as possible, in order to soothe and comfort her mother's last waking hours. She helped her to bed with gentle patience; the restraint imposed upon her by her tender filial love was good for her, though all the time she was longing to be alone to have another wild outburst. When her mother was going off to sleep, Sylvia went to look at her baby, also in a soft sleep. Then she gazed out at the evening sky, high above the tiled roofs of the opposite houses, and the longing to be out under the peaceful heavens took possession of her once more.

'It's my only comfort,' said she to herself; 'and there's no earthly harm in it. I would ha' been at home to his tea, if I could; but when he doesn't want me, and mother doesn't want me, and baby is either in my arms or asleep; why, I'll go any cry my fill out under yon great quiet sky. I cannot stay in t' house to be choked up wi' my tears, nor yet to have him coming about me either for scolding or peace-making.'

So she put on her things and went out again; this time along the High Street, and up the long flights of steps towards the parish church, and there she stood and thought that here she had first met Kinraid, at Darley's burying, and she tried to recall the very look of all the sad, earnest faces round the open grave – the whole scene, in fact; and let herself give way to the miserable regrets she had so often tried to control. Then she walked on, crying bitterly, almost unawares to herself; on through the high, bleak fields at the summit of the cliffs; fields bounded by loose stone fences, and far from all sight of the habitation of man. But, below, the sea rose and raged; it was high water at the highest tide, and the wind blew gustily from the land, vainly combating the great waves that came invincibly up with a roar and an impotent furious dash against the base of the cliffs below.

Sylvia heard the sound of the passionate rush and rebound of many waters, like the shock of mighty guns, whenever the other sound of the blustering gusty wind was lulled for an instant. She was more quieted by this tempest of the elements than she would have been had all nature seemed as still as she had imagined it to be while she was yet in-doors and only saw a part of the serene sky.

She fixed on a certain point, in her own mind, which she would reach, and then turn back again. It was where the outline of the land curved inwards, dipping into a little bay. Here the field-path she had hitherto followed descended somewhat abruptly to a cluster of fishermen's cottages, hardly large enough to be called a village; and then the narrow roadway wound up the rising ground till it again reached the summit of the cliffs that stretched along the coast for many and many a mile.

Sylvia said to herself that she would turn homewards when she came within sight of this cove, – Headlington Cove, they called it. All the way along she had met no one since she had left the town, but just as she had got over the last stile, or ladder of stepping-stones, into the field from which the path descended, she came upon a number of people – quite a crowd, in fact; men moving forward in a steady line, hauling at a rope, a chain, or something of that kind; boys children, and women holding babies in their arms, as if all were fain to come out and partake in some general interest.

They kept within a certain distance from the edge of the cliff, and Sylvia, advancing a little, now saw the reason why. The great cable the men held was attached to some part of a smack, which could now be seen by her in the waters below, half dismantled, and all but a wreck, yet with her deck covered with living men, as far as the waning light would allow her to see. The vessel strained to get free of the strong guiding cable; the tide was turning, the wind was blowing off shore, and Sylvia knew without being told, that almost parallel to this was a line of sunken rocks that had been fatal to many a ship before now, if she had tried to take the inner channel instead of keeping out to sea for miles, and then steering in straight for Monkshaven port. And the ships that had been thus lost had been in good plight and order compared to this vessel, which seemed nothing but a hull without mast or sail.

By this time, the crowd – the fishermen from the hamlet down below, with their wives and children – all had come but the bedridden – had reached the place where Sylvia stood. The women, in a state of wild excitement, rushed on, encouraging their husbands and sons by words, even while they hindered them by actions; and, from time to time, one of them would run to the edge of the cliff and shout out some brave words of hope in her shrill voice to the crew on the deck below. Whether these latter heard it or not, no one could tell; but it seemed as if all human voice must be lost in the tempestuous stun and tumult of wind and wave. It was generally a woman with a child in her arms who so employed herself. As the strain upon the cable became greater, and the ground on which they strove more uneven, every hand was needed to hold and push, and all those women who were unencumbered held by the dear rope on which so many lives were depending. On they came, a long line of human beings, black against the ruddy sunset sky. As they came near Sylvia, a woman cried out,—

'Dunnot stand idle, lass, but houd on wi' us; there's many a bonny life at stake, and many a mother's heart a-hangin' on this bit o' hemp. Tak' houd, lass, and give a firm grip, and God remember thee i' thy need.'

Sylvia needed no second word; a place was made for her, and in an instant more the rope was pulling against her hands till it seemed as though she was holding fire in her bare palms. Never a one of them thought of letting go for an instant, though when all was over many of their hands were raw and bleeding. Some strong, experienced fishermen passed a word along the line from time to time, giving directions as to how it should be held according to varying occasions; but few among the rest had breath or strength enough to speak. The women and children that accompanied them ran on before, breaking down the loose stone fences, so as to obviate delay or hindrance; they talked continually, exhorting, encouraging, explaining. From their many words and fragmentary sentences, Sylvia learnt that the vessel was supposed to be a Newcastle smack sailing from London, that had taken the dangerous inner channel to save time, and had been caught in the storm, which she was too crazy to withstand; and that if by some daring contrivance of the fishermen who had first seen her the cable had not been got ashore, she would have been cast upon the rocks before this, and 'all on board perished.'

'It were dayleet then,' quoth one woman; 'a could see their faces, they were so near. They were as pale as dead men, an' one was prayin' down on his knees. There was a King's officer aboard, for I saw t' gowd about him.'

'He'd maybe come from these hom'ard parts, and be comin' to see his own folk; else it's no common for king's officers to sail in aught but King's ships.'

'Eh! but it's gettin' dark! See there's t' leeghts in t' houses in t' New Town! T' grass is crispin' wi' t' white frost under out feet. It'll be a hard tug round t' point, and then she'll be gettin' into still waters.'

One more great push and mighty strain, and the danger was past; the vessel – or what remained of her – was in the harbour, among the lights and cheerful sounds of safety. The fishermen sprang down the cliff to the quay-side, anxious to see the men whose lives they had saved; the women, weary and over-excited, began to cry. Not Sylvia, however; her fount of tears had been exhausted earlier in the day: her principal feeling was of gladness and high rejoicing that they were saved who had been so near to death not half an hour before.

She would have liked to have seen the men, and shaken hands with them all round. But instead she must go home, and well would it be with her if she was in time for her husband's supper, and escaped any notice of her absence. So she separated herself from the groups of women who sate on the grass in the churchyard, awaiting the return of such of their husbands as could resist the fascinations of the Monkshaven public houses. As Sylvia went down the church steps, she came upon one of the fishermen who had helped to tow the vessel into port.

'There was seventeen men and boys aboard her, and a navy-lieutenant as had comed as passenger. It were a good job as we could manage her. Good-neet to thee, thou'll sleep all t' sounder for havin' lent a hand.'

The street air felt hot and close after the sharp keen atmosphere of the heights above; the decent shops and houses had all their shutters put up, and were preparing for their early bed-time. Already lights shone here and there in the upper chambers, and Sylvia scarcely met any one.

She went round up the passage from the quay-side, and in by the private door. All was still; the basins of bread and milk that she and her husband were in the habit of having for supper stood in the fender before the fire, each with a plate upon them. Nancy had gone to bed, Phœbe dozed in the kitchen; Philip was still in the ware-room, arranging goods and taking stock along with Coulson, for Hester had gone home to her mother.

Sylvia was not willing to go and seek out Philip, after the manner in which they had parted. All the despondency of her life became present to her again as she sate down within her home. She had forgotten it in her interest and excitement, but now it came back again.

Still she was hungry, and youthful, and tired. She took her basin up, and was eating her supper when she heard a cry of her baby upstairs, and ran away to attend to it. When it had been fed and hushed away to sleep, she went in to see her mother, attracted by some unusual noise in her room.

She found Mrs Robson awake, and restless, and ailing;

dwelling much on what Philip had said in his anger against Sylvia. It was really necessary for her daughter to remain with her; so Sylvia stole out, and went quickly downstairs to Philip – now sitting tired and worn out, and eating his supper with little or no appetite – and told him she meant to pass the night with her mother.

His answer of acquiescence was so short and careless, or so it seemed to her, that she did not tell him any more of what she had done or seen that evening, or even dwell upon any details of her mother's indisposition.

As soon as she had left the room, Philip set down his half-finished basin of bread and milk, and sate long, his face hidden in his folded arms. The wick of the candle grew long and black, and fell, and sputtered, and puttered; he sate on, unheeding either it or the pale gray fire that was dying out – dead at last.

CHAPTER XXXIII

AN APPARITION

MRS ROBSON was very poorly all night long. Uneasy thoughts seemed to haunt and perplex her brain, and she neither slept nor woke, but was restless and uneasy in her talk and movements.

Sylvia lay down by her, but got so little sleep, that at length she preferred sitting in the easy-chair by the bedside. Here she dropped off to slumber in spite of herself; the scene of the evening before seemed to be repeated; the cries of the many people, the heavy roar and dash of the threatening waves, were repeated in her ears; and something was said to her through all the conflicting noises, – what it was she could not catch, though she strained to hear the hoarse murmur that, in her dream, she believed to convey a meaning of the utmost importance to her.

This dream, that mysterious, only half-intelligible sound, recurred whenever she dozed, and her inability to hear the words uttered distressed her so much, that at length she sate bolt upright, resolved to sleep no more. Her mother was talking in a half-conscious way; Philip's speech of the evening before was evidently running in her mind.

'Sylvie, if thou're not a good wife to him, it'll just break my heart outright. A woman should obey her husband, and not go her own gait. I never leave the house wi'out telling father, and getting his leave.'

And then she began to cry pitifully, and to say unconnected things, till Sylvia, to soothe her, took her hand, and promised never to leave the house without asking her husband's permission, though in making this promise, she felt as if she were sacrificing her last pleasure to her mother's wish; for she knew well enough that Philip would always raise objections to the rambles which reminded her of her old free open-air life. But to comfort and cherish her mother she would have done anything; yet this very morning that was dawning, she must go and ask his permission for a simple errand, or break her word.

She knew from experience that nothing quieted her mother so well as balm-tea;* it might be that the herb really possessed some sedative power; it might be only early faith, and often repeated experience, but it had always had a tranquillizing effect; and more than once, during the restless hours of the night, Mrs Robson had asked for it; but Sylvia's stock of last year's dead leaves was exhausted. Still she knew where a plant of balm grew in the sheltered corner of Haytersbank Farm garden; she knew that the tenants who had succeeded them in the occupation of the farm had had to leave it in consequence of a death, and that the place was unoccupied; and in the darkness she had planned that if she could leave her mother after the dawn came, and she had attended to her baby, she would walk quickly to the old garden, and gather the tender sprigs which she was sure to find there.

Now she must go and ask Philip; and till she held her baby to her breast, she bitterly wished that she were free from the duties and chains of matrimony. But the touch of its waxen fingers, the hold of its little mouth, made her relax into docility and gentleness. She gave it back to Nancy to be dressed, and softly opened the door of Philip's bed-room.

'Philip!' said she, gently. 'Philip!'

He started up from dreams of her; of her, angry. He saw her there, rather pale with her night's watch and anxiety, but looking meek, and a little beseeching.

'Mother has had such a bad night! she fancied once as some balm-tea would do her good – it allays used to: but my dried balm is all gone, and I thought there'd be sure to be some in t' old garden at Haytersbank. Feyther planted a bush just for mother, wheere it allays came up early, nigh t' old elder-tree; and if yo'd not mind, I could run theere while she sleeps, and be back again in an hour, and it's not seven now.'

'Thou's not wear thyself out with running, Sylvie,' said Philip, eagerly; 'I'll get up and go myself, or, perhaps,' continued he, catching the shadow that was coming over her face, 'thou'd rather go thyself: it's only that I'm so afraid of thy tiring thyself.'

'It'll not tire me,' said Sylvia. 'Afore I was married, I was out often far farther than that, afield to fetch up t' kine, before my breakfast.'

'Well, go if thou will,' said Philip. 'But get somewhat to eat first, and don't hurry; there's no need for that.'

She had got her hat and shawl, and was off before he had finished his last words.

The long High Street was almost empty of people at that early hour; one side was entirely covered by the cool morning shadow which lay on the pavement, and crept up the opposite houses till only the topmost story caught the rosy sunlight. Up the hill-road, through the gap in the stone wall, across the dewy fields, Sylvia went by the very shortest path she knew.

She had only once been at Haytersbank since her wedding-day. On that occasion the place had seemed strangely and dissonantly changed by the numerous children who were diverting themselves before the open door, and whose play-things and clothes strewed the house-place, and made it one busy scene of confusion and untidiness, more like the Corneys' kitchen in former times, than her mother's orderly and quiet abode. Those little children were fatherless now; and the house was shut up, awaiting the entry of some new tenant. There were no shutters to shut; the long low window was blinking in the rays of the morning sun; the house and cow-house doors were closed, and no poultry wandered about the field in search of stray grains of corn, or early worms. It was a strange and unfamiliar silence, and struck solemnly on Sylvia's mind. Only a thrush in the old orchard down in the hollow, out of sight, whistled and gurgled with continual shrill melody.

Sylvia went slowly past the house and down the path leading to the wild, deserted bit of garden. She saw that the last tenants had had a pump sunk for them, and resented the innovation, as though the well she was passing could feel the insult. Over it grew two hawthorn trees; on the bent trunk of one of them she used to sit, long ago: the charm of the position being enhanced by the possible danger of falling into the well and being drowned. The rusty unused chain was wound round the windlass; the bucket was falling to pieces from dryness. A lean cat came from some outhouse, and mewed pitifully with hunger; accompanying Sylvia to the garden, as if glad of some human companionship, yet refusing to allow itself to be touched. Primroses grew in the sheltered places, just as they formerly did; and made the uncultivated ground seem less deserted than the garden, where the last year's weeds were rotting away, and cumbering the ground.

Sylvia forced her way through the berry bushes to the herb-plot, and plucked the tender leaves she had come to seek; sighing a little all the time. Then she retraced her steps; paused softly before the house-door, and entered the porch and kissed the senseless wood.

She tried to tempt the poor gaunt cat into her arms, meaning to carry it home and befriend it; but it was scared by her endeavour and ran back to its home in the outhouse, making a green path across the white dew of the meadow. Then

Sylvia began to hasten home, thinking, and remembering – at the stile that led into the road she was brought short up.

Some one stood in the lane just on the other side of the gap; his back was to the morning sun; all she saw at first was the uniform of a naval officer, so well known in Monkshaven in those days.

Sylvia went hurrying past him, not looking again, although her clothes almost brushed his, as he stood there still. She had not gone a yard – no, not half a yard – when her heart leaped up and fell again dead within her, as if she had been shot.

'Sylvia!' he said, in a voice tremulous with joy and passionate love. 'Sylvia!'

She looked round; he had turned a little, so that the light fell straight on his face. It was bronzed, and the lines were strengthened; but it was the same face she had last seen in Haytersbank gully three long years ago, and had never thought to see in life again.

He was close to her and held out his fond arms; she went fluttering towards their embrace, as if drawn by the old fascination; but when she felt them close round her, she started away, and cried out with a great pitiful shriek, and put her hands up to her forehead as if trying to clear away some bewildering mist.

Then she looked at him once more, a terrible story in her eyes, if he could but have read it.

Twice she opened her stiff lips to speak, and twice the words were overwhelmed by the surges of her misery, which bore them back into the depths of her heart.

He thought that he had come upon her too suddenly, and he attempted to soothe her with soft murmurs of love, and to woo her to his outstretched hungry arms once more. But when she saw this motion of his, she made a gesture as though pushing him away; and with an inarticulate moan of agony she put her hands to her head once more, and turning away began to run blindly towards the town for protection.

For a minute or so he was stunned with surprise at her behaviour; and then he thought it accounted for by the shock of his accost, and that she needed time to understand the unexpected joy. So he followed her swiftly, ever keeping her in view, but not trying to overtake her too speedily.

'I have frightened my poor love,' he kept thinking. And by this thought he tried to repress his impatience and check the speed he longed to use; yet he was always so near behind that her quickened sense heard his well-known footsteps following, and a mad notion flashed across her brain that she would go to the wide full river, and end the hopeless misery she felt enshrouding her. There was a sure hiding-place from all human reproach and heavy mortal woe beneath the rushing waters borne landwards by the morning tide.

No one can tell what changed her course; perhaps the thought of her sucking child; perhaps her mother; perhaps an angel of God; no one on earth knows, but as she ran along the quay-side she all at once turned up an entry, and through an open door.

He, following all the time, came into a quiet dark parlour, with a cloth and tea-things on the table ready for breakfast; the change from the bright sunny air out of doors to the deep shadow of this room made him think for the first moment that she had passed on, and that no one was there, and he stood for an instant baffled, and hearing no sound but the beating of his own heart; but an irrepressible sobbing gasp made him look round, and there he saw her cowered behind the door, her face covered tight up, and sharp shudders going through her whole frame.

'My love, my darling!' said he, going up to her, and trying to raise her, and to loosen her hands away from her face. 'I've been too sudden for thee: it was thoughtless in me; but I have so looked forward to this time, and seeing thee come along the field, and go past me, but I should ha' been more tender and careful of thee. Nay! let me have another look of thy sweet face.'

All this he whispered in the old tones of manœuvring love, in that voice she had yearned and hungered to hear in life, and had not heard, for all her longing, save in her dreams.

She tried to crouch more and more into the corner, into the hidden shadow – to sink into the ground out of sight.

Once more he spoke, beseeching her to lift up her face, to let him hear her speak.

But she only moaned.

'Sylvia!' said he, thinking he could change his tactics, and pique her into speaking, that he would make a pretence of suspicion and offence.

'Sylvia! one would think you weren't glad to see me back again at length. I only came in late last night, and my first thought on wakening was of you; it has been ever since I left you.'

Sylvia took her hands away from her face; it was gray as the face of death; her awful eyes were passionless in her despair.

'Where have yo' been?' she asked, in slow, hoarse tones, as if her voice were half strangled within her.

'Been!' said he, a red light coming into his eyes, as he bent his looks upon her; now, indeed, a true and not an assumed suspicion entering his mind.

'Been!' he repeated; then, coming a step nearer to her, and taking her hand, not tenderly this time, but with a resolution to be satisfied.

'Did not your cousin – Hepburn, I mean – did not he tell you? – he saw the press-gang seize me, – I gave him a message to you – I bade you keep true to me as I would be to you.'

Between every clause of this speech he paused and gasped for her answer; but none came. Her eyes dilated and held his steady gaze prisoner as with a magical charm – neither could look away from the other's wild, searching gaze. When he had ended, she was silent for a moment, then she cried out, shrill and fierce,—

'Philip!' No answer.

Wilder and shriller still, 'Philip!' she cried.

He was in the distant ware-room completing the last night's work before the regular shop hours began; before breakfast, also, that his wife might not find him waiting and impatient.

He heard her cry; it cut through doors, and still air, and great bales of woollen stuff; he thought that she had hurt herself, that her mother was worse, that her baby was ill, and he hastened to the spot whence the cry proceeded.

On opening the door that separated the shop from the sitting-room, he saw the back of a naval officer, and his wife on the ground, huddled up in a heap; when she perceived him come in, she dragged herself up by means of a chair, groping like a blind person, and came and stood facing him.

The officer turned fiercely round, and would have come towards Philip, who was so bewildered by the scene that even yet he did not understand who the stranger was, did not perceive for an instant that he saw the realization of his greatest dread.

But Sylvia laid her hand on Kinraid's arm, and assumed to herself the right of speech. Philip did not know her voice, it was so changed.

'Philip,' she said, 'this is Kinraid come back again to wed me. He is alive; he has niver been dead, only taken by t' press-gang. And he says yo' saw it, and knew it all t' time. Speak, was it so?'

Philip knew not what to say, whither to turn, under what refuge of words or acts to shelter.

Sylvia's influence was keeping Kinraid silent, but he was rapidly passing beyond it.

'Speak!' he cried, loosening himself from Sylvia's light grasp, and coming towards Philip, with a threatening gesture. 'Did I not bid you tell her how it was? Did I not bid you say how I would be faithful to her, and she was to be faithful to me? Oh! you damned scoundrel! have you kept it from her all that time, and let her think me dead, or false? Take that!'

His closed fist was up to strike the man, who hung his head with bitterest shame and miserable self-reproach; but Sylvia came swift between the blow and its victim.

'Charley, thou shan't strike him,' she said. 'He is a damned scoundrel' (this was said in the hardest, quietest tone), 'but he is my husband.'

'Oh! thou false heart!' exclaimed Kinraid, turning sharp

on her. 'If ever I trusted woman, I trusted you, Sylvia Robson.'

He made as though throwing her from him, with a gesture of contempt that stung her to life.

'Oh, Charley!' she cried, springing to him, 'dunnot cut me to the quick; have pity on me, though he had none. I did so love thee; it was my very heart-strings as gave way when they told me thou was drowned – feyther, and th' Corneys, and all, iverybody. Thy hat and t' bit o' ribbon I gave thee were found drenched and dripping wi' sea-water; and I went mourning for thee all the day long – dunnot turn away from me; only hearken this once, and then kill me dead, and I'll bless yo', – and have niver been mysel' since; niver ceased to feel t' sun grow dark and th' air chill and dreary when I thought on t' time when thou was alive. I did, my Charley, my own love! And I thought thou was dead for iver, and I wished I were lying beside thee. Oh, Charley! Philip, theere, where he stands could tell yo' this was true. Philip, wasn't it so?'

'Would God I were dead!' moaned forth the unhappy, guilty man. But she had turned to Kinraid, and was speaking again to him, and neither of them heard or heeded him – they were drawing closer and closer together – she, with her cheeks and eyes aflame, talking eagerly.

'And feyther was taken up, and all for setting some free as t' press-gang had gotten by a foul trick; and he were put i' York prison, and tried, and hung! – hung! Charley ! – good kind feyther was hung on a gallows; and mother lost her sense and grew silly in grief, and we were like to be turned out on t' wide world, and poor mother dateless – and I thought yo' were dead – oh! I thought yo' were dead, I did – oh, Charley, Charley!'

By this time they were in each other's arms, she with her head on his shoulder, crying as if her heart would break.

Philip came forwards and took hold of her to pull her away; but Charley held her tight, mutely defying Philip. Unconsciously she was Philip's protection, in that hour of danger, from a blow which might have been his death if strong will could have aided it to kill.

'Sylvie!' said he, grasping her tight. 'Listen to me. He didn't love yo' as I did. He had loved other women. I, yo' – yo' alone. He loved other girls before yo', and had left off loving 'em. I – I wish God would free my heart from the pang; but it will go on till I die, whether yo' love me or not. And then – where was I? Oh! that very night that he was taken, I was a-thinking on yo' and on him; and I might ha' given yo' his message, but I heard them speaking of him as knew him well; talking of his false fickle ways. How was I to know he would keep true to thee? It might be a sin in me, I cannot say; my heart and my sense are gone dead within me. I know this, I've loved yo' as no man but me ever loved before. Have some pity and forgiveness on me, if it's only because I've been so tormented with my love.'

He looked at her with feverish eager wistfulness; it faded away into despair as she made no sign of having even heard his words. He let go his hold of her, and his arm fell loosely by his side.

'I may die,' he said, 'for my life is ended!'

'Sylvia!' spoke out Kinraid, bold and fervent, 'your marriage is no marriage. You were tricked into it. You are my wife, not his. I am your husband; we plighted each other our troth. See! here is my half of the sixpence.'

He pulled it out from his bosom, tied by a black ribbon round his neck.

'When they stripped me and searched me in th' French prison, I managed to keep this. No lies can break the oath we swore to each other. I can get your pretence of a marriage set aside. I'm in favour with my admiral, and he'll do a deal for me, and back me out. Come with me; your marriage shall be set aside, and we'll be married again, all square and above-board. Come away. Leave that damned fellow to repent of the trick he played an honest sailor; we'll be true, whatever has come and gone. Come, Sylvia.'

His arm was round her waist, and he was drawing her towards the door, his face all crimson with eagerness and hope. Just then the baby cried.

'Hark!' said she, starting away from Kinraid, 'baby's

crying for me. His child – yes, it is his child – I'd forgotten that – forgotten all. I'll make my vow now, lest I lose mysel' again. I'll never forgive yon man, nor live with him as his wife again. All that's done and ended. He's spoilt my life, – he's spoilt it for as long as iver I live on this earth; but neither yo' nor him shall spoil my soul. It goes hard wi' me, Charley, it does indeed. I'll just give yo' one kiss – one little kiss – and then, so help me God, I'll niver see nor hear till – no, not that, not that is indeed – I'll niver see – sure that's enough – I'll never see yo' again on this side heaven, so help me God! I'm bound and tied, but I've sworn my oath to him as well as yo': there's things I will do, and there's things I won't. Kiss me once more. God help me, he's gone!'

CHAPTER XXXIV

A RECKLESS RECRUIT

She lay across a chair, her arms helplessly stretched out, her face unseen. Every now and then a thrill ran through her body: she was talking to herself all the time with incessant low incontinence of words.

Philip stood near her, motionless: he did not know whether she was conscious of his presence; in fact, he knew nothing but that he and she were sundered for ever; he could only take in that one idea, and it numbed all other thought.

Once more her baby cried for the comfort she alone could give.

She rose to her feet, but staggered when she tried to walk; her glazed eyes fell upon Philip as he instinctively made a step to hold her steady. No light came into her eyes any more than if she had looked upon a perfect stranger; not even was there the contraction of dislike. Some other figure filled her mind, and she saw him no more than she saw the inanimate table. That way of looking at him withered him up more than any sign of aversion would have done.

He watched her laboriously climb the stairs, and vanish

out of sight; and sat down with a sudden feeling of extreme bodily weakness.

The door of communication between the parlour and the shop was opened. That was the first event of which Philip took note; but Phœbe had come in unawares to him, with the intention of removing the breakfast things on her return from market, and seeing them unused, and knowing that Sylvia had sate up all night with her mother, she had gone back to the kitchen. Philip had neither seen nor heard her.

Now Coulson came in, amazed at Hepburn's non-appearance in the shop.

'Why! Philip, what's ado? How ill yo' look, man!' exclaimed he, thoroughly alarmed by Philip's ghastly appearance. 'What's the matter?'

'I!' said Philip, slowly gathering his thoughts. 'Why should there be anything the matter?'

His instinct, quicker to act than his reason, made him shrink from his misery being noticed, much more made any subject for explanation or sympathy.

'There may be nothing the matter wi' thee,' said Coulson, 'but thou's the look of a corpse on thy face. I was afeared something was wrong, for it's half-past nine, and thee so punctual!'

He almost guarded Philip into the shop, and kept furtively watching him, and perplexing himself with Philip's odd, strange ways.

Hester, too, observed the heavy broken-down expression on Philip's ashen face, and her heart ached for him; but after that first glance, which told her so much, she avoided all appearance of noticing or watching. Only a shadow brooded over her sweet, calm face, and once or twice she sighed to herself.

It was market-day, and people came in and out, bringing their store of gossip from the country, or the town – from the farm or the quay-side.

Among the pieces of news, the rescue of the smack the night before furnished a large topic; and by-and-by Philip heard a name that startled him into attention.

The landlady of a small public-house much frequented by sailors was talking to Coulson.

'There was a sailor aboard of her as knowed Kinraid by sight, in Shields, years ago; and he called him by his name afore they were well out o' t' river. And Kinraid was no ways set up, for all his lieutenant's uniform (and eh! but they say he looks handsome in it!); but he tells 'm all about it – how he was pressed aboard a man-o'-war, an' for his good conduct were made a warrant officer, boatswain, or something!'

All the people in the shop were listening now; Philip alone seemed engrossed in folding up a piece of cloth, so as to leave no possible chance of creases in it; yet he lost not a syllable of the good woman's narration.

She, pleased with the enlarged audience her tale had attracted, went on with fresh vigour.

'An' there's a gallant captain, one Sir Sidney Smith,* and he'd a notion o' goin' smack into a French port, an' carryin' off a vessel from right under their very noses; an' says he, "Which of yo' British sailors 'll go along with me to death or glory?" So Kinraid stands up like a man, an' "I'll go with yo', captain," he says. So they, an' some others as brave, went off, an' did their work, an' choose whativer it was, they did it famously; but they got caught by them French, an' were clapped into prison i' France for iver so long; but at last one Philip – Philip somethin' (he were a Frenchman, I know) – helped 'em to escape, in a fishin'-boat. But they were welcomed by th' whole British squadron as was i' t' Channel for t' piece of daring they'd done i' cuttin' out t' ship from a French port; an' Captain Sir Sidney Smith was made an admiral, an' him as we used t' call Charley Kinraid, the specksioneer, is made a lieutenant, an' a commissioned officer i' t' King's service; and is come to great glory, and slep in my house this very blessed night as is just past!'

A murmur of applause and interest and rejoicing buzzed all around Philip. All this was publicly known about Kinraid, – and how much more? All Monkshaven might hear tomorrow – nay, to-day – of Philip's treachery to the hero of the hour; how he had concealed his fate, and supplanted him in his love.

Philip shrank from the burst of popular indignation which he knew must follow. Any wrong done to one who stands on the pinnacle of the people's favour is resented by each individual as a personal injury; and among a primitive set of country-folk, who recognize the wild passion in love, as it exists untamed by the trammels of reason and self-restraint, any story of baulked affections, or treachery in such matters, spreads like wildfire.

Philip knew this quite well; his doom of disgrace lay plain before him, if only Kinraid spoke the word. His head was bent down while he thus listened and reflected. He half resolved on doing something; he lifted up his head, caught the reflection of his face in the little strip of glass on the opposite side, in which the women might look at themselves in their contemplated purchases, and quite resolved.

The sight he saw in the mirror was his own long, sad, pale face, made plainer and grayer by the heavy pressure of the morning's events. He saw his stooping figure, his rounded shoulders, with something like a feeling of disgust at his personal appearance as he remembered the square, upright build of Kinraid; his fine uniform, with epaulette and sword-belt; his handsome brown face; his dark eyes, splendid with the fire of passion and indignation; his white teeth, gleaming out with the terrible smile of scorn.

The comparison drove Philip from passive hopelessness to active despair.

He went abruptly from the crowded shop into the empty parlour, and on into the kitchen, where he took up a piece of bread, and heedless of Phœbe's look and words, began to eat it before he even left the place; for he needed the strength that food would give; he needed it to carry him out of the sight and the knowledge of all who might hear what he had done, and point their fingers at him.

He paused a moment in the parlour, and then, setting his teeth tight together, he went upstairs.

First of all he went into the bit of a room opening out of

theirs, in which his baby slept. He dearly loved the child, and many a time would run in and play a while with it; and in such gambols he and Sylvia had passed their happiest moments of wedded life.

The little Bella was having her morning slumber; Nancy used to tell long afterwards how he knelt down by the side of her cot, and was so strange she thought he must have prayed, for all it was nigh upon eleven o'clock, and folk in their senses only said their prayers when they got up, and when they went to bed.

Then he rose, and stooped over, and gave the child a long, lingering, soft, fond kiss.

And on tip-toe he passed away into the room where his aunt lay; his aunt who had been so true a friend to him! He was thankful to know that in her present state she was safe from the knowledge of what was past, safe from the sound of the shame to come.

He had not meant to see Sylvia again; he dreaded the look of her hatred, her scorn, but there, outside her mother's bed, she lay, apparently asleep. Mrs Robson, too, was sleeping, her face towards the wall. Philip could not help it; he went to have one last look at his wife. She was turned towards her mother, her face averted from him; he could see the tear-stains, the swollen eyelids, the lips yet quivering: he stooped down, and bent to kiss the little hand that lay listless by her side. As his hot breath neared that hand it was twitched away, and a shiver ran through the whole prostrate body. And then he knew that she was not asleep, only worn out by her misery, – misery that he had caused.

He sighed heavily; but he went away, downstairs, and away for ever. Only as he entered the parlour his eyes caught on two silhouettes, one of himself, one of Sylvia, done in the first month of their marriage, by some wandering artist, if so he could be called. They were hanging against the wall in little oval wooden frames; black profiles, with the lights done in gold; about as poor semblances of humanity as could be conceived; but Philip went up, and after looking for a minute or so at Sylvia's, he took it down, and buttoned his waistcoat over it.

It was the only thing he took away from his home.

He went down the entry on to the quay. The river was there, and waters, they say, have a luring power, and a weird promise of rest in their perpetual monotony of sound. But many people were there, if such a temptation presented itself to Philip's mind; the sight of his fellow-townsmen, perhaps of his acquaintances, drove him up another entry – the town is burrowed with such – back into the High Street, which he straightway crossed into a well-known court, out of which rough steps led to the summit of the hill, and on to the fells and moors beyond.

He plunged and panted up this rough ascent. From the top he could look down on the whole town lying below, severed by the bright shining river into two parts. To the right lay the sea, shimmering and heaving; there were the cluster of masts rising out of the little port; the irregular roofs of the houses; which of them, thought he, as he carried his eye along the quay-side to the market-place, which of them was his? and he singled it out in its unfamiliar aspect, and saw the thin blue smoke rising from the kitchen chimney, where even now Phœbe was cooking the household meal that he never more must share.

Up at that thought and away, he knew not nor cared not whither. He went through the ploughed fields where the corn was newly springing; he came down upon the vast sunny sea, and turned his back upon it with loathing; he made his way inland to the high green pastures; the short upland turf above which the larks hung poised 'at heaven's gate.'* He strode along, so straight and heedless of briar and bush, that the wild black cattle ceased from grazing, and looked after him with their great blank puzzled eyes.

He had passed all enclosures and stone fences now, and was fairly on the desolate brown moors; through the withered last year's ling and fern, through the prickly gorse, he tramped, crushing down the tender shoots of this year's growth, and heedless of the startled plover's cry, goaded by the furies. His only relief from thought, from the remembrance of Sylvia's looks and words, was in violent bodily action.

So he went on till evening shadows and ruddy evening lights came out upon the wild fells.

He had crossed roads and lanes, with a bitter avoidance of men's tracks; but now the strong instinct of self-preservation came out, and his aching limbs, his weary heart, giving great pants and beats for a time, and then ceasing altogether till a mist swam and quivered before his aching eyes, warned him that he must find some shelter and food, or lie down to die. He fell down now, often; stumbling over the slightest obstacle. He had passed the cattle pastures; he was among the black-faced sheep; and they, too, ceased nibbling, and looked after him, and somehow, in his poor wandering imagination, their silly faces turned to likenesses of Monkshaven people – people who ought to be far, far away.

'Thou'll be belated on these fells, if thou doesn't tak' heed,' shouted some one.

Philip looked abroad to see whence the voice proceeded.

An old stiff-legged shepherd, in a smock-frock, was within a couple of hundred yards. Philip did not answer, but staggered and stumbled towards him.

'Good lork!' said the man, 'wheere hast ta been? Thou's seen Oud Harry,* I think, thou looks so scared.'

Philip rallied himself, and tried to speak up to the old standard of respectability; but the effort was pitiful to see, had any one been by, who could have understood the pain it caused to restrain cries of bodily and mental agony.

'I've lost my way, that's all.'

''Twould ha' been enough, too, I'm thinkin', if I hadn't come out after t' ewes. There's t' Three Griffins near at hand: a sup o' Hollands 'll set thee to reeghts.'

Philip followed faintly. He could not see before him, and was guided by the sound of footsteps rather than by the sight of the figure moving onwards. He kept stumbling; and he knew that the old shepherd swore at him; but he also knew such curses proceeded from no ill-will, only from annoyance at the delay in going and 'seein' after t' ewes.' But had the man's words conveyed the utmost expression of hatred, Philip would neither have wondered at them, nor resented them.

They came into a wild mountain road, unfenced from the fells. A hundred yards off, and there was a small public-house, with a broad ruddy oblong of firelight shining across the tract.

'Theere!' said the old man. 'Thee cannot well miss that. A dunno tho', thee bees sich a gawby.'*

So he went on, and delivered Philip safely up to the landlord.

'Here's a felly as a fund on t' fell side, just as one as if he were drunk; but he's sober enough, a reckon, only summat's wrong i' his head, a'm thinkin'.'

'No!' said Philip, sitting down on the first chair he came to. 'I'm right enough; just fairly wearied out: lost my way,' and he fainted.

There was a recruiting sergeant of marines sitting in the house-place, drinking. He, too, like Philip, had lost his way; but was turning his blunder to account by telling all manner of wonderful stories to two or three rustics who had come in ready to drink on any pretence; especially if they could get good liquor without paying for it.

The sergeant rose as Philip fell back, and brought up his own mug of beer, into which a noggin of gin had been put (called in Yorkshire 'dog's-nose'). He partly poured and partly spilt some of this beverage on Philip's face; some drops went through the pale and parted lips, and with a start the worn-out man revived.

'Bring him some victual, landlord,' called out the recruiting sergeant. 'I'll stand shot.'

They brought some cold bacon and coarse oat-cake. The sergeant asked for pepper and salt; minced the food fine and made it savoury, and kept administering it by teaspoonfuls; urging Philip to drink from time to time from his own cup of dog's-nose.

A burning thirst, which needed no stimulant from either

pepper or salt, took possession of Philip, and he drank freely, scarcely recognizing what he drank. It took effect on one so habitually sober; and he was soon in that state when the imagination works wildly and freely.

He saw the sergeant before him, handsome, and bright, and active, in his gay red uniform, without a care, as it seemed to Philip, taking life lightly; admired and respected everywhere because of his cloth.

If Philip were gay, and brisk, well-dressed like him, returning with martial glory to Monkshaven, would not Sylvia love him once more? Could not he win her heart? He was brave by nature, and the prospect of danger did not daunt him, if ever it presented itself to his imagination.

He thought he was cautious in entering on the subject of enlistment with his new friend, the sergeant; but the latter was twenty times as cunning as he, and knew by experience how to bait his hook.

Philip was older by some years than the regulation age; but, at that time of great demand for men, the question of age was lightly entertained. The sergeant was profuse in statements of the advantages presented to a man of education in his branch of the service; how such a one was sure to rise; in fact, it would have seemed from the sergeant's account, as though the difficulty consisted in remaining in the ranks.

Philip's dizzy head thought the subject over and over again, each time with failing power of reason.

At length, almost, as it would seem, by some sleight of hand, he found the fatal shilling in his palm, and had promised to go before the nearest magistrate to be sworn in as one of his Majesty's marines the next morning. And after that he remembered nothing more.

He wakened up in a little truckle-bed in the same room as the sergeant, who lay sleeping the sleep of full contentment; while gradually, drop by drop, the bitter recollections of the day before came, filling up Philip's cup of agony.

He knew that he had received the bounty-money; and though he was aware that he had been partly tricked into it, and had no hope, no care, indeed, for any of the advantages so liberally promised him the night before, yet he was resigned, with utterly despondent passiveness, to the fate to which he had pledged himself. Anything was welcome that severed him from his former life, that could make him forget it, if that were possible; and also welcome anything which increased the chances of death without the sinfulness of his own participation in the act. He found in the dark recess of his mind the dead body of his fancy of the previous night; that he might come home, handsome and glorious, to win the love that had never been his.

But he only sighed over it, and put it aside out of his sight – so full of despair was he. He could eat no breakfast, though the sergeant ordered of the best. The latter kept watching his new recruit out of the corner of his eye, expecting a remonstrance, or dreading a sudden bolt.

But Philip walked with him the two or three miles in the most submissive silence, never uttering a syllable of regret or repentance; and before Justice Cholmley, of Holm-Fell Hall, he was sworn into his Majesty's service, under the name of Stephen Freeman. With a new name, he began a new life. Alas! the old life lives for ever!

CHAPTER XXXV

THINGS UNUTTERABLE

AFTER Philip had passed out of the room, Sylvia lay perfectly still, from very exhaustion. Her mother slept on, happily unconscious of all the turmoil that had taken place; yes, happily, though the heavy sleep was to end in death. But of this her daughter knew nothing, imagining that it was refreshing slumber, instead of an ebbing of life. Both mother and daughter lay motionless till Phœbe entered the room to tell Sylvia that dinner was on the table.

Then Sylvia sate up, and put back her hair, bewildered and uncertain as to what was to be done next; how she should meet the husband to whom she had discarded all allegiance, repudiated the solemn promise of love and obedience which she had vowed.

Phœbe came into the room, with natural interest in the invalid, scarcely older than herself.

'How is t' old lady?' asked she, in a low voice.

Sylvia turned her head round to look; her mother had never moved, but was breathing in a loud uncomfortable manner, that made her stoop over her to see the averted face more nearly.

'Phœbe!' she cried, 'come here! She looks strange and odd; her eyes are open, but don't see me. Phœbe! Phœbe!'

'Sure enough, she's in a bad way!' said Phœbe, climbing stiffly on to the bed to have a nearer view. 'Hold her head a little up t' ease her breathin' while I go for master; he'll be for sendin' for t' doctor, I'll be bound.'

Sylvia took her mother's head and laid it fondly on her breast, speaking to her and trying to rouse her; but it was of no avail: the hard, stertorous* breathing grew worse and worse.

Sylvia cried out for help; Nancy came, the baby in her arms. They had been in several times before that morning; and the child came smiling and crowing at its mother, who was supporting her own dying parent.

'Oh, Nancy!' said Sylvia; 'what is the matter with mother? yo' can see her face; tell me quick!'

Nancy set the baby on the bed for all reply, and ran out of the room, crying out,

'Master! master! Come quick! T' old missus is a-dying!'

This appeared to be no news to Sylvia, and yet the words came on her with a great shock, but for all that she could not cry; she was surprised herself at her own deadness of feeling.

Her baby crawled to her, and she had to hold and guard both her mother and her child. It seemed a long, long time before any one came, and then she heard muffled voices, and a heavy tramp: it was Phœbe leading the doctor upstairs, and Nancy creeping in behind to hear his opinion.

He did not ask many questions, and Phœbe replied more

frequently to his inquiries than did Sylvia, who looked into his face with a blank, tearless, speechless despair, that gave him more pain than the sight of her dying mother.

The long decay of Mrs Robson's faculties and health, of which he was well aware, had in a certain manner prepared him for some such sudden termination of the life whose duration was hardly desirable, although he gave several directions as to her treatment; but the white, pinched face, the great dilated eye, the slow comprehension of the younger woman, struck him with alarm; and he went on asking for various particulars, more with a view of rousing Sylvia, if even it were to tears, than for any other purpose that the information thus obtained could answer.

'You had best have pillows propped up behind her – it will not be for long; she does not know that you are holding her, and it is only tiring you to no purpose!'

Sylvia's terrible stare continued; he put his advice into action, and gently tried to loosen her clasp, and tender hold. This she resisted; laying her cheek against her poor mother's unconscious face.

'Where is Hepburn?' said he. 'He ought to be here!'

Phœbe looked at Nancy, Nancy at Phœbe. It was the latter who replied,

'He's neither i' t' house nor i' t' shop. A seed him go past t' kitchen window better nor an hour ago; but neither William Coulson or Hester Rose knows where he's gone to.'

Dr Morgan's lips were puckered up into a whistle, but he made no sound.

'Give me baby!' he said, suddenly. Nancy had taken her up off the bed where she had been sitting, encircled by her mother's arm. The nursemaid gave her to the doctor. He watched the mother's eye, it followed her child, and he was rejoiced. He gave a little pinch to the baby's soft flesh, and she cried out piteously; again the same action, the same result. Sylvia laid her mother down, and stretched out her arms for her child, hushing it, and moaning over it.

'So far so good!' said Dr Morgan to himself. 'But where is the husband? He ought to be here.' He went downstairs to make inquiry for Philip; that poor young creature, about whose health he had never felt thoroughly satisfied since the fever after her confinement, was in an anxious condition, and with an inevitable shock awaiting her. Her husband ought to be with her, and supporting her to bear it.

Dr Morgan went into the shop. Hester alone was there. Coulson had gone to his comfortable dinner at his well-ordered house, with his common-place wife. If he had felt anxious about Philip's looks and strange disappearance, he had also managed to account for them in some indifferent way.

Hester was alone with the shop-boy; few people came in during the universal Monkshaven dinner-hour. She was resting her head on her hand, and puzzled and distressed about many things – all that was implied by the proceedings of the evening before between Philip and Sylvia; and that was confirmed by Philip's miserable looks and strange abstracted ways to-day. Oh! how easy Hester would have found it to make him happy! not merely how easy, but what happiness it would have been to her to merge her every wish into the one great object of fulfiling his will. To her, an on-looker, the course of married life, which should lead to perfect happiness, seemed to plain! Alas! it is often so! and the resisting forces which make all such harmony and delight impossible are not recognized by the bystanders, hardly by the actors. But if these resisting forces are only superficial, or constitutional, they are but the necessary discipline here, and do not radically affect the love which will make all things right in heaven.

Some glimmering of this latter comforting truth shed its light on Hester's troubled thoughts from time to time. But again, how easy would it have been to her to tread the maze that led to Philip's happiness; and how difficult it seemed to the wife he had chosen!

She was aroused by Dr Morgan's voice.

'So both Coulson and Hepburn have left the shop to your care, Hester. I want Hepburn, though; his wife is in a very anxious state. Where is he? can you tell me?'

'Sylvia in an anxious state! I've not seen her to-day, but last night she looked as well as could be.'

'Ay, ay; but many a thing happens in four-and-twenty hours. Her mother is dying, may be dead by this time; and her husband should be there with her. Can't you send for him?'

'I don't know where he is,' said Hester. 'He went off from here all on a sudden, when there was all the market-folks in t' shop; I thought he'd maybe gone to John Foster's about th' money, for they was paying a deal in. I'll send there and inquire.'

No! the messenger brought back word that he had not been seen at their bank all morning. Further inquiries were made by the anxious Hester, by the doctor, by Coulson; all they could learn was that Phœbe had seen him pass the kitchen window about eleven o'clock, when she was peeling the potatoes for dinner; and two lads playing on the quay-side thought they had seen him among a group of sailors; but these latter, as far as they could be identified, had no knowledge of his appearance among them.

Before night the whole town was excited about his disappearance. Before night Bell Robson had gone to her long home. And Sylvia still lay quiet and tearless, apparently more unmoved than any other creature by the events of the day, and the strange vanishing of her husband.

The only thing she seemed to care for was her baby; she held it tight in her arms, and Dr Morgan bade them leave it there, its touch might draw the desired tears into her weary, sleepless eyes, and charm the aching pain out of them.

They were afraid lest she should inquire for her husband, whose non-appearance at such a time of sorrow to his wife must (they thought) seem strange to her. And night drew on while they were all in this state. She had gone back to her own room without a word when they had desired her to do so; caressing her child in her arms, and sitting down on the first chair she came to, with a heavy sigh, as if even this slight bodily exertion had been too much for her. They saw her eyes turn towards the door every time it was opened, and they thought it was with anxious expectation of one who could not be found, though many were seeking for him in all probable places.

When night came some one had to tell her of her husband's disappearance; and Dr Morgan was the person who undertook this.

He came into her room about nine o'clock; her baby was sleeping in her arms; she herself pale as death, still silent and tearless, though strangely watchful of gestures and sounds, and probably cognizant of more than they imagined.

'Well, Mrs Hepburn,' said he, as cheerfully as he could, 'I should advise your going to bed early; for I fancy your husband won't come home to-night. Some journey or other, that perhaps Coulson can explain better than I can, will most likely keep him away till to-morrow. It's very unfortunate that he should be away at such a sad time as this, as I'm sure he'll feel when he returns; but we must make the best of it.'

He watched her to see the effect of his words.

She sighed, that was all. He still remained a little while. She lifted her head up a little and asked,

'How long do yo' think she was unconscious, doctor? Could she hear things, think yo', afore she fell into that strange kind o' slumber?'

'I cannot tell,' said he, shaking his head. 'Was she breathing in that hard snoring kind of way when you left her this morning?'

'Yes, I think so; I cannot tell, so much has happened.'

'When you came back to her, after your breakfast, I think you said she was in much the same position?'

'Yes, and yet I may be telling yo' lies; if I could but think: but it's my head as is aching so; doctor, I wish yo'd go, for I need being alone, I'm so mazed.'

'Good-night, then, for you're a wise woman, I see, and mean to go to bed, and have a good night with baby there.'

But he went down to Phœbe, and told her to go in from time to time, and see how her mistress was.

He found Hester Rose and the old servant together; both

had been crying, both were evidently in great trouble about the death and the mystery of the day.

Hester asked if she might go up and see Sylvia, and the doctor gave his leave, talking meanwhile with Phœbe over the kitchen fire. Hester came down again without seeing Sylvia. The door of the room was bolted, and everything quiet inside.

'Does she know where her husband is, think you?' asked the doctor at this account of Hester's. 'She's not anxious about him at any rate: or else the shock of her mother's death has been too much for her. We must hope for some change in the morning; a good fit of crying, or a fidget about her husband, would be more natural. Good-night to you both,' and off he went.

Phœbe and Hester avoided looking at each other at these words. Both were conscious of the probability of something having gone seriously wrong between the husband and wife. Hester had the recollection of the previous night, Phœbe the untasted breakfast of to-day to go upon.

She spoke first.

'A just wish he'd come home to still folks' tongues. It need niver ha' been known if t' old lady hadn't died this day of all others. It's such a thing for t' shop t' have one o' t' partners missin', an' no one for t' know what's comed on him. It niver happened i' Fosters' days, that's a' I know.'

'He'll maybe come back yet,' said Hester. 'It's not so very late.'

'It were market-day, and a',' continued Phœbe, 'just as if iverything mun go wrong together; an' a' t' country customers'll go back wi' fine tale i' their mouths, as Measter Hepburn was strayed an' missin' just like a beast o' some kind.'

'Hark! isn't that a step?' said Hester suddenly, as a footfall sounded in the now quiet street; but it passed the door, and the hope that had arisen on its approach fell as the sound died away.

'He'll noane come to-night,' said Phœbe, who had been as eager a listener as Hester, however. 'Thou'd best go thy ways home; a shall stay up, for it's not seemly for us a' t' go to our beds, an' a corpse in t' house; an' Nancy, as might ha' watched, is gone to her bed this hour past, like a lazy boots as she is. A can hear, too, if t' measter does come home; tho' a'll be bound he wunnot; choose wheere he is, he'll be i' bed by now, for it's well on to eleven. I'll let thee out by t' shop-door, and stand by it till thou's close at home, for it's ill for a young woman to be i' t' street so late.'

So she held the door open, and shaded the candle from the flickering outer air, while Hester went to her home with a heavy heart.

Heavily and hopelessly did they all meet in the morning. No news of Philip, no change in Sylvia; an unceasing flow of angling and conjecture and gossip radiating from the shop into the town.

Hester could have entreated Coulson on her knees to cease from repeating the details of a story of which every word touched on a raw place in her sensitive heart; moreover, when they talked together so eagerly, she could not hear the coming footsteps on the pavement without.

Once some one hit very near the truth in a chance remark.

'It seems strange,' she said, 'how as one man turns up, another just disappears. Why, it were but upo' Tuesday as Kinraid come back, as all his own folk had thought to be dead; and next day here's Measter Hepburn as is gone no one knows wheere!'

'That's t' way i' this world,' replied Coulson, a little sententiously. 'This life is full o' changes o' one kind or another; them that's dead is alive; and as for poor Philip, though he was alive, he looked fitter to be dead when he came into t' shop o' Wednesday morning.'

'And how does she take it?' nodding to where Sylvia was supposed to be.

'Oh! she's not herself, so to say. She were just stunned by finding her mother was dying in her very arms when she thought as she were only sleeping; yet she's never been able to cry a drop; so that t' sorrow's gone inwards on her brain, and from all I can hear, she doesn't rightly understand as her husband is missing. T' doctor says if she could but cry, she'd come to a juster comprehension of things.'

'And what do John and Jeremiah Foster say to it all?'

'They're down here many a time in t' day to ask if he's come back, or how she is; for they made a deal on 'em both. They're going t' attend t' funeral to-morrow, and have given orders as t' shop is to be shut up in t' morning.'

To the surprise of every one, Sylvia, who had never left her room since the night of her mother's death, and was supposed to be almost unconscious of all that was going on in the house, declared her intention of following her mother to the grave. No one could do more than remonstrate: no one had sufficient authority to interfere with her. Dr Morgan even thought that she might possibly be roused to tears by the occasion; only he begged Hester to go with her, that she might have the solace of some woman's company.

She went through the greater part of the ceremony in the same hard, unmoved manner in which she had received everything for days past.

But on looking up once, as they formed round the open grave, she saw Kester, in his Sunday clothes, with a bit of new crape round his hat, crying as if his heart would break over the coffin of his good, kind mistress.

His evident distress, the unexpected sight, suddenly loosed the fountain of Sylvia's tears, and her sobs grew so terrible that Hester feared she would not be able to remain until the end of the funeral. But she struggled hard to stay till the last, and then she made an effort to go round by the place where Kester stood.

'Come and see me,' was all she could say for crying: and Kester only nodded his head – he could not speak a word.

CHAPTER XXXVI

MYSTERIOUS TIDINGS

THAT very evening Kester came, humbly knocking at the kitchen-door. Phœbe opened it. He asked to see Sylvia.

'A know not if she'll see thee,' said Phœbe. 'There's no makin' her out; sometimes she's for one thing, sometimes she's for another.'

'She bid me come and see her,' said Kester. 'Only this mornin', at missus' buryin', she telled me to come.'

So Phœbe went off to inform Sylvia that Kester was there; and returned with the desire that he would walk into the parlour. An instant after he was gone, Phœbe heard him return, and carefully shut the two doors of communication between the kitchen and sitting-room.

Sylvia was in the latter when Kester came in, holding her baby close to her; indeed, she seldom let it go now-a-days to any one else, making Nancy's place quite a sinecure, much to Phœbe's indignation.

Sylvia's face was shrunk, and white, and thin; her lovely eyes alone retained the youthful, almost childlike, expression. She went up to Kester, and shook his horny hand, she herself trembling all over.

'Don't talk to me of her,' she said hastily. 'I cannot stand it. It's a blessing for her to be gone, but, oh——'

She began to cry, and then cheered herself up, and swallowed down her sobs.

'Kester,' she went on, hastily, 'Charley Kinraid isn't dead; dost ta know? He's alive, and he were here o' Tuesday – no, Monday, was it? I cannot tell – but he were here!'

'A knowed as he weren't dead. Every one is a-speaking on it. But a didn't know as thee'd ha' seen him. A took comfort i' thinkin as thou'd ha' been wi' thy mother a' t' time as he were i' t' place.'

'Then he's gone?' said Sylvia.

'Gone; ay, days past. As far as a know, he but stopped

a' neet. A thought to mysel' (but yo' may be sure a said nought to nobody), he's heerd as our Sylvia were married, and has put it in his pipe, and ta'en hissel' off to smoke it.'

'Kester!' said Sylvia, leaning forwards, and whispering. 'I saw him. He was here. Philip saw him. Philip had known as he wasn't dead a' this time!'

Kester stood up suddenly.

'By goom, that chap has a deal t' answer for.'

A bright red spot was on each of Sylvia's white cheeks; and for a minute or so neither of them spoke.

Then she went on, still whispering out her words.

'Kester, I'm more afeared than I dare tell any one: can they ha' met, think yo'? T' very thought turns me sick. I told Philip my mind, and took a vow again' him – but it would be awful to think on harm happening to him through Kinraid. Yet he went out that morning, and has niver been seen or heard on sin'; and Kinraid were just fell again' him, and as for that matter, so was I; but——'

The red spot vanished as she faced her own imagination.

Kester spoke.

'It's a thing as can be easy looked into. What day an' time were it when Philip left this house?'

'Tuesday – the day she died. I saw him in her room that morning between breakfast and dinner; I could a'most swear to it's being close after eleven. I mind counting t' clock. It was that very morn as Kinraid were here.'

'A'll go an' have a pint o' beer at t' King's Arms, down on t' quay-side; it were theere he put up at. An' a'm pretty sure as he only stopped one night, and left i' t' morning betimes. But a'll go see.'

'Do,' said Sylvia, 'and go out through t' shop; they're all watching and watching me to see how I take things; and daren't let on about t' fire as is burning up my heart. Coulson is i' t' shop, but he'll not notice thee like Phœbe.'

By-and-by Kester came back. It seemed as though Sylvia had never stirred; she looked eagerly at him, but did not speak.

'He went away i' Rob Mason's mail-cart, him as tak's t'

letters to Hartlepool. T' lieutenant (as they ca' him down at t' King's Arms; they're as proud on his uniform as if it had been a new-painted sign to swing o'er their doors), t' lieutenant had reckoned upo' stayin' longer wi' 'em; but he went out betimes o' Tuesday morn', an' came back a' ruffled up, an' paid his bill – paid for his breakfast, though he touched noane on it – an' went off i' Rob postman's mail-cart, as starts reg'lar at ten o'clock. Corneys has been theere askin' for him, an' makin' a piece o' work, as he niver went near 'em; and they bees cousins. Niver a one among 'em knows as he were here as far as a could mak' out.'

'Thank yo', Kester,' said Sylvia, falling back in her chair, as if all the energy that had kept her stiff and upright was gone now that her anxiety was relieved.

She was silent for a long time; her eyes shut, her cheek laid on her child's head. Kester spoke next.

'A think it's pretty clear as they'n niver met. But its a' t' more wonder where thy husband's gone to. Thee and him had words about it, and thou telled him thy mind, thou said?'

'Yes,' said Sylvia, not moving. 'I'm afeared lest mother knows what I said to him, there, where she's gone to – I am—' the tears filled her shut eyes, and came softly overflowing down her cheeks; 'and yet it were true, what I said, I cannot forgive him; he's just spoilt my life, and I'm not one-and-twenty yet, and he knowed how wretched, how very wretched, I were. A word fra' him would ha' mended it a'; and Charley had bid him speak the word, and give me his faithful love, and Philip saw my heart ache day after day, and niver let on as him I was mourning for was alive, and had sent me word as he'd keep true to me, as I were to do to him.'

'A wish a'd been theere; a'd ha' felled him to t' ground,' said Kester, clenching his stiff, hard hand with indignation.

Sylvia was silent again: pale and weary she sate, her eyes still shut.

Then she said,

'Yet he were so good to mother; and mother loved him

so. Oh, Kester!' lifting herself up, opening her great wistful eyes, 'it's well for folks as can die; they're spared a deal o' misery.'

'Ay!' said he. 'But there's folk as one 'ud like to keep fra' shirkin' their misery. Think yo' now as Philip is livin'?'

Sylvia shivered all over, and hesitated before she replied.

'I dunnot know. I said such things; he deserved 'em all——'

'Well, well, lass!' said Kester, sorry that he had asked the question which was producing so much emotion of one kind or another. 'Neither thee nor me can tell; we can neither help nor hinder, seein' as he's ta'en hissel' off out on our sight, we'd best not think on him. A'll try an' tell thee some news, if a can think on it wi' my mind so full. Thou knows Haytersbank folk ha' flitted, and t' oud place is empty?'

'Yes!' said Sylvia, with the indifference of one wearied out with feeling.

'A only telled yo' t' account like for me bein' at a loose end i' Monkshaven. My sister, her as lived at Dale End an' is a widow, has comed int' town to live; an' a'm lodging wi' her, an' jobbin' about. A'm gettin' pretty well to do, an' a'm noane far t' seek, an' a'm going now: only first a just wanted for t' say as a'm thy oldest friend, a reckon, and if a can do a turn for thee, or go an errand, like as a've done to-day, or if it's any comfort to talk a bit to one who's known thy life from a babby, why yo've only t' send for me, an' a'd come if it were twenty mile. A'm lodgin' at Peggy Dawson's,* t' lath and plaster cottage at t' right hand o' t' bridge, a' among t' new houses, as they're thinkin' o' buildin' near t' sea: no one can miss it.'

He stood up and shook hands with her. As he did so, he looked at her sleeping baby.

'She's liker yo' than him. A think a'll say, God bless her.'

With the heavy sound of his out-going footsteps, baby awoke. She ought before this time to have been asleep in her bed, and the disturbance made her cry fretfully.

'Hush thee, darling, hush thee!' murmured her mother;

'there's no one left to love me but thee, and I cannot stand thy weeping, my pretty one. Hush thee, my babe, hush thee!'

She whispered soft in the little one's ear as she took her upstairs to bed.

About three weeks after the miserable date of Bell Robson's death and Philip's disappearance, Hester Rose received a letter from him. She knew the writing on the address well; and it made her tremble so much that it was many minutes before she dared to open it, and make herself acquainted with the facts it might disclose.

But she need not have feared; there were no facts told, unless the vague date of 'London' might be something to learn. Even that much might have been found out by the post-mark, only she had been too much taken by surprise to examine it.

It ran as follows:—

'Dear Hester,—

'Tell those whom it may concern, that I have left Monkshaven for ever. No one need trouble themselves about me; I am provided for. Please to make my humble apologies to my kind friends, the Messrs Foster, and to my partner, William Coulson. Please to accept of my love, and to join the same to your mother. Please to give my particular and respectful duty and kind love to my aunt Isabella Robson. Her daughter Sylvia knows what I have always felt, and shall always feel, for her better than I can ever put into language, so I send her no message; God bless and keep my child. You must all look on me as one dead; as I am to you, and maybe shall soon be in reality.

'Your affectionate and obedient friend to command,

'Philip Hepburn.

'P.S.—Oh, Hester! for God's sake and mine, look after' ('my wife,' scratched out) 'Sylvia and my child. I think Jeremiah Foster will help you to be a friend to them. This is the last solemn request of P.H. She is but very young.'

Hester read this letter again and again, till her heart

caught the echo of its hopelessness, and sank within her. She put it in her pocket, and reflected upon it all the day long as she served in the shop.

The customers found her as gentle, but far more inattentive than usual. She thought that in the evening she would go across the bridge, and consult with the two good old brothers Foster. But something occurred to put off the fulfilment of this plan.

That same morning Sylvia had preceded her, with no one to consult, because consultation would have required previous confidence, and confidence would have necessitated such a confession about Kinraid as it was most difficult for Sylvia to make. The poor young wife yet felt that some step must be taken by her; and what it was to be she could not imagine.

She had no home to go to; for as Philip was gone away, she remained where she was only on sufferance; she did not know what means of livelihood she had; she was willing to work, nay, would be thankful to take up her old life of country labour; but with her baby, what could she do?

In this dilemma, the recollection of the old man's kindly speech and offer of assistance, made, it is true, half in joke, at the end of her wedding visit, came into her mind; and she resolved to go and ask for some of the friendly counsel and assistance then offered.

It would be the first time of her going out since her mother's funeral, and she dreaded the effort on that account. More even than on that account did she shrink from going into the streets again. She could not get over the impression that Kinraid must be lingering near; and she distrusted herself so much that it was a positive terror to think of meeting him again. She felt as though, if she but caught a sight of him, the glitter of his uniform, or heard his well-known voice in only a distant syllable of talk, her heart would stop, and she should die from very fright of what would come next. Or rather so she felt, and so she thought before she took her baby in her arms, as Nancy gave it to her after putting on its out-of-door attire.

With it in her arms she was protected, and the whole

current of her thoughts was changed. The infant was wailing and suffering with its teething, and the mother's heart was so occupied in soothing and consoling her moaning child, that the dangerous quay-side and the bridge were passed almost before she was aware; nor did she notice the eager curiosity and respectful attention of those she met who recognized her even through the heavy veil which formed part of the draping mourning provided for her by Hester and Coulson, in the first unconscious days after her mother's death.

Though public opinion as yet reserved its verdict upon Philip's disappearance – warned possibly by Kinraid's story against hasty decisions and judgments in such times as those of war and general disturbance – yet every one agreed that no more pitiful fate could have befallen Philip's wife.

Marked out by her striking beauty as an object of admiring interest even in those days when she sate in girlhood's smiling peace by her mother at the Market Cross – her father had lost his life in a popular cause, and ignominious as the manner of his death might be, he was looked upon as a martyr to his zeal in avenging the wrongs of his townsmen; Sylvia had married amongst them too, and her quiet daily life was well known to them; and now her husband had been carried off from her side just on the very day when she needed his comfort most.

For the general opinion was that Philip had been 'carried off' – in seaport towns such occurrences were not uncommon in those days – either by land-crimps or water-crimps.*

So Sylvia was treated with silent reverence, as one sorely afflicted, by all the unheeded people she met in her faltering walk to Jeremiah Foster's.

She had calculated her time so as to fall in with him at his dinner hour, even though it obliged her to go to his own house rather than to the bank where he and his brother spent all the business hours of the day.

Sylvia was so nearly exhausted by the length of her walk and the weight of her baby, that all she could do when the door was opened was to totter into the nearest seat, sit down, and begin to cry.

In an instant kind hands were about her, loosening her heavy cloak, offering to relieve her of her child, who clung to her all the more firmly, and some one was pressing a glass of wine against her lips.

'No, sir, I cannot take it! wine allays gives me th' head-ache; if I might have just a drink o' water. Thank you, ma-am' (to the respectable-looking old servant), 'I'm well enough now; and perhaps, sir, I might speak a word with yo', for it's that I've come for.'

'It's a pity, Sylvia Hepburn, as thee didst not come to me at the bank, for it's been a long toil for thee all this way in the heat, with thy child. But if there's aught I can do or say for thee, thou hast but to name it, I am sure. Martha! wilt thou relieve her of her child while she comes with me into the parlour?'

But the wilful little Bella stoutly refused to go to any one, and Sylvia was not willing to part with her, tired though she was.

So the baby was carried into the parlour, and much of her after-life depended on this trivial fact.

Once installed in the easy-chair, and face to face with Jeremiah, Sylvia did not know how to begin.

Jeremiah saw this, and kindly gave her time to recover herself, by pulling out his great gold watch, and letting the seal dangle before the child's eyes, almost within reach of the child's eager little fingers.

'She favours you a deal,' said he, at last. 'More than her father,' he went on, purposely introducing Philip's name, so as to break the ice; for he rightly conjectured she had come to speak to him about something connected with her husband.

Still Sylvia said nothing; she was choking down tears and shyness, and unwillingness to take as confidant a man of whom she knew so little, on such slight ground (as she now felt it to be) as the little kindly speech with which she had been dismissed from that house the last time that she entered it.

'It's no use keeping yo', sir,' she broke out at last. 'It's about Philip as I comed to speak. Do yo' know any thing whatsomever about him? He niver had a chance o' saying anything, I know; but maybe he's written?'

'Not a line, my poor young woman!' said Jeremiah, hastily putting an end to that vain idea.

'Then he's either dead or gone away for iver,' she whispered. 'I mun be both feyther and mother to my child.'

'Oh! thee must not give it up,' replied he. 'Many a one is carried off to the wars, or to the tenders o' men-o'-war; and then they turn out to be unfit for service, and are sent home. Philip 'll come back before the year's out; thee'll see that.'

'No; he'll niver come back. And I'm not sure as I should iver wish him t' come back, if I could but know what was gone wi' him. Yo' see, sir, though I were sore set again' him, I shouldn't like harm to happen him.'

'There is something behind all this that I do not understand. Can thee tell me what it is?'

'I must, sir, if yo're to help me wi' your counsel; and I came up here to ask for it.'

Another long pause, during which Jeremiah made a feint of playing with the child, who danced and shouted with tantalized impatience at not being able to obtain possession of the seal, and at length stretched out her soft round little arms to go to the owner of the coveted possession. Surprise at this action roused Sylvia, and she made some comment upon it.

'I niver knew her t' go to any one afore. I hope she'll not be troublesome to yo', sir?'

The old man, who had often longed for a child of his own in days gone by, was highly pleased by this mark of baby's confidence, and almost forgot, in trying to strengthen her regard by all the winning wiles in his power, how her poor mother was still lingering over some painful story which she could not bring herself to tell.

'I'm afeared of speaking wrong again' any one, sir. And mother were so fond o' Philip; but he kept something from me as would ha' made me a different woman, and some one else, happen, a different man. I were troth-plighted wi'

Kinraid the specksioneer, him as was cousin to th' Corneys o' Moss Brow, and comed back lieutenant i' t' navy last Tuesday three weeks, after ivery one had thought him dead and gone these three years.'

She paused.

'Well?' said Jeremiah,* with interest; although his attention appeared to be divided between the mother's story and the eager playfulness of the baby on his knee.

'Philip knew he were alive; he'd seen him taken by t' press-gang, and Charley had sent a message to me by Philip.'

Her white face was reddening, her eyes flashing at this point of her story.

'And he niver told me a word on it, not when he saw me like to break my heart in thinking as Kinraid were dead; he kept it a' to hissel'; and watched me cry, and niver said a word to comfort me wi' t' truth. It would ha' been a great comfort, sir, only t' have had his message if I'd niver ha' been to see him again. But Philip niver let on to any one, as I iver heared on, that he'd seen Charley that morning as t' press-gang took him. Yo' know about feyther's death, and how friendless mother and me was left? and so I married him; for he were a good friend to us then, and I were dazed like wi' sorrow, and could see naught else to do for mother. He were allays very tender and good to her, for sure.'

Again a long pause of silent recollection, broken by one or two deep sighs.

'If I go on, sir, now, I mun ask yo' to promise as yo'll niver tell. I do so need some one to tell me what I ought to do, and I were led here, like, else I would ha' died wi' it all within my teeth. Yo'll promise, sir?'

Jeremiah Foster looked in her face, and seeing the wistful, eager look, he was touched almost against his judgment into giving the promise required; she went on.

'Upon a Tuesday morning, three weeks ago, I think, tho' for t' matter o' time it might ha' been three years, Kinraid come home; come back for t' claim me as his wife, and I were wed to Philip! I met him i' t' road at first; and I couldn't tell him theere. He followed me into t' house – Philip's house, sir, behind t' shop – and somehow I told him all, how I were a wedded wife to another. Then he up and said I'd a false heart – me false, sir, as had eaten my daily bread in bitterness, and had wept t' nights through, all for sorrow and mourning for his death! Then he said as Philip knowed all t' time he were alive and coming back for me; and I couldn't believe it, and I called Philip, and he come, and a' that Charley had said were true; and yet I were Philip's wife! So I took a mighty oath, and I said as I'd niver hold Philip to be my lawful husband again, nor iver forgive him for t' evil he'd wrought us, but hold him as a stranger and one as had done me a heavy wrong.'

She stopped speaking; her story seemed to her to end there. But her listener said, after a pause,

'It were a cruel wrong, I grant thee that; but thy oath were a sin, and thy words were evil, my poor lass. What happened next?'

'I don't justly remember,' she said, wearily. 'Kinraid went away, and mother cried out; and I went to her. She were asleep, I thought, so I lay down by her, to wish I were dead, and to think on what would come on my child if I died; and Philip came in softly, and I made as if I were asleep; and that's t' very last as I've iver seen or heared of him.'

Jeremiah Foster groaned as she ended her story. Then he pulled himself up, and said, in a cheerful tone of voice,

'He'll come back, Sylvia Hepburn. He'll think better of it: never fear!'

'I fear his coming back!' said she. 'That's what I'm feared on; I would wish as I knew on his well-doing i' some other place; but him and me can niver live together again.'

'Nay,' pleaded Jeremiah. 'Thee art sorry what thee said; thee were sore put about, or thee wouldn't have said it.'

He was trying to be a peace-maker, and to heal over conjugal differences; but he did not go deep enough.

'I'm not sorry,' said she, slowly. 'I were too deeply wronged to be "put about;" that would go off wi' a night's sleep. It's only the thought of mother (she's dead and happy, and knows nought of all this, I trust) that comes between me and hating Philip. I'm not sorry for what I said.'

Jeremiah had never met with any one so frank and undisguised in expressions of wrong feeling, and he scarcely knew what to say.

He looked extremely grieved, and not a little shocked. So pretty and delicate a young creature to use such strong relentless language!

She seemed to read his thoughts, for she made answer to them.

'I dare say you think I'm very wicked, sir, not to be sorry. Perhaps I am. I can't think o' that for remembering how I've suffered; and he knew how miserable I was, and might ha' cleared my misery away wi' a word; and he held his peace, and now it's too late! I'm sick o' men and their cruel, deceitful ways. I wish I were dead.'

She was crying before she had ended this speech, and seeing her tears, the child began to cry too, stretching out its little arms to go back to its mother. The hard stony look on her face melted away into the softest, tenderest love as she clasped the little one to her, and tried to soothe its frightened sobs.

A bright thought came into the old man's mind.

He had been taking a complete dislike to her till her pretty way with her baby showed him that she had a heart of flesh within her.

'Poor little one!' said he, 'thy mother had need love thee, for she's deprived thee of thy father's love. Thou'rt half-way to being an orphan; yet I cannot call thee one of the fatherless to whom God will be a father. Thou'rt a desolate babe, thou may'st well cry; thine earthly parents have forsaken thee, and I know not if the Lord will take thee up.'

Sylvia looked up at him affrighted; holding her baby tighter to her, she exclaimed.

'Don't speak so, sir! it's cursing, sir! I haven't forsaken her! Oh, sir! those are awful sayings.'

'Thee hast sworn never to forgive thy husband, nor to live with him again. Dost thee know that by the law of the land, he may claim his child; and then thou wilt have to forsake it, or to be forsworn? Poor little maiden!' continued he, once more luring the baby to him with the temptation of the watch and chain.

Sylvia thought for a while before speaking. Then she said,

'I cannot tell what ways to take. Whiles I think my head is crazed. It were a cruel turn he did me!'

'It was. I couldn't have thought him guilty of such baseness.'

This acquiescence, which was perfectly honest on Jeremiah's part, almost took Sylvia by surprise. Why might she not hate one who had been both cruel and base in his treatment of her? And yet she recoiled from the application of such hard terms by another to Philip, by a cool-judging and indifferent person, as she esteemed Jeremiah to be. From some inscrutable turn in her thoughts, she began to defend him, or at least to palliate the harsh judgment which she herself had been the first to pronounce.

'He were so tender to mother; she were dearly fond on him; he niver spared aught he could do for her, else I would niver ha' married him.'

'He was a good and kind-hearted lad from the time he was fifteen. And I never found him out in any falsehood, no more did my brother.'

'But it were all the same as a lie,' said Sylvia, swiftly changing her ground, 'to leave me to think as Charley were dead, when he knowed all t' time he were alive.'

'It was. It was a self-seeking lie; putting thee to pain to get his own ends. And the end of it has been that he is driven forth like Cain.'

'I niver told him to go, sir.'

'But thy words sent him forth, Sylvia.'

'I cannot unsay them, sir; and I believe as I should say them again.'

But she said this as one who rather hopes for a contradiction.

All Jeremiah replied, however, was, 'Poor wee child!' in a pitiful tone, addressed to the baby.

Sylvia's eyes filled with tears.

'Oh, sir, I'll do anything as iver yo' can tell me for her. That's what I came for t' ask yo'. I know I mun not stay theere, and Philip gone away; and I dunnot know what to do: and I'll do aught, only I must keep her wi' me. Whativer can I do, sir?'

Jeremiah thought it over for a minute or two. Then he replied,

'I must have time to think. I must talk it over with brother John.'

'But you've given me yo'r word, sir!' exclaimed she.

'I have given thee my word never to tell any one of what has passed between thee and thy husband, but I must take counsel with my brother as to what is to be done with thee and thy child, now that thy husband has left the shop.'

This was said so gravely as almost to be a reproach, and he got up, as a sign that the interview was ended.

He gave the baby back to its mother; but not without a solemn blessing, so solemn that, to Sylvia's superstitious and excited mind, it undid the terrors of what she had esteemed to be a curse.

'The Lord bless thee and keep thee! The Lord make His face to shine upon thee!'*

All the way down the hill-side, Sylvia kept kissing the child, and whispering to its unconscious ears,—

'I'll love thee for both, my treasure, I will. I'll hap thee round wi' my love, so as thou shall niver need a feyther's.'

CHAPTER XXXVII

BEREAVEMENT

HESTER had been prevented by her mother's indisposition from taking Philip's letter to the Fosters, to hold a consultation with them over its contents.

Alice Rose was slowly failing, and the long days which she

had to spend alone told much upon her spirits, and consequently upon her health.

All this came out in the conversation which ensued after reading Hepburn's letter in the little parlour at the bank on the day after Sylvia had had her confidential interview with Jeremiah Foster.

He was a true man of honour, and never so much as alluded to her visit to him; but what she had then told him influenced him very much in the formation of the project which he proposed to his brother and Hester.

He recommended her remaining where she was, living still in the house behind the shop; for he thought within himself that she might have exaggerated the effect of her words upon Philip; that, after all, it might have been some cause totally disconnected with them, which had blotted out her husband's place among the men of Monkshaven; and that it would be so much easier for both to resume their natural relations, both towards each other and towards the world, if Sylvia remained where her husband had left her – in an expectant attitude, so to speak.

Jeremiah Foster questioned Hester straitly about her letter: whether she had made known its contents to any one. No, not to any one. Neither to her mother nor to William Coulson? No, to neither.

She looked at him as she replied to his inquiries, and he looked at her, each wondering if the other could be in the least aware that a conjugal quarrel might be at the root of the dilemma in which they were placed by Hepburn's disappearance.

But neither Hester, who had witnessed the misunderstanding between the husband and wife on the evening, before the morning on which Philip went away, nor Jeremiah Foster, who had learnt from Sylvia the true reason of her husband's disappearance, gave the slightest reason to the other to think that they each supposed they had a clue to the reason of Hepburn's sudden departure.

What Jeremiah Foster, after a night's consideration, had to propose was this; that Hester and her mother should come and occupy the house in the market-place, conjointly with Sylvia and her child. Hester's interest in the shop was by this time acknowledged. Jeremiah had made over to her so much of his share in the business, that she had a right to be considered as a kind of partner; and she had long been the superintendent of that department of goods which were exclusively devoted to women. So her daily presence was requisite for more reasons than one.

Yet her mother's health and spirits were such as to render it unadvisable that the old woman should be too much left alone; and Sylvia's devotion to her own mother seemed to point her out as the very person who could be a gentle and tender companion to Alice Rose during those hours when her own daughter would necessarily be engaged in the shop.

Many desirable objects seemed to be gained by this removal of Alice: an occupation was provided for Sylvia, which would detain her in the place where her husband had left her, and where (Jeremiah Foster fairly expected in spite of his letter) he was likely to come back to find her; and Alice Rose, the early love of one of the brothers, the old friend of the other, would be well cared for, and under her daughter's immediate supervision during the whole of the time that she was occupied in the shop.

Philip's share of the business, augmented by the money which he had put in from the legacy of his old Cumberland uncle, would bring in profits enough to support Sylvia and her child in ease and comfort until that time, which they all anticipated, when he should return from his mysterious wandering – mysterious, whether his going forth had been voluntary or involuntary.

Thus far was settled; and Jeremiah Foster went to tell Sylvia of the plan.

She was too much a child, too entirely unaccustomed to any independence of action, to do anything but leave herself in his hands. Her very confession, made to him the day before, when she sought his counsel, seemed to place her at his disposal. Otherwise, she had had notions of the possibility of a free country life once more – how provided for and arranged she hardly knew; but Haytersbank was to let, and Kester disengaged, and it had just seemed possible that she might have to return to her early home, and to her old life. She knew that it would take much money to stock the farm again, and that her hands were tied from much useful activity by the love and care she owed to her baby. But still, somehow, she hoped and she fancied, till Jeremiah Foster's measured words and carefully-arranged plan made her silently relinquish her green, breezy vision.

Hester, too, had her own private rebellion – hushed into submission by her gentle piety. If Sylvia had been able to make Philip happy, Hester could have felt lovingly and almost gratefully towards her; but Sylvia had failed in this.

Philip had been made unhappy, and was driven forth a wanderer into the wide world – never to come back! And his last words to Hester, the postcript of his letter, containing the very pith of it, was to ask her to take charge and care of the wife whose want of love towards him had uprooted him from the place where he was valued and honoured.

It cost Hester many a struggle and many a self-reproach before she could make herself feel what she saw all along – that in everything Philip treated her like a sister. But even a sister might well be indignant if she saw her brother's love disregarded and slighted, and his life embittered by the thoughtless conduct of a wife! Still Hester fought against herself, and for Philip's sake she sought to see the good in Sylvia, and she strove to love her as well as to take care of her.

With the baby, of course, the case was different. Without thought or struggle, or reason, every one loved the little girl. Coulson and his buxom wife, who were childless, were never weary of making much of her. Hester's happiest hours were spent with that little child. Jeremiah Foster almost looked upon her as his own from the day when she honoured him by yielding to the temptation of the chain and seal, and coming to his knee; not a customer to the shop but knew the smiling child's sad history, and many a country-woman would save a rosy-cheeked apple from out her store that autumn to bring it on next market-day for 'Philip Hepburn's baby, as had lost its father, bless it.'

Even stern Alice Rose was graciously inclined towards the little Bella; and though her idea of the number of the elect was growing narrower and narrower every day, she would have been loth to exclude the innocent little child, that stroked her wrinkled cheeks so softly every night in return for her blessing, from the few that should be saved. Nay, for the child's sake, she relented towards the mother; and strove to have Sylvia rescued from the many castaways with fervent prayer, or, as she phrased it, 'wrestling with the Lord.'

Alice had a sort of instinct that the little child, so tenderly loved by, so fondly loving, the mother whose ewe-lamb she was, could not be even in heaven without yearning for the creature she had loved best on earth; and the old woman believed that this was the principal reason for her prayers for Sylvia; but unconsciously to herself, Alice Rose was touched by the filial attentions she constantly received from the young mother, whom she believed to be foredoomed to condemnation.

Sylvia rarely went to church or chapel, nor did she read her Bible; for though she spoke little of her ignorance, and would fain, for her child's sake, have remedied it now it was too late, she had lost what little fluency of reading she had ever had, and could only make out her words with much spelling and difficulty. So the taking her Bible in hand would have been a mere form; though of this Alice Rose knew nothing.

No one knew much of what was passing in Sylvia; she did not know herself. Sometimes in the nights she would waken, crying, with a terrible sense of desolation; every one who loved her, or whom she had loved, had vanished out of her life; every one but her child, who lay in her arms, warm and soft.

But then Jeremiah Foster's words came upon her; words that she had taken for cursing at the time; and she would so gladly have had some clue by which to penetrate the darkness of the unknown region from whence both blessing and cursing came, and to know if she had indeed done something which should cause her sin to be visited on that soft, sweet, innocent darling.

If any one would teach her to read! If any one would explain to her the hard words she heard in church or chapel, so that she might find out the meaning of sin and godliness! – words that had only passed over the surface of her mind till now! For her child's sake she should like to do the will of God, if she only knew what that was, and how to be worked out in her daily life.

But there was no one she dared confess her ignorance to and ask information from. Jeremiah Foster had spoken as if her child, sweet little merry Bella, with a loving word and a kiss for every one, was to suffer heavily for the just and true words her wronged and indignant mother had spoken. Alice always spoke as if there were no hope for her; and blamed her, nevertheless, for not using the means of grace that it was not in her power to avail herself of.

And Hester, that Sylvia would fain have loved for her uniform gentleness and patience with all around her, seemed so cold in her unruffled and undemonstrative behaviour; and moreover, Sylvia felt that Hester blamed her perpetual silence regarding Philip's absence without knowing how bitter a cause Sylvia had for casting him off.

The only person who seemed to have pity upon her was Kester; and his pity was shown in looks rather than words; for when he came to see her, which he did from time to time, by a kind of mutual tacit consent, they spoke but little of former days.

He was still lodging with his sister, widow Moore, working at odd jobs, some of which took him into the country for weeks at a time. But on his returns to Monkshaven he was sure to come and see her and the little Bella; indeed, when his employment was in the immediate neighbourhood of the town, he never allowed a week to pass away without a visit.

There was not much conversation between him and Sylvia at such times. They skimmed over the surface of the small events in which both took an interest; only now and then a sudden glance, a checked speech, told each that there were deeps not forgotten, although they were never mentioned.

Twice Sylvia – below her breath – had asked Kester, just as she was holding the door open for his departure, if anything had ever been heard of Kinraid since his one night's visit to Monkshaven: each time (and there was an interval of some months between the inquiries) the answer had been simply, no.

To no one else would Sylvia ever have named his name. But indeed she had not the chance, had she wished it ever so much, of asking any questions about him from any one likely to know. The Corneys had left Moss Brow at Martinmas, and gone many miles away towards Horncastle. Bessy Corney, it is true, was married and left behind in the neighbourhood; but with her Sylvia had never been intimate; and what girlish friendship there might have been between them had cooled very much at the time of Kinraid's supposed death three years before.

One day before Christmas in this year, 1798, Sylvia was called into the shop by Coulson, who, with his assistant, was busy undoing the bales of winter goods supplied to them from the West Riding, and other places. He was looking at a fine Irish poplin dress-piece when Sylvia answered to his call.

'Here! do you know this again?' asked he, in the cheerful tone of one sure of giving pleasure.

'No! have I iver seen it afore?'

'Not this, but one for all t' world like it.'

She did not rouse up to much interest, but looked at it as if trying to recollect where she could have seen its like.

'My missus had one on at th' party at John Foster's last March, and yo' admired it a deal. And Philip, he thought o' nothing but how he could get yo' just such another, and he set a vast o' folk agait for to meet wi' its marrow; and what he did just the very day afore he went away so mysterious was to write through Dawson Brothers, o' Wakefield, to Dublin, and order that one should be woven for yo'. Jemima had to cut a bit off hers for to give him t' exact colour.'

Sylvia did not say anything but that it was very pretty, in a low voice, and then she quickly left the shop, much to Coulson's displeasure.

All the afternoon she was unusually quiet and depressed.

Alice Rose, sitting helpless in her chair, watched her with keen eyes.

At length, after one of Sylvia's deep, unconscious sighs, the old woman spoke:

'It's religion as must comfort thee, child, as it's done many a one afore thee.'

'How?' said Sylvia, looking up, startled to find herself an object of notice.

'How?' (The answer was not quite so ready as the precept had been.) 'Read thy Bible, and thou wilt learn.'

'But I cannot read,' said Sylvia, too desperate any longer to conceal her ignorance.

'Not read! and thee Philip's wife as was such a great scholar! Of a surety the ways o' this life are crooked! There was our Hester, as can read as well as any minister, and Philip passes over her to go and choose a young lass as cannot read her Bible.'

'Was Philip and Hester——'

Sylvia paused, for though a new curiosity had dawned upon her, she did not know how to word her question.

'Many a time and oft have I seen Hester take comfort in her Bible when Philip was following after thee. She knew where to go for consolation.'

'I'd fain read,' said Sylvia, humbly, 'if anybody would learn me; for perhaps it might do me good; I'm noane so happy.'

Her eyes, as she looked up at Alice's stern countenance, were full of tears.

The old woman saw it, and was touched, although she did not immediately show her sympathy. But she took her own time, and made no reply.

The next day, however, she bade Sylvia come to her, and then and there, as if her pupil had been a little child, she began to teach Sylvia to read the first chapter of Genesis; for all other reading but the Scriptures was as vanity to her, and she would not condescend to the weakness of other books. Sylvia was now, as ever, slow at book-learning; but she was meek and desirous to be taught, and her willingness in this respect pleased Alice, and drew her singularly towards one who, from being a pupil, might become a convert.

All this time Sylvia never lost the curiosity that had been excited by the few words Alice had let drop about Hester and Philip, and by degrees she approached the subject again, and had the idea then started confirmed by Alice, who had no scruple in using the past experience of her own, of her daughter's, or of any one's life, as an instrument to prove the vanity of setting the heart on anything earthly.

This knowledge, unsuspected before, sank deep into Sylvia's thoughts, and gave her a strange interest in Hester – poor Hester, whose life she had so crossed and blighted, even by the very blighting of her own. She gave Hester her own former passionate feelings for Kinraid, and wondered how she herself should have felt towards any one who had come between her and him, and wiled his love away. When she remembered Hester's unfailing sweetness and kindness towards herself from the very first, she could better bear the comparative coldness of her present behaviour.

She tried, indeed, hard to win back the favour she had lost; but the very means she took were blunders, and only made it seem to her as if she could never again do right in Hester's eyes.

For instance, she begged her to accept and wear the pretty poplin gown which had been Philip's especial choice; feeling within herself as if she should never wish to put it on, and as if the best thing she could do with it was to offer it to Hester. But Hester rejected the proffered gift with as much hardness of manner as she was capable of assuming; and Sylvia had to carry it upstairs and lay it by for the little daughter, who, Hester said, might perhaps learn to value things that her father had given especial thought to.

Yet Sylvia went on trying to win Hester to like her once more; it was one of her great labours, and learning to read from Hester's mother was another.

Alice, indeed, in her solemn way, was becoming quite fond of Sylvia; if she could not read or write, she had a deftness and gentleness of motion, a capacity for the household matters which fell into her department, that had a great effect on the old woman, and for her dear mother's sake Sylvia had a stock of patient love ready in her heart for all the aged and infirm that fell in her way. She never thought of seeking them out, as she knew that Hester did; but then she looked up to Hester as some one very remarkable for her goodness. If only she could have liked her!

Hester tried to do all she could for Sylvia; Philip had told her to take care of his wife and child; but she had the conviction that Sylvia had so materially failed in her duties as to have made her husband an exile from his home – a penniless wanderer, wifeless and childless, in some strange country, whose very aspect was friendless, while the cause of all lived on in the comfortable home where he had placed her, wanting for nothing – an object of interest and regard to many friends – with a lovely little child to give her joy for the present, and hope for the future; while he, the poor outcast, might even lie dead by the wayside. How could Hester love Sylvia?

Yet they were frequent companions that ensuing spring. Hester was not well; and the doctors said that the constant occupation in the shop was too much for her, and that she must, for a time at least, take daily walks into the country.

Sylvia used to beg to accompany her; she and the little girl often went with Hester up the valley of the river to some of the nestling farms that were hidden in the more sheltered nooks – for Hester was bidden to drink milk warm from the cow; and to go into the familiar haunts about a farm was one of the few things in which Sylvia seemed to take much pleasure. She would let little Bella toddle about while Hester sate and rested: and she herself would beg to milk the cow destined to give the invalid her draught.

One May evening the three had been out on some such expedition; the country side still looked gray and bare, though the leaves were showing on the willow and blackthorn and sloe, and by the tinkling runnels, making hidden music along the copse side, the pale delicate primrose buds were showing amid their fresh, green, crinkled leaves. The larks had been singing all the afternoon, but were now dropping down into their nests in the pasture fields; the air had just the sharpness in it which goes along with a cloudless evening sky at that time of the year.

But Hester walked homewards slowly and languidly, speaking no word. Sylvia noticed this at first without venturing to speak, for Hester was one who disliked having her ailments noticed. But after a while Hester stood still in a sort of weary dreamy abstraction; and Sylvia said to her,

'I'm afeared yo're sadly tired. Maybe we've been too far.'

Hester almost started.

'No!' said she, 'it's only my headache which is worse to-night. It has been bad all day; but since I came out it has felt just as if there were great guns booming, till I could almost pray 'em to be quiet. I am so weary o' th' sound.'

She stepped out quickly towards home after she had said this, as if she wished for neither pity nor comment on what she had said.

CHAPTER XXXVIII

THE RECOGNITION

FAR away, over sea and land, over sunny sea again, great guns were booming on that 7th of May, 1799.*

The Mediterranean came up with a long roar on a beach glittering white with snowy sand, and the fragments of innumerable sea-shells, delicate and shining as porcelain. Looking at that shore from the sea, a long ridge of upland ground, beginning from an inland depth, stretched far away into the ocean on the right, till it ended in a great mountainous bluff, crowned with the white buildings of a convent sloping rapidly down into the blue water at its base.

In the clear eastern air, the different characters of the

foliage that clothed the sides of that sea-washed mountain might be discerned from a long distance by the naked eye; the silver gray of the olive-trees near its summit; the heavy green and bossy forms of the sycamores lower down; broken here and there by a solitary terebinth or ilex tree, of a deeper green and a wider spread, till the eye fell below on the maritime plain, edged with the white seaboard and the sandy hillocks; with here and there feathery palm-trees, either isolated or in groups – motionless and distinct against the hot purple air.

Look again; a little to the left on the sea-shore there are the white walls of a fortified town, glittering in sunlight, or black in shadow.

The fortifications themselves run out into the sea, forming a port and a haven against the wild Levantine storms; and a lighthouse rises out of the waves to guide mariners into safety.

Beyond this walled city, and far away to the left still, there is the same wide plain shut in by the distant rising ground, till the upland circuit comes closing in to the north, and the great white rocks meet the deep tideless ocean with its intensity of blue colour.

Above, the sky is literally purple with heat; and the pitiless light smites the gazer's weary eye as it comes back from the white shore. Nor does the plain country in that land offer the refuge and rest of our own soft green. The limestone rock underlies the vegetation, and gives a glittering, ashen hue to all the bare patches, and even to the cultivated parts which are burnt up early in the year. In spring-time alone does the country look rich and fruitful; then the corn-fields of the plain show their capability of bearing, 'some fifty, some an hundred fold;'* down by the brook Kishon, flowing not far from the base of the mountainous promontory to the south, there grow the broad green fig-trees, cool and fresh to look upon; the orchards are full of glossy-leaved cherry-trees; the tall amaryllis puts forth crimson and yellow glories in the fields, rivalling the pomp of King Solomon; the daisies and the hyacinths spread their myriad flowers; the anemones, scarlet as blood, run hither and thither over the ground like dazzling flames of fire.

A spicy odour lingers in the heated air; it comes from the multitude of aromatic flowers that blossom in the early spring. Later on they will have withered and faded, and the corn will have been gathered, and the deep green of the eastern foliage will have assumed a kind of gray-bleached tint.

Even now in May, the hot sparkle of the everlasting sea, the terribly clear outline of all objects, whether near or distant, the fierce sun right overhead, the dazzling air around, were inexpressibly wearying to the English eyes that kept their skilled watch, day and night, on the strongly-fortified coast-town that lay out a little to the northward of where the British ships were anchored.

They had kept up a flanking fire for many days in aid of those besieged in St. Jean d'Acre; and at intervals had listened, impatient, to the sound of the heavy siege guns, or the sharper rattle of the French musketry.

In the morning, on the 7th of May, a man at the masthead of the *Tigre** sang out that he saw ships in the offing; and in reply to the signal that was hastily run up, he saw the distant vessels hoist friendly flags. That May morning was a busy time. The besieged Turks took heart of grace; the French outside, under the command of their great general, made hasty preparations for a more vigorous assault than all many, both vigorous and bloody, that had gone before (for the siege was now at its fifty-first day), in hopes of carrying the town by storm before the reinforcement coming by sea could arrive; and Sir Sidney Smith, aware of Buonaparte's desperate intention, ordered all the men, both sailors and marines, that could be spared from the necessity of keeping up a continual flanking fire from the ships upon the French, to land, and assist the Turks and the British forces already there in the defence of the old historic city.

Lieutenant Kinraid, who had shared his captain's daring adventure off the coast of France three years before, who had been a prisoner with him and Westley Wright, in the Temple at Paris, and had escaped with them, and, through

Sir Sidney's earnest recommendation, been promoted from being a warrant officer to the rank of lieutenant, received on this day the honour from his admiral of being appointed to an especial post of danger. His heart was like a war-horse, and said, Ha, ha! as the boat bounded over the waves that were to land him under the ancient machicolated* walls where the Crusaders made their last stand in the Holy Land. Not that Kinraid knew or cared one jot about those gallant knights of old; all he knew was, that the French, under Boney, were trying to take the town from the Turks, and that his admiral said they must not, and so they should not.

He and his men landed on that sandy shore, and entered the town by the water-port gate; he was singing to himself his own country song—

> Weel may the keel row, the keel row, &c.

and his men, with sailors' aptitude for music, caught up the air, and joined in the burden with inarticulate sounds.

So, with merry hearts, they threaded the narrow streets of Acre, hemmed in on either side by the white walls of Turkish houses, with small grated openings high up, above all chance of peeping intrusion.

Here and there they met an ample-robed and turbaned Turk going along with as much haste as his stately self-possession would allow. But the majority of the male inhabitants were gathered together to defend the breach, where the French guns thundered out far above the heads of the sailors.

They went along none the less merrily for the sound to Djezzar Pacha's* garden, where the old Turk sate on his carpet, beneath the shade of a great terebinth tree, listening to the interpreter, who made known to him the meaning of the eager speeches of Sir Sidney Smith and the colonel of the marines.

As soon as the admiral saw the gallant sailors of H.M.S. *Tigre*, he interrupted the council of war without much ceremony, and going to Kinraid, he despatched them, as before arranged, to the North Ravelin, showing them the way with rapid, clear directions.

Out of respect to him, they had kept silent while in the strange, desolate garden; but once more in the streets, the old Newcastle song rose up again till the men were, perforce, silenced by the haste with which they went to the post of danger.

It was three o'clock in the afternoon. For many a day these very men had been swearing at the terrific heat at this hour – even when at sea, fanned by the soft breeze; but now, in the midst of hot smoke, with former carnage tainting the air, and with the rush and whizz of death perpetually whistling in their ears, they were uncomplaining and light-hearted. Many an old joke, and some new ones, came brave and hearty, on their cheerful voices, even though the speaker was veiled from sight in great clouds of smoke, cloven only by the bright flames of death.

A sudden message came; as many of the crew of the *Tigre* as were under Lieutenant Kinraid's command were to go down to the Mole, to assist the new reinforcements (seen by the sailor from the masthead at day-dawn), under command of Hassan Bey, to land at the Mole, where Sir Sidney then was.

Off they went, almost as bright and thoughtless as before, though two of their number lay silent for ever at the North Ravelin – silenced in that one little half-hour. And one went along with the rest, swearing lustily at his ill-luck in having his right arm broken, but ready to do good business with his left.

They helped the Turkish troops to land more with good-will than tenderness; and then, led by Sir Sidney, they went under the shelter of English guns to the fatal breach, so often assailed, so gallantly defended, but never so fiercely contested as on this burning afternoon. The ruins of the massive wall that here had been broken down by the French, were used by them as stepping stones to get on a level with the besieged, and so to escape the heavy stones which the latter hurled down; nay, even the dead bodies of the morning's comrades were made into ghastly stairs.

When Djezzar Pacha heard that the British sailors were

defending the breach, headed by Sir Sidney Smith, he left his station in the palace garden, gathered up his robes in haste, and hurried to the breach; where, with his own hands, and with right hearty good-will, he pulled the sailors down from the post of danger, saying that if he lost his English friends he lost all!

But little recked the crew of the *Tigre* of the one old man – Pacha or otherwise – who tried to hold them back from the fight; they were up and at the French assailants clambering over the breach in an instant; and so they went on, as if it were some game at play instead of a deadly combat, until Kinraid and his men were called off by Sir Sidney, as the reinforcement of Turkish troops under Hassan Bey were now sufficient for the defence of that old breach in the walls, which was no longer the principal object of the French attack; for the besiegers had made a new and more formidable breach by their incessant fire, knocking down whole streets of the city walls.

'Fight your best Kinraid!' said Sir Sidney; 'for there's Boney on yonder hill looking at you.'

And sure enough, on a rising ground, called Richard Cœur de Lion's Mount, there was a half-circle of French generals, on horseback, all deferentially attending to the motions, and apparently to the words, of a little man in their centre; at whose bidding the aide-de-camp galloped swift with messages to the more distant French camp.

The two ravelins which Kinraid and his men had to occupy, for the purpose of sending a flanking fire upon the enemy, were not ten yards from that enemy's van.

But at length there was a sudden rush of the French to that part of the wall where they imagined they could enter unopposed.

Surprised at this movement, Kinraid ventured out of the shelter of the ravelin to ascertain the cause; he, safe and untouched during that long afternoon of carnage, fell now, under a stray musket-shot, and lay helpless and exposed upon the ground undiscerned by his men, who were recalled to help in the hot reception which had been planned for the

French; who, descending the city walls into the Pacha's garden, were attacked with sabre and dagger, and lay headless corpses under the flowering rose-bushes, and by the fountain side.

Kinraid lay beyond the ravelins, many yards outside the city walls.

He was utterly helpless, for the shot had broken his leg. Dead bodies of Frenchmen lay strewn around him; no Englishman had ventured out so far.

All the wounded men that he could see were French; and many of these, furious with pain, gnashed their teeth at him, and cursed him aloud, till he thought that his best course was to assume the semblance of death; for some among these men were still capable of dragging themselves up to him, and by concentrating all their failing energies into one blow, put him to a speedy end.

The outlying pickets of the French army were within easy rifle shot; and his uniform, although less conspicuous in colour than that of the marines, by whose sides he had been fighting, would make him a sure mark if he so much as moved his arm. Yet how he longed to turn, if ever so slightly, so that the cruel slanting sun might not beat full into his aching eyes. Fever, too, was coming upon him; the pain in his leg was every moment growing more severe; the terrible thirst of the wounded, added to the heat and fatigue of the day, made his lips and tongue feel baked and dry, and his whole throat seemed parched and wooden. Thoughts of other days, of cool Greenland seas, where ice abounded, of grassy English homes, began to make the past more real than the present.

With a great effort he brought his wandering senses back; he knew where he was now, and could weigh the chances of his life, which were but small; the unwonted tears came to his eyes as he thought of the newly-made wife in her English home, who might never know how he died thinking of her.

Suddenly he saw a party of English marines advance, under shelter of the ravelin, to pick up the wounded, and bear them within the walls for surgical help. They were so near he could see their faces, could hear them speak; yet he durst not make any sign to them when he lay within range of the French picket's fire.

For one moment he could not resist raising his head, to give himself a chance for life; before the unclean creatures that infest a camp came round in the darkness of the night to strip and insult the dead bodies, and to put to death such as had yet the breath of life within them. But the setting sun came full into his face, and he saw nothing of what he longed to see.

He fell back in despair; he lay there to die.

That strong clear sunbeam had wrought his salvation.

He had been recognized as men are recognized when they stand in the red glare of a house on fire; the same despair of help, of hopeless farewell to life, stamped on their faces in blood-red light.

One man left his fellows, and came running forwards, forwards in among the enemy's wounded, within range of their guns; he bent down over Kinraid; he seemed to understand without a word; he lifted him up, carrying him like a child; and with the vehement energy that is more from the force of will than the strength of body, he bore him back to within the shelter of the ravelin – not without many shots being aimed at them, one of which hit Kinraid in the fleshy part of his arm.

Kinraid was racked with agony from his dangling broken leg, and his very life seemed leaving him; yet he remembered afterwards how the marine recalled his fellows, and how, in the pause before they returned, his face became like one formerly known to the sick senses of Kinraid; yet it was too like a dream, too utterly improbable to be real.

Yet the few words this man said, as he stood breathless and alone by the fainting Kinraid, fitted in well with the belief conjured up by his personal appearance. He panted out,—

'I niver thought you'd ha' kept true to her!'*

And then the others came up; and while they were making a sling of their belts, Kinraid fainted utterly away, and the next time that he was fully conscious, he was lying in his berth in the *Tigre*, with the ship-surgeon setting his leg. After that he was too feverish for several days to collect his senses. When he could first remember, and form a judgment upon his recollections, he called the man especially charged to attend upon him, and bade him go and make inquiry in every possible manner for a marine named Philip Hepburn, and when he was found, to entreat him to come and see Kinraid.

The sailor was away the greater part of the day, and returned unsuccessful in his search; he had been from ship to ship, hither and thither; he had questioned all the marines he had met with, no one knew anything of any Philip Hepburn.

Kinraid passed a miserably feverish night, and when the doctor exclaimed the next morning at his retrogression, he told him, with some irritation, of the ill-success of his servant; he accused the man of stupidity, and wished fervently that he were able to go himself.

Partly to soothe him, the doctor promised that he would undertake the search for Hepburn, and he engaged faithfully to follow all Kinraid's eager directions; not to be satisfied with men's careless words, but to look over muster-rolls and ships' books.

He, too, brought the same answer, however unwillingly given.

He had set out upon the search so confident of success, that he felt doubly discomfited by failure. However, he had persuaded himself that the lieutenant had been partially delirious from the effects of his wound, and the power of the sun shining down just where he lay. There had, indeed, been slight symptoms of Kinraid's having received a sun-stroke; and the doctor dwelt largely on these in his endeavour to persuade his patient that it was his imagination which had endued a stranger with the lineaments of some former friend.

Kinraid threw his arms out of bed with impatience at all this plausible talk, which was even more irritating than the fact that Hepburn was still undiscovered.

'The man was no friend of mine; I was like to have killed him when last I saw him. He was a shopkeeper in a country town in England. I had seen little enough of him; but enough to make me able to swear to him anywhere, even in a marine's uniform, and in this sweltering country.'

'Faces once seen, especially in excitement, are apt to return upon the memory in cases of fever,' quoth the doctor, sententiously.

The attendant sailor, reinstalled to some complacency by the failure of another in the search in which he himself had been unsuccessful, now put in his explanation.

'Maybe it was a spirit.* It's not not th' first time as I've heared of a spirit coming upon earth to save a man's life i' time o' need. My father had an uncle, a west-country grazier. He was a-coming over Dartmoor in Devonshire one moonlight night with a power o' money as he'd got for his sheep at t' fair. It were stowed i' leather bags under th' seat o' th' gig. It were a rough kind o' road, both as a road in character, for there'd been many robberies there of late, and th' great rocks stood convenient for hiding-places. All at once father's uncle feels as if some one were sitting beside him on th' empty seat; and he turns his head and looks, and there he sees his brother sitting – his brother as had been dead twelve year and more. So he turns his head back again, eyes right, and never say a word, but wonders what it all means. All of a sudden two fellows come out upo' th' white road from some black shadow, and they looked, and they let th' gig go past, father's uncle driving hard, I'll warrant him. But for all that he heard one say to t' other, "By ——, there's *two* on 'em!" Straight on he drove faster than ever, till he saw th' far lights of some town or other. I forget its name, though I've heared it many a time; and then he drew a long breath, and turned his head to look at his brother, and ask him how he'd managed to come out of his grave i' Barum churchyard, and th' seat was as empty as it had been when he set out; and then he knew that it were a spirit come to help him against th' men who thought to rob him, and would likely enough ha' murdered him.'

Kinraid had kept quiet through this story. But when the sailor began to draw the moral, and to say, 'And I think I may make bold to say, sir, as th' marine who carried you out o' th' Frenchy's gun-shot was just a spirit come to help you,' he exclaimed impatiently, swearing a great oath as he did so, 'It was no spirit, I tell you; and I was in my full senses. It was a man named Philip Hepburn. He said words to me, or over me, as none but himself would have said. Yet we hated each other like poison; and I can't make out why he should be there and putting himself in danger to save me. But so it was; and as you can't find him, let me hear no more of your nonsense. It was him, and not my fancy, doctor. It was flesh and blood, and not a spirit, Jack. So get along with you, and leave me quiet.'

All this time Stephen Freeman lay friendless, sick, and shattered, on board the *Thesus*.*

He had been about his duty close to some shells that were placed on her deck; a gay young midshipman was thoughtlessly striving to get the fusee out of one of these by a mallet and spike-nail that lay close at hand; and a fearful explosion ensued, in which the poor marine, cleaning his bayonet near, was shockingly burnt and disfigured, the very skin of all the lower part of his face being utterly destroyed by gunpowder. They said it was a mercy that his eyes were spared; but he could hardly feel anything to be a mercy, as he lay tossing in agony, burnt by the explosion, wounded by splinters, and feeling that he was disabled for life, if life itself were preserved. Of all that suffered by that fearful accident (and they were many) none was so forsaken, so hopeless, so desolate, as the Philip Hepburn about whom such anxious inquiries were being made at that very time.

CHAPTER XXXIX

CONFIDENCES

It was a little later on in that same summer that Mrs Brunton came to visit her sister Bessy.

Bessy was married to a tolerably well-to-do farmer who

lived at an almost equal distance between Monkshaven and Hartswell; but from old habit and convenience the latter was regarded as the Dawsons' market-town; so Bessy seldom or never saw her old friends in Monkshaven.

But Mrs Brunton was far too flourishing a person not to speak out her wishes, and have her own way. She had no notion, she said, of coming such a long journey only to see Bessy and her husband, and not to have a sight of her former acquaintances at Monkshaven. She might have added, that her new bonnet and cloak would be as good as lost if it was not displayed among those who, knowing her as Molly Corney, and being less fortunate in matrimony than she was, would look upon it with wondering admiration, if not with envy.

So one day farmer Dawson's market-cart deposited Mrs Brunton in all her bravery at the shop in the market-place, over which Hepburn and Coulson's names still flourished in joint partnership.

After a few words of brisk recognition to Coulson and Hester, Mrs Brunton passed on into the parlour and greeted Sylvia with boisterous heartiness.

It was now four years and more since the friends had met; and each secretly wondered how they had ever come to be friends. Sylvia had a country, raw, spiritless look to Mrs Brunton's eye; Molly was loud and talkative, and altogether distasteful to Sylvia, trained in daily companionship with Hester to appreciate soft slow speech, and grave thoughtful ways.

However, they kept up the forms of their old friendship, though their hearts had drifted far apart. They sat hand in hand while each looked at the other with eyes inquisitive as to the changes which time had made. Molly was the first to speak.

'Well, to be sure! how thin and pale yo've grown, Sylvia! Matrimony hasn't agreed wi' yo' as well as it's done wi' me. Brunton is allays saying (yo' know what a man he is for his joke) that if he'd ha' known how many yards o' silk I should ha' ta'en for a gown, he'd ha' thought twice afore he'd ha' married me. Why, I've gained a matter o' thirty pound o' flesh sin' I were married!'

'Yo' do look brave and hearty!' said Sylvia, putting her sense of her companion's capacious size and high colour into the prettiest words she could.

'Eh! Sylvia! but I know what it is,' said Molly, shaking her head. 'It's just because o' that husband o' thine as has gone and left thee; thou's pining after him, and he's not worth it. Brunton said, when he heared on it – I mind he was smoking at t' time, and he took his pipe out of his mouth, and shook out t' ashes as grave as any judge – "The man," says he, "as can desert a wife like Sylvia Robson as was, deserves hanging!" That's what he says! Eh! Sylvia, but speakin' o' hanging I was so grieved for yo' when I heared of yo'r poor feyther! Such an end for a decent man to come to! Many a one come an' called on me o' purpose to hear all I could tell 'em about him!'

'Please don't speak on it!' said Sylvia, trembling all over.

'Well, poor creature, I wunnot. It is hard on thee, I grant. But to give t' devil his due, it were good i' Hepburn to marry thee, and so soon after there was a' that talk about thy feyther. Many a man would ha' drawn back, choose howiver far they'd gone. I'm noane so sure about Charley Kinraid. Eh, Sylvia! only think on his being alive after all. I doubt if our Bessy would ha' wed Frank Dawson if she'd known as he wasn't drowned. But it's as well she did, for Dawson's a man o' property, and has getten twelve cows in his cow-house, beside three right down good horses; and Kinraid were allays a fellow wi' two strings to his bow. I've allays said and do maintain, that he went on pretty strong wi' yo', Sylvie; and I will say I think he cared more for yo' than for our Bessy, though it were only yesterday at e'en she were standing out that he liked her better than yo'. Yo'll ha' heared on his grand marriage?'

'No!' said Sylvia, with eager painful curiosity.

'No! It was in all t' papers! I wonder as yo' didn't see it. Wait a minute! I cut it out o' t' *Gentleman's Magazine*, as Brunton bought o' purpose, and put it i' my pocket-book when I were a-coming here: I know I've got it somewheere.'

She took out her smart crimson pocket-book, and rummaged in the pocket until she produced a little crumpled bit of printed paper, from which she read aloud,

'On January the third, at St. Mary Redcliffe, Bristol, Charles Kinraid Esq., lieutenant Royal Navy, to Miss Clarinda Jackson, with a fortune of 10,000*l.*'

'Theere!' said she, triumphantly, 'it's something as Brunton says, to be cousin to that.'

'Would yo' let me see it?' said Sylvia, timidly.

Mrs Brunton graciously consented; and Sylvia brought her newly acquired reading-knowledge, hitherto principally exercised on the Old Testament, to bear on these words.

There was nothing wonderful in them, nothing that she might not have expected; and yet the surprise turned her giddy for a moment or two. She never thought of seeing him again, never. But to think of his caring for another woman as much as he had done for her, nay, perhaps more!

The idea was irresistibly forced upon her that Philip would not have acted so; it would have taken long years before he could have been induced to put another on the throne she had once occupied. For the first time in her life she seemed to recognize the real nature of Philip's love.

But she said nothing but 'Thank yo',' when she gave the scrap of paper back to Molly Brunton. And the latter continued giving her information about Kinraid's marriage.

'He were down in t' west, Plymouth or somewhere, when he met wi' her. She's no feyther; he'd been in t' sugar-baking business; but from what Kinraid wrote to old Turner, th' uncle as brought him up at Cullercoats, she's had t' best of edications: can play on t' instrument and dance t' shawl dance; and Kinraid had all her money settled on her, though she said she'd raything give it all to him, which I must say, being his cousin, was very pretty on her. He's left her now, having to go off in t' *Tigre*, as is his ship, to t' Mediterranean seas; and she's written to offer to come and see old Turner, and make friends with his relations, and Brunton is going to gi'e me a crimson satin as soon as we know for certain when she's coming, for we're sure to be asked out to Cullercoats.'

'I wonder if she's very pretty?' asked Sylvia, faintly, in the first pause in this torrent of talk.

'Oh! she's a perfect beauty, as I understand. There was a traveller as come to our shop as had been at York, and knew some of her cousins theere, that were in t' grocery line – her mother was a York lady – and they said she was just a picture of a woman, and iver so many gentlemen had been wantin' to marry her, but she just waited for Charley Kinraid, yo' see!'

'Well, I hope they'll be happy; I'm sure I do!' said Sylvia.

'That's just luck. Some folks is happy i' marriage, and some isn't. It's just luck, and there's no forecasting it. Men is such unaccountable animals, there's no prophesyin' upon 'em. Who'd ha' thought of yo'r husband, him as was so slow and sure – steady Philip, as we lasses used to ca' him – makin' a moonlight flittin', and leavin' yo' to be a widow bewitched?'

'He didn't go at night,' said Sylvia, taking the words 'moonlight flitting' in their literal sense.

'No! Well, I only said "moonlight flittin'" just because it come uppermost and I knowed no better. Tell me all about it, Sylvie, for I can't mak' it out from what Bessy says. Had he and yo' had words? – but in course yo' had.'

At this moment Hester came into the room; and Sylvia joyfully availed herself of the pretext for breaking off the conversation that had reached this painful and awkward point. She detained Hester in the room for fear lest Mrs Brunton should repeat her inquiry as to how it all happened that Philip had gone away; but the presence of a third person seemed as though it would be but little restraint upon the inquisitive Molly, who repeatedly bore down upon the same questions till she nearly drove Sylvia distracted, between her astonishment at the news of Kinraid's marriage; her wish to be alone and quiet, so as to realize the full meaning of that piece of intelligence; her desire to retain Hester in the conversation; her efforts to prevent Molly's recurrence to the circumstances of Philip's disappearance, and the longing –

more vehement every minute – for her visitor to go away and leave her in peace. She became so disturbed with all these thoughts and feelings that she hardly knew what she was saying, and assented or dissented to speeches without there being either any reason or truth in her words.

Mrs Brunton had arranged to remain with Sylvia while the horse rested, and had no compunction about the length of her visit. She expected to be asked to tea, as Sylvia found out at last, and this she felt would be the worst of all, as Alice Rose was not one to tolerate the coarse, careless talk of such a woman as Mrs Brunton without uplifting her voice in many a testimony against it. Sylvia sate holding Hester's gown tight in order to prevent her leaving the room, and trying to arrange her little plans so that too much discordance should not arise to the surface. Just then the door opened, and little Bella came in from the kitchen in all the pretty, sturdy dignity of two years old, Alice following her with careful steps, and protecting, outstretched arms, a slow smile softening the sternness of her grave face; for the child was the unconscious darling of the household, and all eyes softened into love as they looked on her. She made straight for her mother with something grasped in her little dimpled fist; but half-way across the room she seemed to have become suddenly aware of the presence of a stranger, and she stopped short, fixing her serious eyes full on Mrs Brunton, as if to take in her appearance, nay, as if to penetrate down into her very real self, and then, stretching out her disengaged hand, the baby spoke out the words that had been hovering about her mother's lips for an hour past.

'Do away!' said Bella, decisively.

'What a perfect love!' said Mrs Brunton, half in real admiration, half in patronage. As she spoke, she got up and went towards the child, as if to take her up.

'Do away! do away!' cried Bella, in shrill affright at this movement.

'Dunnot,' said Sylvia; 'she's shy; she doesn't know strangers.'

But Mrs Brunton had grasped the struggling, kicking child

by this time, and her reward for this was a vehement little slap in the face.

'Yo' naughty little spoilt thing!' said she, setting Bella down in a hurry. 'Yo' deserve a good whipping, yo' do, and if yo' were mine yo' should have it.'

Sylvia had no need to stand up for the baby who had run to her arms, and was soothing herself with sobbing on her mother's breast; for Alice took up the defence.

'The child said, as plain as words could say, "go away," and if thou wouldst follow thine own will instead of heeding her wish, thou mun put up with the wilfulness of the old Adam, of which it seems to me thee hast getten thy share at thirty as well as little Bella at two.'

'Thirty!' said Mrs Brunton, now fairly affronted. 'Thirty! why, Sylvia, yo' know I'm but two years older than yo'; speak to that woman an' tell her as I'm only four-and-twenty. Thirty, indeed!'

'Molly's but four-and-twenty,' said Sylvia, in a pacificatory tone.

'Whether she be twenty, or thirty, or forty, is alike to me,' said Alice. 'I meant no harm. I meant but for t' say as her angry words to the child bespoke her to be one of the foolish. I know not who she is, nor what her age may be.'

'She's an old friend of mine,' said Sylvia. 'She's Mrs Brunton now, but when I knowed her she was Molly Corney.'

'Ay! and yo' were Sylvia Robson, and as bonny and light-hearted a lass as any in a' t' Riding, though now yo're a poor widow bewitched, left wi' a child as I mustn't speak a word about, an' living wi' folk as talk about t' old Adam as if he wasn't dead and done wi' long ago! It's a change, Sylvia, as makes my heart ache for yo', to think on them old days when yo' were so thought on yo' might have had any man, as Brunton often says; it were a great mistake as yo' iver took up wi' yon man as has run away. But seven year 'll soon be past fro' t' time he went off, and yo'll only be six-and-twenty then; and there'll be a chance of a better husband for yo' after all, so keep up yo'r heart, Sylvia.'

Molly Brunton had put as much venom as she knew how

into this speech, meaning it as a vengeful payment for the supposition of her being thirty, even more than for the reproof for her angry words about the child. She thought that Alice Rose must be either mother or aunt to Philip, from the serious cast of countenance that was remarkable in both; and she rather exulted in the allusion to a happier second marriage for Sylvia, with which she had concluded her speech. It roused Alice, however, as effectually as if she had been really a blood relation to Philip; but for a different reason. She was not slow to detect the intentional offensiveness to herself in what had been said; she was indignant at Sylvia for suffering the words spoken to pass unanswered; but in truth they were too much in keeping with Molly Brunton's character to make as much impression on Sylvia as they did on a stranger; and besides, she felt as if the less reply Molly received, the less likely would it be that she would go on in the same strain. So she coaxed and chattered to her child and behaved like a little coward in trying to draw out of the conversation, while at the same time listening attentively.

'As for Sylvia Hepburn as was Sylvia Robson, she knows my mind,' said Alice, in grim indignation. 'She's humbling herself now, I trust and pray, but she was light-minded and full of vanity when Philip married her, and it might ha' been a lift towards her salvation in one way; but it pleased the Lord to work in a different way, and she mun wear her sackcloth and ashes in patience. So I'll say naught more about her. But for him as is absent, as thee hast spoken on so lightly and reproachfully, I'd have thee to know he were one of a different kind to any thee ever knew, I reckon. If he were led away by a pretty face to slight one as was fitter for him, and who had loved him as the apple of her eye, it's him as is suffering for it, inasmuch as he's a wanderer from his home, and an outcast from wife and child.'

To the surprise of all, Molly's words of reply were cut short even when they were on her lips, by Sylvia. Pale, fire-eyed, and excited, with Philip's child on one arm, and the other stretched out, she said,—

'Noane can tell – noane know. No one shall speak a judgment 'twixt Philip and me. He acted cruel and wrong by me. But I've said my words to him hissel', and I'm noane going to make any plaint to others; only them as knows should judge. And it's not fitting, it's not' (almost sobbing), 'to go on wi' talk like this afore me.'

The two – for Hester, who was aware that her presence had only been desired by Sylvia as a check to an unpleasant *tête-à-tête* conversation, had slipped back to her business as soon as her mother came in – the two looked with surprise at Sylvia; her words, her whole manner, belonged to a phase of her character which seldom came uppermost, and which had not been perceived by either of them before.

Alice Rose, though astonished, rather approved of Sylvia's speech; it showed that she had more serious thought and feeling on the subject than the old woman had given her credit for; her general silence respecting her husband's disappearance had led Alice to think that she was too childish to have received any deep impression from the event. Molly Brunton gave vent to her opinion on Sylvia's speech in the following words:—

'Hoighty-toighty! That tells tales, lass. If yo' treated steady Philip to many such looks an' speeches as yo'n given us now, it's easy t' see why he took hisself off. Why, Sylvia, I niver saw it in yo' when yo' was a girl; yo're grown into a regular little vixen, theere wheere yo' stand!'

Indeed she did look defiant, with the swift colour flushing her cheeks to crimson on its return, and the fire in her eyes not yet died away. But at Molly's jesting words she sank back into her usual look and manner, only saying quietly,—

'It's for noane to say whether I'm vixen or not, as doesn't know th' past things as is buried in my heart. But I cannot hold them as my friends as go on talking on either my husband or me before my very face. What he was, I know; and what I am, I reckon he knows. And now I'll go hurry tea, for yo'll be needing it, Molly!'

The last clause of this speech was meant to make peace; but Molly was in twenty minds as to whether she should accept the olive-branch or not. Her temper, however, was of that obtuse kind which is not easily ruffled; her mind, stagnant in itself, enjoyed excitement from without; and her appetite was invariably good, so she stayed, in spite of the inevitable *tête-à-tête* with Alice. The latter, however, refused to be drawn into conversation again; replying to Mrs Brunton's speeches with a curt yes or no, when, indeed, she replied at all.

When all were gathered at tea, Sylvia was quite calm again; rather paler than usual, and very attentive and subdued in her behaviour to Alice; she would evidently fain have been silent, but as Molly was her own especial guest, that could not be, so all her endeavours went towards steering the conversation away from any awkward points. But each of the four, let alone little Bella, was thankful when the market-cart drew up at the shop-door, that was to take Mrs Brunton back to her sister's house.

When she was fairly off, Alice Rose opened her mouth in strong condemnation; winding up with—

'And if aught in my words gave thee cause for offence, Sylvia, it was because my heart rose within me at the kind of talk thee and she had been having about Philip; and her evil and light-minded counsel to thee about waiting seven years, and then wedding another.'

Hard as these words may seem when repeated, there was something of a nearer approach to an apology in Mrs Rose's manner than Sylvia had ever seen in it before. She was silent for a few moments, then she said,—

'I ha' often thought of telling yo' and Hester, special-like, when yo've been so kind to my little Bella, that Philip an' me could niver come together again; no, not if he came home this very night——'

She would have gone on speaking, but Hester interrupted her with a low cry of dismay.

Alice said,—

'Hush thee, Hester. It's no business o' thine. Sylvia Hepburn, thou'rt speaking like a silly child.'

'No. I'm speaking like a woman; like a woman as finds

out she's been cheated by men as she trusted, and as has no help for it. I'm noane going to say any more about it. It's me as has been wronged, and as has to bear it: only I thought I'd tell yo' both this much, that yo' might know somewhat why he went away, and how I said my last word about it.'

So indeed it seemed. To all questions and remonstrances from Alice, Sylvia turned a deaf ear. She averted her face from Hester's sad, wistful looks; only when they were parting for the night, at the top of the little staircase, she turned, and putting her arms round Hester's neck she laid her head on her neck, and whispered,—

'Poor Hester – poor, poor Hester! if yo' an' he had but been married together, what a deal o' sorrow would ha' been spared to us all!'

Hester pushed her away as she finished these words; looked searchingly into her face, her eyes, and then followed Sylvia into her room, where Bella lay sleeping, shut the door, and almost knelt down at Sylvia's feet, clasping her, and hiding her face in the folds of the other's gown.

'Sylvia, Sylvia,' she murmured, 'some one has told you – I thought no one knew – it's no sin – it's done away with now – indeed it is – it was long ago – before yo' were married; but I cannot forget. It was a shame, perhaps, to have thought on it iver, when he niver thought o' me; but I niver believed as any one could ha' found it out. I'm just fit to sink into t' ground, what wi' my sorrow and my shame.'

Hester was stopped by her own rising sobs, immediately she was in Sylvia's arms. Sylvia was sitting on the ground holding her, and soothing her with caresses and broken words.

'I'm allays saying t' wrong things,' said she. 'It seems as if I were all upset to-day; and indeed I am;' she added, alluding to the news of Kinraid's marriage she had yet to think upon.

'But it wasn't yo', Hester: it were nothing yo' iver said, or did, or looked, for that matter. It were yo'r mother as let it out.'

'Oh, mother! mother!' wailed out Hester; 'I niver thought as any one but God would ha' known that I had iver for a day thought on his being more to me than a brother.'

Sylvia made no reply, only went on stroking Hester's smooth brown hair, off which her cap had fallen. Sylvia was thinking how strange life was, and how love seemed to go all at cross purposes; and was losing herself in bewilderment at the mystery of the world; she was almost startled when Hester rose up, and taking Sylvia's hands in both of hers, and looking solemnly at her, said,—

'Sylvia, yo' know what has been my trouble and my shame, and I'm sure yo're sorry for me – for I will humble myself to yo', and own that for many months before yo' were married, I felt my disappointment like a heavy burden laid on me by day and by night; but now I ask yo', if yo've any pity for me for what I went through, or if yo've any love for me because of yo'r dead mother's love for me, or because of any fellowship, or daily breadliness between us two, – put the hard thoughts of Philip away from out yo'r heart; he may ha' done yo' wrong, anyway yo' think that he has; I niver knew him aught but kind and good; but if he comes back from wheriver in th' wide world he's gone to (and there's not a night but I pray God to keep him, and send him safe back), yo' put away the memory of past injury, and forgive it all, and be, what yo' can be, Sylvia, if you've a mind to, just the kind, good wife he ought to have.'

'I cannot; yo' know nothing about it, Hester.'

'Tell me, then,' pleaded Hester.

'No!' said Sylvia, after a moment's hesitation; 'I'd do a deal for yo', I would, but I daren't forgive Philip, even if I could; I took a great oath again' him. Ay, yo' may look shocked at me, but it's him as yo' ought for to be shocked at if yo' knew all. I said I'd niver forgive him; I shall keep to my word.'

'I think I'd better pray for his death, then,' said Hester, hopelessly, and almost bitterly, loosing her hold of Sylvia's hands.

'If it weren't for baby theere, I could think as it were my

death as 'ud be best. Thcm as one thinks t' most on, forgets one soonest.'

It was Kinraid to whom she was alluding; but Hester did not understand her; and after standing for a moment in silence, she kissed her, and left her for the night.

CHAPTER XL

AN UNEXPECTED MESSENGER

After this agitation, and these partial confidences, no more was said on the subject of Philip for many weeks. They avoided even the slightest allusion to him; and none of them knew how seldom or how often he might be present in the minds of the others.

One day the little Bella was unusually fractious with some slight childish indisposition, and Sylvia was obliged to have recourse to a never-failing piece of amusement; namely, to take the child into the shop, when the number of new, bright-coloured articles was sure to beguile the little girl out of her fretfulness. She was walking along the high terrace of the counter, kept steady by her mother's hand, when Mr Dawson's market-cart once more stopped before the door. But it was not Mrs Brunton who alighted now; it was a very smartly-dressed, very pretty young lady, who put one dainty foot before the other with care, as if descending from such a primitive vehicle were a new occurrence in her life. Then she looked up at the names above the shop-door, and after ascertaining that this was indeed the place she desired to find, she came in blushing.

'Is Mrs Hepburn at home?' she asked of Hester, whose position in the shop brought her forwards to receive the customers, while Sylvia drew Bella out of sight behind some great bales of red flannel.

'Can I see her?' the sweet, south-country voice went on, still addressing Hester. Sylvia heard the inquiry, and came forwards, with a little rustic awkwardness, feeling both shy and curious.

'Will yo' please walk this way, ma'am?' said she, leading her visitor back into her own dominion of the parlour, and leaving Bella to Hester's willing care.

'You don't know me!' said the pretty young lady, joyously. 'But I think you knew my husband. I am Mrs Kinraid!'

A sob of surprise rose to Sylvia's lips – she choked it down, however, and tried to conceal any emotion she might feel, in placing a chair for her visitor, and trying to make her feel welcome, although, if the truth must be told, Sylvia was wondering all the time why her visitor came, and how soon she would go.

'You knew Captain Kinraid, did you not?' said the young lady, with innocent inquiry; to which Sylvia's lips formed the answer, 'Yes,' but no clear sound issued therefrom.

'But I know your husband knew the captain; is he at home yet? Can I speak to him? I do so want to see him.'

Sylvia was utterly bewildered; Mrs Kinraid, this pretty, joyous, prosperous little bird of a woman, Philip, Charley's wife, what could they have in common? what could they know of each other? All she could say in answer to Mrs Kinraid's eager questions, and still more eager looks, was, that her husband was from home, had been long from home: she did not know where he was, she did not know when he would come back.

Mrs Kinraid's face fell a little, partly from her own real disappointment, partly out of sympathy with the hopeless, indifferent tone of Sylvia's replies.

'Mrs Dawson told me he had gone away rather suddenly a year ago, but I thought he might be come home by now. I am expecting the captain early next month. Oh! how I should have liked to see Mr Hepburn, and to thank him for saving the captain's life!'

'What do yo' mean?' asked Sylvia, stirred out of all assumed indifference. 'The captain! is that' (not 'Charley,' she could not use that familiar name to the pretty young wife before her) 'yo'r husband?'

'Yes, you knew him, didn't you? when he used to be staying with Mr Corney, his uncle?'

'Yes, I knew him; but I don't understand. Will yo' please to tell me all about it, ma'am?' said Sylvia, faintly.

'I thought your husband would have told you all about it; I hardly know where to begin. You know my husband is a sailor?'

Sylvia nodded assent, listening greedily, her heart beating thick all the time.

'And he's now a Commander in the Royal Navy, all earned by his own bravery! Oh! I am so proud of him!'

So could Sylvia have been if she had been his wife; as it was, she thought how often she had felt sure that he would be a great man some day.

'And he has been at the siege of Acre.'

Sylvia looked perplexed at these strange words, and Mrs Kinraid caught the look.

'St. Jean d'Acre, you know – though it's fine saying "you know," when I didn't know a bit about it myself till the captain's ship was ordered there, though I was the head girl at Miss Dobbin's in the geography class – Acre is a seaport town, not far from Jaffa, which is the modern name for Joppa, where St. Paul went to long ago; you've read of that, I'm sure, and Mount Carmel, where the prophet Elijah was once, all in Palestine, you know, only the Turks have got it now?'

'But I don't understand yet,' said Sylvia, plaintively; 'I daresay it's all very true about St. Paul, but please, ma'am, will yo' tell me about yo'r husband and mine – have they met again?'

'Yes, at Acre, I tell you,' said Mrs Kinraid, with pretty petulance. 'The Turks held the town, and the French wanted to take it; and we, that is the British Fleet, wouldn't let them. So Sir Sidney Smith, a commodore and a great friend of the captain's, landed in order to fight the French; and the captain and many of the sailors landed with him; and it was burning hot; and the poor captain was wounded, and lay a-dying of pain and thirst within the enemy's – that is the French – fire; so that they were ready to shoot any one of his own side who came near him. They thought he was dead himself, you see, as he was very near; and would have been too, if your husband had not come out of shelter, and taken him up in his arms or on his back (I couldn't make out which), and carried him safe within the walls.'

'It couldn't have been Philip,' said Sylvia, dubiously.

'But it was. The captain says so; and he's not a man to be mistaken. I thought I'd got his letter with me; and I would have read you a part of it, but I left it at Mrs Dawson's in my desk; and I can't send it to you,' blushing as she remembered certain passages in which 'the captain' wrote very much like a lover, 'or else I would. But you may be quite sure it was your husband that ventured into all that danger to save his old friend's life, or the captain would not have said so.'

'But they weren't – they weren't – not to call great friends.'

'I wish I'd got the letter here; I can't think how I could be so stupid; I think I can almost remember the very words, though – I've read them over so often. He says, "Just as I gave up all hope, I saw one Philip Hepburn, a man whom I had known at Monkshaven, and whom I had some reason to remember well" – (I'm sure he says so – "remember well"), "he saw me too, and came at the risk of his life to where I lay. I fully expected he would be shot down; and I shut my eyes not to see the end of my last chance. The shot rained about him, and I think he was hit; but he took me up and carried me under cover." I'm sure he says that, I've read it over so often; and he goes on and says how he hunted for Mr Hepburn all through the ships, as soon as ever he could; but he could hear nothing of him, either alive or dead. Don't go so white, for pity's sake!' said she, suddenly startled by Sylvia's blanching colour. 'You see, because he couldn't find him alive is no reason for giving him up as dead; because his name wasn't to be found on any of the ships' books; so the captain thinks he must have been known by a different name to his real one. Only he says he should like to have seen him to have thanked him; and he says he would give a deal to know what has become of him; and as I was staying two days at Mrs Dawson's, I told them I must come over to Monkshaven, if only for five minutes, just to hear if your good husband was come home, and to shake his hands, that helped to save my own dear captain.'

'I don't think it could have been Philip,' reiterated Sylvia.

'Why not?' asked her visitor; 'you say you don't know where he is; why mightn't he have been there where the captain says he was?'

'But he wasn't a sailor, nor yet a soldier.'

'Oh! but he was. I think somewhere the captain calls him a marine; that's neither one nor the other, but a little of both. He'll be coming home some day soon; and then you'll see!'

Alice Rose came in at this minute, and Mrs Kinraid jumped to the conclusion that she was Sylvia's mother, and in her overflowing gratitude and friendliness to all the family of him who had 'saved the captain' she went forward, and shook the old woman's hand in that pleasant confiding way that wins all hearts.

'Here's your daughter, ma'am!' said she to the half-astonished, half-pleased Alice. 'I'm Mrs Kinraid, the wife of the captain that used to be in these parts, and I'm come to bring her news of her husband, and she don't half believe me, though it's all to his credit, I'm sure.'

Alice looked so perplexed that Sylvia felt herself bound to explain.

'She says he's either a soldier or a sailor, and a long way off at some place named in t' Bible.'

'Philip Hepburn led away to be a soldier!' said she, 'who had once been a Quaker?'

'Yes, and a very brave one too, and one that it would do my heart good to look upon,' exclaimed Mrs Kinraid. 'He's been saving my husband's life in the Holy Land, where Jerusalem is, you know.'

'Nay!' said Alice, a little scornfully. 'I can forgive Sylvia for not being over keen to credit thy news. Her man of peace becoming a man of war; and suffered to enter Jerusalem, which is a heavenly and a typical city* at this time; while me, as is one of the elect, is obliged to go on dwelling in Monkshaven, just like any other body.'

'Nay, but,' said Mrs Kinraid, gently, seeing she was touching on delicate ground, 'I did not say he had gone to Jerusalem, but my husband saw him in those parts, and he was doing his duty like a brave, good man; ay, and more than his duty; and, you may take my word for it, he'll be at home some day soon, and all I beg is that you'll let the captain and me know, for I'm sure if we can, we'll both come and pay our respects to him. And I'm very glad I've seen you,' said she, rising to go, and putting out her hand to shake that of Sylvia; 'for, besides being Hepburn's wife, I'm pretty sure I've heard the captain speak of you; and if ever you come to Bristol I hope you'll come and see us on Clifton Downs.'

She went away, leaving Sylvia almost stunned by the new ideas presented to her. Philip a soldier! Philip in a battle, risking his life. Most strange of all, Charley and Philip once more meeting together, not as rivals or as foes, but as saviour and saved! Add to all this the conviction, strengthened by every word that happy, loving wife had uttered, that Kinraid's old, passionate love for herself had faded away and vanished utterly: its very existence apparently blotted out of his memory. She had torn up her love for him by the roots, but she felt as if she could never forget that it had been.

Hester brought back Bella to her mother. She had not liked to interrupt the conversation with the strange lady before; and now she found her mother in an obvious state of excitement; Sylvia quieter than usual.

'That was Kinraid's wife, Hester! Him that was th' specksioneer as made such a noise about t' place at the time of Darley's death. He's now a captain – a navy captain, according to what she says. And she'd fain have us believe that Philip is abiding in all manner of Scripture places; places as has been long done away with, but the similitude whereof is in the heavens, where the elect shall one day see them. And she says Philip is there, and a soldier, and that he saved her husband's life, and is coming home soon. I wonder what John and Jeremiah 'll say to his soldiering then? It'll noane be to their taste, I'm thinking.'

This was all very unintelligible to Hester, and she would dearly have liked to question Sylvia; but Sylvia sate a little apart, with Bella on her knee, her cheek resting on her child's golden curls, and her eyes fixed and almost trance-like, as if she were seeing things not present.

So Hester had to be content with asking her mother as many elucidatory questions as she could; and after all did not gain a very clear idea of what had really been said by Mrs Kinraid, as her mother was more full of the apparent injustice of Philip's being allowed the privilege of treading on holy ground – if, indeed, that holy ground existed on this side heaven, which she was inclined to dispute – than to confine herself to the repetition of words, or narration of facts.

Suddenly Sylvia roused herself to a sense of Hester's deep interest and balked inquiries, and she went over the ground rapidly.

'Yo'r mother says right – she is his wife. And he's away fighting; and got too near t' French as was shooting and firing all round him; and just then, according to her story, Philip saw him, and went straight into t' midst o' t' shots, and fetched him out o' danger. That's what she says, and upholds.'

'And why should it not be?' asked Hester, her cheek flushing.

But Sylvia only shook her head, and said,

'I cannot tell. It may be so. But they'd little cause to be friends, and it seems all so strange – Philip a soldier, and them meeting theere after all!'

Hester laid the story of Philip's bravery to her heart – she fully believed in it. Sylvia pondered it more deeply still; the causes for her disbelief, or, at any rate, for her wonder, were unknown to Hester! Many a time she sank to sleep with the picture of the event narrated by Mrs Kinraid as present to her mind as her imagination or experience could make it: first one figure prominent, then another. Many a morning she wakened up, her heart beating wildly, why, she knew not, till she shuddered at the remembrance of the scenes that had passed in her dreams: scenes that might be acted in reality that very day; for Philip might come back, and then?

And where was Philip all this time, these many weeks, these heavily passing months?

CHAPTER XLI

THE BEDESMAN OF ST. SEPULCHRE

PHILIP lay long ill on board the hospital ship. If his heart had been light, he might have rallied sooner; but he was so depressed he did not care to live. His shattered jaw-bone, his burnt and blackened face, his many injuries of body, were torture to both his physical frame, and his sick, weary heart. No more chance for him, if inded there ever had been any, of returning gay and gallant, and thus regaining his wife's love. This had been his poor, foolish vision in the first hour of his enlistment; and the vain dream had recurred more than once in the feverish stage of excitement which the new scenes into which he had been hurried as a recruit had called forth. But that was all over now. He knew that it was the most unlikely thing in the world to have come to pass; and yet those were happy days when he could think of it as barely possible. Now all he could look forward to was disfigurement, feebleness, and the bare pittance that keeps pensioners from absolute want.

Those around him were kind enough to him in their fashion, and attended to his bodily requirements; but they had no notion of listening to any revelations of unhappiness, if Philip had been the man to make confidences of that kind. As it was, he lay very still in his berth, seldom asking for anything, and always saying he was better, when the ship-surgeon came round with his daily inquiries. But he did not care to rally, and was rather sorry to find that his case was considered so interesting in a surgical point of view, that he was likely to receive a good deal more than the average amount of attention. Perhaps it was owing to this that he recovered at all. The doctors said it was the heat that made him languid, for that his wounds and burns were all doing well at last; and by-and-by they told him they had ordered him 'home.' His pulse sank under the surgeon's finger at the mention of the word; but he did not say a word. He was too indifferent to life and the world to have a will; otherwise they might have kept their pet patient a little longer where he was.

Slowly passing from ship to ship as occasion served; resting here and there in garrison hospitals, Philip at length reached Portsmouth on the evening of a September day in 1799. The transport-ship in which he was, was loaded with wounded and invalided soldiers and sailors; all who could manage it in any way struggled on deck to catch the first view of the white coasts of England. One man lifted his arm, took off his cap, and feebly waved it aloft, crying, 'Old England for ever!' in a faint shrill voice, and then burst into tears and sobbed aloud. Others tried to pipe up 'Rule Britannia,' while more sate, weak and motionless, looking towards the shores that once, not so long ago, they never thought to see again. Philip was one of these; his place a little apart from the other men. He was muffled up in a great military cloak that had been given him by one of his officers; he felt the September breeze chill after his sojourn in a warmer climate, and in his shattered state of health.

As the ship came in sight of Portsmouth harbour, the signal flags ran up the ropes; the beloved Union Jack floated triumphantly over all. Return signals were made from the harbour; on board all became bustle and preparation for landing; while on shore there was the evident movement of expectation, and men in uniform were seen pressing their way to the front, as if to them belonged the right of reception. They were the men from the barrack hospital, that had been signalled for, come down with ambulance litters and other marks of forethought for the sick and wounded, who were returning to the country for which they had fought and suffered.

With a dash and a great rocking swing the vessel came up to her appointed place, and was safely moored. Philip sat still, almost as if he had no part in the cries of welcome, the bustling care, the loud directions that cut the air around him, and pierced his nerves through and through. But one in authority gave the order; and Philip, disciplined to obedience, rose to find his knapsack and leave the ship. Passive as he seemed to be, he had his likings for particular comrades; there was one especially, a man as different from Philip as well could be, to whom the latter had always attached himself; a merry fellow from Somersetshire, who was almost always cheerful and bright, though Philip had overheard the doctors say he would never be the man he was before he had that shot through the side. This marine would often sit making his fellows laugh, and laughing himself at his own good-humoured jokes, till so terrible a fit of coughing came on that those around him feared he would die in the paroxysm. After one of these fits he had gasped out some words, which led Philip to question him a little; and it turned out that in the quiet little village of Potterne, far inland, nestled beneath the high stretches of Salisbury Plain, he had a wife and a child, a little girl, just the same age even to a week as Philip's own little Bella. It was this that drew Philip towards the man; and this that made Philip wait and go ashore along with the poor consumptive marine.

The litters had moved off towards the hospital, the sergeant in charge had given his words of command to the remaining invalids, who tried to obey them to the best of their power, falling into something like military order for their march; but soon, very soon, the weakest broke step, and lagged behind; and felt as if the rough welcomes and rude expressions of sympathy from the crowd around were almost too much for them. Philip and his companion were about midway, when suddenly a young woman with a child in her arms forced herself through the people, between the soldiers who kept pressing on either side, and threw herself on the neck of Philip's friend.

'Oh, Jem!' she sobbed, 'I've walked all the road from

Potterne. I've never stopped but for food and rest for Nelly, and now I've got you once again, I've got you once again, bless God for it!'

She did not seem to see the deadly change that had come over her husband since she parted with him a ruddy young labourer; she had got him once again, as she phrased it, and that was enough for her; she kissed his face, his hands, his very coat, nor would she be repulsed from walking beside him and holding his hand, while her little girl ran along scared by the voices and the strange faces, and clinging to her mammy's gown.

Jem coughed, poor fellow! he coughed his churchyard cough; and Philip bitterly envied him – envied his life, envied his approaching death; for was he not wrapped round with that woman's tender love, and is not such love stronger than death? Philip had felt as if his own heart was grown numb, and as though it had changed to a cold heavy stone. But at the contrast of this man's lot to his own, he felt that he had yet the power of suffering left to him.

The road they had to go was full of people, kept off in some measure by the guard of soldiers. All sorts of kindly speeches, and many a curious question, were addressed to the poor invalids as they walked along. Philip's jaw, and the lower part of his face, were bandaged up; his cap was slouched down; he held his cloak about him, and shivered within its folds.

They came to a standstill from some slight obstacle at the corner of a street. Down the causeway of this street a naval officer with a lady on his arm was walking briskly, with a step that told of health and a light heart. He stayed his progress though, when he saw the conyoy of maimed and wounded men; he said something, of which Philip only caught the words, 'same uniform,' 'for his sake,' to the young lady, whose cheek blanched a little, but whose eyes kindled. Then leaving her for an instant, he pressed forward; he was close to Philip, – poor sad Philip absorbed in his own thoughts, – so absorbed that he noticed nothing till he heard a voice at his ear, having the Northumbrian burr, the Newcastle inflections which he knew of old, and that were to him like the sick memory of a deadly illness; and then he turned his muffled face to the speaker, though he knew well enough who it was, and averted his eyes after one sight of the handsome, happy man, – the man whose life he had saved once, and would save again, at the risk of his own, but whom, for all that, he prayed that he might never meet more on earth.

'Here, my fine fellow, take this,' forcing a crown piece into Philip's hand. 'I wish it were more; I'd give you a pound if I had it with me.'

Philip muttered something, and held out the coin to Captain Kinraid, of course in vain; nor was there time to urge it back upon the giver, for the obstacle to their progress was suddenly removed, the crowd pressed upon the captain and his wife, the procession moved on, and Philip along with it, holding the piece in his hand, and longing to throw it far away. Indeed he was on the point of dropping it, hoping to do so unperceived, when he bethought him of giving it to Jem's wife, the footsore woman, limping happily along by her husband's side. They thanked him, and spoke in his praise more than he could well bear. It was no credit to him to give that away which burned his fingers as long as he kept it.

Philip knew that the injuries he had received in the explosion on board the *Theseus* would oblige him to leave the service. He also believed that they would entitle him to a pension. But he had little interest in his future life; he was without hope, and in a depressed state of health. He remained for some little time stationary, and then went through all the forms of dismissal on account of wounds received in service, and was turned out loose upon the world, uncertain where to go, indifferent as to what became of him.

It was fine, warm October weather as he turned his back upon the coast, and set off on his walk northwards. Green leaves were yet upon the trees; the hedges were one flush of foliage and the wild rough-flavoured fruits of different kinds; the fields were tawny with the uncleared-off stubble, or emerald green with the growth of the aftermath. The roadside cottage gardens were gay with hollyhocks and Michaelmas daisies and marigolds, and the bright panes of the windows glittered through a veil of China roses.

The war was a popular one, and, as a natural consequence, soldiers and sailors were heroes everywhere. Philip's long drooping form, his arm hung in a sling, his face scarred and blackened, his jaw bound up with a black silk handkerchief; these marks of active service were reverenced by the rustic cottagers as though they had been crowns and sceptres. Many a hard-handed labourer left his seat by the chimney corner, and came to his door to have a look at one who had been fighting the French, and pushed forward to have a grasp of the stranger's hand as he gave back the empty cup into the good wife's keeping, for the kind homely women were ever ready with milk or homebrewed to slake the feverish traveller's thirst when he stopped at their doors and asked for a drink of water.

At the village public-house he had had a welcome of a more interested character, for the landlord knew full well that his circle of customers would be large that night, if it was only known that he had within his doors a soldier or a sailor who had seen service. The rustic politicians would gather round Philip, and smoke and drink, and then question and discuss till they were drouthy again; and in their sturdy obtuse minds they set down the extra glass and the supernumerary pipe to the score of patriotism.

Altogether human nature turned its sunny side out to Philip just now; and not before he needed the warmth of brotherly kindness to cheer his shivering soul. Day after day he drifted northwards, making but the slow progress of a feeble man, and yet this short daily walk tired him so much that he longed for rest – for the morning to come when he needed not to feel that in the course of an hour or two he must be up and away.

He was toiling on with this longing at his heart when he saw that he was drawing near a stately city, with a great old cathedral in the centre keeping solemn guard. This place might be yet two or three miles distant; he was on a rising ground looking down upon it. A labouring man passing by, observed his pallid looks and his languid attitude, and told him for his comfort, that if he turned down a lane to the left a few steps farther on, he would find himself at the Hospital of St. Sepulchre,* where bread and beer were given to all comers, and where he might sit him down and rest awhile on the old stone benches within the shadow of the gateway. Obeying these directions, Philip came upon a building which dated from the time of Henry the Fifth. Some knight who had fought in the French wars of that time, and had survived his battles and come home to his old halls, had been stirred up by his conscience, or by what was equivalent in those days, his confessor, to build and endow a hospital for twelve decayed soldiers, and a chapel wherein they were to attend the daily masses he ordained to be said till the end of all time (which eternity lasted rather more than a century, pretty well for an eternity bespoken by a man), for his soul and the souls of those whom he had slain. There was a large division of the quadrangular building set apart for the priest who was to say these masses; and to watch over the well-being of the bedesmen. In process of years the origin and primary purpose of the hospital had been forgotten by all excepting the local antiquaries; and the place itself came to be regarded as a very pleasant quaint set of almshouses; and the warden's office (he who should have said or sung his daily masses was now called the warden, and read daily prayers and preached a sermon on Sundays) an agreeable sinecure.

Another legacy of old Sir Simon Bray was that of a small croft of land, the rent or profits of which were to go towards giving to all who asked for it a manchet* of bread and a cup of good beer. This beer was, so Sir Simon ordained, to be made after a certain receipt which he left, in which ground ivy took the place of hops. But the receipt, as well as the masses, was modernized according to the progress of time.

Philip stood under a great broad stone archway; the back-door into the warden's house was on the right side; a kind of buttery-hatch was placed by the porter's door on the opposite side. After some consideration, Philip knocked at the closed shutter, and the signal seemed to be well understood. He heard a movement within; the hatch was drawn aside, and his bread and beer were handed to him by a pleasant-looking old man, who proved himself not at all disinclined for conversation.

'You may sit down on yonder bench,' said he. 'Nay, man! sit i' the sun, for it's a chilly place, this, and then you can look through the grate and watch th' old fellows toddling about in th' quad.'

Philip sat down where the warm October sun slanted upon him, and looked through the iron railing at the peaceful sight.

A great square of velvet lawn, intersected diagonally with broad flag-paved walks, the same kind of walk going all round the quadrangle; low two-storied brick houses, tinted gray and yellow by age, and in many places almost covered with vines, Virginian creepers, and monthly roses; before each house a little plot of garden ground, bright with flowers, and evidently tended with the utmost care; on the farther side the massive chapel; here and there an old or infirm man sunning himself, or leisurely doing a bit of gardening, or talking to one of his comrades – the place looked as if care and want, and even sorrow, were locked out and excluded by the ponderous gate through which Philip was gazing.

'It's a nice enough place, bean't it?' said the porter, interpreting Philip's looks pretty accurately. 'Leastways, for them as likes it. I've got a bit weary on it myself; it's so far from th' world, as a man may say; not a decent public within a mile and a half, where one can hear a bit o' news of an evening.'

'I think I could make myself very content here,' replied Philip. 'That's to say, if one were easy in one's mind.'

'Ay, ay, my man. That's it everywhere. Why, I don't think that I could enjoy myself – not even at th' White Hart, where they give you as good a glass of ale for twopence as anywhere i' th' four kingdoms* – I couldn't, to say, flavour my ale even there, if my old woman lay a-dying; which is a sign as it's the heart, and not the ale, as makes the drink.'

Just then the warden's back-door opened, and out came the warden himself, dressed in full clerical costume.

He was going into the neighbouring city, but he stopped to speak to Philip, the wounded soldier; and all the more readily because his old faded uniform told the warden's experienced eye that he had belonged to the marines.

'I hope you enjoy the victual provided for you by the founder of St. Sepulchre,' said he, kindly. 'You look but poorly, my good fellow, and as if a slice of good cold meat would help your bread down.'

'Thank you, sir!' said Philip. 'I'm not hungry, only weary, and glad of a draught of beer.'

'You've been in the Marines, I see. Where have you been serving?'

'I was at the siege of Acre, last May, sir.'

'At Acre! Were you, indeed? Then perhaps you know my boy Harry? He was in the —th.'

'It was my company,'* said Philip, warming up a little. Looking back upon his soldier's life, it seemed to him to have many charms, because it was so full of small daily interests.

'Then, did you know my son, Lieutenant Pennington?'

'It was he that gave me this cloak, sir, when they were sending me back to England. I had been his servant for a short time before I was wounded by the explosion on board the *Theseus*, and he said I should feel the cold of the voyage. He's very kind; and I've heard say he promises to be a first-rate officer.'

'You shall have a slice of roast beef, whether you want it or not,' said the warden, ringing the bell at his own back-door. 'I recognize the cloak now – the young scamp! How soon he has made it shabby, though,' he continued, taking up a corner where there was an immense tear not too well botched up. 'And so you were on board the *Theseus* at the time of the explosion? Bring some cold meat here for the good man – or stay! Come in with me, and then you can tell Mrs Pennington and the young ladies all you know about Harry, – and the siege, – and the explosion.'

So Philip was ushered into the warden's house and made to eat roast beef almost against his will; and he was questioned and cross-questioned by three eager ladies, all at the same time, as it seemed to him. He had given all possible details on the subjects about which they were curious; and was beginning to consider how he could best make his retreat, when the younger Miss Pennington went up to her father – who had all this time stood, with his hat on, holding his coat-tails over his arms, with his back to the fire. He bent his ear down a very little to hear some whispered suggestion of his daughter's, nodded his head, and then went on questioning Philip, with kindly inquisitiveness and patronage, as the rich do question the poor.

'And where are you going to now?'

Philip did not answer directly. He wondered in his own mind where he was going. At length he said,

'Northwards, I believe. But perhaps I shall never reach there.'

'Haven't you friends? Aren't you going to them?'

There was again a pause; a cloud came over Philip's countenance. He said,

'No! I'm not going to my friends. I don't know that I've got any left.'

They interpreted his looks and this speech to mean that he had either lost his friends by death, or offended them by enlisting.

The warden went on,

'I ask, because we've got a cottage vacant in the mead. Old Dobson, who was with General Wolfe at the taking of Quebec,* died a fortnight ago. With such injuries as yours, I fear you'll never be able to work again. But we require strict testimonials as to character,' he added, with as penetrating a look as he could summon up at Philip.

Philip looked unmoved, either by the offer of the cottage, or the illusion to the possibility of his character not being satisfactory. He was grateful enough in reality, but too heavy at heart to care very much what became of him.

The warden and his family, who were accustomed to consider a settlement at St. Sepulchre's as the sum of all good to a worn-out soldier, were a little annoyed at Philip's cool way of receiving the proposition. The warden went on to name the contingent advantages.

'Besides the cottage, you would have a load of wood for firing on All Saints', on Christmas, and on Candlemas days – a blue gown and suit of clothes to match every Michaelmas, and a shilling a day to keep yourself in all other things. Your dinner you would have with the other men, in hall.'

'The warden himself goes into hall every day, and sees that everything is comfortable, and says grace,' added the warden's lady.

'I know I seem stupid,' said Philip, almost humbly, 'not to be more grateful, for it's far beyond what I iver expected or thought for again, and it's a great temptation, for I'm just worn out with fatigue. Several times I've thought I must lie down under a hedge, and just die for very weariness. But once I had a wife and a child up in the north,' he stopped.

'And are they dead?' asked one of the young ladies in a soft sympathizing tone. Her eyes met Philip's, full of dumb woe. He tried to speak; he wanted to explain more fully, yet not to reveal the truth.

'Well!' said the warden, thinking he perceived the real state of things, 'what I propose is this. You shall go into old Dobson's house at once, as a kind of probationary bedesman. I'll write to Harry, and get your character from him. Stephen Freeman I think you said your name was? Before I can receive his reply you'll have been able to tell how you'd like the kind of life; and at any rate you'll have the rest you seem to require in the meantime. You see, I take Harry's having given you that cloak as a kind of character,' added he, smiling kindly. 'Of course you'll have to conform to rules just like all the rest, – chapel at eight, dinner at twelve, lights out at nine; but I'll tell you the remainder of our regulations as we walk across quad to your new quarters.'

And thus Philip, almost in spite of himself, became installed in a bedesman's house at St. Sepulchre.

CHAPTER XLII

A FABLE AT FAULT

PHILIP took possession of the two rooms which had belonged to the dead Sergeant Dobson. They were furnished sufficiently for every comfort by the trustees of the hospital. Some little fragments of ornament, some small articles picked up in distant countries, a few tattered books, remained in the rooms as legacies from their former occupant.

At first the repose of the life and the place was inexpressibly grateful to Philip. He had always shrunk from encountering strangers, and displaying his blackened and scarred countenance to them, even where such disfigurement was most regarded as a mark of honour. In St. Sepulchre's he met none but the same set day after day, and when he had once told the tale of how it happened and submitted to their gaze, it was over for ever, if he so minded. The slight employment his garden gave him – there was a kitchen-garden behind each house, as well as the flower-plot in front – and the daily arrangement of his parlour and chamber were, at the beginning of his time of occupation, as much bodily labour as he could manage. There was something stately and utterly removed from all Philip's previous existence in the forms observed at every day's dinner, when the twelve bedesmen met in the large quaint hall, and the warden came in his college-cap and gown to say the long Latin grace which wound up with something very like a prayer for the soul of Sir Simon Bray. It took some time to get a reply to ship letters in those times when no one could exactly say where the fleet might be found.

And before Dr Pennington had received the excellent character of Stephen Freeman, which his son gladly sent in answer to his father's inquiries, Philip had become restless and uneasy in the midst of all this peace and comfort.

Sitting alone over his fire in the long winter evenings, the scenes of his past life rose before him; his childhood; his aunt Robson's care of him; his first going to Foster's shop in Monkshaven; Haytersbank Farm, and the spelling lessons in the bright warm kitchen there; Kinraid's appearance; the miserable night of the Corneys' party; the farewell he had witnessed on Monkshaven sands; the press-gang, and all the long consequences of that act of concealment; poor Daniel Robson's trial and execution; his own marriage; his child's birth; and then he came to that last day at Monkshaven: and he went over and over again the torturing details, the looks of contempt and anger, the words of loathing indignation, till he almost brought himself, out of his extreme sympathy with Sylvia, to believe that he was indeed the wretch she had considered him to be.

He forgot his own excuses for having acted as he had done; though these excuses had at one time seemed to him to wear the garb of reasons. After long thought and bitter memory came some wonder. What was Sylvia doing now? Where was she? What was his child like – his child as well as hers? And then he remembered the poor footsore wife and the little girl she carried in her arms, that was just the age of Bella; he wished he had noticed that child more, that a clear vision of it might rise up when he wanted to picture Bella.

One night he had gone round this mill-wheel circle of ideas till he was weary to the very marrow of his bones. To shake off the monotonous impression he rose to look for a book amongst the old tattered volumes, hoping that he might find something that would sufficiently lay hold of him to change the current of his thoughts. There was an odd volume of *Peregrine Pickle*,* a book of sermons; half an army list of 1774, and the *Seven Champions of Christendom*.* Philip took up this last, which he had never seen before. In it he read how Sir Guy, Earl of Warwick, went to fight the Paynim in his own country, and was away for seven long years; and when he came back his own wife Phillis, the countess in her castle, did not know the poor travel-worn hermit, who came daily to seek his dole of bread at her hands along with many beggars and much poor. But at last, when he lay a-dying in his cave in the rock, he sent for her by a secret sign known but to them twain. And she came with great speed, for she knew it was her lord who had sent for her; and they had many sweet and holy words together before he gave up the ghost, his head lying on her bosom.

The old story known to most people from their childhood was all new and fresh to Philip. He did not quite believe in the truth of it, because the fictitious nature of the histories of some of the other Champions of Christendom was too patent. But he could not help thinking that this one might be true; and that Guy and Phillis might have been as real flesh and blood, long, long ago, as he and Sylvia had even been. The old room, the quiet moonlit quadrangle into which the cross-barred casement looked, the quaint aspect of everything that he had seen for weeks and weeks; all this predisposed Philip to dwell upon the story he had just been reading as a faithful legend of two lovers whose bones were long since dust. He thought that if he could thus see Sylvia, himself unknown, unseen – could live at her gates, so to speak, and gaze upon her and his child – some day too, when he lay a-dying, he might send for her, and in soft words of mutual forgiveness breathe his life away in her arms. Or perhaps—— and so he lost himself, and from thinking, passed on to dreaming. All night long Guy and Phillis, Sylvia and his child, passed in and out of his visions; it was impossible to make the fragments of his dreams cohere; but the impression made upon him by them was not the less strong for this. He felt as if he were called to Monkshaven, wanted at Monkshaven, and to Monkshaven he resolved to go; although when his reason overtook his feeling, he knew perfectly how unwise it was to leave a home of peace and tranquillity and surrounding friendliness, to go to a place where nothing but want and wretchedness awaited him unless he made himself known; and if he did, a deeper want, a more woeful wretchedness, would in all probability be his portion.

In the small oblong of looking-glass hung against the wall, Philip caught the reflection of his own face, and laughed scornfully at the sight. The thin hair lay upon his temples in the flakes that betoken long ill-health; his eyes were the same as ever, and they had always been considered the best feature in his face; but they were sunk in their orbits, and looked hollow and gloomy. As for the lower part of his face, blackened, contracted, drawn away from his teeth, the outline entirely changed by the breakage of his jaw-bone, he was indeed a fool if he thought himself fit to go forth to win back that love which Sylvia had forsworn. As a hermit and a beggar, he must return to Monkshaven, and fall perforce into the same position which Guy of Warwick had only assumed. But still he should see his Phillis, and might feast his sad hopeless eyes from time to time with the sight of his child. His small pension of sixpence a day would keep him from absolute want of necessaries.

So that very day he went to the warden and told him he thought of giving up his share in the bequest of Sir Simon Bray. Such a relinquishment had never occurred before in all the warden's experience; and he was very much inclined to be offended.

'I must say that for a man not to be satisfied as a bedesman of St. Sepulchre's argues a very wrong state of mind, and a very ungrateful heart.'

'I'm sure, sir, it's not from any ingratitude, for I can hardly feel thankful to you and to Sir Simon, and to madam, and the young ladies, and all my comrades in the hospital, and I niver expect to be either so comfortable or so peaceful again, but——'

'But? What can you have to say against the place, then? Not but what there are always plenty of applicants for every vacancy; only I thought I was doing a kindness to a man out of Harry's company. And you'll not see Harry either; he's got his leave in March!'

'I'm very sorry. I should like to have seen the lieutenant again. But I cannot rest any longer so far away from – people I once knew.'

'Ten to one they're dead, or removed, or something or other by this time; and it'll serve you right if they are. Mind! no one can be chosen twice to be a bedesman of St. Sepulchre's.'

The warden turned away; and Philip, uneasy at staying, disheartened at leaving, went to make his few preparations for setting out once more on his journey northwards. He had to give notice of his change of residence to the local distributor of pensions; and one or two farewells had to be taken, with more than usual sadness at the necessity; for Philip, under his name of Stephen Freeman, had attached some of the older bedesmen a good deal to him, from his unselfishness, his willingness to read to them, and to render them many little services, and, perhaps, as much as anything, by his habitual silence, which made him a convenient recipient of all their garrulousness. So before the time for his departure came, he had the opportunity of one more interview with the warden, of a more friendly character than that in which he gave up his bedesmanship. And so far it was well; and Philip turned his back upon St. Sepulchre's with his sore heart partly healed by his four months' residence there.

He was stronger, too, in body, more capable of the day-after-day walks that were required of him. He had saved some money from his allowance as bedesman and from his pension, and might occasionally have taken an outside place on a coach, had it not been that he shrank from the first look of every stranger upon his disfigured face. Yet the gentle, wistful eyes, and the white and faultless teeth always did away with the first impression as soon as people became a little acquainted with his appearance.

It was February when Philip left St. Sepulchre's. It was the first week in April when he began to recognize the familiar objects between York and Monkshaven. And now he began to hang back, and to question the wisdom of what he had done – just as the warden had prophesied that he would. The last night of his two hundred mile walk he slept at the little inn at which he had been enlisted nearly two years before. It was by no intention of his that he rested at that identical place. Night was drawing on; and, in making, as he thought, a short cut, he had missed his way, and was fain to seek shelter where he might find it. But it brought him very straight face to face with his life at that time, and ever since. His mad, wild hopes – half the result of intoxication, as he now knew – all dead and gone; the career then freshly opening shut up against him now; his youthful strength and health changed into premature infirmity, and the home and the love that should have opened wide its doors to console him for all, why in two years Death might have been busy, and taken away from him his last feeble chance of the faint happiness of seeing his beloved without being seen or known of her. All that night and all the next day, the fear of Sylvia's possible death overclouded his heart. It was strange that he had hardly ever thought of this before; so strange, that now, when the terror came, it took possession of him, and he could almost have sworn that she must be lying dead in Monkshaven churchyard. Or was it little Bella, that blooming, lovely babe, whom he was never to see again? There was the tolling of mournful bells in the distant air to his disturbed fancy, and the cry of the happy birds, the plaintive bleating of the new-dropped lambs, were all omens of evil import to him.

As well as he could, he found his way back to Monkshaven, over the wild heights and moors he had crossed on that black* day of misery; why he should have chosen that path he could not tell – it was as if he were led, and had no free will of his own.

The soft clear evening was drawing on, and his heart beat thick, and then stopped, only to start again with fresh violence. There he was, at the top of the long, steep lane that was in some parts a literal staircase leading down from the hill-top into the High Street, through the very entry up which he had passed when he shrank away from his former and his then present life. There he stood, looking down once more at the numerous irregular roofs, the many stacks of chimneys below him, seeking out that which had once been his own dwelling – who dwelt there now?

The yellower gleams grew narrower; the evening shadows broader, and Philip crept down the lane a weary, woeful man. At every gap in the close-packed buildings he heard the merry music of a band, the cheerful sound of excited voices.

Still he descended slowly, scarcely wondering what it could be, for it was not associated in his mind with the one pervading thought of Sylvia.

When he came to the angle of junction between the lane and the High Street, he seemed plunged all at once into the very centre of the bustle, and he drew himself up into a corner of deep shadow, from whence he could look out upon the street.

A circus was making its grand entry into Monkshaven, with all the pomp of colour and of noise that it could muster. Trumpeters in parti-coloured clothes rode first, blaring out triumphant discord. Next came a gold-and-scarlet chariot drawn by six piebald horses, and the windings of this team through the tortuous narrow street were pretty enough to look upon. In the chariot sate kings and queens, heroes and heroines, or what were meant for such; all the little boys and girls running alongside of the chariot envied them; but they themselves were very much tired, and shivering with cold in their heroic pomp of classic clothing. All this Philip might have seen; did see, in fact; but heeded not one jot. Almost opposite to him, not ten yards apart, standing on the raised step at the well-known shop door, was Sylvia, holding a child, a merry dancing child, up in her arms to see the show. She too, Sylvia, was laughing for pleasure, and for sympathy with pleasure. She held the little Bella aloft that the child might see the gaudy procession the better and the longer, looking at it herself with red lips apart and white teeth glancing through; then she turned to speak to some one behind her – Coulson, as Philip saw the moment afterwards; his answer made her laugh once again. Philip saw it all; her bonny careless looks, her pretty matronly form, her evident ease of mind and prosperous outward circumstances. The years that he had spent in gloomy sorrow, amongst wild scenes, on land or by sea, his life in frequent peril of a bloody end, had gone by with her like sunny days; all the more sunny because he was not there. So bitterly thought the poor disabled marine, as, weary and despairing, he stood in the cold shadow and looked upon the home that should have been his haven, the wife that should have welcomed him, the child that should have been his comfort. He had banished himself from his home; his wife had forsworn him; his child was blossoming into intelligence unwitting of any father. Wife, and child, and home, were all doing well without him; what madness had tempted him thither? an hour ago, like a fanciful fool, he had thought she might be dead – dead with sad penitence for her cruel words at her heart – with mournful wonder at the unaccounted-for absence of her child's father preying on her spirits, and in some measure causing the death he had apprehended. But to look at her there where she stood, it did not seem as if she had had an hour's painful thought in all her blooming life.

Ay! go in to the warm hearth, mother and child, now the gay cavalcade has gone out of sight, and the chill of night has succeeded to the sun's setting. Husband and father, steal out into the cold dark street, and seek some poor cheap lodging where you may rest your weary bones, and cheat your more weary heart into forgetfulness in sleep. The pretty story of the Countess Phillis, who mourned for her husband's absence so long, is a fable of old times; or rather say Earl Guy never wedded his wife, knowing that one she loved better than him was alive all the time she had believed him to be dead.

CHAPTER XLIII

THE UNKNOWN

A FEW days before that on which Philip arrived at Monkshaven, Kester had come to pay Sylvia a visit. As the earliest friend she had, and also as one who knew the real secrets of her life, Sylvia always gave him the warm welcome, the cordial words, and the sweet looks in which the old man delighted. He had a sort of delicacy of his own which kept him from going to see her too often, even when he was stationary at Monkshaven; but he looked forward to the times when he allowed himself this pleasure as a child at school looks forward to its holidays. The time of his service at Haytersbank had, on the whole, been the happiest in all his long monotonous years of daily labour. Sylvia's father had always treated him with the rough kindness of fellowship; Sylvia's mother had never stinted him in his meat or grudged him his share of the best that was going; and once, when he was ill for a few days in the loft above the cow-house, she had made him possets, and nursed him with the same tenderness which he remembered his mother showing to him when he was a little child, but which he had never experienced since then. He had known Sylvia herself, as bud, and sweet promise of blossom; and just as she was opening into the full-blown rose, and, if she had been happy and prosperous, might have passed out of the narrow circle of Kester's interests, one sorrow after another came down upon her pretty innocent head, and Kester's period of service to Daniel Robson, her father, was tragically cut short. All this made Sylvia the great centre of the faithful herdsman's affection; and Bella, who reminded him of what Sylvia was when first Kester knew her, only occupied the second place in his heart, although to the child he was much more demonstrative of his regard than to the mother.

He had dressed himself in his Sunday best, and although it was only Thursday, had forestalled his Saturday's shaving; he had provided himself with a paper of humbugs for the child – 'humbugs' being the north-country term for certain lumps of toffy, well-flavoured with peppermint – and now he sat in the accustomed chair, as near to the door as might be, in Sylvia's presence, coaxing the little one, who was not quite sure of his identity, to come to him, by opening the paper parcel, and letting its sweet contents be seen.

'She's like thee – and yet she favours her feyther,' said he; and the moment he had uttered the incautious words he looked up to see how Sylvia had taken the unpremeditated, unusual reference to her husband. His stealthy glance did not meet her eye; but though he thought she had coloured a little, she did not seem offended as he had feared. It was true that Bella had her father's grave, thoughtful, dark eyes, instead of her mother's grey ones, out of which the childlike expression of wonder would never entirely pass away. And as Bella slowly and half distrustfully made her way towards the temptation offered her, she looked at Kester with just her father's look.

Sylvia said nothing in direct reply; Kester almost thought she could not have heard him. But, by-and-by, she said,—

'Yo'll have heared how Kinraid – who's a captain now, and a grand officer – has gone and got married.'

'Nay!' said Kester, in genuine surprise. 'He niver has, for sure!'

'Ay, but he has,' said Sylvia. 'And I'm sure I dunnot see why he shouldn't.'

'Well, well!' said Kester, not looking up at her, for he caught the inflections in the tones of her voice. 'He were a fine stirrin' chap, yon; an' he were allays for doin' summut; an' when he fund as he couldn't ha' one thing as he'd set his mind on, a reckon he thought he mun put up wi' another.'

'It 'ud be no "putting up,"' said Sylvia. 'She were staying at Bessy Dawson's, and she come here to see me – she's as pretty a young lady as yo'd see on a summer's day; and a real lady, too, wi' a fortune. She didn't speak two words wi'out bringing in her husband's name – "the captain," as she called him.'

'An' she come to see thee?' said Kester, cocking his eye at Sylvia with the old shrewd look. 'That were summut queer, weren't it?'

Sylvia reddened a good deal.

'He's too fause to have spoken to her on me, in t' old way, – as he used for t' speak to me. I were nought to her but Philip's wife.'

'An' what t' dickins had she to do wi' Philip?' asked Kester, in intense surprise; and so absorbed in curiosity that he let the humbugs all fall out of the paper upon the floor, and the little Bella sat down, plump, in the midst of treasures as great as those fabled to exist on Tom Tiddler's ground.*

Sylvia was again silent; but Kester, knowing her well, was

sure that she was struggling to speak, and bided his time without repeating his question.

'She said – and I think her tale were true, though I cannot get to t' rights on it, think on it as I will – as Philip saved her husband's life somewheere nearabouts to Jerusalem. She would have it that t' captain – for I think I'll niver ca' him Kinraid again – was in a great battle, and were near upon being shot by t' French, when Philip – our Philip – come up and went right into t' fire o' t' guns, and saved her husband's life. And she spoke as if both she and t' captain were more beholden to Philip than words could tell. And she come to see me, to try and get news on him.'

'It's a queer kind o' story,' said Kester, meditatively. 'A should ha' thought as Philip were more likely to ha' gi'en him a shove into t' thick on it, than t' help him out o' t' scrape.'

'Nay!' said Sylvia, suddenly looking straight at Kester; 'yo're out theere. Philip had a deal o' good in him. And I dunnot think as he'd ha' gone and married another woman so soon, if he'd been i' Kinraid's place.'

'An' yo've niver heared on Philip sin' he left?' asked Kester, after a while.

'Niver; nought but what she told me. And she said that t' captain made inquiry for him right and left, as soon after that happened as might be, and could hear niver a word about him. No one had seen him, or knowed his name.'

'Yo' niver heared of his goin' for t' be a soldier?' persevered Kester.

'Niver. I've told yo' once. It were unlike Philip to think o' such a thing.'

'But thou mun ha' been thinkin' on him at times i' a' these years. Bad as he'd behaved hissel', he were t' feyther o' thy little un. What did ta think he had been agait on when he left here?'

'I didn't know. I were noane so keen a-thinking on him at first. I tried to put him out o' my thoughts a'together, for it made me like mad to think how he'd stood between me and – that other. But I'd begun to wonder and to wonder about him, and to think I should like to hear as he were doing well. I reckon I thought he were i' London, wheere he'd been that time afore, yo' know, and had allays spoke as if he'd enjoyed hissel' tolerable; and then Molly Brunton told me on t' other one's marriage; and, somehow, it gave me a shake in my heart, and I began for to wish I hadn't said all them words i' my passion; and then that fine young lady come wi' her story – and I've thought a deal on it since, – and my mind has come out clear. Philip's dead, and it were his spirit as come to t' other's help in his time o' need. I've heard feyther say as spirits cannot rest i' their graves for trying to undo t' wrongs they've done i' their bodies.'

'Them's my conclusions,' said Kester, solemnly. 'A was fain for to hear what were yo'r judgments first; but them's the conclusions I comed to as soon as I heard t' tale.'

'Let alone that one thing,' said Sylvia, 'he were a kind, good man.'

'It were a big deal on a "one thing," though,' said Kester. 'It just spoilt yo'r life, my poor lass; an' might ha' gone near to spoilin' Charley Kinraid's too.'

'Men takes a deal more nor women to spoil their lives,' said Sylvia, bitterly.

'Not a' mak' o' men.* I reckon, lass, Philip's life were pretty well on for bein' spoilt at after he left here; and it were mebbe, a good thing he got rid on it so soon.'

'I wish I'd just had a few kind words wi' him, I do,' said Sylvia, almost on the point of crying.

'Come, lass, it's as ill moanin' after what's past as it 'ud be for me t' fill my eyes wi' weepin' after t' humbugs as this little wench o' thine has grubbed up whilst we'n been talkin'. Why, there's not one on 'em left!'

'She's a sad spoilt little puss!' said Sylvia, holding out her arms to the child, who ran into them, and began patting her mother's cheeks, and pulling at the soft brown curls tucked away beneath the matronly cap. 'Mammy spoils her, and Hester spoils her——'

'Granny Rose doesn't spoil me,' said the child, with quick, intelligent discrimination, interrupting her mother's list.

'No; but Jeremiah* Foster does above a bit. He'll come in fro' t' Bank, Kester, and ask for her, a'most ivery day. And he'll bring her things in his pocket; and she's so fause, she allays goes straight to peep in, and then he shifts t' apple or t' toy into another. Eh! but she's a little fause one,' – half devouring the child with her kisses. 'And he comes and takes her a walk oftentimes, and he goes as slow as if he were quite an old man, to keep pace wi' Bella's steps. I often run upstairs and watch 'em out o' t' window; he doesn't care to have me with 'em, he's so fain t' have t' child all to hisself.'

'She's a bonny un, for sure,' said Kester; 'but not so pretty as thou was, Sylvie. A've niver tell'd thee what a come for tho', and it's about time for me t' be goin'. A'm off to t' Cheviots to-morrow morn t' fetch home some sheep as Jonas Blundell has purchased. It'll be a job o' better nor two months a reckon.'

'It'll be a nice time o' year,' said Sylvia, a little surprised at Kester's evident discouragement at the prospect of the journey or absence; he had often been away from Monkshaven for a longer time without seeming to care so much about it.

'Well, yo' see it's a bit hard upon me for t' leave my sister – she as is t' widow-woman, wheere a put up when a'm at home. Things is main an' dear; four-pound loaves is at sixteenpence; an' there's a deal o' talk on a famine i' t' land; an' whaten a paid for my victual an' t' bed i' t' lean-to helped t' oud woman a bit, – an' she's sadly down i' t' mouth, for she cannot hear on a lodger for t' tak' my place, for a' she's moved o'er to t' other side o' t' bridge for t' be nearer t' new buildings,* an' t' grand new walk they're makin' round t' cliffs, thinkin' she'd be likelier t' pick up a labourer as would be glad on a bed near his work. A'd ha' liked to ha' set her agait wi' a 'sponsible lodger afore a'd ha' left, for she's just so soft-hearted, any scamp may put upon her if he nobbut gets houd on her blind side.'

'Can I help her?' said Sylvia, in her eager way. 'I should be so glad; and I've a deal of money by me——'

'Nay, my lass,' said Kester, 'thou munnot go off so fast;

it were just what I were feared on i' tellin' thee. I've left her a bit o' money, and I'll mak' shift to send her more; it's just a kind word, t' keep up her heart when I'm gone, as I want. If thou'd step in and see her fra' time to time, and cheer her up a bit wi' talkin' to her on me, I'd tak' it very kind, and I'd go off wi' a lighter heart.'

'Then I'm sure I'll do it for yo', Kester. I niver justly feel like mysel' when yo're away; for I'm lonesome enough at times. She and I will talk a' t' better about yo' for both on us grieving after yo'.'

So Kester took his leave, his mind set at ease by Sylvia's promise to go and see his sister pretty often during his absence in the North.

But Sylvia's habits were changed since she, as a girl at Haytersbank, liked to spend half her time in the open air, running out perpetually without anything on to scatter crumbs to the poultry, or to take a piece of bread to the old cart-horse, to go up to the garden for a handful of herbs, or to clamber to the highest point around to blow the horn which summoned her father and Kester home to dinner. Living in a town where it was necessary to put on hat and cloak before going out into the street, and then to walk in a steady and decorous fashion, she had only cared to escape down to the freedom of the sea-shore until Philip went away; and after that time she had learnt so to fear observation as a deserted wife, that nothing but Bella's health would have been a sufficient motive to take her out of doors. And, as she had told Kester, the necessity of giving the little girl a daily walk was very much lightened by the great love and affection which Jeremiah Foster now bore to the child. Ever since the day when the baby had come to his knee, allured by the temptation of his watch, he had apparently considered her as in some sort belonging to him; and now he had almost come to think that he had a right to claim her as his companion in his walk back from the Bank to his early dinner, where a high chair was always placed ready for the chance of her coming to share his meal. On these occasions he generally brought her back to the shop-door when he returned to his afternoon's work at the Bank. Sometimes, however, he would leave word that she was to be sent for from his house in the New Town, as his business at the Bank for that day was ended. Then Sylvia was compelled to put on her things, and fetch back her darling; and excepting for this errand she seldom went out at all on week-days.

About a fortnight after Kester's farewell call, this need for her visit to Jeremiah Foster's arose; and it seemed to Sylvia that there could not be a better opportunity of fulfilling her promise and going to see the widow Dobson, whose cottage was on the other side of the river, low down on the cliff side, just at the bend and rush of the full stream into the open sea. She set off pretty early in order to go there first. She found the widow with her house-place tidied up after the midday meal, and busy knitting at the open door – not looking at her rapid-clicking needles, but gazing at the rush and recession of the waves before her; yet not seeing them either, – rather seeing days long past.

She started into active civility as soon as she recognized Sylvia, who was to her as a great lady, never having known Sylvia Robson in her wild childish days. Widow Dobson was always a little scandalized at her brother Christopher's familiarity with Mrs Hepburn.

She dusted a chair which needed no dusting, and placed it for Sylvia, sitting down herself on a three-legged stool to mark her sense of the difference in their conditions, for there was another chair or two in the humble dwelling; and then the two fell into talk – first about Kester, whom his sister would persist in calling Christopher, as if his dignity as her elder brother was compromised by any familiar abbreviation; and by-and-by she opened her heart a little more.

'A could wish as a'd learned write-of-hand,' said she; 'for a've that for to tell Christopher as might set his mind at ease. But yo' see, if a wrote him a letter he couldn't read it; so a just comfort mysel' wi' thinkin' nobody need learn writin' unless they'n got friends as can read. But a reckon he'd ha' been glad to hear as a've getten a lodger.' Here she nodded her head in the direction of the door opening out of the house-place into the 'lean-to,' which Sylvia had observed on drawing near the cottage, and the recollection of the mention of which by Kester had enabled her to identify widow Dobson's dwelling. 'He's a-bed yonder,' the latter continued, dropping her voice. 'He's a queer-lookin' tyke, but a don't think as he's a bad un.'

'When did he come?' said Sylvia, remembering Kester's account of his sister's character, and feeling as though it behoved her, as Kester's confidante on this head, to give cautious and prudent advice.

'Eh! a matter of a s'ennight ago. A'm noane good at mindin' time; he's paid me his rent twice, but then he were keen to pay aforehand. He'd comed in one night, an' sate him down afore he could speak, he were so done up; he'd been on tramp this many a day, a reckon. "Can yo' give me a bed?" says he, panting like, after a bit. "A chap as a met near here says as yo've a lodging for t' let." "Ay," says a, "a ha' that; but yo' mun pay me a shiling a week for 't." Then my mind misgive me, for a thought he hadn't a shilling i' t' world, an' yet if he hadn't, a should just ha' gi'en him t' bed a' t' same: a'm not one as can turn a dog out if he comes t' me wearied o' his life. So he outs wi' a shillin', an' lays it down on t' table, 'bout a word. "A'll not trouble yo' long," says he. "A'm one as is best out o' t' world," he says. Then a thought as a'd been a bit hard upon him. An' says I, "A'm a widow-woman, and one as has getten but few friends:" for yo' see a were low about our Christopher's goin' away north; "so a'm forced-like to speak hard to folk; but a've made mysel' some stirabout* for my supper; and if yo'd like t' share an' share about wi' me, it's but puttin' a sup more watter to 't, and God's blessing 'll be on 't, just as same as if 't were meal." So he ups wi' his hand afore his e'en, and says not a word. At last he says, "Missus," says he, "can God's blessing be shared by a sinner – one o' t' devil's children?" says he. "For the Scriptur' says he's t' father o' lies."* So a were puzzled-like; an' at length a says, "Thou mun ask t' parson that; a'm but a poor faint-hearted widow-woman; but a've allays had God's blessing somehow, now a bethink me, an' a'll share it wi' thee as far as my will goes." So he raxes* his hand across t' table, an' mutters summat, as he grips mine. A thought it were Scriptur' as he said, but a'd needed a' my strength just then for t' lift t' pot off t' fire – it were t' first vittle a'd tasted sin' morn, for t' famine comes down like stones on t' head o' us poor folk: an' a' a said were just "Coom along, chap, an' fa' to; an' God's blessing be on him as eats most." An' sin' that day him and me's been as thick as thieves, only he's niver telled me nought of who he is, or wheere he comes fra'. But a think he's one o' them poor colliers, as has getten brunt i' t' coal-pits; for, t' be sure, his face is a' black wi' fire-marks; an' o' late days he's ta'en t' his bed, an' just lies there sighing, – for one can hear him plain as dayleet thro' t' bit partition wa'.'

As a proof of this, a sigh – almost a groan – startled the two women at this very moment.

'Poor fellow!' said Sylvia, in a soft whisper. 'There's more sore hearts i' t' world than one reckons for!' But after a while, she bethought her again of Kester's account of his sister's 'softness;' and she thought that it behoved her to give some good advice. So she added, in a sterner, harder tone – 'Still, yo' say yo' know nought about him; and tramps is tramps a' t' world over; and yo're a widow, and it behoves yo' to be careful. I think I'd just send him off as soon as he's a bit rested. Yo' say he's plenty o' money?'

'Nay! A never said that. A know nought about it. He pays me aforehand; an' he pays me down for whativer a've getten for him; but that's but little; he's noane up t' his vittle, though a've made him some broth as good as a could make 'em.'

'I wouldn't send him away till he was well again, if I were yo'; but I think yo'd be better rid on him,' said Sylvia. 'It would be different if yo'r brother were in Monkshaven.' As she spoke she rose to go.

Widow Dobson held her hand in hers for a minute, then the humble woman said,—

'Yo'll noane be vexed wi' me, missus, if a cannot find i' my heart t' turn him out till he wants to go hissel'? For a wouldn't like to vex yo', for Christopher's sake; but a know what it is for t' feel for friendless folk, an' choose what may come on it, I cannot send him away.'

'No!' said Sylvia. 'Why should I be vexed? it's no business o' mine. Only I should send him away if I was yo'. He might go lodge wheere there was men-folk, who know t' ways o' tramps, and are up to them.'

Into the sunshine went Sylvia. In the cold shadow the miserable tramp lay sighing. She did not know that she had been so near to him towards whom her heart was softening, day by day.

CHAPTER XLIV

FIRST WORDS

It was the spring of 1800.* Old people yet can tell of the hard famine of that year. The harvest of the autumn before had failed; the war and the corn laws had brought the price of corn up to a famine rate; and much of what came into the market was unsound, and consequently unfit for food, yet hungry creatures bought it eagerly, and tried to cheat disease by mixing the damp, sweet, clammy flour with rice or potato meal. Rich families denied themselves pastry and all unnecessary and luxurious uses of wheat in any shape; the duty on hair-powder was increased; and all these palliatives were but as drops in the ocean of the great want of the people.

Philip, in spite of himself, recovered and grew stronger; and as he grew stronger hunger took the place of loathing dislike to food. But this money was all spent; and what was his poor pension of sixpence a day in that terrible year of famine? Many a summer's night he walked for hours and hours round the house which once was his, which might be his now, with all its homely, blessed comforts, could he but go and assert his right to it. But to go with authority, and in his poor, maimed guise assert that right, he had need be other than Philip Hepburn. So he stood in the old shelter of the steep, crooked lane opening on to the hill out of the market-place, and watched the soft fading of the summer's eve into night; the closing of the once familiar shop; the exit of good, comfortable William Coulson, going to his own home, his own wife, his comfortable, plentiful supper. Then Philip – there were no police in those days, and scarcely an old watchman in that primitive little town – would go round on the shady sides of streets, and, quickly glancing about him, cross the bridge, looking on the quiet, rippling stream, the grey shimmer foretelling the coming dawn over the sea, the black masts and rigging of the still vessels against the sky; he could see with his wistful, eager eyes the shape of the windows – the window of the very room in which his wife and child slept, unheeding of him, the hungry, broken-hearted outcast. He would go back to his lodging, and softly lift the latch of the door; still more softly, but never without an unspoken, grateful prayer, pass by the poor sleeping woman who had given him a shelter and her share of God's blessing – she who, like him, knew not the feeling of satisfied hunger; and then he laid him down on the narrow pallet in the lean-to, and again gave Sylvia happy lessons in the kitchen at Haytersbank, and the dead were alive; and Charley Kinraid, the specksioneer, had never come to trouble the hopeful, gentle peace.

For widow Dobson had never taken Sylvia's advice. The tramp known to her by the name of Freeman – that in which he received his pension – lodged with her still, and paid his meagre shilling in advance, weekly. A shilling was meagre in those hard days of scarcity. A hungry man might easily eat the produce of a shilling in a day.

Widow Dobson pleaded this to Sylvia as an excuse for keeping her lodger on; to a more calculating head it might have seemed a reason for sending him away.

'Yo' see, missus,' said she, apologetically, to Sylvia, one evening, as the latter called upon the poor widow before going to fetch little Bella (it was now too hot for the child to cross the bridge in the full heat of the summer sun, and Jeremiah would take her up to her supper instead) – 'Yo' see, missus, there's not a many as 'ud take him in for a shillin' when it goes so little way; or if they did, they'd take it out on him some other way, an' he's not getten much else, a reckon. He ca's me granny, but a'm vast mista'en if he's ten year younger nor me; but he's getten a fine appetite of his own, choose how young he may be; an' a can see as he could eat a deal more nor he's getten money to buy, an' it's few as can mak' victual go farther nor me. Eh, missus, but yo' may trust me a'll send him off when times is better; but just now it would be sendin' him to his death; for a ha' plenty and to spare, thanks be to God an' yo'r bonny face.'

So Sylvia had to be content with the knowledge that the money she gladly gave to Kester's sister went partly to feed the lodger who was neither labourer nor neighbour, but only just a tramp, who, she feared, was preying on the good old woman. Still the cruel famine cut sharp enough to penetrate all hearts; and Sylvia, an hour after the conversation recorded above, was much touched, on her return from Jeremiah Foster's with the little merry, chattering Bella, at seeing the feeble steps of one, whom she knew by description must be widow Dobson's lodger, turn up from the newly-cut road which was to lead to the terrace walk around the North Cliff, a road which led to no dwelling but widow Dobson's. Tramp, and vagrant, he might he in the eyes of the law; but, whatever his character, Sylvia could see him before her in the soft dusk, creeping along, over the bridge, often stopping to rest and hold by some support, and then going on again towards the town, to which she and happy little Bella were wending.

A thought came over her: she had always fancied that this unknown man was some fierce vagabond, and had dreaded lest in the lonely bit of road between widow Dobson's cottage and the peopled highway, he should fall upon her and rob her if he learnt that she had money with her; and several times she had gone away without leaving the little gift she had intended, because she imagined that she had seen the door of the small chamber in the 'lean-to' open softly while she was there, as if the occupant (whom widow

Dobson spoke of as never leaving the house before dusk, excepting once a week) were listening for the chink of the coin in her little leathern purse. Now that she saw him walking before her with heavy languid steps, this fear gave place to pity; she remembered her mother's gentle superstition which had prevented her from ever sending the hungry empty away, for fear lest she herself should come to need bread.

'Lassie,' said she to little Bella, who held a cake which Jeremiah's housekeeper had given her tight in her hand, 'yon poor man theere is hungry; will Bella give him her cake, and mother will make her another to-morrow twice as big?'

For this consideration, and with the feeling of satisfaction which a good supper not an hour ago gives even to the hungry stomach of a child of three years old, Bella, after some thought, graciously assented to the sacrifice.

Sylvia stopped, the cake in her hand, and turned her back to the town, and to the slow wayfarer in front. Under the cover of her shawl she slipped a half-crown deep into the crumb of the cake, and then restoring it to little Bella, she gave her her directions.

'Mammy will carry Bella; and when Bella goes past the poor man, she shall give him the cake over mammy's shoulder. Poor man is so hungry; and Bella and mammy have plenty to eat, and to spare.'

The child's heart was touched by the idea of hunger, and her little arm was outstretched ready for the moment her mother's hurried steps took her brushing past the startled, trembling Philip.

'Poor man, eat this; Bella not hungry.'

They were the first words he had ever heard his child utter. The echoes of them rang in his ears as he stood endeavouring to hide his disfigured face by looking over the parapet of the bridge down upon the stream running away towards the ocean, into which his hot tears slowly fell, unheeded by the weeper. Then he changed the intention with which he had set out upon his nightly walk, and turned back to his lodging.

Of course the case was different with Sylvia; she would have forgotten the whole affair very speedily, if it had not been for little Bella's frequent recurrence to the story of the hungry man, which had touched her small sympathies with the sense of an intelligible misfortune. She liked to act the dropping of the bun into the poor man's hand as she went past him, and would take up any article near her in order to illustrate the gesture she had used. One day she got hold of Hester's watch for this purpose, as being of the same round shape as the cake; and though Hester, for whose benefit the child was repeating the story in her broken language for the third or fourth time, tried to catch the watch as it was intended that she should (she being the representative of the 'hungry man' for the time being), it went to the ground with a smash that frightened the little girl, and she began to cry at the mischief she had done.

'Don't cry, Bella,' said Hester. 'Niver play with watches again. I didn't see thee at mine, or I'd ha' stopped thee in time. But I'll take it to old Darley's on th' quay-side, and maybe he'll soon set it to rights again. Only Bella must niver play with watches again.'

'Niver no more!' promised the little sobbing child. And that evening Hester took her watch down to old Darley's.

This William Darley was the brother of the gardener at the rectory; the uncle to the sailor who had been shot by the press-gang years before, and to his bed-ridden sister. He was a clever mechanician, and his skill as a repairer of watches and chronometers was great among the sailors, with whom he did a very irregular sort of traffic, conducted often without much use of money, but rather on the principle of barter, they bringing him foreign coins and odd curiosities picked up on their travels in exchange for his services to their nautical instruments or their watches. If he had ever had capital to extend his business, he might have been a rich man; but it is to be doubted whether he would have been as happy as he was now in his queer little habitation of two rooms, the front one being both shop and workshop, the other serving the double purpose of bed-room and museum.

The skill of this odd-tempered, shabby old man was sometimes sought by the jeweller who kept the more ostentatious shop in the High Street; but before Darley would undertake any 'tickle'* piece of delicate workmanship for the other, he sneered at his ignorance, and taunted and abused him well. Yet he had soft places in his heart, and Hester Rose had found her way to one by her patient, enduring kindness to his bedridden niece. He never snarled at her as he did at too many; and on the few occasions when she had asked him to do anything for her, he had seemed as if she were conferring the favour on him, not he on her, and only made the smallest possible charge.

She found him now sitting where he could catch the most light for his work, spectacles on nose, and microscope in hand.

He took her watch, and examined it carefully without a word in reply to her. Then he began to open it and take it to pieces, in order to ascertain the nature of the mischief.

Suddenly he heard her catch her breath with a checked sound of surprise. He looked at her from above his spectacles; she was holding a watch in her hand which she had just taken up off the counter.

'What's amiss wi' thee now?' said Darley. 'Hast ta niver seen a watch o' that mak' afore? or is it them letters on t' back, as is so wonderful?'

Yes, it was those letters – that interlaced, old-fashioned cipher. That Z. H. that she knew of old stood for Zachary Hepburn, Philip's father. She knew how Philip valued this watch. She remembered having seen it in his hands the very day before his disappearance, when he was looking at the time in his annoyance at Sylvia's detention in her walk with baby. Hester had no doubt that he had taken this watch as a matter of course away with him. She felt sure that he would not part with this relic of his dead father on any slight necessity. Where, then, was Philip? – by what chance of life or death had this, his valued property, found its way once more to Monkshaven?

'Where did yo' get this?' she asked, in as quiet a manner as she could assume, sick with eagerness as she was.

To no one else would Darley have answered such a question. He made a mystery of most of his dealings; not that he had anything to conceal, but simply because he delighted in concealment. He took it out of her hands, looked at the number marked inside, and the maker's name – 'Natteau Gent, York'* – and then replied,—

'A man brought it me yesterday, at nightfall, for t' sell it. It's a matter o' forty years old. Natteau Gent has been dead and in his grave pretty nigh as long as that. But he did his work well when he were alive; and so I gave him as brought it for t' sell about as much as it were worth, i' good coin. A tried him first i' t' bartering line, but he wouldn't bite; like enough he wanted food, – many a one does now-a-days.'

'Who was he?' gasped Hester.

'Bless t' woman! how should I know?'

'What was he like? – how old? – tell me.'

'My lass, a've summut else to do wi' my eyes than go peering into men's faces i' t' dusk light.'

'But yo' must have had light for t' judge about the watch.'

'Eh! how sharp we are! A'd a candle close to my nose. But a didn't tak' it up for to gaze int' his face. That wouldn't be manners, to my thinking.'

Hester was silent. Then Darley's heart relented.

'If yo're so set upo' knowing who t' fellow was, a could, mebbe, put yo' on his tracks.'

'How?' said Hester, eagerly. 'I do want to know. I want to know very much, and for a good reason.'

'Well, then a'll tell yo'. He's a queer tyke, that one is. A'll be bound he were sore pressed for t' brass; yet he out's wi' a good half-crown, all wrapped up i' paper, and he axes me t' make a hole in it. Says I, "It's marring good king's coin; at after a've made a hole in't, it'll never pass current again." So he mumbles, and mumbles, but for a' that it must needs be done; and he's left it here, and it t' call for 't to-morrow at e'en.'

'Oh, William Darley!' said Hester, clasping her hands tight together. 'Find out who he is, where he is – anything – everything about him – and I will so bless yo'.'

Darley looked at her sharply, but with some signs of sympathy on his grave face. 'My woman,' he said 'a could ha' wished as you'd niver seen t' watch. It's poor, thankless work thinking too much on one o' God's creatures. But a'll do thy bidding,' he continued, in a lighter and different tone. 'A'm a 'cute old badger when need be. Come for thy watch in a couple o' days, and a'll tell yo' all as a've learnt.'

So Hester went away, her heart beating with the promise of knowing something about Philip, – how much, how little, in these first moments, she dared not say even to herself. Some sailor newly landed from distant seas might have become possessed of Philip's watch in far-off latitudes; in which case, Philip would be dead. That might be. She tried to think that this was the most probable way of accounting for the watch. She could be certain as to the positive identity of the watch – being in William Darley's possession. Again, it might be that Philip himself was near at hand – was here in this very place – starving, as too many were, for insufficiency of means to buy the high-priced food. And then her heart burnt within her as she thought of the succulent, comfortable meals which Sylvia provided every day – nay, three times a day – for the household in the market-place, at the head of which Philip ought to have been; but his place knew him not. For Sylvia had inherited her mother's talent for housekeeping, and on her, in Alice's decrepitude and Hester's other occupations in the shop, devolved the cares of due provision for the somewhat heterogeneous family.

And Sylvia! Hester groaned in heart over the remembrance of Sylvia's words, 'I can niver forgive him the wrong he did to me,' that night when Hester had come, and clung to her, making the sad, shameful confession of her unreturned love.

What could ever bring these two together again? Could Hester herself – ignorant of the strange mystery of Sylvia's heart, as those who are guided solely by obedience to principle must ever be of the clue to the actions of those who are led by the passionate ebb and flow of impulse? Could Hester herself? Oh! how should she speak, how should she act, if Philip were near – if Philip were sad and in miserable estate?

Her own misery at this contemplation of the case was too great to bear; and she sought her usual refuge in the thought of some text, some promise of Scripture, which should strengthen her faith.

'With God all things are possible,'* said she, repeating the words as though to lull her anxiety to rest.

Yes; with God all things are possible. But ofttimes He does his work with awful instruments. There is a peacemaker whose name is Death.

CHAPTER XLV

SAVED AND LOST

HESTER went out on the evening of the day after that on which the unknown owner of the half-crown had appointed to call for it again at William Darley's. She had schooled herself to believe that time and patience would serve her best. Her plan was to obtain all the knowledge about Philip that she could in the first instance; and then, if circumstances allowed it, as in all probability they would, to let drop by drop of healing, peacemaking words and thoughts fall on Sylvia's obdurate, unforgiving heart. So Hester put on her things, and went out down towards the old quay-side on that evening after the shop was closed.

Poor Sylvia!* She was unforgiving, but not obdurate to the full extent of what Hester believed. Many a time since Philip went away had she unconsciously missed his protecting love; when folks spoke shortly to her, when Alice scolded her as one of the non-elect, when Hester's gentle gravity had something of severity in it; when her own heart failed her as to whether her mother would have judged that she had done well, could that mother have known all, as possibly she did by this time. Philip had never spoken otherwise than tenderly to her during the eighteen months of their married life, except on the two occasions before recorded: once when she referred to her dream of Kinraid's possible return, and once again on the evening of the day before her discovery of his concealment of the secret of Kinraid's involuntary disappearance.

After she had learnt that Kinraid was married, her heart had still more strongly turned to Philip, she thought that he had judged rightly in what he had given as the excuse for his double dealing; she was even more indignant at Kinraid's fickleness* than she had any reason to be; and she began to learn the value of such enduring love as Philip's had been – lasting ever since the days when she first began to fancy what a man's love for a woman should be, when she had first shrunk from the tone of tenderness he put into his especial term for her, a girl of twelve – 'Little lassie,' as he was wont to call her.

But across all this relenting came the shadow of her vow – like the chill of a great cloud passing over a sunny plain. How should she decide? what would be her duty, if he came again, and once more called her 'wife'? She shrank from such a possibility with all the weakness and superstition of her nature; and this it was which made her strengthen herself with the re-utterance of unforgiving words; and shun all recurrence to the subject on the rare occasion when Hester had tried to bring it back, with a hope of softening the heart which to her appeared altogether hardened on this one point.

Now, on this bright summer evening, while Hester had gone down to the quay-side, Sylvia stood with her out-of-door things on in the parlour, rather impatiently watching the sky, full of hurrying clouds, and flushing with the warm tints of the approaching sunset. She could not leave Alice: the old woman had grown so infirm that she was never left by her daughter and Sylvia at the same time; yet Sylvia had to fetch her little girl from the New Town, where she had been to her supper at Jeremiah Foster's. Hester had said that she should not be away more than a quarter of an hour; and Hester was generally so punctual that any failure of hers, in this respect, appeared almost in the light of an injury on those who had learnt to rely upon her. Sylvia wanted to go and see widow Dobson, and learn when Kester might be expected home. His two months were long past; and Sylvia had heard through the Fosters of some suitable and profitable employment for him, of which she thought he would be glad to know as soon as possible. It was now some time since she had been able to get so far as across the bridge; and, for aught she knew, Kester might already be come back from his expedition to the Cheviots. Kester was come back. Scarce five minutes had elapsed after these thoughts had passed through her mind before his hasty hand lifted the latch of the kitchen-door, his hurried steps brought him face to face with her. The smile of greeting was arrested on her lips by one look at him: his eyes staring wide, the expression on his face wild, and yet pitiful.

'That's reet,' said he, seeing that her things were already on. 'Thou're wanted sore. Come along.'

'Oh! dear God! my child!' cried Sylvia, clutching at the chair near her; but recovering her eddying senses with the strong fact before her that whatever the terror was, she was needed to combat it.

'Ay; thy child!' said Kester, taking her almost roughly by the arm, and drawing her away with him out through the open doors on to the quay-side.

'Tell me!' said Sylvia, faintly, 'is she dead?'

'She's safe now,' said Kester. 'It's not her – it's him as saved her as needs yo', if iver husband needed a wife.'

'He? – who? O Philip! Philip! is it yo' at last?'

Unheeding what spectators might see her movements, she threw up her arms and staggered against the parapet of the bridge they were then crossing.

'He! – Philip! – saved Bella? Bella, our little Bella, as got her dinner by my side, and went out wi' Jeremiah, as well as could be. I cannot take it in; tell me, Kester.' She kept trembling so much in voice and in body, that he saw she could not stir without danger of falling until she was calmed; as it was, her eyes became filmy from time to time, and she drew her breath in great heavy pants, leaning all the while against the wall of the bridge.

'It were no illness,' Kester began. 'T' little un had gone

for a walk wi' Jeremiah Foster, an' he were drawn for to go round t' edge o' t' cliff, wheere they's makin' t' new walk reet o'er t' sea. But it's but a bit on a pathway now; an' t' one was too oud, an' t' other too young for t' see t' water comin' along wi' great leaps; it's allays for comin' high up again' t' cliff, an' this spring-tide it's comin' in i' terrible big waves. Some one said as they passed t' man a-sittin' on a bit on a rock up above – a dunnot know, a only know as a heared a great fearful screech i' t' air. A were just a-restin' me at after a'd comed in, not half an hour i' t' place. A've walked better nor a dozen mile to-day; an' a ran out, an' a looked, an' just on t' walk, at t' turn, was t' swish of a wave runnin' back as quick as t' mischief int' t' sea, an' oud Jeremiah standin' like one crazy, lookin' o'er int' t' watter; an' like a stroke o' leeghtnin' comes a man, an' int' t' very midst o' t' great waves like a shot; an' then a knowed summut were in t' watter as were nearer death than life; an' a seemed to misdoubt me that it were our Bella; an' a shouts an' a cries for help, an' a goes mysel' to t' very edge o' t' cliff, an, a bids oud Jeremiah, as was like one beside hissel', houd tight on me, for he were good for nought else; an' a bides my time, an' when a sees two arms houdin' out a little drippin' streamin' child, a clutches her by her waist-band, an' hauls her to land. She's noane t' worse for her bath, a'll be bound.'

'I mun go – let me,' said Sylvia, struggling with his detaining hand, which he had laid upon her in the fear that she would slip down to the ground in a faint, so ashen-grey was her face. 'Let me, – Bella, I mun go see her.'

He let go, and she stood still, suddenly feeling herself too weak to stir.

'Now, if you'll try a bit to be quiet, a'll lead yo' along; but yo' mun be a steady and brave lass.'

'I'll be aught if yo' only let me see Bella,' said Sylvia, humbly.

'An' yo' niver ax at after him as saved her.' said Kester, reproachfully.

'I know it's Philip,' she whispered, 'and yo' said he wanted me; so I know he's safe; and, Kester, I think I'm 'feared on him, and I'd like to gather courage afore seeing him, and a look at Bella would give me courage. It were a terrible time when I saw him last, and I did say——'

'Niver think on what thou did say; think on what thou will say to him now, for he lies a-dyin'! He were dashed again t' cliff an' bruised sore in his innards afore t' men as come wi' a boat could pick him up.'

She did not speak; she did not even tremble now; she set her teeth together, and, holding tight by Kester, she urged him on; but when they came to the end of the bridge, she seemed uncertain which way to turn.

'This way,' said Kester. 'He's been lodgin' wi' Sally this nine week, an' niver a one about t' place as knowed him; he's been i' t' wars an' getten his face brunt.'

'And he was short o' food,' moaned Sylvia, 'and we had plenty, and I tried to make yo'r sister turn him out, and send him away. Oh! will God iver forgive me?'

Muttering to herself, breaking her mutterings with sharp cries of pain, Sylvia, with Kester's help, reached widow Dobson's house. It was no longer a quiet, lonely dwelling. Several sailors stood about the door, awaiting, in silent anxiety, for the verdict of the doctor, who was even now examining Philip's injuries. Two or three women stood talking eagerly, in low voices, in the doorway.

But when Sylvia drew near the men fell back; and the women moved aside as though to allow her to pass, all looking upon her with a certain amount of sympathy, but perhaps with rather more of antagonistic wonder as to how she was taking it – she who had been living in ease and comfort while her husband's shelter was little better than a hovel, her husband's daily life a struggle with starvation; for so much of the lodger at widow Dobson's was popularly known; and any distrust of him as a stranger and a tramp was quite forgotten now.

Sylvia felt the hardness of their looks, the hardness of their silence; but it was as nothing to her. If such things could have touched her at this moment, she would not have stood still right in the midst of their averted hearts, and murmured something to Kester. He could not hear the words uttered by that hoarse choked voice, until he had stooped down and brought his ear to the level of her mouth.

'We'd better wait for t' doctors to come out,' she said again. She stood by the door, shivering all over, almost facing the people in the road, but with her face turned a little to the right, so that they thought she was looking at the pathway on the cliff-side, a hundred yards or so distant, below which the hungry waves still lashed themselves into high ascending spray; while nearer to the cottage, where their force was broken by the bar at the entrance to the river, they came softly lapping up the shelving shore.

Sylvia saw nothing of all this, though it was straight before her eyes. She only saw a blurred mist; she heard no sound of waters, though it filled the ears of those around. Instead she heard low whispers pronouncing Philip's earthly doom.

For the doctors were both agreed; his internal injury was of a mortal kind, although, as the spine was severely injured above the seat of the fatal bruise, he had no pain in the lower half of his body.

They had spoken in so low a tone that John Foster, standing only a foot or so away, had not been able to hear their words. But Sylvia heard each syllable there where she stood outside, shivering all over in the sultry summer evening. She turned round to Kester.

'I mun go to him, Kester; thou'll see that noane come in to us, when t' doctors come out.'

She spoke in a soft, calm voice; and he, not knowing what she had heard, made some easy conditional promise. Then those opposite to the cottage door fell back, for they could see the grave doctors coming out, and John Foster, graver, sadder still, following them. Without a word to them – without a word even of inquiry – which many outside thought and spoke of as strange – white-faced, dry-eyed Sylvia slipped into the house out of their sight.

And the waves kept lapping on the shelving shore.

The room inside was dark, all except the little halo or

circle of light made by a dip-candle. Widow Dobson had her back to the bed – her bed – on to which Philip had been borne in the hurry of terror as to whether he was alive or whether he was dead. She was crying – crying quietly, but the tears down-falling fast, as, with her back to the lowly bed, she was gathering up the dripping clothes cut off from the poor maimed body by the doctors' orders. She only shook her head as she saw Sylvia, spirit-like, steal in – white, noiseless, and upborne from earth.

But noiseless as her step might be, he heard, he recognized, and with a sigh he turned his poor disfigured face to the wall, hiding it in the shadow.

He knew that she was by him; that she had knelt down by his bed; that she was kissing his hand, over which the languor of approaching death was stealing. But no one spoke.

At length he said, his face still averted, speaking with an effort.

'Little lassie, forgive me now! I cannot live to see the morn!'

There was no answer, only a long miserable sigh, and he felt her soft cheek laid upon his hand, and the quiver that ran through her whole body.

'I did thee a cruel wrong,' he said, at length. 'I see it now. But I'm a dying man. I think that God will forgive me – and I've sinned against Him; try, lassie – try, my Sylvie – will not thou forgive me?'

He listened intently for a moment. He heard through the open window the waves lapping on the shelving shore. But there came no word from her; only that same long shivering, miserable sigh broke from her lips at length.

'Child,' said he, once more. 'I ha' made thee my idol; and if I could live my life o'er again I would love my God more, and thee less; and then I shouldn't ha' sinned this sin against thee. But speak one word of love to me – one little word, that I may know I have thy pardon.'

'Oh, Philip! Philip!' she moaned, thus adjured.

Then she lifted her head, and said,

'Them were wicked, wicked words, as I said; and a

wicked vow as I vowed; and Lord God Almighty has ta'en me at my word. I'm sorely punished, Philip, I am indeed.'

He pressed her hand, he stroked her cheek. But he asked for yet another word.

'I did thee a wrong. In my lying heart I forgot to do to thee as I would have had thee to do to me. And I judged Kinraid in my heart.'

'Thou thought as he was faithless and fickle,' she answered quickly; 'and so he were. He were married to another woman not so many weeks at after thou went away. Oh, Philip, Philip! and now I have thee back, and——'

'Dying' was the word she would have said, but first the dread of telling him what she believed he did not know, and next her passionate sobs, choked her.

'I know,' said he, once more stroking her cheek, and soothing her with gentle, caressing hand. 'Little lassie!' he said, after a while when she was quiet from very exhaustion, 'I niver thought to be so happy again. God is very merciful.'

She lifted up her head, and asked wildly, 'Will He iver forgive me, think yo'? I drove yo' out fra' yo'r home, and sent yo' away to t' wars, wheere yo' might ha' getten yo'r death; and when yo' come back, poor and lone, and weary, I told her for t' turn yo' out, for a' I knew yo' must be starving in these famine times. I think I shall go about among them as gnash their teeth for iver, while yo' are wheere all tears are wiped away.'*

'No!' said Philip, turning round his face, forgetful of himself in his desire to comfort her. 'God pities us as a father pities his poor wandering children; the nearer I come to death the clearer I see Him. But you and me have done wrong to each other; yet we can see now how we were led to it; we can pity and forgive one another. I'm getting low and faint, lassie; but thou must remember this: God knows more, and is more forgiving than either you to me, or me to you. I think and do believe as we shall meet together before His face; but then I shall ha' learnt to love thee second to Him; not first, as I have done here upon the earth.'

Then he was silent – very still. Sylvia knew – widow

Dobson had brought it in – that there was some kind of medicine, sent by the hopeless doctors, lying upon the table hard by, and she softly rose and poured it out and dropped it into the half-open mouth. Then she knelt down again, holding the hand feebly stretched out to her, and watching the faint light in the wistful loving eyes. And in the stillness she heard the ceaseless waves lapping against the shelving shore.

Something like an hour before this time, which was the deepest midnight of the summer's night, Hester Rose had come hurrying up the road to where Kester and his sister sate outside the open door, keeping their watch under the star-lit sky, all others having gone away, one by one, even John and Jeremiah Foster having returned to their own house, where the little Bella lay, sleeping a sound and healthy slumber after her perilous adventure.

Hester had heard but little from William Darley as to the owner of the watch and the half-crown; but he was chagrined at the failure of all his skilful interrogations to elicit the truth, and promised her further information in a few days, with all the more vehemence because he was unaccustomed to be baffled. And Hester had again whispered to herself 'Patience! Patience!' and had slowly returned back to her home to find that Sylvia had left it, why she did not at once discover. But, growing uneasy as the advancing hours neither brought Sylvia nor little Bella to their home, she had set out for Jeremiah Foster's as soon as she had seen her mother comfortably asleep in her bed; and then she had learnt the whole story, bit by bit, as each person who spoke broke in upon the previous narration with some new particular. But from no one did she clearly learn whether Sylvia was with her husband, or not; and so she came speeding along the road, breathless, to where Kester sate in wakeful, mournful silence, his sister's sleeping head lying on his shoulder, the cottage door open, both for air and that there might be help within call if needed; and the dim slanting oblong of the interior light lying across the road.

Hester came panting up, too agitated and breathless to ask

how much was truth of the fatal, hopeless tale which she had heard. Kester looked at her without a word. Through this solemn momentary silence the lapping of the ceaseless waves was heard, as they came up close on the shelving shore.

'He? Philip?' said she. Kester shook his head sadly.

'And his wife – Sylvia?' said Hester.

'In there with him, alone,' whispered Kester.

Hester turned away, and wrung her hands together.

'Oh, Lord God Almighty!' said she, 'was I not even worthy to bring them together at last? And she went away slowly and heavily back to the side of her sleeping mother. But 'Thy will be done' was on her quivering lips before she lay down to her rest.

The soft grey dawn lightens the darkness of a midsummer night soon after two o'clock. Philip watched it come, knowing that it was his last sight of day, – as we reckon days on earth.

He had been often near death as a soldier; once or twice, as when he rushed into fire to save Kinraid, his chances of life had been as one to a hundred; but yet he had had a chance. But now there was the new feeling – the last new feeling which we shall any of us experience in this world – that death was not only close at hand, but inevitable.

He felt its numbness stealing up him – stealing up him. But the head was clear, the brain more than commonly active in producing vivid impressions.

It seemed but yesterday since he was a little boy at his mother's knee, wishing with all the earnestness of his childish heart to be like Abraham, who was called the friend of God, or David, who was said to be the man after God's own heart, or St. John, who was called 'the Beloved.'* As very present seemed the day on which he made resolutions of trying to be like them; it was in the spring, and some one had brought in cowslips; and the scent of those flowers was in his nostrils now, as he lay a-dying – his life ended, his battles fought, his time for 'being good' over and gone – the opportunity, once given in all eternity, past.

All the temptations that had beset him rose clearly before him; the scenes themselves stood up in their solid materialism

– he could have touched the places; the people, the thoughts, the arguments that Satan had urged in behalf of sin, were reproduced with the vividness of a present time. And he knew that the thoughts were illusions, the arguments false and hollow; for in that hour came the perfect vision of the perfect truth: he saw the 'way to escape'* which had come along with the temptation; now, the strong resolve of an ardent boyhood, with all a life before it to show the world 'what a Christian might be;'* and then the swift, terrible now, when his naked, guilty soul shrank into the shadow of God's mercy-seat, out of the blaze of His anger against all those who act a lie.

His mind was wandering, and he plucked it back. Was this death in very deed? He tried to grasp at the present, the earthly present, fading quick away. He lay there on the bed – on Sally Dobson's bed in the house-place, not on his accustomed pallet in the lean-to. He knew that much. And the door was open into the still, dusk night; and through the open casement he could hear the lapping of the waves on the shelving shore, could see the soft grey dawn over the sea – he knew it was over the sea – he saw what lay unseen behind the poor walls of the cottage. And it was Sylvia who held his hand tight in her warm, living grasp; it was his wife whose arm was thrown around him, whose sobbing sighs shook his numbed frame from time to time.

'God bless and comfort my darling,' he said to himself. 'She knows me now. All will be right in heaven – in the light of God's mercy.'

And then he tried to remember all that he had ever read about, God, and all that the blessed Christ – that bringeth glad tidings of great joy unto all people* had said of the Father, from whom He came. Those sayings dropped like balm down upon his troubled heart and brain. He remembered his mother, and how she had loved him; and he was going to a love wiser, tenderer, deeper than hers.

As he thought this, he moved his hands as if to pray; but Sylvia clenched her hold, and he lay still, praying all the same for her, for his child, and for himself. Then he saw the sky redden with the first flush of dawn; he heard Kester's long-drawn sigh of weariness outside the open door.

He had seen widow Dobson pass through long before to keep the remainder of her watch on the bed in the lean-to, which had been his for many and many a sleepless and tearful night. Those nights were over – he should never see that poor chamber again, though it was scarce two feet distant. He began to lose all sense of the comparative duration of time: it seemed as long since kind Sally Dobson had bent over him with soft, lingering look, before going into the humble sleeping-room – as long as it was since his boyhood, when he stood by his mother dreaming of the life that should be his, with the scent of the cowslips tempting him to be off to the woodlands where they grew. Then there came a rush and an eddying through his brain – his soul trying her wings for the long flight. Again he was in the present: he heard the waves lapping against the shelving shore once again.

And now his thoughts came back to Sylvia. Once more he spoke aloud, in a strange and terrible voice, which was not his. Every sound came with efforts that were new to him.

'My wife! Sylvie! Once more – forgive me all.'

She sprang up, she kissed his poor burnt lips; she held him in her arms, she moaned, and said,

'Oh, wicked me! forgive me – me – Philip!'

Then he spoke, and said, 'Lord, forgive us our trespasses as we forgive each other!' And after that the power of speech was conquered by the coming death. He lay very still, his consciousness fast fading away, yet coming back in throbs, so that he knew it was Sylvia who touched his lips with cordial, and that it was Sylvia who murmured words of love in his ear. He seemed to sleep at last, and so he did – a kind of sleep, but the light of the red morning sun fell on his eyes, and with one strong effort he rose up, and turned so as once more to see his wife's pale face of misery.

'In heaven,' he cried, and a bright smile came on his face, as he fell back on his pillow.

Not long after Hester came, the little Bella scarce awake in her arms, with the purpose of bringing his child to see him ere yet he passed away. Hester had watched and prayed through the livelong night. And now she found him dead, and Sylvia, tearless and almost unconscious, lying by him, her hand holding his, her other thrown around him.

Kester, poor old man, was sobbing bitterly; but she not at all.

Then Hester bore her child to her, and Sylvia opened wide her miserable eyes, and only stared, as if all sense was gone from her. But Bella suddenly rousing up at the sight of the poor, scarred, peaceful face, cried out,—

'Poor man who was so hungry. Is he not hungry now?'

'No,' said Hester, softly. 'The former things are passed away – and he is gone where there is no more sorrow, and no more pain.'

But then she broke down into weeping and crying. Sylvia sat up and looked at her.

'Why do yo' cry, Hester?' she said. 'Yo' niver said that yo' wouldn't forgive him as long as yo' lived. Yo' niver broke the heart of him that loved yo', and let him almost starve at yo'r very door. Oh, Philip! my Philip, tender and true.'

Then Hester came round and closed the sad half-open eyes; kissing the calm brow with a long farewell kiss. As she did so, her eye fell on a black ribbon round his neck. She partly lifted it out; to it was hung a half-crown piece.

'This is the piece he left at William Darley's to be bored,' said she, 'not many days ago.'

Bella had crept to her mother's arms as a known haven in this strange place; and the touch of his child loosened the fountains of her tears. She stretched out her hand for the black ribbon, put it round her own neck; after a while she said,

'If I live very long, and try hard to be very good all that time, do yo' think, Hester, as God will let me to him where he is?'

* * * * *

Monkshaven is altered now into a rising bathing place. Yet, standing near the site of widow Dobson's house on a summer's night, at the ebb of a spring-tide, you may hear the waves come lapping up the shelving shore with the same ceaseless, ever-recurrent sound as that which Philip listened to in the pauses between life and death.

And so it will be until 'there shall be no more sea.'*

But the memory of man fades away. A few old people can still tell you the tradition of the man who died in a cottage somewhere about this spot, – died of starvation while his wife lived in hard-hearted plenty not two good stone-throws away. This is the form into which popular feeling, and ignorance of the real facts, have moulded the story. Not long since a lady went to the 'Public Baths'* a handsome stone building erected on the very site of widow Dobson's cottage, and finding all the rooms engaged she sat down and had some talk with the bathing woman; and, as it chanced, the conversation fell on Philip Hepburn and the legend of his fate.

'I knew an old man when I was a girl,' said the bathing woman, 'as could niver abide to hear t' wife blamed. He would say nothing again' th' husband; he used to say as it were not fit for men to be judging; that she had had her sore trial, as well as Hepburn hisself.'

The lady asked, 'What became of the wife?'

'She was a pale, sad woman, allays dressed in black. I can just remember her when I was a little child, but she died before her daughter was well grown up; and Miss Rose took t' lassie, as had always been like her own.'

'Miss Rose?'

'Hester Rose! have yo' niver heared of Hester Rose, she as founded t' alms-houses for poor disabled sailors and soldiers on t' Horncastle road? There's a piece o' stone in front to say that "This building is erected in memory of P. H." – and some folk will have it P. H. stands for t' name o' th' man as was starved to death.'

'And the daughter?'

'One o' th' Fosters, them as founded t' Old Bank, left her

a vast o' money; and she were married to distant cousin of theirs, and went off to settle in America many and many a year ago.'

THE END

APPENDIX A

'THE KEEL ROW' AND RHYMES OF NORTHERN BARDS

AFTER her father's death in March 1829 Elizabeth Gaskell paid an extended visit to the home of his former tutor, a Unitarian minister in Newcastle-upon-Tyne, The Revd William Turner. The visit is believed to have provided much useful material for *Ruth* (1853) but it also served to renew the future novelist's connections with Northumbria (her father's family roots were in Berwick-on-Tweed). It is possible, too, that it was at this period that Mrs Gaskell became familiar with the Newcastle song 'Weel may the Keel row' which she used virtually as a signature tune for Kinraid in *Sylvia's Lovers.* The song, with a variant, was printed as the opening poem in the important collection *Rhymes of Northern Bards: being a curious Collection of old and new Songs and Poems, Peculiar to the Counties of Newcastle upon Tyne, Northumberland and Durham*, edited by John Bell, and published by him in Newcastle in 1812. These two versions are reprinted here, together with 'The Sandgate Lassie's Lament' from the same volume. This last poem deals with the impressment of a sailor called Johnny (the name of the hero of 'The Keel Row'), purports to be the lament of a betrothed girl, and is the work of a poet who shares Sylvia's surname.

WEEL MAY THE KEEL ROW

As I cam thro' Sandgate, thro' Sandgate, thro' Sandgate,
As I cam thro' Sandgate, I heard a lassie sing,
Weel may the keel row, the keel row, the keel row,
Weel may the keel row, that my laddie's in.

He wears a blue bonnet, blue bonnet, blue bonnet,
He wears a blue bonnet, a dimple in his chin:
And weel may the keel row, the keel row, the keel row,
And weel may the keel row, that my laddie's in.

THE NEW KEEL ROW

by T. T. – To the old Tune.

Whe's like my Johnny,
Sae leish, sae blithe, sae bonny,
He's foremost 'mang the mony
  Keel lads o' Coaly Tyne;
He'll set or row so tightly,
Or in the dance so sprightly,
He'll cut and shuffle slightly,
  'Tis true – were he not mine.

Weel may the keel row,
The keel row, the keel row,
Weel may the keel row,
  That my laddie's in:
He wears a blue bonnet,
A bonnet, a bonnet,
He wears a blue bonnet,
  A dimple in his chin.

He's ne mair learning,
Than tells his weekly earning,
Yet reet frae wrang discerning,
  Tho' brave, ne bruiser he;
Tho' he no worth a plack is,
His awn coat on his back is,
And nane can say that black is
  The white o' Johnny's ee.

Each pay-day nearly,
He takes his quairt right dearly,
Then talks O, latin O, – cheerly,
  Or mavies jaws away;
How caring not a feather,
Nelson and he together,
The springy French did lether,
  And gar'd them shab away.

Were a' kings comparely,
In each I'd spy a fairly,
An' ay wad Johnny barly,
He gets sic bonny bairns;
Go bon, the queen, or misses,
But wad for Johnny's kisses,
Luik upon as blisses,
Scrimp meals, caff beds, and dairns.

Wour lads, like their deddy,
To fight the French are ready,
But gie's a peace that's steady,
And breed cheap as lang syne;
May a' the press gangs perish,
Each lass her laddy cherish:
Lang may the Coal Trade flourish
Upon the dingy Tyne.

Breet star o' Heaton,
Your ay wour darling sweet'en,
May blessings leet on
Your leady, bairns, and ye;

God bless the King and Nation.
Each bravely fill his station,
Our canny *Corporation*,
Lang may they sing wi' me,

Weel may the keel row, &c.

THE SANDGATE LASSIE'S LAMENT

by Henry Robson.

They're prest my dear Johnny,
Sae sprightly and bonny, –
Alack! I shall ne'er mair d'weel, O:
The kidnapping squad,
Laid hold of my lad,
As he was unmooring the keel, O;
O my sweet laddie,
My canny keel laddie,
Sae handsome, sae canty, and free, O;
Had he staid on the Tyne,
Ere now he'd been mine,
But oh! he's far over the sea, O.

Should he fall by commotion,
Or sink in the ocean,
(May sick tidings ne'er come to the *Key*, O)
I could ne'er mair be glad,
For the loss of my lad
Wad break my poor heart, and I'd *dee*, O!
O my sweet laddie, &c.

But should my dear tar
Come safe from the war,
What heart-bounding joy wad I feel, O;
To the church we wad flee,
And married be,
And again he shall row in his keel, O.
O my sweet laddie, &c.

O my sweet laddie,
My canny keel laddie,
Sae handsome, sae canty, and free, O:
Tho' far from the Tyne,
I still hope he'll be mine,
And live happy as any can be, O.
O my sweet laddie, &c.

APPENDIX B

A REVISED CHRONOLOGY FOR SYLVIA'S LOVERS

As Graham Handley noted in the August issue of *Notes and Queries* for 1965 'there is an error in the straightforward chronology of *Sylvia's Lovers* which ... indicates some loose stitching in the historical fabric so carefully woven by Mrs Gaskell'. The opening of Chapter 2 of the novel purposefully but, as it proves, inaccurately informs us that Sylvia and Molly Corney set out for Monkshaven 'early in October of the year 1796'. In Chapter 12, after some fifteen months have passed, Philip disappointedly leaves the Corneys' party and hears the bells of Monkshaven church ring out 'a welcome to the New Year 1796'. The conflict in these two dates is the most obvious pointer to the fact that the chronology of the early chapters is at fault, though, as Graham Handley points out, the mention of certain historical events in Chapter 14 might well increase the unease of an alert reader. The middle of the novel moves us forward steadily in time without giving us precise indications of the date at which the events are supposedly set. It is March in Chapter 18 when Kinraid disappears, and May in the subsequent chapter. Chapter 22 moves us from summer to November, and Chapter 23, describing the assault on the Randyvowse, takes place on 23 February of a year we might suppose to be either 1797 or 1798. It is March when Daniel Robson is committed for trial at York (Chapter 27) and April when his widow and daughter return to Haytersbank in Chapter 28. In Chapter 32, a good year after Sylvia's marriage to Philip (their baby is old enough to be taken out for long walks) Mrs Gaskell tells us that it is the spring of 1798, and, in preparing us for Kinraid's reappearance in Chapter 33, we learn that it is three years since he vanished.

From this point on the novel's chronology can be accurately measured by reference to the historical events that the novelist weaves into her story and which she herself dates carefully. If Kinraid had been captured by the French at Havre-de-Grace while taking part in Sir Sidney Smith's raid on the port (as we are told he did in Chapter 34) he cannot have returned to England until the spring of 1798 for Sir Sidney himself did not reach London until 8 May of that year. The dating of Chapter 33 would appear to be accurate, therefore, and we can further conclude that Kinraid must have been seized by the press-gang in March 1795. That date would also tally with his volunteering to join Sir Sidney Smith's boarding-party in April 1796. It is also possible consequently to correct the date of the opening of the story to October 1793 and that of Daniel Robson's execution to March 1797. Graham Handley's suggestion that the Randyvowse might have been burned in February 1793 must also be corrected, though the 23rd did not fall on a Saturday in 1797.

The final chapters of the novel follow a correct chronological sequence after Kinraid's return in Chapter 33. Chapter 37 takes us from Christmas 1798 to May 1799, and Chapter 38, which describes the events at the siege of Acre, is properly dated to the fifty-first day of the siege, 7 May. Philip returns to England in September 1799 and leaves St. Sepulchre's in February 1800. He arrives in Monkshaven in April and dies there in the summer of the same year.

APPENDIX C

THE TEXTS OF THE FIRST AND ILLUSTRATED EDITIONS OF SYLVIA'S LOVERS

MOST of the changes in the dialect spoken by characters made in the second edition of *Sylvia's Lovers* in March 1863 are attempts to render more faithfully Yorkshire as opposed to Lancashire speech. A collation of the first and second editions of the novel reveals a consistent move away from words or sounds which have too much of the Lancashire ring which would have been familiar to readers of *Mary Barton* or *North and South.* Thus 'th'' become 't'', 'ye' or 'you' become 'yo', 'father' 'feyther', 'ever' and 'never' 'iver' and 'niver', 'there' 'theere', 'in' 'i'', 'don't' 'dunnot', 'must' 'mun', 'with' 'wi'', 'right' 'reet', and 'night' 'neet'. These changes were maintained and extended in the *Illustrated Edition* which is the basis of the text of the present edition. To demonstrate the extent of these changes I have selected three heavily revised passages of dialogue rather than attempted to record each alteration in turn. Some of the variants between the first and second editions are noted by J. G. Sharps in his *Mrs Gaskell's Observation and Invention* (Linden Press 1970) Appendix V (pp. 587–592).

1. Chapter 30 pp. 345–6

a. *First Edition*

'There, that's poetry for ye as I larnt i' my youth. But there's a deal to be said as cannot be put int' po'try, an' yet a cannot say it, somehow. It would tax a parson t' say all as I've getten i' my mind. It's like a heap o' wool just after shearing time; it's worth a deal, but it tak's a vast o' combing, and carding, and spinning afore it can be made use on. If a were up to t' use o' words, a could say a mighty deal; but somehow a 'm tongue-teed when a come to want my words most, so a 'll only just mak' bold t' say as a think yo've done pretty well for yo'rsel', getten a house-full of furniture' (looking around him as he said this), 'and vittle and clothing for t' axing, belike, an' a home for t' missus in her time o' need; an' mebbe not such a bad husband as a once thought yon man would mak'; a 'm not above saying as he's mebbe better nor a took him for; – so here's to ye both, and wishing ye health and happiness, ay, and money to buy yo' another, as country folk say.'

b. *Illustrated Edition*

'Theere, that's po'try for yo' as I larnt i' my youth. But there's a deal to be said as cannot be put int' po'try, an' yet a cannot say it, somehow. It'd tax a parson t' say a' as a've getten i' my mind. It's like a heap o' woo' just after shearin' time; it's worth a deal, but it tak's a vast o' combin', an' cardin', an' spinnin' afore it can be made use on. If a were up to t' use o' words, a could say a mighty deal; but somehow a'm tongue-teed when a come to want my words most, so a'll only just mak' bold t' say as a think yo've done pretty well for yo'rsel', getten a house-full o' furniture' (looking around him as he said this), 'an' vittle an' clothin' for t' axing, belike, an' a home for t' missus in her time o' need; an' mebbe not such a bad husband as a once thought yon man 'ud mak'; a'm not above sayin' as he's, mebbe, better nor a took him for; – so here's to ye both, and wishin' ye health and happiness, ay, and money to buy yo' another, as country folk say.'

2. Chapter 34 p. 385

a. *First Edition*

'And there's a gallant captain, one Sir Sidney Smith, and he'd a notion o' going right into a French port, and carrying off a vessel from right under their very noses; and says he, "Which of you British sailors 'll go along with me to death or glory?" So Kinraid stands up like a man, and "I'll go with you, captain," he says. So they, and some others as brave, went off, and did their work, and choose whativer it was, they did it famously; but they got caught by them French, and were clapped into a prison in France for iver so long; but at last one Philip – Philip something (he were a Frenchman, I know) – helped 'em to escape, in a fishing-boat. But they were welcomed by the whole British squadron as was in the Channel for the piece of daring they'd done in cutting out t' ship from a French port; and Captain Sir Sidney Smith was made an admiral, and him as we used to call Charley Kinraid, the specksioneer, is made a lieutenant, and a commissioned officer in t' King's service; and is come to great glory, and slep in my house this very blessed night as is just past!'

b. *Illustrated Edition*

'An' there's a gallant captain, one Sir Sidney Smith, and he'd a notion o' goin' smack into a French port, an' carryin' off a vessel from right under their very noses; an' says he, "Which of yo' British sailors 'll go along with me to death or glory?" So Kinraid stands up like a man, an' "I'll go with yo', captain," he says. So they, an' some others as brave, went off, an' did their work, an' choose whativer it was, they did it famously; but they got caught by them French, an' were clapped into prison i' France for iver so long; but at last one Philip – Philip somethin' (he were a Frenchman, I know) – helped 'em to escape, in a fishin'–boat. But they were welcomed by th' whole British squadron as was i' t' Channel for t' piece of daring they'd done i' cuttin' out t' ship from a French port; an' Captain Sir Sidney Smith was made an admiral, an' him as we used t' call Charley Kinraid, the specksioneer, is made a lieutenant, an' a commissioned officer i' t' King's service; and is come to great glory, and slep in my house this very blessed night as is just past!'

3. Chapter 43 pp. 473–4

a. *First Edition*

'Yo'll have heard how Kinraid – who's a captain now, and a grand officer – has gone and got married.'

'Nay!' said Kester, in genuine surprise. 'He never has, for sure!'

'Ay, but he has,' said Sylvia. 'And I'm sure I don't see why he shouldn't.'

'Well, well!' said Kester, not looking up at her, for he caught the inflections in the tones of her voice. 'He were a fine stirring chap, yon; and he were allays for doing summut; and when he found he couldn't have one thing as he'd set his mind on, I reckon he thought he must put up wi' another.'

'It would be no "putting up,"' said Sylvia. 'She was staying at Bessy Dawson's, and she came here to see me – she's as pretty a young lady as yo'd see on a summer's day; and a real lady, too, with a fortune. She didn't speak two words without bringing in her husband's name, – the "captain," as she called him.'

'And she came to see thee?' said Kester, cocking his eye at Sylvia with the old shrewd look. 'That were summut queer, weren't it?'

Sylvia reddened a good deal.

'He's too fause to have spoken to her on me, in t' old way, – as he used for t' speak to me. I were nought to her but Philip's wife.'

'And what t' dickins had she to do wi' Philip?' asked Kester, in intense surprise; and so absorbed in curiosity that he let the humbugs all fall out of the paper upon the floor, and the little Bella sat down, plump, in the midst of treasures as great as those fabled to exist on Tom Tiddler's ground.

Sylvia was again silent; but Kester, knowing her well, was sure that she was struggling to speak, and bided his time without repeating his question.

'She said – and I think her tale were true, though I cannot get to t' rights on it, think on it as I will – as Philip saved her husband's life somewhere nearabouts to Jerusalem. She would have it that t' captain – for I think I'll niver call him Kinraid again – was in a great battle, and were near upon being shot by the French, when Philip – our Philip – came up and went right into t' fire o' t' guns, and saved her husband's life. And she spoke as if both she and t' captain were more beholden to Philip than words could tell. And she came to see me, to try and get news on him.'

'It's a queer kind o' story,' said Kester, meditatively. 'A should ha' thought as Philip were more likely to ha' gi'en him a shove into t' thick on it, than to help him out o' t' scrape.'

'Nay!' said Sylvia, suddenly looking straight at Kester; 'yo're out there. Philip had a deal o' good in him. And I dunnot think as he would have gone and married another woman so soon, if he'd been i' Kinraid's place.'

'An' yo've niver heerd on Philip sin' he left?' asked Kester, after a while.

'Niver; nought but what she told me. And she said that t' captain made inquiry for him right and left, as soon after that happened as might be, and could hear niver a word about him. No one had seen him, or knowed his name.'

'Yo' never heard of his going for to be a soldier?' persevered Kester.

'Niver. I've told yo' once. It were unlike Philip to think o' such a thing.'

'But thou must ha' been thinking on him at times in a' these years. Bad as he had behaved hissel', he were t' father o' thy little one. What didst ta think he had been agait on when he left here?'

b. *Illustrated Edition*

'Yo'll have heared how Kinraid – who's a captain now, and a grand officer – has gone and got married.'

'Nay!' said Kester, in genuine surprise. 'He niver has, for sure!'

'Ay, but he has,' said Sylvia. 'And I'm sure I dunnot see why he shouldn't.'

'Well, well!' said Kester, not looking up at her, for he caught the inflections in the tones of her voice. 'He were a fine stirrin' chap, yon; an' he were allays for doin' summut; an' when he fund as he couldn't ha' one thing as he'd set his mind on, a reckon he thought he mun put up wi' another.'

'It 'ud be no "putting up,"' said Sylvia. 'She were staying at Bessy Dawson's, and she come here to see me – she's as pretty a young lady as yo'd see on a summer's day; and a real lady, too, wi' a fortune. She didn't speak two words wi'out bringing in her husband's name, – "the captain," as she called him.'

'An' she come to see thee?' said Kester, cocking his eye at Sylvia with the old shrewd look. 'That were summut queer, weren't it?'

Sylvia reddened a good deal.

'He's too fause to have spoken to her on me, in t' old way, – as he used for t' speak to me. I were nought to her but Philip's wife.'

'An' what t' dickens had she to do wi' Philip?' asked Kester, in intense surprise; and so absorbed in curiosity that he let the humbugs all fall out of the paper upon the floor, and the little Bella sat down, plump, in the midst of treasures as great as those fabled to exist on Tom Tiddler's ground.

Sylvia was again silent; but Kester, knowing her well, was sure that she was struggling to speak, and bided his time without repeating his question.

'She said – and I think her tale were true, though I cannot get to t' rights on it, think on it as I will – as Philip saved her husband's life somewheere nearabouts to Jerusalem. She would have it that t' captain – for I think I'll niver ca' him Kinraid again – was in a great battle, and were near upon being shot by t' French, when Philip – our Philip – come up and went right into t' fire o' t' guns, and saved her husband's life. And she spoke as if both she and t' captain were more beholden to Philip than words could tell. And she come to see me, to try and get news on him.'

'It's a queer kind o' story,' said Kester, meditatively. 'A should ha' thought as Philip were more likely to ha' gi'en him a shove into t' thick on it, than t' help him out o' t' scrape.'

'Nay!' said Sylvia, suddenly looking straight at Kester; 'yo're out theere. Philip had a deal o' good in him. And I dunnot think as he'd ha' gone and married another woman so soon, if he'd been i' Kinraid's place.'

'An' yo've niver heared on Philip sin' he left?' asked Kester, after a while.

'Niver; nought but what she told me. And she said that t' captain made inquiry for him right and left, as soon after that happened as might be, and could hear niver a word about him. No one had seen him, or knowed his name.'

'Yo' niver heared of his goin' for t' be a soldier?' persevered Kester.

'Niver. I've told yo' once. It were unlike Philip to think o' such a thing.'

'But thou mun ha' been thinkin' on him at times i' a' these years. Bad as he'd behaved hissel', he were t' feyther o' thy little un. What did ta think he had been agait on when he left here?'

EXPLANATORY NOTES

Half-title. Oh for thy voice . . . Behind the veil: the novel's epigraph, suggested by ECG's daughter, Meta, is derived from Section LVI of Tennyson's *In Memoriam*:

> O life as futile, then, as frail!
> O for thy voice to soothe and bless!
> What hope of answer, or redress?
> Behind the veil, behind the veil.

Page 1. (1) *Monkshaven*: Whitby, the original of Monkshaven, straddles the mouth of the river Esk on the coast of Yorkshire midway between the Humber and the Tyne. The town is dominated still by the ruins of its ancient Abbey. There were only some 11,000 inhabitants in 1860.

(2) *a throneless queen*: this would appear to be a reference to Mary, Queen of Scots who never in fact visited Whitby. It is possible, however, that the 'throneless queen' is Eanfled, daughter of King Edwin of Northumbria and widow of King Oswy who retired to Whitby Abbey in the late seventh century. Her daughter, Aelfled, was Abbess.

(3) *the German Ocean*: the North Sea. The term 'German Ocean' was current until the late nineteenth century.

Page 3. (1) *staithes*: wharfs. The term is of Scandinavian origin and is used to describe the quays of Whitby.

(2) *scaur*: cliff.

Page 4. *old man*: southernwood (artemisia abrotanum). See p. 231 note 1.

Page 6. *Lord Thurlow*: Edward Thurlow, first baron Thurlow (1731–1806) was appointed solicitor-general in 1770, attorney-general in 1771 and Lord Chancellor in 1778. The story of his arrest by the press-gang in Long Acre (*not* Tower Hill) is found in Vol. VII of Lord Campbell's *Lives of the Lord Chancellors* (1845–1847): 'When Attorney-General, for some reason or another, by way of frolic, he had disguised himself as a sailor . . . he was seized by a press-gang, and, his oaths being at variance with his protestations that he was a *gentleman*, they carried him to their rendezvous at the Tower'.

Page 10. (1) *1796*: although ECG failed to correct this date it would seem from the evidence of the novel's own later time-scheme that it begins in the autumn of 1793. See Appendix B.

(2) *Sylvia Robson*: in his *History of Whitby* of 1817 The Revd George Young mentions that there were some ten or twelve Whitby families of the name of Robson and some nine called 'Corney'. ECG had also been in correspondence with an old Whitby resident, John Corney, who had sent her information on the riot of 1793.

Page 12. *a little sultana*: Sylvia is sitting cross-legged in the Turkish manner.

Page 14. *the great deep:* possibly a reminiscence of Psalm 36:6.

Page 16. (1) *skeps*: baskets.

(2) *a lamiter*: a cripple.

(3) *Resolution*: a successful Whitby whaler of 291 tons of this name is recorded in Young's *History*.

Page 17. *specksioneer*: the chief harpooner on a whaler. The specksioneer also directed the flensing or cutting up of the whale's blubber. There was no whaler called the *Good Fortune* registered at Whitby.

Page 19. *the Keel row*: see Appendix A.

Page 20. *huxters*: small tradesmen.

Page 21. *Foster's shop*: ECG appears to have based the Fosters on the Quaker brothers Jonathan and George Sanders who owned a prosperous grocery and sail-cloth maker's business in Church St., Whitby. They had started a bank in 1779.

Page 23. *Coulson. . . Hester Rose*: ECG had lodged with a family named Rose during her visit to Whitby in 1859 but had already used the name 'Hester Rose' in her Christmas Story *The Crooked Branch*, published in *Household Words* in 1859. The surnames Foster and Rose are both noted as common by Young in his *History of Whitby.* A William Colson was Abbot of Whitby from 1475–1499.

Page 28. *Randyvowse*: a tavern used as a rendezvous by the Press Gang.

Page 30. *fishing cobles*: flat-bottomed, square-sterned fishing-boats chiefly used on the north-east coast of England.

Page 31. (1) *Mr John*: in the first edition of the novel ECG mistakenly calls the owner of the parlour 'Jeremiah' though she has already told us that Jeremiah Foster lives 'on the other side of the water'. This mistake, which runs throughout the chapter, was corrected in the second edition.

(2) *like the very heathen*: Psalm 2:1.

Page 34. *sea-wrack*: seaweed cast up on the shore.

Page 36. (1) *clap-bread*: oat-meal cake, beaten thin and baked hard.

(2) '*Turf cakes*' *and* '*singing hinnies*': a turf cake is baked in a covered pan among the ashes of a peat fire. A singing hinny is a currant-cake cooked on a girdle and said to emit a singing sound while cooking.

(3) *bishopped*: burnt in cooking.

Page 37. *Hollands*: Hollands-gin.

Page 40. *When I gived my vote*: the original of Monkshaven, Whitby, only became a borough in 1832 with the passing of the Reform Bill. Its MP from 1847–59 was the great engineer Robert Stephenson.

Page 46. (1) *dree*: difficult, or, as the word is explained in Chapter 9 of *Mary Barton*, 'long and tedious'.

(2) *Madame de Maintenon*: Françoise d'Aubigné, Marquise de Maintenon (1635–1719) was governess to Louis XIV's children and the king's mistress. He secretly married her in 1684. Her difficult task of amusing a man 'who was not amusable' is described in the *Mémoires* of the duc de Saint-Simon.

Page 47. *fause*: shrewd.

Page 48. (1) *cachinnation*: loud laughter.

(2) *strike*: a measure generally approximating to a bushel, but in some areas varying from half a bushel to two or four bushels.

Page 50. (1) *fettling*: mending.

(2) *silk-buttons*: cloth covered buttons were prohibited by a statute of 1721 in order to encourage the manufacture of metal buttons.

Page 51. *a kind of domestic Jupiter*: Robson, like Jupiter, seeks to be all-knowing and not dependent upon his wife for information.

Page 55. *Darley*: according to Young's *History of Whitby* a William Darley was overseer for the poor of the village of Ruswarp in 1817.

Page 61. *galraverging*: gadding about.

Page 62. *scrimpit*: scrimped.

Page 63. (1) *the coming winter's rages*: the opening words of the song from Act IV sc. 2 of Shakespeare's *Cymbeline*:

Fear no more the heat o' the sun,
Nor the furious winter's rages.

(2) *that church*: St. Nicholas's Church is closely based on the parish church of St. Mary at Whitby. St. Nicholas is the patron saint of sailors.

Page 64. *sudden death*: from the Litany in the Book of Common Prayer: 'From lightning and tempest; from plague, pestilence, and famine; from battle and murder, and from sudden death, *Good Lord deliver us.*'

Page 65. (1) *the church stair*: according to Young there were only 190 stairs (with resting places at different distances' in 1817 but by 1860, shortly after ECG's visit, a guidebook states that the number of steps had risen to its original number of 196.

(2) *the accustomed time for the funerals*: Young notes that 'the usual hour of burial at Whitby is 3 o'clock pm from michaelmas to lady-day, and 5 o'clock during the rest of the year; but several of the genteel families bury in the morning, at 7 or 8 o'clock'.

Page 66. (1) *within ear-shot of the pulpit*: once again ECG draws directly on the fine unrestored interior of St. Mary's at Whitby for her description of St. Nicholas's. The earlier reference to the fact that 'there was no wood-work' implies a lack of medieval as opposed to later ecclesiastical fittings.

(2) *friend and follower of Wesley*: John Wesley, who died in 1791, had been an almost annual visitor to Whitby and had preached at the opening of the Methodist Chapel there in June 1788. In 1784 he had noted that 'the Society [of Methodists] here may be a pattern to all England.'

Page 67. *In the midst of life we are in death:* one of the sentences directed to be said or sung at the graveside in the Order for the Burial of the Dead in the Book of Common Prayer.

Page 68. *the glorious Revolution*: the Revolution of 1688 by means of which William III replaced James II on the English throne.

Page 69. *It is the Lord's doing*: 'This is the Lord's doing: and it is marvellous in our eyes.' Psalm 118:23.

Page 73. *such a Quaker*: Friends hold that war and violence are contrary to the precepts and spirit of the Gospel.

Page 74. *Mason on Self-Knowledge and Law's Serious Call:* John Mason (1706–63), a Presbyterian minister in Surrey and London, published his *Self-Knowledge; Shewing the Nature and Benefit of that Important Science and the Way to Obtain It* in 1745. It had reached its fourteenth edition by 1791. The Anglican divine, William Law (1686–1761) published his *Serious Call to a Devout and Holy Life* in 1728. It became a profound influence on eighteenth-century spirituality and especially on Wesleyanism. The fifteenth edition appeared in 1805.

Page 75. *the number of the elect*: those believed to be chosen by God for eternal salvation to the exclusion of others. Sylvia is worrying about the implications of a commonly held Calvinistic doctrine.

Page 76. *dread the grave as little as her bed*: the third stanza of the Evening Hymn by Bishop Thomas Ken (1637–1711):

> Teach me to live, that I may dread
> The grave as little as my bed;
> Teach me to die, that so I may
> Rise glorious at the awful day.

Page 82. (1) *First Day*: Sunday. Alice is avoiding the term she regards as having pagan connotations.

(2) *a creepie-stool*: a low stool.

Page 84. *gnashing o' teeth*: Luke 13:28.

Page 85. *Martinmas*: the feast of St. Martin, 11 November.

Page 87. *multitudinous rush*: doubtless a remembrance of the 'multitudinous seas' of *Macbeth* Act II sc. 2.

Page 91. *for I loves the tossin' say*: I have been unable to find a printed source for this 'sea ditty'.

Page 94. (1) *the lover of Jess MacFarlane*: the song is to be found in Volume 2 of Robert Archibald Smith's *The Scottish Minstrel* (six volumes 1821–4):

> I took it in my head
> To write my luve a letter
> But alas! She canna read,
> And I like her a' the better (verse 3)

(2) *dip-candle*: a candle made by repeatedly dipping a wick in melted tallow.

Page 96. (1) *t' give a pair o' gloves to*: gloves are a traditional betrothal present and may be given by the woman to the man or *vice versa*.

(2) *mim*: prim, demure.

Page 97. *cranching*: a variant on crunching.

Page 98. *the duty on salt*: salt-duties were first exacted in Britain in 1702 and had been revived in 1732. They were bitterly attacked during the closing years of the eighteenth century as being an imposition which hit the poor hardest. They were considerably reduced in 1823, but only finally removed in 1825.

Page 99. *th' ship John of Hull*: many of the details of whaling in the north Atlantic are derived from William Scoresby's *An Account of the Arctic Regions, with a History and Description of the Northern Whale-Fishery* (1820). A boat named the *John* is mentioned by Scoresby, but it was registered at Greenock. The stories concerning the dangers of icebergs and Robson's account of falling into the sea closely follow Scoresby.

Page 100. (1) *reeved*: securing the rope by passing it through a hole, ring or block.

(2) *moulds*: earth.

Page 101. '*What is your name, M or N?*': the opening question of the Prayer Book Catechism. The response is correctly abbreviated as 'N or M', 'N' representing 'name', and 'M' (a double N) 'names'.

Page 102. *dwined away*: pined away.

Page 103. *Aimwell*: a ship named the *Aimwell* of 263 tons was registered as a whaler at Whitby according to Young.

Page 107. *farred*: put far off, removed.

Page 108. *barm*: the froth formed on the top of fermenting malt liquors, used to leaven bread.

Page 111. (1) *fain*: glad, fond.

(2) *keep a calm sough*: say nothing; keep quiet.

Page 115. *on t'Side*: the Side was formerly the principal street of Newcastle-upon-Tyne, leading up from the bridge to the parish church of St. Nicholas. Despite its steepness it contained the houses of the city's chief merchants.

Page 123. (1) *pined as a Methody preacher after a love-feast*: Methodists revived the early-Christian custom of an *agape* or love-feast from *c*. 1738. A long sermon and prayer were integral to what was basically a meal shared as a sign of brotherly-love.

(2) *statute fair*: the annual fair at which servants or labourers were hired.

Page 124. *marlock*: frolic, lark about.

Page 127. (1) *lile*: little.

(2) *kittle*: difficult. ECG may have found the word in Charlotte Brontë's *Shirley* (1849) Chapter 18.

Page 133. *watch-night*: originally a monthly service held by Methodists extending over midnight, but in later use specifically a service held on New Year's Eve.

Page 134. *Mavor's Spelling-book*: William Mavor (1758–1837) first published his *English Spelling Book* in 1801. It was already in its 32nd edition by 1826.

Page 135. (1) *Yates and Peels... the parsley-leaf*: chintzes and calicoes had originally been imported from India but were commonly imitated by eighteenth-century English textile printers. From *c.* 1752 copper-plates began to supersede wood-blocks, but plate-printing was possible in only one colour at a time, green being produced by printing yellow over blue (though the colour faded with time). A single process for printing 'solid' green was only invented in 1809, thus stimulating the introduction of complex patterns involving green tones such as the 'parsley-leaf'. Printing by mechanical rollers was not general until *c.* 1815. 'Yates and Peels', properly the firm of Howarth, Yates and Peel, was a prominent Lancashire calico-printer's. A founder of the firm, Sir Robert Peel, was the father of the statesman of the same name.

(2) *palempours*: or palampores are patterned Indian Chintz bed-covers.

Page 143. *Niver fash thysel'*: 'Don't worry about it'.

Page 145. *vanitas vanitatum*: vanity of vanities; *Ecclesiastes* 1:2.

Page 149. *stawed*: stalled or simply 'full'. The same expression is used in Chapter 13 of *Cranford*.

Page 152. *jorum*: a bowl of punch.

Page 154. *the new year, 1796*: again an uncorrected error. ECG had told us in Chapter 2 that the story had begun in October 1796. This would seem to be New Year 1795. See Appendix B.

Page 155. *apples o' Sodom*: the belief that the fruit of Sodom was beautiful to look at but vile to taste is based on Deuteronomy 32:32–3 (where the fruits are called vines). For the 'apples' of Sodom see *Paradise Lost* X, 560–5.

Page 156. *hope had come in the morning*: Psalm 30:5. 'Heaviness may endure for a night, but joy cometh in the morning'.

Page 162 *throng*: busy.

Page 167. *The oppressive act against seditious meetings*: a reference to the Two Acts of 1795: the Treasonable and Seditious Practices Act (which extended the law of Treason to spoken and written words) and the Seditious Meetings Act (which restricted meetings and political lectures). The parliamentary debates prior to the passing of the Acts are recorded in the volumes of the *Annual Register* for 1795 and 1796.

Page 168. (1) *the young Corsican warrior:* in September 1795 Napoleon's name had been erased from the list of general officers in Paris. In the spring of 1796, however, the success of the Italian Campaign had firmly restored his reputation and his influence over the Directory of Revolutionary France.

(2) *the Corresponding Society*: the London Corresponding Society was founded in January 1792 with affiliations throughout Great Britain in order to promote universal suffrage and annual parliaments. The 'correspondance' was between societies rather than with France. The founder of the London society, Thomas Hardy, was arrested in May 1794 on a charge of high treason. Committee members were seized and imprisoned in April 1796 and the society was formally suppressed in July 1799.

Page 169. *And they did begin... per quarter*: all of these topics of discussion are recorded in the volumes of the *Annual Register* for 1795 and 1796.

Page 177. *shippen*: cow-house. ECG spells the word as 'shippon' throughout the first edition of the novel.

Page 178. *druv e'en King Solomon silly*: probably a reference to Ecclesiastes 7:25–9.

Page 179. *afterings*: the milk drawn last from a cow.

Page 181. (1) *bearing away the bell at church*: taking the first place for beauty.

(2) *stripping*: extracting the milk remaining in the cow's udder after the normal milking process.

Page 182. *teem*: empty into an appropriate vessel.

Page 185. (1) *fremd*: strange, or, more precisely, a non-member of the household.

(2) *my master's out*: the first edition has 'measter'. ECG seems to be giving Bell Robson a Cumberland as opposed to a Yorkshire pronunciation.

Page 187. (1) *gaum-like*: sensible.
(2) *bingy*: curdled; sour.

Page 188. *leading manure*: carting and spreading manure as fertilizer.

Page 190. *stubs*: worn horse-shoe nails.

Page 191. *bandanas*: coloured silk handkerchiefs with spots of white or yellow forming a design and produced by tying knots in parts of the cloth to prevent them receiving colour during the dyeing process. Originally of Indian origin.

Page 192. '*damn the faults we have no mind to*': a reminiscence of a couplet from Samuel Butler's *Hudibras* (I.213–14):

Compound for sins, they are inclin'd to
By damning those they have no mind to.

Page 197. *Davis' Straits*: lying between Greenland and Baffin Island. The straits were discovered by the navigator John Davis in 1585.

Page 205. *Hazael*: when the prophet Elisha foretells that Hazael will become king of Syria, Elisha weeps 'knowing the evil that he will do unto the children of Israel'. Hazael affrontedly replies 'Is thy servant a dog, that he should do this great thing?' (2 Kings 8:13). In the first edition of the novel ECG mistakenly accredits the statement to Gehazi, Elisha's servant, though the quotation was evidently a favourite one.

Page 213. '*Norroway over the foam*': from the version of the ballad 'Sir Patrick Spens' published in Volume 3 of Scott's *Minstrelsy of the Scottish Border* (1803 ed.):

To Noroway, to Noroway,
To Noroway oer the faem;
The king's daughter of Noroway
'Tis thou maun bring her hame.

Page 225. *wafered*: sealed by means of a wafer, a small disc of flour mixed with gum.

Page 227. *to say nothing . . . Haytersbank*: before the introduction of the penny post it was usual for the recipient rather than the sender to pay for a letter.

Page 228. *Mordecai sitting in Haman's gate*: according to the Book of Esther when Haman was advanced by King Ahasuerus only the exiled Jew, Mordecai, refused to do him reverence. 'Then went

Haman forth that day joyful and with a glad heart: but when Haman saw Mordecai in the king's gate, that he stood not up, nor moved for him, he was full of indignation against Mordecai' (Esther 5:9.)

Page 230. *LOVED AND LOST*: the chapter-title is derived from Tennyson's *In Memoriam* (XXVII):

> I hold it true, whate'er befall;
> I feel it, when I sorrow most;
> 'Tis better to have loved and lost
> Than never to have loved at all.

Section LVI of the same poem provides the epigraph for the novel as a whole.

Page 231. (1) *southernwood and sweetbriar*: southernwood, the 'old man' mentioned in Chapter I, was formerly much cultivated for medicinal purposes, having stimulant, antiseptic and detergent properties. It was also used as a remedy for various women's ailments. The sweet-briar, a species of eglantine, was grown for its scent as much as for its petals and hips, both of which were used in the kitchen.

(2) *hen-and-chicken daisies*: a variety of compound daisy.

Page 238. *John's*: here and throughout the chapter the first edition text has 'Jeremiah'. The mistake was remedied in the second edition.

Page 241. *melling wi'*: meddling with, concerned with.

Page 244. *moithering*: worrying, bothering. Alice's reference is to Matthew 22:30.

Page 245. (1) *Sorrows of Werther*: ECG is correct in her assertion of the popularity of English versions of Goethe's *Die Leiden des jungen Werthers* (1774). It was first translated in 1779 and editions followed annually until 1785. Other translations appeared in 1786, 1789, 1794, 1801 and 1802. William Blake jestingly notes in his 'An Island in the Moon' (1784–5) that *Werther* was as much a necessary part of his 'Miss Filligreework's' personal furniture as her hats and gloves.

(2) *Law's Serious Call*: see p. 74 note 1.

(3) *Klopstock's Messiah*: the German poet Gottlieb Friedrich Klopstock (1724–1803) published his *Messias* in three parts between 1749 and 1773. The first fifteen books were translated into English in 1763–66 and proved steadily popular as devotional reading.

Carlyle, writing in 1824, nevertheless regarded this translation as 'hacked and mangled' distorting the epic into a 'theosophic rhapsody'.

(4) *Complete Farrier*: possibly *The Experienced Farrier*, first published in 1678.

Page 246. *Jacob's... service for Rachel*: Genesis 29:18–30.

Page 254. *the famous maxim of Rochefoucault*: de la Rochefoucault's *Maxime* 99: 'Dans l'adversité de nos meilleurs amis nous trouvons toujours quelque chose qui ne nous déplait pas.'

Page 257. *pea-jacket*: a short overcoat of coarse cloth commonly worn by sailors.

Page 261. (1) *his forcing his way in*: in all editions published before the Illustrated Edition this reads ungrammatically '*their* forcing *their* way in'.

(2) *t' some purpose*: according to Mrs Ellis H. Chadwick these were the actual words used by William Atkinson, the original of Daniel Robson, at the Whitby Riot of 1793. They had been communicated to ECG by a Mrs Scott of Whitby whose grandfather had been present on the occasion. (*Mrs Gaskell: Homes, Haunts and Stories*, 1913, p. 259).

Page 265. *all their money was gone*: all earlier editions have 'all their money was done'.

Page 266. (1) *treacle-posset*: a hot drink made of treacle and cider or milk.

(2) *hoasts*: coughs.

Page 271. *clem*: starve.

Page 273. *making a coil*: making a fuss.

Page 275. *keep ward*: keep guard.

Page 278. *dang*: strike.

Page 282. *Bridewell*: originally a royal palace off Fleet Street in London, converted into a house of correction in the sixteenth century. The name was later commonly applied to any gaol.

Page 285. *4th section of 1 George I, statute 1, chapter 5*: the famous 'Riot Act' of 1714 (repealed in 1967) provided that if twelve or more persons unlawfully riotously assembled and refused to disperse within an hour after the reading of a specified portion of it by a competent authority, they should be considered as felons.

Page 288. *a tax-cart*: or 'taxed-cart'; a two-wheeled open cart drawn by a single horse. A reduced duty was charged on it due to its use generally for agricultural or trade purposes.

Page 296. ***main***: very much.

Page 297. *comforter*: a long woollen scarf.

Page 298. *maskit*: drawn, infused.

Page 300. *Botany Bay*: the first transportation of convicts to Botany Bay was in May 1787. The discontinuation of the practice was announced to Parliament in February 1853.

Page 304. *The Farmer's Complete Guide*: *The Farmer's Compleat Guide, through all the Articles of his Profession* was first published in 1760.

Page 308 (1) *the real question*: in all earlier editions of the novel the last sentences of this paragraph read:

> 'Some of this very natural indignation might possibly be expressed and interwoven into the counsel's speech for the defence. It was their only chance, since Simpson's evidence was conclusive as to the part Robson had taken; and indeed there was no use attempting to prove an alibi. But again, the worst was, that, in a recent trial at Bristol, – in late events at Hull, – the court and magistrates had almost behaved as though they were advocates against the prisoner; and the judge might so behave as to quench any counsel who might attempt to stir up the sympathies of the jury in any matter in which Government had a direct interest.'

The information about trials at Bristol and Hull was probably provided by the MP for Hull, General Perronet Thompson with whom ECG was in correspondence about impressment. She changed this paragraph after hearing from an anonymous correspondent that she had made a mistake 'in old Daniel's trial, in representing the counsel for the *defence* as making a *speech* for the prisoner. Whereas, at the time, they were not allowed to do so; only to watch the case and examine witnesses.' [Letters 521]. Her correspondent was possibly J. D. Coleridge.

(2) *forty miles*: all earlier editions have 'twenty miles'. Forty miles is a nearer estimation of the distance between Whitby and York.

Page 310. *we are dust*: Psalm 103:14.

Page 311. *redd theirselves up*: clear themselves up.

Page 313. '*Be the day weary... even-song*': a variant on the proverb 'Be the day never so long, at length cometh evensong.'

Page 315. *Our God, our help in ages past*: the opening line of Isaac Watt's paraphrase of Psalm 90 generally begins 'O God, our help in ages past'.

Page 316. '*Old Grouse in the gun-room*': a reference to Act II sc. I of Goldsmith's *She Stoops to Conquer*: 'Your worship must not tell the story of ould Grouse in the gun-room. I can't help laughing at that... We have laughed at that these twenty years'.

Page 320. *greeting*: weeping.

Page 323. *dateless*: stupefied, deranged.

Page 329. '*close at his ear*': a reminiscence of *Paradise Lost* IV 800: 'Squat like a toad, close at the ear of Eve'.

Page 337. '*From him... turn not thou away*': a misquotation of Matthew 5:42: 'Give to him that asketh thee, and from him that would borrow of thee turn thou not away.'

Page 338. *shandry*: properly a shandryan, a kind of chaise with a hood.

Page 341. '*sit in her parlour and sew up a seam*': a variant on the nursery rhyme:

> Curly locks, curly locks
> Wilt thou be mine.
> Thou shalt not wash dishes
> Nor yet feed the swine;
> But sit on a cushion
> And sew a fine seam
> And feed upon strawberries
> Sugar and cream.

Page 342. (1) '*white work*': fine white embroidery on white fabric (linen, lawn, muslin etc.).

(2) '*ox and the ass*': domestic animals traditionally mentioned together possibly because of the reference to them in the tenth commandment (Exodus 20:17).

Page 345. '*Long may ye live ... Pro-ge-ny*': a traditional blessing on a marriage. In a letter to Mary Howitt (18 August 1838) ECG describes the use the verses were put to at her own wedding at Knutsford in Cheshire in 1832.

Page 349. *pattens*: wooden overshoes an inch or two in height enabling the wearer to step dry-shod through mud or water.

Page 355. *flytin'*: chiding, finding fault with.

Page 357. *a Cumberland 'statesman'*: a term peculiar to Cumberland and Westmorland, though generally synonymous with 'yeoman' in other counties. A land-owner who works his own land.

Page 358. *Scarby Moorside*: in earlier editions of the novel ECG has 'Kirby Moorside'. She changed the name of the village in response to a comment from James Dixon of November 1863. Dixon had pointed out that there was an actual village called Kirby Moorside some 20 miles from Whitby in the North Riding of Yorkshire. She did not, however, alter Philip's reference in Chapter 6 to the fact that the Robsons worship at 'Kirk Moorside'.

Page 359. (1) *'A crust of bread and liberty'*: the last line of Pope's 'An Imitation of the Sixth Satire of the Second Book of Horace':

> 'Give me again my hollow Tree!
> A Crust of Bread and Liberty.'

(2) *the west side of the town*: earlier editions have '*north* side'. This too was changed at the suggestion of James Dixon. ECG replied to his letter apologizing that, having only been in Whitby for a fortnight, and 'in such cloudy November weather that I might very easily be ignorant of the points of the compass if I did not look at a map'.

Page 360. *western*: all earlier editions have 'northern'.

Page 374. *balm-tea*: an infusion of the leaves of the lemon balm (melissa officinalis) believed to promote relaxation and sound sleep.

Page 385. *Sir Sidney Smith*: Sir William Sidney Smith (1764–1840) boarded and captured a French lugger at Havre-de-Grace in April 1796. The lugger was taken in tow with Smith and his boarding-party on it, but was attacked by the French and forced to surrender. Three officers and sixteen men were imprisoned on landing. Smith was removed to the Temple at Paris but managed to escape by means of forged papers and reached London on 8 May 1798. The 'Philip somethin'' referred to is the Royalist exile and officer in the engineers, Colonel Phélypeaux, who assisted in Sir Sidney's escape.

Page 388. *'at heaven's gate'*: the song from *Cymbeline* Act II scene 3:

'Hark, hark, the lark at heaven's gate sings,
and Phoebus gins arise.'

Page 389. *Oud Harry*: a euphemism for the Devil.

Page 390. *gawby*: idiot.

Page 393. *stertorous*: characterized by neavy snoring.

Page 404. *Peggy Dawson's*: the surname 'Dawson' is also possibly derived from Young's *History of Whitby*, for a sailor named William Dawson is noted as living to the advanced age of 96. Dawson died in 1811.

Page 407. *land-crimps or water-crimps*: the impressment of men for service on land or at sea.

Page 410. *Jeremiah*: all earlier editions have 'John'.

Page 414. *'The Lord bless thee . . . shine upon thee'*: this commonly used blessing is derived from Numbers 6:24–5.

Page 424. *7th of May, 1799*: French troops under Napoleon had attacked Acre in July 1798 and had begun the siege of the city in March 1799. They had breached the wall but were repulsed by the Turkish garrison, supported by a British squadron off-shore. A major assault began in early May and was only finally abandoned on the 27th of the month. ECG derives much of her information about the siege from the *Annual Register* for 1799, a volume which contains both extended accounts of the action and Sir Sidney Smith's despatches from the *Tigre*.

Page 425. '*some fifty, some an hundred fold*': a misquotation of the end of the parable of the sower (Matthew 13:8): 'some an hundredfold, some sixtyfold, some thirtyfold'.

Page 426. *the Tigre*: Sir Sidney Smith's flagship was of eighty-four guns.

Page 427. (1) *machicolated*: walls constructed with a projecting parapet through which stones or molten lead could be poured on assailants.

(2) *Djezzar Pacha*: The Turkish governor of Acre.

Page 431. '*I niver thought you'd ha' kept true to her*': even this crucial short sentence was slightly revised in the second edition. The first edition has: 'I niver thought you would ha' kept true to her!'.

Page 433. *Maybe it was a spirit*: this anecdote is typical of ECG's interest in folk-story and local legend, though its source is uncertain.

The dialect in this passage was heavily revised in the second edition suggesting even more clearly that the sailor is a northerner rather than a Devonian.

Page 434. *the Theseus*: there is no record of an explosion on board HMS *Theseus* though Sir Sidney Smith reported in his despatches that seven private marines were listed as wounded between 9 and 20 May 1799.

Page 451. *a heavenly and a typical city*: Alice is somewhat narrowly citing the belief derived from the Epistle to the Galatians (4:26) that the new Covenant freed Christian believers from earthly allegiance to a holy city. They were instead citizens of a heavenly city; the earthly Jerusalem, being in bondage, is contrasted to the 'type' of the celestial Jerusalem 'which is the mother of us all'. St. John's vision in the Book of Revelation of the New Jerusalem 'coming down from God out of heaven' (Chapter 21) further reinforces the distinction between the two cities.

Page 459. (1) *the Hospital of St. Sepulchre*: in his walk northward from Portsmouth Philip has evidently reached Winchester (with its 'great old cathedral'). The 'Hospital of St. Sepulchre' is modelled on that of St. Cross, a mile south of Winchester. St. Cross was not, however, founded 'in the time of Henry V' by a 'knight who had fought in the French wars' but by Bishop Henry de Blois in the year 1136. It was refounded in the mid-fifteenth century by Cardinal Beaufort who added an 'Almshouse of Noble Poverty'. Every traveller passing by St. Cross, as by St. Sepulchre's, is allowed to partake of the 'Wayfarers' Dole' consisting of a horn of beer and a slice of bread.

St. Cross had gained a certain notoriety in 1808 as the result of a scandal concerning the abuse of the Mastership, a scandal on which Trollope is believed to have drawn for his novel *The Warden* published in 1857. ECG seems not to want to imply any opprobrium towards the warden of her own charitable foundation.

(2) *manchet*: a small loaf or roll of fine wheaten bread.

Page 460. *th' four kingdoms*: i.e. England, Scotland, Ireland and France. George III's hereditary, if somewhat empty, claim to the throne of France was not surrendered until 1801.

Page 461. *company*: the first edition has 'regiment'. This was altered in the second edition both here and in Chapter 42.

Page 462. *the taking of Quebec*: on 13 September 1759.

Page 465. (1) *Peregrine Pickle*: Smollett's novel was first published in 1751.

(2) *the Seven Champions of Christendom*: it would seem that it was unlikely that Philip would have found the legend of Guy of Warwick in *The Seven Champions of Christendom* for this last traditionally recounted the stories of the seven patron saints of western Europe (SS George, Denis, James, Anthony, Andrew, Patrick and David). The standard printed version in English was produced throughout the seventeenth and eighteenth centuries.

It is just possible, however, that ECG is thinking of a chap-book version of the *Seven Champions* bound together with a copy of the equally popular *History of the Famous Exploits of Guy, Earl of Warwick*. The legend of Guy was first written down in the twelfth century and survives in ballad form as well as in prose. Introducing the poem in the Third Volume of his *Reliques of Ancient English Poetry* in 1765 Bishop Percy noted that 'the history of sir Guy, tho' now very properly resigned to children, was once admired by all readers of wit and taste: for taste and wit had once their childhood'. The version of the story given by ECG closely follows standard versions of Guy's relationship with his wife Phillis (or Felice) though it omits the account of the Earl's fight with the giant Colbrand which is reputed to have taken place at Winchester close to where Philip is supposedly reading about it.

Page 469. *black*: the first edition has 'bleak'.

Page 473. *Tom Tiddler's ground*: a children's game in which one player is 'Tom Tiddler' with a territory marked by a line drawn on the ground. Other players attempt to run over this territory crying 'We're on Tom Tiddler's ground, picking up gold and silver'.

Page 475. *Not a' mak' o' men*: not all kinds of men; not many men.

Page 476. (1) *Jeremiah*: the first edition has 'John'.

(2) *t' new buildings*: the late eighteenth century saw a considerable expansion of Whitby to the west of the River Esk. The extension of Flowergate, known as 'New Buildings' was described by Young in his *A Picture of Whitby and its Environs* (1824) as the finest street in the town, consisting 'only of one row of houses; but all of them handsome, and some magnificent'. The 'grand new walk' around the cliffs which Kester mentions is typical of the 'improvements' taking place at the turn of the century and which

mark the transition from a town based on whaling to a watering-place.

Page 479. (1) *stirabout*: porridge made by stirring oatmeal into boiling water or milk.

(2) *t' father o' lies*: John 8:44.

Page 480. *raxes*: stretches.

Page 481. *the spring of 1800*: it is likely that the details of the 'hard famine' were derived from the *Annual Register* and from surviving witnesses.

Page 486. '*tickle*': difficult, complex.

Page 487. '*Natteau Gent, York*': presumably an invention of ECG's.

Page 489. (1) *With God all things are possible*: Matthew 19:26.

(2) *Poor Sylvia!*: the first edition has 'Poor little Sylvia'.

Page 490. *fickleness*: the first edition has 'feebleness'.

Page 496. *wheere all tears are wiped away*: Revelation 21:4.

Page 498. *Abraham . . . David . . . 'the Beloved'*: Isaiah 41:8, I Samuel 13:14, John 13:23, John 19:26.

Page 499. (1) *the 'way to escape'*: I Corinthians 10:13: 'There hath no temptation taken you but such as is common to man: but God is faithful, who will not suffer you to be tempted above that ye are able; but will with the temptation also make a way to escape that ye may be able to bear it'.

(2) '*what a Christian might be*': probably a reminiscence of Addison's celebrated death-bed resolve to summon Lord Warwick ('a young man of very irregular life') to see 'how a Christian can die'.

(3) *unto all people*: Luke 2:10.

Page 502. (1) '*there shall be no more sea*': Revelation 21:1: 'And I saw a new heaven and a new earth: for the first heaven and the first earth were passed away: and there was no more sea.'

(2) '*Public Baths*': the baths at Whitby were erected in 1826.

mark the machinery in a given place on winding, or a starting place.

Page [illegible]: [illegible] porridge made by [illegible] oatmeal [illegible] boiling water or milk.

[illegible]

Page [illegible]: [illegible]

Page [illegible]: [illegible] were [illegible] from the [illegible] and [illegible]

Page [illegible]: [illegible] complex.

Page [illegible]: [illegible]

Page [illegible]: [illegible]

[illegible]

Page [illegible]: [illegible]

Page [illegible]: [illegible]

Page [illegible]: [illegible]

[illegible]

[illegible]

[illegible]

Page [illegible]: [illegible]

[illegible]

Make You Remember

MACY BECKETT

Published by arrangement with NAL Signet Eclipse,
a member of Penguin Group (USA) LLC.
A Penguin Random House Company.

First published in Great Britain in 2014
by HEADLINE ETERNAL
An imprint of HEADLINE PUBLISHING GROUP

1

Cataloguing in Publication Data is available from the British Library

ISBN 978 1 4722 2080 6

Offset in Palatino by Avon DataSet Ltd,
Bidford-on-Avon, Warwickshire

Printed and bound by CPI Group (UK) Ltd, Croydon, CR0 4YY

Papers used by Headline are from well-managed forests
and other responsible sources

HEADLINE PUBLISHING GROUP
An Hachette UK Company
338 Euston Road
London NW1 3BH

www.headlineeternal.com
www.headline.co.uk
www.hachette.co.uk

Make You Remember

Chapter 1

Devyn Mauvais looked at the gratitude in her client's rheumy eyes and said the most expensive words in recent history. "Now, don't you worry about my fee, hon. Your happiness is payment enough." Then she helped the old woman tuck a folded twenty back into the pocket of her tattered housedress, along with the talisman she'd just "bought."

"Thank you, child." The woman wrapped her bony arms around Devyn's waist, bringing with her the scent of arthritis cream. "You do your mama proud, God rest her."

No, not really. Mama would spin in her grave if she knew her oldest daughter was peddling sacred oils and ritual kits out of her living room. The first rule she'd taught Devyn was that it's bad juju to profit from helping others. Out of habit, Devyn crossed herself while patting her client's back.

After walking the woman to her car, Devyn returned to her sagging front porch, where her gaze landed on the brand-new sign affixed near the screen door. In odd contrast to the faded aluminum siding, the sign announced: EFFECTIVE IMMEDIATELY, A FEE OF $20 PER HOUR WILL BE CHARGED FOR ALL SPIRITUAL CONSULTATIONS. POTION, SPELLS, AND CANDLE PRICES ARE AVAILABLE UPON REQUEST. INQUIRE WITHIN OR BOOK AN APPOINTMENT AT MAUVAISVOODOO.COM.

God, she had a Web site. Could she possibly sink any lower?

She threw open the front door and tried to ignore the prickle of shame tugging at her stomach. A month ago, she never would have accepted a cent for reading the bones. Funny how quickly life could spiral out of control when you lived paycheck to paycheck. Since she'd lost her temp job at the Lord of the Springs mattress store, bad juju was the least of Devyn's worries.

The rent was overdue, her cupboards were bare, and for the past week, she'd parked her Honda behind a Dumpster a few blocks away in a game of hide-and-seek with the repo man. She'd even resorted to "borrowing" wireless Internet from the trailer park across the street, something no twenty-seven-year-old woman should ever have to do.

But not even *she* was desperate enough to take grocery money from little old ladies.

"Yet," she muttered.

Checking her cell phone, Devyn noted she had five minutes before her last appointment of the day, some out-of-towner named Warren Larabee who'd prepaid online via credit card. In preparation, she lit a stick of incense, then mixed a satchel of herbs, coins, and ancestral soil from Memère's tomb for a Good Fortune charm. Nine times out of ten, that was what men wanted. The other was "natural male enhancement," which she couldn't provide. If the flag wouldn't fly, there was something wrong with the pole, and that was a job for the doctor.

She was a Mauvais, not a magician.

At six o'clock on the button, a gentle rapping sounded at her door, and she ushered a middle-aged man with a thick salt-and-pepper crew cut into her living room. He wore a business suit and an easy smile that told Devyn he wasn't a true believer in voodoo. With his relaxed posture, both hands tucked loosely inside his pockets, it looked like he'd come here to bring the word of the Lord. Not that she needed it. A devout Catholic, she'd chaired the Saint Mary's fish fry six years running.

In any case, it was obvious that Warren Larabee hadn't come here for a reading. Devyn's eyes found the Louisville Slugger she kept propped in the corner. The man seemed harmless, but creepers came in all sorts of packaging.

"Mr. Larabee?" She swept a hand toward the sofa while taking the opposite chair. "What brings you in?"

He ignored her question and smiled while assessing her strapless red minidress and black stiletto pumps. "You're not what I expected."

Devyn laughed when she imagined what he must be thinking: that for an extra fee, she would offer spiritual *and* sexual healing. "Trust me, I don't usually wear this to meet clients. My ten-year high school reunion is tonight." And if she wanted to make it in time for the complimentary open bar—which she did—she'd have to rush out the door as soon as this appointment ended.

"Well, you look lovely," Warren said. "I'm sure you'll make your classmates green with envy."

"Isn't that what we all want?" Joking aside, she folded both hands in her lap and got down to business. "You're not here for a charm, are you?"

"Very perceptive." He nodded his approval like a proud parent. "No, I'm here to offer you an opportunity."

Visions of sales pitches danced in Devyn's head, but she suppressed an eye roll. "You paid for an hour. How you use it is your prerogative."

"I own Larabee Amusements," he said. "Maybe you've heard of it?"

Devyn shook her head.

"We sell sightseeing packages in cities all over the country." He shifted forward to rest both elbows on his knees. "Celebrity mansion tours in Hollywood, honky-tonk pub crawls in Nashville, boat trips in the Everglades, that sort of thing."

"And let me guess," Devyn said. "You're branching out in New Orleans?"

"No, that market's already saturated. We're opening a franchise right here in Cedar Bayou." He lifted a shoulder. "It's only twenty minutes away, and the town has a rich history. I can't believe nobody's capitalized on it yet."

"If you're looking for investors, I can't help you." Devyn had already depleted her nest egg by helping her sister get the Sweet Spot bakery off the ground. Several years later, they were finally breaking even, but not doing well enough to keep Devyn from assembling lunches from free samples at the grocery store.

"That's not why I'm here," he assured her with a lifted palm. "I'd like to hire you."

She perked up. Now he had her attention. "To do what?"

"You're Devyn Mauvais," he said as if that fact had slipped her mind. "Direct descendant of Juliette Mauvais, the most feared voodoo queen in Louisiana history. From what I hear, the locals are still afraid to speak her name." Warren pointed to Memère's portrait on the wall, where Juliette looked down her nose at them, her full lips curved in a smirk. With her smooth olive skin and exotic eyes, she'd been the most beautiful woman in the bayou, but anyone who trifled with her did so at their own peril. There was a local family—the Dumonts—who knew it firsthand, even after a hundred years.

"You look like her," Warren said.

Devyn gave a dismissive laugh. "Not as much as my sister. Those two are the living spit."

"But enough that you could pass for Juliette if you wore traditional period clothing and a headdress." Warren paused as if for dramatic effect, then made jazz hands. "Just imagine how chilling a haunted cemetery tour would be if you were the one leading it."

Devyn's stomach sank. This wasn't the kind of opportunity she'd hoped for. She would rather spend all day asking *You want fries with that?* than lead gawking tourists to her great-great-grandmother's resting place so they could pose for cheesy pictures in front of her tomb.

"There's more," Warren added when she didn't respond. "I'll set you up in a shop near the cemetery so you can sell"—he thumbed at the rows of dressed candles on display—"your little trinkets when the tour is over."

"Wait just a minute." She held up an index finger. "Little *trinkets*? This is my heritage you're talking about, not some Tupperware party."

Warren's eyes flew wide. "Of course. I didn't mean to offend."

"Well, you did."

"But in addition to a generous salary, you'd make tips from the—"

"No, thank you." Devyn reminded herself that she'd earned twenty dollars listening to this drivel, which would make a small dent in the electric bill. But that was a bargain for this man, and she'd had enough. "Not even for tips."

Warren fell silent, taking in the peeling paint on the walls as if to ask *Seriously, lady? Don't you need the cash?* "If the salary is an issue, we can negotiate."

"Do you need spiritual guidance, Mr. Larabee?" When he lowered his brows in confusion and shook his head, she added, "Then I'm afraid our appointment is over."

To his credit, Warren didn't push. He fished a business card from his shirt pocket and set it on the coffee table. He then stood up and offered his palm. "I'll be in town until Halloween, so take a few weeks to think about it. I hope you'll change your mind."

Devyn shook his hand and walked him to the door, but that was as far as her courtesy extended. Warren gave a final wave, then strode to the sleek Mercedes parked at the curb. Seconds later, he was gone, taking his job offer with him.

Devyn blew out a breath and told herself she'd made the right choice. Selling a few satchels of gris-gris during a time of need was one thing, but cashing in on her heritage was another. No amount of money was worth her dignity.

So why was she still on the porch, watching his Mercedes fade into the distance?

She shook her head to clear it and went back into the house for a quick lipstick touch-up. There was free booze awaiting her in the Cedar Bayou High gymnasium, and she was overdue for a good time.

Devyn parked her Honda behind a Salvation Army clothing receptacle at the rear of the school, then locked the doors and paused to admire her reflection in the driver's-side window.

She had originally planned to skip the reunion, but that was before she'd found this amazeballs Gucci dress for thirty dollars at a thrift store in New Orleans. Fire-engine red and so short it barely covered her butt, it hugged her curves like it was hand-stitched for her—by angels. The only thing wrong with it was a tiny spot of ink on the side hem, but who cared?

It was Gucci!

This dress almost made her forget how far she'd fallen. Maybe she didn't have a job or a family of her own, but her body was still bitchin'—if she did say so herself—and one out of three wasn't bad.

Devyn clicked across the parking lot and through the school's back door, her peep-toe stilettos echoing in the narrow hallway. She had a sway in her hips tonight, the kind only a custom-fitted designer dress could inspire. Even Jenny Hore—appropriately pronounced *whore*—would eat her heart out. The one girl in school unfazed by the last name Mauvais, Jenny had made it her unholy mission to steal everything that mattered to Devyn: her lunch money, her project ideas, her spot on the varsity cheer squad—even her junior-year boyfriend, Slade Summers, may they both rot in hell.

With any luck, Jenny and Slade had aged horribly and grown miserable in each other's company. The prospect put an extra pep in Devyn's step as she approached the sign-in station.

The table was unmanned, so she scanned the rows of name-tag stickers for her own. When she didn't find it, she picked up the attendance clipboard and ran her fingernail down the class roster.

"Excuse me, Miss," said a familiar baritone voice before its owner plucked the clipboard from Devyn's hands. "That's mine."

Instantly, her jaw clenched. She slid a glare toward

the voice, which brought her eye-level to a gray polo stretched tight over the broadest chest in Cedar Bayou. She would know. From there, she craned her neck toward the ceiling and met a pair of arrogant green eyes smiling beneath a thatch of auburn hair. Mirrored sunglasses were pushed atop his head, despite the fact that the sun had set an hour ago. His name tag said HELLO, MY NAME IS INIGO MONTOYA, but she knew better. This overgrown muscle head was Beau Dumont: high school football star, ex-marine, class demigod, and a constant pain in her ass since the day he'd returned to town a few months ago.

"I was hoping you'd stay home," she said. "But then, who would the idiot masses have to worship?"

His gaze took a leisurely stroll up and down her body. "With you in that dress, nobody's going to notice little ol' me."

The compliment didn't touch her. She'd learned a long time ago that Beau's pretty words carried no weight. She sneered at his clipboard. "Who put you in charge?"

"Why wouldn't I be in charge? I was voted Most Likely to Succeed."

"What's that?" She leaned in, cupping an ear. "Most Likely a Sleaze? I'd say that sounds about right."

Beau chuckled low and deep, then lifted a dark curl from her shoulder. He rubbed it between his thumb and index finger before using the end to tickle her cheek. "You didn't always think I was sleazy, Dev."

Devyn's knees softened, and she discreetly grasped

the folding table for support. "That was before you—" *said you loved me and disappeared for almost a decade.* "Left me on the hook for what we did after graduation."

His lips slid into a crooked grin that used to make her panties fall off, back when she'd naïvely thought she could break the curse that had turned all Dumont men into liars, cheats, and runners. Now that cocky grin made her palm itch to smack him upside the head.

"Best night of my life," he said.

She narrowed her eyes. "That's because you weren't the one who got arrested."

"Aw, now. I said I was sorry for that." He pulled her name tag from his pocket and began scanning her dress for a place to stick it. "Besides, I heard the charges were dropped."

Devyn snatched the name tag from him. "Bite me."

"Any time you want." Beau tipped her chin, leaning close enough to fill the space between them with the scents of shaving cream and male body heat. "I still remember all the delicious places you like to be nibbled, Kitten."

Kitten.

The casual use of her old nickname sent fire rushing through Devyn's veins. She batted away his hand. "In your dreams. The only thing giving you a good time tonight is your hand. It's a match made in heaven. Not even *you* can ruin that relationship." She whirled toward the gymnasium and strutted away, shaking her moneymaker to give him a sweet view of what he was missing—what he had abandoned ten years ago.

Screw Beau Dumont and his big, gorgeous chest. She was *so* over him.

She reminded herself of that as she strode into the gym, where the bleachers were folded against the walls and the basketball hoops were cranked toward the ceiling. The decorating committee had covered several rows of cafeteria lunch tables with white linen and a scattering of balloon clusters, transporting her back to a time when her greatest worry was which outfit would make a boy's jaw drop.

Aside from her financial woes, it would seem she'd come full circle.

Streamers crisscrossed the dimly lit room, and Snoop Dogg's "Drop It Like It's Hot" played from someone's iPod docking station in the corner. It was like prom night all over again, except for the standing bar erected near the floor mats. She made a beeline for the booze, and once she had a lemon drop martini in hand, she scanned the room for a familiar face.

"Dev!"

A woman's shout drew Devyn's attention to a small group gathered on the opposite side of the gym. She squinted in the dim lighting and recognized Margo and some of the other cheerleaders who'd moved away from the bayou after graduation. When Devyn waved, Margo bounced with excitement, then cringed and cradled her pregnant belly between both hands.

"Hey," Devyn said, joining Margo with outstretched arms.

After a long hug, Margo pulled back to look at

Devyn. "You're stunning. I hate you." But her warm smile promised the opposite.

"Oh, please." Devyn flapped a hand and patted her friend's swollen tummy. "You're absolutely glowing. Congratulations! Is this your first?"

"Our third," Margo said and introduced her husband. One by one, each woman in the group did the same until they glanced at Devyn and paused expectantly.

She held up her naked left hand. "Still single." The girls followed with a chorus of *Good for you* and *Nothing wrong with that*, but a shadow of pity softened their tone. "My sister, Allie, got married, though," Devyn said, shamelessly deflecting. "Just a couple of months ago, to Marc Dumont."

That made eyebrows rise. Until recently, no Dumont man had made it to the altar since the day Memère jinxed their line. Few people believed in the curse, but firsthand experience had shown Devyn it was like thunder—impossible to see, but very real. She still didn't know how Marc had broken the hex, but for her sister's sake, she was glad that he did. Allie's feet hadn't touched the ground since their Vegas wedding.

"Maybe Beau's next," said Margo with a teasing elbow nudge. She nodded toward the gym doors. "He's been watching you since you walked into the room."

Devyn glanced over her shoulder and saw him standing there, the top of his head barely clearing the doorway as he leaned against the jamb and folded his muscled arms. He winked at her, and she turned back to Margo with an eye roll. "Don't hold your breath."

From there, the discussion turned to careers. Devyn learned that her old cheer squad had gone on to become Web designers, freelance writers, and stay-at-home moms. When her turn came to share, Devyn played it off with a carefree shrug. "I haven't quite decided what I want to be when I grow up."

Everyone laughed and Devyn was able to unclench her shoulders. Margo had just pulled out her iPhone to show everyone pictures of her children when she glanced across the room and squealed in delight. "Jenny's here! And Slade!"

Devyn smoothed the front of her dress, sucked in her tummy, and turned slowly toward the gym entrance to catch a glimpse of her nemesis. Would Jenny's eyes have grown dull, darkened by circles of exhaustion? Had her golden hair faded with time and too much chemical processing? Would Slade have lost half his hair and gained a hundred pounds?

As it turned out, no.

The pair strutted into view looking better than ever, damn it.

Jenny tossed a curtain of glossy blond hair over one shoulder, rocking a designer halter dress paired with knee-high stiletto boots. Even in the dim lighting, a set of obscenely large diamond studs winked from her earlobes, and she made sure everyone spotted the quilted Chanel bag on her shoulder. Slade was dressed more like a Greek billionaire than the soccer stud that Devyn remembered. Whatever the pair had been up to these past ten years, they had clearly made more money than the Rockefellers.

Those bastards.

After a round of hugs and hellos, Jenny pinned Devyn with a critical gaze. "Well, if it isn't Devyn Mauvais. Bless your little heart."

Whatever. Every Southern girl knew that was code for "Go die in a fire."

Devyn smiled sweetly. "Well, if it isn't my favorite *Hore*."

"Actually, it's Summers now." Jenny thrust forward her left hand to display a diamond approximately the size of the moon.

Devyn quietly sipped her martini, but her lack of enthusiasm didn't stop Jenny from launching into a story about her sunset wedding ceremony on a private beach just outside Cabo San Lucas. For the next ten minutes, she spun a tale of nauseating excess that had the whole group transfixed. Even Beau Dumont had ambled over to hear the details.

Devyn had long since tuned out the prattle, so she was caught off guard when Jenny abruptly stopped and pointed at her.

"What?" Devyn asked.

Jenny covered her mouth to stifle a giggle. "Nice dress, Dev."

Devyn stood a bit straighter and smiled. "Thanks. I picked it up for a steal."

"I know," Jenny said. "From the Tulane Avenue Goodwill, right? That's where I donated it." She leaned down to inspect the side hem. "Yep. There's the stain I never could get out."

Devyn stopped breathing.

"It looks cute on you, though," Jenny added with a shrug that said, *But not as good as it looked on me.* "One girl's trash is another girl's treasure, right?"

At once, Devyn felt the weight of two dozen gazes shifting in her direction. Her upper body went numb, as if she had slept with both arms tucked beneath her pillow and cut off her circulation. Several charged beats passed in silence before she forced a wide grin and toasted her enemy. "Are you calling a Gucci design trash? I do believe that's blasphemy."

A few people chuckled, but it was a *this is getting awkward* kind of laugh.

Jenny smoothed her fingers possessively through Slade's hair. "You crack me up, Dev. Always have."

Maybe it was the public humiliation, or maybe it was the martini, but something hijacked Devyn's vocal cords and forced her to blurt out, "That's what my boyfriend says."

Oh, shit. What had she just done?

"Hey." Margo delivered a good-natured shove. "You didn't say anything about a boyfriend. Spill! I want to hear all about him."

"Yes," Jenny said as if sniffing blood in the water. "Spill."

It took a moment for Devyn to find her voice. "He's . . . great. Big and gorgeous and super sweet. We're crazy about each other."

"Is he local?" asked Margo.

"Uh . . . kind of."

"Kind of?" Jenny asked with an arched brow. "What's his name?"

Yeah, you idiot, Devyn chided herself. *What's his name?* "I can't say. We're keeping things on the down-low." Double shit! Who actually said *on the down-low* anymore?

"What does he do for a living?" asked Margo.

Devyn said the first thing that came to mind. "He owns a business." When that didn't seem to satisfy anyone, she fumbled. "I can't say anything more, or you'll know who he is."

The triumphant smile that curled Jenny's lips said she knew it was a lie. And clearly she would take great pleasure in raking Devyn over the coals. "Oh, come on," Jenny crooned. "Give us a hint. We won't tell." She glanced around at her friends. "Will we?"

Everyone shook their heads and peered at Devyn, waiting for her to speak. Her eyes locked with Beau's for one interminable moment, the intensity behind his gaze hot enough to tighten her stomach. Why did he have to be here to witness this? She had always hoped to make him sorry one day, but he probably thought he'd dodged a bullet when he ditched her all those years ago.

"Go on," Jenny prodded. "Tell us who he is."

Devyn's palms began to sweat. This was like a nightmare, only worse. Because she would rather deliver a naked speech in front of the whole school than admit she'd invented a fictitious boyfriend. Just when she opened her mouth to dig herself a deeper hole, Beau crossed through the center of the group and stood by her side.

Slipping an arm around her waist, Beau pulled her hard against him and announced, "It's me. I'm Dev's boyfriend—*and* her boss."

Chapter 2

Beau kept going and hoped like hell no one realized he was talking out of his ass.

"That's why we had to keep it quiet," he said. "Dev's managing the education center on my riverboat, and I didn't want anyone thinking she earned the job on those pretty little knees." He delivered a hard smack to her bottom. "Isn't that right, Kitten?"

Devyn squeaked at the physical contact, fisting her martini glass almost hard enough to shatter it. When she swiveled her ice-blue gaze to his, he couldn't tell whether she wanted to kiss him or drive one of those pretty little knees between his legs.

"Mmm-hmm," she forced out. "Plus, there's all that bad blood between our families."

"A hundred years' worth," he agreed. "But now that Marc and Allie have tied the knot, why not go public?"

Margo bounced on her toes, pointing a wild finger at them. "I knew it! I could tell from the way you were watching her!"

Beau playfully ruffled Devyn's curls. "What can I say? The flame never died. I got back to town and we picked up right where we left off," he said as he waggled his eyebrows. "Except it's a thousand times hotter. I can't keep her off me—she's an animal in the sack."

The corners of Devyn's mouth tightened. "I'm just making up for lost time, Sugar Dumplin'. You know, that whole decade we missed out on."

He ignored the jab and lifted his Sam Adams toward that bitch, Jenny Hore. "I don't care where her dress came from, it's going to look great on my bedroom floor tonight." Then he tipped back his bottle for a deep pull.

Dev pinched his back hard enough to make him yelp. "I can't wait," she said. "Did you remember to take your little blue pill?"

Beau coughed and sputtered beer into his fist. She knew damn well he didn't have any performance issues, and that shit was hitting below the belt. "Come on, baby," he said as he set down their drinks and nodded toward the dance floor. "They're playing our song."

Slade Summers wrinkled his forehead. "Your song is 'Bump n' Grind'?"

"Yeah." Beau thumbed at Devyn. "It's her stripper jam. She loves to dance for me."

"Lucky bastard."

"You said it, man." Beau went in for a fist bump, but Devyn tugged him away before it connected.

"That's enough, honey," she said. "Nobody wants to hear what I have to do to get your Magic Stick to stand—"

"Great seeing you again," Beau boomed while ushering Dev away from the group. When they were out of earshot, he whispered, "What the hell? I'm trying to help you."

"My stripper jam?" she hissed. "You had to go there?"

"What about that Viagra comment?" He pulled her into a dance, his hands sliding around her waist while she reluctantly locked both wrists around his neck. "I don't need a pill to get my Magic Stick standing, which I'm sure you remember all too well."

She shot him a smile full of poison. "Methinks the gentleman doth protest too much."

"Yeah?" he asked. "Methinks you weren't protesting all those times I had you wide open on the riverbank begging for my—"

"Bless your heart, Beau Dumont," she interrupted, eyes cold enough to freeze the balls off a brass monkey. "Bless it right out of your chest."

He chuckled to himself. "I don't think you really mean that."

"Then maybe you're even more stupid than I thought."

Ouch. It seemed Kitten had her claws out tonight.

Beau remembered a time when Devyn talked sweetly to him—in the months before graduation, when they were young and head over heels in lust. She had spent countless hours wrapped around him, all softness and light. They'd hiked and fished and skinny-dipped before making love in the tall grass and walking home with chigger bites in some really interesting places.

Those were the best days of his life; so naturally, he'd bolted.

For the first time since leading Devyn to the dance floor, he became aware of her nearness, the way their fused bodies moved in an effortless, synchronized rhythm. It had always been like this with her. They'd had their fair share of problems, but rhythm wasn't one of them. Of their own volition, his hands slid from her waist to find their favorite resting spot at the base of her spine, right where the curve of her ass began. With her heated skin pressed so close, he realized she still smelled the same, like honeysuckle and sex. He'd missed that scent.

He'd missed *her*.

Devyn seemed to sense the shift in his mood, because she peered up at him and lifted one eyebrow in warning. "Listen," she began, then hesitated. "About what happened with Jenny . . ."

"I think the words you're looking for," he said, dipping his mouth an inch from hers, "are *Thank you, Beau. You're my hero.*"

She pushed him back. "Whatever. Thank you."

"You're welcome."

Devyn's icy mask faltered as she studied him beneath a fringe of thick lashes. "Why'd you do it?"

Beau shrugged. "Jenny's an asshole. Back in high school, she came on to me in the boys' locker room, and when I shot her down, she spread an ugly rumor about my mama."

"Oh, yeah." Dev sucked a sympathetic breath through her teeth, and for a moment, they were friends again. "I remember that. Nobody believed her, you know."

"Good." Beau was used to folks flapping their gums about his daddy. The old dirty bastard had six sons by five different women, including a baby due in December. But Beau's mama was innocent in the whole mess. The only mistake she'd made was loving the wrong man. "Still pissed me off, though."

"Not to change the subject," Dev said, "but when are we going to break up? I need to quit that fake job, too."

"Whoa, now. Not so fast." He really did need an educational director for the next cruise. Devyn wasn't a certified teacher, but she'd spent some time in college training as one. Plus, now that her sister had married Beau's brother, they were practically family. She would fit right in with the rest of the crew. "You can dump me any time you want, but the job's not fake. You start next week."

"Excuse me?" She pulled back and cocked her head. "You can't be serious."

"Careful, Kitten," he said, nodding toward the group. "We're supposed to be madly in love, remember?"

With an exasperated sigh, she rested her cheek on his chest. The affectionate gesture did nothing to soften the acid in her voice, and in the blink of an eye, their temporary friendship came to an end. "I'm not setting foot aboard that floating garbage heap. Especially not with you."

"Watch it," he warned. Trashing the *Belle* was almost as bad as talking smack about his mama. "I saved your hide back there, and you're going to repay the favor. Our director's on maternity leave. I only need you for a couple of weeks."

"Not happening."

"What's the problem?" Beau asked. "Allie told me you lost your job. The salary for this position is more than what your old temp agency paid." Once again, Devyn should be thanking him, not digging in her heels.

"Maybe I don't want to work under you." Then she emphasized, "Or *be* under you."

An automatic grin formed on his lips. It sounded an awful lot like she didn't trust herself around him. To test his theory, Beau lowered his mouth to her right ear, which he recalled was more sensitive than the left. "Afraid you won't be able to keep your hands off me?"

She shivered in his arms and said, "You wish," but her breath hitched, rendering the words powerless.

Beau brushed his lips over her earlobe before taking it gently between his teeth. In response, Devyn released a sigh that sent a jolt of lust straight to his Jockeys. "Then you have no reason to worry," he murmured. "I'll see you first thing Monday morning . . . unless you want to admit to your friends that we lied."

The song ended, and they ceased their lazy sway.

Devyn looked up at him, her blue eyes charged with a mingling of desire and loathing, mostly the latter. "All right," she said. "But only for two weeks, then consider us even."

"See, that wasn't so hard, was it?" he said, noting that his Magic Stick certainly was. That soldier was all too happy to be back in Dev's company. Beau gave a slight nod toward her friends. "We can go over there if you want. But I'm warning you, any more mentions of little blue pills and I'll tell them about your recent spanking fetish."

"Forget it," she said, her shoulders sagging in defeat. "I'm just going home to burn this dress."

Beau couldn't blame her. For show, he settled a hand at her lower back. "Come on. I'll walk you to your car."

She shifted a glare at him. "Not necessary."

"What kind of boyfriend would I be if I didn't walk you out?"

"Fine." She sighed, kicking off her high heels and handing them over. "A good boyfriend would hold my stilettos."

They reached her table and she shoved her purse at him. "And my bag."

Beau grumbled under his breath. This fake boyfriend thing was for the birds. Here he was holding a purse, and he wasn't even getting fake lucky tonight. As long as she didn't ask him to buy a box of tampons. That was where he drew the line.

After a round of good-byes to their old friends, Devyn and Beau walked out the back door and crossed the parking lot. He didn't know where she was leading him, though. Once they made it to the rear of the lot, it became clear there were no cars out there.

"Oh, no," Devyn moaned, jogging a full rotation around a Dumpster-sized clothing donation bin before stopping and hanging her head. "It's gone. He must have followed me here when I left the house."

"Who followed you?" Beau glanced around the parking lot. Years of military training kicked his senses into high gear as he checked the grounds for any visible threat. The area looked secure. "Did someone steal your car?"

Instead of answering him, Devyn crouched into a ball and wrapped both arms around her knees.

"Do I need to call the police?" he said.

"No. Nobody stole my car. And don't mention this to my sister. I mean it—not a word."

She looked so small and broken curled up like that, vulnerable in a way Beau hadn't seen since his return to town. The new Devyn allowed nothing to chip her cold facade. Strange as it seemed, he was kind of relieved to see a flash of weakness from her. It proved she was still human under all that armor. But when he rested a comforting hand on her shoulder, she shrugged it off.

"Are you going to tell me what's happening here?" he asked.

She stood and brushed off her hands, and just like that, her icy shields went up. "Here's what's happening, Dumont. You're going to be a good boyfriend and drive me home. But first, you're going to pick up a bottle of Bacardi from the grocery. And a box of Tampax."

Monday morning, Beau awoke with the sun. He poured his coffee into a thermos and rolled down the windows in his old Chevy Tahoe while driving to the *Belle*'s docking station in downtown New Orleans.

Autumn had mercifully stolen half the humidity from the air, so he enjoyed the cool breeze while it lasted. Around here, crisp oxygen was a delicacy. He felt around the front seat for his sunglasses before realizing they were resting on top of his head. Squinting against the windshield's glare, he pushed his glasses into place and wondered how his fake girlfriend planned on getting to work today.

He had finally gotten Dev to admit that her car had been repossessed, a tidbit he'd promised to keep under wraps. Out of the kindness of his fake boyfriend heart, he'd offered to pick her up, but Devyn had scoffed and claimed she didn't want "any kind of ride" from him. Never mind that her gaze had flickered to his lap when she'd said it.

As long as she arrived with the rest of the staff, let the stubborn minx find her own way into the city. If he didn't see her curly head aboard the *Belle* by nine thirty, he would personally drive back to her house and haul her in over his shoulder. He caught himself grinning at the mental image.

This was going to be a fun couple of weeks.

When he pulled into the dock parking lot, he cut the

Chevy's engine and took a few minutes to gaze at the *Belle* through fresh eyes—the eyes of a soon-to-be co-owner. When Daddy had retired, he'd made Marc captain and deeded over the boat, which was the sensible thing to do at the time. There was no resentment for it on Beau's part. He had left the family business for a military enlistment, followed by half a decade of private contract work that had earned him a nice six-figure nest egg. All the while, Marc had stayed in Cedar Bayou and busted his ass to keep the *Belle* thriving. Marc had deserved the reins their daddy had handed him.

But things were different now.

Ten years living in crowded barracks and dusty hovels had shown Beau where he belonged, and it was right here in the bayou with the half brothers he'd left behind. He was looking to put down roots, and as it happened, Marc was seeking an investor to share the burden so he could spend more time with his new bride. Beau had the money and the inclination. It was a win-win.

Assuming they could get along . . .

Like most brothers, Beau and Marc had a tendency to bust each other's balls. Add the fact that their daddy had bounced back and forth between their mamas' beds for decades, and it was a wonder any of the Dumont brood had survived the animosity of their teenage years. But they were older and wiser now, and the *Belle* was a really big boat. With four expansive decks and hundreds of interior suites, she was larger than some motels. And if that wasn't enough room for two brothers' egos, they had worse problems than sibling rivalry.

Beau crossed the ramp onto the main deck, his shoes clattering over the metal grates until every bird within earshot startled and took flight. That sound used to make his chest tight, back when summers aboard this boat had felt more like a prison sentence than a seasonal job. It had taken ten years of dodging bullets overseas for him to realize how good he'd had it right here. Today he found himself smiling as he jogged up the steps to the second-floor dining room, where the scents of freshly cleaned carpet and touch-up paint greeted him.

Today the *Belle* felt like home.

The family meeting was already under way, four Dumonts gathered in their usual spot near the executive bar. Marc occupied the chair at the head of the table, but the real boss of this operation was the curly-headed pastry chef in his lap, Allie Mauvais-Dumont. The pair had thwarted a hundred-year curse with "perfect faith" in their love, and as corny as that sounded, it was mighty sweet to see them together. In fact, Marc was so busy rubbing his wife's back that he didn't notice Beau moving up behind him.

Beau kissed his sister-in-law on the cheek and took the seat beside her. Then he tugged a lock of his brother's idiotically long, wavy hair and dispensed some well-deserved ribbing. "Sorry, Captain. Now that Allie's around, you're not the prettiest girl on board anymore."

Marc laughed, not even bothering to raise his middle finger. That was a man in love, right there. "It's all right," he said. "Because next to you, I still look like a million bucks." He extended a hand, palm up. "And speaking of money . . ."

Beau pulled a cashier's check from his wallet and slid it toward his little brother while Alex and Nicky leaned across the table to gawk at it. Their blond brows lifted in perfect synchronization, the word *whoa* forming on their lips. Identical twins, they were the only Dumont brothers who shared the same mama, a Swedish beauty who had caught their daddy's eye for the better part of a year. Unlike the rest of the tawny-skinned clan, Alex and Nick's looks favored their mother's, with light hair, blue eyes, and a perpetual sunburn.

"I'm in the wrong business," Nick said, shaking his head in envy.

"No shit," Alex agreed. "If the marines pay that well, then sign me up."

The money Beau had invested wasn't even half of his savings, but in Alex and Nick's eyes, because they were fresh out of college and subsisting on ramen noodles and Milwaukee's Best, it probably seemed like a fortune.

"Hate to break it to you, but you wouldn't make much as enlisted men," he told his brothers. "The real money's in contract work, and you'll have to earn every last cent of it." To prove it, he lifted his T-shirt to show them the shrapnel scar from a dirty bomb he'd had the misfortune of encountering during one of his tours.

That's when Marc's half sister, Ella-Claire, happened to join them. "It's not even five o'clock, and Beau's already busting out a six pack?" She teasingly wolf whistled at his exposed abs and took the chair on the other side of her brother.

Marc shot daggers at Beau. "Put down your damn shirt." Even though Ella-Claire didn't share a drop of blood with the other Dumonts, they were all expected to treat her like family. Which they did. But try telling that to Marc, who thought everyone was out to defile her. Alex must have known it all too well. He scooted his chair a few inches away from Ella, lest he brush her leg and incur the captain's wrath.

"Let's get the meeting started," Marc said. He launched into a status report—everything from the functionality of the train linkage to the new staff members he had hired. He said that Worm, their kid brother, couldn't work the upcoming trip due to school, but he'd bus tables on the weekend dinner cruises. "Allie's agreed to stay on as pastry chef," Marc said and paused to kiss his wife's hand. "And I managed to sweet-talk Chef Therein on board to replace Beau in the galley." He nodded at Beau. "The money our brother invested will update the state suites and fix the plumbing issues from last season's possum invasion."

"And we'll add a few upgrades to the casino," Beau

said. "Which I'll be managing, along with general security. I can even pilot the boat if I have to."

"That reminds me." Marc pointed a ballpoint pen at Alex and Nick. "Make sure the staff knows that Beau's co-owner now. What he says goes. We eventually want to get to the point where he and I can seamlessly switch off as captain."

"You got it," the twins said in unison.

"Speaking of which," Beau said, "there's something I should mention. My first act as co-owner was hiring someone to fill in managing the education center."

A flash of annoyance passed over Marc's features, but he recovered quickly and took a silent moment—probably to unclench his ass cheeks. "Oh, yeah? Anyone I know?"

Beau leaned back to assume a casual pose in hopes that his body language might soften the inevitable shit storm to come. "Devyn," he muttered and took a sip of coffee.

"Devyn . . ." Marc trailed off, waiting for a last name.

"You know." Beau raised his thermos toward the woman who could almost pass for Dev's twin. "Allie's sister."

Allie's eyes nearly bugged out of her head while everyone else at the table drew a collective breath. Marc's voice sounded half strangled when he clarified, "Devyn *Mauvais*?"

Beau played it cool. "Does your wife have another sister named Devyn?"

"The same girl who threw a drink in your face at the wedding reception?" Alex asked.

Laughing, Nicky elbowed his twin. "That shit was priceless."

Beau shot his brothers a glare. "Okay, so she's not my biggest fan right now." And in all honesty, Beau had come on too strong at the reception. "But I know she can—"

"She kind of scares me," Ella-Claire interrupted.

"Hell, she scares everyone," Marc said, staring at Beau as if he'd sprouted horns. "Devyn Mauvais sends her exes to urgent care, and you want her working with the passengers' kids?"

"That was a coincidence," Allie piped up. "All six times."

"But still!"

"Look," Beau said. "I know Dev's a little . . . intense. But you don't know her like I do. She used to tutor little kids after school, and she had a way of explaining things that made sense to them." He had faith that the old Devyn was still alive—maybe buried deep, but still in there somewhere. "I'm sure she'll do a good job."

Marc shared a concerned glance with his wife. "I get where you're coming from," he said to Beau. "I really do. But come on. You're thinking with the wrong head."

Beau couldn't contain a sarcastic laugh. "What a coincidence. Because a few months ago, we were all saying the same thing about *you* when Chef Regale refused to work with the pretty pastry chef you hired." Beau glanced at Allie to drive his point home. "The one sitting in your lap right now."

"That's different," Marc ground out. "Allie was qualified for the job."

"No arguments there," Beau said. "But I recall telling you to keep it in your pants—that it was a bad example to sleep with a staffer. So don't preach to me about thinking with the wrong head. No offense, Allie," he added with an apologetic wave. "You know we all love you."

"None taken," she mumbled, cheeks darkening as she glanced at her lap.

Marc's jaw tightened. Like a snorting bull, he sucked an audible breath through his nose.

"Here we go. Pay up." Ella-Claire held a hand toward Alex, who begrudgingly slapped a five-dollar bill into her palm. "I knew you two couldn't go five minutes without fighting."

"We're not fighting," Beau told her. "We're debating."

The look Marc gave him said he was debating tossing Beau overboard. "If you're so confident in your choice, let's put it to a vote. All in favor of hiring Devyn to manage the education center—and all the infants, toddlers, and preschoolers in it—raise your hands."

Beau glanced around the table. Only one hand went up: Allie's. She shrugged and told her husband, "She's my sister. Dev's always been there when I needed her, and she takes a lot of pride in what she does. If she's committed to this, you can trust that she'll go all in."

Marc blew out a long breath. He took a while to think it over before slashing a hand through the air.

"No. I like Devyn, but I'm not comfortable putting her in charge. Anyway, it would be a slap in the face to everyone who's got seniority."

"How about a compromise, then?" Allie offered. "What if we move Mrs. Grayson to the director position and put Devyn in charge of the eight-to-twelve-year-old group?"

A few seconds ticked by in silence. With a twist of his lips, Marc conceded, "I guess that could work."

Beau thought it over and nodded. "I can agree to that."

"Then it's settled," Marc said, though the darkness in his voice contradicted his words. If he didn't need Beau's money so badly, he would have probably given back the check and resumed his dictatorship over the boat. "Let's get on track. We have a lot to discuss."

From there, the conversation turned to subjects like sanitation and supplies, but the mood never bounced back. Shoulders were stiff, eyes were downcast, and when Marc adjourned the meeting, everyone rattled off a list of to-dos and scattered like buckshot. Even Allie invented an excuse about calling the chef to coordinate meal plans, but Beau knew she used the same dessert menu for the whole season.

Once they were alone, Beau turned to Marc. He had to be sure that fancy white captain's hat wasn't so firmly cemented onto his brother's head that it couldn't be shared. "Are you sure you can handle this?"

"*This* being what, exactly?"

"All of it. Me being here, calling the shots without your blessing."

"You think I can't take a partner at the helm?"

Beau flashed a palm. "Just sayin'."

"Look, you made a decision from an emotional place," Marc said. "It was a mistake, and I don't regret calling you out on it. I'll do it again if I have to, which I'm sure I will."

"That goes both ways, Captain."

"Damn right, it does." Marc sniffed a teasing laugh. "Know what else goes both ways?"

"Enlighten me."

"Not sleeping with the staff." Folding his arms, Marc parroted Beau's words from the cruise when Allie had first come on board. "She's your employee now, and you've got no business chasing her skirt. So keep it in your pants, big brother." Then he clapped Beau on the arm and walked away, calling over his shoulder, "Good luck with that."

Beau grumbled, "Asshole" under his breath and stalked outside to the second-floor deck, where he let the breeze cool his temper by a few degrees.

Beau's motives for hiring Devyn had nothing to do with getting laid. He had seen her in action senior year when she'd volunteered at Cedar Bayou Elementary. Even though she'd grown a thicker skin since then, she was still the same girl who'd baked a giant sheet cake and divided it up to help the students understand fractions when nothing else had worked. If he closed his eyes, he could still see the sparkle of pride in her gaze when she'd told him about that day's lesson. She was so radiant it felt like staring at the sun.

Okay, if he was being honest, he *did* like the idea of being close to her for the next two weeks, but that didn't mean he was thinking with his dick.

When a flashy Mercedes Benz pulled into the parking lot, Beau forgot his troubles, the security specialist in him taking over. The black sedan parked beside his beat-up Chevy and cut the engine, but nobody on staff drove a car like that. The driver had probably taken a wrong turn. Beau strode toward the bow ramp for a closer look, and the passenger door opened, revealing a familiar shapely leg.

It was Devyn's. He'd slung that same leg over his shoulder enough times to know.

But who had given her a ride? Resting both elbows on the deck rail, he leaned down and squinted to bring the driver into focus. One masculine wrist was slung over the steering wheel, but he couldn't see anything more. Then Devyn shifted, leaning against the man in what looked a lot like a cuddle.

A completely irrational surge of jealousy heated Beau from his scalp to his toes. He had no claim on Devyn, but that didn't stop him from grasping the rail with both hands to suppress the urge to charge down the stairs and tear off the driver's-side door. A few deep breaths later, Beau finally regained control of his body.

What the hell was wrong with him? He needed to get his shit together.

His brother was right about one thing—Beau was in command now, and it was time to act like it. He had no business making hotheaded decisions . . . like grabbing his fake girlfriend by the shoulders and kissing her into a frenzy right there in front of Mercedes Man.

No, that was a bad idea. Instead, Beau stayed put and watched the pair from a distance . . . because he had a right to know what was going on with his employee.

He was just being a responsible boss. Nothing wrong with that.

Chapter 3

"One more signature, right here." Warren Larabee pointed to the bottom of the W-9 form, and Devyn leaned in to scrawl her name on the proverbial dotted line. She tried not to press against his shoulder, but in the car's close quarters, it couldn't be helped. He inspected the tax document and tucked it into a manila file folder. "We're all set. Call me when the cruise is over, and we'll work out the details."

"Sounds great," Devyn said, though she certainly didn't *feel* great about this decision. Her stomach had lurched and twisted ever since she'd picked up Warren's business card last night. "Thanks for the ride, by the way."

"No problem." He grinned at her while scratching the stubble along his jawline. "But I have to ask. What changed your mind about the cemetery tour?"

Oh, nothing really. Having my car repo'd. Wearing someone else's dress to my reunion. The overdue rent notice stapled to my door. My ex getting a front row seat for all of it. "Just had a change of heart."

"Huh." Warren didn't seem to buy her excuse, but he wasn't complaining. "Well, whatever the reason, I'm glad to have you on the team. Welcome to Larabee Amusements."

They said good-bye, and Devyn watched him drive away before she faced her new workplace. Then her heavy stomach sank another inch.

To anyone else, the *Belle of the Bayou* would seem like a Mark Twain fantasy come to life. Its wood decks were waxed to a high gloss and lined with oversize rocking chairs. Each outward-facing room was framed by an arch of freshly painted white latticework, which contrasted brilliantly against the massive red paddle wheel anchoring the stern and the dual black smokestacks stretching toward the sky. As historical reproductions went, the *Belle* was at the top of her class.

But Devyn saw this boat for what it really was: a lion's den.

And the biggest beast of them all was standing on the second-level deck glaring at her as if she'd already let him down. She checked her watch and yelled, "Save the lecture, Dumont. I'm ten minutes early."

Wood planks squeaked beneath Beau's considerable weight as he clomped down the stairs to meet her at the head of the ramp. The way he narrowed those hazel green eyes at her made Devyn wonder if she had dressed inappropriately. She didn't see a problem with her khaki skirt and floral T-shirt, but what did she know?

"It's business casual until the cruise next week, right?" she asked.

He ignored the question and jutted his chin toward the parking lot. "Who was that?"

"Who?" She glanced over her shoulder at the vacant asphalt.

"That guy who drove you here."

The mere mention of Warren Larabee had her gaze dropping to the tips of her white canvas sneakers. She wasn't ready to admit to anyone—not even her sister—that she had accepted a job to lead cemetery tours. It was too shameful. So she returned Beau's glare and squared her shoulders. "None of your business, that's who." Then she skirted his massive body and stepped onto the deck. "Why don't you just point me in the right direction so I can start my job?"

He didn't say anything at first. But when he was done staring her down, he abruptly turned and strode inside without a word. She followed, wondering what had crawled up his butt so early this morning.

She instantly regretted thinking about his butt.

Against Devyn's will, her focus locked onto the rock-hard contours of his backside displayed beneath thin, faded jeans that cupped him in all the right places. From there, she watched his long, powerful legs move through the halls in strides so brisk she scurried to keep up. As spectacular as it was, his lower half paled in comparison to the muscled planes of his back and a pair of shoulders so broad they stretched the fabric of his T-shirt to near transparency.

Damn it. Why did he have to look so scrumptious?

Devyn was no angel. She'd partied with her fair

share of men over the years, but it would take three standard hotties to equal one Beau Dumont. He had the most strikingly male physique she'd ever seen. It was what had drawn her eye when they'd first met in high school. She'd been a junior varsity cheerleader, and he'd been the captain of the football team. She remembered standing on the sidelines admiring him during one of the games when she should have been doing toe-touches. He had a body that said *Don't worry, baby. You're safe. Nothing can hurt you while I'm around.*

It was a shame that what was inside didn't match his outside appearance. Because no girl was safe in Beau Dumont's presence.

He led her across a wide lobby to the check-in desk, which was labeled the PURSER'S STATION. A twenty-something brunette with a shoulder-length ponytail stood behind the counter and squinted at her computer. Devyn recognized the girl as Ella-Claire, Marc's half sister. Their paths had crossed a time or two since the wedding, and she seemed nice enough.

"Hey, darlin'," Beau said to Ella. "Can you take care of Miss Mauvais's paperwork?"

Ella flicked a glance at Devyn before offering Beau a warm smile. Seriously warm. As in the sufficient temperature to bake an apple pie. "For you?" she chirped. "Anything."

Oh, barf.

Devyn didn't know why she cared, but the whole exchange left her feeling queasy. Maybe it was all the Bacardi she drank over the weekend. She was pushing thirty now, and she couldn't hold her liquor like she used to.

Ella-Claire handed Devyn a clipboard full of papers. "I'll get you a staff polo. What's your size?"

"Medium," Beau answered for her.

After a knowing smile and a wink—yes, an actual wink—Ella trotted off to the back room to retrieve a shirt. When she returned, she slid it across the counter and started talking with Beau about onshore excursions in Natchez.

While filling out her paperwork, Devyn recalled that Marc and Ella-Claire shared the same mom but had different fathers, while Beau and Marc shared the same dad, but had different mothers. Which meant that Beau wasn't actually related to the pretty young thing. *Wonder if he's nailed her yet,* Devyn thought. With his track record, it seemed likely.

Not that she cared or anything.

Devyn had just finished signing her second W-9 of the day when blond twins, who both resembled a young Matt Damon, strode behind the counter and began rifling through the cabinets. She'd met the pair at her sister's wedding reception, but she couldn't remember their names or tell them apart, so she secretly referred to them as Thing One and Thing Two.

"Hey there, gorgeous," said Thing One, making more eye contact with Devyn's chest than anything else. "Welcome aboard. I'm Nick. If you need anything—and I mean *anything*—I'm your man."

Devyn plastered on a sickly sweet grin. "Hi, Nick. Quit staring at my tits, or you'll be wearing this clipboard like an enema."

Thing Two burst out laughing and slapped his twin brother on the back. "I like her. Good call, Beau."

Beau didn't seem to think Devyn was quite as hilarious, but his lips twitched and his gaze sparkled when it landed on hers. For no reason at all, Devyn's pulse hitched. Probably that second cup of coffee. Yeah, that had to be it.

Beau must have completely gotten over whatever was irritating him, because he grinned as he led her away from the lobby and toward the education center at the heart of the boat.

"You'll bunk with a roommate once the cruise starts," he explained as they wound their way through the narrow halls. "There's not much space, so pack light."

"Can I bunk with Allie?"

"You can try," he said. "But I don't think Marc's bed is big enough for the three of you."

Devyn's cheeks heated. "Sometimes I forget they're married."

"Don't worry," Beau said with a hint of sarcasm. "You'll have plenty of reminders when you're around them twenty-four seven."

She was about to ask if Allie was here today when Beau ushered her inside a room that resembled a daycare center. A few travel cribs lined the far wall with a changing station in the corner. On the opposite side of a movable room partition stood a rectangular classroom table. Squishy foam alphabet tiles carpeted the floor, and a glance at the ceiling revealed paper chains strung from corner to corner.

Why had he brought her in here?

"There's been a small change of plan," Beau said. "We're putting you in charge of the oldest group, the eight-to-twelve-year-olds."

"Oldest group?" she repeated in a daze.

"There aren't many on this trip. You won't have more than ten, and that's assuming their parents drop them off every day. Some folks don't."

Devyn swallowed hard. This wasn't the kind of education center she'd had in mind. She'd pictured a mini museum where she would hand out pamphlets and recite historical facts for passengers who gave a shit about things like that.

Clearly, she'd been wrong.

She envisioned the room at full capacity, dozens of shrieking rug rats varying in age from infants to twelve-year-olds, each demanding attention for a very specific set of needs. This was a problem. Devyn didn't even like kids. They were exhausting and selfish and they smelled like peanut butter and warm cheese.

"I'm a babysitter?" she asked. "For two solid weeks?"

The way Beau's mouth dropped open made her think she'd offended him. "There are no babysitters here. We offer more than child care. You'll be teaching the kids about river travel, everything from the history of steamers in the Civil War to the math and science behind steam engines. We've got a collection of lesson plans all ready to go."

Okay, so a *glorified* babysitter. "This isn't what I expected."

"What did you think I was hiring you to do?"

After she explained it to him, Beau shook his head. "We already have an onboard historian—our pawpaw."

"Your grandpa?" They actually let that cantankerous old geezer interact with the public? "The same guy who brews moonshine and sells it in baby food jars at the farmer's market?"

Beau scratched the back of his neck and took a sudden interest in his shoes. "Yeah, that's him."

"Isn't there somewhere else you can use me?"

When Beau glanced up, a hint of mischief twinkled in his eyes. "I can think of a dozen delightful ways to use you, Kitten. But the only staffer I need is right here in the center."

Devyn slumped against the doorjamb and sighed, too deflated to think of a witty comeback. She could barely tolerate two hours in the company of little kids, let alone two weeks. The worst part was that after this assignment lurked an equally soul-sucking job of playing dress-up and leading strangers to her ancestors' graves. There seemed to be no end in sight to her troubles, no second chances.

This was her life now.

"Don't look so excited," Beau said, his tone flat.

"It's just . . ."

"This isn't what you expected," he finished.

"Yeah." She pulled in a fortifying breath. "But don't worry. I'll survive. I can handle almost anything for two weeks."

"Nice attitude." Beau's mood shifted, darkening while he folded both arms across his chest. "Because that's what every kid wants—to feel like a temporary burden for you to survive."

She spun on him. "How dare you try to dump a guilt trip on me! I didn't ask for this. You strong-armed me into coming here, remember?"

"Yeah." He closed the distance between them until they stood an inch apart, with the set of his shoulders every bit as tight as his mouth. Even though she hadn't done anything wrong, his heated stare made Devyn want to hide her face. "I thought this job would be good for you."

He couldn't be serious. "Good for me, how?"

Beau pointed at the miniature chairs surrounding the classroom table. "This was your dream once—and you were good at it. Maybe you've forgotten, but I haven't. I was hoping you could reconnect with that old passion and do something with your life."

She matched his stubborn stance, folding her arms and refusing to look at him. What Beau didn't seem to comprehend was that high school was a long time ago. A lot had changed since then. Including herself.

Beau cupped her chin and turned her to face him. "I know how you bounce from one dead-end job to the next. Allie told me. You're floundering, Dev."

"No, I'm not."

"Yes, you are. And you're better than that."

She pushed away his hand, but she couldn't refute his words. There was truth in his statement—the kind of raw honesty that settled in her lungs and choked her.

"Spend the day here," he said. "Go through the lesson plans. Decide whether this is something you think you could be good at. If it's not, I'll let you off the hook." He lowered his head and used his eyes to deliver an ultimatum. "All or nothing. I won't let you half-ass it. Are we clear?"

Devyn nodded.

"I'll be in the casino installing some new slots," he said. "Come find me when you make up your mind."

"Baking soda?"

Devyn stepped inside the walk-in pantry and scanned the shelves until she found what she was looking for. She pulled back the industrial-sized plastic lid and peered inside. "Half a can."

"I'll add it to the list." Allie scribbled on her notepad.

After an hour of skimming riverboat-themed craft ideas and rolling her eyes at cheesy historical role-playing activities, Devyn had snuck out of the education center to the boat's galley to help her sister inventory ingredients. The task wasn't exactly a thrill ride, but at least she was in good company. Besides, she had spent so much time at the Sweet Spot bakery that she felt at home with flour in her hair and Crisco beneath her fingernails.

"I wish I could work in here with you," Devyn said.

"That makes a hell of a lot more sense than sticking me in the romper room."

Instead of weighing in with her opinion, Allie bent over her notepad and pretended to study the list she'd made—the one with only a handful of items on it.

Something was up.

"What?" Devyn asked. "Spit it out."

Allie bit her lip and glanced up with an apology in her mismatched amber-gray eyes. "I know you're not happy in the education center, and I can empathize. During the last cruise, I had to serve drinks in the casino because Chef Regale wouldn't let me in the galley. It was demeaning. But Beau really went to bat for you this morning to get you that position."

"What?" That made no sense. Beau had practically forced her into taking the job, which implied that he was desperate. Allie made it sound like there were a swarm of applicants.

"At the family meeting," Allie said, "there were a few . . . well . . . *concerns* about letting you work with the kids. But Beau wouldn't back down. It caused a fight, and things are still kind of awkward between the brothers."

Devyn's lips parted. "Nobody wants me here?" She sounded hurt, even to her own ears, though she didn't know why she cared. She didn't even like the Dumonts.

"I want you here," Allie promised. "Beau does, too. But the rest of the family"—she cringed and spoke her next words through her teeth—"they think you're a little scary."

"Me?" Devyn repeated, pointing at herself. "I'm not scary!"

Allie tipped her head and raised a brow. "Did you or did you not threaten to shove a clipboard up Nicky's ass?"

"Psh, that doesn't count," Devyn said with a flick of her wrist. "The skeevy bastard had it coming."

"Maybe, but you could have handled it like a professional." Allie tucked her pencil behind one ear. "And Ella-Claire is afraid you don't like her."

Devyn splayed both hands. "But I didn't do anything!"

"That's exactly the point," Allie said. "You didn't smile or shake her hand or show any interest in her as a person. What was she supposed to think?"

Allie was wrong about one thing. Devyn *had* shown an interest in Ella-Claire, but only as it applied to Beau. She still wanted to know if the two had done the deed. "Okay, so I could have been a little friendlier. But that doesn't mean I'm a terrifying monster who eats children."

"I know that." Allie's face broke into a gentle smile, and she crossed the galley to rest a hand on Devyn's shoulder. "You're my best friend and the finest person I've ever met. Look at how you helped me get the Sweet Spot off the ground. You could have done anything with the money Mom and Dad left us, but you used it to help buy the shop." Her eyes misted over.

Allie was such a softie. If she discovered the sad state of Devyn's bank account, she'd probably take out a second mortgage on the bakery and give back that money. Which was why she couldn't find out.

"Any good sister would have done the same," Devyn mumbled.

"Don't be so sure," Allie said. "You're special, whether or not you believe it. I want everyone else to see the real you, but first you have to let them in. It wouldn't kill you to lighten up, either."

Even if Devyn agreed with her sister's advice, which she didn't, what was the point of forging friendships with a family who had spent the last century using and discarding women? Memère had jinxed their line for a reason—her Dumont lover had ditched her at the altar, and all these years later, the men in that clan still couldn't keep it in their pants. Just look at Beau's dad. That sleaze had enough offspring to populate a small country.

The doubt must have shown on Devyn's face, because Allie said, "They're good people. Even Beau. I know it hurt when he ran out on you—I was there to pick up the pieces—but he's not that same selfish boy anymore. He's trying to make amends. And he has faith in you."

For some odd reason, that burned even worse than hearing that his brothers didn't want her here. Devyn's chest grew heavy when she remembered the disappointment on Beau's face and the way his voice had gone soft when he'd given her the option to quit. She hated that Beau had the power to make her feel ashamed, but he did.

"You should stay and give it a try," Allie said. "What's the worst that can happen?"

"I could get pinkeye. That stuff runs rampant in day cares."

"Never killed anyone."

"What about norovirus? I could die from dehydration."

"The nurse has meds for that."

"The boat could sink."

Allie playfully shoved Devyn's shoulder. "Then we'll go down together. It'll be way more interesting than dying of old age."

A smile played across Devyn's lips. Leave it to Allie to put things in perspective. "Okay, but if we have a *Titanic* moment, you'd better not let me go like Rose did to Jack."

"Never. You're stuck with me." Allie gathered her in a hug.

"Can you handle inventory on your own?" Devyn asked. "I need to find Beau."

"Go ahead." Allie offered a gentle push toward the door to make her point. "But be sweet to him, okay? He really did—"

"Go to bat for me," Devyn finished. "Yeah, yeah. I know."

What she didn't know was why he'd fought so hard. Refusing to give it any further thought, she left the galley and followed the signs to the casino on the second floor. When she reached the double doors, she steeled herself and walked inside.

The noise of Metallica greeted her on the stereo, along with the vibrant greens of felt-covered blackjack tables and the flash of neon beer signs. Even with the overhead lights turned on and the rows of electronic slots lying dormant, Devyn was so visually overwhelmed that it took a moment to spot Beau in the back of the room near the bar. He didn't notice as she approached, so she kept her footsteps quiet and watched him work.

A sheen of sweat had glued Beau's T-shirt to his skin as he hauled an outdated video poker machine from the bar and replaced it with a new one featuring wizards or maybe a vampire theme. It was hard to tell because Devyn was too distracted by the man installing it. His powerful biceps bunched as he repositioned the heavy machinery. He was so completely male that it stopped Devyn in her tracks. He must have sensed her watching, because he turned and widened his eyes in surprise.

"Hey." Beau lifted the front of his shirt and used it to wipe the sweat from his face. "I didn't hear you come in."

God help her. His flat slab of a belly was even harder than she remembered, all rippling muscle with a dusting of dark hair that encircled his navel and dipped below the waistband of his jeans. In another lifetime, she'd spent hours lying beside him in the cool shaded grass and let her fingernails trace that happy trail to where it ended. Which had resulted in a whole lot of heavy breathing. Her body remembered all too well.

Even now, her blood warmed with recognition and sent heat pooling south of the border.

Damn her Judas lady bits.

"You done?" he asked, pointing at his exposed stomach. "Or do you want another minute?" When she answered by way of her middle finger, he tugged down his shirt. "So, did you make a decision?"

"Yeah," she said. "I'm sticking around."

"Really?" The way his whole face lit up told her he wasn't expecting that answer. "I'm glad to hear it."

Devyn studied her fingernails and pretended that his reaction didn't cause her heart to swell. "What can I say? I love a challenge."

"Come up with your own lesson plans if you want," he said. "Let Ella-Claire know if you need any supplies, but try to keep it to a small list. We're on a budget."

"Sure." The room began to feel small with the two of them standing there, Beau smiling at her like she'd just told him he won the Powerball. She took a step back, and then another. But she couldn't leave before saying one last thing. "Thanks, by the way."

"For what?"

"Allie told me what you did. I don't know why you want me around so badly, but I'm glad you stood up for me."

A crooked grin tugged Beau's lips as he leaned an elbow on the bar. "Why, Devyn Mauvais. Are you being nice?"

She heaved a sigh. Why did he have to go and ruin

it? "Enjoy it while you can. This is a onetime deal." Then she left the sweaty caveman to his work and returned to the education center.

She'd rock this job, if for no other reason than to spite the Dumonts.

Chapter 4

When the day came for the *Belle* to embark on a two-week tour of the Mississippi, Devyn reported for duty wearing a frilly lace-up corset dress instead of her uniform of a staff polo and khakis. Her costume wasn't the most historically accurate of reproductions—in fact, she looked more like a pirate's wench than a proper lady of the Victorian era—but the kids in the education center wouldn't know that. They'd see her outfit and beg to dress up themselves; then she'd launch into an enthralling history lesson that would captivate them for the rest of the afternoon.

That was the goal, anyway.

But first she needed to get her room assignment and drop off her duffel bag. When she approached the purser's desk, Ella-Claire glanced up from her computer and did a double take.

Devyn smiled, remembering her sister's words about lightening up. "History by immersion," she said. "We're playing dress-up in the center today."

"Aww." Ella tipped her head as if admiring a puppy. "What a fun idea."

Fun wasn't the word Devyn had in mind, but whatever. She dug into her dress pocket and handed over a tiny red satchel tied with yellow string, a peace offering to make up for their shaky first encounter. "I made some gris-gris for you. It's for love and luck."

Ella brought a grateful hand to her breast, her gaze softening. "Allie used to make these for me, but she quit."

"I know," Devyn said.

The fact that Allie had abandoned their heritage was a bone of contention between them. Allie claimed she had never believed in voodoo, that she'd faked the rituals and told her clients what they needed to hear to help them change. She called it self-fulfilling prophesy. Devyn called it faithlessness. Tomato, to-*mah*-to.

"She said this kind was your favorite."

"Thanks," Ella said. Still beaming, she pocketed her gift. "That was thoughtful of you."

"Anyway, I need my room assignment so I can get settled in." Devyn hoped her roommate didn't snore. She was a light sleeper, and if the Dumonts thought she was scary now, they should see her after a bout of insomnia.

Instead of looking up the information, Ella watched her in silent contemplation. When she spoke, her words were tentative. "There's an open spot in my room. If you want it."

Luckily, Devyn was able to maintain her smile, despite mingled feelings on the offer. Ella-Claire seemed like a sweet girl, but if they had both slept with Beau . . . well, that could make for an awkward two weeks on the water. However, there was no way to decline the invitation without hurting Ella's feelings, so in the end, the decision made itself.

Devyn made a show of widening her eyes in enthusiasm. "Really? That would be awesome! Allie's told me so many wonderful things about you."

"You, too!" Ella said as she flashed a thousand-watt smile that made Devyn instantly regret any negative thoughts she'd had about the girl. Ella was so excited that her ponytail was swinging. "Here," she said, handing over an old-fashioned key on a string. "Staff rooms are down below. We're in lucky number thirteen. I already took the bottom bunk, so I hope you don't mind the top."

Bunk beds? Devyn suppressed a sigh. What was next, days-of-the-week underpants and juice boxes? "That's my favorite," she lied smoothly. "See you around, roomie."

She made her way down to room thirteen and unlocked the door. When she let herself inside, she nearly banged her shins on the bed frame. She had assumed the rooms would be small, but this was more like a closet. Between the bunks and a single dresser pressed against the side wall, there was barely enough room to turn around. And she had to share this space with a roommate?

Good thing she wasn't claustrophobic.

She tossed her duffel onto the top mattress and noticed an adjoining doorway. It seemed they had their own bathroom. That was something to be grateful for . . . or so she thought. A peek inside showed nothing but a miniature sink and a standing shower stall, the whole bathroom no bigger than an airplane lavatory. Where was the toilet?

She texted the question to her sister.

Moments later, Allie replied, *Check behind the shower curtain.*

Devyn pulled aside the plastic panel and gasped out loud. Her fingers flew over the cell phone screen. *Are you f-ing kidding me? A toilet in the shower??? That's so wrong!*

Biting her lip, she glanced at her duffel bag. She hadn't unpacked it yet. If she hurried, she might be able to give her resignation and escape before the boat pulled away from the dock.

I know, right? Allie texted. *Even the suites are like that. You get used to it after a while.*

"Not friggin' likely," Devyn muttered. *We can drink when we're off duty, right? Because I'm going to need a stiff one later.*

Allie replied, *That's what SHE said.* ☺

A much-needed laugh shook Devyn's chest. *You're warped. Wish me luck today.*

You make your own luck.

No arguments there. And since there was no use in delaying the inevitable, Devyn headed to the education center for her first day of "school."

She found the room empty, which didn't surprise her because the passengers were still boarding. The quiet was exactly what she needed to calm her jittery pulse, so she used the lull to her advantage by arranging a variety of hats and old-style vests on the table, along with the scavenger hunt worksheets she'd prepared. She had just finished going over her plans for the day when heavy footsteps drew her attention to the doorway.

Only one person could make such a clatter walking on foam tiles, and when she turned to face him, her already unstable pulse skipped a beat. Beau was in uniform—wearing a gold-embellished white dress shirt and coat over freshly-pressed slacks, a black tie knotted at the base of his broad neck. The effect was strikingly debonair, even with sunglasses pushed atop his head.

Clearly God was trying to test her.

Grinning like the devil himself, Beau appraised her costume, and in a few smooth strides, he closed the distance between them. Devyn knew she should back up, but he held her captive with his mesmerizing green gaze, and her feet refused to budge. He smelled delicious in his unique way. Familiar, like Irish Spring soap and store-brand shampoo. No frills for this man.

"Nice." His words dripped honey while he dragged an index finger slowly down the length of her corset laces, then all the way back up again. "*Very* nice."

Devyn's corset stays must have been too tight, because it took a moment to catch her breath. "You're not too painful to look at either."

"Not too painful?" he repeated with a deep chuckle. "Enough with the wild praise, darlin'. You're making me blush."

Darlin'. Like that meant anything. He said it to all the girls, including Devyn's new roommate. The reminder helped snap her out of whatever lusty haze she'd fallen into. She smacked his hand and skirted the table to gain some distance. "I've got a job to do, so if you don't mind . . ."

"Not at all." In one quick motion, he snagged her fingers and bent to sweep a kiss over her knuckles. His eyes never left hers, and she felt the touch of his lips in more places than just her hand. "I'll be back to check on you later."

Before she could tell him not to bother, he strode from the room.

Devyn blew out a breath and tried to refocus. She tracked down ten pencils and clipboards, just in case all of her students showed up for the scavenger hunt, but an hour passed without the pitter-patter of any feet, little or otherwise. Eventually the room director, who doubled as one of the infant caregivers, joined her.

Mrs. Grayson explained that most passengers would keep their children with them on the first day, to acclimate them to the new environment. "The only people who'll make drop-offs today," she confided behind her hand, "are the ones who don't want their kids here."

"But if the parents want to be alone, why bring the

kids at all?" Devyn had seen the brochures, and more specifically, the fare breakdown. Two weeks aboard the *Belle* cost more than the same number of nights at a top-notch Caribbean resort. And kids weren't free.

Mrs. Grayson turned up her palms. "It happens. More often than not, because of custody arrangements or last-minute changes of plan."

"Ah." Devyn understood. "It's Mom's week to have the kids, and Dad can't keep them."

"Something like that."

As it turned out, the woman nailed it. When the first—and only—children shuffled into the education center that afternoon, they were brothers tagging along on a honeymoon with their mom and brand-new stepdad. Devyn didn't know which was worse, having to bring your kids on your honeymoon, or being the kid. Because, seriously. How awkward.

The first boy, a shaggy-haired nine-year-old in a Super Mario Bros. T-shirt, crept into the room in baby steps while scanning his surroundings. When his gaze landed on the video gaming station in the back corner, he stood a bit straighter and lengthened his stride until he stood before Devyn with a hopeful grin.

But his big brother clearly resented being here. Wearing a Saints ball cap and a frown, the twelve-year-old sauntered forward with both hands shoved in his pockets and gave an eye roll that said, *I'm too old for this shit.*

Devyn felt him loud and clear. *Welcome to my world, kid.* She brightened her smile and invited the boys to join her at the table, where she'd arranged all her materials. "I'm Miss Mauvais, and I'm glad you came. It was getting too quiet in here."

The younger one pointed at the gaming station. "Do you have *Super Smash Brothers Brawl*?"

Devyn blinked at him. Was he speaking English?

Without asking permission, he bolted to the corner and tore open the plastic bin of games, then started digging through dozens of cases. His brother shuffled over in his Converse Chucks and picked through a second bin. Neither had seemed to notice her costume, or maybe they just didn't care. Devyn looked to Mrs. Grayson for guidance, but found none. The woman told Devyn she was taking her lunch break and left her alone with the boys.

She watched them pluck a case from the bin and inspect the gaming disk for scratches. When the older brother moved to turn on the Nintendo, she stopped him.

"Here's the thing . . ." Devyn took the game from them and set it next to the television. "I know it's vacation, but I'm supposed to teach you something." She glanced at the information cards their mother had filled out. "In fact, I have to sign some forms telling your school what you learned on this trip, or your absence won't be excused."

Both boys groaned.

"Hey," she said, resting a hand on her heart. "I don't make the rules."

"But this is supposed to be fun," whined the younger boy. "Mom promised."

"I'll make you a deal," Devyn said. "For every two minutes you spend with me, I'll give you one minute on the Nintendo. That should give you about an hour to play after the main lesson."

The older brother pursed his lips in consideration, obviously doing that math. "Together or separate?"

"Together," she said. "There's only one console, so you'll have to pick two-player games anyway."

He heaved an epic sigh worthy of the most angst-ridden tween. "Fine. Whatever." He gave his brother a knowing look. "It's not like we have a say in *any* of this."

Devyn had a feeling the kid was referring to more than just a history lesson. "I hear your mom got married. That's exciting, huh?"

A glare was his only reply.

Devyn didn't let it get her down. With this age group, sulking was par for the course. "It was nice of her to bring you on the honeymoon. My parents never took me anywhere."

When neither boy responded, she decided to dispense with the pleasantries. "Here." She handed them each a clipboard, then swept a hand over the dress-up clothes on the table. "Pick an outfit and we'll get this party started."

The nine-year-old—whose name was Will, according to his information card—eagerly snatched up a satin top hat and a gentlemanly vest and put them on. But his older brother, Jason, was having none of that nonsense. He folded his arms and cocked his head to the side in the unmistakable gesture for *Oh, hell naw.*

"Or not," she mumbled.

The first item on the scavenger hunt list was to learn the emergency exit that led outside to the lifeboats. Devyn showed the boys how to follow the signs to the main deck, and for the next couple of hours, she led them on an activity-based tour of the most useful parts of the boat: the main dining hall, the purser's desk, the library, the theater, and the recreation room. When she caught Jason checking his watch, she took the brothers to the pilothouse to watch Marc drive the *Belle*. Even Devyn was impressed by the gadgetry on display, but instead of admiring the control panels or asking to blow the steam whistle, the boys checked the time and told her they'd earned an hour on the Nintendo.

Devyn was forced to admit she'd lost the battle. With a heavy heart, she accompanied her students back to the education center, where they spent the rest of the afternoon playing an old video game they admittedly didn't even like. The figurative cherry on her sundae of failure was when Beau dropped in to check on her, exactly as he'd promised.

She hugged a clipboard to her chest as he took the seat across from her at the table. "It's not what you think," she said, nodding toward the noises of *BOING, BOING, BOING, BWOOP!* "They earned that game."

"Relax, hon." Beau rested an arm on the back of a vacant chair beside him, easy like Sunday morning. And it would be easy for him. He'd spent half his childhood on this boat. "You don't know what I'm thinking."

"Spare me. These kids are neck-deep in Mario World, and you think I'm not doing my job."

He laughed under his breath, shaking his head. "Not even close."

"Oh, yeah?" She leaned toward him with a challenge in her voice. "What, then?"

An impish grin played on his lips. "Maybe I saw you a few hours ago when you walked through the lobby," he said, reaching across the table to take her clipboard, his voice lowering to a whisper. "Maybe I noticed how freakin' hot you were in that dress, and I couldn't get you out of my head all day. Maybe I walked in here and imagined undoing all those laces . . . with my teeth." He wagged his brows. "Maybe that's what I was thinking."

Devyn's cheeks grew warm when she imagined him untying her corset laces, but in her fantasy, Beau used his strong, dexterous hands. The tips of his fingers would be rough when they brushed her skin, and her breasts would fit perfectly within his big palms—she remembered that detail quite well.

"Wouldn't surprise me." Devyn let her curls fall forward, hoping to conceal the blush he'd brought to her face. "Your mind's always in the gutter."

"Not always," he objected. "Only when you're around."

She didn't believe that—once a Dumont, always a Dumont.

Deciding to derail that train of thought, she turned her attention to the boys. "Anyway, I had to bribe them to participate in my lesson. From the way they acted, you'd think I was dragging them over fifty yards of broken glass."

"Give yourself some slack," Beau said. "They're kids on vacation. Everyone needs some down time."

Devyn supposed he was right, but she hated that the boys would leave here and dread returning in the morning. "Still. How do I make it fun for them?"

Beau shrugged and stated the obvious. "They're boys." When she gave him a *No shit, Sherlock* glare, he added, "Appeal to what boys like."

"And what's that?"

He cracked his knuckles and thought about it. "When I was that age, I was into country music, video games, football, and girls. Not necessarily in that order."

Devyn grabbed her clipboard away from him. "Real helpful, thanks."

"Oh, and blowing things up. That's some good, clean, redneck fun, right there."

"You're a regular genius," she said with an eye roll. "However can I repay your sage advice?"

When he grinned, she quickly amended, "Don't answer that."

Laughing, Beau stood from the table and ruffled her

hair. "You'll be fine. Just dip a little deeper into your bag of tricks, that's all."

"You make it sound so simple," Devyn said as she straightened her curls and slouched. What she needed was more tricks in her bag.

"They're boys. It doesn't get any simpler than that."

But he was wrong.

Over the next three days, Devyn dug all the way to the bottom of her bag of tricks, to no avail. Her lesson on the math and science of paddle-wheel propulsion was a bust, the kids tuned out her informative lecture on the economy of interstate trade, and one boy actually nodded off while playing the "boat race" board game she'd spent all day building.

She was officially tapped out.

"How about crafts?" suggested Ella-Claire one night from the bottom bunk. "Maybe a scrapbook of their trip? The students can color pictures and keep a journal for a keepsake to take home."

Devyn shifted on her mattress to dodge a rogue spring poking her hip. "These kids are too old for crafts. They're in that weird in-between age when they're too young to sit still for lectures but too mature for crayons and finger paint. I'm competing for their attention with Mario and Luigi, and I'm getting my ass kicked."

"Well, in all fairness, they do have Princess Peach."

"And Yoshi."

"Yeah," Ella said. "The deck is totally stacked against you."

A series of musical knocks rapped at the door, followed by a man's voice. He sounded close, as if he'd pushed his lips against the crack between the door and the wall. "Elles-Bells," he called. "You awake?"

"Elles-Bells?" asked Devyn.

"It's Alex. Mind if I let him in?"

"Go ahead. All my interesting parts are covered."

Ella flipped back her blanket and answered the door . . . wearing nothing but a T-shirt that barely covered her panties, something that didn't escape Devyn's notice. When Ella turned on the light and let Thing Two inside, her wardrobe choice didn't escape his notice either. His eyes flew cartoonishly wide and locked on to Ella's legs.

"You could have told me you weren't decent," he said, still staring.

"Dork." Playfully, Ella shoved him in the shoulder. But unlike the casual touches she gave the other Dumont brothers, this one lingered. She threaded an arm through his and peered up at him with more than just warmth in her gaze—this was full-on heat. Interesting. "You saw a lot more than this when we went tubing on Saturday."

A dopey smile broke out on Thing Two's face. "*And* when we went fishing the weekend before that. God bless that little string bikini of yours." He parked his backside on the edge of the dresser and seemed to notice Devyn for the first time. When he spotted her, his brows jumped like she'd caught him doing something wrong, and he detangled his arm from Ella's. Very interesting. "Oh," he said with a shaky wave. "Hey, Devyn."

She waved back and propped on one elbow to study him. Devyn was no behavioral analyst, but it seemed like Thing Two had a *thing* for Marc's half sister. Devyn pointed back and forth between the pair. "You two are . . ." She trailed off, thick with the implication.

"Friends," Thing Two said quickly, and with a bit more emphasis than necessary.

"Best friends," Ella clarified. "Since we were kids."

"Uh-huh." Best friends with benefits, probably. "How sweet."

While Thing Two and Ella-Claire huddled around his iPhone to watch a funny video he'd found online, Devyn pulled her own cell from beneath her pillow.

Ella-Claire and Alex, she texted her sister, *are they an item?*

A few minutes later, Allie texted back. *Officially? No. Marc would lose his shit. None of the brothers have laid a hand on Ella. Unofficially? Yeah, they're both totally sprung. It's kind of cute.*

Devyn found herself smiling, but not out of joy for the secret lovers currently giggling at the latest SNL digital short. She smiled because of the other thing Allie told her: if none of the Dumont brothers had touched Ella-Claire, it meant Ella and Beau hadn't knocked boots. Devyn shouldn't mind either way, but there was no denying that her chest felt lighter than it had five minutes ago.

Don't be a sap, she criticized inwardly. *This doesn't mean anything.*

To dial down her excitement a few notches, she forced herself to recall the morning after graduation, when she'd awoken naked and alone in a two-person sleeping bag, hungover and snuggling the school mascot she and Beau had "liberated" the night before from its pen. She'd trusted Beau with her heart, and he'd skipped town without so much as a good-bye. A six-word note had arrived in the mail from boot camp a couple of weeks later, but his half illegible *Sorry, Dev, I joined the Marines* was no consolation for what she'd suffered.

He'd hurt her once, and he would do it again if she gave him the chance.

Her sister's words turned over in her head. *He's not that same selfish boy anymore. He's trying to make amends. And he has faith in you.*

Was that true?

Devyn didn't know. But no matter how hard she tried to push Beau Dumont out of her thoughts, she drifted to sleep dreaming about one of her happiest memories—their first date.

Instead of defaulting to dinner and a movie, Beau had borrowed his pawpaw's boat and motored them to his top-secret fishing hole, the one he'd never even shared with his brothers. The fact that he trusted her with something so special made Devyn's heart flutter, and she couldn't stop sneaking sideways glances at his full mouth as they dangled their poles in the water. It was a perfect spring evening, the low sun sharpening the angles of Beau's masculine cheekbones and bringing out the reddish hues in his hair.

He was breathtaking.

"Any nibbles?" he whispered, nodding at her motionless fishing line.

Devyn shook her head. She wanted to talk to him, but the nervous butterflies in her tummy had stolen her voice.

"Soon," he promised, then winked and nearly made her ovaries explode. "This place is magical. The fish can't resist me here."

Devyn couldn't imagine a living creature resisting Beau in *any* location, but instead of saying so, she blushed and gazed out at the water.

He was right. Within minutes, she hooked a five-pound catfish. The gleam of admiration in Beau's eyes made her want to throw it back and catch an even bigger one, but she reeled in the fish and settled against Beau's chest when he moved behind her.

"Nice catch," Beau murmured in her ear as he pulled the hook free. "You're a natural."

Devyn turned to look at him. "I can't take the credit. Like you said, this place is enchanted."

His lips slid into a crooked grin, and just like that, she was done for. He glanced at her mouth for one infinite moment while her heart thumped in anticipation of his next move. Then, right there, with a squirming catfish in hand, Beau kissed her for the first time.

It was remarkably tender—a light brush of lips that lingered, making her feel like the most cherished girl in the bayou. When he pulled back, he smiled down at her and whispered, "Magical."

She agreed. Something was blooming between them... something unearthly. And she loved every minute of it.

Chapter 5

"Come on, cowboy," Beau muttered to himself. "Keep your hands where I can see 'em."

Pressing his nose against the one-way glass, Beau squinted across the casino to the high-dollar poker table, where a gambler in his mid-forties and wearing a black Stetson kept dropping one hand into his lap. Anyone with a lick of common sense knew better than to do that, especially the professionals. Beau supposed it was possible the cowboy had a case of jock itch, but he doubted it.

He checked the closed circuit television feed on the monitor affixed to the wall, but the overhead view was no better. For the life of him, he couldn't tell whether the gambler was innocently digging in his pocket for a stick of gum or swapping out cards. If the guy was cheating, he was as subtle about it as a bullhorn.

Beau checked the floor for Nicky, spotting him making the rounds near the craps table. He called his brother's cell and watched him answer it.

"Be cool," Beau said. "But I don't like what I'm seeing at the high stakes poker table. Check out the guy in the black cowboy hat."

Nick had worked the casino floor since the day he'd turned twenty-one, so he knew to rotate casually and flick a glance in that direction. He pretended to wave his congratulations to a slot winner while reporting to Beau. "Dark wash jeans, black Laredos, nursing a whisky sour, and a little twitchy?"

Damn, that boy was good. "You got it."

"Want me to pay him a visit?"

"Yeah, but be friendly." They needed to proceed with caution. Each passenger had paid a pretty penny for two luxurious, stress-free weeks on board the *Belle*, and Beau's first priority was keeping the customers happy and coming back for more. Word of mouth advertising was king, and nothing would turn off a return traveler faster than an insult . . . like a false accusation of cheating. "Bring the table a round of drinks," he said. "Some complimentary sandwiches, too. That should get you plenty close."

"I'm on it."

While Nick put in his order at the bar, Beau watched the overhead feed. He made a mental note to talk with the blackjack dealer about the tipping procedure. He didn't suspect the woman of anything shady, but once in a while, a gambler would slide over a chip to tip her, and she'd neglect to tap it on the table before dropping it in her shirt pocket. It was standard practice to help Beau identify legitimate money leaving the table, and she should know better. Aside from that, everything looked kosher. There were barely any vacant stools at the gaming tables, and all the slots were occupied.

That was what Beau liked to see.

He noticed Nicky balancing a tray on one arm and making his way to the poker table. With a disarming smile, Nick set a drink in front of each player. If Beau hadn't been looking for it, he never would have noticed his brother's gaze dipping into the cowboy's lap. After handing out a few sandwiches, Nick strode back to the bar and disappeared off camera into the storage area, which meant he would soon be joining Beau in the security room.

The door opened and Nick slid inside with a laugh. "Well, he's cheating, but not on us."

"Translation, please?"

Nicky held up his left hand. "Dude's wearing a wedding band, and he's sexting his mistress. Or maybe the girl's just a booty call. I can't be sure, but he's certainly looking to hook up with someone named Jill."

Beau let out a breath, both relieved the guy wasn't scamming the house and annoyed by the infidelity. Having grown up watching his mama's heart shatter after each of his daddy's indiscretions, he had no tolerance for assholes who fooled around. He hated his dad for keeping Mama on the hook all those years, coming around every so often to spend a night or two, staying just long enough to get her hopes up again. Despite popular opinion, breaking up really wasn't hard to do.

If you didn't want to be with your lover, you should end it before moving on.

Beau glanced out the one-way glass at the cowboy, who'd just glanced into his lap to tap another text. He wanted to give the guy the benefit of the doubt.

"How do you know he's not sexting with his wife?" he asked.

"Easy," Nick said. "Because his last message said *I'll meet you in your suite as soon as my wife falls asleep.*"

Beau shook his head in contempt. "Dickhead."

Nicky shrugged and checked his own messages, seemingly unbothered by the stranger's behavior. Probably because the twins' mama had wised up and kicked Daddy to the curb shortly after she gave birth. Then she'd married a pharmacist and never looked back. Nick and Alex had escaped the fate of most Dumont boys, winding up with a white picket fence. They didn't understand how it was for Marc, Beau, and little Jackson—or Worm, as folks called him. The three of them knew the shame of wanting to protect their mothers and falling short. No doubt the new baby that Daddy had sired would learn soon enough, too.

Poor kid.

Beau realized he was clenching his jaw, so he took a deep breath and shook off thoughts of his father. The old man wasn't worth it.

"Hey," he said to Nicky. "Take over for me, will you? I'm cutting out for a break." It was four thirty, and if he hurried, he could catch the end of Devyn's lesson before the education center closed for the day. Seeing her gorgeous face never failed to cheer him up, and recently she gave him two smiles for every glare—progress.

"You got it, boss."

On his way out, Beau crossed through the casino and discreetly offered a few of the high rollers free tickets to an offshore excursion in Natchez. Then he left behind the plinking noise of slot payouts and stepped into the blissful silence of the hallway. When he reached the education center, he inched open the door and tiptoed inside.

Devyn had tacked a diagrammed steam engine poster to the wall, and she stood beside it, pointing to the high pressure cylinder. "Exhaust steam comes from here . . ." She trailed off and blew a lock of hair from her eye, then sighed when she noticed two boys playing rock-paper-scissors under the table.

"Can we play Nintendo now?" asked the oldest kid in the group, a blond who crossed his arms and slouched in his chair.

The girl next to him asked, "When's my mom coming?"

Beau took a knee on the foam tiles beside the table. When Devyn noticed him, she attempted a grin, but it didn't reach her eyes. She looked like she needed a hug.

"Can we go outside again?" lisped the youngest boy.

"No, I want to finish explaining how the *Belle*'s engine works," Devyn said. "Don't you think it's awesome that something as simple as steam can power this big boat?"

The kids provided their answer in the form of silence.

Devyn hooked a thumb at the poster. "After the steam leaves this chamber . . ." She paused again and locked eyes with him, and then something new sparked behind her gaze. Her lips parted in thought for a few moments before she said, "You know what? Forget this. Who likes to blow stuff up?"

Backs straightened and eyebrows rose. Scattered cries of *Yeah!* and *Me!* and *I do!* filled the room while Beau's stomach dropped an inch. Where was Devyn going with this?

"Blowing up something is called an explosion," she explained. "Does anyone know what the opposite of 'explode' is?"

The slouchy kid said, "Implode."

"Exactly." Devyn bent low to make eye contact with her now-attentive class. "Who wants to see me make a Coke can implode using the power of steam?"

Every hand in the room shot up.

"Okay, then." She pointed to Beau with a grin so infectious it lifted the corners of his own mouth. "Mr. Dumont, would you like to be my assistant?"

"Yes, ma'am." He pushed up from the floor and rubbed his hands together, relieved that she had no plans to ignite the boat. "Just tell me what to do."

"I saw an electric hot plate in the break room," Devyn said. "I'll need that and a pot of cold water. A pair of tongs, too. Oh, and an empty Coke can."

"Hot plate, tongs, cold water, Coke," he repeated. "Be right back."

Ten minutes later, he returned with the supplies and helped Devyn set up her experiment on the table while the kids sat at a safe distance, cross-legged on the floor. She put a small amount of water in the Coke can and set it on the burner to boil, then placed the pot of cold water in the center of the table. When a light mist wafted up from the can, she held a piece of black paper behind it so the kids could see the steam.

"Look," Devyn said, holding her palm over the can. "It's just a tiny bit of steam. Not even enough to burn me."

It was five o'clock, and several parents had filed into the room to pick up their little ones. Beau welcomed them to take a seat beside their kids, and soon Devyn had a captive audience of nearly twenty onlookers.

"Now watch what happens when I turn it upside down in the pot of cold water." Using the tongs, she clasped the bottom of the Coke can. "The temperature difference is going to create a vacuum and make the can . . ." She leaned forward and raised an expectant brow.

"Implode!" shouted the kids.

"That's right." She paused, heightening the anticipation. "Is everyone ready?"

The children nodded.

"Count down with me," Devyn said. "Three . . . two . . . one!"

She turned the can upside down, and the instant it touched the surface of the water, a loud *THWOOP!* thundered in the air, making the kids jump. Just like that, the can was decimated, completely crushed as if she'd taken a sledgehammer to it. Devyn held her tongs forward to show everyone.

Wild applause broke out from the audience. From the look of admiration in the kids' eyes, you'd think Devyn had summoned fire from her hands. She flourished the crushed can and took a bow.

"Thank you," she said with a playful wink. "I'm here all week. Don't forget to tip your server."

The oldest kid perked up and begged, "Do it again!"

"Tomorrow," Devyn promised. "I'll plan some other steam projects, too. So be here bright and early."

The children nodded eagerly and bounced on their toes, still chattering about the experiment as their parents led them into the hallway. Once the center had vacated, Beau told the director, "I'd like a word with Miss Mauvais. You can go on to supper, and I'll make sure to lock up when we leave." After Mrs. Grayson made her exit, Beau shut the door behind her and turned to Devyn.

"That was amazing," he said. "You knocked it out of the ball park."

She waved him off with a grin.

"How did you come up with the idea?"

A glow radiated from Dev's face, the unmistakable pride of a job well done. "I saw someone run the same experiment my freshman year in college, but I'd forgotten all about it. Then you came in, and I remembered what you said about blowing things up." She used a hand to mimic an explosion. "Boom. It triggered a memory."

"And you made fun of my *sage advice,*" he teased. "Guess I'm useful for something, after all."

"Very useful." The joy shining behind her gaze made Beau's chest tight. He couldn't recall any reward greater than seeing her this happy. "Thank you, Beau."

Beau. She'd said his name.

Such a simple thing, and yet the gentle sound of it on her tongue lit him up like the Vegas strip. A surge of emotions swelled inside his lungs, and he acted without thinking. He eliminated the distance between them and took Devyn's face between his hands. Then he fulfilled his greatest fantasy from the last ten years—he kissed her.

Her lips were every bit as soft as he remembered, the honeyed taste of her mouth so achingly familiar that it gave him chills, even after all this time. If he thought the *Belle* felt like home, it was nothing compared to kissing Devyn.

Now he was home.

Despite the drive to take more, he didn't rush. Instead, he moved with deliberate care to give her a chance to respond, and when she opened to him, he explored her thoroughly with slow, sensual licks that had her groaning into his mouth.

Locking both arms around his neck, Dev stood on tiptoe and angled her head to deepen the kiss. The tip of her soft tongue stroked his while every inch of her body crushed against him. Beau's tenuous grasp on control snapped in half. He fisted her shirt and hugged her closer while he plundered her mouth with a decade's worth of bottled-up passion.

Suddenly, he couldn't get enough. It was as if a vacuum had opened up inside him, just like the flattened Coke can, and nothing but Devyn could fill the void. Every drop of blood in his body turned hot and rushed between his legs, every part of him begging to be inside her. He made love to her mouth, stopping only long enough to steal a ragged breath.

Before he knew what he'd done, he'd pushed her against the wall and lifted her by her ass so she could wrap her legs around him. She wasted no time in hooking her ankles behind his back and straining against the ridge of his erection. A shock of pleasure tore through his groin and ricocheted down the length of his thighs. He swallowed a curse and rocked into her.

At the contact, Devyn made the same adorable mewling sound that had earned her nickname back in high school. It was the hottest fucking noise on the planet, and Beau damn near blew in his pants.

"Kitten," he whispered against her mouth. "I missed you."

She pulled back, panting. Her eyes were thick with lust, her lips slick and swollen. She opened her mouth to speak but shut it again and darted a glance at the wide display windows lining the front wall. Then she nodded toward the other side of the room.

"Supply closet," she said. "Hurry."

Devyn's wish was his command.

Careful not to trip over discarded toys and games, he carried her to the closet and threw open the door. A glance inside made him wonder if they would both fit.

Shelves cluttered with Play-Doh, paints, and craft supplies lined the closet walls on three sides with a vacuum cleaner taking up half the floor space. There wouldn't be room to turn around, but he didn't much care. He ducked his head and wedged their bodies inside, then shut the door, enveloping them in darkness.

Devyn didn't miss a beat. With her legs still wrapped around his waist, she unbuttoned his dress coat and rubbed her hands up and down his chest, sucking in a breath as if she'd just seen the Grand Canyon for the first time. He wanted to touch her too, ached to feel the weight of her breast in his palm. Beau supported her with one arm and tried slipping his free hand up the front of her shirt, but he banged his elbow on the shelf and knocked an object to the floor with a *thunk*. For an instant, he worried there might be paint seeping onto the carpet, but then Devyn started grinding again, and she wiped his mind clean of everything but the sweet pressure building behind his fly.

"Damn, baby." He nuzzled the side of her neck and gently nipped her delicate flesh. "You feel so good."

"Mmm," she agreed, digging her heels into his backside for more leverage.

Beau's eyes had adjusted to the darkness, and he pulled back to gaze at her. He repeated, "I missed you. Tell me you missed me, too."

Dev's teeth flashed as she grinned at him. "You talk too much." She leaned closer and licked his top lip. "I think you've forgotten what your tongue is for."

Beau chuckled. Maybe she wasn't ready to forgive

him, but it was hard to be disappointed while she was riding his jock. Beau used a thumb to tease her nipple to a tight point, wishing like hell she'd worn that flimsy lace-up dress instead of a shirt and pants. And wishing twice as hard that he'd brought a condom. If he had, he'd be inside her right now.

"There's not enough room in here, Kitten," he murmured. "But if you come back to my suite, I'll peel off your clothes and make you eat those words." Then he traced the shell of her ear with his tongue to show that he still knew how to use it. "And you'll know what you've been missing."

She groaned, writhing in his arms. "It's unearthly," she whispered. "Just like the first time."

"What?" he asked.

"Nothing. Enough with the chitchat. Shut up and finish what you started."

Devyn would get no arguments from him. He kissed her, pressing her against the shelving while he thrust between her thighs in an imitation of what he wanted to do with her in bed.

Each stroke made him harder than the last, and soon the tight space was filled with the sounds of labored breathing and groans of pleasure. It occurred to him that he'd left the center door unlocked, and anyone who walked in would overhear. But Beau couldn't bring himself to care. All that mattered was release from the pressure building low in his gut.

When Devyn began panting and arching wildly against him, he quickened the tempo until she made the whimpering noise that'd always told him she was on the brink. Kisses turned clumsy as they moved together in a frenzied rhythm, the friction of their bodies making Beau throb until he couldn't hold out any longer. He remembered how Devyn liked it, so he squeezed her ass hard while rotating his hips in circles, and she came undone.

Digging her nails into his shoulders, she tipped back her head and muffled a cry while riding out her orgasm. Her ecstasy spurred his own, and seconds later, Beau bucked against her with a low groan. Violent spasms of pleasure erupted between his thighs, and he saw stars as he spilled in hot release. He rested his head against the base of Devyn's neck, his heart thundering so loud it rang in his ears. The quakes kept racking him long after his climax ended, and he rocked into her until every drop was wrung from his core.

He regained use of his brain by gradual degrees, and when his world righted itself, he was grinning like a dope and so satisfied he could have floated away on a breeze.

"Holy shit," he breathed. "We've still got it."

"I know, right?"

He kissed her forehead and gave quiet laugh. "Only you."

"*Only me* what?" she asked defensively.

"Could make me come so hard . . . or in my pants." It was going to be an uncomfortable walk back to his cabin. "It's like senior year all over again. Remember that time we snuck into the janitor's closet during study hall? I had to go to football practice with cold, wet boxers. Couldn't run worth a damn, and the coach chewed my ass."

Devyn didn't seem to enjoy hearing that. Instead of laughing with him, she detangled her legs and planted both feet on the floor, then pressed a palm to his chest in a silent message to give her some space. "I need to clean up out there."

Her abrupt reaction stunned him into a beat of silence. "You okay?"

"Fine," she insisted. "But it's cramped in here. I can't breathe."

As soon as he opened the door and took a step back, she slipped around him and began picking up toys from the floor with the single-minded determination of a lady on a mission. She didn't even pause to let her eyes adjust to the light. In seconds, she'd collected an armful and deposited the toys in the nearest bin. Beau moved forward to help her, but she extended a palm like a traffic cop.

"I've got this," she said. "You probably have a lot to do, so you can go."

Was that a dismissal? It sure sounded like one.

"Hey." He tried to catch her gaze, but she wouldn't look at him. "What's wrong?"

She folded a board game in half and shoved it inside a box. "Nothing."

"Did I hurt you?"

"Of course not."

"You came before I did, right?"

"Yes. It was great, thanks."

It was great, thanks? What was this, a business transaction?

Beau retraced his steps, trying to figure out where he'd gone wrong. Everything was fine until he'd mentioned senior year. He figured their past wasn't quite water under the bridge, but bringing up one of their best times together shouldn't have caused her to shut down.

He snagged her by the elbow. "Talk to me. Are you all right?"

When she spun on him, there was defiance in her eyes. "I'm always all right." She pointed a little red fire truck at him and repeated, "Always. I've been fine for the last ten years, and there's nothing wrong with me now."

"Why are you mad at me?" he asked. "You told me to finish what I started, and I did."

"I'm not mad at you." She threw the truck into the bin with enough force to send another toy bouncing out to the floor.

"Funny," he said. "When I woke up this morning, I didn't have 'dumbass' tattooed on my forehead." He pointed at his temple. "Is it on there now?"

She glared at him.

"I'm not an idiot, Dev. Tell me what I did wrong."

Devyn spent the next couple of minutes in silence, scurrying about the room and tidying up while Beau stood there with his arms folded, refusing to budge until she answered him. After she was finished, she stowed the electric burner inside the closet they'd recently vacated and closed the doors with a gentle *click*. She kept her back to him when she finally spoke.

"You didn't do anything wrong." Her voice was soft but wounded, like she was fighting off tears. But when he moved to join her, she extended an arm to keep him at a distance. "It's been a long day. Just go, all right?"

No. Nothing about this felt all right. "You're making me worried."

"Look, we had a good time." Her voice wasn't soft now, the frost on her tongue virtually cooling the room by a few degrees. "The fact that I don't want to cuddle afterward doesn't mean there's anything wrong with me. I'm not a clinger. I never was."

Beau wasn't stupid, and he knew what she was doing—pushing him to leave. He didn't want to walk away, but clearly she had no intention of lowering her defenses. If he stayed, it would only antagonize her. "Fine, I'll go. But I'm gonna check on you later."

She sniffed a dry laugh. "I'm not going to jump overboard because of you, Dumont. No need to flatter yourself."

A spark of anger flared in his chest. After what he'd done on graduation night, he expected to work hard to earn back Devyn's trust. But that didn't mean he would be her personal whipping boy. He walked behind her, stopping when he noticed her shoulders stiffen. He bent to her ear and said, "Since I came back to town, I've done nothing but help you, and you've thrown it in my face every time. I don't know what crawled up your ass, but come find me when you're ready to apologize. I'll be waiting."

Then he buttoned his coat, reclaimed his Man Card, and stalked back to his room to change clothes. It was a cold, sticky walk up the stairwell, which perfectly matched his mood.

So much for feeling satisfied.

Chapter 6

"This is your third batch." Allie pulled a wire basket from the deep fryer and shook bits of breaded okra onto a clean plate, then dusted them with garlic salt and parmesan cheese, just like Mama used to do. She slid the plate across the gleaming stainless steel island. "After this, the kitchen is closed, so you'd better go on and tell me what's bothering you."

Devyn pulled another beer from the industrial-sized fridge and popped the top. She took a long gulp, but all the beer and comfort food in the world wouldn't push down the self-loathing lodged in her throat. "I'm weak." She took another swig and added, "And pathetic."

"Oh, come on. Weak?" Allie pushed a stool to the opposite side of the island and took a seat. "This coming from the girl who tracked down my fifth-grade bully and gave him an atomic wedgie on the playground?"

Devyn smiled at the memory. The kid had outweighed her by fifteen pounds, but she'd had the height advantage, which had come in handy for tugging the waistband of his tighty-whities over his head. "Hey, nobody messes with my sister."

"Or *my* sister," Allie said. "So tell me what's wrong."

A frown replaced Devyn's smile, and she shoved a bite of okra into her mouth.

Allie pointed back and forth from the beer to the fried okra. "This has man trouble written all over it."

"Beau," she mumbled around her food. "Who else?"

"What did he do?"

"Strangely enough, it's not what he did," Devyn said. "It's what I did."

"Okay, so what did you do?"

Devyn used a fork to stab at the innocent chunks of okra. "After graduation, when he made all those promises and then skipped out on me, I swore I'd never take him back."

She had spent more time than she wanted to admit fantasizing about how he'd drop to his knees and beg for a second chance. In her daydreams, she had scoffed and told Beau to go to hell, then climbed inside her silver Maserati and sped away with her hot Italian boyfriend. So much for that. "He's back in town less than a month. A few crooked smiles and a handful of pretty words, and I'm dry humping him in the day-care closet."

Allie's eyes flew wide. "You did what in the where?"

"You heard me."

Devyn recalled the night of her high school reunion,

when Beau had told everyone their song was "Bump n' Grind." How appropriate. "Tell me that's not the weakest, most pathetic thing ever."

Allie's lips twitched in a poorly concealed grin as she reached for the okra. Clearly she wasn't taking this seriously. "You got some over-the-clothes action from a big, hunky guy. I'd say that's the opposite of pathetic."

"Not just any big, hunky guy, and you know it," Devyn said, raising the beer to her lips, but then she slammed the bottle back onto the steely counter. "When he kissed me, I forgot about everything I felt ten years ago—the fear when I couldn't find him, the embarrassment of being the last to know he joined the marines, the heartbreak when I realized he was gone forever. All of it just vanished."

Until afterward, when he'd mentioned the time they had fooled around in the janitor's closet. Then all those old emotions had come rushing back in a tidal wave that'd nearly had her in tears.

"Cut yourself some slack," Allie said. "You two loved each other once. Those were powerful feelings, and it sounds like neither of you really moved on."

"Maybe." But still, Devyn hated herself for how Beau had snapped his fingers and she'd come—no pun intended—faster than a bullet train. "It gets worse. He didn't like the way I acted when we, you know, were done, so he laid a guilt trip on me." She shook her head in disbelief. "After dumping me like a load of garbage, he weaseled his way between my legs again and somehow *I'm* the bad guy."

"Why are you the bad guy?"

Devyn hunched over her plate and mumbled, "I was kind of mean to him."

"Kind of?"

"Okay, totally mean. But I didn't know what to do," Devyn said, helplessly turning up her palms. "I was freaking out, and I needed to be alone. He wouldn't take a hint. He wanted to stand around and talk about the 'good old days'"—she made air quotes—"which weren't all that good, trust me."

"So you bit his head off," Allie said with a nod. "I know how you operate."

"Hey," Devyn said. That stung. "Whose side are you on anyway?"

Allie didn't hesitate to say, "Yours. Always yours. Never doubt that." She folded both arms and rested them on the island. "But you have a habit of striking out when you feel cornered or threatened. What I don't think you understand is that Beau's not a threat to you."

"How do you know?" Devyn asked, because deep down, she felt threatened and her instincts had never led her astray. "Nothing's changed." When Allie took a breath to argue, Devyn cut her off. "All right, so maybe Beau's changed. Maybe he's a new man with good intentions. But the curse is still the same. It's only a matter of time before he screws me over again, because that's what Dumont men do."

Allie rolled her eyes. "Not this nonsense."

"Yes, this *nonsense*." After everything that had happened, Devyn couldn't believe her sister still denied the curse. "The Dumont men are hexed. Don't try to blame parental example and self-fulfilling prophesy, because the women get married and ride off into the sunset—just not the guys."

"There's a perfectly good explaina—"

"Not to mention," Devyn interrupted, "the freaky stuff that happened to Marc when you two got serious." At the wedding reception, Marc had confided that each time he'd tried asking Allie to move in with him, he was unable to speak the words. He had said it was like having an invisible pillow stuffed over his face. "And when he wanted to marry you, every imaginable force of nature stood in his way."

"A coincidence," Allie said. "Nothing more."

"Oh, yeah? What about Memère's ring?" It was no coincidence that Marc had stumbled upon the engagement ring his great-great-grandfather had given their great-great-grandmother before the old fool had ditched her at the altar and suffered a curse for it.

"He was in the right place at the right time."

"Fine," Devyn said, because she'd saved her best argument for last. "Then explain the birthmark."

Exactly as expected, Allie didn't have anything to say to that.

Each Dumont man was born with a wine-colored splotch on the skin above his heart. Marc's birthmark had mysteriously disappeared on his wedding night while his brothers had retained theirs. It was how Devyn knew he'd broken the curse only for himself, not the entire family.

Allie scowled, obviously trying to come up with some psychobabble scientific explanation for what she stubbornly refused to acknowledge. "I haven't figured that out yet. But I'm sure there's a logical reason for it."

"There *is* a logical reason," Devyn said. "Memère's hex."

"Fine." The flatness of Allie's tone warned she was switching tactics. "For argument's sake, let's say there actually is a hex on the Dumonts."

That wasn't hard to do. "Okay."

"Marc and I proved that it can be broken."

"It wasn't easy, though."

"No, it wasn't," Allie agreed. "But nothing worthwhile ever is." She paused to munch on a bite of fried okra, then reached across to steal a sip of beer. "Remember how hard you tried to break the curse for me and Marc?"

Devyn nodded.

"Why not do the same for yourself?"

Because there were plenty of fish in the sea—fish without baggage. "What makes you think I want to?"

Allie glanced at the two empty plates of comfort food, cocking a brow as if no further explanation was necessary.

"Okay, so Beau and I have chemistry," Devyn admitted. "Truckloads of it. But that's not enough to make a relationship last. And besides, I couldn't break the curse for Marc. He had to do it himself."

"Purest faith shall set you free," Allie said, reciting the last line from Memère's spell. Her gaze turned soft, and

for a moment, she sounded like a believer. "All the two of you need is faith."

Whatever. All Devyn needed was to get off this boat and back to her regular life—the one that didn't include Beau Dumont. Which reminded her . . . "Hey, I've been meaning to tell you something."

"Is it how wonderful I am?"

"Well, that's a given," Devyn said smiling, but she kept her gaze fixed on an empty beer bottle. "About a week ago, a guy offered me a job and I took it."

"That's great!"

"Yeah," Devyn said, resolving to be positive. "It's a unique opportunity, and the owner's excited to have me on the team."

"What kind of job is it?"

Devyn cleared her throat and studied her fingernails. "I'm going to lead haunted graveyard tours in Cedar Bayou," she said; then she chanced a peek at her sister.

For a pregnant beat, Allie froze and her lips parted. She quickly recovered with a congratulatory smile, but her original reaction spoke volumes. "How perfect is that? Nobody knows more about Memère's history than you do."

"Mmm-hmm." Suddenly Devyn didn't want to talk about her new job anymore. Even her sister, who had little esteem for their voodoo heritage, recognized the shame of exploiting it. "Just wanted to let you know."

"I'm happy if you're happy," Allie said, reaching across the island to offer a gentle nudge. "But you're not exactly turning cartwheels."

Devyn shrugged and picked up one last bite of okra. "It's money."

She popped the morsel in her mouth, but her appetite had died, so she tossed it back onto the plate. "Thanks for the snacks. I'm heading to bed."

"Hope you feel better in the morning," Allie said. "If not, come back and I'll make Mama's warm bread pudding with an extra dash of lemon. That always cheers me up."

Devyn hugged her sister and turned to go, but her footsteps were heavier than before. She was pretty sure not even bread pudding could fix what ailed her.

Devyn didn't sleep well that night, or the night afterward. She tossed and turned on her narrow bunk. Just when the lazy haze of slumber would begin to wash over her, she'd see the hurt in Beau's eyes and jerk awake while his words echoed in her head.

Come find me when you're ready to apologize. I'll be waiting.

"Fat chance." Devyn punched her pillow to fluff it, then faced the ceiling. She hadn't done anything wrong. She hadn't asked him to kiss her, and she hadn't asked for this job. He'd muscled his way into her life without permission. He was the one who owed her an apology—ten years' worth of *I'm sorry*—not the other way around.

So why was guilt chewing a hole in her stomach?

"Damn you, Beau Dumont," she whispered in the darkness. "Damn you for making me feel like this. And damn myself for giving you the power to do it."

Ella-Claire stirred from the bottom bunk, mumbling in her sleep and smacking her lips, so Devyn kept quiet and tried to lie still. Sleep finally took her as the blackness of night gave way to the purple bruise of morning, and the alarm sounded way too soon for her weary body.

She washed in a daze, too exhausted to cast her usual scowl at the shower-toilet, and she made for the coffee station in the dining hall before her hair was even dry.

While stirring her creamer, she couldn't help discreetly scanning the passengers and crew for the object of her angst. It wasn't hard to spot him. Beau stood a full head and shoulders above everyone else, his white uniform a stark contrast against a sea of polo shirts and button-downs as he entered the room. He smiled and nodded *good morning* to everyone in his path, but he didn't spare a glance in Devyn's direction when he topped off his travel thermos with black coffee.

He stood close enough to fill her space with the mingled scents of roasted Colombian beans and aftershave. It was a pleasing homey smell, evoking memories of Sunday mornings with her family. Devyn leaned behind him to toss her sugar packet in the trash. Ready to bury the hatchet, she brought a cardboard cup to her lips and faced Beau to give him a chance to acknowledge her.

But he didn't.

Instead, he screwed on his thermos lid and turned to

leave. He waved at everyone but her and strolled out the door without looking back. The bite of rejection made Devyn's shoulders round forward. He was really going to do this—freeze her out until she apologized. For the thousandth time, she wondered why Beau's approval mattered so much to her. Clearly she needed professional help.

Fine, she thought. *Let him stew a while. I'm not apologizing.*

She lasted all of eight hours.

When five o'clock rolled around and the education center emptied, Devyn was ready to jump out of her skin. Each minute had ticked by in torturously slow degrees until it felt like time was going in reverse. All day, her focus had been shot. It had taken three tries to get her candle-powered mini steamboat to work, because Beau had dominated her brain and clumsied her fingers.

She refused to examine the reasons why, but she couldn't stand knowing he was upset with her. It didn't mean she wanted a repeat performance of their closet adventure, and it didn't mean she wanted to be friends. She would make her apology quick and sterile, and then things could go back to normal.

As normal as they ever were.

After cleaning up and preparing her materials for the next day, Devyn walked to the casino, figuring she'd find Beau there. She stopped in front of the double doors to take a fortifying breath and wipe her clammy palms on her pants. She could do this—be the bigger person. Five minutes of eating crow would restore her sanity.

It was a worthy trade.

Shaking back her hair, she strode inside. An overload of sensations smacked her in the face as she scanned the crowded room for Beau's stubborn auburn head. Between the flashing lights, the clamoring machines, and the boisterous cheering from the craps table, she had to make three passes before realizing he wasn't there.

A hand tapped her on the shoulder, and she spun around to find Thing One smiling at her. She knew it was him because he still hadn't learned to keep his gaze away from her boobs.

"Looking for the boss man?" he asked.

Devyn nodded. "Where is he?"

"In the security room," he said, pointing to a swinging door behind the bar. "Go through the storage area; then it's the first door on the right."

She followed his directions and strode toward the bar. Her knees trembled and her heart pounded the closer she got to the storage area, but she pushed open the door without hesitation.

Ripping off the Band-Aid, and all that.

To her surprise, Beau was already waiting for her. The door to the security room was open, and he leaned against the jamb with both arms folded across his chest, his face a blank mask. He'd removed his jacket and rolled up his sleeves, revealing muscled forearms that heightened her anxiety level. It wasn't easy to meet his chilly gaze, but she forced herself to look him in the eyes.

"How did you know I was here?" she asked.

Beau nodded behind him. "One-way glass. I saw you coming."

"Oh." She cleared her throat and blotted her palms again. "Is this a bad time? Because I can come back later."

To his credit, Beau didn't stare her down or make her grovel. He kept his expression impassive, but moved out of the way and swept a hand to invite her inside.

The security headquarters was about the same size as her bedroom, but at least ten degrees warmer thanks to a table full of computer equipment and a flat-screen monitor hanging on the wall. That explained why Beau had removed his jacket.

While he shut the door and dragged over a folding chair, Devyn glanced out the one-way glass and wondered what had gone through his mind when he'd watched her cross the casino floor. She had expected him to gloat or at least offer one of his signature smirks, but he was being unusually mature. She wasn't sure if that would make her apology easier or not.

"Have a seat," he said, lowering to his swiveling office chair.

Devyn preferred to stand, so she walked behind the

chair and gripped its metal back for support. Beau didn't seem to mind, probably because they were eye level now. Since delaying the inevitable wouldn't make this any easier, she jumped right in.

"You know why I'm here," she said, staring out the glass without seeing anything. "I was upset, and I shouldn't have taken it out on you. I'm sorry. You didn't deserve that."

He didn't say anything at first, just shifted on his seat. When he spoke, there was no trace of resentment in his tone. "Thank you. I know that wasn't easy."

"I can admit when I'm wrong."

"But still."

"Yeah," she conceded. "Nothing between us is ever easy."

He blew out a breath and seemed to relax a bit. "Can I ask what I did to make you mad? Because I keep replaying it in my mind, trying to figure out where I went wrong. It's been driving me crazy. Whatever I did, I promise I wasn't trying to upset you."

Devyn's heart warmed with the knowledge that their spat had affected both of them. She met his gaze, humbled by the concern she saw there. It gave her the courage to tell him the truth. "It's my issue. I don't like thinking about our past. Reminiscing about old times might make you laugh, but for me, memory lane is paved with land mines and broken glass."

"Was it really that bad?" He blinked at her. "I know I messed up, but—"

"You hurt me, Beau." Devyn couldn't believe she'd just said that out loud. She had spent so much time pretending otherwise, but it felt good to admit the truth, like dropping a barbell she'd carried for too long. "And everything is tainted because of that. Even the good times."

He stood from his chair and reached for her, but seemed to think better of it. "I'm really sorry, Dev. I wish I could make you understand how much I regret leaving." While keeping his distance, he paused until he caught her eye. "I panicked and I ran. We can blame the curse or my own immaturity, but either way it was wrong. I've spent the last decade kicking my own ass for ruining what we had, and I never got you out of my head." He tapped his temple and repeated, "Never. I don't think I ever will."

Devyn squeezed the metal chair while her eyes prickled. She didn't want to hear how much he'd missed her. All she had come here to do was apologize and leave. If Beau kept going on like this, she would have to shut him down by admitting something she'd kept buried from everyone, even her sister. Devyn had refused to think about it for the last decade. In fact, she'd done such a good job at blocking the memory that it didn't seem real anymore.

"Let me try to make amends," he went on. "Can't we start over? We'll go as slow as you want. I'll take you out to dinner and I promise I won't lay a hand on—"

"You don't get it." Devyn's voice cracked, and she paused to blink back tears. "There's more."

Beau shook his head in confusion.

She filled her lungs and announced, "You got me pregnant."

"What?" He braced one hand on the wall while his jaw went slack. Stammering, he tried several times to get the words out. "When? Why didn't you say anything?"

"I didn't know at first. I took a test the same day your letter came in the mail." She lifted a shoulder. "Then I got my period a few days later, and then there was no reason to tell you. What was the point? You were long gone, and we were over."

Silently, he lowered to his chair.

"But those three days before the miscarriage? They were awful." Devyn drew a shuddering breath. "Not because I was young and alone. I knew my family would help with the baby and the military would garnish your wages. I'd have enough support to get by. That wasn't what scared me."

Beau just stared at her, so she blotted her eyes and went on. "What scared me the most was knowing what happens to the kids in your family. And to their mothers. You left me behind to travel the world, and I was just another Dumont castoff, tied to you forever by a baby you would've ignored except on holidays, assuming you happened to be in town."

Beau's voice was barely audible when he asked, "Did you really think that?"

"Yes. I got a glimpse of what could have been," Devyn said. "This might sound hateful, and I don't mean any disrespect, but I almost ended up like your mama. I don't want that for myself. No man is worth it."

Not even the only man she'd ever loved.

Devyn took a deep breath and continued. "That's why we can't start over. That's why I don't want to reminisce about sneaking off to the janitor's closet. If I could erase all that from my memory, I would."

Judging by the lack of color in his cheeks, Beau hadn't quite absorbed the news yet. Devyn understood. At eighteen, it had taken her two full hours to acknowledge the second blue line on her pregnancy test. She had kept staring at it like the results might change if she blinked enough times.

"Look, I didn't come here to lay anything heavy on you," she said. "I just want you to know where we stand—and why I can't go back." Then she corrected, "Why *we* can't go back. I don't want that kind of life."

Beau dragged a hand over his face and stared into empty space for so long that he seemed to have forgotten she was there. She took that as her cue to leave.

"I'm sorry for snapping at you the other day. That's all I came here to tell you."

When he didn't answer, she folded her chair and leaned it against the wall, then quietly let herself out.

Devyn had thought that apologizing to Beau would make her feel better, but when she stepped into the casino, each electric chirp pierced her skull like a jackhammer. It was as if she had shed her skin, and now her nerves were exposed. Needing to escape, she jogged across the floor and didn't stop until she'd reached the ship's galley.

With moisture welling in her eyes, she asked her sister, "Is that offer of bread pudding still on the table?"

Allie dropped her cup of flour and rushed to offer a hug. "Oh, honey. You bet it is. And ice cream, too."

Chapter 7

During recon training, the marines had tested the limits of Beau's body and mind to the breaking point through a series of drills most men couldn't survive. He'd suffered in silence for three months of the most grueling physical exertion imaginable, like *The Longest Day*, an eighteen-hour test of endurance where he had puked and dry heaved so much it was a wonder his stomach hadn't ruptured. But that was child's play compared to the nighttime exercises. Exhausted from a full day of swimming, running, and towing boats with his bare hands, he had been ordered to hold his position in pitch darkness while his instructors attacked him with blank artillery and tear gas.

It was goddamned terrifying.

With no gas mask, he'd used his sweat-soaked T-shirt to cover his mouth and nose, fighting the urge to retreat to the next sand dune for a breath of clean air. His eyes and throat had burned hotter than hellfire, panic had surged through his veins, and it was the most unnatural thing in the world to lie there and breathe that poison.

He kind of felt that way now—suffocated and confused.

Conflicting emotions of anger, loss, and shame pressed against his lungs to smother him as real as the tear gas that had brought him to his knees. The longer he sat in the security room, the harder his pulse rushed. His muscles tensed, and his blood boiled. He wanted to fight someone, but he didn't know why.

Who was he even mad at?

Not Devyn. She hadn't done anything wrong. And yet the mental echo of her words made him want to punch a hole in the wall.

I almost ended up like your mama.

He sucked a breath through his nose and shot to his feet, then paced a circuit around the room in an effort to burn off some rage. What in the ever-loving hell was wrong with him?

Two quick knocks sounded from the door, and Nicky poked his head inside. His blond brows shot up, telling Beau how crazy he must look. "You okay?" Nick asked. "Devyn ran out of here like the room was on fire."

Beau couldn't worry about her right now. He needed to get out of here and blow off some steam.

"Take over for a while, will you? I'm going to the gym."

"Sure." Nick seemed concerned, but he clearly knew better than to pry. "Take the rest of the night off if you want. I'll pull Alex from the purser's desk. We can hold down the fort."

On his way out the door, Beau clapped his brother on the arm and said, "Thanks." Then he charged upstairs to his suite while avoiding eye contact with everyone he passed.

After changing clothes, he jogged to the gym, pleased to find it empty. He glanced at the clock and realized it was dinnertime, which meant he would have the place to himself for a solid hour or two. Beau scanned the workout equipment to find the right outlet. Soon he spotted it—a red punching bag hanging from the ceiling in the corner of the room. His lips curved and his fists clenched in anticipation.

Perfect.

Two hours later, Beau's knuckles were raw and he could barely lift his arms, but he felt nearly human again. He swiped the back of his hand across his forehead and geared up for one last swing, a grand finale with all his weight behind it. When his right hook connected with the bag, a loud smack echoed through the gym, and one of the bag's reinforcement straps tore, causing it to hang from the ceiling at a skewed angle.

Beau swore under his breath. He should have quit while he was ahead.

"See?" said a male voice from behind him. "This is why we can't have nice things."

Marc strode into view with his jacket slung over one arm and his captain's hat in hand. He must have come off duty in the pilothouse, because he'd loosened his tie and undone the first few buttons of his dress shirt.

Beau didn't need to ask how his brother had ended up here.

"Nicky ratted me out."

"More or less," Marc said. He took a seat on one of those silly Nautilus machines that women used to work their inner thighs—the kind that spread their legs wide open. "He asked me to check on you. Said he hasn't seen you this pissed since the day I broke your nose."

Beau chuckled dryly, remembering the first and last time he had ever dissed Marc's mother. Deep in his teenage heart, he'd known better, but he'd cracked a joke about the woman to score a laugh with his friends. "I deserved that."

"Yes, you did," Marc agreed. "But let's not change the subject. Nick also said you had a fight with Devyn."

"That's not true."

"You sure?" Marc said, standing as he grabbed a clean towel from a nearby table. He handed it to Beau while wrinkling his nose in distaste. "You need a shower."

"The answer is yes," Beau said. He used the towel to wipe down his sweaty face. "To both of those statements. Dev and I aren't fighting." And he sure as hell needed a shower. He smelled like roadkill.

"Okay." The way Marc drew out the word sounded like he didn't buy it. "Then why the bloody knuckles? What did that innocent punching bag ever do to you?"

Beau glanced down and noticed a smudge of blood

across the back of his right hand. Again, he wished he had quit before that final throw that broke the bag. He grabbed a clean towel and wrapped it around his knuckles while stalling for an excuse. Beau honestly didn't know what to say, because he didn't understand what had come over him.

"Spit it out," Marc said.

Beau sat on the matted floor and flicked a glance at his brother. The two of them had never been close—in fact, they'd spent most of their teenage years at each other's throats—but they had a lot in common, like a deadbeat dad. It prompted him to ask, "Did you ever worry that you'd turn out like the old man?"

From the way Marc's chin dropped, he wasn't anticipating that question. He glanced down at his captain's hat, perhaps recalling all the years their father had worn it. "Maybe a little. I never wanted to repeat his mistakes. That's why I always kept it wrapped when I took a woman home."

Beau sensed that his brother had left something unsaid. "But . . . ?"

"But Allie pointed out something when we were dating," he said, leaning forward to rest both elbows on his knees. "She said I was exactly like Daddy, just without all the kids." He sniffed a humorless laugh. "I didn't like hearing that, but she was right. I fooled around with half the parish and never stayed with one woman long enough to make it count. The only difference between me and Daddy was I had nothing to show for it."

"So in all those years," Beau said, "you never slipped one past the goalie?"

"Not that I know of."

"What if you had?"

"Gotten some girl pregnant?"

"Yeah." Beau pretended to inspect the bruised knuckles on his left hand. "What would you have done?"

Marc shrugged. "The right thing, I guess. I would've manned up and taken care of the kid."

"Would you have married the mother?"

A look of incredulity crossed Marc's face, along with a nervous grin. "Let's not get carried away. That's a really bad reason to get married. I would have made sure she was taken care of." Then he clarified, "Financially, I mean. I wouldn't have used her as a permanent booty call the way Daddy did with our mamas."

Beau was glad to hear that. "I would have married her."

Marc cocked his head. "Married who?"

Uh-oh. He hadn't meant to say that out loud. "No one in particular," he lied. "If I'd gotten a girl in trouble, I would have tried to make an honest go of it. That's all I was sayin'."

Marc scrutinized him for a long moment. "Is there anything you want to tell me?"

Beau pushed up from the floor. "Nope."

"So you're all right?"

"Yep," he said, hooking a thumb at the battered punching bag. "You can take that out of my wages, Captain. I'm off to the shower."

Marc waved a hand in front of his nose. "It's about damn time."

A grin lifted the corners of Beau's mouth. Though he'd never admit it, he was glad Nicky had sent Marc down here. This chat had helped him understand what had been eating him, and more important, what he needed to do about it.

On his way back to his suite, he sent Devyn a text. *I need to talk to you. My room in twenty minutes. Won't take long, promise.*

Devyn's cell chimed from her back pocket to announce an incoming text. With a bowl of bread pudding in one hand, she used the other to retrieve her phone and swipe the glass. Her heart jumped when she read the message, and she hid the screen so Allie couldn't see.

"What does Beau want?" Allie asked from the other side of the island. "That was him, right?"

Damn it. "How did you know?"

Allie toasted her with a glass of milk. "It's the *Oh, shit!* face. You only make it when he's around." She took a bite of her own bread pudding. "So what did he want?"

"To talk."

"That's probably a good idea."

"To talk in his *suite.*"

A devilish smile spread over Allie's face. "A very good idea."

"No, it's a very bad idea."

Devyn hadn't told her sister about the miscarriage.

For all Allie knew, Beau wanted to talk about the weather. But that wasn't what he had in mind, and Devyn had no interest in dredging up those memories. She had finally calmed down after three desserts. Besides, the last place she needed to meet Beau was in his bedroom. They'd be horizontal before the door clicked shut. "You know what happens when we're alone."

Allie rolled her eyes. "It's not like your pants will come flying off the second you cross the threshold."

"Psh." Close enough.

"Tell you what," Allie said. "Go talk to him. If you're not back here in half an hour, I'll come up there and knock on his door. And I won't stop until one of you answers."

"You would do that? Run booty interference?"

"Just one of the many services I offer."

Devyn began to take her sister's suggestion seriously. After the bomb she had dropped on Beau, it was only natural that he'd have questions. And aside from bedrooms—and closets—there weren't many private places to talk aboard the boat. "Okay," she decided. "But you might have to use some muscle to get me out of there."

"Seriously?"

"Yes, seriously," she said. Her sister didn't understand the power of Beau's sexual magnetism. "Promise that you'll make me leave, no matter what."

"Fine," Allie said flatly. "I promise."

"Just give me a few minutes to get up there."

Devyn made a pit stop in her room to splash cool water on her face. It didn't do much to alleviate the puffiness beneath her reddened eyes, but the refreshing chill gave her a much needed energy boost.

Soon she was standing in front of Beau's door, every bit as nervous as when she had come to apologize earlier that evening. Beau certainly did have a way of making her heart race. She'd probably burned off a serving of bread pudding just standing here working up the courage to knock.

She held her breath and rapped her knuckles on the door. Moments later, the door swung open and that breath whooshed out in a rush as Devyn fought to keep the shock from parting her lips.

Beau stood there . . . wearing nothing but a towel.

Oh, God. She was screwed.

"I said twenty minutes," he told her, gripping the white terrycloth at his waist. "I'm not dressed yet."

Yes, she could see that. In fact, she could see a lot of things, like the contours of his muscled shoulders and broad chest, his hair-encircled nipples tightened to hard buds. Her own traitorous nipples puckered to match. Her gaze was held hostage by the overwhelming masculinity of him, from the thick column of his neck down to his lean, powerful legs. He must have just stepped out of the shower, because water droplets rested along the ridge of his pectorals, and the scent of soap carried into the hall. Even with a burgundy stain over his heart and battle scars marring his flesh, he was a glorious sight to behold.

Devyn swallowed hard. "My bad," was all she could say.

"Come on in."

He turned and strode into the room, and she followed, reluctantly shutting the door behind her. Maybe she should have told Allie to come in fifteen minutes. A lot could happen in half an hour.

Don't be stupid, Devyn chided herself. *You can handle this.*

But then Beau dropped his towel, revealing the hard curves of his naked ass, and a wave of desire slammed into her with so much force she stumbled back a step. "Holy Mother of God," she cried, still unable to look away. "You could have warned me!" Her fingers twitched to grab those muscled cheeks and hold on tight.

"What's the big deal?" Beau continued digging through his dresser drawer until he found a pair of athletic shorts and pulled them on. "It's nothing you haven't seen before."

"Common courtesy," she said. "I don't run around naked in front of *you*."

He glanced over his bare shoulder with the crooked grin that had always been her kryptonite. "Feel free. It wouldn't bother me in the least."

Devyn took a moment to close her eyes and refocus. When she opened them, she did her best to train her gaze on his face. "You wanted to talk."

"Yes." His playful smile disappeared and he took a seat on the edge of the bed. He gestured for her to join him. "Thanks for coming. I wasn't sure if you would."

Devyn didn't want to sit beside him, so she scanned the room for a less dangerous position. His suite was about three times the size of hers, but it was still small enough to put her within an arm's reach no matter where she sat. She chose a cushioned chair in the corner. A couple of feet of distance was better than nothing.

Devyn folded her arms. "I know it was a shock, telling you about the pregnancy like that. I figured you'd need some time to process. I mean, there was never an actual baby. But still."

"But still," he agreed. "There was. For a few weeks, at least."

Devyn had never allowed herself to think of the baby that way. It was less painful to say her period had shown up late than to admit she and Beau had conceived a child and then lost it. "So, are you okay?"

"I am now. But I was mixed up at first. Took a while to figure out why."

"It's probably scary," she said. "Knowing how close you came to being a dad."

"No, that's not it." Beau shifted on the mattress, leaning forward to lock their gazes. "But before we go any further, I want to say I'm sorry you had to face that alone. I should have been there when you took the test. Hell, I should have bought it from the store and held your hand while we waited for the lines to show up. If I could change that, I would."

She nodded to accept his apology. "It was a long time ago."

"I'm sorry all the same," he said. "And what shook

me today wasn't the fact that we almost had a baby. It was that you thought I'd handle the situation like my old man. I'm not him. I would have stepped up, Dev."

Devyn didn't doubt that he believed it, but she wasn't so sure Beau would've done right by her. "It's easy to sit here ten years later and say what you would have done."

"No." He shook his head, his expression deadly serious. "I hated what my dad did to my mama. I watched him break her. I still can't stand to be in the same room with him. I hate that I have his eyes, his smile, or any part of his DNA." In challenge, he pointed a finger at her. "Did I ever mess around behind your back while we were dating?"

Devyn shrank back. "I don't think so."

"The answer is *no*. I don't cheat, and that's because I'm nothing like him." Beau's cheeks had reddened, and he stopped to suck in a few breaths. "If you'd written to me and said you were pregnant, I would have sent for you. It would've been *me* who broke the curse for the first time, not Marc. I would've married you, hexes be damned, and I would have loved that baby. Because I loved you."

He waited until she looked up at him before speaking again. "I need you to know that."

Devyn wrung her hands and willed away the telltale prickle behind her eyes. She was done crying over this man. "You and me, married fresh out of high school?" She scoffed. "We wouldn't have lasted six months."

"Maybe," he said. "Maybe not. But I would've bent over backward to try and make it work. Don't doubt that."

Why was he bringing this up? Did he enjoy twisting her heart, making her reopen wounds that had nearly healed?

"Well, it doesn't matter anyway. What's done is done, and the pregnancy was over as soon as it began."

"It *does* matter," he said. Pushing off the bed, Beau knelt at her feet and braced both hands on the armrests of her chair, essentially trapping her in place. "You said we can't start over because you don't want my mother's life. This is me telling you that won't happen."

Now she saw where he was going with this. For a split second, Devyn understood how Beau had felt all those years ago when he'd panicked and skipped town. Her heart rushed and she would have fled if she weren't blocked by two hundred pounds of solid man. He was too close, the heat from his exposed skin settling over her, weakening her resolve.

"If you don't want to give me a second chance, then fine," he said, taking one of her hands between both of his, so strong and warm. "I'll respect that. But make your choice for the right reasons, not because you're afraid I'll turn into my father. I'm not him, and I never will be."

Devyn needed space, but she couldn't bring herself to push him away—not even when he tipped their foreheads together and slid his rough palms up the length of her arms.

"Do you hear me, Dev?" he murmured while trailing his fingertips along her jawline. "Say you believe me."

Against her will, Devyn's hands gravitated to the inside bend of Beau's elbows, then traced the rock-hard curves of muscle all the way to his shoulders. His skin was hot and smooth beneath her fingers, an oh so familiar sensation she'd missed for far too long. Her knees parted an inch, and then another, allowing him to nudge his massive body in between. She didn't want to run anymore. Instead, she locked both legs around Beau's hips to hold him there.

"Please." He cradled her face while his lips brushed hers in a whisper kiss. "Tell me."

Letting her eyelids flutter shut, Devyn nodded within the confines of his powerful hands. "I believe you."

Using the tip of his tongue, he traced her bottom lip and she instantly opened for him. But he teased her with his mouth, nipping at her without getting too close, forcing her to lean forward and chase his tongue. "Do you want this?" he asked with another brush of lips. "I need to hear that you want me."

"Yes," Devyn said. She could do this—indulge in some steamy action with her ex—as long as she kept her feelings out of the equation. So she threw her arms around Beau's neck and thrust her tongue into his mouth in a kiss that turned from hot to scintillating in an instant. Groaning, he pulled her into a crushing embrace and captured her mouth like a soldier headed for war. Her lips throbbed, but she wanted it harder. Desperation overtook her, and she clawed at his shoulders as if to pull herself inside him.

Beau tugged her hips out of the chair, and before she knew what had happened, Devyn was flat on her back while a wall of delicious muscle pressed her into the carpet. He parted her thighs and settled between them, then slid the full length of his erection against her from base to tip and back again. Pure pleasure had her bowing back with a gasp, but she wanted more than dry friction this time.

She wanted everything.

"Inside me," she ordered, reaching between them to unbutton her pants. "Right now."

Beau didn't argue. He pushed aside her hand and took over. In seconds, he had her zipper down, and he roughly shoved her pants to her ankles, where they remained trapped against her shoes. Her panties soon followed. She started to kick them off, but Beau touched her for the first time in earnest, and she was helpless to do anything but moan with the pleasure.

"Mercy," he whispered, spreading moisture over her folds in an erotic massage. "You're already wet for me." He made a male noise of appreciation and repeated, "So wet."

She opened wider for him and shamelessly begged with her hips. When he skimmed a thumb over her sensitive bud, she made an embarrassing mewing noise and rocked against his hand. Propping on one elbow, he studied her while barely dipping a finger inside, playing at her entrance until she grew aching and swollen with need. In turn, she reached into his shorts and curled a hand around the steely length of him, and then stroked his shaft, teasing him with a feather touch that drew beads of arousal to the tip.

Their breathing came in ragged gasps for the next few minutes as they locked eyes and drove each other toward the brink. When a sheen of sweat had broken out across Beau's forehead, he asked, "Are you on the Pill?"

"I have an IUD."

"Do you want me to get a condom?"

"No." Devyn couldn't wait that long. Tugging him closer, she used his satin head to stroke the juncture of her thighs until Beau groaned and nudged inside an inch. That first luscious invasion felt so good that Devyn's toes curled in her shoes.

"More," she pleaded. "Hurry."

But Beau took his time, using his plump tip to stretch her so slowly she had to bite her lip to contain a scream. "God, baby." His eyes clenched tightly as he struggled for control. "You feel so good it's unreal."

Panting, she rolled her hips to take him an inch deeper when someone pounded on the bedroom door and yelled her name. "No!" Devyn cried, suddenly remembering the instructions she'd given her sister. "No, no, no!"

Confused, Beau glanced at the door. "Ignore it. Whoever it is, they can come back later."

Another series of knocks sounded, followed by Allie's voice. "Answer the door, Devyn. I'm not going away until you do."

"It's okay," Devyn shouted to her sister. "Forget what I said before. I'm fine."

"No dice," Allie said, pounding her fist harder. "I'm not leaving without you. Don't make me call Marc to bring the master key, because I will!"

Devyn looked at the virile body braced above her, especially the long, thick erection poised between her thighs, and she gave a pitiful whimper. She told Beau, "We have to stop for a minute."

After taking in the situation, he gaped with disbelief. "You told her to come here and cockblock me?"

"Kind of." Devyn scooted away from him and tugged up her pants. "Just wait, and I'll get rid of her."

Beau pulled up his shorts and pushed to his knees with a grunt of frustration. "You never cease to amaze me, Dev."

"Hold that thought." Without bothering to zip her khakis, she rushed to the door and opened it a crack. Allie peered back at her, gripping her hips like a maiden aunt, guardian of virtue. "Go away," Devyn hissed. "I don't need you."

Before she could shut the door, Allie wedged her shoe inside. "A deal is a deal. You're coming with me."

"No, I mean it—"

Allie flashed a palm. "If you change your mind, Beau will still be here in the morning." Delivering a pointed look, she added, "*After* you've had a chance to clear the hormones out of your system."

"Please let me stay? I promise I'll never ask you for anything, ever again."

"Begging won't work."

"Pleeeeeeease?"

"Come quietly, or I'll drag you out by force."

"Pretty please with a cherry on top?"

"Not even with whipped cream and sprinkles."

Devyn let her head thunk against the wall. "You're not going to leave, are you?"

"Nope, so you might as well tell him good-bye."

Why did Allie have to be such a good sister?

"Fine," Devyn sighed. "Give me a second."

"I'll give you ten."

Of course, Beau had overheard the entire conversation. He was standing out of view against the side wall, watching her like he didn't know whether to ruffle her curls or wring her neck. "You've got to go," he said flatly.

"Yeah, sorry."

He blew out a dry laugh that assured he wasn't angry, only frustrated. He moved in and pressed a chaste kiss to her cheek. "It's okay. I told you we could take it slow, and I meant that. I've got all the time in the world."

When Devyn slipped into the hall and shut the door

behind her, Allie made a show of inspecting her wrinkled pants and untucked shirt.

"Tsk, tsk." Smiling, Allie gave a disapproving shake of her head. "You're so easy."

Devyn slung an arm around her sister's neck as they strode toward the stairwell. "You have no idea."

Chapter 8

Everything changed after that night.

Logically, Devyn knew she should stay away from Beau. She fully acknowledged that she was playing with fire, and since he'd burned her once, he would probably do it again. But try telling that to her raging libido.

Beau had given her a taste of perfection, and now a hunger had opened up so deep inside her that it eclipsed everything else. He'd even dominated her sleep, appearing in dreams to stroke her with his masterful fingers and impale her with his iron shaft. She had awoken from each fantasy gasping, suspended a hairsbreadth from climax and unable to do a damn thing about it because Ella-Claire was a light sleeper.

If there was a female equivalent for blue balls, Devyn had it.

As the days passed, she found herself rationalizing a relationship with Beau—nothing serious, of course. No flowery poems or *I love you*s or promises of forever. She would keep it casual and guard her heart. She'd even reflected that a fling would be good for her health. Didn't scientists claim that orgasms released endorphins and decreased stress? Who couldn't use a few more endorphins? Maybe if she took things nice and slow—seriously slow, as in molasses speed—there was no harm in letting Beau try to earn back her trust.

Right?

But it seemed like she was trying too hard to convince herself, which usually meant something was wrong. For that reason, she avoided him and threw all her energy into her job at the education center. Or she tried to, at least. There was no escaping Beau in such close quarters. Their paths crossed several times a day, like at the coffee station each morning.

Right now, he stood so near that the sleeve of his starched white jacket brushed her bare elbow. Devyn focused on peeling back the foil lid to her creamer, but the intoxicating scent of Beau's aftershave had her fingers slipping. As he took his first sip of coffee, she slid a covert glance at him to watch the muscles work in his throat. Her heart rushed at the sight, sending heated blood to some pretty interesting places. No man had a right to look so sexy this early in the morning.

"Want some help with that?" he asked.

Devyn nearly dropped her creamer. "No, thanks. I've got it."

Beau's lips quirked in a grin when he caught her staring at his neck. He lowered his voice to a deep rumble that flowed over her like warm honey. "How'd you sleep last night?"

"Fine," she lied. "You?"

"Like a baby." Leaning another inch into her space, he murmured in her ear, "I've got that great big suite all to myself. Gives me plenty of room to spread out naked on my king-sized bed."

Devyn's eyes closed while her skin pricked into goose bumps.

"Wouldn't mind sharing it, though," he added. "If you asked me real nice. But I can't guarantee you'll get much sleep. In fact, I promise you won't."

The creamer slipped from her hands and plunked to the table. Without missing a beat, Beau picked it up and handed it to her, then told her to have a great day and strode from the room.

Damn it. He was enjoying this, the arrogant bastard . . . the delicious, hard-bodied, toe-curling arrogant bastard.

Devyn shook her head to clear it. Forget the creamer, she would drink her coffee black today. She grabbed an apple turnover and headed for the education center, but she realized halfway down the hall that she'd forgotten a handout on her dresser. When she returned to her room and opened the door, she drew back in shock, sending coffee sloshing over the rim of her cardboard cup.

Ella-Claire sat on the dresser while Thing Two braced his hands on either side of her hips and leaned in for a kiss. At the interruption, they flinched and turned toward Devyn with noticeably different reactions—guilt from him, sexual frustration from Ella-Claire. By now,

Devyn could recognize the symptoms of a woman unfulfilled.

"Uh," Thing Two stammered, giving a fake business-like nod at Ella. "I think we got that lash out of your eye."

"Oh, come off it," Devyn said. She shut the door and pointed in a silent request to her handout, which was stuck under Ella's butt. "She didn't have anything in her eye. You were macking on your half brother's half sister." God, that sounded even more absurd when she said it out loud. "Your secret's safe with me. But don't insult my intelligence by pretending nothing's going on. Just sack up and own it."

It seemed her advice was wasted on Thing Two. He mumbled an excuse about running payroll and promptly bolted from the room.

Ella handed over the sheet of paper while deflating like an old balloon.

"Sorry about that," Devyn said. "If I'd known you wanted to be alone, I would have come back later. Next time, hang something on the door like a hat or a hair elastic so I'll get the message."

"It doesn't matter." Ella-Claire sank back against the dresser. "Even if he *had* finally kissed me, I doubt he would ever do it again."

"Wait a minute." Devyn had assumed the two were already getting it on. They shot off so many sparks she expected someone to lose an eye. "You haven't kissed yet?"

Ella shook her head, sending her ponytail into motion. "Nothing more than a peck on the cheek. I was telling the truth when I said Alex and I are best friends."

Wow, Devyn's smutty radar was off. "But you want more?"

The girl shrugged and picked at her manicure. "Yes. Maybe. I always had feelings for Alex, but I kept him in the friend zone. He was a player, just like his brothers," she said, glancing at Devyn. "You know, a typical Dumont guy."

"Yeah," Devyn deadpanned. "I know."

"But in the last few months, he's changed. Matured. He takes on extra duties around here instead of hitting the bars, and he hasn't been with anyone since the time he and Nicky accidentally slept with the jazz singer."

Devyn shook her head in disbelief. Only a Dumont man could end up in the middle of an unintentional three-way.

"It's a long story," Ella said. "Anyway, I've started to think there could be hope for him, that maybe he'd end up more like Marc and less like their dad."

"But you're worried about the curse," Devyn said, completely understanding. It was a valid concern.

Ella flapped a hand. "I don't believe in all that."

You should. "Then what's the problem?"

"It's Marc," Ella said with a frustrated sigh. "He can barely stand for any of his brothers to look at me. If he found out that Alex almost kissed me, he'd throw him overboard. I'm not even kidding."

"I get that." Devyn had felt protective of her own sister when Allie had gotten involved with a Dumont.

"But you're an adult, and sooner or later he needs to respect your wishes."

"That's what I keep telling Alex, but he idolizes Marc," Ella said, staring at the door as if replaying how quickly Thing Two had fled the scene. "I don't think he's scared of what Marc might do to him. I think he's afraid of disappointing his big brother." She drew a stuttered breath. "But what about me? Why don't I matter? Why is it okay to disappoint his best friend?"

Devyn felt a prickle of sympathy for the girl. If Thing Two wasn't ready to pursue a relationship with Ella, it would seem he hadn't matured all that much. Devyn crossed the small room and unzipped her duffel bag, then found a sachet of gris-gris. She had mixed a batch last night to untangle her own muddled emotions.

Handing the pouch to Ella-Claire, she said, "Here, this is for clarity of heart, so keep it in your pocket. It will help lead you in the right direction, but you'll have to do some of the work yourself."

Ella nodded for her to go on.

"It's time to have a 'Come to Jesus' talk with Thing Two." At the girl's puzzled expression, Devyn corrected, "I mean with Alex. Be clear about what you want, and tell him to make a choice—no more straddling the line. Either he's in, or he's out. But don't let him string you along." She gave Ella's arm an encouraging squeeze. "You're a smart, beautiful young woman, and if he's not willing to fight for you, then he's not worthy."

Ella smiled and a tear spilled down her cheek. There

was gratitude in her gaze, but fear too, like she already knew what Alex's response would be and she didn't want it confirmed.

"Be strong," Devyn told her. "Don't settle for less than what you deserve."

When Ella promised to take the advice to heart, Devyn left for the education center, where her counseling skills came in handy for the second time that day.

Jason, the older sibling of the honeymoon crashers, sat on the floor in the corner of the room, slouched against the wall with the bill of his Saints ball cap pulled down over his eyes. On a typical day, he dragged into the room with a heavy sigh and an eye roll, but a reluctant smile would follow once Devyn set up a science experiment. This morning something was clearly wrong. He had never looked so dejected.

Nearby, his younger brother immersed himself in *Super Mario World*, fingers flying over the control buttons, his tongue pressed against the corner of his mouth while his gaze stayed fixed on the television screen. Nothing out of the ordinary with that one.

None of her other students had arrived, so she sat beside Jason in the corner and tipped up his hat. "Hey, there," she said. "You okay?"

His eyes met hers for an instant before he jerked down the bill. "I don't feel good. I just want to be left alone."

She touched his cheek with the back of her hand, noting that he didn't feel warm. "Do I need to send you to the infirmary?" Her instincts said no, but it was worth asking.

Jason brought both knees to his chest and shook his head.

"Should I page your mom?"

The boy made a noise of contempt. "She probably wouldn't come. She's too busy with Dave." He said *Dave* like it was the foulest of swears, which explained a lot.

"Ah." Blended family angst. That was a hard transition to make, and Devyn didn't envy any of them. "Sounds like you're not a fan of your new step-dad. He seems like a nice guy to me."

Another grunt.

"I don't know Dave that well," Devyn said, "but I've noticed something important about him that makes me think he's a good man."

Slowly, Jason lifted the bill of his cap and peered at her. "Like what?"

"The way he looks at your mom." Devyn gave a serious nod. "When they come to drop you off and pick you up, he acts like she's the only woman on the boat." She thumbed toward the infants on the other side of the partition. "When Cameron's mom showed up yesterday in a bikini top, every guy in the room stared at her. But your step-dad didn't even notice. He was too busy holding your mom's hand and kissing the top of her head."

Jason made a *yuck* face. "He always does that."

"Seems like he really loves her." When the boy shrugged with indifference, Devyn asked, "Isn't that what you want? Someone who thinks your mom is the most important person in the world?"

Jason dodged the question. "*He's* not the most important person to her. That's me and my brother."

"Of course." Now Devyn understood the root of the problem. Jason felt displaced. "And that will never change. A mother's love for her children is like nothing else on earth. But you know what?"

"What?"

"Someday you and your brother are going to grow up and leave home." She knew the boy wouldn't believe her if she said so, but there would soon come a time when his mother was no longer the center of his world. "Eventually, you'll start your own family. And think how lonely your mom would be if she didn't have your step-dad to keep her company."

That seemed to get through to him. Jason pursed his lips and stared at the foam-tiled floor for a few moments. "I'll always take care of her, no matter what."

"I know you will," Devyn said. "But you'll have a job and a wife and kids. That will take up a lot of your time." When he didn't respond, she gently tweaked his ball cap. "Don't you want your mom to have a best friend who loves her? Someone to make her happy when you're not there?"

"I guess."

"Then maybe give Dave a break. Maybe give your mom one, too. Starting a brand-new family is kind of hard, and they're going to need your help—especially as the big brother. William looks to you as an example. If you treat your step-dad like a friend, he'll do the same." She nudged him with her elbow. "What do you think?"

Jason peeked up with understanding in his eyes. "Yeah, I guess I can do that."

"Good," she told him. "That's the best wedding present you could give your mom." Devyn threw a glance at Will. "Now let's peel your brother off the Nintendo and set up an experiment."

Jason grinned up at her. "First, can we implode another Coke can?"

"You bet." Then she added the usual disclaimer, "As long as you explain the science behind it."

"I can do that in my sleep," he boasted. Then he said something that melted Devyn's heart. "'Cause you're a real good teacher."

"Thanks for taking such good care of the boys," Jason's mother said at pick-up. "It's like I get my own class every night because they can't stop talking about what they learned. I wish they were this excited about school back home."

"It's my pleasure." And Devyn meant every word. She'd grown to enjoy her time in the center—the light of discovery in the children's eyes, and the increasing admiration behind their smiles. A couple of the students had even pilfered flowers from the lobby vases to give her each morning, which touched her more deeply than she wanted to admit. "See you tomorrow."

As she waved good-bye and began tidying the room, a fierce warmth glowed beneath Devyn's breastbone. It had been such a long time since she'd felt the sensation that it took her a few moments to identify what it was—pride.

She smiled to herself and studied the hand-drawn maps the children had made that afternoon, each stop along the Mississippi labeled according to nineteenth-century trade. Will's depiction of a beaver pelt looked more like a Brillo Pad, but at least he'd understood the significance of fur as currency.

She was good at this. Really good. And more than that, she liked it.

The cell phone vibrated in Devyn's pocket, interrupting her reverie. She didn't recognize the incoming number and hesitated before answering.

"Hello?"

"Hi," said a man's voice. "It's Warren Larabee."

Instantly, the glow inside Devyn's chest morphed into a chill of dread. She'd been so distracted lately that she had forgotten about the job that awaited her back home.

"Miss Mauvais?" he asked when she didn't respond. "Is this a bad time?"

"Not at all," she said with a manufactured smile. "I just finished my shift, so your timing is perfect."

"Good. I wanted to run something past you real quick." Warren launched into a spiel about the graveyard tour and how excited the team was to script a reenactment of Memère's botched wedding day. "Juliette was jilted at the altar by a local, right?" Warren asked. "Edward Dumont? He's buried at the same cemetery."

"Yes," Devyn said. "Then she cursed his line so the men in that family would never find lasting love."

"Uh-huh. The team wants to know if you have any-

barely moving, not making a sound. That's no way to fuck." When she elbowed him in the ribs, he corrected, "I mean, make love."

She stood on tiptoe and peered at the gamblers as if picturing a secret tryst. "I don't see anywhere remotely private enough to pull it off."

Beau left his chair and settled behind her, near enough to catch the floral scent of her shampoo. He rested one hand on her waist and used the other to point out the window. "Right back there," he said into her ear, "near the corner. Someone standing behind that machine is out of sight."

Devyn relaxed into him, bringing the firm cushion of her ass against his fly, and Beau nearly swallowed his tongue. "Except for the ceiling cameras," she pointed out.

All the blood in his body funneled toward his crotch. Devyn's nearness—the warm press of her body and her intoxicating scent—scrambled his thoughts until his words stumbled out in a disjointed murmur against her earlobe. "People . . . tend to forget"—he cleared his throat—"the cameras."

She must have sensed the shift in him, because she stilled for a moment before releasing a shaky breath. "Do they?"

"Oh, yeah," he moaned. He wanted to bury his nose in her curls, so he did. She surprised him by tilting her head aside to bare her neck. Taking full advantage, he nuzzled the patch of skin below her ear and took her waist between both hands. She smelled of sweetness and sex, which wasn't helping the problem growing inside his pants. "It's easy to get caught up in the moment."

She arched her lower back just enough to brush his erection with her bottom. "Distracted by the rush."

"Uh-huh," he said while squinting his eyes shut. As if that would stop the desire from engorging him. He shouldn't have lit this match. The last thing he needed was another night spent with a cramp in his gut. "Listen," he said, groaning when she ground against him again. "I said we could go as slow as you wanted. . . ."

She took his hands and guided them to her breasts.

God bless, she wasn't making this easy. He couldn't stop his palms from molding to her softness. The heavy weight of her breasts was so deliciously familiar, filling his hands to perfection. He skimmed both thumbs over her nipples, pleased to find them already erect. She wanted him, and he loved that.

"And I meant it," he said. "We don't have to rush."

"Mmm," she hummed, bowing back for a heavier touch. "Slow is good."

Then she blew everything to hell by reaching behind her to stroke his erection. She cupped him hard and slid her palm gradually down to his base before sliding it back to the tip, where she circled the underside of his sensitive head with one fingernail. "I like it slow."

He groaned and thrust into her grasp, hoping like crazy she wasn't toying with him. He was hard enough to pound nails. "Baby, you're killing me."

Still stroking him, she used her free hand to cover

his, encouraging him to massage her nipples. When he rolled them between his fingers, she whimpered, tipped back her head to rest on his chest, and said, "What a wonderful way to die."

The last thing Beau wanted to do was stop, but that was exactly what had to happen unless she intended to take him all the way.

"Where's this going, Dev?"

She peered over her shoulder with a hunger in her gaze that matched his own. Her cheeks had grown flushed; her lips parted as she locked eyes with him and asked, "Are there cameras in this room?"

Beau shook his head. "Not a single one."

She blinked up at him, so beautiful it almost hurt to look at her. In that moment, he would have shaved twenty years off his life to have Devyn for one night—to peel off her clothes and consume every inch of her. To make up for the ten years he'd wasted living outside of her bed. Beau held his breath and waited for an answer.

"Good," she said. "Then hurry up and kiss me."

Chapter 10

Devyn didn't need to tell him twice.

Before she had a chance to blink, Beau took her cheek in one hand. She turned her face and arched her neck, rising to meet him while he lowered his mouth to hers. At the contact, she released a whimper that revealed how desperately she wanted him, but she didn't care. She was beyond pride. Her body had taken the wheel, and it was veering full throttle toward the massive, hard man behind her.

One touch had her skin burning with fever, and when the tip of his tongue flicked against her upper lip, chills rushed over Devyn's body. All her cares fell away until there was only Beau—his mouth firm and commanding as he explored her with a seeking tongue. A wave of desire settled between her thighs until she was so hot she could have combusted.

No one kissed like Beau Dumont. No one on earth.

When she broke free for air, he lifted her curls and slid his open mouth down the side of her throat, nibbling a trail to the weak spot at the top of her shoulder. There, he sucked her mercilessly while drawing her close with one powerful arm. Devyn pressed a hand against the window and bit her lip to contain a moan. She wanted to face him, to nestle their bodies together as tightly as she could, but then she glanced through the glass and locked eyes with a stranger on the other side.

A smoldering thrill shot up the length of Devyn's thighs.

In the instant before she remembered the stranger couldn't see them, she feared the man had caught her in the act. She envisioned what he would have seen—Beau kneading one of her breasts and biting her neck while she reached behind to palm his erection. For the briefest of moments, she had thought someone was watching her.

And surprisingly, she'd liked it.

The hint of danger heightened her sensations, each touch twice as erotic as before, and she finally understood the appeal of public sex. It was dangerous and forbidden. Which was hot as hell.

Still gazing out the window, she guided Beau's hand over her hips and whispered, "Touch me."

He made a noise of raw male hunger and tugged the hem of her skirt to her waist, then used a thumbnail to trace swirls around the source of her need, teasing her through the thin fabric of her panties. "Both hands on the glass," he ordered. "I'm not getting off in my pants this time, Kitten."

She did as she was told.

"I'm going to finish inside you," he promised. "But first," he said as his thumb pressed her swollen bud and made her gasp, "you'll come for me." He held the pressure and moved in a circle, rubbing tension into her core. "Again and again, until you can't stand up. By the time I'm ready to make love to you, there won't be a bone left in your body . . . except mine."

Devyn moaned and widened her stance. She was halfway there.

He tucked his hand inside her panties and took her breath away with the delicate play of his fingers. They taunted and probed, sliding between her wet folds with a lethal precision that had her panting Beau's name. He knew what he was doing, knew her body like a favorite song, and he strummed her chords until every muscle in her legs tensed in anticipation of release. Her hands squeaked against the window, a chorus of desperate noises rising from her throat. When she shifted her gaze to meet the eyes of a woman checking her reflection in the mirror, a flare of heat blossomed within her and Devyn went flying over the edge.

She came down slowly to find that Beau had followed the direction of her gaze into the casino. There was a devilish smile in his voice when he pressed his lips to her ear and whispered, "It feels like they're watching us, doesn't it?"

Devyn nodded, unable to form a coherent sentence.

"Did you like that?"

She swallowed and nodded again.

"Then let's try something." After removing her panties, he sat her on the edge of a tall rolling chair and swiveled it to face the window. Then he sank to his knees in front of the chair and propped her left heel on his shoulder. "I want you to pretend we're back there in the slots, hiding in the corner while I remind you what my tongue is for."

She wanted to tell him to wait a few minutes, that she was too sensitive after her climax, but then he licked her soft and slow, and she was powerless to do anything but lie back and surrender to his mouth.

Pure pleasure washed over her as he sucked and nibbled, pausing only long enough to utter a curse and tell her how good she tasted. He dragged the tip of his tongue back and forth over her throbbing flesh while she held tightly to the chair and moaned with inexplicable bliss. When she spread wider for him, he used two fingers to dip inside and stretch her by gradual degrees until he pushed all the way in and pulled back out again. Devyn remembered his instructions, but she couldn't pretend she was anywhere but right here, riding his long fingers while he sucked her to orgasm.

She came hard and fast, crying out into the room without a care for who might overhear. She was too far gone. Her inner walls convulsed around his pistoning fingers until the tremors ceased and she slumped back in the chair, utterly boneless.

Exactly as he'd promised.

Beau nipped at her inner thigh before rising from the floor and giving her a look that would melt steel. He licked off each of his fingers and spoke in a lust-roughened voice. "You're so fucking sweet, Dev. You always were."

The heat behind his gaze sent a new shiver of desire down her spine. She glanced at the enormous bulge straining the front of his pants and reached for the zipper. "Now it's my turn to taste you."

"Unh-uh." Wickedly, he grinned and shook his head. "You'll have to take a rain check. I want inside you. Right now."

She tried to stand, but her knees wobbled and gave out, sending her plunking back to the chair.

This seemed to please him. Beau smiled while unbuttoning his pants. "Didn't I say you wouldn't be able to stand up? I'm a man of my word."

Swamped by satisfaction, Devyn couldn't fire a witty comeback. Instead, she mirrored his smile and watched as he lowered his zipper to free his erection. His skin was stretched tight over a delightfully long, wide shaft. He was the living embodiment of masculinity, so big and strong and hard. Despite the two orgasms he'd given her, heat pooled low in Devyn's belly, making her go tingly in all the right places. Her body wanted him—*needed* him—and she was more than ready to take him in.

She spread her thighs for him, and he stepped in between, then gathered her in his arms. "Wrap your legs around my waist," he said. "I'm going to fuck you against the window, with all those people on the other side."

A charge of anticipation unfurled between her legs. The whole experience was so wrong, but in the best way. She couldn't recall the last time sex had made her feel so alive. She clung to Beau's shoulders and locked both ankles at the base of his spine while he grabbed her by the hips and pressed her bare bottom to the glass. The cold shock made her breath catch, but she quickly recovered when he nudged his rounded head inside her.

"Oh, God," she groaned while her eyelids slammed shut. The pleasure. There was no describing it. He'd given her only an inch, and she was already on the verge of coming. "More," she pleaded.

He pulled out to the tip and slid in halfway, until her body protested at the pressure of his girth. Beau hissed through his teeth and held there, trembling with need while she stretched to accommodate him. Then he pulled back and sank in a fraction more, working inside her gradually until he rocked his hips one last time and buried himself to the base.

Devyn held her breath and willed her inner muscles to relax. God, she was so full—so unbelievably full. She hadn't had a man this big in years, not since the last time she and Beau had made love, and the delirious invasion came with a stitch of pain.

"Are you okay?" he asked against her lips.

She nodded. "Just give me a second."

He kissed her in a gentle sweep of lips that told her to take all the time she needed. When her passage had adjusted, she squeezed her inner muscles and ground against him. "Go slow," she whispered.

And he did. He cradled her hips between his powerful hands and moved in and out in a lazy, fluid motion that had her neck arching against the window. He watched her carefully, gauging her reaction. "Is this all right?"

"Yes." *Oh, yes.* Feeling him so deep and hard inside her was the truest form of ecstasy she'd ever known. With his iron shaft gliding so smoothly between her legs, Devyn was much better than all right.

Until he gave her that intense look—the one that said this wasn't just sex.

"Dev . . ." he whispered, then pulled in a shaky breath. Unable to say anything more, he burned her up with his gaze and tipped their foreheads together. In response, her heart swelled and cracked as if to allow him inside, baring herself in a way she hadn't done since graduation night.

Right before he'd abandoned her.

She couldn't keep this up. He was taking too much. But when she let her lids flutter closed to escape the connection, Beau halted his movements.

"Look at me," he whispered. "No hiding. I want all of you." She rolled her hips, but he pressed her hard against the window to keep her immobile. "Want me to stop?"

"No," she cried, hating herself for her weakness even as she strained forward for more friction. She opened her eyes. "Don't you dare."

"That's a good girl."

Beau rewarded her with a rotation of his hips, smiling

when her eyes rolled back in rapture. He quickened the tempo of his thrusts, and she matched each one. Keeping their gazes locked, she dug her fingertips into his shoulders and held tight as the tension built low in her core. She raced toward climax to alleviate the sweet agony, telling herself this didn't mean anything, that she could give Beau her body and keep her soul hidden.

Even though it felt like a lie.

Beau gasped, his rigid control beginning to crack. She could tell he was near the brink, and she was nearly there herself. "Come for me," he murmured, squeezing her ass with those strong fingers. "I want to feel it, Dev."

Then he angled his hips and plunged hard, hitting exactly the right spot. She cried out and begged him to do it again. So he did, over and over, filling the small room with the squeak of her bare skin against the glass and the ragged pull of breath into their lungs. Each slow, slamming thrust increased the pressure until it finally broke into a molten release that sent sparks bursting down her legs. She buried her face in his shoulder and sobbed an incoherent strand of curses as she clenched around his pumping shaft.

"God damn," Beau growled with his forehead pressed to the window. "You feel so fucking good, I can't—" He cut off, and with one final slam of his hips, he stiffened and spilled into her with a low groan. For several heartbeats, he continued swearing under his breath until he placed a kiss below Devyn's ear. "Unreal," he whispered. "That was unreal."

"Mmm," she agreed. It always had been—sex with Beau was never the problem. What came afterward was a different story. "It really *is* a Magic Stick."

He laughed and pulled back to look at her, so happy that it put a hitch in Devyn's pulse. "Abracadabra, honey."

"And you're so modest, too," she teased. "The whole package."

"Let's make some more magic." He kissed her, soft and sweet. "Stay with me tonight. I've got that great big bed—plenty of room to strip you down and tend to anything I missed." In demonstration, he took her breast in hand and swept a thumb over her nipple. "I still haven't kissed you here."

The sweep of his thumb was going to turn her on again if he didn't stop. Devyn had no regrets for what she and Beau had done, but she needed some distance. Her body might be able to handle another round with him, but she couldn't say the same about her heart. If she spent the night in his bed, he would have her wide open and desperate, and he'd make her look into his eyes until he branded her. She wasn't ready for that, wasn't sure if she ever would be. Shaking her head, she unwrapped her legs from around his hips, sucking in a sharp breath of pain when he withdrew.

Maybe her body couldn't handle another round, after all.

"Sore?" he asked, handing over her panties.

It took a couple of tries to get her wobbly legs inside her bikini briefs. "Yeah. It's been a while for me."

He zipped up and smoothed his shirt, trying unsuccessfully to hide a prideful grin. "Stay the night anyway. I won't lay a hand on you."

She arched a disbelieving brow.

"Okay," he conceded, "I might. But I'll be gentle, and you know I'll make it good."

Yes, she knew. But that wasn't the issue. "Not tonight."

"Hey." He stopped what he was doing and took her face between his hands. "Are we all right?"

"Just all right?" she asked. "Didn't we agree that we're magical?"

"You know what I mean."

"We're okay, Dumont." To reassure him, she stood on tiptoe and kissed his nose. "And we're still on for tomorrow. Come get me when lunch is ready."

"At least let me walk you to your room."

She palmed his chest. "No way, not while you're wearing that dopey grin. The whole staff will know what we've been up to."

That dopey grin widened. "You're glowing too, by the way."

Devyn didn't doubt it. And truth be told, that scared her.

So she told him good-bye and returned to her room on shaky knees, for once relieved at the sight of her lumpy, narrow bunk. There, she was safe.

The next morning, the staff formed a line near the bow ramp to wave to the passengers as they left for their daylong excursions in Natchez. In between shaking hands and wishing guests a great day, Beau kept catching Devyn's eye, flashing a secret smile that affected her more than she wanted to admit. The heat in his stunning green eyes made her heartbeat catch, and when she returned to her room to change, she found herself taking extra care with her makeup and deliberating over what to wear.

She finally decided on jeans and a simple, snug-fitting blouse in Beau's favorite color—blue—and let her curls hang loose around her shoulders. She even skipped the antifrizz serum because it felt sticky, and Beau loved playing with her hair. Every choice she made was out of consideration for him.

That's how she knew she was in trouble.

At around noon, he knocked on the door, looking good enough to eat in paper-thin denim and a short sleeve T-shirt that hugged the contours of his muscled chest. He must have come straight from the galley, because he carried the scent of baked bread on his clothes. When a wide smile lifted the corners of his lips, he made her mouth water in more ways than one.

"You look beautiful," he said.

"You're kind of easy on the eyes yourself."

He laughed and lifted a wicker picnic basket for show. "As much as I'd love to stand here and soak up your ridiculous compliments, our lunch is getting cold." Extending an elbow, he asked, "Ready?"

She grabbed her handbag, and they linked their arms to set off toward the dock. At the head of the ramp, they crossed paths with Thing One and Thing Two, but for once, Devyn couldn't tell the twins apart because each man kept his gaze respectfully above the neck. This was unusual, not that she was complaining. Since they were still in uniform, she glanced at their name tags to differentiate between them.

"Hot date?" Nick asked with a crooked grin.

The question didn't faze Beau. "Jealous?"

"Hell, yeah. I'm stuck here running payroll for this guy," he hitched a thumb at his twin, "while he gallivants around Natchez with Ella-Claire."

Alex smiled. "He lost a bet, fair and square."

"I don't know about *fair*," Nick mumbled.

Ignoring his twin brother's complaint, Alex turned to Devyn. "Is Ella still getting ready? She needs to shake her tail feather, or we're going to miss our tour."

Devyn tipped her head in confusion. Ella had been up and out before breakfast. She hadn't even joined the staff that morning to bid farewell to the guests. "She left hours ago. I assumed she was with you."

"No." His blond brows pinched together. "I haven't seen her since yesterday." When he pulled out his cell phone and texted Ella, she didn't reply. A wrinkle of disappointment creased his forehead, and for the briefest of moments, Devyn felt sorry for him. Until she remembered her conversation with Ella-Claire—and the hurt in the young woman's eyes.

It seemed that Ella had drawn a line in the sand. Good for her.

Devyn put the matter behind her as she and Beau

strode down the ramp and onto the dock parking lot. The unyielding pavement felt so good beneath her feet that she stamped her heels a few times against the asphalt, enjoying the energy that resonated up her shins.

Beau cast an amused glance at her. "Better?"

"Much." She pulled in a deep breath of Mississippi air and turned her face to the sun, its rays heating her skin despite autumn's arrival. It was the perfect day for shore leave—clear and ever so breezy with the faint scent of mown grass drifting on the wind.

She turned to Beau and found him watching her with a grin. He shook his head in a slight gesture of disbelief. "I could look at you all day and never get my fill."

Her face heated, so Devyn did what she knew best—she deflected. "Where are we eating?"

"Over there a ways," he said, jutting his chin toward a grassy easement about fifty yards upriver. "It's not a proper park, but there are a few picnic tables overlooking the river. Should be more private than anything we'll find in town."

He surprised her by taking her hand as they walked onward. His fingers felt so perfect when they were laced between hers that Devyn couldn't bring herself to pull away. She enjoyed feeling anchored to him like this, so she swung their joined hands between them and savored the caress of the sun on her shoulders until they reached the first wooden picnic table and settled on opposite sides.

"What did you pack in here?" she asked, lifting the lid to peek inside.

Beau lightly smacked her hand. "Sit down and relax," he said, pulling a bottle from the basket and twisting off the top. "Here, have a beer."

"Nice." She tipped it back for a deep pull. She didn't know how he managed it, but the beer was ice-cold. "Doesn't matter what else is in there, this lunch is already a winner."

He unpacked the contents: two paper-wrapped packages, a pair of dill pickle spears, half a cheesecake, and a sack of breaded bits she couldn't identify. Then he pointed to the first bundles. "Gourmet grilled cheese sandwiches. Smoked provolone and cured bacon on artisan bread with sun-dried tomato pesto."

"Oh, my God," she moaned. That sounded like heaven. "I just had an orgasm in my mouth."

Beau waggled his brows. "Only one? You know that's not enough for me," he said as he shook the bag, rustling the bread crumbs inside. "Allie told me you love fried okra, so I put a spin on your mama's recipe. Gave it a little kick."

"You do love spice."

"Who doesn't like it hot?" he asked with a wink while opening the bag. "Try one."

She didn't need further persuading. The mixture smelled amazing, like peppers and salted garlic. When she popped a bite in her mouth, the flavors burst across her tongue, and she made a noise of pleasure. "You've got skills, Dumont," she mumbled around the okra. "Mad skills."

"Wait till you try the grilled cheese," he said as he

unwrapped both their sandwiches and grabbed a beer for himself. "You'll fall down at my feet in worship."

Devyn chuckled while she sank her teeth into the crispy bread, but by the time she finished her first bite, she wasn't laughing anymore. The smoky cheese and bacon provided the perfect contrast to the sweet tang of sun-dried tomatoes. Her taste buds were weeping with joy as she devoured the sandwich with no lady-like grace whatsoever. She wished she had an extra stomach so she could keep eating—it was that good.

"Wow," she said, wiping her mouth. "Ex-marine, security specialist, casino pit boss, gourmet chef. Is there anything you can't do?"

"Apparently, I can't get you to spend the night with me," he complained, tipping his beer bottle toward her. "How about it, Kitten? I'm awful lonely in that suite by myself."

Before she could tell him no, the rumble of a nearby vehicle drew her attention to the street. Then, as if it were a scene from her own personal nightmare, a Larabee Amusements tour bus motored past them and turned toward the heart of town. Here she was, having the best culinary experience of her life with a hard-bodied stud begging her to share his bed, and the moment was ruined by the reminder of what awaited her at home.

"There's no escaping it," she said to herself.

Beau watched the bus until it drove out of sight. His voice was full of caution when he said, "You have options, you know."

Devyn propped her chin in one hand, irritated with herself for letting something as trivial as a passing tour bus ruin her lunch. "Not as many as you think."

"Come on, Dev," Beau said. "I've seen you in the education center. You were born to teach. It's not too late to go back to school."

She laughed at the absurdity of it. "How am I supposed to support myself through four years of college *and* pay for tuition and books?" she asked. That ship had sailed long ago. "Most states require teachers to get a masters degree on top of that. I can feel my blood pressure rising just thinking about it."

"So you bite the bullet for a few years," Beau said. From the flippancy in his tone, you'd think they were discussing a cardio workout. "The reward will be worth it."

"And the tuition?" she asked.

"Student loans and grants."

"Sure," she deadpanned. He made it sound so simple. "And who's going to pay my rent while I'm in class all day?"

"It won't be easy—"

"So far, that's the first logical thing to come out of your mouth."

"But there are ways to make it work," he said, ignoring her. "Split rent with a roommate, get a job that fits your hours, look for programs that let you take classes online. If you want it bad enough, you'll figure out a solution."

"Maybe I don't want it that badly." She enjoyed

teaching, but not enough to spend another four years living like a pauper. For once, Devyn wanted to go to dinner without checking the credit balance on her MasterCard. She wanted to feel like an adult, not a college kid. "I appreciate your concern, but just drop it, okay?"

Beau clenched his jaw, but he didn't push. He drew a deep breath through his nose and blew it out. "I care about you. Sue me."

Devin smiled and threw a bread crumb at him. "Thank you. Now, new subject."

"Okay, how about this," he said as he upped the ante by flicking a chunk of okra at her. "Let's talk about the curse."

That caught her off guard. She wasn't sure if she liked this topic any better.

"Specifically," he added, "how we're going to break it."

"*We?*" she asked. No, she definitely didn't like where this was going.

"Yeah, I want you to help me."

Devyn bought herself a few seconds by finishing her beer, but by the time she'd swallowed the last drop, she was no closer to forming a response than before. Months ago, she had tried helping Marc and Allie break the curse . . . and failed. In the end, the only thing that had worked was Marc's determination to marry Allie at any cost. Devyn didn't want to think about marriage—especially not to the man who'd crushed her heart.

When she didn't answer, Beau nudged her across the table. "Hey, take a breath."

She hadn't realized she was holding it.

"I'm not asking for a Vegas wedding," he said. "Just a little help from a friend."

Devyn chanced a glance at him. He'd begun shredding the paper wrapping from his sandwich, a telltale sign that this wasn't an easy request for him to make.

"Growing up," he went on, "I didn't exactly have the *Leave it to Beaver* experience. But I want that someday—a wife and a family, all my kids under one roof. I want to eat pancakes on the weekends and coach little league. I want the picket fence."

The idea of Beau married to another woman, smoothing his hands possessively over her pregnant belly, made Devyn's chest ache. But she refused to dwell on why she felt that way. "I don't know how much good I can do. The Dumonts have the power to undo the hex, not me."

"Purest faith shall set you free," he quoted from Memère's curse. "But what does that mean? What does it look like? I don't understand, and that's where you come in."

Devyn pursed her lips and stared at her beer bottle as if Sam Adams might come to life and tell her what to do. Logically, she knew there was no harm in doing a little digging, but that didn't stop her stomach from pulling into a knot.

"Did I mention," Beau said, pointing at their dessert, "that I brought cheesecake?"

Devyn smiled and shook off whatever shadow had passed over her. Beau was right—he wasn't asking for much. Besides, after all the things he'd done for her, she owed him a favor. "Oh, well that changes everything."

"So you'll do it?"

"You *did* give me an orgasm in my mouth . . ."

"Among other places."

"True," she agreed. "All right, Dumont. I'll help you break the hex."

"Thanks, Dev." His grateful smile made her go all gooey inside. "This means a lot."

"No problem," she said, reminding herself that this wasn't a big deal. "That's what friends are for."

Chapter 11

Beau sipped his iced tea and studied the flat-screen television, analyzing the footage he'd missed a few days ago when he was otherwise occupied with Devyn. The roulette table was still underperforming, and his instincts told him one of the employees was skimming chips. The problem was that in order to pull off the scheme for any significant amount of money, the perp needed a partner—someone working in the cash-out station who would look the other way and trade those chips for greenbacks. It was bad enough to have one thief on the payroll, but a conspiratorial partnership was a whole other level of betrayal. Thinking about it made Beau's fists tighten, and he squinted at the recorded feed in determination to nail the bastards.

But then he spotted Devyn's image, and his focus blew to hell.

She had been walking toward the exit, her hair still mussed from his fingers, and she threw a glance over her shoulder toward the one-way glass where moments before, he'd held her there and made them both dizzy with pleasure. He paused the footage to freeze her in place, then zoomed in to read her expression. Her lips were parted, her eyes glassy beneath a furrowed brow. It didn't take a brain surgeon to identify the emotion etched onto her features.

She was afraid.

That didn't surprise him. He'd sensed her reluctance to let go when she refused to look him in the eyes during lovemaking. Since that night, they'd had sex three more times, but it wasn't the same as it had been in the security room—just a few stolen moments in supply closets and dark corners, with Devyn continuing to refuse to stay the night with him. She was holding back; that was clear. But still, it stung to see the evidence of her anxiety in high definition.

Beau supposed he couldn't blame her. She'd loved him once, and he had made her suffer for it. Trust was earned. Regaining hers would take time.

Luckily, he had plenty of that.

His cell phone buzzed to announce a new text, and he smiled. Devyn must be on her lunch break. He checked the screen and saw that he was right.

Meet me in my room, she told him, *and I'll give you something a lot more filling than a grilled cheese sandwich.*

If Beau had his choice, he'd meet her in his suite and spend all day worshipping her body. But since she wasn't ready for that, he'd take whatever he could get.

I'm on my way, he promised. *Don't start without me.*

* * *

Twenty minutes later, Devyn was on all fours, coming harder than a runaway train while he thrust into her from behind. It didn't escape Beau's notice that she was refusing to have face-to-face sex with him, but with her inner muscles clenching around him like a liquid fist, he couldn't bring himself to give a shit. He slammed into her one last time and growled, erupting in a climax he felt all the way to the soles of his feet.

Once he caught his breath, Beau skimmed a loving hand over the bare ass cheeks peeking out from beneath Devyn's skirt. He pulled out slowly and tucked himself back into his pants.

"Much better than a grilled cheese," he agreed. "But I'll be hungry again in a few hours."

Laughing, she retrieved her panties from beneath the bed. "More like a few minutes."

"You know me well." And because of that, she probably knew what was coming next. "Stay with me tonight."

"I can't." She didn't meet his gaze when she pulled on her underwear and lowered her skirt. "I have a roommate, remember? Ella-Claire will notice if I'm missing."

"She's a big girl. I'm pretty sure she had 'the talk' with her mama."

"You're my boss," Devyn reminded him. "We're not supposed to be sleeping together."

Beau didn't bother arguing that he'd already outed himself as her boyfriend at the class reunion, or that Marc knew they were involved and had begrudgingly accepted it. Because that wasn't the real reason she avoided sharing his bed. Instead, he threw her a teasing grin and pleaded, "Come on. All this sneaking around is making me feel cheap."

She folded her arms and returned his smile. "Want me to buy you dinner next time? I can probably scrounge up some flowers, too."

"You're breakin' my heart, darlin'."

"Mmm," she said, crawling toward him. She laced her fingers behind his neck and kissed him until he couldn't tell which way was up. "And yet," she whispered against his lips, "you keep coming back for more."

Beau couldn't deny it, but that didn't mean she had him by the short and curlies. He took back a handful of the power by nibbling his way down the side of her neck while massaging her breast. He grazed the top of her shoulder with his teeth, using one finger to circle her nipple until Devyn whimpered and strained against him. Until she spread her legs and rocked against his thigh. Until he knew he could have her again.

Then he stood up and told her good-bye.

Later that night, she made him pay.

"Dev," he groaned from inside the linen closet, where he stood against a shelf of bath towels while she knelt at his feet, teasingly flicking her tongue over the tip of his erection. She'd been torturing him with whisper licks for what felt like an hour, and now he was so painfully hard that she may have broken his dick.

"Damn it," he swore. "You'll be the death of me."

The thin strip of light leaking inside from the hallway wasn't enough to illuminate the closet, but he could hear the smile in her voice. "I don't want to kill you, Dumont." She wrapped a loose hand around his shaft, barely skimming him as she pumped up and down. "In fact, I'm kind of attached to some of your finer parts."

"Then prove it," he hissed, gripping the shelf behind him.

"Tsk, tsk, tsk." With her fingernails, she brushed the sensitive patch of skin behind his balls, making his jock twitch. "I didn't hear the magic word."

"Please," he said in a rush. This was a matter of life and death. Now was *not* the time for saving face. "Please, Dev."

She pretended to consider his request, then quickly sucked a bead of moisture from his engorged tip before she pulled back, letting the cool air replace her blazing mouth. Beau clenched his teeth, regretting with every fiber of his soul that he'd teased her earlier that day.

Payback was a bitch.

And apparently, Devyn knew it. She rose to her feet and faced him, taking his throbbing length in her hand. "You're so hard," she mused. "Is there someplace you'd like to put this?"

Beau snapped.

Grabbing her around the waist, he sank to the floor and took her with him until she straddled his lap. He shoved up her skirt, hooked a thumb around the crotch of her panties, and positioned himself at the base of her slick entrance. Then, curling an arm behind Devyn's body, he tugged her down while he thrust upward, filling her with a liquid ease that ripped a moan from both their throats.

"Yeah," he murmured. "Right there."

She rode him slowly at first, building to a desperate tempo that was sure to leave rug burns on her knees. So he rolled her to the floor and slung her legs over his shoulders. The new position must have hit her hot spot, because she mewled and cried and cursed as he rocked in and out of her. Between her primal noises of pleasure and the slap of their colliding hips, it was a wonder half the boat couldn't hear them.

Not that he particularly gave a damn at the moment.

"Now it's your turn to beg," he said, pausing to grind a deep rotation against her. "Let's hear the magic word, Kitten."

Her voice was a low whine. "I hate you."

He chuckled to himself. "I don't think so. I think you're loving one of my *finer parts* right now."

"Please," she whispered. Her breaths came in shallow gasps. "Please don't stop."

He didn't make her ask again, mostly because he couldn't hold out for much longer. Drawing on his last shreds of energy, Beau drove into her hard and fast. They came together in a rush of sensation so powerful that he may have left his own body. It was hard to tell, because he was still dizzy with the intoxicating feel of her sex when they untangled their limbs a few moments later.

"Wow," she breathed, adjusting her clothes. "Just wow."

"Seconded." He felt in the darkness for her hand, then gave it an affectionate squeeze. But when he tried to wrap his arm around her, Devyn planted a hasty kiss at his temple.

"I'll text you tomorrow at lunch," she said, moving to her feet before he'd even zipped his pants. She opened the closet door, blinding him with a flash of light from the hallway before she shut it again.

And then she was gone.

What the hell?

Beau sat there, utterly dumbstruck as he tried to process the hasty escape. He was only joking when he'd said their hookups made him cheap, but damned if he didn't feel a little used right now. Was it his imagination, or had they taken a step backward? Each time with Devyn seemed brasher than the last, a series of hit-and-runs with her doing all the running. She was pulling away emotionally and using him to get off.

That's when it struck him—they weren't making love anymore. They were fucking. And not affectionate fucking, either. This was down and dirty, biting and clawing, teasing and swearing, animal sex. The no-strings-attached kind. And as hot as it was, Beau had come too far with Devyn to let their relationship mutate into some one-dimensional friends with benefits arrangement.

He wanted more.

Which meant no more booty calls.

"Shit." His Magic Stick wasn't going to like that, but it would have to take one for the team. "Be strong, big guy," he muttered to his crotch. "Keep your eye on the prize."

"You've got to be strong." Devyn gripped Ella-Claire's upper arms. "Don't cave now, not when he's finally getting a glimpse of what life is like without you."

Ella jutted out her bottom lip. "But I miss him."

"That's good," Devyn said with an encouraging nod. "I'm sure he misses you too. Think about how miserable you are." When Ella's mouth pulled into a frown, Devyn added, "Now imagine Alex feeling the same way."

"How is this supposed to make me feel better?"

"Well, it doesn't," Devyn admitted. "But it's important that Alex realizes two things."

Ella made a *go ahead* motion with her hand.

"First, he has to know you're serious—that you're not making empty threats when you tell him to fish or cut bait," Devyn advised. The same rule applied in the education center. If her students acted the fool and she threatened a consequence, she always had to follow through on it. "If you keep taking him back, he'll learn that you don't mean what you say."

"And second?"

"He's taking you for granted." Devyn paused to let the words sink in. "Some people have to lose what they love in order to appreciate it. Alex might be one of those people. If so, this distance is just what the doctor ordered."

Ella blinked her big blue eyes and puffed a sigh.

"What did Alex say when you told him you wanted more?" Devyn asked.

The girl's shoulders sagged. "He was totally logical about the whole thing. He said he's attracted to me too, but if we cross the line, it could ruin our friendship and mess up the whole family dynamic."

Devyn didn't say so, but she thought Alex had made a valid argument.

"He asked me to imagine what would happen if we dated and then broke up," Ella continued. "How tense and awkward it would be, especially because we all work together. And how things would never be the same between him and Marc."

"Alex would be risking a lot," Devyn pointed out. "More than you, because Marc holds him to a different standard. And you two are barely out of college. The odds that you'll take your friendship to the next level and stay together forever are pretty slim."

Ella folded her arms and made a noise of offense. "A minute ago, you were telling me to stay strong and make him suffer. Now you're agreeing with him. Whose side are you on?"

"Yours, believe it or not." As much as Devyn wanted to see Ella-Claire with the guy of her dreams, she needed to understand all the possible consequences instead of letting her heart call the shots. "By default, a relationship with Alex won't be easy. Have you considered that?"

Ella answered with a question of her own. "Do you

know how hard it is to stand back and watch him with other girls? To be his friend and pretend I don't care when someone slips a phone number in his pocket? Or to laugh it off when I hear one of his brothers tease him about his dates?"

Devyn thought back to her picnic with Beau, when she'd pictured him with a wife and a family that didn't include her. "I can imagine."

"I can't keep going on like this," Ella said. "It hurts too much. Either we take it to the next level, or we go our separate ways so I can move on. Our family dynamic is screwed no matter what, because something has to change. That's what you and Alex don't understand."

"Aw, honey." Devyn squeezed Ella's shoulder, her heart aching for the girl. "I get it. And my original advice still stands. If you want to give Alex an ultimatum, then hold your ground. I hope you get what you want."

A tear spilled from her lashes and trailed down her cheek. "Why does this have to be so hard?"

"Because," Devyn said, "we don't appreciate what comes for free."

The next day, Devyn inhaled her turkey on rye and jogged to her room while trying not to choke on a bite of lettuce. Her lunch break was only forty-five minutes long, and she had already wasted a few of those precious minutes on actual lunch.

Which wasn't what she hungered for.

After letting herself inside, she wrapped a hair elastic around the doorknob in a silent message for her roommate, then undressed down to her matching bra and panty set—black lace, sure to put some extra giddy-up in Beau's pulse. She took a seat on the dresser and sent him a quick text.

I'm in my room, and all my clothes are on the floor, she typed. *The door's unlocked for you. . . .*

His response was almost instantaneous. *I'll be there in five.*

Devyn checked her watch and smiled when Beau made it there in three minutes, not five. Just as she expected, his eyes bulged at the sight of her, but then he shut the door behind him, and something in his expression shifted. Cooled. He raised his gaze to hers and stood near the wall instead of planting himself between her parted thighs.

She hadn't seen that coming.

The longer he stood there silently staring her down, the more exposed Devyn felt. What was taking him so long? Were they going to do this, or not?

"We need to talk," Beau said, tucking both hands in his pockets. "Maybe you should put on your clothes."

Devyn's lungs emptied as her skin flushed with the unchecked embarrassment of rejection. Here she was, on display for him in a few strategically placed scraps of lace, and he suggested she get dressed? Her ears had heard him, but her mind was a little slow on the uptake. Beau had been all over her like a duck on a june bug since he'd come back to town, and now he didn't want her anymore?

"Aw, now." He gave a sympathetic tilt of his head. "Don't look at me like that."

Devyn gasped before she could stop herself. How was she looking at him? Because the only thing more pathetic than rejection was showing how much it hurt. She scrambled off the dresser and lunged for her pants, which lay on the floor with one leg turned inside out. She'd wanted Beau so badly that she hadn't taken the time to undress like a normal person. No, she'd torn the clothes off her body like they were made of acid. Devyn cursed herself as she punched an arm through her khakis in a desperate attempt to right them.

"Stop." Beau snatched away the pants and tossed them over his shoulder. He was in full uniform, and when his gold-embellished coat brushed her bare stomach, she felt naked in an exaggerated way, like she was standing in Times Square in nothing but her birthday suit. "Look at me, Dev."

When she shoved against him with both hands, he wrestled her until she was facing the mirror, then wrapped his powerful arms around hers and held her immobile. Her breathing was heavy as she glared at his reflection, but she didn't bother to struggle. Beau was a tank—six and a half feet of solid muscle. Any attempt to wriggle free would be a waste of energy.

"Let go," she ordered. "You're the one who told me to get dressed."

"Not like this. Hear me out first."

"Okay, talk."

But of course he didn't do that. He stood there and

watched her, easy as you please, until she calmed down enough to unclench her shoulders. Only then did he begin.

"It's not that I don't want you," he said. "Because I do."

She scoffed at him. "Like I care."

"*I* care."

As if to demonstrate, he gathered her hair aside and placed a kiss on her shoulder, holding her gaze as he did. Then he smoothed a rough palm over the outside swell of her hip and continued past her waist, all the way up to her rib cage. Gently, he massaged one breast through her bra before pulling down the stretchy lace to expose her nipple. It pebbled against her will, proving how *very much* she cared.

With a low grumble of appreciation, he circled the puckered tip with his thumb. "I want you more than I want air." And he showed her by pressing the evidence against her backside. "But I'm not a teenager anymore, Dev. I want more than a few minutes with you inside a dark closet. I want everything."

When he licked his fingers and used them to tug at her nipple, Devyn sealed her lips to trap a moan. But that didn't stop wet heat from pooling in her belly, radiating downward until the flesh between her thighs ached.

"I want to spread you out on my bed," he went on, "and strip you naked. Then I'm going to kiss you here." Lightly, he pinched her nipple. "And here," he said, winding a southbound finger over her belly button.

"And especially here." His hand dipped into her panties, where he stroked her halfway to oblivion.

As much as Devyn tried to hide it, desire played across her face, lowering her lids and bringing a blush to her cheeks. Beau's breaths quickened against her neck as he watched the reflection of his fingers playing between her legs. He felt so good—*too* good—and she hated that only Beau had the power to make her lose herself.

"After that," he said, "I'm going to make love to you, and I'll take my sweet time. Then we'll fall asleep while I'm still inside you—and the next time you wake up, you'll already be moaning my name."

At that moment, with Beau rubbing hot tension into her core, she would have agreed to anything if it would make him keep going. And he must have known it, because he pulled his fingers free and took a moment to suck them clean.

"But until then," he told her, "I won't settle for quick and dirty sex." He held her gaze in the mirror as he bent his mouth to her ear. "Just knock on my door when you're ready for the real deal. I'll make you glad you came."

Several minutes later, long after Beau had left her alone and unsatisfied, Devyn stared at her reflection and tried to pinpoint what was bothering her . . . aside from the ache of desire between her legs. There was something else needling at her consciousness, but it was just beyond her grasp.

Realization hit a while later, when she was in the

education center waiting for the kids to return from lunch. Beau had cut her off and issued an ultimatum—exactly like she'd told Ella-Claire to do. Which implied Devyn had done something wrong. She was the fickle partner.

But she hadn't seen herself that way.

She didn't fear commitment or monogamy. Devyn could totally see herself settling down someday and having children. In holding back from Beau, she was only protecting herself from a proven flight risk.

There was nothing wrong with that.

And much like the trouble brewing between Alex and Ella-Claire, there were two sides to the story, two valid reasons for each partner wanting a different outcome. In demanding that she spend the night with him, Beau didn't realize how much he was asking of her. Or maybe he understood and simply didn't care. Either way, she wouldn't be knocking on his bedroom door any time soon.

"Or at all," she clarified to herself. "Like, ever."

Because much like Pandora's box, once she opened that door, there would be no closing it.

Chapter 12

In the two days that followed, Devyn spent her evenings in the galley under the pretense of helping her sister with the baking. In truth, she needed to stay busy. Idle hands were the devil's playground, and if left to their own devices, Devyn's hands would soon find their way into Beau's pants like magnets to steel.

Steel.

That described him all too well, and suddenly she blushed at the recollection of how magnificent he had felt inside her, so hard and deep. She shut down that train of thought and put more weight behind her rolling pin, flattening the pastry dough for tomorrow's breakfast turnovers.

"Hey," she said to her sister. "Can I ask you something?"

"No." Allie shook her head and eyed her sarcastically over a bowl of blackberries. "You're not allowed to talk while providing free labor. Shut up and get back to work."

Devyn snagged a berry from the bowl and tossed it into her mouth, earning her a reproachful look. "Let's imagine that the unthinkable happened, and you lost the bakery and all your income. No insurance money, no emergency fund. You've got nothing to cushion the fall except a paycheck or two."

Allie frowned. "Okay."

"Now imagine that the restaurant of your dreams offered to make you head pastry chef, but they won't give you the job until you graduate from culinary school. And they won't help pay for the tuition or any of your living expenses—it's all on you. Would you do it?"

"Go back to school?"

Devyn nodded. "Knowing that you wouldn't have two nickels to rub together for the next four years, and you'd be up to your neck in student loan debt by the time you graduated."

Allie blew out a low whistle and thought about it for a while before saying, "I don't think so. I'd probably spend more time on the *Belle*. Our dining hall manager is retiring soon, so maybe I'd take over that position."

Devyn didn't know why, but her sister's answer disappointed her. "You wouldn't miss the bakery?"

"Sure I would," Allie said, adding a scoop of sugar to her berries. "But I can still do that here."

"What if you couldn't?" Devyn asked. "If being a pastry chef on the *Belle* wasn't an option, would you go to culinary school then?"

With her lips pursed, Allie considered the question

before shaking her head. "Probably not. I like baking, but I don't have to do it for a living. I could cook at home for my family and not feel like I'm missing out. Besides, I like working here on the boat with Marc. It keeps us close." She giggled to herself. "And he loves nooners. I wouldn't get any of those if I went away to school."

Devyn was beginning to see that comparing her situation to Allie's was an *apples vs. oranges* kind of thing. Allie was a Dumont now, which meant she had a guaranteed job aboard the *Belle*. She was invested here, so supporting the family business was satisfying enough—in more ways than one.

But Devyn wasn't a part of anything larger than herself, which was both liberating and scary in equal measure. She had the freedom to go wherever the wind took her, but no safety net if the wind quit blowing and dropped her out of the sky.

"Why do you ask?" Allie said. "Do you want to go to culinary school?"

"No. Just thinking, that's all."

"About wh—" Allie's eyes went round with realization. "Oh, my god. You're thinking about getting your teaching degree! Devyn, that's great! Do it!"

Devyn held up a floury hand. "Take a chill pill. I'm not *seriously* thinking about it, just giving it a teensy-weensy bit of consideration."

It was only because Beau had planted the bug in her ear. Now that he'd cut her off from the good stuff, she had more free time to kick around those types of thoughts.

"I'm not actually going to do it."

"Why not?"

Devyn scoffed. She couldn't believe her sister had to ask. "For the same reason you wouldn't do it if you lost the bakery. I'm already broke as a joke. With a tuition bill and no way to work full-time, I'll be flat-out destitute—for at least four years. And then there'll be student loan debt after that."

"But they have programs for that," Allie said. "One of my wedding cake clients last year was a teacher. We got to talking, and she told me the government paid off half her student loans because she taught science in a qualifying school."

"A qualifying school?" Devyn asked with an arched brow. "In other words, the kind no one else wants to work at?"

"Oh, please." Allie flapped a hand. "You could handle the toughest students. Besides, those are the kids who need you most. You could make a difference in their lives. Isn't that what you always wanted growing up?"

Yes, it was. And the unique challenge of teaching at-risk students appealed to Devyn more than she let on. That kind of work would never be dull, and the rewards would extend way beyond a paycheck. She felt a brief glimmer of hope—a faint stirring of warmth within her breast—that her dream had come back to life.

But then reality set in.

Four long years of classes, homework, exams, and internships. That subtle stirring of warmth grew cold. In order to become a teacher, she'd first have to be a student. The whole thing was too overwhelming to consider.

"I'm not going back to school," she said in a tone that closed the topic for debate. "It's too late for that."

"Okay . . ." Allie dragged out the word, clearly not letting Devyn off the hook so easily. "But what about the haunted cemetery tours? It's none of my business how much Warren Larabee offered to pay you, but is this a career? Or is it just a job? Because if it's only another temporary job, you're going to find yourself facing this same problem next year. And the year after that. At some point, you have to settle into an occupation for the long haul. Which means you might as well finish your degree now."

"You don't have a degree," Devyn pointed out.

"I don't need one," Allie said. "But if I *did*, I'd suck it up and go back to school."

Devyn pretended to focus on cutting the dough into strips while reflecting on Warren's salary offer. The amount had seemed generous at the time—considering she'd just come home to an overdue rent notice stapled to the front door—but was it enough to support her in the long term? She imagined herself in forty years, hunched over and leading the haunted tour with a walker. Not a pretty sight. Maybe she should negotiate for a bigger piece of the pie.

She was brainstorming ways to ask for a raise when Nick poked his head inside the galley. She knew it was him because a few days ago, she'd noticed that his left eyebrow arched a bit higher than the right, giving the illusion that he always had something naughty on his mind. Which, knowing him, was probably the case.

"Hey, Dev," Nick said. "The boss man wants to see you."

"Great." Devyn blew out a breath, not bothering to ask which of her bosses had summoned her. She knew. "What does he want?"

"Dunno."

"Where is he?"

"Where else? In the security room."

Devyn brushed the flour from her hands and untied her apron. "All right. I'll head up there in a minute."

"He's in a shit mood," Nick warned. "Just sayin'."

A flicker of concern passed through her. It took a lot to get Beau riled up. Devyn wondered what had happened to ruin his mood, and she found herself quickening the pace to wash her hands so she could get to him faster. Maybe she should take some iced tea and his favorite dessert, too.

"Do we have any pecan pie left from supper?" she asked Allie.

Her sister grinned knowingly. "In the fridge."

Beau liked his pie warm, so Devyn heated up a slice and topped it with a scoop of vanilla bean ice cream, then filled a travel cup with iced tea and set off for the casino. As usual, he saw her coming through the one-way glass and already had the security room door open for her when she arrived.

Beau might have been in a dark mood before, but when he spotted the rich ice cream melting over warm pecan pie, his eyes brightened. "Is that for me?"

Devyn held it out to him, along with the cup. "This, too. I heard you're having a rough night."

When he took the offerings, he watched her for several charged moments with so much gratitude that Devyn tingled all over. She knew she shouldn't be sending mixed messages, but she couldn't bring herself to not care for him. Making Beau smile like this—especially after a hard day—brought her a deep sense of satisfaction, similar to the way she felt after a grand slam lesson in the education center.

"Thanks." He took his pie to the swiveling chair parked in front of the observation window and sat on half of the seat, then motioned for her to share the spot beside him. "This'll take the edge off."

There wasn't much space next to his big body, but Devyn settled in best as she could and peered through the glass. The casino was at half capacity, probably because the theater shows were in progress, so she could see all the way to the craps table at the rear of the room. While Beau ate his pie, she studied the passengers, some laughing at their losses while others sat at the gaming tables with the laser focus of seasoned gamblers. Muffled noises of electronic chirps and cheers filtered into the room to punctuate the occasional scrape of Beau's fork against the plate. It was kind of nice sitting there beside him, enjoying his body heat and a few minutes of quiet company.

Once he'd finished his pie, Devyn asked, "Feel better?"

"Much," he said as he wrapped a casual arm around her and pulled her in for a hug. "That was real sweet of you."

"What happened today? Want to talk about it?"

He huffed a sigh and pointed out the window. "See the employee manning the roulette wheel?"

Devyn brought the man into focus—tall and lanky, mid-thirties, brown hair. He wore a red staff polo shirt and a natural smile that said he genuinely enjoyed his job. "What about him?"

"I'm pretty sure he's skimming chips. I've been watching him for days, and I can't figure out how he's doing it," Beau said, setting down his cup with enough force to shake the computer table. "It's driving me crazy."

That came as a surprise to her. Devyn didn't know the guy, but he had one of those honest faces, the kind she tended to trust automatically. "How do you know it's him?"

"Because his table has been underperforming." Beau explained how part of his job involved tracking each table and gaming machine to make sure they generated the predicted income. "There's only one reason for a steady drop like that."

"But how do you know he's the one stealing?" she asked.

"He's the only one who mans that table."

"What about during his lunch break?"

"We shut it down for the hour," Beau said. "The casino doesn't see much action during lunch, so it doesn't pay to get another employee to cover it."

Devyn leaned forward to study the man more closely. Compared to the other dealers, all business with their tight mouths and their chilly gazes, he seemed so friendly. He even bent down to pick up a woman's handbag for her when she dropped it—a sweet gesture, but a bit naïve as it left the table unsupervised for a split second. That made Devyn wonder if someone else had noticed the man's helpful nature . . . and taken advantage of it.

"What if it's a passenger?" Devyn asked. "Or more than one passenger working together?" She could envision it: one partner distracting the dealer while the other covertly palmed a handful of chips from the table. If they did it right, they could bend over the chips to hide the act from the ceiling cameras.

Beau grunted in doubt. "I don't know. These folks aren't breezing in here from off the street. They've paid a shitload of money for their tickets. I can count the number of times on one hand that we've busted a guest for stealing."

Devyn shrugged. "Rich people steal sometimes. For the thrill of it."

"Yeah, but still."

"Couldn't hurt to check out the footage again," she said. "Look at it from a different perspective. You might notice something you missed before."

"I guess," he said, peering down at her, so close to her that their lips nearly touched. His gaze dropped to her mouth, but he made no move to kiss her. Devyn didn't know whether to feel relieved or annoyed. She liked kissing him. "Want to help?" he asked.

When she didn't answer right away—because she was too busy brooding over why he wouldn't kiss her—he saved the moment by adding, "I miss having you around."

"Yeah?" she asked, a smile flittering across her lips.

"That's the real reason I sent Nicky to get you," Beau said as he coiled a lock of her hair around his finger and flashed a crooked grin that made her stomach flip. "Just because we're not sleeping together doesn't mean we can't hang out." He made his eyebrows bob. "Though I'm happy to correct that first part whenever you want."

Devyn laughed and reclaimed her hair, glad to hear that he wanted her, though she shouldn't have cared either way. "I'll help look at the security tapes, Dumont. But you're sleeping alone tonight."

He set up the recorded feed on the big screen monitor, and for the next hour, Devyn watched the footage while Beau surveyed the casino through the window. She looked for anything out of the ordinary—guests repeatedly knocking items to the floor or monopolizing the roulette dealer's attention—but so far it all seemed aboveboard.

When her eyes couldn't take the strain any longer, she promised to return tomorrow. Beau gave her a gentlemanly kiss on the hand before they parted, but there was nothing tame about the hunger in his gaze when his lips brushed her knuckles. If his intent was to keep her awake half the night, he accomplished his goal. It was stubborn determination, and maybe a little bit of pride, that kept Devyn in her bunk.

The next night didn't yield any breakthroughs either, but she enjoyed spending the evening curled up beside Beau on their shared chair, his powerful arm wrapped around her so sure and steady. To pass the time while they studied the footage, they talked about where they'd traveled since high school and their favorite places to visit. It turned out they were both partial to beaches. Beau told her about Hisaronu Bay in Turkey, two stretches of sandy beach with aquamarine waters and a nearly constant breeze perfect for windsurfing.

"I want to take you there someday," he said, as if making plans together for the future was a foregone conclusion.

Devyn wasn't sure how she felt about that, so she kept the conversation moving. "My favorite is Caneel Bay in Saint John. I took a private charter there from Saint Thomas and spent the day snorkeling." She didn't mention that she'd taken the trip with an ex. "It's warm and gorgeous, and getting to the Virgin Islands is easy because you don't need a passport."

From there, they compared their favorite movies and discovered they were both fans of slapstick comedies, specifically Monty Python films and spoofs like Austin Powers.

"Monty Python's *Holy Grail* is the funniest thing

ever committed to film," Beau declared. "Especially the scene where King Arthur asks the French guard to join his quest to find the grail—"

"And the guard says, *We already have one,*" Devyn interrupted with a giggle-snort. "Best line ever!"

"I was just going to say the same thing," Beau said, smiling down at her in wonder. "I can't believe you like that movie. How did I never know that about you?"

Devyn propped her chin on his chest and returned his smile. "Well, we didn't do a whole lot of talking when we dated."

"True," he said with a chuckle. "And I guess we fell into the same pattern here on the boat."

"You know what they say about old habits . . ."

"Mmm," he agreed. He kissed her forehead and returned his attention to the recorded feed on the monitor. "I'm glad we're finally getting to know each other. I like you, Devyn Mauvais."

She grinned and settled into his embrace, utterly content for the first time in recent memory. "You're not so bad either, Dumont."

The following night, they were sharing stories of their most embarrassing moments when Devyn noticed something strange on the monitor. She sat up and leaned closer to the screen, then asked Beau to pause the footage.

"Look right there," she said, pointing to a familiar cowboy hat. It was the married asshole who had hit on her last week. The man leaned a hip against the roulette table to place a bet, which wasn't what bothered her. "Now check this out." She indicated a busty young blonde standing across from the cowboy, placing a wager of her own.

"What about them?" Beau asked.

"They're not a couple, or at least they don't act like it." She'd noticed while observing the casino floor that the cowboy was a loner. Aside from an occasional tip of his hat, he didn't engage in conversation with the other gamblers. "I've never seen them talk."

"Okay . . ."

"But they keep coming to the roulette table and standing right across from each other." That struck Devyn as odd. "Why would two strangers feel the urge to play roulette at exactly the same time—and assume the same positions at the table?"

Beau wrinkled his forehead and played the overhead feed in slow motion. For the next several minutes, they scrutinized every frame containing the couple, but didn't turn up any evidence of theft. The cowboy lost two bets and ambled off to the nearest blackjack table while the blonde strode to the bar for a glass of wine.

Devyn didn't have a lick of proof, but her instincts blared a red alert. "Something's up with those two," she muttered to herself. "I can feel it."

"Maybe she's Jill," Beau said.

"Who's Jill?"

"His mistress." Beau explained how he and Nicky had checked out the guy for suspicious behavior at the poker table, and glimpsed a text message to his lover.

"He's not a total idiot, but apparently not enough to canoodle in public with the other woman."

Devyn wasn't convinced. "Do you have a smaller camera? Something I can wear, or plant near the roulette wheel?"

Beau shook his head.

She slid him a disbelieving glare. "What kind of ex-military security buff doesn't have a spy cam?"

He shrugged. "The kind running security on a historic riverboat."

"Well, the ceiling cameras aren't cutting it." She needed a way to get a low, hands-level view of the dealer's chips, since that's where any theft was likely coming from. "How late does the cowboy usually hang around?"

"Till closing," Beau said. "He's a big player."

In more ways than one, the cheating jerk. Devyn had an idea to get a closer look. It wasn't the most brilliant plan she'd ever concocted, but it was worth a shot. "I'm guessing employees aren't allowed to gamble here or fraternize with guests, right?"

"Not if they want to keep their jobs."

"I'm going back to my room to change," she said. "Tell Nicky that I'm going to hang out on the floor for a while, and not to bother me."

Beau eyed her while folding both arms over his massive chest. "Why? What have you got up your sleeve?"

"Nothing," Devyn said with a wink. "*Yet.*"

Twenty minutes later, she was back in the casino wearing a push-up bra and her lowest cut blouse, the one that showed enough boob to stop traffic. It also had long sleeves that flared at the wrist . . . perfect for concealing a handheld camera, or in her case, a cell phone with video capacity.

She scanned the room for a black cowboy hat and found it bent over the roulette wheel. Perfect timing. Devyn made her way to the opposite side of the table, not surprised to find the blonde there. The woman pulled a ten-dollar chip from her sequined clutch and bet on red. Devyn settled beside the blonde and pretended to study the wheel, then bent just enough at the waist to bring her cleavage into prime view for anyone facing her.

It didn't take long for the cowboy to notice. Devyn didn't make direct eye contact, but through her periphery, she could see him ogling. So she stood there and let him get his fill. The blonde made a sound of annoyance, barely audible, but loud enough to tell Devyn the woman didn't like competing for the cowboy's attention.

So the two *were* involved. At least that suspicion was confirmed.

"Last call for bets," the dealer announced. After a few players tossed down their chips, he waved a hand over the table. "No more wagers."

All eyes were on the tiny white roulette ball—even the dealer's—when he put it in motion. Discreetly, Devyn tapped her cell phone screen, setting it to record while she angled the camera lens toward the dealer's chips and pretended to watch the circling ball. It bounced a few times and landed on black, causing half the table to groan and the other half to cheer. But Devyn didn't stick around to watch the payout. She had what she'd come for.

She strode away toward the bar and rejoined Beau in the security room.

Beau stared at her half-exposed chest while greeting her at the door. "Interesting wardrobe choice. Not that I'm complaining, mind you."

Devyn glanced down at the girls, grinning at her partners in crime. "They got the job done. Anyone facing me was too distracted to notice this." She held up her cell phone. "Now let's see if I caught anything good."

Huddling around her small screen, they watched the recording with bated breath. The footage was a bit shaky, and she'd captured only half the dealer's chip rack in the video frame, but it was the right half. The shadow of a sequined clutch passed over the stacks, and then a set of slim, fair fingers quickly slipped beneath it to capture a single one-hundred-dollar chip. The theft wasn't grand enough to alert the dealer, but quite the haul when spread out over the course of an evening. Or a week. The pair had probably scammed thousands by now.

"Well, son of a bitch," Beau muttered. "You were right."

Devyn cupped an ear. "Come again? I didn't hear you."

Laughing, he took her face between his hands and

gently tipped back her head. He held her gaze for a few heartbeats, giving her a chance to pull away. When she didn't, he murmured, "You were right," and then kissed her, soft and slow.

Beau didn't crowd her, and he didn't rush. He tasted her with shallow licks that served to multiply her hunger instead of sate it. Devyn hadn't truly realized until then how much she'd missed this—his warmth, his strength, the feeling of safety within his arms. The kiss turned her knees soft, and when he pulled back, it was way too soon.

He skimmed a thumb over her bottom lip and whispered, "I'd better go find Marc."

Dizzied by the rush of sensation, it took Devyn a moment to understand. "Oh, right. So you can call the police."

"Mind if I borrow your phone?" Beau asked. "I need the video."

She handed it over. Now seemed like the time to leave, but she couldn't control her feet. They remained planted firmly in front of Beau's hard body. "Need anything else?"

He flashed a downright scandalous grin that answered the question, then stepped around her and left to find his brother. Alone in the security room, Devyn heard the mental echo of Beau's words from days earlier.

Knock on my door when you're ready for the real deal. I'll make you glad you came.

As if to make the decision for her, Devyn's hands

curled into fists—prepared to knock on thin air if it would bring him back to her. She didn't know how much longer she could hold out.

It was going to be a long night.

Chapter 13

They never caught Cowboy Casanova on camera, but the bastard's girlfriend sang like a diva as soon as Beau and Marc pulled her into the security office and showed her the evidence of her theft.

Jill confessed that her role in the scheme was to palm one chip at a time, then pass off the haul to her lover so he could cash them out at the end of the night. Being a high roller, the cowboy wouldn't raise any suspicions with a few hundred-dollar chips in his possession. The couple had agreed to split the earnings, and they'd done it for a cheap thrill—just like Devyn had said.

"I always knew that guy was a bubble off level," Beau told Marc while watching the police handcuff the pair of lovers. Since the *Belle* wouldn't dock in Saint Louis for another day, Marc had made an emergency stop south of the city. "Never pegged him for a thief, though."

Under the dim glow of the dock lighting, Marc nodded at the cowboy's wife as she followed the police down the bow ramp, already on her cell phone with a local attorney. "I can't believe she's gonna bail him out."

Beau had no trouble believing it. His mother would have done the same thing. Some people had more loyalty than sense.

"Anyway," Marc said, clapping Beau on the shoulder. "I'm heading back to the pilothouse. Tell Devyn thanks for me."

"Will do."

Beau imagined all the sinfully creative ways he'd like to thank Devyn for her help and they made his johnson twitch. But he kept those thoughts to himself as he returned to his suite for the night. He'd finally drawn her out of her protective shell, and the last thing he planned to do was lose ground by pushing too hard.

She would come to him when she was ready.

Once he returned to his suite, he distracted himself with a warm shower before slipping on a pair of boxer briefs and turning off the light. He was halfway to the bed when someone knocked on his door.

It was probably Marc. The police had promised to call with a case number and the name of the investigator they'd be working with. Beau swung open the door and felt his eyebrows jump. He hadn't expected to find Devyn on the other side, shifting on her socked feet and blinking at him as if she'd come to the wrong room.

She wore long pajama pants paired with a tank top, and because Beau was a red-blooded man with a functioning pair of eyes, he immediately noticed that she wasn't wearing a bra. Her pert nipples puckered beneath the white cotton top, which was so transparent she might as well not bother wearing it.

Jesus, she'd walked through the halls in this getup?

"Get in here." He ushered her inside while glancing up and down the hallway. "I hope no one saw you."

She furrowed her brow in confusion. "Why?"

"Your top," he said. "It's practically see-through. What are you doing running around in your pajamas anyway?"

Her lips parted, and she gaped at him while her cheeks darkened. "You . . . you said . . ." Abruptly, she turned and reached for the doorknob. "Never mind."

Realization struck Beau between the eyes like a hollow-point bullet, leaving his brain foggy and his heart scrambling to catch up. Had she come here for *him*? Still stunned, he slapped a palm against the door to keep her from opening it.

"Wait a minute," he said. "Did you come to spend the night?"

Still facing away, she tensed her shoulders.

"Damn it, Dev. Don't torture me." He flipped on the light so he could read her body language. "If that's why you're here, you'd better say so."

"Maybe it was a bad idea," she whispered.

Bracing his other hand on the door, he leaned in to press the length of his body against her, then bent low enough to nuzzle her ear. "There's nothing to be afraid of," he murmured. A shiver passed through her at the contact, telling him she didn't want to leave. "I promise I won't bite . . . hard."

She peeked at him and pulled her hair to one side. "What if I ask you to?"

By way of answer, he sank his teeth into the curve of her shoulder and made her gasp. He soothed the injury with his tongue while skimming both palms down the length of her bare arms. When she was pliable enough to sink to the floor, he turned her to face him.

"Do you want to be here?" he asked.

She nodded. "You know I do."

"If we get in that bed," he said, "you won't leave until the sun comes up. Understood?"

Her pale blue eyes came alive with desire, and she nodded again.

"And you'll do everything I say."

Judging by her sudden intake of breath, she seemed to like that. "Yes. Everything."

"Good," he said, jutting his chin toward the other side of the room. "Go pull back the covers. Then take off your clothes and lie down on your back." He stayed where he was, leaning a shoulder against the wall to watch her carry out his commands while he grew harder by the instant.

Her movements were slow and seductive as she tugged back the comforter and top sheet. Facing away from him, she peeled off her tank and dropped it to the floor. Her pajama bottoms and lacy panties soon followed. She stayed like that for another heartbeat before coyly glancing at him over one shoulder.

"On the bed," Beau told her. "Faceup."

With a flush of excitement on her cheeks, she crawled across the mattress and settled somewhere in the middle, then lay back, resting her head on his pillow.

Saints alive, she was breathtaking.

Beau had seen her naked before, many times. But the decade they'd spent apart had rounded her hips and thickened her thighs, making her painfully feminine in a way no eighteen-year-old could compete. The teenage Devyn had been sexy—no doubt about it—but the grown-up Devyn would bring any man to his knees.

This was a woman, not a girl.

"Raise your arms." His voice had darkened with lust. "Grab the headboard and stretch out so I can see all of you."

When she did as she was told, Devyn arched her back like a cat, lifting her exposed breasts in a tantalizing offer he couldn't refuse. Beau left his place by the wall and stretched out on the bed beside her, propping on one elbow to admire the view. The scent of vanilla lotion carried on her flushed olive skin, so warm and smooth and tempting. He longed to strip off his briefs and lower himself onto her, but Beau had waited ten years for this moment. Even if it killed him, he would take his time and savor each sensation.

"Close your eyes," he whispered, and she obeyed.

Starting at her throat, he trailed a worshipful hand down her chest until he reached the outside swell of her breast. There, he skimmed his knuckles over her velvet skin and then took her fully into his palm, lightly squeezing, testing the delicious weight of her. A growl of appreciation rumbled in his throat.

"You're beautiful, Devyn." So beautiful that he almost couldn't stand it. Looking at her was like trying to stare at the sun. He bent his mouth to her ear and breathed, "Even more spectacular than I remember."

The last time he'd tasted her pink nipples, he was too young to appreciate their unmatchable texture—smooth enough to shame silk—or how instantly they'd bead inside his mouth. Now he knew what he'd been missing, and he took one between his lips to reacquaint himself.

At the gentle tug of suction, she gasped and bowed back for more. Beau gave it to her, sucking hard and deep before using his teeth to scrape each pebbled tip. When he raised his head to admire the wet peaks of her swollen breasts, Devyn's eyes were clenched shut, and a deep patch of color stained her cheeks. Still holding to the headboard, she pressed her thighs together and murmured, *"Beau."*

He'd taken some hard blows to the chest during his time with the marines, but nothing rocked him like the sound of his name on Devyn's tongue. Nothing on earth. He watched her writhe in need, and it fed his own desire. He didn't want to tease Devyn or make her beg. Tonight was different. He wanted to give her everything he had, to make her climax until she drowned with pleasure.

"Open your legs," he ordered. When her thighs trembled slowly apart, he ordered, "All the way."

She spread wide open for him, and Beau sat up to appreciate the thatch of dark curls between her thighs. He turned his gaze lower, to the delicate folds where she glistened with arousal.

"I love making you wet," he said. "When I see how badly you want me, it makes me so hot I can't think straight."

Gently, he stroked the core of her, letting his fingers slip and slide over her heated cleft until she mewled and opened even wider for him. He slid a finger inside, groaning at the satiny resistance of her entrance, so hot and tight. He couldn't wait to feel it clenching around his erection. He pulled out and added a second finger, then pumped her slowly, purposely avoiding her swollen bundle of nerves while he watched her chest heave with ragged breaths. Only when she'd soaked the sheet beneath her bottom did he press his thumb to her clitoris.

Devyn cried out. So he did it again.

"Do you want to come now?" he asked.

She licked her lips and nodded furiously.

He sat between her thighs and used both hands in tandem, one spreading her folds and massaging her stiff bud while with the other, he plunged his fingers deep inside, stretching and twisting and driving her toward the edge. When her orgasm hit, she tensed her thighs, lifting her hips off the mattress and giving him an erotic view of the whole thing. Beau could see the muscles of her sex contracting around his drenched fingers, and he damned near lost his mind.

"Fuck," he muttered. It was the hottest experience of his life.

He couldn't wait to feel it again, this time on his tongue. As soon as her inner walls stopped pulsing, he positioned himself flat on the bed with his face between her thighs. Then without hesitation, he lapped at her sensitive flesh.

Devyn drew a sharp breath, but she didn't ask him to stop. After a few moments, she relaxed again and gave a sigh of contentment. "I can't believe how good that feels," she said on a strained breath. "Please don't stop."

There was no chance of that happening. He couldn't believe how good she tasted, like salted caramel and raw sex, and he wouldn't have stopped for all the secrets of the universe. He used his tongue to delve deep before tracing the outline of her swollen bud, then repeated the pattern until she moaned and arched her hips against his willing mouth. When her throaty cries grew pleading, he sucked her hard while pushing his fingers inside her, and she climaxed again in a burst of wet heat. He kept going until the very last shudder passed through her. Only then did he consider his own needs.

Panting, Beau pushed onto all fours and looked down at her damp thighs. Devyn was primed and dripping, more than ready to take all of him in one hard thrust. His jock throbbed, and he tugged off his briefs. He had to be inside her—now.

But when he lowered himself between her legs, she

released the headboard and pushed a weak hand to his chest. "Just a minute," she said.

"Honey, unless the room's on fire"—and probably not even then—"I can't wait any longer."

Understanding dawned in her eyes, and she wrapped her fingers around his erection. She stroked him from tip to base, easing his agony with a firm grip. "It's my turn. I want to taste you."

Beau shook his head. It was too late for that.

"Please," she asked while squeezing him. "We've got all night. Let me get on my knees for you." She licked her lips and whittled away at his resolve. "Then tell me what to do. I liked that."

"Shit," he hissed. She wasn't making it easy to say no. The idea of Devyn's lips wrapped around him, his commands turning her on as she slid her mouth up and down his shaft, was too tempting to resist. He drew a deep breath to regain control, then sat on the edge of the bed with his feet resting on the floor. Pointing to the carpet, he told her, "Down here."

In the languid movements of a highly satisfied woman, she slipped off the bed and knelt on the floor with her little feet tucked beneath her. When she peeked up at him through her lashes and awaited instructions, she was the perfect combination of innocence and siren. It was like a scene ripped straight from his fantasies.

"Grab me at the base," he told her in a husky voice he barely recognized as his own. She curled a palm around him, and he ordered, "Tighter."

She strengthened her grip, and a bead of arousal rose to the surface. She glanced at it and back to him with a question in her eyes, so he gave her permission with a nod.

Her tongue swept a hot trail over the head, and then she sucked his tip hard enough to tear a groan from Beau's throat. He had no patience for taunting licks, so he told her to take him fully into her mouth, and she did—with gusto.

The blazing, liquid glide of her lips was perfection. With each dip, she took him so deeply that he bumped the back of her throat. Then she rose, inch by inch, up the length of him using fierce suction. The tight press of her mouth sated the ache between his legs, and for the next several minutes, he threaded a hand in her hair to guide her movements, keeping the rhythm slow and the pressure hard because he had no intention of coming in her mouth tonight.

"That's enough," Beau eventually told her. "Get back on the bed." He wanted more than simple pleasure. He wanted everything.

A renewed desire shone in Devyn's gaze when she settled on the mattress and held out her arms. Beau didn't have to tell her to look at him. Her eyes remained fixed on his as he lowered between her dampened thighs and settled atop her, supporting his weight on one elbow. He kissed her swollen lips and whispered, "Wrap your legs around me."

Her smooth calves locked around his waist, and he cupped her cheek, waiting for the emotional connection she'd denied him over the past week. It came gradually, a softening behind her gaze that deepened with each of their shared heartbeats, until she laced both arms around his neck and regarded him with a familiar tenderness he hadn't seen in years. It shook him, down to his very foundation.

"There you are," he whispered against her lips, and thrust into her.

She gasped, lashes lowering to her cheeks.

Beau clenched his jaw to trap a groan.

God, the pleasure. There was no comparison.

She was a liquid furnace, gripping him inside and out as he pulled back and rocked into her. Each slippery stroke drove him halfway to insanity, but then she opened her eyes again and grounded him. Surrendered to him. Their breathing mingled, and their bodies moved together in flawless synchronization while she gazed at him in awe.

"I missed this," he told her. "God, I missed it so much."

Her eyes went misty, and she finally admitted, "I did, too. I missed you, Beau."

Just like that, he was a goner. If there was any piece of his heart he'd set aside for safekeeping, she owned it now. She owned all of him, destroyed him with nothing more than a few words and a soft gaze.

He drove into her with a new fury, as if he could join them forever if he plunged deep enough. She matched his every thrust, rolling her hips and squeezing him with her inner muscles as the tension built to the point of no return. Her moans grew strangled in a way that told him she'd climax at any moment.

"Stay with me," he panted. "Look at me when I make you come."

Half delirious, she nodded and kept their eyes locked. When her inner walls began to spasm, he slammed into her and let go, and they flew over the edge with a mingled cry of release. In that moment of shared ecstasy, Beau could swear that he saw into her soul.

He'd never felt anything like it.

When they came back down, he refused to release her—not even to turn off the bedroom light. If he had his way, he'd never let her go again. Rotating them to the side, he held her tightly in his arms, and they lay like that until sleep took them.

At several points during the night, they awoke to make love again—first in the bed, and then in the shower, and finally on the plush armchair before returning to the bed. Each time, Beau had demanded real intimacy from Devyn, and to his surprise, she didn't object. She gave herself to him freely, and by the sun's first rays, they were so tangled up in each other that Beau couldn't tell where she ended and he began.

The faint glow emanating from the window told Beau it was nearly time to get up, and a glance at the bedside alarm clock confirmed it. He muttered a curse and buried his nose in Devyn's curls, which smelled of his shampoo. It made him smile. He enjoyed the lingering evidence that she'd stayed here and used his things.

Used *him* in every way imaginable.

But that wasn't really true. She hadn't used him, not like before. What they'd shared last night was more than sex, and he couldn't wait to do it again. He loved waking up with her sleepy head resting on his chest and her faint snuffles punctuating the silence. And taking her whenever he wanted was pretty damned sweet, too. He'd had a perpetual woody since she'd knocked on his door in those flimsy pajamas.

Even now, after a night of erotic gluttony, he was stiff and growing more engorged by the second. To relieve the pressure, he thrust against Devyn's thigh, but it wasn't enough. Luckily for both of them, they had a little time to play.

Careful not to wake her, he teased her nipple through the bed sheet—a light circling of his thumb that puckered her to a tight point—while he bent to kiss her ear. When she woke up, he wanted her already wet and throbbing. It didn't take long before he got his wish. Devyn came to with a soft moan and rocked against his hip.

"Mornin'," he said against her temple.

"Mmm." Her greeting was more of a purr. She propped her chin on his chest and blinked at him with a smile that melted every organ inside his body. "What time is it?"

Beau turned her to the side and settled close behind,

then reached between her legs to stroke her with nothing but his fingertips. He was greeted with slick heat, and his chest rumbled in response. "Early enough," he said, thrusting against her gorgeous ass.

She made a lusty noise and guided his other hand to her breast. "You're a machine, Dumont."

He nibbled her shoulder and asked around his teeth, "Is that a problem?"

"There are no problems," she said while grinding her bottom against him. "Only opportunities."

Beau chuckled to himself. He'd said that to her during the first trying days in the education center. But he didn't want to think about work right now, not when he had a raging hard-on and Devyn's writhing body begging to take it all in.

"Open your legs for me," he murmured, tugging her outside knee.

When she parted her thighs, he nudged the tip of his erection inside and played at her entrance, feeding her desire with shallow strokes while he tickled her clitoris. He imagined she'd be tender this morning, and he didn't want to slam into her like an animal. So he let her set the pace, holding still while she backed onto his shaft one gentle inch at a time. When she was nearly seated at the base, he wrapped an arm around her and thrust deep.

Beau grunted as every nerve ending between his legs crackled alive. The sensations were almost too much to bear—the silken texture of Devyn's sex, her luscious scent, the breathy sounds of arousal rising from her throat. He held her closer and rode her faster, working her with his fingers because he wasn't going to last.

Her whimpers built to a cry of ecstasy as her secret muscles quaked around him. He followed her over the edge in a heart-stopping climax that left him slick with sweat and heaving for breath.

"God damn," he whispered once his voice had returned. "I swear it gets better every time."

Unable to speak, Devyn moaned in agreement.

The alarm beeped from the bedside table, and Beau silenced it with the side of his fist. He didn't want to leave the haven of this bed, but they'd never make it out of his suite if they didn't hit the shower soon. If past events were any indication, he'd be hard again in five minutes.

"Come on." He pushed to a sitting position and glanced down at her. She was sprawled on her back with a blush on her cheeks and a sheen of satisfaction in her eyes, her curly hair fanning across his pillow. It was a damned fine sight. "Let's get cleaned up, then grab some coffee."

Devyn groaned with a pouty lower lip, then broke into a stretch that arched her back off the mattress. Her nipples tightened, and Beau felt the hitch low in his gut. Jesus, she was too sexy for her own good. Maybe they had time for one more round. . . .

"Oh, no you don't." She must have read the desire

on his face, because she held up a finger and scooted to the opposite side of the bed. "You'll make us late." She winced as she stood from the mattress. "Plus, I'm sore in places I swear didn't exist before last night."

Beau couldn't stop a prideful grin from curving his mouth. He held up both hands in surrender. "I'll be on my best behavior."

"Liar." Devyn scanned the floor for her clothes, then gathered them up. "I'm not showering with you."

"Aw, come on, Kitten. Don't you want to conserve water? It's the environmentally responsible thing to do. . . ."

"Nice try," she said while stepping into her panties. "But I don't have a toothbrush or a change of clothes. It makes more sense to go back to my room while the halls are still quiet."

She was right, but Beau didn't like it. "Fine. But bring some things with you when you come back tonight."

Devyn paused with her tank top slung around her neck. She arched one brow. "Who said I was coming back tonight?"

Smiling, he darted up from the bed and captured her waist. He dragged her back and sank onto the mattress with her straddling his lap. Before she had a chance to wriggle free, he closed his mouth over one nipple and drew it in with gentle suction. He tugged her hips downward until her most sensitive spot brushed his, and within seconds, she was at his mercy.

"God, you're good," she whispered. When he released her nipple, she tipped their foreheads together and trailed her fingers through his hair. Her blue gaze was on fire with far more than simple lust—she glowed with the possibility of second chances. "Yes, Dumont. I'll be back."

Chapter 14

Just as Devyn rounded the corner and reached her room, Ella-Claire strode out the door looking bright-eyed, bushy-tailed, and ready for the day in her crisp white purser's uniform. The instant her gaze met Devyn's, she gripped one hip and smiled.

"Well, well, well," Ella said, purposely blocking the doorway. "There's my long lost roomie." With a teasing shake of her head, she assessed Devyn's wrinkled pajamas. "You naughty girl. I know the Walk of Shame when I see it. Do I even need to ask whose bed you shared last night? Or will Beau be wearing the same goofy smile as you?"

Devyn glanced up and down the hall, relieved to find it empty. "Say it a little louder, why don't you?" Despite her critical words, she couldn't stop herself from laughing. A night of nonstop orgasms tended to have that effect on a girl. "I don't think the people on the third floor heard all the dirty details."

All teasing stopped, and Ella-Claire pressed a heartfelt hand to her chest. "Look at you. You're glowing."

Devyn didn't doubt it. Only minutes ago, Beau'd had her nipple in his mouth while she straddled yet another one of his impressive erections. She touched her fingers to her cheeks, feeling the heat that infused them. "I need a cool shower."

"That won't help," Ella said. "You're in love with him."

Devyn's jaw dropped.

"Go ahead and deny it," Ella added in challenge. "But I won't believe a word. You've got it bad—both of you."

"Do me a favor and keep that talk to yourself. There's no reason to start throwing around labels," Devyn said as she nudged aside her nosy roommate and opened the door. "I need a shower."

Ella waggled her brows. "I'll bet you do." She waved and strode down the hall, calling over her shoulder, "I'd say *see you later*, but we both know you won't be sleeping here tonight."

Devyn didn't bother arguing. It was true—she would spend the night in Beau's bed. And the night after that, and probably all foreseeable nights to come. Beau had put a force on her, stronger than a jolt of electricity and twice as hot.

Was it love?

Devyn didn't know, and she didn't particularly care. Whatever this was, she wanted more of it—for however long it lasted. Which likely wouldn't be long, considering a Dumont man was involved. But she banished those thoughts, refusing to let them harsh her glow. She liked feeling giddy for a change, so she held on to her happiness tightly as she hopped into the shower, where she sang off-key without a care for who might overhear.

An hour later, she was styled to perfection, though the effects of her under-eye concealer could go only so far. She strode to the lower dining hall for a much-needed cup of coffee and stopped short at the entrance. Beau stood there waiting for her with a smile on his face and two cardboard cups in hand. His eyelids seemed heavier than usual, but the drowsy effect heightened his rugged, masculine appeal. Only he could look this hot after a night of sleep deprivation.

It wasn't fair.

Beau raised one cup. "Already got you covered. I thought we could drink our coffee on the deck."

Though touched by the gesture, Devyn eyed the cup with skepticism. She was picky about how she took her coffee. "Two creamers, three—"

"Three sugars, and a dash of vanilla syrup," he finished. "I know."

"Wow," she said, taking the cup and inhaling the heavenly scent of roasted beans and sweet vanilla. Based on the smell, he'd totally nailed it. "Impressive."

He wrapped an arm around her shoulder and guided her down the hall. "I've been paying attention."

That made her smile. She'd paid attention, too. "You

mostly drink yours black, but sometimes you dump in a random amount of sweetened creamer. Sometimes sugar, but not always." There was no rhyme or reason to his method.

"What can I say?" he asked while pushing open the door to the main deck. "I'm a man of mystery."

She laughed and preceded him outside, where a crisp morning breeze greeted her. The riverbank smelled of wood smoke and fallen leaves, a unique scent of autumn that got her pulse hitching in anticipation of football games and roasting turkeys. She rested a hand on the railing and gazed out at the churning water behind the paddle wheel.

"Trying to keep the ladies guessing?" she asked when Beau settled close beside her.

"Nope." He sipped his coffee and added, "Just one lady."

Devyn used her cup to hide a grin. "Oh, yeah? Is she special?"

Beau didn't answer right away, but then he used a large finger to tilt her face toward his. He kissed her in a light brush of lips and pulled back to offer that lopsided grin—the one that turned her insides to pudding every single time. "*Special* doesn't begin to describe her. She's spectacular."

Devyn's heart quivered. That's when she knew she was hooked far beyond the force of physical attraction. Scarier still, she didn't want to retreat. Beau had replaced her center of gravity, making it impossible to escape his pull, so she nestled into his embrace and they sipped their coffee in contented silence.

For the first time in over a decade, she felt truly at home.

"I want to talk about something," Devyn said that night as she crushed a bag of gingersnaps for her sister's apple streusel topping. She pointed the heavy wooden rolling pin at Allie. "But you have to promise not to give me any shit."

Allie held up a paring knife in oath, her fingers damp from slicing apples. "Consider this a Zero Shit Zone."

"Okay." Devyn blew out a breath. "I want to learn everything I can about Memère's curse on the Dumonts."

Allie rolled her eyes so hard she might have viewed her own brain. "Not this again."

"Hey! You promised."

With a resigned nod, Allie went back to chopping apples. "All right. We can talk about Memère's curse," then mumbled, "even though it's just superstition that snowballed into a multigenerational pattern of dysfunction."

Devyn snickered. "It's cute how you can't contain your psychobabble. Is there a name for that? Probably some kind of compulsive disorder . . ."

"Yeah, yeah," Allie said. "What do you want to know?"

"Everything you can tell me." All that Devyn recalled about the curse was that Edward Dumont had ditched Memère at the altar. In a fit of rage, Memère had hexed him with the words *Fickle love rots your family tree. None but purest faith shall set you free.* Beyond that, the woman left no instructions for breaking the curse.

Allie shrugged. "You read the old letter to Edward Dumont. Everything I know about the hex is in there."

"But what about Memère?" Devyn asked. "I want to know more about her—anything that will help me understand what she was thinking that day. Didn't you find her journal during the move to Marc's place?"

"Mmm-hmm."

"What was in it?"

Allie shivered as if someone had walked over her grave. "Scary stuff. Our great-great-grandma was *not* a nice lady."

"So what did Edward Dumont see in her?"

A wry smile lifted Allie's lips as she took a bite of apple. "He was a man. What do you think?"

"Ah." Devyn should have known. Some things never changed, like the power of mind-blowing sex. "It was hot between them?"

"Not just hot," Allie said. "According to her journal, she and Edward were *combustible beyond measure*."

Devyn wolf-whistled. "You go, Memère!"

"From there," Allie continued, "it turned to love. But Edward's family didn't approve of the match. They came from old money, and I guess Memère wasn't pedigreed enough for them. She didn't write a lot about it, but from what I gather, it took a while for her to convince Edward that they could be happy without his family's blessing."

"Let me guess," Devyn said. "Edward's family threatened to cut him out of the will."

Allie shook her head. "She didn't say. All she wrote was that they agreed to marry in secret, and after the wedding day, she never wrote about him again. Not a single word." Allie gave a sad sigh. "But I noticed a difference in the tone of her entries. After that, she was just so . . ."

"Angry?"

"More like bitter. She stopped making love charms for a while. The only reason she started again was because it was her biggest moneymaker. I'm surprised she ever got married."

While Devyn rolled her wooden pin over another bag of gingersnaps, she processed what she'd learned about Memère, stretching out the scant information like saltwater taffy to gain more insight into the hex. One detail stood out to Devyn—Memère had to convince Edward that they didn't need his family's blessing. It implied that their approval meant a lot to him, or perhaps it was their money he cared about. Either way, he'd turned his back on love because he feared it wasn't enough.

Purest faith shall set you free.

Edward Dumont had lacked faith in love.

But how was that knowledge going to help Beau?

When it came to matters of the heart, he was fearless. He'd held nothing back. In fact, he'd been pushing for more since he came back to town. He seemed to genuinely want a future with her.

For now, Devyn thought. *There's no telling what he'll do in the end.*

She'd never expected him to bolt after graduation, and he had claimed to love her then. Maybe his faith wasn't as strong as she assumed.

"Does any of that help?" Allie asked, drawing Devyn back to present company.

Devyn gave her bag of gingersnaps one final whack before tossing it aside and releasing a long sigh. "Not really."

"You're overthinking this." Allie offered an apple slice, but Devyn waved it off. "Beau's a changed man, and he's obviously crazy about you. Why not give him another chance and see where it goes?"

That was easy for Allie to say—she didn't believe in the curse. "Because that'd just be a temporary fix. Why should I get more attached to him if he decides to cut and run again?"

If she wanted to be with him in the long term—and that was a big *if*—then they had to break the hex.

"Hon, listen." Allie rested a sticky hand on Devyn's shoulder, then realized what she'd done and pulled it back. "I know you want to control the outcome, but you can't. There's no curse—and there's no mystical cure-all that will make your fears disappear. You've got to trust Beau. He might hurt you again, or he might make you deliriously happy. You'll never know unless you try."

"But—"

Allie flashed a palm. "No *buts*. Love's always a risk."

Devyn didn't care what Allie said; the curse was real. Just look at Beau's mama—for nearly three decades, she'd been risking her heart for his father. And what good did it do? She was alone, pining after him while he shacked up with a woman half his age—a woman pregnant with his sixth child. Allie was definitely right about one thing: Devyn couldn't control the outcome.

And she hated that.

She finished the streusel topping, then wrapped up a few cookies and tucked them in her pocket to take to Beau. After swinging by her room for her backpack—which she'd stuffed with clean clothes and toiletries—she set off for his suite. If she couldn't control forever, she'd enjoy the here and now.

Halfway to the stairwell, she passed Alex, who she imagined was headed for her room. To save him the effort she said, "Ella's not in there."

Alex came to a slow halt, his shoulders hunched as he exhaled a long breath. "Of course she's not. She's avoiding me like I'm a case of herpes."

Devyn took a step toward the stairwell, but the dejection in his voice stopped her. The last thing she wanted to do was get in the middle of someone else's drama—she had enough of her own—and yet she couldn't leave him. Not like this.

"Want to talk about it?" she asked.

"No," he said, then immediately contradicted himself. "But has she told you anything? Like what I did to make her so mad? I don't know how to fix this, because she won't talk to me. I don't even pass her in the hall anymore. It's like she's invisible."

Figuring they should keep their voices low, Devyn joined him and leaned against the wall. "Well, you know she wants more than friendship, right?"

Another sigh. "Yeah."

"I can tell you're attracted to her," Devyn said. "But does it go any deeper than that? Do you love her?"

Alex looked at her with those deep blue eyes, and for a moment, his face transformed. His gaze turned soft. A half smile formed on his lips, tugging a dimple into view. It was easy to see how Ella-Claire had fallen for him.

"She means the world to me," he said.

"That doesn't answer my question," Devyn pointed out. "Ella-Claire wants to hear those three magical words."

No longer the lovesick puppy dog, Alex sniffed a laugh, his eyes dancing with mischief. "*Put it anywhere*? Those are my three favorite words."

Devyn shook her head at the pervert, doing her best not to laugh because she didn't want to encourage him. "You're such a Dumont."

"Thanks."

"It wasn't a compliment." Folding her arms, she delivered a stern look. "Let's get back on track."

"Okay," he said with an apologetic wave. "Go ahead."

"Ella told me all the reasons you want to stay in the Friend Zone, and believe me, I understand. You made some good points. I actually agree with you."

Alex's blond brows jumped. "Finally, someone who gets it!"

"I do," she assured him with a pat on the arm. "But none of that matters, because love isn't logical. Ella-Claire can't just turn off her feelings and be your best friend again. She can't watch you move on with someone else. It's too painful."

He fell silent for a few beats. "But I'm not dating anyone."

"For now," she said. Seeing how young and attractive Alex was, Devyn knew he wouldn't stay single for long. And neither would Ella. "Put yourself in her shoes. Do you want to think about her in bed with another man?"

Alex thrust forward a palm as if to block the image. "Don't put those kinds of thoughts in my head!"

"Maybe that's part of the problem. You think she'll always stick around because you don't see her as a grown woman with needs and desires." While he processed that, she added, "Bottom line: the two of you can't be friends. Either you're in, or you're out, so figure out what you want and make peace with the consequences. Because no matter what you choose, there will be consequences."

Alex stared at the carpet between his feet. Since he

clearly had some soul-searching to do, she gave him one of Beau's cookies and left him alone with his thoughts.

She jogged up the stairs two at a time and found herself bouncing on her toes when she reached Beau's door. A surge of butterflies tickled her chest when he answered, and she saw her excitement reflected in his honest smile. He was still in uniform, but he'd removed his tie and unbuttoned his dress shirt to midchest. She'd never seen anyone more handsome, even with those ridiculous sunglasses resting atop his head.

"It's about time," he said, glancing at his watch. "I think you enjoy torturing me."

In consolation, she handed over the remaining cookie—white chocolate macadamia nut, his favorite. "I came as fast as I could."

He took the cookie and devoured it in two bites. "You're forgiven," he said with his mouth full, then ushered her inside his suite.

Devyn stood on tiptoe and pulled the sunglasses off his head. "What is it with you and these things? Was the glare inside the casino too blinding?"

After washing down his cookie with a swig of bottled water, he shrugged out of his dress jacket and slung it onto the nearest chair. "I covered the afternoon shift in the pilothouse. Marc's backup guy got sick, and until we know whether it's contagious, we're quarantining him to his room."

"Ah. Good thinking." In such close quarters, stomach bugs ran rampant on ships like this one. She tossed his sunglasses onto his discarded dress jacket and asked, "Do you like piloting the boat?"

He shrugged. "It's a nice change, but I don't really—"

"Care what the job is," Devyn finished. "You just like being here with your family."

Beau grinned. "You probably think that's cheesy."

She closed the distance between them and threaded her fingers behind his broad neck. Beau didn't have any wild career ambitions or a hunger for power. He'd made the people he loved the priority in his life, and she thought that was sexy as hell.

"There's nothing cheesy about you, Dumont." She rose up to kiss him and then said, "*Saucy*, maybe. But not cheesy."

From somewhere in the distance, a woman's voice crooned, smooth and slow, and the sounds of jazz filtered into the room. Devyn rested a cheek on Beau's chest and listened to the song for a few sultry beats.

"Live music from the main deck," Beau said.

"Mmm."

He took her hand in his and wrapped an arm around her waist, drawing her nearer. Then he led her in a dance—a lazy sway with their feet barely moving across the floor. It was more of a caress than anything else, but Devyn didn't mind. In fact, she liked it. Any excuse to be close to Beau was good enough for her.

When the song ended, he kissed her forehead and murmured, "I've been thinking about the curse."

She tipped back her head to study him, but he stared

across the room, his expression blank. "About what, specifically?"

"I still want you to help me break it." He met her gaze, and there was no mistaking the concern etched onto his striking features. "It took a long time to get another chance with you. I don't want anything driving us apart again."

The old Devyn would have said Beau was getting ahead of himself, that she hadn't promised him anything beyond a full night in his bedroom. But he'd changed her. Now she shared his hope. She didn't want their time together to end.

"I'm doing my best," she said, then told him what she'd learned about Edward Dumont. "Love wasn't enough for him. That's where the *purest faith* line came from. But I don't know how else I can help. I can't make you believe, not deep down, the way it counts."

He didn't say anything after that, just gathered her to his chest and smoothed a hand over her hair while they finished their dance. The music stopped, and he wordlessly peeled off her clothes.

When he took her to bed, he loved her stronger than before. Not hard enough to hurt her, but with a passion that took her by surprise. He withheld his own climax for what seemed like hours as he made her come again and again. It wasn't until she was too weak to wrap her legs around his waist that he finally let go. After, he held her tightly throughout the night. Devyn wasn't sure what to make of his behavior.

Either Beau had absolutely no faith in their future, or enough to last a lifetime.

Chapter 15

"Here you go." Devyn signed the elementary school vacation form and handed it to Will, then scrawled her signature on the middle school version and slid it across the table to his older brother, Jason. "I can honestly say that you two learned a lot on this trip." She winked. "And that you were a pleasure to have in class. I'm going to miss you guys."

"Me, too," Will said with an adorable gap-toothed grin. "Since it's our last day, can we play *Super Mario World*?"

"I want to crush some more Coke cans," Jason added. "Can we do that, too?"

"Anything you want," she said. "It's your party."

Devyn poured the contents of two soda cans into paper cups for the brothers, then invited them to dig into the pizza she'd special-ordered from the galley. Since the boat would dock in New Orleans in a few hours, most parents had elected to keep their children.

Which meant Devyn and the boys had the education center to themselves to celebrate in style.

Well, in twelve-year-old-boy style.

But she'd come to appreciate the *beep beep bwoop* noises of *Mario World* and the laughter of her two favorite students. She had forgotten how much fun children could be, and she hated for the trip to end.

While sinking her teeth into a slice of pepperoni pizza, she darted a glance at the front of the room, where rows of windows looked out into the hallway. Beau had promised to eat lunch with them, but he was twenty minutes late. She pulled out her cell phone and sent him a quick text.

The pizza was getting cold, so we started without you. There's still plenty left, and I'm wearing that lace-up corset dress you like . . .

A few minutes later, he replied. *Sorry, can't make it. It's madness at the purser's desk. I'm stuck here for a while, but have an extra slice for me.*

Devyn's heart sank. In the grand scheme of things, lunch in the education center was no biggie, but she couldn't shake the feeling that something was wrong. A shadow of unease had gradually crept over her all day, similar to the heaviness in the air before a storm. Her instincts told her trouble was brewing, and she was rarely wrong.

She and Beau had discussed what would happen when the *Belle* docked. They would continue to see each other. In fact, they'd scheduled a date tomorrow night to listen to a jazz band at Beau's favorite bar.

They'd even had the big exclusivity talk—no easy feat for any couple. There was no reason to worry.

But Devyn couldn't help it. She was worried.

She forced the prickle of anxiety to the back of her mind and gave the brothers her full attention. After stuffing themselves with pizza and ice cream sundaes, the boys parked in front of the Nintendo, and she cheered them on through a dozen levels. Then she let Jason hold the tongs during the steam-powered can-crushing experiment.

The afternoon passed in a whirlwind of games, crafts, and dress-up, and the next thing Devyn knew, the boys' mother came to sign them out. One quick hug from Will and a wave from Jason, and then they were gone.

Devyn stood facing the door for a few beats, stunned by the abrupt quiet.

Slowly, she turned and surveyed the center, starting with the empty travel cribs on the far wall and ending on the opposite side of the room, where a pile of historic dress-up clothes rested beside two decimated Coke cans.

Her stomach grew heavy, and she found herself hesitating to clean up the mess. It wasn't until the boat came to a stop that she tossed Jason's soda cans into the recycling bin and put away Will's silk top hat and vest. She disposed of their leftover food and dishes, then tidied the room until there was no choice but to leave.

With a sigh, she closed the door and returned to her room to pack.

Now that all the passengers had left, an eerie silence

descended over the *Belle* like fog creeping across a graveyard. Gone were the constant footsteps and the rumble of the steam engine, the sounds of laughter and the paddle wheel's steady whir. It was strange how quickly she'd grown accustomed to the motion and noise. Her room key seemed unnaturally loud when she slid it into the lock and opened the door.

She stopped short.

A travel suitcase rested on the bottom cot, and Ella-Claire bent over it, punching handfuls of dirty clothes inside with enough force to shake the bunk bed. She snatched a toiletry bag from the dresser and threw it on top of the laundry, where it bounced off and tumbled to the floor.

"Shit," the girl muttered, then simply stood and hung her head.

Devyn had never known her roommate to swear . . . or abuse cosmetics. It looked like Alex had come to a decision, but not the one Ella-Claire had hoped for. Devyn picked up the cosmetics bag and tucked it inside the suitcase. "What did he say?"

Ella drew a hitched breath and blew it out, clearly hanging on by a thread. "Exactly what I expected him to say. He cares for me, but we can only be friends."

"Aw, hon." Devyn held out her arms and Ella rushed inside, promptly breaking down in sobs. While Ella's shoulders shook, Devyn rubbed her back and made gentle shushing noises. "I'm so sorry. Love sucks."

Ella nodded, then drew back and used a shirtsleeve to dab at her eyes. "I'll drink to that."

"If it makes you feel any better, I can tell from the way Alex talks about you that he's completely smitten."

"It doesn't help," Ella said. "If anything, that makes it worse. He knows we could be happy together, but he won't try because he doesn't want to upset his family. It means I'm not enough for him."

Chills broke out at the base of Devyn's neck. She'd heard this story before—from the pages of her great-great-grandmother's journal. Devyn had originally sympathized with Alex's concerns, but now she saw the real problem.

"He doesn't have faith in love," Devyn said blankly. She couldn't believe she hadn't seen it before. "And you can't fix that."

Ella braced both palms on the dresser and stared at her reflection in the mirror. "What am I going to do?" Her voice was a thick whisper, so devoid of hope that it put a lump in Devyn's throat. "I love this job, but how can I stay here? Seeing him every day is going to kill me."

"Hey, now," Devyn said. She gripped her friend's hand and gave it a fortifying squeeze. "I know it hurts, but a broken heart never killed anyone."

Ella laughed without humor. "Yet."

"This is what you're going to do." Meeting Ella's gaze in the mirror, Devyn kept her tone firm in an unspoken message of strength. "Call your very best friends to come over, and tell them to bring chocolate and booze. Then take the weekend to wallow. Lock yourself inside your apartment and eat Ben & Jerry's for breakfast.

Watch sad movies. Sing Alanis Morissette songs. Yell, cry, draw mustaches on Alex's pictures—whatever makes you feel better. But when the weekend is over, it's time to suck it up and rejoin the living."

Ella nodded, and another tear spilled free.

"You're such a sweet girl." Devyn gave her friend's ponytail a light tug. "Don't let this change you."

"Thanks for the support," Ella said with a sniffle. "But maybe a change is exactly what I need."

Devyn asked what she meant by that, but Ella smoothly switched the subject to Beau, so they packed their bags while swapping old stories about him. When Devyn had finished clearing out her things, she hugged Ella one more time.

"Stay strong," Devyn said. "And call me. In fact, let's meet for drinks next week."

"It's a date."

"I know you're not a hardcore believer," Devyn said, "but if you want me to read the bones for you or mix a special gris-gris bag, just say the word."

"I might take you up on that." She smiled weakly. "Thanks, Devyn. I'm glad we got to know each other."

"Me, too," Devyn said, and meant it.

After donning a pair of sunglasses to hide her puffy eyes, Ella wheeled her suitcase out the door. Then she was gone, too.

Devyn's shoulders slumped.

This was like graduation day all over again, her favorite people parting ways. Sure, many of them were local, but how often would their paths cross once life interfered? She was lucky if she saw her own sister once a week.

At least she had an evening with Beau to look forward to. And since he'd promised her a ride home, she grabbed her backpack and duffel and set off to find him.

Twenty minutes later—after a wasted trip to his suite, the casino, the purser's office, and the pilothouse—she took a seat on one of the main deck rocking chairs and texted for him to meet her there.

Lulled by the warm breeze and the sounds of water slapping against the boat, Devyn lost track of time. A while later, she recognized the heavy clomp of Beau's shoes coming down the outside staircase and she glanced over her shoulder to wave at him.

He looked a little worse for wear with his tie crooked and his hair mussed. A pen was tucked precariously behind one ear, competing for space beside the sunglasses perched on top of his head, and he had a yellow Post-it note stuck to his sleeve. But despite the obvious rough day, his eyes shone bright with excitement when he spotted her.

Devyn returned his infectious smile, relieved by his reaction. "Either you had a great day," she told him, "or you're really glad it's over. Which one?"

Chuckling, Beau pulled the pen from behind his ear. "Neither," he said as his gaze landed on the laces of her corset dress. He used his pen to point at her. "But it's getting better by the second."

Devyn teasingly dragged an index finger down the

length of her laces. "Take me home, and you can finally undo these with your teeth."

He sucked in an apologetic breath. "I'll have to take a rain check. There's an avalanche of paperwork, time sheets, and accounting reports to deal with. As soon as I drop you off, I've got to come right back. I'll probably spend the next couple of nights here, too." He lowered to her height and cupped her cheek. "Sorry, Kitten."

"No, it's fine." That familiar sensation of worry crept over her again, but she forced it back. Beau wasn't making excuses. There was work to be done. "Are we still on for tomorrow night?" When he blinked in confusion, she reminded him, "The jazz band."

"Oh, right." He smacked his forehead. "Yeah, we're good. I can get away for a few hours."

"We can cancel, if you want."

"No," he insisted. "I wouldn't miss it."

"If you're sure . . ."

"One thousand percent."

There was just one thing Devyn didn't understand. If Beau's chaotic day was about to stretch into the week from hell, why was he smiling? He wasn't getting laid for at least forty-eight hours. If anything, he should be in tears.

"Not that I'm complaining, but why the happy face?" she asked. "When you came down here, it looked like you had good news."

"I do." He slung her backpack over one shoulder and grabbed her duffel, then laced their fingers together and led her toward the bow ramp. "Awesome news. This is going to change everything."

Devyn wasn't sure she liked the sound of that, but she tried to match his excitement. "Don't keep me in suspense."

"I just finished talking to Allie."

"Oh, yeah? About what?"

"About you."

When she slid him a wary glance, he explained, "You know, your issues with going back to college."

Devyn resisted the urge to roll her eyes. "Yes, and as you pointed out, they're *my* issues. I appreciate your concern, but you and my sister need to mind your own—"

"You haven't heard the best part," he interrupted. "I was thinking of ways I could help, and then I realized that since Allie moved in with Marc, her old apartment above the bakery is empty."

"I could have told you that. She's going to rent it to the—"

"No, she's not." Beau squeezed their linked hands. "I talked her into letting you stay there for free."

Devyn stumbled and came to a clumsy halt. "You did what?"

"Think about it," he said. "You're part owner of the shop, so it makes sense to let you crash there. Now you can move out of your place and use that money for tuition." He grinned so widely it crinkled the skin around his eyes. "You don't have to worry about rent until after you graduate."

Like she'd taken a soccer ball to the stomach, Devyn struggled to draw breath. She'd hidden her money problems from Allie for good reason, and it was mortifying to think that Beau had disclosed something so sensitive behind her back. Her cheeks flushed hot when she imagined what he'd probably said—how her car had been repossessed and the rent was a month overdue. That she could barely support herself, even though she was pushing thirty.

Did Beau and Allie think she needed a handout?

"I can't believe you did that," she finally said.

Beau beamed, clearly pleased with himself. "It was no big deal."

"No." She jerked free from his grasp. "I can't believe you went to my sister and begged for charity. Do you have any idea how that makes me feel?"

His smile disappeared.

"If I'd wanted to stay at the bakery," she continued, her voice rising a notch, "I would have asked Allie myself. But I didn't. And there's a reason for that." Living in her own rental house, even with its sagging front porch and a back door that didn't lock, gave her some semblance of integrity. Of independence. She had no intention of giving that up. "Who the hell do you think you are?"

"Dev." Still dazed, Beau shook his head. "I had no idea that—"

"I might not have a car," she ground out. "Or nice furniture or fancy clothes. And yes, I'm a little behind on the bills. But that doesn't mean I want a knight in shining armor to ride to my rescue. I don't need a hero!"

"I wasn't trying to be a—"

"Bullshit!" She held an index finger an inch from his nose. "That's exactly what you're trying to do—fix all my problems. I'm not a child."

How could he see this as anything other than an act of betrayal? Beau should have come to her with his idea instead of going over her head. Besides, she'd told him in no uncertain terms that she wasn't returning to college. "Damn it, I don't want to go back to school, and that's my decision to make. Not yours. Mine!"

He dropped her duffel bag and splayed both hands. "But you were happy in the education center. I can tell you don't want to lead cemetery tours for that Warren guy."

"So what?" she demanded. "The decision is still mine."

"But part of that decision had to do with money. I thought if we removed that obstacle . . ."

"No. There is no *we* in this choice." The longer she stood there watching his dumbfounded expression, the higher her blood pressure climbed. He still had no clue what he'd done wrong, so she said, "Don't think that because we're sleeping together, you get to make life decisions for me."

"I don't think that!"

"You know what? Forget it." She sighed, holding out her hand. "Give me my backpack."

He furrowed his brow, thumbing toward the parking lot. "Stop it, Dev. Let me drive you home."

When he didn't surrender the backpack, she wrestled it away from him. It took a few tries, but he eventually gave up the fight and let her jerk it from his shoulder. "I'm taking a cab."

"Don't be ridiculous. You know how far Cedar Bayou—"

She cut him off with a fierce glare and said, "I swear to God, if you say that I don't have money to waste on a taxi, I will turn you from a bull to a heifer with one kick." The corset dress didn't allow much range of motion, but she could work around that. "Don't test me, Dumont!"

Wisely, Beau shut his mouth and handed her the duffel bag. He didn't say a word or chase after her when she stormed off the boat, another smart move on his part.

Without looking back, Devyn continued across the dock parking lot and crossed the street toward the French Quarter. She would never admit it, but Beau was right—she couldn't afford a taxi ride to Cedar Bayou. As soon as she was out of sight of the *Belle*, she pulled out her cell phone and sent a text to her sister.

DON'T MENTION THIS TO BEAU, but I need a ride home. I'll be at the Sweet Spot. Meet me there as soon as you can. PS: Thanks, but I'm not taking the apartment.

Devyn pocketed her phone and set off for the bakery, hoping the staff had plenty of freshly baked brown sugar pecan scones. She was going to need one. Or a dozen.

Beau scrubbed a hand over his face and checked the clock on the purser's office wall. He felt like he'd been running accounts for a week, but only two hours had passed since Devyn's explosive tirade. He couldn't focus on profits and losses while the image of her icy-blue glare burned behind his retinas. Groaning, he pushed away a stack of paperwork and rotated his neck to disperse the tension that had his muscles tangled in knots.

Marc glanced up from his laptop, then studied Beau with a shit-eating grin. "I heard you got your ass handed to you by your girlfriend. Do you need a hug?"

Beau flashed a hand gesture that told his little brother exactly what he could do with that hug. "Who told you that?"

"Let's see . . ." Marc peered at the ceiling in contemplation. "I heard it from Alex, who heard it from Nicky, who heard it from a housekeeper he's probably banging, who heard it from a server, who heard it from the porter that saw the whole thing."

"Jesus," Beau muttered while pinching his temples. "This place is worse than high school."

"That's not the best part," Marc said with a smirk that was going to get his ass kicked if he didn't knock it off. "According to the entertainment staff, the whole thing was your fault."

"Mine?" Beau asked, pointing at himself. Unbelievable. That old saying was true: no good deed went unpunished. "How do they figure I'm the bad guy?"

"Well, that's where the story breaks down. One version says you got busted sweet-talking a dancer from the stage show, and another claims it was a guest," he said, his grin widening. "But I know you better than that. I think you opened that big trap of yours, and something moronic tumbled out. How close am I?"

Folding his arms, Beau leaned back in his chair and returned his brother's sneer. "You're off by a mile, as usual."

Marc swept a permissive hand over his laptop. "Then enlighten me."

"You know what my big crime was?" Beau asked, secretly glad for the opportunity to talk through his frustrations. He'd tried tracking down Allie, but she'd left an hour ago to run an errand. "I tried to help Dev achieve her dream." He released a humorless laugh while holding up both palms like a robbery victim. "Get a rope and call the lynch mob."

"Mmm-hmm." The twist of Marc's lips said he wasn't convinced. "What would she say if I asked for her side of the story?"

Beau could still hear the fury in Devyn's voice. Tension began clawing a ragged trail into his head, and he reminded himself to unclench his jaw. "She's stubborn."

"You didn't answer my question."

Beau puffed a sigh. "She'd say it's none of my business." Which, if you asked him, was ass backward. He cared for Devyn, so of course her happiness was his business—it was at the top of his priority list. As it should be.

"Why don't you tell me exactly what you did to *help?*" Marc said. "Then I'll tell you where you went wrong."

"Fine." Beau supposed it couldn't hurt to get an outside opinion. So he told his brother everything, starting with what happened at the Cedar Bayou reunion, where he learned how much financial trouble Devyn had fallen into.

"That's why I offered her a job in the education center," he said, then went on to explain her transformation working with the kids.

Everything was going fine until he told Marc, "Money's the biggest problem in getting her back to college, so I started thinking of ways to handle her expenses. . . ."

But when he said the words out loud, it kind of sounded like he'd overstepped his boundaries. That's when Beau felt the first pinprick of awareness in the gut, a needling sensation that told him he might have made a mistake. Money was a touchy subject. If he were the one with no cash, would he want Devyn brainstorming solutions for him—and talking to other people about it?

"And?" Marc prompted.

"Uh," Beau stammered. "So I talked with Allie. . . ."

Suddenly a new image of Devyn flashed in his mind, not the furious diva who'd threatened his manhood before stomping off the boat, but the wide-eyed beauty blinking up at him in shock. *I can't believe you went to my sister and begged for charity. Do you have any idea how that makes me feel?*

"Aaaaand?" Marc prompted again.

"Shit," Beau said, letting his head drop into his hands. For the first time, he saw how clearly he'd missed the mark. He'd gone to Allie with the purest of intentions, but in doing so, he'd taken the power from Devyn and had embarrassed her in the process. Of course she was angry. She had every right to be. "I'm an idiot."

Marc nodded and said, "Glad I could help you reach that conclusion." He tapped his cell phone and held it forward to display the red RECORD button. "Can you say that again? I'm sure you'll give me a reason to replay this soon enough."

The teasing words flew to the periphery of Beau's mind. He looked back and forth from the piles of paperwork to Marc. "Think you can handle this? I've got to go find her and apologize."

His brother considered the request for a few silent beats. "You know that private booking we've got in a couple weeks?"

"The big wedding?"

"Yeah," Marc said, pointing at the ledgers. "I'll run these reports if you'll pilot the boat during the charter. Allie and I are overdue for some time off."

For a fleeting moment, it occurred to Beau that trading one night of work for an entire weekend of nonstop responsibility wasn't a fair shake, but he wasn't exactly in a position to negotiate. "It's a deal."

"Sweet." Marc rubbed his palms together, then pointed a finger at Beau. "You're off the hook tonight. Have fun groveling."

Beau speared his brother with a glare. "Real helpful. I don't remember giving you this much shit when you mucked it up with Allie. In fact, I called in a bunch of favors to track her down in Vegas."

"You know I'm just yanking your chain," Marc said. "Good luck, man. How hard did you screw the pooch?"

Well, he'd wounded Devyn's pride, so . . . "DEFCON one."

Marc winced. "Might want to swing by the jeweler's on your way to Devyn's place. Richman's stays open late. Tell them to show you the estate pieces—Allie's crazy about that stuff."

That wasn't a bad idea. "Thanks. I'll do that."

"See you tomorrow," Marc said, his tone growing serious. "And don't sweat this. Anyone with eyes can tell Devyn's crazy about you. Whatever you did, I'm sure the damage isn't as bad as you think."

Beau grabbed his phone and wallet, nodding in agreement. He'd worked too hard for a second chance with Devyn to give up now. One way or another, he'd fix this.

Chapter 16

Before Devyn even unlocked the front door, she dropped her duffel bag and used her bare hands to pry the MauvaisVoodoo.com sign off the outside wall. Her grunts and swears drew a few curious gazes from the sidewalk, but she didn't care. With an extra tug, most of the sign tore free, leaving the plastic corners firmly nailed to the siding. That was good enough for her. She marched to the side of the porch and chucked the sign into the recycling bin.

Once she let herself inside, she leaned against the door and stared blankly into the living area, where nothing but the faint drone of the refrigerator greeted her. If she thought the *Belle* was quiet, that was nothing compared to the void she faced in her own home. The scents of sacred oils and herbs from the dressed candles nearby brought a moment's relief, but a wave of loneliness soon swept it away.

She missed Beau.

Make no mistake, he still wasn't forgiven. But she

and Allie had stopped for drinks on the long drive home, which had given her time to cool off. She couldn't forget Allie's parting words: *Go easy on him, okay? He went about it the wrong way, but his heart was in the right place. He's not happy unless you're happy. When you think about it, the whole thing is actually kind of sweet.*

Devyn disagreed on the last point—there was nothing *sweet* about humiliation—but honestly, she knew she'd overreacted. And now that she'd had time to think about it, she understood that Beau had touched a nerve. He was right; she didn't want to lead graveyard tours, and bringing it up had triggered an eruption of negative emotions. But no matter what he said, college wasn't in the cards for her. The haunted tour was her best option.

Maybe she should call Warren Larabee to ask for a raise. Since she was going to debase herself for a living, she might as well make decent money doing it.

She was halfway to the coffee table to retrieve his business card when a knock sounded from the front porch. Figuring it was Allie, she swiveled on her heel and threw open the door.

But it wasn't her sister.

Beau held forward a bundle of orange gerbera daisies, her favorite. He wore an apology on his face—written in the creases between his eyes and the downward pull of his mouth. Even his broad shoulders slouched in contrition. He couldn't have looked more regretful if he'd tried, but he spoke the words anyway. "I'm awful sorry, Dev."

Just like that, all of Devyn's residual anger melted. She met him on the porch and stood on tiptoe to wrap both arms around his neck. The crinkle of cellophane warned she was crushing the flowers, but neither of them minded. Beau embraced her with enough force to lift her feet off the planks. He carried her inside the house, then kicked the door shut and held her close, his nose buried deep in her curls as if they'd been apart for a century instead of a few hours.

They clung to each other for a while, until Beau apologized again and told her what an idiot he'd been. Devyn pulled back to look at him, taking his face between her hands.

"I'm sorry, too," she said. "I shouldn't have blown up at you like that."

He lowered her feet to the floor and tossed the flowers onto the end table. "I can't believe I went to Allie without talking to you first. Baby, I swear I didn't—"

"I know." She held a finger to his lips. "You didn't mean any harm."

"That's not an excuse."

No, it wasn't. But Devyn needed to put the scuffle behind them. She couldn't stand it when she and Beau were at odds. "Let's forget it, okay? I don't want to fight."

"Me neither." Beau took her by the hand and led her to the sofa, where he settled as close to her as he could get. He kept her hand and pressed it between both of his, peering at her with a new intensity that made her tummy flutter. "I've been thinking. . . ."

When he trailed off, she nodded for him to continue.

"About us." He licked his lips nervously. "About our past, and more important, our future."

"Okaaay," she said, drawing out the word because she didn't know where he was going with this.

"Dev, this is going to sound crazy, but bear with me." Drawing a deep breath, he reached into his coat pocket and produced a black felt jewelry box. He opened it, and then time stood still. Because nestled in the box was a gleaming platinum ring. And not just any ring. A round diamond solitaire—at least two carats with the chunky facets of an old miner cut. It caught the meager light from the window and sprayed prisms onto Devyn's lap.

She stared at the ring and stopped breathing. Beau was right; he'd lost his mind.

"I want to get married," he told her. He must have noticed the lack of movement in her chest, because he squeezed her hand and ordered, "Inhale."

She filled her lungs, but she couldn't manage to blink. Her gaze remained fixed on the sparkling stone that had just turned her world upside down. Like the oleander blossom, it was beautiful but dangerous. A commitment like this—and at such an early stage in their relationship—could ruin everything. What was Beau thinking? They'd been together for only a week, and a tumultuous one at that.

"Just hear me out." He set the ring box on the coffee table. When her gaze followed it, he cupped her chin and turned her to face him. His eyes warmed with a sincerity she couldn't ignore, so she laced their fingers together and gave him the benefit of the doubt.

"I'm listening," she said.

"Devyn, I love you." His announcement was firm and clear, so full of certainty that it made her pulse jump. "I didn't always do a good job of showing it, but I'm not that boy anymore." He brought their linked hands to his chest, where his heart pounded every bit as fiercely as hers. "We spent a lot of time apart, and in all those years, I never loved anyone but you. I couldn't hide from my feelings. Every night, it was your face I saw when I closed my eyes. You haunted me."

Devyn's bottom lip trembled and her vision went blurry. She had never admitted it, but he'd haunted her, too. She'd spent their decade apart with a steady rotation of filler boyfriends, but none of them could make her forget Beau. No matter how hard she'd tried to exorcise his memory, the image of his crooked smile and the echo of his laughter had lingered like a stain on her soul.

"Do you love me?" he asked.

A tear spilled free when she nodded, her voice a wet whisper. "Yes."

He smiled as if he'd glimpsed heaven. "I want to hear it."

She cleared the thickness from her throat. "I love you, Beau. That's not the problem. I never stopped."

"Then marry me." In one brisk motion, he dropped to one knee. His grasp on her hand was warm and strong, full of promise. "I already know you're the one

I want. If you feel the same way, then why should we wait? Let's start our life together, right now."

"Right now?" A sudden dizziness swirled at her temples. She'd barely walked in the front door—hadn't even changed out of her costume—and Beau was proposing that they elope?

"Well, not right now," he corrected with a laugh. "We'll have to get a marriage license, and then I imagine there's a few days' waiting period, but still . . ."

A sobering thought occurred to Devyn. She'd seen this same light in Beau's eyes after graduation, when they'd planned their future together and sealed it with a night of wild lovemaking. She'd believed him then, and his change of heart had come with no warning—an abrupt shift that had knocked the wind out of her for years to come. She couldn't let that happen again. It would kill her.

"Maybe we should slow down," she said. "I don't want you to wake up tomorrow and regret anything. If we're right for each other, there's no reason to—"

He cut her off with a soft kiss. When he broke away, he delivered a sober look that said he understood her fears. "I won't run away again, Dev. I'm not a naïve kid who's excited about playing house with his girlfriend. I'm a grown man who wants you for my life partner." He squeezed her hand tightly. "The curse won't stop me this time, because I have all the faith in the world that we're meant to be."

Devyn hesitated. She wanted to trust him, and yet . . .

"Baby, I give you my word," he said. "I'll never leave. I'd sooner cut off my right arm than hurt you."

"I don't know." She glanced at the glittering diamond tucked into its velvet bed and then back to Beau, searching for something she couldn't name.

He placed her palm above his heart. "If there's one perfect truth in this world, it's that we were made for each other. Let me show you. Please marry me."

Devyn's blood chilled with doubt, but she couldn't say no. She wanted to believe him more than she wanted the sun to rise. Extending her left hand, she told him, "All right. I'll marry you."

"Really?" His face broke into a smile of sheer joy, and in the span of a few heartbeats, he had the ring on her finger. The platinum felt surprisingly cold and heavy, but Devyn told herself she'd get used to it. "I'm going to make you so happy," he promised. "Starting right now."

Before she had a chance to ask how long he could stay, he delivered a slow, drugging kiss that had her skin flushing with fever. Still kneeling, he parted her thighs and situated himself in between, then his fingers went to work on the corset laces of her bodice.

She broke from the kiss and helped him out of his jacket. "What about your paperwork?"

"Forget it," he said, admiring the line of cleavage displayed beneath the first loose stays. "I'm yours for the whole night." Then he bent to her ear, whispering, "And every night after that for the rest of my life."

Or at least until he gets bored with me.

No! Devyn clenched her eyes shut, silencing her inner skeptic. Beau loved her, and he had purest faith. That was enough to break the hex. "I like the sound of that," she told him, and bent her neck to welcome the hot slide of his mouth.

"Mmm," he agreed while biting her shoulder. "Me, too."

In seconds, the sultry rush of sensations made it impossible to think about anything but pleasure. When using his teeth proved too slow, Beau attacked the rest of her laces with his fingers until he had her exposed.

Groaning in appreciation, he kneaded one breast with his palm while drawing her opposite nipple into his mouth. Devyn barely had time to tip back her head before his hand disappeared beneath her dress and skimmed the inside of her thigh. She opened for him, and he stroked her into a panting, moaning frenzy.

Still kneeling, he shucked her panties to the floor and unzipped his fly. "Sorry, hon," he said while he tugged her to the edge of the sofa cushion. "We'll take it slow the next round."

Devyn didn't mind; she was more than ready for him. She spread herself wide and fisted the fabric at her sides while Beau slid gently to the hilt. Then something shifted in his gaze, and he slammed into her with fury. He made love to her hard and fast, until they came together in violent spasms of release.

As promised, the next round lasted for hours. He carried her upstairs and undressed them both before laying her on the bed and cherishing her body with his mouth. Sometime after midnight, Beau held her close and rested her newly adorned left hand over his chest. Devyn watched the diamond glimmer with the rhythmic rise and fall of his rib cage. *Beautiful and dangerous, like white oleander.* When her eyelids grew heavy and drifted shut, she promised herself that nothing was wrong.

Devyn knew she was dreaming because her mama sat on the edge of the mattress and smoothed the hair back from her forehead. The only time she saw her mother was in dreams, and she cherished each fleeting moment, even if it was nothing but a subconscious fantasy.

"Time to get up, baby," Mama said, her amber-colored eyes smiling beneath the dark riot of curls she'd never been able to tame. "You overslept."

Devyn pushed to her elbows and glanced at the bedside alarm clock, but it was missing. Her entire bedroom had undergone a snowy transformation, furnished with whitewashed pine and decorated in white linen. Even the walls were painted stark white. The room looked vacant and sterile, nothing like her style.

"What time is it?" she asked.

"Almost eight." Mama stood and backed toward the door, beckoning for Devyn to follow. "The school bus will be here in five minutes, and you haven't packed anyone's lunch."

In an instant flood of realization, Devyn remembered that she had four children. Her pulse hitched, and she threw back the covers, then grabbed her bathrobe and rushed downstairs to the kitchen.

Four lunch boxes rested on the counter beside an industrial-sized tub of Skippy and a loaf of bread. Devyn flew into action, spreading peanut butter over the first slice, but the bread tore with each sweep of the butter knife. She grabbed another slice, but no matter how many times she tried, she couldn't make a single sandwich.

"Hurry," Mama urged. "We don't have much time."

Devyn sensed her children scurrying behind her in the kitchen. She couldn't see their faces, but their rapid-fire cries filled the room.

"I can't find my backpack!"

"Did you see my planner?"

"I need help double-knotting my shoes!"

"Where's my library book?"

Devyn's heart thumped in panic. She couldn't worry about any of that until she knew her children would be fed. She ran to the pantry, finding it empty. Why didn't they have any food?

"You'll have to buy your lunches at school," she told them.

"They can't," Mama said. "Their accounts are overdrawn, don't you remember?"

Suddenly, Devyn recalled the overdue notice that had come in yesterday's mail. She owed the cafeteria fifty dollars, and she didn't have the money to pay the charges. From somewhere outside, a bus honked its horn, and chaos erupted in the kitchen as the children pleaded with her to finish their sandwiches.

In desperation, Devyn looked around. "Where's Beau?" she asked her mother. "Why isn't he helping me?"

Mama tipped her head in sympathy, her mouth pulling into a frown. "Oh, honey." She pointed at the refrigerator, where a note was taped beside a rainbow finger painting. "He left that for you."

As if moving underwater, Devyn struggled to reach the note. When she pulled it free, it was identical to the letter he'd sent after graduation. *Sorry, Dev. I joined the Marines.*

"No," she whispered. "He promised he'd never leave."

Mama rested a hand on her shoulder, though it brought no comfort. "I'm sure he meant it at the time. But things change, baby. People change. Nothing lasts forever."

An ache opened up inside Devyn's chest, quickly turning into a vacuum of suffering unlike anything she'd ever known. Tears flooded her vision, and she doubled over while sobs racked her body. She never imagined she could hurt this badly. She cried and cried, but the grief never ceased. Because deep down, she knew Beau wasn't coming back this time—and that she'd never be whole again.

Mercifully, the dream ended and she awoke with a gasp. She bolted upright in bed, still clutching the spot above her breast where an imaginary ache threatened to tear her in half.

The movement startled Beau awake. "What's wrong?" He blinked against the early-morning rays and scanned the room for signs of trouble.

"Bad dream," she said, panting.

He released a sleepy chuckle. "Lord, honey. You almost gave me a heart attack."

It was hard to feel sorry for him with this unholy pressure tightening around her ribs. She couldn't shake off the ghost of sadness that had followed her into reality.

"Come here." Beau wrapped her in his strong embrace. She was still irrationally mad at him for abandoning their family that didn't even exist, but she rested her head on his shoulder and let him rub her back until the fear subsided. "Want to tell me about it?" he asked.

"No," she said firmly. If she discussed the nightmare, it might cement into a memory. The only thing she could do was hope the images would fade, like many of her other dreams.

"Then we should probably get up," Beau said, leaning aside to check the clock. "I want to apply for our marriage license before I head back to the *Belle*. How does that sound?"

"Sounds perfect," Devyn said. She took a deep breath and blew it out. Maybe holding the license in her hands would make their engagement seem more real. "I'll get the coffee started."

"Wait," he said, catching her by the wrist. "Just let me bring this up one more time, and then I promise I'll drop it."

"*Beau.*" She wasn't in the mood for another fight. "I'm not going back to school."

"I know," he said. "But you'll be a Dumont soon. I thought you might want a permanent job in the education center. If you don't, that's fine. I'll support you in whatever—"

"Yes!" The offer sent Devyn bouncing in place, and she didn't need another instant to think about it. This was just the boost she needed after her horrible dream. She couldn't imagine anything better than doing what she loved alongside her favorite people. "I'll call Warren and tell him the deal's off."

She was halfway to the door when Beau called out and stopped her again.

"I love you," he said with a grin that lit her up inside.

Devyn returned his smile. "Love you, too."

As she padded down the stairs, she inwardly scolded herself. *See? I told you everything would be fine.*

She reminded herself of that two days later when the simple act of picking out a wedding cake made her hyperventilate. The bakery walls spun around her like a carnival fun house. Only it wasn't fun at all. She sat down and put her head between her knees, willing herself not to vomit inside her sister's shop.

"Here." Allie shoved an empty piping bag over Devyn's nose and mouth. It smelled like butter cream frosting. "Now relax and breathe, nice and slow."

Devyn did as she was told, and in a few minutes,

her lips stopped tingling. She handed back the bag. "Thanks. I don't know what came over me."

Allie watched her for a few moments, then closed the photo album of cake designs and squatted down to meet Devyn's eyes. "I'm going to ask you a question, and I want you to be honest with me." To show how serious she was, she extended a pinkie.

Devyn hooked their little fingers in a silent oath. "Promise."

"Is this what you really want?" Allie asked, nodding at a catalog of cake toppers. "You haven't been yourself the last couple days, and you don't seem very happy for a woman who's about to marry the love of her life."

"I do want to marry Beau," Devyn said. "I swear. I love him so much it hurts."

"Then what's the problem?"

"I think it's the dreams." Devyn pressed two fingers against her temples to drive out the negativity that had invaded her sleep since the night of Beau's proposal. "I keep having nightmares that he's going to skip out on me. I know it's not real, but it's messing with my head."

"Dreams can be a manifestation of your fears," Allie said. "Deep down, maybe you don't trust him."

"I should have known you'd go all *psychoanalyst* on me," Devyn said as she narrowed her eyes at her sister. Secretly, she wondered if Allie had a point though. "Beau's given me every reason to believe he can break the hex. He's got way more faith than Marc did."

"This has nothing to do with hexes," Allie said. "You haven't let go of the past."

"Of course I have," Devyn said. Satisfied that she wouldn't faint, she stood up from her chair and grabbed her purse. "Prewedding jitters are normal. I just need to power through it." She reached for her sister's hand and said, "Come on. Let's go look at wedding dresses." If that didn't warm her cold feet, nothing would.

Allie glanced down at the pastry bag. "Are you sure you're up to it?"

"Up to it?" Devyn asked, scoffing. "I've been waiting for this my whole life."

"All right, but I'm bringing the bag." Allie stuffed it in her pocket. "Just in case."

Twenty minutes later, they strode through the front door of New Orleans's swankiest bridal shop, not that Devyn could afford anything in there. But she knew she'd feel better after trying on a few designer gowns—all she needed was Gucci, her drug of choice.

As they waded through a sea of fluffy white tulle and delicate lace, a tiny spark of excitement flared to life inside Devyn's tummy. But right on the heels of excitement came a flashback from her first nightmare. Then she wasn't in the bridal shop anymore. She was inside her vacant bedroom, surrounded by white linens, white furniture, bare white walls. A sudden crush of emptiness gripped her in its icy fingers, and she struggled to catch her breath.

"No," Devyn whispered, blindly reaching out for something stable. "Not again."

Allie guided her to a cushioned loveseat. "It's okay.

Breathe," she said, pushing the icing bag to Devyn's mouth. "Nice and slow, just like before."

A middle-aged sales clerk appeared and offered a bottle of water, but Devyn waved her off. "Thanks, but I'll be fi—"

"Oh, my God!" Allie screeched. "Your hands!"

Devyn glanced down at her hands and gasped in horror. A scattering of pink welts had risen on her skin, and her fingers had begun to swell. She dropped the icing bag like it was on fire and cried, "What's happening to me?"

"Is your ring platinum?" the sales clerk asked. When Devyn nodded, the woman urged, "Take it off. Hurry!"

At first, Devyn didn't understand. But then she remembered that it was nearly impossible to cut through platinum. If her hands swelled any bigger, she might lose her ring finger. She tugged at the band, but it wouldn't budge.

"Here," Allie said, producing a tube of lip balm from her purse. She squeezed a dollop of petroleum jelly onto Devyn's finger, and together, they worked the lubricated band back and forth until it finally slipped free and plunked to the floor.

"Thank God," Devyn said as she released a shaky breath, pressing a hand to her chest. "That was close."

Allie wrapped the greasy engagement ring in a tissue and tucked it inside Devyn's purse. Then she took Devyn's swollen hands and turned them over, inspecting them. "You still don't have any allergies, right?"

"Not a single one."

Allie looked up, her gaze serious. "This is psychosomatic, Dev."

"Psycho what?"

"The swelling, the hives, the dizziness and nightmares," Allie said. "You're doing this to yourself. The wedding is stressing you out to the point that it's making you sick."

More than anything, Devyn wanted to argue that it wasn't true. But the lump rising in her throat warned that her sister was dead-on. Then, like a sign from beyond, the blotches disappeared from her skin and the swelling receded. She'd removed Beau's ring, and her body had quit rebelling against her.

No matter how hard Devyn tried to pretend otherwise, this engagement wasn't right. She loved Beau, and she wanted to be with him, but she couldn't marry him—at least not now. Tears burned behind her eyes, and she pressed her lips together to contain a sob. She didn't want to fall apart in public.

Allie tugged her to standing and led her to the car, then drove to the last place on earth Devyn wanted to show her face—the *Belle*.

"You have to tell him," Allie said when she put the car in park and turned off the engine.

Devyn hung her head. She understood what had to happen, but she didn't know if she had the strength to go through with it. This was going to break Beau's heart.

And hers, too.

Chapter 17

Beau knew something was wrong the instant Allie walked into the purser's office and locked her mismatched eyes on him. Her skin had paled a shade or two, and she gnawed on her bottom lip like it was a strip of beef jerky.

"What's the matter?" he asked. "It's not the gaming board, is it? Because I faxed over those pages from the ledger."

Her gaze dropped to the floor. "You need to talk to Devyn. She's in the parking lot."

Stomach dipping, he pushed away from the desk. "Is she okay?"

Allie nodded, but she wouldn't look at him. "She's not hurt or anything."

Interesting choice of words.

Beau had a bad feeling about this, but he swallowed his dread and jogged outside to the main deck. He spotted Devyn sitting on the hood of an old sedan, but much like her sister, she wouldn't meet his gaze. He made his way down the bow ramp, and when he strode near enough to see her folded hands, he noticed she wasn't wearing her engagement ring.

His already leaden stomach sank another inch.

The remaining few steps between them seemed to last a thousand years, because deep in his gut, Beau knew what she'd come here to say. But he refused to think the words because he was afraid that would make them true. Maybe there was a logical explanation for the slump of her shoulders and the way she stared at the ground. Perhaps she'd lost the ring and was afraid to tell him. He held on to that hope and joined her at the car, choosing to remain standing because his instincts warned him to maintain some distance.

"What's going on?" he asked. "Allie said you wanted to talk."

Devyn nodded and lifted her face. That's when any last shreds of hope drifted away on the breeze. Her pale blue eyes were bloodshot from crying, her lids puffy and smudged with mascara. But even more daunting was the expression behind those eyes: shame mingled with sorrow. She looked like she wanted to crawl into a hidey-hole and stay there forever.

Beau's extremities went numb. She was breaking up with him.

The realization must have shown on his features, because Devyn wrapped both arms around herself and tipped her head to the side while fresh tears welled beneath her lashes. He wanted to plead with her, but the mere act of pulling air into his lungs was all he could manage.

"I'm so sorry; I can't do it," she told him in a strangled whisper. She reached into her pocket and pulled out his ring—wrapped in a Kleenex, as if it were something filthy that she couldn't bear to touch. Her hand trembled as she held it forward. "But I do love you."

Beau made no move to take the ring. He didn't want it. "Then what's the problem?"

Sniffling, she unwrapped the bundle and used the tissue to dab at her nose. When she finally spoke, it was to the diamond instead of him. "Love's not enough."

He didn't understand. Of course it was enough. "What more do you need?"

Devyn covered her face with both hands, muffling her voice when she shook her head and said, "I don't even know."

Beau hesitated twice to touch her, afraid that if he did, whatever remained of their relationship would pop like a soap bubble. He steeled himself and pulled her palms away from her eyes. "Dev, none of this makes sense. You have to tell me what's wrong—that's the only way I can fix it."

"But that's the thing," she said, splaying one hand in helplessness. "You can't fix this. Nobody can."

"Is it the curse? Is that what's got you so wound up?"

"It used to be." She rested both elbows on her knees and stared out at the water, a shadow passing over her countenance. "But then I realized we're not safe, even if we break Memère's hex. Breaking her spell would let us get married, but it doesn't guarantee anything beyond that. There's no promise of forever. We can still grow apart." Another tear slipped down her cheek, and she scrubbed it away with her fist. "You can still leave me."

"But I won't."

She whipped her head toward him. "You don't know that."

"Damn it, Devyn," he said. "Yes I do!"

"How?" she demanded. "You can't see the future. Maybe this is what you want now, but people change. What guarantee do I have that you won't get the itch to run again?"

Beau couldn't believe they were having this conversation. "Have I given you any reason to believe I'm not in this for the long haul?"

Biting her lip, she shook her head.

"Have I so much as *looked* at another woman since I came back to town?"

"No, but—"

"But nothing," he interrupted, a flicker of anger rising inside him. "I've done everything I can to prove that I'm serious. For God's sake, Devyn, I asked you to be my wife! It doesn't get any more serious than that. At some point you're going to have to trust me."

She took a sudden interest in the pavement.

"Can you do that?" he asked.

A full minute of charged silence hung between them, providing her answer.

Beau pinched the bridge of his nose and expelled a long breath. He wanted to shake Devyn's shoulders until she felt the certainty of his commitment, but he couldn't force her to believe in him any more than he could stop the earth from turning. Faith had to come from within, and he didn't have enough for the both of them.

"If you can't trust me," he said, "then we don't have a future. I don't know what else to say."

Apparently, neither did Devyn.

She pushed off the car hood and stood before him, then pressed the ring into his palm. Her fingers were cool and stiff, with no hint of the affection that had once filled her touch. She closed his hand around the metal and left him with one last apology before she strode across the parking lot.

And then she was gone.

Beau didn't know how long he stood there—maybe five minutes, maybe ten—blinking back the heat that expanded behind his eyes. He'd awoken that morning halfway to being married to the woman of his dreams. Now he was alone. He couldn't believe how quickly he'd lost it all. His rib cage felt like a jack-o'-lantern, scooped out of everything that had once made him complete. Worst of all was the knowledge that he couldn't do a damned thing about it.

At some point, he put one foot in front of the other

and blankly made his way back onto the boat, seeing nothing, hearing nothing.

Feeling nothing.

Devyn's cell phone rang from beside her at the kitchen table. The screen read *Belle of the Bayou*, so she continued sipping her coffee and let the call go to voice mail.

It wasn't Beau on the other end of the line, she was confident of that. In the week that had passed since the breakup, he'd made no effort to contact her. Not that she blamed him. But she didn't want to talk to anyone on the *Belle*. The association hit too close to home, too near her bruised heart for comfort. Even cashing her paycheck had brought tears to her eyes, because giving up that simple piece of paper had severed her last ties to the boat . . . and to Beau.

No, she corrected. *Not to him.* As long as her sister was a Dumont, Devyn would be tethered to Beau in that way. Surely their paths would cross on occasion; there was no preventing it. And she couldn't expect him to stay single forever. Someday she'd have to watch him move on with another woman.

A sudden coldness overtook Devyn, and she tugged the lapels of her robe together. She eyed her steaming mug, but she knew that all the coffee in the world wouldn't thaw the chill inside her.

She'd lost her sun.

The phone rang again, but this time it showed *Warren Larabee* calling. Figuring her day couldn't get any worse, Devyn swiped the screen and answered.

"Miss Mauvais," he said, sounding surprised. "I'm glad I caught you."

The way he spoke to her, you'd think she had a life. Little did he know she hadn't left the house—or her bathrobe, for that matter—in days. "You barely did," she lied. "I was on my way out the door. What can I do for you?"

"I'll make this quick, since we're both on the run." In the background, his car shifted gears. "I know you said you're not interested in graveyard tours, but I couldn't leave town without trying to change your mind one last time."

She opened her mouth to speak, but he beat her to it.

"If you'll reconsider," he said, "I'd be willing to offer you a partnership."

Devyn almost dropped the phone in her coffee. "Come again?"

"Just for the Cedar Bayou location, mind you," he clarified. "But this would mean more creative control. And certainly more money."

"But I can't invest anything. All my funds are tied up in my sister's bakery."

"You don't have to spend a cent," he told her. "Your last name is what you'd bring to the table. What do you say?"

For a few beats, she couldn't say anything. Then she stammered, "Uh . . . I'm sorry. You caught me off guard. It sounds like a generous offer, but I'm in shock."

He laughed as if he liked the sound of that. "Listen, I'm on my way to the airport. But I left a signed contract with my New Orleans attorney. If you're interested, all you have to do is swing by his office and countersign it. There's a clause that voids the agreement if it's not executed within three days, so you have until then to think it over."

Devyn thanked him and took down the name of his attorney, then said good-bye. She sat there and stared at the phone in her hand, still unable to believe he'd offered her a full partnership—with no investment. A smile pushed up the corners of her mouth.

Maybe her luck had finally changed.

It took every bit of her inner strength to wait twenty-four hours, but Devyn forced herself to think through all the implications of signing Warren's contract. The only thing holding her back was pride, but self-respect wouldn't pay the rent. When she couldn't come up with a logical reason not to go through with the deal, she dressed in her finest—and only—business suit and called a taxi to shuttle her to the lawyer's office in New Orleans.

Twenty minutes later, she strode through the front door of Rylon & Associates and checked in with the receptionist, a pretty young brunette wearing a pantsuit and a bun that made her look more like a granny than a recent college graduate.

You're one to criticize, Devyn thought. *Once you take this deal, you'll have to dress up like your great-great-grandmother every night.*

She shook off the observation and forced a grin.

"Make yourself comfortable," the receptionist said, sweeping a hand toward a cluster of cushioned armchairs. "Mr. Rylon's last appointment ran a bit longer than expected, but he'll be with you shortly. Can I get you anything to drink? Some coffee, maybe?"

"Coffee would be great. Thanks."

"How do you take it?"

"Two creamers, three sugars, and a dash of—" Devyn cut off, not wanting to sound like a prima donna. "You know what? Never mind. Water will be fine."

"Coming right up."

Devyn settled in the middle seat and tried to ignore the nervous flutters in her belly. The contract waiting for her in the next room was legally binding, which meant she couldn't change her mind again. On the one hand, Warren had offered her a lot more money than she felt she deserved. She'd be crazy to turn him down. But once she signed on the dotted line, her fate was sealed, and that scared her more than she wanted to admit.

"Here you go." The receptionist placed a chilled bottle of water on the table, along with the newest copy of *People*. "Thought you might like something to read while you wait."

That was exactly the kind of distraction Devyn needed. She reached for the magazine but paused when a uniformed delivery man walked in the door, carrying the most exquisite floral arrangement she'd ever seen—tall and elegant with a sampling of orchids ranging in color from pale pink to rich fuchsia.

The receptionist's face broke into a smile as if she already knew the flowers were for her. "Delivery for Angie?" she asked the man.

He checked the envelope secured to the vase, then handed her the arrangement. "Yes, ma'am."

When the receptionist—Angie, presumably—carried the vase to her desk, Devyn followed to admire the orchids. She lovingly touched one delicate petal and told the woman, "They're gorgeous."

Angie beamed. "My fiancé has excellent taste in flowers."

"Congrats on the engagement." A prickle of envy stabbed at Devyn, but she ignored it. "When's the big day?"

"Tomorrow," the woman said. "But it's a weekend destination wedding, and we leave this afternoon. In fact, I'm slipping out in a few minutes."

Devyn leaned in to smell the orchids. "Well, this arrangement is spectacular. Either your fiancé did something very naughty, or you did something very nice."

Grinning, Angie blushed and averted her gaze. "No, it's nothing like that. Today's his last radiation treatment." She shrugged. "It might not sound very romantic, but we celebrate every milestone we can."

"Radiation?" Devyn asked, drawing back a bit. "Does he have cancer?"

"Hodgkin's lymphoma." Angie's smile faltered and returned to her lips with a little less brightness. "The prognosis isn't good—he's got about six months. That's why we moved up the wedding date."

Devyn's hand flew to her chest. "I'm so sorry." She felt awful for bringing it up, and even worse for the young woman and her fiancé. "I shouldn't have said anything."

"It's all right. I don't mind talking about it." Studying the floral arrangement, Angie separated a few stems and seemed to recover a fraction of her earlier cheer. "We get a lot of questions, especially from our families. They don't understand why we're having such a lavish ceremony." She rolled her eyes, and for a moment, she resembled a typical bride. "I know what they're thinking: why spend so much money on a marriage that can't last? But look at all the divorces around here. Nobody faults *them* for having the wedding of their dreams. At least I'll mean it when I say *till death do us part*."

In awe, Devyn studied the young receptionist. Angie was quite possibly the bravest person she'd ever met. This woman would be a widow before her first anniversary, and yet here she was, planning her nuptials and celebrating the little time they had left. If Devyn were in the same position, she'd probably distance herself from her partner so his death wouldn't hurt as badly when it happened.

How did Angie cope with the knowledge that her husband would be gone so soon? Devyn remembered the grief from her dreams. She couldn't imagine facing that agony. Though it was none of her business, she had to ask, "Are you scared?"

Angie didn't hesitate. "Terrified."

"Then why are you doing this?"

A soft grin curved Angie's lips. Tears pooled in her eyes, but they looked like the happy kind. "Because he's my other half. I'd rather have six amazing months with him than a lifetime of mediocrity with any other man."

Devyn was moved by the love in that statement. Her gaze had grown misty, so she dabbed at the corners of her eyes. "Then I'm happy for you. I know the wedding will be perfect."

"Thanks," Angie said. "I'm trying really hard to protect my joy. And that means focusing on the present, not the future."

The desk phone rang, and she paused to answer it. When she hung up, she nodded toward the hallway and said, "Mr. Rylon is ready. I'll walk you to his office."

"Oh." Devyn had nearly forgotten why she was here. "Right."

Angie led the way down the hall to a corner office, where a bespectacled gentleman sat behind a mahogany desk and a mountain of paperwork. "Unless you need anything," Angie told the man, "I'm going to head out now."

He glanced up and smiled. "Have a wonderful wedding. Take plenty of pictures, and don't hurry back. We'll hold down the fort for as long as you need."

Angie waved good-bye and shut the door, and then the mood shifted from tear-jerking poignancy to business as usual. Devyn reached across the desk to shake the attorney's hand. He had a warm grip and a friendly face that reminded her of Mr. Rogers, but the transition was too abrupt. She couldn't stop thinking about the receptionist, and more specifically, what she'd said about living in the present and—

"Miss Mauvais?" Mr. Rylon said. "Did you hear me?"

"Pardon?"

"Have you had a chance to review the contract?" he asked. "Warren said he was going to e-mail it to you."

"Uh . . ." Devyn had lost her Internet access when the trailer park across the street finally wised up and changed their Wi-Fi password. "No, I never got it. Must've gone to my spam folder."

"Not a problem." He opened a manila file and pulled out a stack of papers, then handed them across the desk. "Go ahead and look this over. Let me know if you have any questions."

They both took their seats, and Devyn began reading the first page of the contract. But she didn't make it past the third paragraph before her mind started drifting back to her conversation in the lobby.

He's my other half. I'd rather have six amazing months with him than a lifetime of mediocrity with any other man.

Devyn had never thought about it that way. But the more she turned the words over in her mind, the more she felt the truth behind them—a warm certainty that spread all the way to the bottom of her heart.

She'd never loved another man besides Beau, and she doubted she ever would. Assuming she met someone else and married him, would her life partner be nothing more than a cardboard stand-in for the one she truly wanted? And if so, how was that fair to anyone involved?

Devyn had always considered herself fearless, never hesitating to stand up to the schoolyard bullies of the world, but maybe she wasn't so brave after all. Was she really willing to settle for less than the love of her life simply because it might crush her if the relationship ended?

By breaking the engagement, that was exactly what she had done—refused to give Beau her whole heart for fear that he'd break it again. But what was the point of playing it safe if she spent the rest of her life unfulfilled, trapped in a prison of fear?

"Oh, my God," she whispered, staring through the words on the page. "Purest faith shall set you free." Beau hadn't lacked faith—she had. "I'm a coward."

"Beg your pardon?" Mr. Rylon peered at her from above the rim of his glasses. "Did you have a question?"

"No," she murmured. "Just talking to myself."

She buried her nose in the contract and pretended to scan its pages while her mind reeled with the power of her discovery. Beau was her other half, and more important, he was worth the risk. If they married, their union might last fifty years, or it might crumble after six months. But she would rather completely share her soul with him and risk the pain than hide and stay safe.

So now that she knew she'd made a mistake in letting him go, how was she going to repair the damage? She'd broken his heart, and she'd done a dirty job of it.

Devyn set her jaw. She wasn't sure what to do next,

but she wouldn't earn another chance with Beau by sitting in this office. She slapped the contract on the attorney's desk and abruptly stood from her chair. "I have to go."

Mr. Rylon scrunched his forehead and studied the unsigned pages. "Is there a problem?"

"Yes," she called while throwing open the office door. "And I'm going to fix it or die trying."

As she jogged down the hallway, the attorney called out to her, warning her that the contract would expire in less than forty-eight hours. Devyn couldn't bring herself to care. All that mattered was reaching Beau. She would figure out what to say to him when the time came. She had faith—for the first time in over a decade—that he was her future.

She rushed outside and glanced up and down the street for a taxi, but there were none in sight. So she set off on foot toward the dock, never mind that it was over a mile away. Devyn was powered by determination, and she'd crawl to the *Belle* if she had to.

However, three blocks later, her feet cramped inside their four-inch patent leather bindings. She'd picked the wrong shoes for a trek across the city. Taking a seat on the nearest bench, she pulled out her cell phone and called a taxi . . . praying she had enough remaining credit on her MasterCard to cover the fare.

When the cab pulled up to the curb, she practically flung herself into the backseat and said, "To the riverboat dock, and lay rubber."

The driver nodded and they took off like a shot. He

ran every yellow light—and even a few red ones—but they still arrived at the dock parking lot a few minutes too late. The *Belle* had already pulled away from the ramp and churned downriver.

"Damn it," she swore. "A dinner cruise."

"No," the driver said. "It's a wedding party—they won't be back until Sunday afternoon. I just drove a few of the groomsmen here about half an hour ago."

Devyn muttered another curse and paid the driver. She had enough credit for the fare, but not for a trip to Cedar Bayou, so she stepped onto the parking lot and watched him drive away. There was only one thing to do.

Hey, she texted Allie. *I need another ride home.*

While waiting for her sister to arrive, Devyn sat at the curb and considered her next move. She could call Beau and apologize, but that didn't seem adequate for what she'd done. What she needed was to make a grand gesture—something that would *show* him the depth of her faith.

She bit her lip and brainstormed for the next several minutes. By the time her sister's car turned onto the lot, Devyn had an idea. It was a move so daring that she'd never be able to show her face in Cedar Bayou again if it didn't work. But if this didn't prove her faith, nothing would. Devyn gulped a breath and prepared to set her plan in motion.

It was time to be brave.

Chapter 18

"Of all the private charters," Beau grumbled to himself while increasing the engine speed to seven knots, "it had to be a wedding."

He wasn't one to begrudge another man his happiness, but *damn*. The wound was still fresh, for crying out loud. Walking aboard the boat—its deck rails wrapped in twinkling lights and floral garlands—was like immersing his lacerated heart in a bucket of salt water.

At least he didn't have to participate in the ceremony, or worse, perform it. Part of his upgrade to co-captain had meant becoming a licensed officiate. In his current mood, he'd need a fifth of scotch to join anyone in holy matrimony, and he doubted the couple would appreciate him slurring their vows or calling them by the wrong name.

Two decks below, the rehearsal dinner was in full swing. Beau tried not to imagine the scene, but he could almost hear the tinkling laughter and the clink of crystal champagne flutes as family and friends toasted the happy couple. His temples ached, and he reminded himself to unclench his jaw. It should be *him* down there with Devyn tucked by his side, surrounded by his idiot brothers while they delivered good-natured jeers over aged whiskey.

But it wasn't him, and that left a bitter taste on his tongue.

The setting sun sliced through the pilothouse window, momentarily distracting him from his troubles. Beau slid his Ray-Bans in place and calculated what time he'd reach the first port and dock for the night. Not for another two hours. Until then, he was stuck in here with no one to talk to, no radio, no television . . . no distractions from Devyn's ghost.

Lord have mercy, it was going to be a long weekend.

His cell phone buzzed from his breast pocket. It was a text from Ella-Claire, who'd landed the unfortunate job of head party planner for the festivities. When they'd crossed paths in the purser's office earlier that afternoon, she hadn't looked any happier to be here than he was. By now, Beau recognized the mask of heartbreak, and she'd worn it well. He didn't know which bastard had put that sadness in her gaze, but he intended to find out and pay that man a visit.

Take a break for a few minutes, she messaged. *You should be here to toast the bride and groom.*

Beau groaned so loud he expected the windows to rattle.

As if she'd heard him, Ella added, *You're the acting captain. It's your duty.*

"Shit," he muttered. This was the last thing he needed right now, but Ella was right. He had to sack up and do his job. *I'll be there as soon as we dock,* he told her. *Remind me to kick Marc's ass for talking me into this.*

I'll hold him down for you, she said. *As long as I get in some good swings, too.*

It's a deal.

When Beau strode inside the formal dining hall, it was to the tune of "The Way You Look Tonight," played by a live band the couple had hired for the weekend. He didn't know what these people did for a living, but they'd spared no expense. Pink linens and elaborate orchid centerpieces adorned each table, with at least a hundred guests dining on bourbon-grilled salmon and filet mignon. The wait staff darted smoothly between clusters of partygoers, ensuring that each guest had a flute of custom-made strawberry champagne in hand. Even the small parquet dance floor was transformed beneath the sparkle of a disco ball affixed to the ceiling.

Must be nice to have that much cash to burn. *And a willing woman to burn it on,* he thought. Wiping all traces of envy from his face, he scanned the room for Ella-Claire until he spotted her arranging punch glasses at the dessert table.

He nodded a few polite hellos, intentionally taking the long way around the room to avoid interacting with more guests than he had to. Ella glanced up and met his gaze, then ladled out a serving of punch for him.

"Here," she said, keeping her voice low. "I wish you were off duty, so I could give you something stronger. This can't be easy for you."

Beau didn't want to talk about his short-lived engagement. He had one mission: get in, make his toast, and get the hell out. "Where are the bride and groom?"

Ella linked an arm through his and rotated him toward the center of the room. As discreetly as possible, she pointed to a lone couple swaying on the dance floor. "Right there. Michael and Angela, but they go by Mike and Angie."

One glance at the couple, and all the envy Beau had once felt for them slid down his throat and settled in his stomach like a bowling ball. Clearly the groom was sick. Not the kind of sick that landed a man in bed for a few days, but the kind that would send him to his maker—and soon, judging by the look of him. The man's head was clean-shaven, his skin dull. And while his tuxedo jacket might've concealed his emaciated frame, he couldn't hide the hollows in his cheeks. Beau didn't know how much time the young lovers had left, but the bride clung to her fiancé's shoulders as if a stiff breeze might carry him away.

The pair couldn't be a day over twenty-two, barely old enough to drink and certainly too young for anything this heavy. They should be buying a fixer-upper and clipping coupons, not facing the end of their journey together.

"Aw, shit," he muttered. "Life isn't fair."

Ella rested her cheek on his arm and gave a sad sigh.

"No, it sure isn't. I heard he's got six months, best-case scenario."

"Damn." Beau shook his head and watched the bride and groom gaze soulfully into each other's eyes. He couldn't change the young couple's fate, but he could do his part to make this the best weekend of their lives. "Tell the staff to double their efforts—more smiles, more Southern hospitality. There's a bonus for whoever goes above and beyond. And I'm comping the fare for this trip as a wedding gift from all of us. If Marc has a problem with it, I'll cover the expense myself."

"I think that's a great idea," Ella said. "Want me to dim the lights so you can make a toast?"

"Not yet. Let them finish their dance." The closeness they shared was more important than a few token words from a stranger. "They won't get nearly as many as they deserve."

There wasn't a dry eye on the boat the next day when Mike and Angie exchanged rings and said *I do*. During the minister's pronouncement, even Beau had to face the breeze and blink a few times to clear his vision. The ceremony had put his troubles in perspective, and though he still ached for Devyn, he'd let go of his bitterness.

And that helped, a little.

While the wedding guests celebrated in the formal dining hall, Beau piloted the *Belle* upriver at a leisurely pace, occasionally blowing the steam whistle in an unspoken signal for the bride and groom to kiss. He sent texts back and forth to Ella-Claire to make sure the reception was going smoothly, and instructed the maids to deck out the honeymoon suite with every romantic weapon in their arsenal.

All in all, it was a good day.

Soon after the autumn sun slipped over the horizon, Ella peeked inside the pilothouse wearing the first genuine smile he'd seen on her in weeks. He couldn't help grinning back.

"What?" he asked.

She held up a single sheet of paper. "A fax came in for you. I thought you'd like to see it right away."

Beau's smile flattened. "If it's from the gaming board—"

"Just read it," she interrupted, thrusting the paper at him. "I'll give you some privacy, but text me when you're ready to crack open a bottle of sparkling cider. I want to be the first person to toast you."

Then she backed out of the control room and shut the door, leaving him alone. Beau turned on the overhead light and read the fax.

The honor of your presence is requested
at the marriage of
Devyn Rebecca Mauvais
and
Beau Christopher Dumont
Sunday, the third of November
at eight o'clock in the evening
Saint Mary's Church
Cedar Bayou, Louisiana
RSVP by the second of November

Confused, Beau continued to a handwritten addendum at the bottom of the page, where he recognized Devyn's loopy script.

> *I'll be waiting at the altar in front of all our family and friends, wearing my mother's dress and ready to give you my whole heart. Turns out it was yours all along. No need to RSVP because I have faith—the purest kind—that you'll be there with me. I love you, and I can't wait to begin our life together.*
>
> *Yours always,*
> *Dev*

He stared at the paper for the longest time, half expecting the text to disappear, or for a celebrity to jump out from beneath the control panel and announce that he'd been pranked. But the words stayed right where they belonged, and not a creature stirred inside the pilothouse except the pilot. After a few minutes of stunned silence, Beau allowed himself to believe that the invitation was real.

And he didn't need another second to think it over.

A chortle of laughter arose from his chest while his body broke out in delicious goose bumps. Never in a million years did he expect to receive a faxed invitation to his own wedding, but he wasn't complaining. Devyn wanted him, and that was all that mattered. Besides, nothing between them had been conventional, so why would their wedding day be any different? As long as the wedding *night* went off without a hitch, he'd be a happy man.

With a face-splitting grin, Beau reached up and pulled the steam whistle, then hollered to everyone within earshot, "I'm getting married!"

"I'm getting married." Devyn sighed, using a fingernail to trace the photo of the cake she'd selected—a two-tier red velvet with cream cheese frosting. "Can you believe it?"

Giggling, Allie nodded from her spot behind the bakery sales counter. "Actually, I can. Because you keep reminding me every five minutes."

"I'm happy," Devyn said, and shimmied her hips. "Sue me."

"Not a chance. *This* is the reaction I wanted from you the last time you got engaged." Allie held up two plastic cake toppers, first a traditional bride and groom, then a pair of wedding bells. "Which one? Sorry for the lack of options, but these are all I've got in stock, and we don't have time for a special order."

"I don't know. Which is cheaper?"

Devyn was on a serious budget. She'd sold her flat-screen TV to a neighbor for a couple hundred bucks, and that was all she had to spend on the entire event: alterations for Mama's dress, secondhand wedding bands, decorations, invitations, food. Thank goodness Beau had paid for the marriage license weeks ago, or that would've taken a significant chunk out of her funds.

Narrowing her eyes, Allie chided, "They're both free, just like the cake."

Devyn pointed at the bells.

"Okay." Allie scribbled some notes on her order pad. "Did you hear back from Father Durand about the fellowship hall?"

"Yep, we can use it—no charge."

All those years of chairing the Saint Mary's fish fry had finally paid off. At first, Father Durand had refused to officiate the wedding on such short notice. But when she told him the alternative was a trip to town hall for a civil ceremony, he'd begrudgingly waived the Pre-Cana classes and offered the use of church facilities.

"And since the wedding is after dinnertime, we can get away with just cake and punch, right?"

Allie pursed her lips in consideration. "We should offer a few appetizers, too. I'm sure we can put something together on the cheap."

"What about decorations? I bought a ton of votives from the Dollar Store, but is that enough?" she asked, wishing she had enough money for flowers. Why did pretty things have to cost so much?

"With a few fall touches—like some whole pumpkins and colorful leaves—I think it'll look classy and understated."

"Good. I was hoping you'd say that."

"And the invitations?" Allie asked, pointing at her checklist.

"Got 'em to the post office first thing yesterday morning and sweet-talked Mrs. Sheen into adding them to the truck before the deliveries went out." Since most of their guests lived in town, the invitations had likely arrived that same afternoon. "I called anyone outside the bayou to let them know . . . including that jerkface, Jenny Hore."

Allie wrinkled her nose. "You want her to come?"

"You bet your sweet ass I do." Nothing said *purest faith* like inviting your high school rival to a wedding in which the groom wasn't a guaranteed participant. "Slade, too."

Allie chewed the pencil eraser and studied Devyn for a few beats. "Aren't you just the slightest bit worried that Beau won't come?"

"Nope," Devyn said. "He loves me. He'll be there."

"But how do you know he even got your fax?"

Devyn held up her cell phone. "Because Ella-Claire RSVP'd with regrets that she can't make it. She's working the same charter as Beau, so if she saw the fax, that means he did, too."

"You're gutsy," Allie said, arching an appreciative brow. "I'll give you that."

Devyn decided to take it as a compliment, though she wasn't sure it was meant that way. She checked the time on her phone and noted she was late for her appointment with the seamstress. "I'm off to my fitting. Thanks again for letting me have Mama's dress."

"Of course you should have her dress," Allie said. Moisture began to well in her eyes, and she blinked it away. "Mama would want you to wear it. That way, a part of her can be with us tomorrow."

Devyn fanned her own eyes. "Okay, enough of that. I don't want to get mascara all over her Chantilly lace."

After an over-the-counter hug and a reminder to meet at her house later for an evening of appetizer preparations, Devyn left the Sweet Spot and walked two blocks to the alterations shop. As much as she tried fighting back tears, she completely lost it when she stood before the full-length mirror in her mother's gown.

The white silk sheath with its lace overlay hugged her curves to the waist before flaring out above a hidden petticoat and continuing to the floor. Its capped sleeves had been modernized to slip off her shoulders, but the dress still brought back memories of the wedding portrait that had hung at the top of the stairs in her childhood home. She looked like her mama, and that filled her with more happiness than her body could hold. It was all she could do to keep breathing.

"Your bust is larger," the seamstress said, sweeping a wrinkled hand along the side of Devyn's chest. "So I had to pull apart the seams and add a new panel of fabric. It's not a perfect match, but I don't think anyone will notice." She lifted Devyn's elbow in demonstration. "I hid it beneath your arm, see?"

Devyn rotated in front of the mirror, pretending to inspect the lace at her sides, but all she could see was a blur of white. "It's perfect," she whispered. "Thank you."

Now she truly felt like a bride.

"Do I look like a respectable groom?"

Appraising his reflection in the pilothouse window,

Beau straightened his black bowtie and then turned to face Ella-Claire. He didn't have a tux onboard the *Belle*, and once he docked in New Orleans that afternoon, there wouldn't be time to have his suit cleaned and pressed before the wedding. So he'd opted to wear his formal captain's uniform—starched white slacks and coat paired with a matching black cummerbund and tie. He hoped it was dapper enough, but having no idea what kind of ceremony Devyn had planned, there was no way to tell.

Ella tipped her head and put her hand on her hip, scanning him before delivering a teasing wink. "Well, I don't know about *respectable*, but that's not something you can fix with a tuxedo."

"Very funny."

"You know I'm just messing with you," she said, and stood on tiptoe to kiss his cheek. "You're the handsomest Dumont groom I've ever seen."

Beau laughed. Over the last hundred years, the only other Dumont groom to make it to the altar was Marc, who'd sported one hell of a black eye at his Vegas wedding. "I'm not so sure that's a compliment."

"I've seen the way Devyn looks at you," Ella said. "You could show up in your pawpaw's ratty overalls and she wouldn't care."

Beau brushed a bit of lint off his sleeve. "I just want our wedding day to be memorable."

"Stop fidgeting." Ella-Claire lightly smacked his hand. "You look perfect. And even if you didn't, it's the marriage that counts, not the wedding. Devyn understands how rare it is when the love of your life actually loves you back. She knows how lucky—" Cutting off, Ella cleared her throat and dropped her gaze to the floor.

"Aw, hon." He held out his arms for a hug, but she waved him off with a lame excuse about not wanting to get makeup on his jacket. "At least tell me whose ass I need to beat."

Instead of answering, she changed the subject. "We're about to serve a late lunch. You want me to send up a plate of chicken or ham?"

Beau gave her a look that said he wouldn't be deterred. Whoever had hurt her was going to pay. Maybe he should ask Alex for the guy's name. If anyone knew the details of Ella's personal life, it would be him. The two had been best friends for ages. Hell, Alex would probably want to confront the asshole, too.

"Which one?" she pressed.

"Chicken."

"And we're still on schedule to dock at five thirty?"

"Yes, ma'am."

"Good," she said, and patted his chest. "I'm really happy for you, Beau."

He'd just opened his mouth to thank her when the emergency weather radio affixed to the control panel screeched an alert for a severe thunderstorm warning. "What the hell?" he muttered, glancing through the front window at the clear blue sky. He stepped around Ella to check the radar, which had shown nothing significant that morning. Now a mass of greens and reds drifted into view on the screen to show incoming rain.

"How bad is it?" Ella-Claire asked.

Tapping the keyboard, Beau zoomed out to get a feel for the size of the storm. He swallowed a curse. The system continued all the way to New Orleans, following the river's path as if it knew he was coming. There was no way he'd make it back to Cedar Bayou by eight o'clock tonight—not in this squall. In fact, if the lightning was as bad as it looked, he should probably find the nearest port and evacuate the boat.

"Really bad," he said. "Doesn't look like I'm getting married tonight."

Chapter 19

"Do me a favor," Beau said to Ella-Claire while scanning the map for the nearest docking point. As soon as he found the contact information, he pulled out his cell and dialed the port authority. "We don't have much time before this thing's right on top of us. Get on the phone and find somewhere for the guests and crew to hang out until the storm passes. See if you can hire some buses to meet us at the dock. Then call Devyn and explain what's happening. Tell her I'm sorry, and that I'll touch base with her as soon as the boat's evacuated. Maybe we can have the wedding tomorrow."

Ella nodded. "I'm on it."

Twenty minutes later, after receiving permission from the nearest port authority to dock, Beau turned on the intercom and made an announcement to the entire boat. "Attention, everyone. I'm afraid there's some nasty weather ahead, and we're going to have to stop until the worst of it passes. We should arrive at the next port in about thirty minutes. At that time, I need everyone assembled in the formal dining hall and ready to move to a secure location."

He pushed the *Belle* to full throttle and hoped like hell that the storm was moving slower than they were. The wind kicked up and dark clouds knitted together to block the sun, but at least the rain continued to hold off. He was within ten minutes of their destination when his radar flickered and went dead. The computer immediately followed, and upon closer inspection, Beau noticed that all his electronic equipment had died.

"Damn," he muttered to himself. Whatever lay ahead must be some seriously nasty shit.

A knock sounded at the door, and Ella-Claire stepped inside. "I've got good news and bad news."

"Start with the good," he said. "Then work your way down."

"The city gave us permission to use the community center, and they've agreed to send a few buses to shuttle us there. They say the power's already out, but they've got a backup generator so we won't be sitting in the dark the whole time. I've got the staff brainstorming activities to keep the guests entertained."

"Excellent." That took care of his most immediate concern. "What's the bad news?"

Ella sucked an apologetic breath through her teeth. "I wasn't able to reach Devyn. My phone died right when I was about to make the call."

"I'll do it." But when Beau pulled out his cell phone, it showed NO SIGNAL.

"No one has service," Ella said. "I checked with the

whole staff—even the guests. I can't get a connection on the *Belle*'s outgoing line either. And no fax. We're totally incommunicado."

"Just my friggin' luck." Beau heaved a sigh. "I'll have to call her from the port."

But the bad news kept coming when he docked the *Belle*.

The sky opened up on top of Beau and his passengers as they jogged down the bow ramp and onto the city buses idling at the rear of the parking lot. One guest slipped and sprained her ankle, and another had an asthma attack—a mild one, thank God, because there wasn't a working telephone with which to call nine-one-one. Even the landlines were down; Beau had checked at the port office when he'd first dropped anchor.

"Maybe there's a working phone at the rec center," Ella shouted over the howling wind while shielding her eyes from a sideways rain that seemed to defy gravity.

"Doubtful," Beau shouted back, then peeled a wet blade of grass off his forehead. He pointed at the first bus. "Go with this group and get settled in. I'm gonna stay here and see if the port authority can radio the sheriff in Cedar Bayou." Come hell or high water—and with the river rising so quickly, the second part was guaranteed—Beau had to get word to Devyn before the wedding. He couldn't let her think he'd ditched her at the altar.

Ella nodded, then boarded the first bus. The remaining staff filled the second shuttle, and when Beau saw them safely off the property, he turned and ran toward the port authority office. The sky was black as pitch, making it difficult to see fallen tree limbs and debris flying through the air. By the time he threw open the office door, Beau was soaked to the skin and wearing more leaves than the trees.

"I need to get a message to Cedar Bayou," he said to the old-timer kicked back behind his desk, reading a magazine by the light of a battery-powered lantern. "It's an emergency."

The man turned up a palm. "Sorry, son. The electrical storm knocked out everything, even my police scanner." With a shake of his head, he pointed to the heavens. "I've been here thirty years, and I've never seen anything like it."

Beau raked a hand through his soggy hair and grappled for a plan B. If he couldn't send a message to Devyn, he'd have to find a way to make it to the church on time. He hated to leave behind the *Belle*'s guests and crew, but his backup pilot could transport them home. Plus, he did have Ella-Claire there to ensure that things went smoothly. Considering he'd already comped the cruise fare, he figured that nobody would complain.

"Then I'll have to drive there," Beau said. "Where's the nearest place to rent a car?"

"Well, there's an Avis not too far from here, but that won't help you."

"Why not?"

The old man hooked a thumb toward his radio

equipment. "Because the last thing I heard before the scanner went dead was the mention of a twenty-car pileup on the interstate. The highway patrol probably shut it down by now, and I don't imagine the back roads are any better. We get a lot of flash floods around here."

Beau's stomach dipped into his boxer-briefs. "So there's no way for me to get home?"

"Not unless you can fly," the man said, then flinched when a windblown object *thunked* against the outside wall. "And I wouldn't recommend that either."

Like a scene ripped from his nightmares, Beau stood there dripping wet and helpless. The weather in Cedar Bayou was probably fine, and a squall in another state wouldn't make the news. Devyn would be waiting for him at the altar in front of half the town, oblivious to the fact that he wasn't coming.

Beau imagined how she might feel when the minutes ticked by in painfully awkward silence, their guests staring at her and whispering that history was repeating itself. Abandonment was her greatest fear, and he was about to bring it to fruition—in front of an audience. Even if Devyn forgave him, she'd never fully recover. It would take another decade to regain her trust, assuming she ever let her guard down again.

"God help me," Beau whispered to himself. "It can't happen like this."

Devyn pressed a hand to her belly, which felt like it was about to sprout wings and fly to Canada. The act caused her to drop a pair of candle tapers to the chapel floor, where they broke in half against the hardwood. She stifled a curse, not wanting to swear in the Lord's house.

Allie slanted her a glance while pushing a long white taper into the standing candleholder at the altar. "Nervous?"

"A little," Devyn admitted, bending down to pick up the pieces.

Overall, nothing was wrong. The sanctuary looked lovely, decked out in dozens of simple brass candelabra and a lacey white runner adorning the aisle. She and Allie had just finished decorating the fellowship hall and had set up the cake. Their mother's freshly steamed gown was hanging in the dressing room along with a matching veil borrowed from a friend. But despite the fact that everything had gone according to plan, Devyn couldn't shake her jitters.

"It's natural," Allie said. "All brides feel this way on their wedding day, and that's under *normal* circumstances."

Devyn propped a hand on her hip. "Are you saying my wedding's abnormal?"

Allie's eyes went wide. "No, it's beautiful. But you have more reason to feel nervous because you haven't spoken to the groom in weeks. Technically, you don't even know that he's coming. That has to be weighing on your mind."

"It's not bothering me at all," Devyn insisted, and she meant every word. She had perfect faith that he would be there. "I think I'm more worried about the guests. I haven't had much time"—or money—"to put this together. No one wants to be known for having a tacky wedding."

"Baby, you're talking to the queen of tacky weddings," Allie said with a smile. "I was married in a bikini, remember?"

Devyn snickered at the memory. As maid of honor, she'd worn a bathing suit and leopard print sarong. "Your point?"

Allie set down an armful of candles and gave Devyn's hand a hearty squeeze. "A wedding lasts for a few minutes, but a marriage lasts a lifetime. Look at the big picture."

Devyn returned the squeeze. "You're right. I've got Beau, and that's all that matters."

Allie nodded as if to get down to business. "Now let's finish up in here so I can get started on your hair and makeup."

A hopeful smile curved Devyn's lips. Once she dolled herself up and changed into Mama's gown, all of this would begin to feel real.

"There has to be a way," Beau said while staring out the window into the blackness. A bolt of lightning struck in the distance, momentarily illuminating the raging river, its surges snatching limbs and debris from the parking lot like a greedy child. "I can't stand here and do nothing."

"Once in a while," the old man said from his desk,

"Mother Nature likes to remind us who's boss. I know you want to reach your fiancée, but I'm afraid the Mississippi's got the upper hand tonight."

Beau couldn't argue with that—he'd never seen the river so angry—but his mind kept working to find a solution. Instinctively, he knew there was a way to reach Devyn, and he'd find it if he kept trying.

A few minutes later, a small searchlight pierced the darkness. Beau pressed his forehead to the window and squinted at the half-submerged parking lot, where a speedboat rocked in the current. The passenger holding the light swiveled it to and fro, probably looking for a place to tie off the boat while they sought shelter from the storm.

"There's a small craft out there," Beau said to the old-timer. "I'm going to give them a hand."

When Beau stepped outside, it was to a gust of wind that knocked the hat from his head and sent it flying. He waded through the ankle-deep water, which quickly grew more forceful as he approached the boat. By the time he found an anchor for the craft—in the form of a streetlamp—the water covered his thighs, and it took all his strength to stay on his feet.

"Ahoy!" he shouted above a crack of thunder. The driver glanced at him, and Beau yelled, "Toss me a rope, and I'll tie you off."

As soon as he had the boat secured, he helped the driver and passenger inside the port office. The lantern's glow revealed a middle-aged couple, their dark hair slicked to the sides of their faces. They said the storm had caught them off guard and ten miles from home.

"If the lightning weren't so bad," the husband said, "I'd push ahead. The *Flying Lass* is the fastest boat I've ever owned." He glanced longingly into the parking lot. "My girl's going to take a beating out there."

His wife used her hand like a squeegee to remove the water from her face. "Boats are replaceable. People aren't."

Still gazing into the darkness, the man grunted in reluctant agreement.

That's when Beau realized how he could reach Cedar Bayou—on the very river he'd fled an hour ago. "You say the *Lass* is quick?" he asked, nearly cringing at the stupidity of the plan forming in his mind.

"Quick?" The man scoffed. "She'll pass *quick* and leave it spinning in her wake."

"Is she gassed up?" Beau asked.

"Yeah, why? You think I should dump the fuel tanks in case lightning strikes?"

Beau ignored the question because he didn't have a second to waste. "I'm the pilot and co-owner of the *Belle of the Bayou*, the big steamer docked out there."

"Okay," the man said, furrowing his brow.

"I'm telling you this," Beau said, "because I need to borrow your boat."

The port authority official nearly tipped back in his chair. "*What?* Are you out of your mind?"

Again, Beau ignored the question. "Ten years ago, I almost ruined the best thing that ever happened to me when I ran out on my girlfriend. It took a long time, but I finally convinced her to give me another chance, and eventually, to be my wife. Our wedding's set to take place in a couple hours, and I've got no way to tell her about the storm. If I don't show up, there'll be no coming back from that. She'll think I aband—"

"Listen, mister. I sympathize with you," the boat owner interrupted. "I really do. But if I give you the keys to the *Lass* and you wind up getting yourself killed out there, I'd never forgive myself."

"One way or another, I'm getting home tonight." Beau thumbed toward the parking lot. "If I have to, I'll wander up and down the riverbank until I find another boat. Seems to me, the *Lass* is the safest option. If you lend her to me, you'll be giving me my best shot." He pulled in a breath and hoped for a miracle. "What do you say?"

For the longest time, the man stared out the window. When he met Beau's gaze, it was with a disbelieving shake of his head. He pulled a key float from his pocket and slapped it in Beau's palm. "Godspeed, you crazy SOB."

After ninety-seven bobby pins—yes, Devyn counted—Allie secured one final curl in place and announced, "Now for the veil."

"Can I look yet?"

"Nope," Allie said. "Let's wait until we get the dress on so you can see the full effect."

Devyn bounced one high heel against the floor, but she sat obediently while Allie pinned the veil in place at the back of her updo. The noise of mingled voices carried from the sanctuary into the dressing room, telling Devyn that the guests had begun to arrive. Her pulse kicked into high gear, and she wiped her clammy palms on her robe. She wondered if Beau was in the opposite dressing room feeling the same butterflies of nervous anticipation.

It was like Allie had read her mind. "I told Marc to text me as soon as Beau gets here. So far, no word."

Devyn checked the time on her cell phone. The ceremony was scheduled to begin soon. "He's cutting it close."

"Time for lipstick." Allie used a finger to tilt Devyn's face toward the ceiling. "I've always heard you're supposed to do this before putting on the dress, just in case you drop the tube."

"If you're trying to distract me," Devyn said, "it's not working."

"Shh. Keep your mouth still."

Devyn parted her lips long enough to receive a coat of Flaming Vixen, and then she said, "Maybe I should ask Marc to call him." Immediately, she changed her mind. "No, that doesn't show perfect faith. I just need to calm down and trust that he'll be here." She peeked up and resisted the urge to gnaw on her freshly painted bottom lip. "Right?"

"I know what you need," Allie said. She opened one of the bottles of Chardonnay they'd brought for the reception and poured a generous serving into a plastic cup. "Bottoms up."

Devyn drained the cup and held it out for a refill,

then finished that one, too. The wine did its job, allowing her shoulders to sink from her ears down to their normal position.

Allie unzipped the plastic protector around Mama's dress and lovingly lifted it from the hanger. After shedding her robe, Devyn stepped inside the gown, slipped her arms in the sleeves, and waited for her sister to fasten the back.

"Ready?" Allie asked, and rotated Devyn to face the mirror. "Now tell me that's not a radiant bride."

Devyn gasped when she caught a glimpse of the dark-haired beauty in the mirror. Raven curls spilled from her French twist, peeking out beneath a white veil of delicate lace. Her eyes were dusted with shimmery shadow, her cheeks blushing a shade lighter than her lips. She looked classic and elegant, like she'd stepped out of a copy of *Modern Bride*. Devyn barely recognized herself.

"Thank you," she whispered to her sister. "You're good."

"Psh," Allie said with a dismissive wave. "You made my job easy."

A peal of laughter rang out from the sanctuary, and Devyn glanced at the wall separating her from the guests. There was no more putting it off—it was time to face her friends. She didn't know why the prospect put a hitch in her pulse, but it did. "I should go out there," she said. "I told Beau I'd be waiting at the altar."

Allie checked her cell phone, then pursed her lips in consideration. "Still nothing from Marc."

"Maybe he forgot to text you."

"You go ahead," Allie said with a nod toward the chapel. "I'll check the other dressing room and see if the groom's here." But first, she handed over a cluster of gerbera daisies in jewel tones of burgundy and orange. "I know we said 'no flowers,' but I had this made for you. Every bride needs a fresh bouquet."

After a hug, Allie slipped into the second dressing room while Devyn followed the hallway leading to the front of the sanctuary. She peeked out at the rows of pews populated by smiling, chattering friends, and her heart lifted. These people loved her, and they'd come out tonight to show their support. There was nothing to fear. Keeping that in mind, she summoned a smile and approached the first pew.

Too bad Jenny and Slade were seated there.

"I see you went with white," Jenny said, raking a gaze over Devyn's gown. She sniffed a dry laugh. "Interesting choice."

Devyn fought the urge to smash her bouquet in Jenny's face, instead tightening her smile and keeping her voice chipper. "It was my mother's dress."

"Hmm." Jenny tipped her head and returned the fake grin. "At least it's not *my* gown. I donated it to the Goodwill along with that red Gucci, so you could have easily picked it up on your last scavenging mission."

"Bless your sweet little heart," Devyn said, when what she really wanted to do was knock that Hore into next week. "And thanks for coming."

"We wouldn't miss it." Jenny patted her husband's leg. "Would we, babe?"

Slade quit staring at his iPhone and jerked to attention. "Where's Beau?"

Devyn peered around the chapel but didn't see him. She spotted Allie talking with Marc at the rear of the room, darting frequent glances out the open doors into the parking lot. "Running a bit late," Devyn said. "He'll be here any minute."

With the throttle wide open, Beau hauled ass downriver. Each raindrop stung his face like a tiny missile, but he'd faced worse pain than that in recon training. What really kept his heart pounding was the lightning. White-hot bolts struck the trees lining the riverbank, followed by a deafening boom that rattled his teeth. One surge hit so close that he felt a charge of electricity crawl over his skin.

He damned near wet himself.

The worst part was that he knew he'd never make it to the ceremony on time, and he had no idea how long Devyn would wait for him. All he could do was keep his head down, hold on tight, and hope that the *Lass* had enough gasoline in her tanks to get him to the New Orleans dock where he'd parked his SUV . . . and that lightning didn't strike him dead before then.

Another mile into his journey, the searchlight affixed to the front of the boat illuminated a shadowy object ahead, so he slowed the engines and approached with caution. A tree had fallen into the river and lay partially submerged. If he hadn't spotted it in time, the boat would've been gutted. Carefully, he motored around it and uttered a prayer of thanks.

He kept his speed in check after that, squinting against the rain while he scanned the muddy water for obstacles. He knew it was the safe thing to do, but he couldn't stop picturing Devyn standing at the altar, staring at the chapel doors for his arrival. Every moment he hesitated was another beat of agony for her. He checked his cell phone to see if his service had been restored, but the screen was dead. Likely because the cursed thing was soaking wet.

An hour later, his fingers ached from clenching the steering wheel, and his muscles were stiff enough to crack granite. An occasional sputter from the engine warned him that he'd nearly depleted his gas supply, but the rain had lightened to a drizzle, and the *Belle*'s docking station appeared in the distance. A bubble of hope expanded inside Beau's chest. Once he reached his SUV, he could be in Cedar Bayou within twenty minutes—fifteen if the traffic cops weren't watching.

After hitching the *Lass* to the dock, Beau hit the pavement running and patted his coat pockets for his key fob. Then his footsteps came to a gradual halt as realization set in. He'd left his car keys in the captain's quarters onboard the *Belle*.

"Shit!"

He growled in frustration and slammed the heel of his hand into the driver's-side window. The glass didn't break, but it gave him an idea. Beau had two choices: either siphon the gas from his vehicle's tank, then use it to pilot the boat downriver to Cedar Bayou, or he could break the SUV window and hotwire the engine.

He knew the second option would get him to the chapel faster, so he didn't spend another second debating what to do.

Beau scanned the parking lot for a heavy object, eventually settling on a broken cinder block near the sidewalk. He'd just retrieved the block and held it above his head to smash the rear passenger window when he heard a man's voice shout, "Freeze! Throw down your weapon and get on the ground!"

Father Durand raised his wrinkled hands and announced, "Go in peace and serve the Lord," to which the congregation responded in unison, "Thanks be to God."

Devyn pretended to scratch her cheek while sneaking a covert glance over her shoulder toward the chapel's rear entrance. She'd pleaded with the priest to perform the wedding Mass first, separate from the ceremony, in order to give Beau more time, but he still wasn't here. She plucked a hymnal from beneath her pew and caught Father Durand's eye, then held up the volume in a silent message.

"Uh," Father Durand said before understanding flashed in his gaze. "Please rise and join me in singing 'Gathered in the Love of Christ.'"

The assembly obeyed, but Devyn noticed half of them peering around the sanctuary in confusion. Clearly it hadn't escaped anyone's notice that the groom was missing, and she didn't know how much longer she could keep stalling. While mouthing the words to the hymn, Devyn peeked to her left at Allie, who in turn peered around Marc's arm at his cell phone. After checking the screen, Marc shoved the phone in his pocket with a bit too much force, and Allie furrowed her brow. Their reactions told Devyn everything she needed to know: Beau hadn't checked in.

The hymn ended far too soon, and Father Durand stood at the pulpit in silence while looking to her for direction. God bless that man, she would owe him a hundred fish fries to make up for this. She cleared her throat and said, "The groom is a bit delayed. How about we sing 'A Marriage Blessing'?"

The priest nodded slowly, then led the hymn.

Allie leaned close, pressing her lips to Devyn's ear. "Baby, I know you have faith," she whispered. "But it's past nine o'clock. We can't keep singing hymns all night."

"Just a little bit longer," Devyn whispered back. "I know he'll be here."

But when "A Marriage Blessing" ended, Beau's father and his pregnant girlfriend left their pew and headed for the exit. Encouraged by the defectors, Alex and Nick ducked their heads and followed up the aisle.

"Wait!" Devyn shouted. "Sit back down! Beau's on his way. Give him a few more minutes!"

Beau's father had the decency to pause while the other guests scurried around him and out the door. He gestured at his girlfriend's bulbous belly as if to say, *She can't take these hard pews any longer,* then gave an apologetic wave and left.

"No," Devyn whispered to herself. "Let's sing one more—"

"Miss Mauvais," the priest interrupted. His eyes were round with sympathy when she faced him. "Can I speak with you, please?"

She spun toward the group and held up both palms. "Everyone stay put!" Then she hitched up her gown and jogged up the steps to the altar. "Father, I know this looks bad. But I promise that—"

"Child, I'm sorry," he said with a shake of his gray head. "I have to release the congregation. If the groom has been detained, I can marry you another day."

"Please," she began until noise from behind distracted her. Devyn turned to find that half the assembly had snuck out while her back was turned. Each time a guest left their pew, it seemed to spur two more into action, and within seconds, only a few people remained.

Ironically, Jenny and Slade were among the last to leave. They stood in unison, and when Devyn locked eyes with her nemesis, her stomach turned heavy. She'd expected Jenny to gloat or laugh—at least to deliver her signature sneer—but her expression was thick with pity. She held up a hand and mouthed the word *sorry* before turning and following the others.

That's when Devyn's vision finally blurred with tears. She could handle Jenny's cruelty—it'd always been a sign that the girl was threatened by her—but not sympathy.

Anything but that.

Soon the only people who remained were Allie, Marc, and the priest. Nobody spoke for the longest time. Devyn stood at the altar, staring at her bouquet of orange and red daisies. The logical part of her brain told her to leave—that Beau wasn't coming. But her heart begged her to stay. Even after two hours of practically holding her guests hostage, she still believed he would come.

Maybe she was a fool.

"Hon," Allie said. "Father Durand needs to lock up." She held out a hand. "Come with me. I want you to stay at our place tonight."

A tear slipped down Devyn's cheek, and her voice cracked. "But I know he's coming."

Marc's eyes turned to slits. "You two go ahead to the house. I'm gonna track down my brother. Whether or not I let him live remains to be seen."

A breath hitched inside Devyn's chest, turning to a sob when she realized there was nothing more she could do. She wasn't going to get married tonight. Nodding in defeat, she tossed her bouquet to the floor and strode away from the altar. Allie met her in the aisle and wrapped her in a hug.

Marc patted her back and started to speak, but he cut off when the noise of sirens approached. The wail grew progressively louder until red and blue lights flashed through the church's windows. Then the rear doors busted open with a *clunk* and an enormous man bolted inside the sanctuary.

"Dev!" he shouted. "Thank God you're still here!"

Devyn's jaw dropped. She never would've recognized Beau if he hadn't spoken first. He was soaked to the skin, his filthy uniform plastered to his body while mud caked his cheeks. If she looked closely, she could make out the imprint of an oak leaf stuck to his head.

She wanted to ask what'd happened, but the joy of seeing him rendered her temporarily speechless. He hadn't abandoned her—nothing else mattered.

"Big electrical storm," he panted, lumbering closer. "Knocked out all the phones. I had to evacuate the *Belle* in Mississippi. Then I borrowed a speedboat and made it to New Orleans."

A pair of young police officers followed him inside. One of them grinned and added, "We caught him trying to bust out the window in his car. It's a good thing he had ID on him, otherwise, we'd have taken him in."

"An electrical storm?" Devyn repeated, bringing a hand to her breast. "You could have been killed."

"That's what we told him," said the second officer.

Ignoring everyone but Devyn, Beau strode forward until he stood close enough for her to smell the cool, musty river on his clothes. He reached down and took her hand, his grip wet but firm. "Kitten," he said, gazing at her as if nothing else existed. "I would die a thousand times before missing my chance to marry you."

Devyn's eyes welled with fresh tears, but these were the happy kind. Careful not to ruin her mother's dress, she stood on tiptoe and kissed him lightly on the lips—the only spot not covered in mud.

"You know," Father Durand said from his place at the altar, "we have more than enough witnesses to perform the ceremony. . . ."

Beau peered at her and smiled. "What do you say? I know I'm not much to look at, but if you don't mind—"

"*But* nothing," Devyn said, matching his grin. "You're the most breathtaking groom I've ever seen, and I can't wait to be your wife. Let's get married!"

Chapter 20

With her face glowing and framed by dark curls, Devyn was so beautiful that Beau had a hard time catching his breath. A tiny smudge of mascara shadowed her eyes, proof that he'd made her cry, and he longed to wipe away the evidence with his thumb. But since his hands were muddy, he stroked her palm and gazed at her with all the love in his heart—which was nearly more than he could contain.

"If it is your intent to enter into marriage," the priest said, "declare your consent before God and His church."

That was Beau's cue. "I, Beau Christopher Dumont, take you, Devyn Rebecca Mauvais, to be my wife." No words had ever tasted as sweet. "I promise to be faithful to you in good times and bad, in sickness and in health, and to honor you for all the days of my life."

When she repeated the vow, Beau feared that the joy expanding beneath his breastbone might literally burst him at the seams. He didn't know what he'd done to deserve such happiness, but he was grateful all the same.

Minutes later, Marc reached into his breast pocket and handed over a simple band of white gold. Devyn must have picked it out on her own, because they hadn't had a chance to visit the jeweler together. The engagement ring he'd given her—the one she'd given back—was tucked beneath a stack of socks in his top dresser drawer. He couldn't wait to put it back on her hand. In the meantime, Beau slipped the dainty wedding band on her finger and said, "Take this ring as a sign of my love and fidelity."

Devyn did the same, adorning his dirty finger with a band of gleaming metal. It was a damned fine sight, and he imagined his face would be beaming if it weren't buried beneath a layer of muck.

Finally came the moment Beau had been waiting for—the pronouncement: verbal proof that he and Devyn belonged to each other.

The priest gave them a wide smile. "Insomuch as Devyn and Beau have consented to live together in holy matrimony, having promised their love for each other with these vows, I declare that they are husband and wife." Then he bent at the waist and said to Beau, "Congratulations. You may kiss your bride."

Beau's first instinct was to embrace his wife and kiss her into next week, but he didn't want to stain her dress. It was all Devyn had left of her mother. So he tipped Devyn's chin with one finger and lightly brushed her lips while applause broke out from their meager audience.

"Go change out of that gown, Mrs. Dumont," he whispered against her mouth. "Then I'll give you a proper kiss."

"It's a deal, Mr. Dumont," she whispered back. "And by the way, there's a set of clean clothes for you in the groom's dressing room."

Thank God for Devyn's meticulous planning, because Beau's uniform was beginning to feel like a wetsuit of crushed ice. "I wish I'd known that before the ceremony."

Devyn shook her head. "I wasn't letting you out of my sight until we said *I do*. Now you can change."

Marc piped up, wearing a smile that oozed mischief. "Not yet. I want photographic evidence that I wasn't the ugliest groom in Dumont family history."

Allie gasped, then smacked her husband on the arm.

"Can't argue with that," Beau said. Chuckling, he stood near Devyn and posed for a photo. "I caught a glimpse of my reflection in the car window back in New Orleans. It's a wonder the cops didn't shoot me on sight."

The officers laughed, and after they agreed to stay for cake, Beau reluctantly parted from Devyn to change clothes. He hated to be away from her, so he made it quick—scrubbing his face and hands in the sink, then shucking off his wet uniform in favor of the pressed suit she'd brought over from his place. He still didn't resemble a proper groom, but if Beau had his way, his clothes would adorn the floor of a hotel suite within the hour.

When he met Devyn in the fellowship hall, she was filling two cups of punch for the officers. She wore jeans and a pink T-shirt with BRIDE printed across her chest, and she'd removed the veil but kept her curls pinned in place so they spilled gradually around her cheeks. Beau leaned against the doorjamb for a moment and simply took her in, all smiles and warmth and laughter.

He couldn't believe she was his.

As if she sensed him watching, Devyn glanced over her shoulder. An instant smile appeared on her lips, and she ran toward him with outstretched arms. He pulled her tightly against his chest to savor her soft curves. Suddenly, something deep inside clicked into place, making him whole when he hadn't even realized he was lacking. Beau filled his lungs with her scent of honeysuckle, and then he gave her the kiss she deserved—deep and thorough with a passion that wasn't fit for polite company.

It didn't take long for objections to arise from the peanut gallery.

"Aw, come on," Marc said. "There's a priest here, for Crissakes." His wife elbowed him hard in the ribs, so he crossed himself while tipping his head in apology to Father Durand. "Sorry, Father."

The old man checked his watch. "You're forgiven, but perhaps we should cut the cake. I'm running late for an anointing at the hospital."

"Oh," Devyn said, taking Beau's hand and leading him toward the cake. "I almost forgot."

Allie snapped pictures while they fed each other a bite of red velvet cake. Beau had never liked the act of "smashing," so he slid his fork carefully between Devyn's parted lips, and she did the same. Afterward, Marc lifted his champagne flute in a toast.

"To my big brother and his beautiful bride," he said with a genuine smile. "Beau, we haven't always seen eye to eye, but I want you to know that I'm proud to call you my friend. You're a good man, and you're going to make an even better husband. Devyn, welcome to the family. We're a crazy bunch, but we love you, and I promise that life with us will never be boring."

"I can confirm that," Allie added.

Beau's heart warmed. It was hard to believe that this time last year, he hadn't been on speaking terms with his brother. So much had changed, and he was thankful for that, too.

"To Devyn and Beau," Marc said.

The rest of the group echoed his words, and the clinking of crystal followed. Allie cut a slice of cake for everyone, and within minutes, each plate was clean. The police officers were the first to go. They shook Beau's hand and kissed Devyn's cheek, then congratulated them and left to resume their patrol.

Devyn presented a small wrapped gift to the priest and promised to lock the fellowship hall. The man offered a quick prayer of benediction and said good-bye, leaving Allie and Marc as their last remaining guests.

"You two get the honeymoon started," Allie said. "We'll handle the cleanup."

"Take my car." Marc tossed his keys across the room. "We'll make do with Allie's until you guys get back."

Beau wasn't going to argue with that. After a round of hugs, he scooped Devyn into his arms and carried her to the door. Just when they reached the threshold, she stopped him and made one last request of her sister.

"Hey, do me a favor and run an announcement in the *Cedar Bayou Gazette* with our wedding picture, then mail a clipping to Jenny Hore. She'd better not be nice to me the next time our paths cross."

Beau didn't understand that last bit, but he didn't spend another second dwelling on it. He carried Devyn into the parking lot, and before you could say *Just Married*, they were on the main road leading to the highway.

"Where to?" he asked. "The airport? The moon? I'll take you anywhere you want."

Devyn leaned to the side, resting her head on his shoulder. "I made reservations for us in Baton Rouge."

"Nice." They could make the drive in a little over an hour. "I'm glad we're honeymooning on dry land. I've had my fill of the water."

"Hurry up and get us there," she whispered in his ear. "Because I want my fill of *you*."

"Yes, ma'am." Beau found the interstate and laid rubber. "My wife gets what she wants."

It was all Devyn could do to keep her hands to herself at the check-in counter and then the elevator to their suite on the third floor. During the drive to Baton Rouge, a gradual longing had settled in her bones until she couldn't think of anything except Beau inside her, making them one flesh. She'd never needed him so desperately, and the instant he opened the door, she started pulling off his suit jacket.

"Hold up," he said, extending a hand to keep her in the hallway. "I want to do this right." He swept her into his arms and carried her across the threshold, then kicked the door shut. "There," he murmured against her mouth while setting her down. "Now feel free to rip off my clothes."

She accepted his invitation, peeling off both of their shirts. When she went to work on his trousers, he stopped her.

"I need a shower," he said. "Want to join me?"

By way of answer, she stripped naked and led the way into the bathroom. Moments later, they were standing beneath a steaming spray, locked at the lips while Devyn soaped him up in all her favorite places.

She imagined how she must look, with mascara running down her face and her updo ruined, but she didn't give it a second thought. Instead, she ran her palms over her husband's chiseled chest, down his flat abdomen, over his muscular thighs, and finally to the powerful erection pressed to her belly.

She grasped him at the base and stroked him hard enough to draw a groan of pleasure from his throat. A new desire overtook her, this time to taste him. After rinsing the soap from his body, Devyn sank to her knees and took him fully into her mouth in one brisk motion that had him gasping out loud. Tipping back his head, Beau braced himself against the tile wall and let her take what she needed. She licked and sucked, working him with each long slide of her lips, savoring the sweetness of his skin and the salty beads of arousal rising to his tip until he made her stop.

"No more," he ordered, and tugged her to standing. His eyes were heavy with lust, but there was something else there: the same all-consuming need that burned her from the inside out. They'd made love many times before, but this was different.

Bigger, somehow.

He took one of her breasts in his palm, then lowered to draw her nipple deep into his mouth. She felt the pull of each wet tug directly between her legs, and he must have known it, because he used two fingers to sate the ache, slipping and sliding over her sensitive flesh before dipping inside to tease her until she throbbed.

Beau growled with desire and pushed his shaft between the slick passage of her upper thighs. "God, Dev. I want you right now, but our first time shouldn't be in the shower."

Releasing a soft laugh, she hitched a leg around his hip, then took him in her hand and guided his plump head inside her. Her toes curled at the sensation, and she strained to take him deeper. "Baby, our first time was more than a decade ago, right on the riverbank where anyone could've caught us."

"I remember," he said, and inched deeper. "I wanted

to take you somewhere private, but you were so wet, and you felt so damned good that I couldn't tell whether I was coming or going."

"Mmm." She recalled the sensation all too well. "We couldn't stop."

"Like now."

"Just like now."

Beau rocked into her one luscious inch at a time, and with a final upward glide, he filled her completely. They shared a low groan and locked eyes. In that moment, they were so connected in body and spirit that Devyn couldn't tell where her flesh ended and his began. It was a new emotion—beautiful and so strong that her rib cage hurt.

"I love you," Beau said while he held her hips between his massive palms and pulled out to the tip. She wanted to tell him the same, but when he thrust impossibly deeper, all she could do was make an embarrassing mewling sound. "And I love that noise," he added with a primal rotation of hips that sent her eyes rolling back. "Make it again, Kitten."

She didn't have to try. With each rhythmic stroke, each slow grind, a chorus of animalistic sounds arose from her lips. In desperation, she reached out blindly for traction so she could move with him, but her wet fingers slid off the tile. So she sank her fingernails into Beau's shoulders and panted while he rocked into her so slowly she feared her knees might buckle. Then he held her gaze and quickened the tempo, deepening his thrusts and driving her toward the edge. Soon her lower back was pressed against the wall as he slammed into her, one loud clap of flesh and then another filling the steamy room.

Sweet pressure built between Devyn's legs, increasing until she sobbed with mingled agony and bliss. Beau held inside her to gyrate his hips, and the pain burst into spasms of ecstasy. She came so hard that her vision went black for a moment, and when she focused again, it was to the sight of Beau's green eyes on her. She saw complete adoration there when he bucked against her one final time and let go.

As he came deep within her, Devyn told him, "I love you more."

After that, she went limp as a dishrag.

Beau took her in his powerful arms and turned off the water, then carried her to the king-size bed, where he tucked her beneath the covers and joined her. In the light streaming from the bathroom, she noticed the change in the skin above his heart for the first time.

"Your birthmark," she whispered, stroking the spot with her thumb. "It's gone."

He glanced down and grinned. "Good riddance. I never liked that thing."

"I guess we really did break the hex."

"Of course we did," he said. "Was there ever any doubt?"

They both knew the answer to that question. There *had* been doubt on Devyn's part, and it'd nearly driven them apart. A shiver rolled over her skin when she remembered how close she'd come to letting fear and insecurity keep her from a fulfilling life with her true companion.

"Yes," she answered. "But I promise it'll never happen again. Beau, I'm sorry for ever doubting—"

"Shh." He pressed a finger to her mouth and settled atop her, using a knee to part her thighs. "No apologies allowed on our wedding night." A hint of amusement danced in his gaze. "Have you forgotten what your tongue is for?"

Smiling, Devyn opened for him and slipped both hands possessively over his broad back. *This is my husband,* she thought. *Now and forever.* It seemed she didn't have room for any more happiness, but that wouldn't stop her from trying. "I might need a reminder."

"Lucky for both of us," he said, "I love making you remember."

The last thing she saw before his head dipped beneath the covers was a flash of dimples. Then he kissed a trail down her belly until he reached his destination.

After that, there was no more talking.

Epilogue

Beau spotted Devyn staggering up the bow ramp with an armload of textbooks, so he rushed to help her. He took the volumes and peered at the one on top of the stack. *Science Content for Secondary Students*. It sounded boring, but he'd never admit that and risk giving her a reason to change her mind again. "How exciting," he said instead. "You're on your way to being a licensed teacher!"

She rolled her eyes but couldn't conceal a smile. "In four years."

"Maybe three," he reminded her. "If you take a full summer schedule."

"We already talked about this." As they climbed the outside steps, she shielded her eyes and admired the sparkle of sunlight dancing on the river. The wind tossed her curls, and her lush pink lips spread into an appreciative smile. It stunned Beau into a beat of silence, and he wondered if he'd ever get his fill of looking at her. Probably not. "I'm taking summers off to work in the education center during high season," she said. "My mind's made up."

He knew better than to argue. And truthfully, he liked the idea of them spending summers together aboard the *Belle*. In their nearly three weeks as husband and wife, he'd had to leave her for only one overnight charter, and that was one night too long.

"And by the way," she added, "you don't want to know how much those textbooks cost."

A receipt peeked out from between the pages, so Beau pulled it free and scanned the total. He nearly dropped the whole stack. A hundred dollars per book? She was right—he didn't want to know. "Well," he said. "I guess you can't put a price on education."

Devyn stood on tiptoe to kiss his cheek. "Actually, you can. The university is really good at it."

They made their way to the captain's suite on the top floor, where they usually camped out when Beau was on duty. After depositing her textbooks, they linked hands and headed back down the stairs to the formal dining hall's executive bar, where a family meeting was already in progress.

At once, Beau sensed that something was wrong.

Allie sat beside Marc, dabbing her eyes with a tissue while her husband stared blankly at a piece of paper in his hand. On the other side of the table, Alex and Nicky wore dazed expressions, their twin blond brows lifted and their blue eyes wide. The only sound in the room was the steady *whir* of a refrigerator behind the bar. Not only that, but the head purser was absent.

"What's the matter?" Beau asked, glancing from person to person. "Where's Ella-Claire?" Everyone at the table avoided his gaze, so he pulled up a chair and repeated the question while Devyn settled on his lap.

Marc scrubbed a hand over his face, then slid a piece of paper across the table. At first glance, it looked like an ordinary business letter, but then Beau recognized Ella-Claire's signature at the bottom. He held it up so Devyn could read it at the same time.

Dear Marc and family,

Please accept this letter of resignation from my position as head purser aboard the Bell of the Bayou, *effective immediately. I'm sorry for not being able to give you more notice, but I have accepted another position out of town, and they requested that I start right away.*

Thank you for your support and understanding, both now and for the past decade. I have loved working alongside all of you, and I will miss you deeply. However, I'm at a point in my life where a change is needed, and I trust you to respect that.

Take care of one another while I'm away.

Much love,
Ella-Claire

Beau fisted the paper as his jaw went slack. Just days ago, he'd seen Ella when she had brought a gift to the house—a framed wedding portrait and an "Our First Christmas" ornament for the upcoming holiday. Now she was gone, just like that.

It didn't seem real.

But as the seconds passed, he recalled her behavior on the last charter, and the puzzle pieces clicked into place. Anger flushed his cheeks because he knew exactly why she'd left. He shook the letter at Marc. "This is because of that asshole she was dating."

Marc sat straighter. "What asshole?"

"I don't know," Beau admitted. "She wouldn't give me his name, but I could tell that he messed with her head." He pointed the letter at Alex, her best friend. "Did she tell you anything about this guy?"

Before Alex had a chance to answer, Devyn spoke up. "I think we should mind our own business and do what Ella asked of us: respect her choice. She's a grown woman, and she knows what she wants."

Nicky waved her off. "Screw that. If someone hurt her, I'll have his ass."

"Not before me, you won't," Marc said in a low growl.

"Let's not get ahead of ourselves," Allie said, but then the table erupted in a riot of conversation and arguments, each voice raised in an effort to be heard.

It went on for several minutes until Alex stood up from the table so quickly that his chair tipped over. His typically fair skin flushed dark when he locked eyes with Marc and yelled, "It was me. I'm the asshole. Are you happy now?"

Allie and Devyn shared a sideways glance that told Beau this wasn't news to either of them. But he sure hadn't seen it coming. "What're you talking about?" he asked.

Alex never took his gaze off Marc when he answered. "Ella wanted to be more than friends, but our brother made it perfectly clear that I couldn't touch her. So I told her no." His tone was charged with contempt when he added, "Looks like you got what you wanted."

"Don't twist my words," Marc ground out. If he clenched his jaw any harder, he'd break his face in half. "This is *not* what I wanted."

"Bullshit! You've been riding my ass for months about keeping away from her."

"Damn straight—because I don't want you *riding* my kid sister!"

Devyn held up both palms and said, "Everyone needs to calm down." But the staring match didn't end until she said, "Ella-Claire talked to me about this."

Marc whipped his head around. "And you didn't make her stay?"

"She didn't tell me she was leaving town," Devyn said. "But even if she had, I would have let her go. I know she's your little sister, but she's not a child, Marc. She knew that pursuing a relationship with Alex would have consequences, but she was willing to accept it because she's been in love with him for years. Maybe she resigned because she doesn't need a big brother to protect her from the things she wants in life. Have you considered that?"

The room fell silent and everyone went back to avoiding one another's eyes.

It was Alex who spoke first. "You can have my resignation, too." And then he strode from the table.

"Wait a minute," Marc objected. "We haven't talked about—"

"I'm done talking." Alex never slowed his steps, leaving them with one final message before he disappeared out the door. "At least to you."

Well, add that to the list of things Beau didn't see coming today.

"Wonderful." Marc threw his hands in the air. "Now we're missing our head purser and our personnel director."

"*And* your half brother and sister," Allie reminded him in a chiding voice.

His shoulders drooped an inch. "That, too."

Beau wrapped an arm around Devyn's waist and bent his mouth to her ear. "Your first day back on the job," he whispered, "and you've already caused a mutiny, Mrs. Dumont."

"It'll be all right in the end." For a while, she peered quietly out the port window. "Alex learned something today that took me a long time to figure out, too."

"What's that?"

She looked at him and her gaze turned soft. "Some things are worth the risk."

Beau placed a kiss on her nose. "I'm proud of you."

"For what?" she asked.

"For turning down Larabee's partnership and going back to school." He knew she hadn't taken the easy road, and he respected her for that. "It'll pay off in the end."

She looked confused at first, but then realization dawned in her eyes. "That's not the risk I was talking about."

"Then what was it?"

"You," she said, locking both arms around his neck. "It took me a long time to make peace with the fact that I can't control the future. We might have one year together, or fifty. But I'll cherish each moment, because it's a gift."

Her words made him go all warm inside. Just when he thought Devyn couldn't make him any happier, she outdid herself. "I'm a lucky man," he told her.

"The luckiest," she agreed, then proved it by leaning in to kiss him.

Beau brushed her lips with his and whispered, "There was never any risk, Kitten. I've been yours since our first date."

"Ditto." She grinned as if replaying the memory, and Beau could swear that he heard the chirp of bayou crickets from his old fishing hole. "Something happened that night. It was . . ."

She paused until their eyes met, and then they answered in unison, a smile on both their faces.

"Magical."

Make You Blush

Welcome to the Louisiana Bayou, where hopeful hearts go to great lengths to change their luck in love...

Joy McMasterson appears to have it all: a high-flying career, a swanky home and high-society parents who present her with endless eligible bachelors. But Joy's had just about enough.

Rebelling, Joy visits voodoo priestess Allie Mauvais and leaves armed with a love potion and a whole new attitude. When she finds herself in a tattoo parlour with the drop-dead gorgeous owner, she knows two things: the chemistry between them can't be ignored and there's not a chance she could take Ryan home to her parents.

Will Joy take the leap and surrender to the simmering passion?

'Heart, passion, and laughter'
ROMANTIC TIMES